The Flowers of Ballygrace

The Flowers of Ballygrace

Geraldine O'Neill

First published in Great Britain in 2006 by Orion,
an imprint of the Orion Publishing Group Ltd.

1 3 5 7 9 10 8 6 4 2

All the characters in this book are fictitious, and any resemblance
to actual persons living or dead is purely coincidental.

A CIP catalogue record for this book is available from the British Library.

ISBN-13: (trade paperback) 978 0 7528 7251 3
(hardback) 978 0 7528 7250 6
ISBN-10: (trade paperback) 0 7528 7251 6
(hardback) 0 7528 7250 8

Typeset by Deltatype Ltd, Birkenhead, Merseyside

Printed in Great Britain by Clays Ltd, St Ives plc

The Orion Publishing Group's policy is to use papers that are natural,
renewable and recyclable products and made from wood grown in
sustainable forests. The logging and manufacturing processes
are expected to conform to the environmental regulations
of the country of origin.

The Orion Publishing Group Ltd
Orion House
5 Upper Saint Martin's Lane
London WC2H 9EA

1057

www.orionbooks.co.uk

To Christopher and Zoe
Wishing you both
Health, wealth and happiness
And much love.

Acknowledgements

A warm thanks to all the staff at Orion, and a special mention to Genevieve Pegg, who worked with me on *The Flowers of Ballygrace*, in Kate Mills' absence.

Thanks to my ever-supportive agent, Sugra Zaman, and the staff at Watson Little.

I'm also indebted to the people of Daingean, Co. Offaly, who co-operated with me in the Grand Canal 200 project, which formed the basis of this book. I'd like to give a special mention to the late Andy Mangan from Rochfortbridge, who gave his time, memories and photographs for the canal project.

Thanks to Siobhan McCormack and Olive Heffernan for involving me in the community project and for their help with the displays etc.

As always, thanks to my greatest supporter, Mike, for his enduring love and patience.

Those undeserved joys
which come uncalled
and make us more pleased
than grateful –
are they that sing.

HENRY DAVID THOREAU

Chapter 1

≈∞≈

The air was sweet with summer scents from the trees and the spindly wild blossoms, as Kate Flowers cycled along the tow-path from her family cottage in Ballygrace to Tullamore town. The afternoon sunlight brought a glinting shimmer to the normally dull canal, and several times the unaccustomed heat gave Kate a silly urge to strip off to her underwear, jump in and splash about as she had often done when she was a young girl. But having reached the age of twenty, she had long since learned to temper her spontaneity over such things.

Even though it was quiet at this particular stretch of the canal, you never knew who was lurking about – watching and listening. And it would just be her luck for another cyclist or a fisherman to suddenly appear from behind a hedge or a tree at the wrong moment. She shook her head at the thought, her curly black ponytail bouncing on her shoulders, knowing that such a thing would ruin her reputation for ever. And that was the last thing she or her widowed mother needed. Her older brother Brendan was doing a good enough job of ruining the family's reputation without Kate adding to it.

She dismounted the bike now to push the sturdy high-Nellie over a small, steep bridge. When she reached the middle point on the bridge, she leaned the bike against the wall and sat down on a flat smooth stone to look down at the canal. There was no sign of the pair of swans that had made their home there this last few weeks.

She walked across the bridge now to look at the opposite side, and after a few moments, a smile spread across her full lips as she spotted the white shapes close by the canal bank.

She watched them for a while, then she suddenly looked at her

1

watch. She would have to get a move on or the best of the meat would be gone in the butcher's, and then Brendan would give out to her about how he paid for all the food that was put on the Flowers' table, and the least she and her mother could do was to make sure that it was of a decent standard.

Kate Flowers tucked a stray ringlet of jet-black hair back into her thick ponytail, as she studied the contents of her wicker shopping basket. 'I think that's everything . . .' she said, her brow furrowed in concentration.

'I suppose you'll be going to the Maypole Dance down at Ballygrace canal tonight?' Mrs O'Neill said, as she handed over the neatly wrapped package of sausages to add to the pound of rashers, the black and white pudding and the three sirloin steaks already in Kate's basket. The large, thick slice of steak was for Brendan and the two smaller slices for Kate and her mother, Mary.

'Oh . . . I'm not sure,' Kate replied, handing over the two half-crowns, and doing her best not to be drawn into the older woman's inquisition.

'Oh, you don't want to be missing a good night out,' the butcher's wife went on. 'Sure, all the young ones from Ballygrace and thereabouts will be at it, and all the fine-looking young bucks from around the place.' She went over to the till now, then a few moments later came back to count Kate's change into her hand. 'It's one of the best dance nights of the summer, and they're giving it to be a fine mild evening.'

'I'll see . . .' Kate said vaguely, putting the coins into her small, black leather purse. 'I don't like leaving my mother on her own for too long.'

'And how is Mary?' Mrs O'Neill asked, folding her chunky arms on top of the glass counter. She was a good advert for her husband's meat business, looking well fed with rosy red cheeks. 'Is she keeping well in herself?'

'Grand,' Kate said, giving a terse little smile. 'She's a lot better.'

'Ah sure, your poor mother would be fine enough on her own for a few hours. It wouldn't do her the slightest bit of harm.' She lowered her voice. 'And I'm sure she would be delighted to see you out enjoyin' yourself and maybe meeting up with a nice fella to look after the pair of ye. It's a lonely oul' spot down there by the canal, and you shouldn't have any problem gettin' a lad – a good-looking girl like yourself . . .'

'Oh, we're grand as we are,' Kate said quickly, lifting the basket from the counter. 'We have Brendan out there with us at the weekends.'

'It's not the same,' Mrs O'Neill told her, shaking her head gravely. 'You need a man there night and day.' She leaned forward in a conspiratorial manner. 'And anyway, between you and me, I think Brendan will be finding himself a wife one of these days. He's got a good steady job on the canal boats and he's one of the finest dancers in the area. Sure, the girls are only mad for him.'

'Thanks, Mrs O'Neill,' Kate said crisply, turning towards the door, her face flushed with embarrassment. The last thing she wanted to hear was about Brendan finding himself a wife when the whole town knew that he had found himself a wife at the last Maypole Dance.

The only trouble was it was another man's wife.

Chapter 2

K ate drew the back of her hand across her brow to wipe the splashes from it, then plunged both hands back into the depths of the basin of lukewarm water, feeling for her little brown-handled vegetable knife amongst the rings of carrot and parsnip peelings. When she found it, she began to chop half of a large purple and cream turnip.

'The range is good and hot,' her mother said. 'Will I put the potatoes on now?'

Kate looked over her shoulder at the clock on the shelf above the hot stove. It was nearly five o'clock and Brendan would be in at any time. 'I suppose we could have them started,' she said. 'If you just put the pan to the cool end of the cooker, then they can be doing slowly.' She paused. 'Are you sure it's not too heavy for you? D'you want me to lift it?'

'I can manage it grand,' her mother reassured her. 'And I need to start doing a bit more around the place.' Mary got slowly out of her high armchair beside the range – too slowly for a woman in her mid-forties – and went over to the table. She lifted the pan of potatoes and carried it over to the hot stove, putting it down on the cast-iron top, then moving the lid to sit at a slight angle, which would allow the steam to escape without causing pressure that would make the water boil over.

Sitting back down in her armchair, she gave a little sigh from the slight exertion.

'Are you feeling all right?' Kate checked, a concerned crease on her brow.

'Grand,' Mary said, smiling and patting her thickly coiled dark hair, which was now sprinkled with grey. 'Thanks be to God I'm feeling that little bit better every day.' Nine weeks before she had been in Tullamore Hospital to have her gall bladder removed, and she was still recovering. A thick rope-like scar now wove its way from high up on her chest to low on her stomach. She had only been out of hospital a few days when the wound had become infected, and it had made the whole ordeal even worse than it should have been, leaving her in a frail condition. The physical set-back had also triggered off Mary's old nervous problems, leaving her low in energy and confidence.

Kate looked out of the widow by the sink to see if there was any sign of Brendan yet, then she turned to the wooden board and started chopping the hard orange turnip into small square shapes. The boat was mooring at Ballygrace for the night, and then it would continue its journey down to Banagher in the morning with the lads that were on for the weekend.

Brendan would be more ready for this break than usual as the previous weekend had been very windy and he had been stuck down in Shannon Harbour until the Saturday afternoon. The boats hadn't dared go any further until the winds had died down.

Brendan had come in that Saturday night complaining bitterly about the hold-up and eager to make up for the drinking and socializing he'd missed the previous night. Kate had covered her head with the blankets when she'd heard him stumbling in, singing and muttering to himself, in the early hours of the morning. He'd moaned and groaned getting up for Mass on the Sunday morning,

4

and had then spent most of the day back in bed before heading out to the pub again in the evening.

But this weekend would be different. The weather was fine and warm and he would be in better form all round, Kate told herself. She went over to the painted white dresser and lifted the pan she used for the vegetables and in a few moments she had it filled two-thirds of the way up with the small pieces of turnip and carrots and parsnips that would hopefully bring a smile to her brother's face. She had prepared his favourite meal: steak, floury potatoes with butter and mixed root vegetables.

The potatoes were just coming to the boil when Kate heard voices coming up the path towards the cottage. She rushed over to the window, frowning, hoping that it wasn't visitors who would end up drinking tea and chatting while the dinner slowly dried up. As usual, there was only enough of a dinner for the three of them, and the family would have to sit it out until the visitors left. The manners they were accustomed to in the Flowers household wouldn't have allowed them to eat while visitors looked on.

Kate didn't know whether to be relieved or annoyed when she saw that it was indeed her brother Brendan, her confusion caused by the fact that he had brought unexpected company along with him – unexpected company that would need feeding. She stepped back from the window, throwing her hands up in the air in a silent gesture of frustration, then she walked to the door to let them in.

'Here she is!' Brendan said in a jovial tone as she lifted the latch. 'Kate Flowers – the best looking girl down this end of the canal! A Flower by name and a flower by nature.'

Kate pinned a tight smile on her face – even though she could have killed him – and opened the door wide in the sort of welcoming gesture that her brother expected on a Friday.

Brendan came in first, greasy in his dark working clothes, followed by a companion in similar garb, carrying a small holdall in one hand and a dark suit on a hanger in the other. Kate lifted her head as the fellow came through the door, and suddenly she was looking into the bluest eyes she had ever seen – possibly made bluer by the grimy sweat on his unexpectedly handsome, smiling face.

'Michael O'Brien,' he said, holding his hand out. 'I'm pleased to meet you, Kate.'

Her breath was suddenly whipped away and the blood rushed to redden her sallow-skinned cheeks. 'Pleased to meet you, Michael,' she said, in a halting, stumbling fashion.

'I hope you don't mind . . .' he said in a rich and low voice, nodding towards the kitchen where Brendan was now, chatting and laughing with his mother. 'I hope it's not inconvenient for you . . . but he nearly dragged me back with him. I was supposed to be staying on the boat until we went out this evening, and I would have made a bite for myself.' He gave a little shrug. 'It was only a few forms to be filled out for the brewery, but I suppose they can be done just as easy in the morning before we get to Tullamore.'

'You're very welcome,' Kate said, ushering him in. Considering he looked only around about her own age, it immediately struck Kate that there was something different about her brother's workmate. He was just above medium height with light brown hair, but it was the face and the bright eyes that made him stand out. There was something in his eyes, which were deep and serious, that made him seem older.

And in those few moments, as he had paused by the door, Kate instinctively knew that Michael O'Brien understood all about Brendan and the way he was. And that he understood what it must be like for Kate and her mother to have to live with him.

While Brendan introduced his workmate to his mother, Kate filled the large tin basin with hot water from the steaming kettle on the range, then lifted a bar of soap from the dish at the sink and a couple of squares cut from an old towel and carried them into her brother's room.

Most evenings – unless he was very drunk – Brendan had a strip-wash to the waist in his bedroom and changed into fresh underclothes and an old but clean shirt and trousers; she presumed his friend would do the same.

'And what parish are your family in?' Mary Flowers asked, her face now lit up and smiling. She enjoyed having company and made the most of it, asking him questions about his home and his family and enquiring about anyone she knew who lived in their area.

Michael O'Brien told her that he lived a couple of miles outside of Tullamore and then he told her how many were in his family and all about the farm they had.

'And did you not fancy workin' full time on the farm?' Mary asked, curious.

'The canal suits me grand,' he said, 'and I help out on the farm when I have time off.'

'The best of both worlds,' Mary said, nodding her head in agreement.

After the men went into the bedroom, Kate bustled back and forth between the table and the range, adding sausages and strips of bacon to the frying pan to stretch the meal to accommodate a fourth – and probably hefty – appetite. She then set another place at the table and busied herself, buttering slices of the brown soda bread that her mother had baked that morning.

The bedroom door opened and Brendan appeared wearing only his trousers and a white beard of shaving-soap on his face. 'Did you get the new blades for the razor?' he asked Kate.

She turned to the window-sill to lift the small chemist's bag and handed it to him.

'Ah, you'll make some fella a nice wife one day!' he said, winking at her.

'I'm sure I will,' she retorted, raising her dark arched eyebrows, 'so long as it's not a slave they're looking for! I've had enough of that kind of craic from you.'

'Oooh!' he said, laughing aloud now. 'We'll have to watch ourselves, Michael. No man is safe around her when she's got the oul' temper up!'

As he turned back into the bedroom – and just before the door closed – Kate caught sight of Michael O'Brien in the old, mottled wardrobe mirror. Like Brendan, he was stripped to the waist, with his broad, muscular back to her, oblivious to her stare as he lathered soap around his face and neck and then under his arms.

Suddenly feeling flustered, Kate turned back to the preparations for the meal. Apart from her brother, she had never seen a man engaged in such a personal act at close range. It made her feel all hot and embarrassed.

'Michael's a lovely fella, isn't he?' her mother said, coming over to inspect the frying pan. She decided that the sausages were done well enough on the bottom now and turned them over with a wooden spoon. 'And I'd say he's from a good family, because he has a nice speaking voice and a lovely manner about him, doesn't he?'

'Very nice,' Kate said, buttering the last slice of soda bread and then coming over to put the plate in the middle of the table. She was still trying to push the captivating picture of the boatman's bare chest and his strong arms out of her mind.

Mary Flowers' voice lowered to a whisper. 'Would you say he's a good-lookin' young lad? Is he the type that the girls would go for?' She gave a girlish giggle. 'I think he's very good-lookin' anyway—'

'Mammy!' Kate hissed, shooting a glance at the bedroom door. 'He'll hear you!'

Mary gave a little sigh, but her eyes were full of amusement. 'Sure, it's not as if I'm sayin' anything wrong – I'm only complimenting him. Where's the harm in that?'

'He would be mortified if he heard you saying such a thing.'

'Oh, devil a bit of it!' Mary said, prodding the sausages with a fork to check if they were cooked right through.

A short while later the two lads emerged from the room, their hair damp and slicked back, their faces well scrubbed and glowing. Mary motioned them to sit down at the table as Kate put bowls of potatoes and mixed vegetables and a jug of thick onion gravy on the table. She then set a hot plate of steak and sausage and rashers in front of their guest and another in front of Brendan.

Michael O'Brien now had one of the smaller steaks and Kate and her mother shared the other. In spite of the exasperation she had felt earlier at having to stretch the meal to another place, Kate felt quite satisfied with the full plates she had managed to come up with.

The men both had large glasses of milk, which had been cooled in a bucket of cold water in the small pantry, and she and her mother had smaller glasses of red lemonade. Kate went back to the plates on the top of the range and served her mother next and herself last. Eventually, she came to sit at the small square table, across from Michael O'Brien, her mother and brother at either side of her.

'Are you all set for the Maypole dancing in Ballygrace tonight?' Brendan said, reaching over to flick the back of his sister's raven-black hair.

'I haven't decided . . .' Kate said, still feeling hot and slightly

8

flustered from the cooking. She glanced at her mother, unsure as to whether she would feel happy leaving her on her own.

'Of course she'll go now,' her mother answered for her. She smiled encouragingly at Kate, but her eyes were flickering across in their guest's direction. 'Won't you? You can go with the two Daly girls.'

Noelle and Sarah Daly lived in an old farmhouse just a five-minute walk down the canal path from the Flowers' cottage. Noelle was the same age as Kate, and Sarah a year younger.

Brendan guffawed. 'She won't get too many dances going with that pair of red-headed heifers,' he said, shaking his head.

'*Heifers!*' Kate gasped, practically choking the word out. 'When did you last have your eyes tested, Brendan Flowers? Noelle and Sarah both have lovely figures.'

'She may as well stay at home as go dancin' with that Daly pair,' Brendan continued, studiously avoiding his sister's steely eye. 'I wouldn't take them around the floor if they were the last two women left in the place.'

'And what makes you think that they'd even consider dancing with an amadán like you?' Kate snapped. 'They have plenty of fellas asking them to dance.' She was grateful to have the Daly girls for company since her best friend, Maura, had become engaged to a lad from Tullamore at Christmas, and no longer went out on her own to dances or the pictures. Anytime they met up now all Maura could talk about were the things she was planning to make or save up for, for her bottom drawer.

Brendan shrugged carelessly and laughed now at Kate's bad temper. Insults from his sister were like water off a duck's back, and anyway, he enjoyed riling her.

'Ah, Brendan,' Mary Flowers admonished lightly, 'you shouldn't be telling lies like that about Noelle and Sarah. They're two lovely looking girls – everybody says how striking they are with their beautiful red hair and their lovely figures. And even if they weren't particularly good-looking, there's more to people than that. Looks aren't everything, you know.'

'True enough,' Brendan remarked, winking over at his work-mate. 'I suppose you don't need to look at the mantelpiece when you're pokin' the fire. Isn't that right, Mickey?' He laughed heartily now at his own joke.

While her mother gave a little exasperated sigh and raised her eyes to the ceiling, Kate's cheeks burned at his crude remark, but she bit back the sharp retort on the tip of her tongue because of their guest. She glanced across at Michael O'Brien and saw him give Brendan a wry smile and shake his head – but there was no laughter in his eyes.

'C'mon now, you must be starving.' Mary held the bowl of potatoes out to their guest.

'This is a grand meal and I'm grateful to ye both for it,' the boatman said quietly, taking three large, hot potatoes and putting them on a small saucer at the side of his dinner plate. He lifted the well-worn, ivory-handled knife and proceeded to peel the bursting skin from the potatoes. He did it deftly and quickly.

Kate stole a glance at him and was surprised to notice how delicate his long tapering fingers looked – more like a pianist's or an artist's hands than a boatman. She was even more surprised to notice how clean they were for a man used to the oily, grimy work on the canal boats.

She took the potatoes from her mother now and after putting two on her saucer, she cut into her small piece of steak, checking that it wasn't over-cooked. Brendan liked everything well done with any fatty bits crispy, and she hoped that Michael O'Brien liked it the same way.

'Do you enjoy the dancing yourself, Michael?' Mary Flowers enquired now.

He nodded and smiled, politely finishing chewing a piece of meat before answering. 'Ah, yes,' he said, nodding his fair hair. 'I love the bit of music.'

'And do you play anything at all?' Mary asked, her eyes bright with interest.

'Sure he has an oul' guitar that he carries on the boat,' Brendan cut in. 'He never goes anywhere without it.'

'Indeed! I'd love to hear you play,' Mary said. She leaned over and touched Kate's elbow. 'Wouldn't you, Kate?'

Kate suddenly became conscious that she had hardly broken breath to her brother's friend. 'What do you play?' she said, looking across the table at him.

'Everything and anything,' he said, smiling directly back at her. 'New and old.'

'And will you be playing at the dance tonight?' Kate's mother said.

'Ah, no doubt I will,' Michael O'Brien said. 'I'll probably join in with a few oul' tunes.'

'Oh, Kate, you'll have to go now,' the older woman said, joining her hands together as though in prayer. 'Sure, it'll be a great night altogether with the fine weather and the music and everything. All the young ones between Ballygrace and Daingean will be there.'

'What about you?' Kate asked her mother.

'I'll be grand,' Mary assured her. 'I'm better every day.' She gestured towards the empty fire in the grate, which would be lit later in the evening. 'I'll be sitting there quite happy listening to the radio and reading my magazine, and lookin' forward to you coming home to tell me all that's happened.'

'I'm not sure . . .' Kate swallowed hard, feeling as though she were under a spotlight with all eyes on her.

'Mammy's right,' Brendan chipped in, making things even worse. 'You'll turn into an oul' maid before you know it. You'll leave it too late and then when you look around all the best fellas will be gone.'

'Don't heed him,' Mary said, waving her hand dismissively in her son's direction. She turned to Kate. 'You can wear that fancy blue frock your Auntie Rose bought you when we were over in Stockport,' Mary suggested now. 'It looks absolutely lovely with your good brooch in the centre.' She clapped her hands together. 'Oh, I used to love going to the Maypole dances when I was a girl – I loved the music and the dancing and seeing all the people that were there. I even loved the cycling back and forward to it with my dancing shoes tied up on the back of the bike.' She gave a little sigh. 'Oh, I wish I was your age again and able to go out and about and enjoy myself.'

Kate listened now, thinking how relieved she was that her mother was back to her old chatty, cheery self. She had always been grateful to have such an easy-going, pleasant-natured mother, and Maura and the Daly girls had always told her how lucky she was, as their mothers were far more serious and at times fairly cross.

'Before I was married,' Mary happily rattled on, 'I used to go to summer dances at the crossroads in Clare with my sister and the other local girls. Oh, the grand nights we had!' Her eyes were suddenly youthful again – full of the girlish memories. 'I tell you, there wouldn't be a single Saturday night when I'd sit in if there was a dance I could go to – or to the pictures.' She roared with laughter now. 'I even enjoyed getting all dressed up and going to the church with my sister and the girls when the Missions were on. Anything to get out of the house. Oh, the young ones have the time of their life and they don't realise it until they're too old to enjoy it any more.'

Kate knew her mother must have had precious few years for dancing after she married a much older man when she was only eighteen, leaving behind her native County Clare and the large family that she grew up in. Her sister Rose was now in Stockport near Manchester, others were in London and several of her brothers had left for America years ago, and since then she'd only seen them at her parents' funerals.

She was married two years when Brendan came along, and he was followed a few years later by Kate.

'Your mother's right,' Michael O'Brien said, looking directly at Kate now. 'Life's too short to waste time.' He nodded over at Brendan. 'And she'll be guaranteed at least two dancing partners over the evening, won't she?'

Kate felt a little flutter of excitement at the thought of Michael O'Brien's strong arms leading her around the wooden platform that was built especially for the Maypole dance every year. 'Well . . . I'll think about it.'

Mary gave a little whoop of delight. 'That's it now, Kate!' she laughed. 'You'll have to go – sure, you have no excuse not to go – and the lads agree!'

After she had dressed and coaxed her black curly hair into what she thought was a slightly more fashionable style, Kate went into Brendan's bedroom to check her reflection in his wardrobe mirror – since it was the only full-length mirror in the house.

As she looked at her reflection, she gave a little sigh of relief and her shoulders relaxed for the first time in hours. She looked fine. And with a little touch of powder and lipstick she was confident enough to know she'd look more than fine.

She smoothed a stray curl down, wondering if Michael O'Brien had thought that she was particularly good-looking. She could tell by the way he looked at her and spoke to her that he was comfortable with her, but he had only seen her in her old working skirt and blouse. The way he had smiled at her made her think that he definitely liked her – but she couldn't tell whether it was in a sisterly way or whether there might be more to it.

What would he think when he saw her in the blue dress with the scooped neck, which went a little lower than she usually dared, and the big broad belt, with the sparkly brooch pinned in the middle of the neck? She didn't know enough about him to guess how he would react.

But Kate knew one thing – *she* definitely liked *him*. He was the nicest looking boy and the nicest mannered boy she'd ever met. None of the local boys that she'd gone out with had stirred her interest the way her brother's friend did.

'Oh, Kate – you look beautiful!' her mother said when she came out of the room. 'You'll be the belle of the ball tonight, so you will.'

'I wouldn't go that far,' Kate laughed, pleased with the compliment, 'but the dress is gorgeous, isn't it?'

'Your Auntie Rose has a great eye when it comes to clothes,' Mary nodded. 'And she knew the colour would look well on you.' She studied her daughter now. 'A paler blue would have looked wishy-washy on you with your dark hair, but that deep blue looks just perfect.'

Kate went over to the kitchen table where she had her navy clutch bag that matched her wedge-heeled navy sandals and she took out her powder compact and lipstick. She dabbed a coat of the light tan powder on her face and neck – going down well into her cleavage – and then she applied a coat of deep pink lipstick.

Mary looked appraisingly at her daughter now. 'You should put a bit of that stuff on that makes your eyelashes look longer,' she suggested. 'It looked lovely when you wore it over in England.'

'Mascara?' Kate said, raising her eyebrows. She never really gave make-up a thought unless she was going out. Most of the time her face was scrubbed clean, and the only beauty preparations she used were a little Anne French or Nivea Creme. 'Maybe I'll put a little bit on. I think it's in the dressing-table drawer.'

She went into the bedroom that she shared with her mother and came out a few moments later with the little square black box. 'You have to be really careful with this stuff,' she told her mother, going over to the sink. She dampened the little brush under the tap and rubbed it over the hard black surface of the mascara block, and then, when she'd worked it into a bit of a paste, she carefully brushed it onto her top lashes and after letting them dry, onto her bottom ones.

'Perfect,' Mary Flowers said. 'You'll knock Michael O'Brien dead on his feet the way you look tonight.'

'Mammy!' Kate hissed, her face flushing. She fiddled about with her brooch now for something to do. 'There will be plenty of beautifully dressed girls there, he won't necessarily be interested in me.'

Her mother's eyes were sparkling with delight – almost as if it was herself going to the dance. 'I'll be waiting up for you to hear every bit of news.'

Chapter 3

꧁꧂

The two Daly girls were ready and waiting when Kate knocked at their door, and almost tumbled out on top of her. 'Oh, you two look nice,' she said, noting that they were both wearing bright, flowery frocks and had obviously spent time curling their straight, strawberry-blonde hair and pinning it back with fancy hair clasps.

Once again, it passed through Kate's mind that Brendan's cruel comments about the sisters were totally uncalled for. They were neither fat nor unattractive, and they always had plenty of lads lining up to dance with them any time she was out with them. And she knew for a fact that Brendan had asked Noelle to go to the pictures last summer, but because of her father's moods, she had let him down at the last minute, and he'd never got over it.

Noelle had called up to the house and embarrassedly tried to explain about her father, but Brendan – his ego bruised – had brushed her aside. He'd not had a good word for the girls – particularly Noelle – ever since.

It had been on the tip of her tongue to say as much when he had started his bad-mouthing about them earlier on, but it could have led to a serious row and apart from having a guest to consider, she knew her mother wasn't up to that kind of thing.

'Quick!' Noelle hissed, catching Kate by the arm and propelling her back towards the gate. 'Daddy's in a fierce bad humour and he nearly stopped us goin' to the dance. Keep moving in case he takes it into his head to bring us back.'

Kate felt a sudden stab of alarm at the thought of Matt Daly coming after them and she quickened her step to match her friends. He was a severe-looking man at the best of times and Kate certainly didn't want to get on the wrong side of him.

Not for the first time, Kate offered up a silent prayer of gratitude that she didn't have a ferocious father at home to contend with. As far as she remembered, her own father had been a gentler kind of man – she certainly had no memories of him ever shouting and bawling the way Matt Daly went on. She had vague recollections of him out on the tow-path teaching her how to ride a bicycle and showing her a bird's nest – not the kind of things that the Daly girls' father would ever do. Kate realised that she was lucky, for her mother was well-known for her easy-going manner – but she reckoned she had more than her fair share of family problems when it came to Brendan.

'You shouldn't have said anything about us wearing the new dresses to the dance!' Noelle said accusingly to her sister as they scurried along. 'You know what he's like when he's in a fierce bad humour!'

'What's he bothered about? Sure, they're not even new!' Sarah snapped back.

'Isn't that the whole point?' Noelle sighed loudly. 'He says he doesn't want us wearin' oul' cast-offs from Mammy's rich relations in America.'

'Pity about him!' Sarah said, thrusting her arm through Kate's now. 'The dresses are lovely and have hardly been worn *and* they fit us perfectly. We couldn't afford to buy this style up in Dublin, so I'll be wearing them and I don't care what he says.' She turned to Kate. 'You don't realise how lucky you are having a quiet house up there. There's times I really envy you...'

'Definitely,' Noelle agreed. 'And I know there's times you must miss not having a father around, Kate – but I don't think you'd swap places with us when Daddy's in bad form.'

Kate gave a little shrug, thinking how Brendan annoyed her at times, but she kept quiet since it was the two girls he'd been going on about earlier on. Besides, her brother was more of an irritant and a nuisance with drink, and he did have a good side, even if he didn't always show it.

'You both look lovely,' she said instead, smiling at them. 'Your hairstyles are very elegant altogether.' She was desperate to lighten the tone of the evening. She hadn't been to a dance for ages and since she had decided to go earlier this evening, she had gradually begun to feel all young and excited again – the way she used to, the way she did up until her mother's illness.

And she knew the fact that Michael O'Brien would be at the dance had added another touch of excitement to the whole event.

'And you look gorgeous, too, Kate, in that lovely blue dress,' Noelle said. 'But then you always do. I wish my hair was naturally curly like yours. We've spent ages doing ours with curlers and setting lotion.'

'You wouldn't want my hair,' Kate laughed, shaking her curly black mane. 'It's got a will of its own and will only go the one way – and it takes half the day to dry.'

'Who was the fine-lookin' fella I saw walkin' up to the house with your Brendan?' Sarah suddenly cut in. 'I saw them when I was out in the yard getting a bucket of turf.'

'Michael O'Brien – he works on the boats along with Brendan,' Kate said lightly. 'I only met him this evening for the first time myself . . .'

'Are they going to the dance tonight?'

'Oh, you know Brendan,' Kate sighed. 'He wouldn't miss a dance if he could help it.'

'And his friend – what kind of a fella is he?' Noelle asked, all interested. Her sister had mentioned seeing him earlier on but she had been busy ironing her dress at the time and hadn't paid that much attention. 'Is he married or single?'

'He's nice enough and I'm sure he's single,' Kate replied carefully. 'He'd have said if he was married. My mother gave him the Spanish Inquisition about his family and everything and he didn't say anything about being married.'

'Ah, but did you get the impression he might be courting anybody?' Noelle asked. 'If he's as good-lookin' as Sarah says, he'll likely be spoken for already.'

Kate's face darkened as it suddenly dawned on her that she hadn't a clue whether Michael O'Brien had a girlfriend or not. 'Now that,' she said, feeling a bit strange at the thought, 'I don't know at all.'

'In that case,' Sarah said, 'we'll have to make it our business to find out tonight.'

'And if he's attached to anybody else,' Noelle added, 'then we'll just have to look elsewhere.'

Half an hour later the girls rounded a bend on the canal tow-path and there in front of them was the old stone bridge at Ballygrace. Through the gap underneath the bridge they could see the crowd that was already gathered around the stage that had been erected the previous afternoon, along with a good-sized wooden platform for dancing.

'It's going to be a grand night,' Noelle prophesied in a low voice. 'And there will be an even bigger crowd in an hour's time.'

'Do you think Brendan and his friend will be there already?' Sarah checked, craning her neck to see if she could recognise anyone in the distance.

Kate smiled and shrugged. She had been thinking the very same thing herself. 'I doubt it,' she answered. 'I would imagine that Brendan will be holding up the bar in the pub for a while yet.'

'He's a bit of a rake, your Brendan,' Sarah laughed. 'A demon for the girls and the drink.'

'He's certainly not as quiet and shy as he used to be back in school,' Noelle added wryly.

Kate felt her face flush at her friend's comment, but there was no point in being annoyed with her neighbour for saying anything about Brendan, and Sarah hadn't spoken in a sneering way. Besides, the two sisters were always open enough with her about their father. Every family, Kate supposed, had their problems.

And anyway – didn't the dogs in the street know what her brother was like? Not that it mattered – Brendan Flowers didn't give a damn what people thought of him or his carry-on. He just sailed on regardless. Although Kate was grateful that he seemed to have quietened down a bit in the past year – since the episode at the Maypole dance with the woman from Edenderry. She reckoned that he must have had a run-in with her husband or maybe he got a fright when he sobered up and realised the risk he'd taken. But Kate knew that her brother still had that undependable streak. She would just have to hold her head up proudly and learn not to care what people thought either. Not caring what other people thought was a lesson she had been working on for a long time – and one she still hadn't mastered. But she would keep on trying.

There was no other option.

The three girls walked along the tow-path, chattering about previous dances they'd been to, who was courting who locally, and discussing plans they had for the summer. They weren't going anywhere very exciting, the Dalys told Kate, but they were going to spend the fortnight they both had off from work up in Dublin with their aunt. Kate told them about her planned visit to her Aunt Rose in Stockport.

'Oh, you're lucky,' Sarah said. 'I'd love to go over to England sometime.'

'I'd love to go to America,' Noelle said. 'Our aunties and uncles out there have said they could get us work and everything.' She sighed. 'One of these days when I've saved up the fare I'll just up and go.'

'You may take me with you!' Sarah announced. 'I couldn't stick it in the house if you weren't there.' Then suddenly she shrieked out loud. 'Feck!' she said, coming to a standstill. 'A bloomin' ould blackberry briar has ripped my stockings and scratched my legs to bits.'

The two other girls halted and gathered around her to examine the damage.

'Your dress hides the ladder in your stocking,' Noelle told her sister.

'And the scratches don't look too bad,' Kate said sympathetically. 'Here,' she said, taking a clean hanky from her handbag. It was newly ironed and pressed into a small neat square. 'Use that to clean up the blood.'

They spent a few moments attending to her minor wounds and when it was decided that she was patched up sufficiently, they resumed their walk towards the Maypole stand. They could hear the sound of music in the distance, and as they grew nearer they could see the group of local musicians sitting on the stage with accordions and banjos and large round tambourines.

'Oh look!' Noelle said, her voice high with excitement. 'There's the mineral table set up as well.' She craned her neck further. 'And there's a good few fellas gathered there already.'

Brendan's opinion of the two Daly girls obviously wasn't shared by the other males already at the dance, who lost no time in taking them on the floor as soon as the music got into full swing. The curvaceous, red-haired girls were both good dancers and although they appeared initially shy and a bit awkward, they had something about them that drew certain local fellows.

The sort of fellows that grew up in families with values similar to the Daly household, and knew that the down-to-earth girls would make good partners for them. The sort of fellows that were taking their chances with the girls early on in the evening before the young, confident bucks appeared – buoyed up with drink – and took over the whole show.

The sort of fellows that knew they had no chance with the likes of Kate Flowers.

Kate stood at the side of the dance floor watching Noelle and Sarah as they moved around the floor in their American dresses, keeping perfect time with the old-fashioned waltz. She wasn't alone and she wasn't bothered about not getting asked up to dance at the beginning of the night. She knew most of the other girls who were there – patiently sipping their bottles of lemonade through stripey paper straws, and watching in the distance for the other, more exciting lads to come walking along the banks of the Ballygrace canal.

The lads that were still holding up the bar in the pubs in Ballygrace.

The lads like Brendan Flowers.

Around ten o'clock, when the light was beginning to fade, the dance started to move into full swing. The dance floor was now packed and Kate found herself up on the wooden platform for one waltz and half-set after another. There were so many people there that it was getting more and more difficult to waltz without bumping into someone, although no one really minded. It only added to the fun and light-heartedness of the evening.

She had just finished a dance and was rather breathlessly thanking her partner – a fellow she knew vaguely from Daingean – when she felt a tap on her shoulder. She turned around and found herself looking up into Michael O'Brien's smiling, handsome face.

'Would you care for a dance, Miss Flowers?' he said lightly, taking her hand as though she had already agreed. Then he led her into the middle of the wooden platform as the band struck up a slow waltz. 'I'd hoped we might get to dance a bit earlier,' he told Kate as he slipped one hand around her slim waist.

'I wouldn't say Brendan was in any hurry to leave the pub,' Kate said ruefully, lifting her gaze upwards, and when her eyes met his, her heart quickened.

He gave a slow smile as though he knew what she was feeling. 'Ah well, that's Brendan for you . . . but then you know him better than anyone I suppose, being his sister?'

'I certainly do,' Kate stated, with an edge to her voice, 'and at times that's to my misfortune.'

He smiled again and gently squeezed her hand. 'Ah, he's not the worst.'

And then, as he guided her into the dance and around the floor, Kate suddenly felt lighter and easier, and after a little while, she began to feel that maybe Brendan wasn't the worst. Other couples joined them on the floor now and as they danced around they fell into a comfortable silence, enjoying the music and feeling the cool night air on their faces.

Halfway through the dance Kate felt a little friendly dig in her back and she turned her head to see Sarah dancing past, smiling and rolling her eyes meaningfully in Michael O'Brien's direction.

'Who's that?' Michael said, laughing.

'Sarah Daly,' Kate replied, 'one of the girls that I came with tonight. She's one of the sisters that Brendan was going on about. The ones he was calling heifers.'

'Oh . . .' Michael said, nodding his head. He glanced back at the red-headed Sarah again and shrugged. 'I don't know what he was going on about, she looks nice enough to me.'

'She is,' Kate said, her dark curls bobbing up and down in emphasis. 'There's not a thing wrong with her or her sister.' Then, just as she was about to tell Michael O'Brien just what she thought of her brother, she felt a hand grasp her roughly at the side of her waist. She turned sharply to find Brendan's grinning, leering face looking into hers.

'Gotcha!' he said, roaring with laughter, 'You were both looking fierce serious there for the minute – who were you givin' out about now?'

'The big, stupid amadán that lives in our house!' Kate said smartly, slapping his hand away. Then she manoeuvred her partner around and led him off in the opposite direction well away from her brother. 'That fella drives me mad like nobody else!' she said. 'And he's even worse when he's had a drink.'

'He's a grand worker,' Michael O'Brien said, 'and easy to get along with on the boat. Better than most of the others. He'd always do you a good turn if he could.'

Kate looked up at him now, just as the dance came to an end. 'Good,' she said in a quieter voice now. 'I'm glad he's all right out of the house, especially for Mammy's sake. She's always worrying about him.'

'Brothers and sisters often have their differences,' he went on now, still holding her in his arms. 'But often, as they get older, they find it easier . . .'

Kate nodded slowly. Then a thought suddenly struck her. 'Does he complain badly about me?'

The boatman smiled and shook his head. 'Not at all – I've never heard him say a bad word about you or your mother. He only has the height of praise.' He squeezed the top of her arms now in a mildly teasing gesture. 'He told me that all the fellas from Ballygrace to Tullamore were after you, but that there was nobody good enough for you.'

'You're a real diplomat, I'll say that for you,' Kate said, laughing. He was staring at her again and she suddenly felt self-conscious, as though it looked as if she was hanging about – waiting for something. Waiting for him. 'Oh, and thanks for the dance.' She eased out of his grip now, and made a very obvious gesture of scanning the crowds for her friends.

'You're not going already, are you?' he said, reaching out to catch her hand in his. 'I thought we might have a few more rounds of the floor.'

Kate looked back at him and she could suddenly feel his blue eyes burning into hers. All traces of jocularity were gone out of them, replaced by a deep seriousness. Then, when his grip tightened on hers, she moved back towards him and, when his arms encircled her waist drawing her into him, her breathing quickened.

The band struck up 'Forget Me Not' and she was suddenly being led around the wide wooden platform again, her blue skirt whirling around her and Michael O'Brien's body very, very close to hers.

This time they danced in silence – all thoughts of Brendan forgotten – their steps in perfect time with the music and with each other. And as she moved, Kate Flowers was wholly conscious of every single short breath she took.

After a while his head gradually bent towards her and then she felt his smooth cheek come to rest against hers, and then she suddenly remembered the glimpse she had of him in the bedroom mirror earlier on that evening scraping the stubble from his face. Something deep in the pit of her stomach stirred and when he moved still closer to her she knew that he felt exactly the same.

When that dance ended and the next – and they were still together – Kate knew that something momentous had walked into their house and into her life that day. Something that was meant to happen. Something that would change everything.

And later, when all daylight had vanished and only the watery light from the fledgling new moon was left, Michael O'Brien leaned towards her and closed his eyes and kissed Kate Flowers full on the lips.

Chapter 4

❧

Mary Flowers threw six dry, brittle pieces of black turf on the fire, dusted her hands together and then lifted her book from the mantelpiece. She sat back down in her comfortable armchair, which was well padded with an old quilt and two cushions, and in a few moments she was back with Cathy and Heathcliff in the tortured, romantic world of *Wuthering Heights*.

As far back as she could remember, she had filled any empty hours with a book of some sort, but lately – since her illness – she had taken comfort in the romance of the books she had read as a girl. The romance she had dreamed of, that had never been part of her own life. The romance that had evaded her when she was married off at barely eighteen to an older man.

Kate carefully lifted the latch on the wooden gate and came up the stone path to the cottage as quietly as she could. Then – very slowly – she turned her key in the lock.

'Is that you, Kate?' her mother called from the fireside, an eager tone in her voice.

'It is,' Kate replied, coming inside. 'I was going quiet in case you might be in bed.'

'Not a bit,' Mary Flowers said, leaning forward with the poker to turn over a few larger pieces of the brightly burning turf. 'I dozed for a while earlier, but I've been wide awake for a good hour or more.' She looked up at the clock on the mantelpiece – it was going on for one o'clock. She made no censorial comment, because it wasn't bad for a dance in Ballygrace – sometimes they went on until three or four in the morning. 'How did you get on at the dance? Did you enjoy yourself?'

'I'd a good enough night,' Kate said, coming over to lay her bag and long blue gloves on the pine table she scrubbed several times a day.

'And who did you come home with?'

Kate smiled. 'Michael O'Brien walked me back.' Then, feeling her cheeks redden, she came across the stone floor to check the kettle by the side of the fire.

'Oh, Kate!' Mary Flowers exclaimed delightedly, her pale face lighting up. 'Sure, I knew it! I knew well he liked you by the way he was looking at you.'

Kate felt the side of the hot kettle. 'Is it long boiled?'

'Not ten minutes ago,' he mother answered quickly, desperate for more information. She gestured towards the crane hook. 'I kept the fire going so you could have a cup of tea when you came in.'

Kate bent down to hang the kettle on the hook now and eased it back into the fire until it was directly over the hottest part.

'He's a lovely lad, isn't he?' Mary went on, her hands joined together. 'And good-lookin' – very good-lookin'! I can't believe that Brendan brought such a grand fellow home with him.'

Kate straightened up now and went over to sit on the chair at the other side of the fire. 'He's a very nice fellow,' she agreed. Then her eyes lit up. 'A very good guitar player and singer and a fine dancer. He joined in with the musicians near the end of the night for a few tunes. We had a great time.' She felt her stomach tighten again as she remembered his strong arms around her and the way his warm mouth had felt on hers.

'Did he ask to see you again?'

Kate nodded, her raven curls bobbing up and down. 'He asked me to go for a walk with him on Sunday afternoon. He has to take the boat down to the maltings in Banagher tomorrow morning, but he says he'll be back late Sunday morning.'

'Lovely! Why don't you ask him to come for his dinner again?'

Kate pursed her lips together in thought. 'Is it not a bit too soon? I don't want to give him the impression that I'm desperate . . .'

'Do you like him, Kate?' Mary said, her brow furrowed.

'Sure, he's grand.'

'I mean do you . . . do you *fancy* him like?'

Kate laughed now and rolled her eyes to the ceiling. '*Mammy!*' she hissed. 'That's not the kind of question a mother should be asking her daughter.'

'I'm only lookin' out for you,' Mary said, leaning across to pat Kate's knee. She took a deep, slow breath. 'You see . . . I don't want you makin' any mistakes – missing any chances. It's not easy to find a good-looking, dependable young man, and the dark winters especially can be long and lonely out in the country.' She paused again. 'Especially if you pick the wrong one.'

Kate stared at her mother now, a startled look in her eyes.

Suddenly realising she had said too much, Mary Flowers lifted the poker and rattled it about amongst the hot embers. 'I'll get the fork and make us a bit of toast now.'

The two women were laughing heartily at Kate's description of an old farmer in Wellington boots covered in cow-dung who had asked every girl at the dance to get up on the floor with him.

'I'm over forty years of age, and even I wouldn't have danced with him!' Mary Flowers said, giggling like a young girl.

Then, as the gate latch sounded, their laughter came to an abrupt halt.

'*Brendan*,' Kate said in a low voice.

'How was he?' her mother said quickly. 'Not too bad, I hope.'

'Good enough form when I last saw him on the dance floor. He hadn't hands enough, grabbing this one and that one.'

The door opened. 'What's all this?' Brendan Flowers greeted them, a distinct edge to his voice – the edge that told them once again he'd drunk too much. 'What's all the great hilarity about?'

'Ah, just chat,' Mary said, her eyes darting across to catch her daughter's. The main objective now would be for them all to get to bed without any rows. 'There's fresh tea in the pot if you want a cup . . .'

'I hope it wasn't me ye were skittin' and laughing about,' Brendan said, coming into the middle of the room.

'An' what would we be laughing at you for?' Kate said, trying to keep an even tone in her voice.

'It wouldn't be the first time,' Brendan said, swaying as he took off his suit jacket.

'Will I cut you a slice of cake to go with the tea?' Mary asked, holding the teapot up.

'Aw . . . go on,' he said, as though he were doing her a great favour by agreeing.

As she watched her brother weave his way into the middle of the room, Kate made the instant decision to take herself off to bed and well out of his way. 'You can sit in here by the fire if you want,' she said, standing up. 'I'm heading off to bed.'

'I see you and Mickey hit it off well,' he said, sinking into the chair like a heavy sack of potatoes being deposited on the floor.

Kate suddenly remembered what Michael O'Brien had said about her brother being one of the hardest workers he knew. Then it dawned on her that apart from being fairly jarred, Brendan was probably simply worn out after a long week on the barge and going straight into a night of drinking and dancing. 'He's a very nice lad,' she said cautiously, not knowing which way he would turn now. There was no telling with him as his moods fluctuated.

'Ah, he's all right,' Brendan said, scratching his head. He took a cup of tea from his mother, spilling a few drops on the stone floor as he did. Then he took the small plate from her with a thick slice of fruitcake – the cake she hoped would sweeten his temperament.

Kate went into the bedroom and got her bottle of Anne French face milk and a piece of cotton wool. She poured a few drops of the runny white liquid on one side of the cotton wool and rubbed it over her face, then she turned it over to the clean side and did the same thing again. She knew she should go to bed and wait until the morning to hear what Brendan had to say about Michael O'Brien, until he was sober – but she couldn't help herself. She wanted to hear what Michael thought of her *now*. She wanted to hear before she went to bed so she could lie awake for a while running through every bit of the night in her mind. She wanted to hear any compliments or nice things that he had to say about her.

'I looked in at the barge on my way home,' Brendan eventually said. 'Just checkin' that things were okay for them headin' off in the mornin' . . .'

'And were you talking to Michael?' Mary Flowers asked now, almost as eager to hear about him as her daughter.

Brendan took a good bite of the cake and then chewed it for a few moments. 'We had a bit of an óul' chat . . . about this and that. Nothin' in particular. Although I did hear one bit of interestin' information earlier on in the day . . .'

'Oh?' Mary said, raising her eyebrows.

He took another bite of the fruitcake, then he looked over towards the open bedroom door. 'Bad news for you, Kate,' he said, raising his voice enough for her to hear him. 'It seems he's not a free man. Michael O'Brien has another girl in Tullamore. He's more or less spoken for.'

As she listened to his words, Kate felt as though a bucket of cold water had just been poured over her. Barefoot now, she walked across the bedroom floor and closed the door. Then she went back and sank down on her single bed, trying to take in all that her brother had said.

She had been sure that something special had happened between her and Michael tonight. Surely she wasn't that naïve and stupid that she had imagined his interest? Surely she hadn't read something into the situation that wasn't there?

She could hear her mother asking Brendan questions about his workmate and she knew that in a few minutes she would come into the bedroom to try to console her – and it was the last thing that Kate wanted.

It was quite obvious that she had been stupid and gullible and she felt bad enough without her mother picking over the bones of it. Silently, she took off the blue dress and her underclothes and pulled on her white cotton nightdress and got into bed.

Chapter 5

Kate pinned the last pillowcase on the washing-line and then stepped back to check that all the items now blowing in the breeze were in the proper order – from the two large sheets – in decreasing size – down to two of Brendan's white hankies. No matter how big a hurry she was in for her chores, she had this niggling little urge inside that made her try to do everything as perfectly as she could.

She had been up since seven o'clock this morning, which was early for a Saturday. A night of tossing and turning and mulling over the situation with Michael O'Brien had left her unable to sleep properly, and now she could feel that she was not altogether firing on four cylinders.

After organising boiled egg and brown soda bread, Kate realised that she didn't feel at all like eating it, and she had taken her mother a tray into the bedroom with the breakfast she had made for herself.

'You're up very early, Kate,' Mary had said, propping two feather pillows behind her to allow her to sit up and eat. 'Are you all right?' she'd added, studying her carefully. Her voice had dropped to just above a whisper. 'Did Brendan upset you last night . . . what he said about Michael?'

'I'm grand, Mammy,' Kate had said, giving a bright, stiff smile. She'd bustled about, checking that her mother was sitting comfortably and in the right position to eat her breakfast.

But Mary had not been fooled. She knew that Kate was putting on a show. It was rare that Kate made any comment on lads she met at dances or any she knew locally. The fact that she'd chattered away so easily about her evening with Brendan's workmate, and how well they'd got on walking back to the cottage at night, told her that her daughter had finally met someone who she thought might be special.

Kate had busied herself around the cottage, trying to keep her mind off Michael O'Brien, and as soon as her mother came out of the bedroom dressed for the day, she flew in past her to strip the bed. 'It's going to be another glorious day,' Kate had called back to her, 'so we might as well get the bedclothes out early. I'll have them ironed and back on the bed by the afternoon.'

'There's no rush, Kate,' Mary had said, her brows down. 'And there's a clean set of sheets and pillowcases for my bed in the press.'

'Well, I have the water all boiled now in pots on the range,' Kate had told her, coming back into the kitchen with a bundle of bedclothes. The determined look on her daughter's face had told Mary that there was no point in arguing with her. She knew that Kate would rush about now from one household task to the next – keeping busy so that she didn't have time to sit and mull over the situation.

Watching her, Mary Flowers had felt a wave of guilt wash over her. She knew that a clever girl like Kate shouldn't be wasting all her time on domestic jobs like this. There was a time when Kate had been full of ambitions to train as a nurse – even to travel over to England to stay with her Aunt Rose and do her nursing in the local hospital in Stockport. But all those dreams had come to a halt when Mary took ill with her nerves a few years back when she was going through the change of life. It was just after Brendan had started work on the boats and there was only the two females left in the house for most of the week.

Mary wasn't quite sure herself what had been wrong, but she had started to take these queer turns that left her heart racing, leaving her breathless and shaking and feeling that she might drop down to the ground in a dead faint at any time. One nightmare trip to Dublin on the train with Kate – to find an outfit for a neighbour's wedding – had left her so frightened that she had not ventured that far ever since. The attack had started on the train going up and continued until they found a little tea-room in O'Connell Street. Eventually, Kate had insisted that they go into the bar of the

Gresham Hotel and had almost to drag her mother inside as she felt it was much too posh and not at all 'for the likes of us'.

Kate had told her quite firmly that they were as well dressed as anybody else and that it looked much better for them to go into a nice hotel and be served a drink at the table than go into one of the men's bars in a side-street. She had ordered her mother a large brandy – explaining to the understanding waiter that her mother wasn't feeling too well – and thankfully it did the trick in calming her down.

Afterwards, they walked to Clery's Department Store where they found a nice suit for Mary for the wedding and then they'd had lunch in a plain but decent restaurant that they both felt at home in. They'd walked around the shops in O'Connell Street until Mary felt another strange turn coming on and then they'd hurried for the bus to take them back to Heuston Station for an earlier train than they'd planned. Before setting off on the train, Kate had insisted that her mother had another little brandy to help her get through the journey.

The following day they went to see Dr Kelly who examined Mary thoroughly and told her that it was probably due to her coming up to the change of life, and reassured her that many women had similar symptoms that would eventually fade away as she got older.

The funny turns had gradually decreased both in severity and in regularity, but it had taken nearly four years, during which time Kate had remained at home looking after her mother. By the time Mary had become more confident, she suddenly developed stomach problems which led to the gall bladder operation. All the while Kate remained in the small cottage with her mother, having taken over the majority of the household chores.

Mary had looked at her daughter, wanting to go over to her and put her arms around her – but instinctively feeling that it might just be the wrong thing. It was such a pity that Michael O'Brien wasn't free because it would be the answer to a prayer if Kate met a nice local lad and got married. Especially a lad that Brendan got on well with.

But it didn't look as if Michael O'Brien was the answer to anything, if he already had a girl waiting in the wings.

Instead of comforting her daughter, Mary had got on with

helping her to carry the smaller containers of boiling water over to the big stone sink where Kate would soak and then scrub the bed linen with a heavy bar of soap. She would then go through the gruelling procedure of rinsing the sheets several times in cold water before feeding them bit by sodden bit through the old heavy mangle.

Brendan's bedroom door had suddenly opened and he came out, tousle-headed and cross. 'How's a man supposed to sleep with all that racket going on?' he said, rubbing his hands through his dark, wiry hair. Then he glanced down at the pile of washing on the stone floor and shook his head. 'Oh no ... not feckin' scrubbing and cleaning at this hour of the mornin' before I've even had a bite to eat? Not on a Saturday mornin' when I'm looking for a bit of peace?'

Mary had moved as quickly as she could and guided him over to one of the armchairs by the empty grate that Kate had cleaned out earlier on. 'Sit over here and I'll bring you a nice cup of tea and a bit of bread while I get the breakfast going for you,' she said in a soothing tone. 'The range is good and hot and it won't take long getting a fry ready for you. Would you like three or four sausages?' She moved over to the larder to get out the wrapped packages from the butcher's shop.

'Four,' Brendan replied in a disgruntled fashion, 'and whatever else you have goin'.'

'I'll do you a few nice crispy rashers and some black and white pudding,' Mary said, smiling ingratiatingly at him. 'How will that do you?'

'Ah, go on,' he said, suddenly smiling back as she knew he would. She knew how to get around the petulant little boy in him. 'An' I'll have a couple of eggs and some fried bread while you're at it.'

Kate had continued steadfastly with her work, completely ignoring her brother's moans and groans as her mother bustled happily around cutting lumps of butter into the frying pan in which she would fry his breakfast.

Kate was well used to Brendan's form on weekend mornings and knew he would come out of the foul mood as his hangover gradually disappeared, although privately she thought her mother was partly to blame for pandering to his bullish ways.

As she looked at the washing swaying backwards and forwards on the line now, Kate wondered if her father could possibly have had a nature like Brendan's, and whether her mother had got around his moods in the same way as she did with her son. It all seemed such a long time ago since he had been alive and part of the family and Kate couldn't remember much about it. She could clearly recall her father being present on certain occasions like her first Holy Communion – but there were other memories that were very woolly and vague.

All in all, she knew he was a quieter and easier man than Brendan, but then he'd been much older and wouldn't have the bull-headed ways of a younger man. And he had never frightened her in any way – she would have remembered that.

She couldn't remember him ever running around or playing with them or anything like that, and he'd always seemed much older than any of her friends' fathers. Old but kind, she decided.

'What about a nice bit of fried bread with a couple of rashers, Kate?' her mother suggested as she came back in from the garden. 'You'll need to have something before going into Tullamore this afternoon.' She nodded at the hissing rashers in the large black frying pan. 'It's nearly ready, another couple of minutes or so.'

Kate paused for a moment, considering the situation. She didn't feel hungry at all, but she knew it was foolish to be cycling three or four miles and back again on an empty stomach. 'You're right, I suppose I should eat a bite now if I'm going to be gone a while,' she said quietly.

Brendan looked up from the table at his sister, a beaming smile on his face. 'Would you be a good girl and pick me up an *Independent* while you're in and a couple of pairs of the plain socks I like from Gayle's shop?'

Kate raised her eyes to the heavens. 'You know I hate going into that shop,' she sighed, sitting down at the table opposite her brother. 'I can't stand the fella that owns it.'

'Oh Kate,' her mother said, laughing, 'you're very hard to please. Sure, Oliver Gayle is a grand fella – he can't do enough for you when you go into the shop.' A faraway look came into her eyes – the kind of look Mary usually reserved for film stars and famous singers. 'And he's always immaculately dressed.'

'So well he might be,' Brendan scoffed, 'an' it's us that's payin' for his fancy suits and ties with the prices that he charges.'

'Ah, but he's far nicer to serve you than any of the ones in the other men's shops, and he's a fine-looking fella as well,' Mary stated.

'I don't care how nice he is when he's serving you, he's still smarmy and he gives me the creeps,' Kate said adamantly. She shook her dark curly head. 'The minute a woman appears in the shop he's all over them, and he's always touching your hand and your arm and looking deep into your eyes.'

'Ah, go on with you!' Brendan laughed, leaning across the table to prod Kate's arm. 'You women are all the same – ye love it! Ye love it when a man gives ye a bit of attention.'

Kate pulled her arm away, giving a loud sigh. 'Well, you'd know all about that – you being such a ladies' man from what I hear.' And she just stopped herself from adding, *And your friend's not up to much either, stringing me along and telling me lies.*

Brendan's brows came down and his eyes darkened. 'And what have you been hearin' then? Who's been blackguarding me?'

Mary shot Kate a warning look, and then she busied herself putting the bacon and fried bread on a plate.

'Well?' Brendan demanded, looking from his sister to his mother. 'Who's been talking about me?'

Kate moved over to the cupboard to get a knife and fork, considering whether she felt like an argy-bargy with her brother this morning. 'Oh, forget it,' she suddenly decided, 'sure, I was only half-codding you.'

He paused for a moment, thinking, then he shook his head. 'You women are all the feckin' same – ye say one thing and mean another. And it's not fair – for us lads are left like eedjits trying to make sense of it all.'

Mary came across to the table with Kate's plate and a smaller plate with two extra sausages and crispy rashers, which she set down beside Brendan. 'Eat that up now and it'll do you good,' she told him encouragingly. She looked at Kate behind Brendan's back and rolled her eyes in exasperation. 'Then maybe you should have another hour or two lying down. It's a long, hard oul' week when you're back on that barge.'

Brendan speared one of the sausages with his fork. 'True,' he said in a more congenial tone. He liked to know the women appreciated him for his work efforts at least. 'A few more hours wouldn't do me any harm, and it might leave me fresher for the few hours out tonight.'

Kate took a bite of her fried bread and wondered what girl Michael O'Brien would be seeing tonight. Presumably he had a girl in all the canal towns he passed through. Well, she thought, he needn't waste his time stopping off to see me when he's passing through Ballygrace again.

Chapter 6

'**A**re you sure you're up to walking all the way to the church, Mammy?' Kate asked anxiously for the second time.

'I'm positive,' Mary Flowers said, checking that her hat was straight in the dressing-table mirror. She was dressed in her good blue Sunday outfit with her white hat and clutch bag and matching white sandals, and her sunny, almost back-to-her-old-self reflection gave her a small boost of confidence. 'If we take it nice and easy and I lean on the bike I'll be grand.' She gestured towards the window. 'And it's a lovely summer's morning, the fresh air will do me the world of good, not to mention being back inside the church. I've hated missing going regularly to Mass.'

'We've plenty of time,' Kate said, pulling on her white cotton gloves. She had her thick black hair loose over her shoulders topped with a straw hat that was adorned with a small bunch of cherries, which picked up the colour in her red gingham dress.

'What about Brendan?' Mary said in a low voice, looking at his closed bedroom door. 'You know he can be funny at times if you don't wait for him.'

'We're off!' Kate called, guiding her mother towards the front door. 'We'll be walking slow if you want to catch up.'

'On ye go,' he called back in a mocking, sing-songy voice. 'I'm well able to walk to Mass on my own. I don't need to be chaperoned by you pair of beauties.'

'It's not chaperoning that fellow needs,' Kate hissed in a low voice, 'it's more like stringing up!'

'Oh, Kate,' her mother gasped, lifting the latch, 'you shouldn't be saying things like that about your brother.'

'What he doesn't hear won't harm him,' Kate said, straightening her straw hat. 'And if it wasn't for upsetting you, I'd be quite happily saying it straight to his face.'

'There's a pair of ye in it,' her mother laughed, trying to keep it light. 'And there's times when I think one's nearly as bad as the other.'

'Don't!' Kate told her mother as they went out the door. 'I'd be stringing myself up if I thought I was remotely like Brendan.'

The two women went around the side of the cottage to get their bikes, laughing and shaking their heads.

'I'm doing not bad at all now, sure I'm not,' Mary Flowers panted as they came around the corner to face the canal bridge at Ballygrace. 'Only a few weeks ago I wouldn't have been fit to walk even this length.'

'You've done just grand,' Kate reassured her. 'And we'll stop up at the bridge to give you a bit of a rest.'

They walked on silently for a few minutes, wheeling the bikes as they went along. Then, when they came up the tow-path and rounded the corner of the bridge, they came to a standstill – Mary's breath coming in short pants as she gripped the handlebars of her old bike. Kate leaned her own bike against the wide stone bridge and then came over to take her mother's bike from her. 'Are you all right?' she asked anxiously.

Mary nodded her head slowly without speaking as she endeavoured to catch her breath.

They both stood for a while in companionable silence, Kate leaning on the bridge and looking down to the canal and then her gaze moved off over the water to the trees and fields beyond.

'Have you decided what you're going to do about Michael O'Brien?' her mother suddenly asked, her voice more even.

Kate turned to face her, shrugging. 'Sure, what's there to do?' she said, attempting to sound light-hearted.

'But you said you'd arranged to meet him this afternoon . . .'

Kate felt her throat start to tighten. 'Wouldn't I be some class of a fool to be meeting up with him when he has another girl on the go?' She turned towards her bike, fiddling about with the saddle-bag strap. 'It doesn't matter anyway. Sure, I hardly knew him at all. We've only known each other a couple of days.'

'But there are times when it doesn't take long to know someone,' her mother said. 'Sometimes you can just tell you're going to get on.'

Kate gave a little dismissive sigh. She went to the handlebars of the bike now. 'Are you up to walking on yet?'

Mary nodded her head and turned towards her own bike. She knew by Kate's tone that the subject was now closed.

When the Mass was finished, Kate and Mary Flowers emerged from the cool, dark church into the bright sunlight, blessing themselves with water from the holy water font on their way out.

As they went out into the churchyard, several women from the village came towards them. 'Mrs Flowers, we're delighted to see you out and about,' the oldest woman said. 'And you're looking more like your old self.'

Mary beamed at them. 'Thanks very much,' she said, nodding her head. She gestured towards Kate. 'I've been well looked after, so I have . . . better than any nurse.'

'And aren't you lucky?' the woman said. 'I hear she's a great worker, she'll have everything done for you.'

Kate gave an embarrassed smile now, awkward at being the centre of attention. 'The fine weather makes a difference,' she said, looking up at the blue sky. 'Everybody feels better.' Then, suddenly, she was aware of a figure coming from the side door of the church straight towards her. She turned to look and when she saw who it was, her whole body stiffened.

All the other women stopped talking and turned to see who had caught Kate's attention. It was Michael O'Brien, smart in his dark Sunday suit trousers and white shirt and tie.

'Hello, Kate,' he said, smiling broadly at her. The confident look slid from his face when he saw the blank look on hers. He turned towards her mother now. 'Mrs Flowers . . .'

'Hello, Michael,' Mary Flowers said, giving him the same beaming smile she had given the women. Although she was slightly anxious at how Kate was going to react, she instantly decided that their differences weren't anything to do with her. She had enough on her plate keeping the peace between her son and daughter without getting involved in their romances. 'Isn't it a grand morning?' She looked at the other women. 'This is Michael O'Brien from Tullamore . . . he works on the boats with Brendan.'

'How are ye all?' he said, smiling politely at the women, then he turned towards Kate, lowering his voice. 'The boat got back earlier this morning, and I thought I'd go to Mass in Ballygrace and catch you coming out . . .' He moved a few feet away from the group, his eyes firmly fixed on her now.

Kate looked back at him – feeling totally trapped – knowing her every move was being closely scrutinised by the group of chattering women. Not in a harmful way, because these particular women were pleasant enough, they would just be watching in the interested way that local village people habitually did.

Wordlessly, she moved away from the group so that he had to follow her out towards the gate. 'I didn't expect to see you at all today,' she said in a tight voice when they were out of earshot of her mother and the other women. 'I thought you might have business in Tullamore or some other place.'

His brow deepened. 'But I thought we had arranged to meet up? I thought we said on Friday night that we might go for a walk out this afternoon . . .'

A hot, angry feeling came over Kate, the sort of feeling that usually came over her when she was annoyed at her brother. A feeling that she usually squashed outside the house as she knew it didn't show a good side of her. But on this occasion the anger was too strong to ignore. And anyway, she didn't care about Michael O'Brien seeing her worst side now. 'And how many other girls do you go for walks with?' she said in a clipped tone. 'By all accounts you have a particular girl in Tullamore.'

He stared at her now, surprise stamped all over his face. Then he found his voice – albeit a quiet, defensive one. 'And might I ask where you got that bit of information from?'

'Where I got it from is none of your business,' Kate retorted sharply. 'But you needn't think that you'll be walking out with me in Ballygrace when you're walking out with another girl in Tullamore.'

'You're wrong,' he told her, 'and whoever told you that can account for it to me. That's not the way I would operate at all.' He shook his head. 'Not at all.'

Kate felt her throat tighten, suddenly doubting her earlier accusations.

'Don't tell me – I suppose it was my good workmate, Brendan?' he said, raising his eyebrows and pursing his lips. 'He's the only one that knows either of us particularly well.' When he saw the hesitation in Kate's eyes, he knew he was on the right track. 'Is he at this Mass?' he said, looking around the busy churchyard.

'He could be gone home by now,' she said quietly, her gaze dropping to the ground.

He reached out now and took her by the arm, scanning the crowds. 'He can't be gone too far.' His grip was neither weak nor tight – but the look on his face was determined. 'Come on,' Michael O'Brien said in a low voice, 'we'll sort this business out immediately.'

Kate made a small, discreet movement, trying to wriggle out of his grasp, without drawing any attention to them. Then she came to a sudden halt as she spotted Brendan over by the side gate, laughing and chatting with some of the local fellows he often had a drink with.

Michael O'Brien followed her gaze. 'That's grand,' he said, letting go of her arm. He waved now, to catch his workmate's attention. Brendan signalled that he'd seen them and was on his way over shortly. 'We'll see what he has to say for himself.'

There was no mistaking the righteousness that the boatman was feeling about his character and integrity being questioned. And Kate knew that there wasn't the slightest hesitation or hint of reluctance about him facing Brendan.

Kate could see now that she had been played for a fool by her brother, and her anger and indignation were now replaced by embarrassment and foolishness. 'There's no need,' she blustered. 'I shouldn't have paid any attention to him . . . it doesn't matter.'

'Well, he can't cause trouble and be allowed to get away with it,' Michael said, smiling openly now as Brendan came towards them. 'That wouldn't be a good way for us to be starting off, would it? He needs to know exactly where he stands where yourself and myself are involved – wouldn't you agree?'

Kate looked at him in a bemused fashion, amazed at his forthrightness. She had summed him up as a much quieter person than this determined man who now stood in front of her.

'Grand morning,' Brendan said loudly to all he passed on his way over to them. Then he came to stand in front of them, all cheery-faced and hail-fellow-well-met. 'Well, Mickey, how's she cuttin' this morning?'

'Not too well, as it happens,' Michael O'Brien replied in a smooth, confident manner. He moved closer to Brendan, folding his arms high up on his chest. 'Kate seems to have got the opinion that I'm walking out with another girl from Tullamore.' There was a little pause. 'You wouldn't happen to know where she got that idea from at all, would you?'

The grin froze on Brendan's face as he realised his workmate was serious. 'Ah sure . . .' he said, shifting his gaze to Kate now. 'Ah sure, that was only a bit of oul' codding . . . I was only having her on – the way brothers and sisters go on, like.'

'There was no codding about it at all!' Kate butted in furiously, her brown eyes glinting with rage. 'When you told me that Michael was already spoken for, you were deadly serious. Don't try back-tracking now because my mother will vouch for me there. She heard the way you were carrying on, and she knew I had no intentions of meeting up with Michael again after what you told me.'

Brendan's face flushed, but he wasn't about to make a show of himself arguing with his sister in the churchyard where there were still plenty of people around. He shrugged and turned back to Michael O'Brien. 'Sure, you know these women . . . how tempera-mental and moody they can be. The way they carry on, takin' everything very serious altogether.'

'No, Brendan,' Michael O'Brien said, his voice lower and deeper, 'I don't know anything about the women at all. I've no reason to be concerned about them. From what I can see, it's *you* that seems to be acting all temperamental and awkward.'

Brendan stepped back, his face well and truly shocked. Surely this wasn't the mild-mannered boatman he spent most of his working week with? The man who was easy-going and didn't take offence at anything. He looked now at his workmate's squared shoulders and tense face. Surely Michael O'Brien wasn't taking his sister's side against him? 'Ah, it was only a bit of oul' craic . . . no harm meant,' he said, his eyes darting from one to the other, not sure which way to go. If it had only been Kate he wouldn't have wasted his time on any explanations about an oul' joke – she could have feckin' well liked it or lumped it – but he didn't want to display that side of himself in front of his workmate. Equally, he didn't want to appear a total fool. 'I suppose I was thinkin' about the two young ladies that often wait for you at the lock-gate when we're passing through Tullamore.'

'Friends of my sister,' the boatman replied curtly, 'and I told you that when you made suggestive remarks about them at the time. There's absolutely nothing in it.'

'Well, in my opinion, one of them certainly has an eye for you,' Brendan countered. 'Ye could tell the way she was lookin' at you . . . I thought there might be something more to it.' He gestured towards Kate. 'Don't forget, this is me sister we're talking about here. I was only looking out for her.'

Kate sighed and threw her eyes heavenwards. Since when had Brendan taken to defending her? To suggest it, he was obviously getting desperate.

'That's not the point,' Michael persisted, quietly but firmly. 'You still had no business telling Kate I had another girl when I don't. If you had any concerns about how I was treating your sister, you should have had a quiet word with me when we were on the boat. That would have been the right way to handle it.'

There was a pause. 'Ah well,' Brendan said, looking slightly injured now, 'it seems me good intentions have obviously been misplaced.'

'It might be a lesson to keep your good intentions to yourself in future,' Kate snapped, unable to hold back any longer. 'Instead of poking your nose in—'

Michael put his hand on her arm. 'I think there's been enough said now,' he said quietly. 'The point has been made, we won't make it any worse.'

Brendan felt a wave of relief, grateful that his workmate was back on his side, and delighted to hear someone else putting his fiery sister back in her place. 'Anyway,' he said, grinning at Michael O'Brien, 'there's been no great harm done, has there? Aren't ye both all cosy together again now?' He gestured upwards to the blue sky. 'You'll have a fine afternoon out walking ... they're givin' very good weather out on the radio—'

'Well, that all depends on how Kate feels about it now,' Michael cut in, refusing to be swayed by Brendan's attempts at being light-hearted. 'After all this nonsense she might decide she's better off having nothing to do with me.' He turned back to Kate now, his eyebrows raised questioningly.

Before Kate had a chance to say anything, Brendan started off again.

'Ah sure, Kate's not a bit like that,' he blustered, his chin jutting out awkwardly and his whole demeanour one of acute embarrass-ment. 'She knows me well enough to know there was no harm intended.'

Kate found herself watching her brother closely – almost scrutinising him – because it had just dawned on her that she had never seen him in this kind of situation before. He had never before been called to account for his moodiness and casually thrown smart remarks. He never gave a thought to his nasty comments as they passed from his brain straight to his lips. He certainly had not given much thought to the hurt the remarks caused where his mother and sister were concerned.

But Michael O'Brien was now driving the issue of Brendan's attitude home in no uncertain terms. As she observed her brother now – almost squirming under his workmate's criticism – Kate suddenly realised with some surprise that Brendan reserved this uncaring attitude for women only. He wasn't going to erupt as he did at home and shout the odds in front of another male. He wasn't going to reveal the bullying side that would make him go down in the estimation of a decent, respectful man.

'How do you feel now you know the truth?' Michael said quietly, putting his hand on Kate's arm. 'Are you willing to give it a go?'

Kate looked at Brendan and was amazed at how anxious he looked and how desperate he was for her to rescue him from this embarrassing situation. Her immediate instinct was to rush in and say everything was fine and they should just forget all about it – but something held her back. If she behaved towards him as she always did – the indulgent way her mother encouraged for peace's sake – he would be back to his old ways in no time. Instead, her brows came down into a frown. 'Grand,' she said in a slightly strangled voice as though it were paining her to agree. 'After all, it wasn't a fault on the part of you or me. We'll just put this whole thing down to a misunderstanding . . . since it's unlikely to happen again.'

She didn't meet Brendan's eyes because she wasn't at all sure how long this lesson would last, and she couldn't tell whether it was something he would learn from and not repeat or whether he had just given in on this particular occasion.

Michael nodded and smiled back while the cringing Brendan stifled a sigh of relief.

'Michael!' Mary Flowers said, rushing over to the group now. 'Why don't you come back home with us now and have a bit of Sunday dinner?' She beamed at Kate. 'Sure, there's enough in that big chicken for the four of us, isn't there?'

'If you're sure?' Michael said, his face lightening up now. 'I wouldn't want to be imposing—'

'Imposing me arse!' Brendan said, clapping his hands together. 'You'll come and have your dinner with us and let that be an end to the arguin'.' His words were spoken with such an assuredness it could have been thought that he was actually the person cooking the meal.

Kate glanced over at the boatman now and a broad smile broke out over her beautiful face. There was nothing more she would like than to have him sitting opposite her at the table again.

There was nothing more she would like than to have him sit at the table with her every day for the rest of her life.

Chapter 7

Brendan was on his best behaviour back at the cottage, rushing to lift roasting dishes out of the oven, helping to drain the big pan of boiling potatoes and offering Michael the Sunday paper to read. Kate's mother was in great spirits, having managed the trip back and forwards to Mass without any great trouble, the bit of a chat with various people outside the church and then having company with them for the meal. All that and Brendan in an unrecognisably good mood – a very rare Sunday indeed.

Kate couldn't remember her mother being so bright and uplifted, and as she busied herself in the kitchen, making gravy and dicing and mashing vegetables, her thoughts flitted from Michael O'Brien to the career ambitions she had abandoned when her mother became ill.

She wondered now if it was possible that she might resurrect her childhood dream of training to be a nurse? If her mother continued to progress like this – and Brendan had finally copped himself on and become more sensible – maybe she could apply for a place in one of the Dublin hospitals when they were doing their next round of recruitment. And if the little bit of money her mother had generously offered her wasn't enough to pay for her training, maybe she could apply to one of the Manchester hospitals as her Aunt Rose had suggested.

Kate knew that she couldn't consider anything at this stage of the year, and it was early days where her mother's health was concerned – but there was a definite improvement. Maybe next spring she would be well enough to manage the house again on her own.

'Can I do anything for you?'

Kate's heart leapt into her throat. Michael O'Brien's voice was soft and he was standing so unexpectedly close that she almost dropped the colander of steaming vegetables into the old stone sink. 'I'm grand ... thanks,' she said over her shoulder. But her hands were suddenly shaking at his nearness.

'Well, let me know if I can give you a hand with anything ...'

'Actually,' she said, brushing away an unruly strand of hair with the back of her hand, 'if you could put this dish of vegetables on the table for me.' She tipped the mixed turnips and carrots into a small china tureen that had been a wedding present of her grandmother's.

Then, as she concentrated on slicing the golden-skinned chicken and carefully portioning it out on four white plates – two large servings for the men and two smaller ones for herself and her mother – she was aware of the boatman's eyes following her every move.

All thoughts of nursing and moving abroad suddenly dissipated from Kate Flowers' mind, replaced by the memory of Michael O'Brien's half-naked reflection in the bedroom mirror.

Then, just before she went to join the others at the table, she quickly turned on the rattly copper tap and splashed cold water up on her burning cheeks to cool them down.

'Now you two head off out for yourselves,' Mary Flowers said as Kate started to collect the empty pudding dishes. 'I'll clear up here while you're gone.' Then, anticipating Kate's reaction, she added, 'And you needn't worry, I'll take it nice and easy. I'm sure Brendan will give me a hand to lift the big black kettle over to the sink.'

'Indeed and I will,' the newly mannered Brendan confirmed, as if doing household chores came as natural to him as breathing. 'If there's anythin' to be lifted and laid then I'll be the man to see to it.'

Mary glanced quickly over at Kate, biting her bottom lip to stop herself from laughing out loud. *How long will it last?* was the unspoken question hanging between mother and daughter.

For the first ten minutes as they walked along the tow-path, conversation between the couple was slightly stilted and veered towards safe, mundane subjects like the weather and the lovely flowers growing on the banks of the canal.

Kate found it hard to be as relaxed and natural as she had been the night of the Maypole dance, as she felt both embarrassed and guilty that she had been taken in by Brendan's lies. She knew she should broach the subject with Michael O'Brien soon and make some kind of an apology, but she just couldn't seem to find the right words. She walked along, slightly self-consciously, fiddling every so often with her handbag or reaching up to adjust her curly dark hair or the angle of her straw hat.

'You look lovely, Kate; I'm proud to be seen out walking with you,' Michael suddenly said as they came to a bend in the canal where there was a makeshift bench. He reached for her hand now and wordlessly guided her over to the seat. They sat close to each other, Kate's hand still warm in his grasp.

She was surprised that his hand felt fairly smooth for a workman and not as rough and thorny as her brother's hands or the other local lads she had danced or walked out with. Brendan and the others were the kind of fellows who rushed into everything and probably used their hands in situations they should check out first. Situations like pulling at prickly bushes or rough grass when they were tying up the boat, or reaching out for pieces of timber that had loose splinters or maybe the odd nail sticking out. Brendan would think nothing of tipping at a smouldering sod of turf with his fingers if it was too near the front of the fire and throwing smoke into the room. He would also stick his blackened hands into the frying pan to grab at a sausage when he didn't have the patience to wait until it was put out on the plate for him. The odd cut or blister would be nothing at all to the likes of Brendan Flowers.

Instinctively Kate knew that Michael O'Brien would never do anything like that. He struck her as a careful sort of man who would take a few seconds to examine something before lifting or touching it. The sort of man who would work out the best angle to approach a job, rather than charging at it like a bull at a gate.

But then, she thought, that was the difference between her brother's nature and his workmate's nature. And the difference in their natures showed in the palms of their hands.

'I was just thinking,' the boatman said in a quiet voice now, 'how very welcome your mother has made me in her house, and it occurred to me that maybe you might like to come out to my own homeplace some Sunday afternoon?'

Kate glanced up at him, more than a little surprised at the suggestion. 'Is it not a bit too soon for that?' she whispered. 'We hardly know each other . . .'

'Well,' he said smiling, 'I've met your mother and brother.'

'But that's different, you work with Brendan . . . you knew him well enough before you met me.'

'That's true,' he said, nodding. Then he smiled and raised his eyebrows. 'Although I don't know how fond he'll be of me after this morning . . .'

Kate felt her throat tighten with embarrassment just thinking about the scene that had occurred outside the church. 'I'm really sorry about that . . .' she blustered. 'But the way he said it . . .' She sighed and shook her head. 'That fella's a demon when he has drink in him and sometimes worse the following day when he has a bad hangover . . . he could say anything. And I'm a bigger fool for believing him.'

'Water under the bridge,' he said, laughing. 'I know it wasn't your fault. I know Brendan too well by now to be surprised at anything he says or does. He's a good worker, but when he has a drink in him he's like a spoilt child.'

'There's times when he could do with a good clatter around the head to knock a bit of sense into him,' Kate said with surprising venom. 'Mammy wasn't hard enough on him when he was younger, and he thinks he can get away with anything.'

'God, I didn't know you were such a vicious woman! I'll have to be very careful I don't do anything to upset you.'

An embarrassed flush crept over Kate's neck and face now, indicating that she knew she had gone a bit too far. She dropped her gaze, trying to focus on the cheery little white and yellow daisies that were growing amongst the wild grass.

Then, Michael O'Brien suddenly burst out laughing and, startled, Kate looked up at him. Within seconds, she was leaning against him laughing heartily too. His arm stole around her and he gathered her in close to him, both still shaking slightly with laughter. Then, their bodies suddenly became still and their faces became serious. Kate closed her eyes and Michael O'Brien's lips came to gently press on hers.

Chapter 8

A month later, on a damp and dull Sunday afternoon, Michael O'Brien cycled out to the Flowers' cottage by the canal. After a cup of tea and a slice of apple tart, he and Kate cycled into Tullamore for Kate to meet the rest of the O'Brien family.

Things had developed quite quickly between Kate and Michael, and he had now become almost part and parcel of the Flowers household. Any evenings he was moored up at Ballygrace Canal, he cycled or walked out to the Flowers' cottage to spend the evening with the family – often when Brendan chose to spend his time in the local pub as opposed to going home. Even if he only had an hour or two to spare on his way back up to Dublin or down to Shannon Harbour, he would call in whenever he could.

Kate's mother's health had gone from strength to strength – aided by the summer sunshine – and she was now able to help Kate with most of the household chores and enjoy the light gardening and pottering about that she had missed for so long.

The atmosphere in the house had improved out of all recognition since Michael O'Brien had started courting Kate, and Mary Flowers was lifted out of herself with the extra company and the light-hearted banter that went on in the house between Kate, Michael and Brendan.

Brendan Flowers had been himself. There were days when he was his good, improved self – particularly when Michael O'Brien was around – and there were days when he was his contrary, awkward old self with Kate and Mary. But all in all there was an improvement, and that made a good enough difference to his mother and sister.

Mrs O'Brien opened the door as soon as Michael and Kate dismounted their bikes and were heading towards the black-painted door. The thin, tallish woman smiled and shook Kate's hand and took the box of Milk Tray chocolates she had brought with a quiet 'thank you', then ushered them into the dark hallway of the sombre grey-stoned farmhouse. As she walked along the passageway between the older woman and Michael, Kate gave fleeting glances at groups of framed photographs that appeared to be taken at a priest's ordination and dotted amongst them was a variety of holy pictures and holy water fonts.

'I have the table set in the parlour for us,' Agnes O'Brien said, opening a door at the bottom of the hallway. The slightly musty room – with its green and wine flowery wallpaper and heavy, dark-red curtains – was no brighter than the hallway, and Kate couldn't help comparing their own bright, airy little cottage very favourably with it. Again, dark, sombre religious pictures and church-style candlesticks were the only decorative features.

The long, narrow dining table had a heavy green velvet tablecloth with fringes on it, and several large old china plates sat in the middle of it, with white pan sandwiches neatly cut into triangles, sliced brown and white soda bread, scones and a large apple tart.

There were also small dishes with butter and jam and what looked like honey. Formal china cups and saucers and plates were set at all eight places.

'You might look into the kitchen to your father and Thomas and the girls to say you're here, Michael,' Mrs O'Brien said, nodding towards the hallway. Then, when they were on their own, she turned to Kate. 'We don't go in for anything too fancy here,' she said quietly. 'All plain home-baking.' She gestured towards the table. 'Michael said you would have had your dinner already . . .'

'Oh, this is grand,' Kate rushed in, 'and I'm very grateful to you for going to all this trouble.' She waved her hand towards the plates. 'It looks lovely . . .'

There was a small silence.

'Well, I believe that Michael has been making himself very much at home in your own place,' the older woman said with a little edge to her voice.

Kate felt her face reddening, recognising the critical tone. 'That was on account of him working with my brother, Brendan, on the boats.' Then she added rather lamely, 'That's how we met . . .'

'Indeed,' Agnes O'Brien said, raising her eyebrows as if the information was a complete surprise to her. She glanced towards the door, hearing footsteps coming along the hallway. 'Well, I feel obliged that we should return your mother's hospitality . . . especially if this business between yourself and our son is to continue. We can't have him sitting eating dinners at other people's tables without returning the compliment.'

Kate suddenly found herself holding her breath. Being told that her visit was nothing more than an obligation wasn't the kind of welcome she had hoped for.

A little wave of relief washed over her now as Michael came into the room followed by his father, three sisters and his older brother.

'I'd like you all to meet Kate Flowers,' he said in a formal voice, striding across the room to stand by her side. She thought for a second that he might take her arm or put his hand casually on her shoulder, as he often did when he was in her mother's house, but he stood quite separately, his hands by his side. And when she glanced at him she noticed that he was standing in a stiff, erect manner – almost like a soldier on guard. A very defensive soldier.

Kate's heart sank lower. There was definitely something wrong, and she had a horrible feeling growing inside her stomach that it was *her*.

The older man looked flustered and his eyes kept darting from his wife to Michael, while the sisters and brother were mainly looking at the floor.

Kate instinctively felt that they had obviously decided – before even meeting her – that they didn't like her and certainly didn't feel she was a suitable companion for Michael.

The silence was suddenly broken as Peter O'Brien came forward with his hand stretched out. 'I'm delighted to meet you, Kate . . .'

Kate somehow managed to smile and meet his firm handshake. 'I was just thanking Mrs O'Brien for inviting me,' she said in a small, strangled voice.

The older man turned now to the younger group behind him. 'And this is Thomas, and my daughters Helen, Sinéad and Patricia.'

The three girls moved forward to shake Kate's hand in a limp, self-conscious kind of way and as she looked at each one in turn, she thought how nice they all looked, but how very, very serious. Especially the oldest girl, Helen, who Kate noticed had not once met her eyes since she had come into the room.

'We might as well all sit down,' Agnes O'Brien said. 'If you'd like to sit down here, Kate,' she said, indicating one of the chairs in the centre of the table beside her.

Without waiting to be told where to sit, Michael pulled out the chair next to his guest.

Once again a silence descended on the room and Kate prayed with all her heart that someone would put the radio on in the background like they always did in her own home.

But there was nothing to kill the silence. Only the liquid gurgling sound as Agnes O'Brien poured eight cups of tea from the large, heavy teapot.

Eventually, as the sandwiches and the other items on the plates were passed around, some semblance of polite conversation started up.

'Michael was saying that you live down at Ballygrace Canal,' Mrs O'Brien said, pouring a thin stream of milk from a china jug into her teacup.

Kate quickly tried to swallow her bite of egg and onion and salad cream sandwich, but for a horrified moment she felt her throat close over and she thought she might go into a coughing fit. She swallowed again, harder, and gave a little cough and thankfully her throat cleared. 'Yes,' she confirmed with a fixed little smile. 'I live with my mother and my brother . . .'

'And your father?' Peter O'Brien enquired.

'He died when I was young.' Kate stared down at the remainder of her sandwich, feeling terribly awkward. This was excruciating for her and it must surely be equally embarrassing for the family.

'Oh, I'm sorry now . . .' he said, looking rather taken aback. Kate wondered why Michael hadn't explained at least *that* to them. Surely he must have told them a little bit about her? Even just the important bits like her father – just enough to avoid the obvious pitfalls.

'I thought I'd mentioned that,' Michael said, frowning, as though he had read her thoughts. 'I'm sure I explained that there was only the three of them.'

'And is it a house or a cottage you live in?' Agnes O'Brien continued, clearly not thrown off her tack by the uncomfortable information about Kate's father.

'A cottage,' Kate confirmed, her voice now firm and her head high. If they were going to compare her background and small ordinary home to this large, rambling farmhouse, then it was just too bad.

Chapter 9

Mary Flowers looked around the sparkling kitchen with no small sense of satisfaction. Everything was washed, dried and put back in its place, and done with an energy and enjoyment she hadn't felt this long time. The kitchen table that she had scrubbed down was now dry save for a few damp patches. She stared thoughtfully at the bare table for a few moments and then, spurred on by the lovely afternoon sunshine, she went over to the small press beneath the sink. She rummaged around for a few moments and then emerged triumphantly clutching a cream porcelain vase decorated with tiny green sprigs of shamrock.

Then, after rinsing off the dust under the cold tap, she left the vase upside down in the sink to drain, lifted the black-handled scissors from their hook and went out into the garden to find something pretty and colourful to brighten up the table.

There was a nice blue-flowering bush over in the corner of the garden that Seamus had planted the summer they got married and there was a yellow rose bush beside it, which she remembered him planting sometime later. Every few years he had added more bushes or plants until the bit of garden at the front and side of the house was comfortably full, but still easy enough to maintain during the busy summer months when there was turf to be reared and brought home.

As Mary clipped a few small branches from the blue bush, she thought of Seamus Flowers' hands having planted it and then tended it over the years, along with all the other shrubs and trees. A little wave of sadness washed over her because she knew well that Seamus had only planted all these bright and colourful fripperies to please her. Not that he had actually come out and said it of course.

Seamus Flowers wasn't given to shows of emotion or anything akin to it. But she knew that until her arrival at the cottage there had only been a few scant hedges in the front and not much else.

And she had made sure she voiced her pleasure at his efforts, and would notice the flush of delight on his face as she paused to examine the newly opening rose buds or when she pointed out how far the clematis had spread across the side of the white-washed cottage walls since the previous year.

He had the same glow of pride when he presented her with a basket of the first new potatoes of the year and bunches of carrots and parsnips and big wide-leafed cabbages with the earth still clinging to them. And then there were the mushrooms that he got up early to pick in the warm summer mornings and the rabbits that he caught in snares and carried home, skinning and cutting them for her because he knew that Mary couldn't bear to do it.

Seamus would laugh when she shuddered at the sight of the poor dead things, but he never did it in a mocking way.

Mary looked at the yellow roses now and decided that they needed another week or two to grow to full size. Instead she cut a few of the large-headed pink peonies, which she thought would look well with the blue. Then, after a little walk around the garden, she made to go back into the cottage, thinking again how sad it was that she had never really been able to love Seamus Flowers the way she had always dreamed of loving her husband as a young girl.

Just as she went to step back in through the front door, she heard the sound of young female voices coming along the canal path. She paused to see who it was, not wishing any local people who were out for a Sunday stroll to think she was purposely avoiding them. Local people could be funny if they felt they were being snubbed, and Mary Flowers was the last one to be accused of snubbing anyone.

'Grand day, Mrs Flowers,' Noelle Daly called in a cheery voice.

'Is Kate in?' Sarah, her younger sister, called next. 'We thought she might like to come out for a bit of a stroll with us.'

Mary's eyes lit up. 'Ah, girls,' she said, coming towards them waving her blooms, 'did youse not know she was walking out with Michael O'Brien this afternoon?' Then, she laughed. '*Cycling* I should say,' she corrected herself. 'They've actually cycled out to his homeplace this afternoon.'

'Oh,' Noelle said, her eyes wide now, 'it's sounding very serious altogether if she's going out to meet the mammy and daddy.'

'Do you think so?' Mary said, feeling a little knot of excitement in her stomach as she thought of her daughter's romance. It would be lovely to have Michael O'Brien visiting on a regular basis, especially with the effect it had on Brendan's humour. She opened the little gate now. 'Why don't ye come in and have a cup of tea with me? The kettle won't take five minutes to boil up again.'

'Are you sure?' Sarah Daly said, glancing at her sister to check whether she wanted to go in or not.

'We wouldn't want to keep you back from your gardening or anything,' Noelle said, smiling and tossing her red hair back over her shoulder.

'Ah sure, I wasn't doing any gardening at all,' Mary laughed. 'I was only picking a few oul' flowers to put in a vase.' She beckoned them to follow her into the cottage. 'With Kate gone off and Brendan down at the pub, I only have myself for company so I'd be delighted to have the pair of ye to chat – to hear any news ye have.'

The girls sat down at the table while Mary left the bunch of flowers in the sink.

'If you don't mind me passing remarks – you're looking very well, Mrs Flowers,' Noelle said, as Mary put the kettle back on the fire to boil and then went to the press to get three mugs and a packet of digestive biscuits which she knew the girls liked.

'Mind ye passing remarks?' Mary laughed. 'Not at all. I'm delighted that you think I look well.' She lifted out a small side plate and put half a dozen of the biscuits on it and then placed it on the table. 'I'm actually feelin' grand,' she told them. 'I think this nice weather is helping.' She lifted the vase from the draining board and turned the tap on to fill it up, and then she carefully put the blue blooms in and then added the pink peonies.

'Oh, they're absolutely lovely!' Sarah exclaimed, leaning over to smell them.

'I thought they might brighten the place up a bit,' Mary said, her spirits lifted with all the compliments. She liked nothing better than to have people in and around the house – especially young girls. It reminded her of growing up in County Clare with her sisters and brothers and the nights they would sit around the kitchen table or by the fire chatting and laughing. But there had been no more girlish laughter after she married Seamus Flowers and moved up to County Offaly.

Oh, she couldn't deny there had been pleasant, cosy evenings sitting by the fire with Seamus, and nice summer's evenings when they had gone for strolls by the canal. There had been lovely family times when they had Brendan and Kate – and even the odd church dance – but the girl in her had gone. She had gone far, far too early. She was buried deep underneath the responsibility for her older husband and motherhood at eighteen years of age.

Mary had gone back to her homeplace in County Clare every summer, but although she enjoyed seeing her parents and family it had never been the same. The younger ones treated her as an adult now and every summer there were fewer and fewer of her brothers and sisters around as they all eventually scattered to America or different parts of England.

Now, with her parents long dead, Mary Flowers was the only remaining member of her immediate family left in Ireland.

She tried not to dwell on the past too often, and she had had several holidays over to her sister Rose in Stockport and had met up with her two brothers and sister from London on a couple of occasions when they came up to Rose's.

And in a few weeks' time she would be going over there with Kate again, as Rose had already sent the boat and train tickets for them. This year she was really going to enjoy herself because it might be the last chance she would have of going on holiday with Kate. If things continued with Michael O'Brien, she mightn't want to go on holiday with her mother again. Things could change very easily and very quickly.

A little feeling of panic fluttered somewhere in her chest.

Sufficient unto the day, Mary told herself. She still had Kate for the time being and the volatile Brendan, who she couldn't see leaving home in the foreseeable future.

And this afternoon she had Kate's friends to keep her company.

She took a few deep breaths as the doctor had advised and distracted herself from the panicky feelings.

As she poured the tea and handed around the biscuits, and listened to the girls talking about a dance they had been to the night before, Mary Flowers gradually began to forget all her anxieties and after a while she was laughing and chatting like a young one herself.

Chapter 10

After the tea and sandwiches were over, Michael's three sisters – who had remained almost silent throughout the meal – left the table. The younger two, Sinéad and Patricia, had each given Kate a brief smile as they slid past her end of the table, but Helen had only nodded vaguely in her direction without actually looking at her. Within a couple of minutes Michael's brother Tom left too, saying he wanted to look in on a sickly calf.

Kate didn't know whether to be relieved they had gone or to be more anxious that she and Michael were now left with Mr and Mrs O'Brien and their attempts at conversation.

'It must be nice and peaceful living by the canal,' Michael's father suddenly said. 'I used to fish there when I was a lad . . . and I often took Michael and Thomas fishing when they were young.'

'It is a lovely place to live,' Kate agreed, and when she looked across the table at the older man she was surprised to see an odd, distant look on his face, as though his thoughts were far from the table and the people around it.

'I think it's one of the reasons I always wanted to work on the boats,' Michael said in his calm voice. 'I loved watching them going up and down when we were sitting on the canal banks, wondering where they were going to and imagining all the towns that they passed through.' He gave a small laugh. 'I thought it was the most exciting job you could have – waking up on the boat in a different place every morning.'

A silence descended on the table like a heavy black cloud.

'That's fine for you to say,' Agnes O'Brien said in a thin, strained voice, 'but if your brother felt the same, we'd be struggling here to run the farm and see to everything.'

Michael's face darkened. 'I do more than my share when I'm at home,' he said, his gaze moving from his mother to his father.

'It's not the same as being here all the time,' she said in a dismissive tone. Then, when he went to speak again she deliberately cut across him, turning towards Kate. 'How do you and your mother manage in the winter without a man? How do you manage for turf and that kind of thing?'

Kate felt her face redden, knowing that there was some kind of an argument going on here, but not at all sure what it was. 'Brendan and the neighbours all work together to bring the turf home in the summer and then Mammy and me bring the turf in from the shed as it's needed.' She paused. 'Brendan is home most weekends, and if he's not there when a heavy job is needed to be done, then we can always ask one of the neighbours. We wouldn't be stuck.'

'And what if Brendan was to get married?' Agnes O'Brien asked, her eyebrows raised. 'That's bound to happen at some stage in the future . . .'

Kate felt a tightness in her chest. 'I suppose that's something we'll work around when it happens . . . but my mother and myself are quite self-sufficient. There's very little we can't do for ourselves.'

'And do you think that Brendan would bring a wife into the

cottage?' Mrs O'Brien went on, clearly making a point. 'Or would he be in a position to look for a house for himself?'

Kate felt almost bewildered now, for the questions that were being fired at her were questions she'd often asked herself in the dark of the night when she either couldn't sleep or had awakened much too early. They were questions she had never even voiced to her mother or to Brendan, for fear of receiving answers she might not like to hear – answers that might have real consequences where her future was concerned. *What if Brendan was to bring a wife home?* There certainly wouldn't be room for her in the small cottage and there would hardly be room for her mother.

'I really don't know – we've never really thought about it . . .' she fumbled, feeling terribly embarrassed and awkward.

Agnes O'Brien gave a long, low sigh and when she spoke again there was a weary tone to her voice. 'I suppose these are things that no family likes to think about, but if we're not prepared for it, anything could happen . . . especially when there's houses and land involved.'

'Land and money mean more to some people than they do to others,' Michael suddenly stated with a distinct edge to his voice.

'That's all right to say when it hasn't affected you yet,' his father put in now. 'But there's very few men who would walk away from a house and farm that have been in the family for years.'

'And while it's grand to be able to do what suits you here and now,' Agnes O'Brien added, 'you have to look to the future.'

'I *am* looking to the future,' Michael stated, his blue eyes narrowed and flinty with annoyance. He paused for a few moments, obviously uneasy, then he reached across and touched Kate's arm. 'I think Kate and I will head off now,' he said abruptly, scraping his chair back against the floor. 'It's looking a bit cloudy, and we don't want to chance getting drowned.'

Kate moved out of her chair as quickly as was decently possible, trying not to show her relief. 'Thanks for the tea and the lovely sandwiches,' she said, pinning a tight little smile on her face, although her stomach was churning. *Never*, she thought, *will I ever set foot in this miserable house again!*

Michael went striding ahead of her to get their coats from the formidable mahogany coat-stand that dominated the hallway.

'It was very nice meeting you...' Agnes O'Brien said as they moved out into the corridor.

'And you,' Kate said, her throat almost closing over to make her choke on the lie.

Michael came towards her holding out her coat. Just as she turned to slip her arms into the sleeves, his father suddenly came rushing from behind and roughly pushed both Kate and Mrs O'Brien out of his way and into the coats on the stand. Both women gasped in shock at being knocked off their feet and turned to look at him.

'Whatever's the matter, Peter?' Agnes O'Brien snapped accusingly.

'I need to get some air...' he said in a strangled voice, going towards the front door. 'I don't feel too good...' He staggered against the wall now, knocking a picture from its hook and then blindly groped around for the latch on the door.

'For God's sake, would you watch where you're going!' Mrs O'Brien said in an anxious voice.

Michael moved swiftly down the hallway after his father but was moments too late as Peter O'Brien finally managed to open the door. And after taking only two steps into the cool evening air, he crashed down onto the ground outside.

Chapter 11

❧

'So, what's the news around the town, girls?' Mary Flowers said eagerly, looking from one red-haired sister to the other. Out of all the young ones in the families along the canal-line, she had always liked these two girls the best.

'Well,' Noelle said hesitantly, 'I've actually got a bit of news of my own this time – I've been offered a position up in Dublin.'

'Oh?' Mary Flowers said, her eyebrows shooting up in surprise. 'And what kind of a position would that be, Noelle?'

'Housekeeping for a doctor.'

'A *doctor*!' Mary Flowers repeated, in a very impressed tone.

'And up in Dublin.' Her eyes widened. 'Oh, Noelle, wouldn't that be lovely for you? Working for a doctor in a big fancy house in Dublin. Wouldn't that be a lovely job?'

Noelle nodded. 'It sounds grand all right . . . it's a *lady* doctor. She's not married or anything, she lives on her own.'

'Ah now, a *lady* doctor,' Mary said, smiling knowingly. 'That makes all the difference – a huge difference.' She paused, cocking her head to the side. 'And d'you mind me askin' how it all came about?' she said, carefully dipping the edge of her digestive biscuit into her tea.

'My Auntie Delia,' Noelle replied, taking a sip from her cup. 'Her friend was working there, going in and out every day, but the doctor wants somebody to live in.'

'And I suppose your auntie's friend couldn't live in herself?' Mary checked, thoroughly enjoying the story. She had often wished she'd had the chance to see a bit more of the world and maybe have had a job like that where she only had to look out for herself, and not have the responsibility of a husband and a family.

'Not very often. She has a family and an elderly father to look after at home,' Noelle explained. 'She has to be home to make the dinner for them in the evening and get the younger ones off to bed.'

'Of course,' Mary said, nodding her head understandingly. The same sad story as herself. 'She couldn't be living in a doctor's house all the time when she had a family at home.' She took a sip of her tea. 'And when do you have to let them know?'

'I've to phone up to my Auntie Delia tomorrow morning, and she'll let her friend know, who'll tell the doctor.'

'And when would you have to go? When would you be starting work?'

'I suppose I can start as soon as I like . . .'

There was a little pause.

'And have you decided yet?' Mary asked. 'And what do your mammy and daddy think?' She reached over to the plate for another biscuit. This was the most interesting news she'd heard in a long time. Although there were often people from Ballygrace heading off to Dublin for work or even over to England, it had been a while since anyone she knew well had gone.

'I think I'll take the job,' Noelle said, glancing over at Sarah who had remained silent throughout the conversation. 'Sure, there's nothing to keep me here. There's nobody who would miss me at all.'

'Ah now, Noelle,' Mary said, pulling an exaggeratedly hurt face. 'Surely you don't mean that?'

Sarah shook her head and then shrugged her shoulders. 'She's always at that, saying nobody cares about her . . .'

'Dear, dear, dear,' Mary Flowers muttered into her cup. 'Sure the whole family down there would miss you – and *we* would miss you.'

'After a while, none of ye would miss me,' Noelle said, suddenly sounding like a young schoolgirl. 'And your Brendan certainly wouldn't miss me . . . he can't stand the very sight of me.'

'*Brendan?*' Mary said, aghast at the suggestion. She wondered what Brendan had done to upset their neighbour. Sadly, she wasn't a bit surprised to hear he might have upset anyone. He was well capable of it.

Noelle looked across the table at her sister – who glowered back at her – and they were both uncomfortably silent for a moment. There was obviously some kind of tension between the girls, not uncommon from what Kate had told her mother. As often as they got on, they could just as easily snipe and dig at each other.

'I hope Brendan hasn't ever said anything to offend ye, girls,' Mary said, shaking her head. 'I know he can be a bit of a brat at times, especially when he has drink taken . . . but he doesn't mean any harm. He's a pure devil at the coddin'. He does the very same thing to Kate, he drives her mad at times.'

'Well anyway,' Noelle said, not commenting on Brendan one way or the other, 'I'm going to take the job. I think it will be a grand change from Ballygrace or Tullamore – it will let me see a bit more of the world.'

'It certainly will,' Mary agreed, 'but have you chatted it out with your mother and father? Are they agreeable about you leavin' home?'

Noelle shrugged. 'They don't seem to mind . . . and they've been saying that me and Sarah need to get some kind of a job soon.'

'You can always come home for visits,' Mary said soothingly, 'can't she, Sarah?'

Sarah nodded. 'Once a month.'

'Once a month . . .' Mary repeated. 'That's not too bad, sure the weeks will fly in. And you'll get to see a bit of Dublin. Did your aunt say which part of Dublin the doctor has the house in?'

'Ballsbridge,' Noelle confirmed. She reached over for another digestive biscuit. 'My Auntie Delia says it's out Donnybrook way.' She gave a little shug. 'I've never been out that way, so I don't know where it is. She says you can get a bus out to it from Grafton Street.'

'Oh, I'm sure,' Mary agreed. 'The buses go out to all the parts of Dublin at all times of the day.' She shook her head vigorously, her eyes wide. 'It's not like the country at all – it's a different world altogether.'

'She'll get paid at the end of the month,' Sarah suddenly said, tossing her pale red hair over her shoulder, 'and she'll have *two* different kinds of apron to wear.'

'*Uniform*,' Noelle corrected her. 'It's a dress and an apron and a little hat. She said I've to wear a plain one in the morning for gettin' the breakfast and doing the jobs like the fires and cleaning, and then a frilly, fancier one in the afternoon for answering the door and the phone.'

'Oh, the *phone*!' Mary said, looking impressed all over again. 'I suppose you'll have to learn how to speak nice to all the other doctors and the patients. Is the surgery near the house?'

'No,' Noelle informed her, 'she has a surgery in the centre of Dublin with her two brothers – they're doctors as well, but they live in a different part from the woman doctor.'

'Imagine!' Mary said, clasping her hands together now. 'Three doctors in the one family. I suppose their father and mother were doctors, too. Oh, I bet they'll have a lovely posh house.' She finished her tea, a faraway look in her eyes.

'Well, I suppose we better be going or we won't get any walk at all,' Noelle said, standing up. 'Thanks for the tea and biscuits, Mrs Flowers, it was lovely.'

'Oh, ye're very welcome, girls,' she said accompanying them to the door. 'I'll tell Kate to call down and see you. I'd say she'll get a bit of a land when she hears you're off to Dublin, Noelle.' She patted Sarah on the shoulder. 'And I'd say you'll certainly miss her, too.'

Sarah shrugged. 'I might go off to work somewhere myself,' she said, tossing her hair in an almost childish manner. 'My Auntie

Delia says she'll look out for a job in a nice shop that might suit me, because I don't fancy the idea of skivvyin' in a big house for somebody that thinks they're better than me.'

'Would you listen to Lady Muck?' Noelle said, rolling her eyes at Mary. All three stood at the cottage gate now, happily prolonging the conversation. 'She thinks she's as good as a doctor now.' She jostled her sister with her elbow, half-irritated and half-joking. 'Nobody would take you for free, because when it comes to housework you're the last flaming hope.'

Then, suddenly hearing footsteps and whistling, they all turned around.

'Who's the last hope?' Brendan Flowers said, a beaming smile on his handsome, tanned face.

'Ah, sure the girls are only at the coddin' with each other,' his mother said, relieved that he didn't seem too jarred. She scanned his face for signs of his mood, and concluded that he was still at the pleasant, amiable stage as opposed to the moody argumentative one. 'Noelle here is telling me that she's heading off to Dublin to start a new job. She's going to be working in a big fancy house lookin' after a doctor.'

Noelle's face instantly flushed as he turned to look at her.

'Is she now?' he said slowly, his smile fading. 'And when are you going?'

Noelle looked down at the ground, and scuffed with her sandal at a deeply imbedded stone. 'I'm not sure,' she muttered. 'It's not all agreed yet . . .'

'She came around to let Kate know,' Mary put in.

'That was good of her,' Brendan said, still staring at Noelle with narrowed eyes.

'I was just sayin' how she'll be missed,' Mary rattled on. 'It won't be the same around here without you. It won't be the same at all, will it, Brendan? Losing one of our nicest neighbours.'

'Ah well,' he said, pushing past the females now, 'I suppose Ballygrace isn't good enough for her now . . . I suppose she'll have her sights set on higher things. All us simple folk around the canal wouldn't be interestin' enough for her.'

'Ah, go away with you, Brendan!' Mary said, waving her hand as though to shoo him away. 'Don't pay any heed to that fella, Noelle

– he'd nearly drive you mad. Wasn't that just what I was telling you earlier? He's a devil to live with when the humour is on him.'

Noelle went around the other side of the gate now, looking far off down the shimmery silver canal. 'We'll head off now, Mrs Flowers,' she said, her voice unusually soft and low.

Sarah went off behind her. 'Tell Kate we'll see probably see her tomorrow.'

'I will indeed,' Mary said, closing the little gate behind them. 'And I'll be seein' you girls.'

The two sisters walked on a few yards, their auburn hair reflecting the golden lights of the sun, and then they both turned to give their neighbour a cheery wave before speeding up to a good step.

Mary waved back at them – her heart sinking a little as she thought of Noelle leaving and maybe never coming back to live around here again. And her sister, too, would probably follow behind her. Things were changing, Mary thought, changing fast – and maybe not for the better.

She sighed to herself and then she turned towards the cottage and Brendan, wondering what had made him be so ignorant to poor Noelle Daly.

Chapter 12

~∞~

Peter O'Brien was pronounced dead on Sunday evening. Kate and her mother sat up late that night, going over and over the tragic events that had happened out at the O'Briens' but Kate was still deeply shocked.

'I'll go with you to the funeral,' Mary Flowers offered as they sat down at the kitchen table to have breakfast on Monday morning, both in pyjamas and dressing-gowns. 'Brendan will be there as well.'

Kate slowly nodded. 'Thanks . . .' She lifted the porridge pot and used a wooden spoon to half-fill two bowls for them. She then carefully poured cold milk on top of the hot oats to cool it down.

'None of this is your fault, Kate,' her mother suddenly said, reaching her hand across the table to cover Kate's. 'The man had a weak heart. Brendan was able to tell us that last night. It's just bad luck that it happened when you were out at the house. It could have happened any time.'

'I know,' Kate replied, fiddling with a stray black ringlet, 'but unfortunately it did happen when I was there, and it happened at the end of a terrible visit.' She stopped, the memory of the awful scene making her catch her breath. 'God, it was terrible! You could have cut the atmosphere with a knife ... the whole family absolutely hated me.' She shook her head. 'I don't know what they were expecting, but I was obviously a big disappointment. Mr and Mrs O'Brien certainly didn't think I was good enough for their son and the sisters and brother weren't any better.'

'I can't believe it,' Mary said, squeezing her daughter's hand. 'We can't be that different to them, surely? Hasn't Michael got the same job as Brendan?'

Kate lifted her gaze to the whitewashed ceiling. 'From what I could gather, they weren't too impressed with Michael working on the canal. They sounded as though they thought he should be at home helping on the farm. They kept going on and on about it.'

'But when he was here he talked all about how he helped on the farm when he had time off from the boats,' Mary stated. 'He gave the impression that he spent most of his time off helping out at home.'

Kate shrugged her shoulders. 'Maybe the O'Briens aren't happy with Michael spending some of his spare time with a girl ...' She reached for a spoon to start on her porridge, although with everything whirling through her mind, she had little appetite. 'Although I have a notion they don't have a problem with him having a girlfriend – I'm sure it's a problem because it's *me*.'

Mary shook her head, finding the whole business confusing and upsetting.

'Well, I can't understand it at all,' she muttered. 'I know we're not exactly like the *Quality* or anything, but the Flowers have always been known to be respectable ...'

'I'll go to the funeral,' Kate decided, 'but I'm not going anywhere near the house.'

'But what about Michael?' Mary asked. 'You will keep going out with him, won't you?'

Kate put the spoon down into the bowl. 'It might not be my decision – it all depends on whether he listens to his family or goes his own way. We'll have to see what happens . . . he's going to be needed at home now that his poor father has gone.'

Noelle Daly called up to the cottage in the afternoon to confirm that she'd accepted the job in Dublin and Mary Flowers and Kate made a big show of congratulating her and wishing her well, although they both knew they would miss her very much. Then, all three grew more serious as Kate once more related the tragic events of the previous evening.

'God, Kate!' Noelle gasped, looking from Kate to her mother. 'What did you all do when he collapsed down dead on the ground?'

Kate looked up to the ceiling, feeling awful as she recounted the whole scene again. 'Well,' she said, 'Mrs O'Brien went into a kind of shock at first. She just stood staring at him with her hands over her mouth, so I ran over and tried to help Michael.'

'What did you do?' Noelle asked.

Kate suddenly went very pale, and her stomach started to churn. She wasn't at all sure if she wanted to say out loud what she'd done, because the memory of it had kept her awake a good bit of the night. But then – as she'd reasoned with herself on and off since it had happened – she'd have automatically done the very same thing whoever it had been. She had only met Peter O'Brien a few hours earlier, but she knew that she would have done the same thing if it had been a complete stranger in the street in Tullamore.

She dropped her eyes to the empty teacup in front of her. 'I gave him the kiss of life . . .'

'Did you, Kate?' her mother said, her mouth open in shock. 'You never said last night . . . you never said anything about trying to save his life.'

'Where did you learn how to do that?' Noelle's eyes were wide with amazement.

'I did a first-aid course at evening classes a few years ago . . .' Kate sighed and shrugged her shoulders. 'It didn't do him any good,' she said, her voice almost a whisper, 'he was already dead.'

'It was still fierce brave of you,' Noelle said, patting her friend's arm. 'I wouldn't have had the faintest idea what to do ... I'd probably have collapsed on the ground along with him.'

'And me too,' Mary Flowers added enthusiastically, then she bit her lip to stop herself laughing at Noelle's dramatic comment, because she knew that Kate wouldn't find anything remotely funny about the situation at all.

Later on, Kate and Noelle walked into Ballygrace to get Mass cards for the O'Brien family and to pick up odds and ends from the shops.

'They say that bad luck comes in threes,' Kate said ruefully as they walked along. 'Michael O'Brien's father dropped dead right in front of me last night, and now you're going away and I'll hardly ever see you. I wonder what's going to be the next terrible thing to happen?'

'That's only oul' superstition,' Noelle told her, linking her arm through Kate's. 'And anyway, I'll get a weekend off a month, and if I don't like the job I'll come straight back home.'

'You'll like it,' Kate said ruefully. 'You've always wanted to get away from here.'

'It's not the place,' Noelle told her. 'Ballygrace is grand. It's our house that's the big problem. When we're all stuck inside you feel as though you don't have an inch of space to yourself.' She shook her face. 'And Daddy drives me mad – he's terrible when he's in bad humour. He swings from one mood to the next in minutes. You never know how you're going to find him. Something you tell him today could be fine and grand, and tomorrow he could hit the roof over it.'

'Sounds a bit like our Brendan,' Kate snorted. 'Although thankfully he's improved a bit recently.' Her voice dropped. 'But that might all die down when Michael O'Brien isn't around so often ...'

Noelle looked sharply at her. 'You don't know ...'

'Well,' Kate said, giving a little smile, 'I hardly think things are going to improve after what's happened.' She patted her friend's hand. 'Forget about the O'Briens and all of that. I'm more interested in hearing about your new job and all the exciting things you'll get up to in Dublin.'

Chapter 13

K ate was standing with the iron in her hand staring out of the window, far across the canal, when she heard the unfamiliar sound of an engine, and a few moments later she saw the black car come into view.

Her heart leapt into her mouth: cars never came to their part of the canal and instinctively she felt it was something serious. Her mother had gone out for a short visit to an elderly couple – Mrs and Mrs Flaherty – who lived further along the tow-path. Mary had promised Mrs Flaherty that she would give her a few cuttings from a trailing, flowering plant that the old lady had admired, and when she was tidying up the garden earlier on, she had snipped a few pieces of the plant for her along with a small bunch of summer roses.

Brendan was also out of the house, working on the boat, and wasn't due back until that evening. He normally wouldn't have been home until Friday, but he had arranged to have the following day – Wednesday – off for the funeral.

Kate put the iron down on the table and stared out at the car, waiting to see who would emerge and what the nature of their business would be. A knot of anxiety came into her chest when she saw Michael O'Brien climb out of the vehicle, dressed very soberly in his dark suit and black tie. Her heart started to beat quicker when, instead of coming in through the gate, he went around to the other side of the car to open the passenger's door.

Kate's hand flew to her mouth as Agnes O'Brien emerged from the car now, dressed from head to toe in black, her face white and stony. Instead of rushing to the door to greet them – as somewhere at the back of her mind she knew she should – Kate stood grounded to the spot for a few moments longer.

Then, she quickly reminded herself that this woman had just suffered a huge shock and tragedy and could not possibly appear any other way than she did. She was hardly likely to be smiling and happy only days after her husband had dropped dead. Which then begged the question in Kate's mind as to why she would come out this afternoon to visit her or anyone in her family?

Had she come to tell Kate to stay away from the funeral? Or maybe she had come to tell her in no uncertain terms to stay well away from her son. Agnes O'Brien had made it very, very clear on Sunday afternoon that she hadn't approved of Kate and didn't feel she and Michael were a suitable match.

Maybe the older woman thought that Kate hadn't got the message and needed to hear it a second time, face to face.

She had no more time for thinking as Michael opened the gate to let his mother through, and they both came up the path towards the door. As though just realising that she would have to let them into the house, Kate rushed to put the iron down on the draining-board at the sink, pausing for a second to check her appearance in Brendan's small shaving-mirror. She registered the flushed look on her face and instantly wished she'd had time to dab her powder puff over it and put on a touch of lipstick, but there was no point in even thinking that. She tucked a few stray curls into her thick black plait, smoothed down her plain, brown-checked summer dress and walked towards the door.

'I hope we haven't called at an inconvenient time ...' Agnes O'Brien said in a thin, strained voice, as they stood facing Kate on the doorstep. Her pale blue eyes held Kate's for just a second, and then they flitted nervously over to her son.

'My mother wanted to have a private word with you,' Michael said in his soft, calm way, his eyes searching her face.

Kate looked back at him for a second or two, trying to read his thoughts – but failing. She didn't have the slightest clue as to why they had driven down the narrow, bumpy tow-path to their cottage.

There was a moment's pause, and then Michael cleared his throat and reached a hand to straighten his black tie.

Kate suddenly felt flustered, realising she was keeping them standing at the door. 'You're both very welcome,' she said, sweeping the door open wide.

'I won't beat about the bush,' Agnes O'Brien said, when they were all seated at the kitchen table. Michael had taken the chair at the end of the table while the two women sat opposite each other, both

66

with arms resting on the top and hands joined together as though in prayer. 'I've come first to apologise to you for not giving you a warmer welcome at our house, and secondly to thank you for doing what you did to try to save my husband's life.'

Kate looked down at her hands, too embarrassed to meet the older woman's gaze. 'That's all right,' she said quietly. 'I was only doing what anyone would have done under the circumstances...'

'No,' Mrs O'Brien said, sounding quite emphatic, and her hands were tapping on the table in a restrained kind of way to further make the point. 'I think it was a very brave thing to do, especially when the rest of us were so shocked and unable to do anything at all.'

Kate lifted her eyes. 'I'm only sorry that it didn't help...'

Agnes O'Brien took a very deep breath that then escaped in a shuddering sigh. 'You couldn't have done any more – he was probably gone before he hit the ground.' Her voice dropped further. 'The doctor said it could have happened any time, it seems it was that kind of thing. No warning...'

There was another pause, where Kate suddenly felt compelled to fill the silence. 'Can I offer you a cup of tea ... or coffee?' Her mind worked quickly, as she tried to remember whether they still had the remains of a bottle of Camp coffee in the press which held all the dry foods near the fireplace. Michael's mother was sure to ask for coffee, and it would be nowhere to be found – probably thrown out long ago through lack of use.

'No thank you,' Mrs O'Brien said in a low voice. 'To be honest, we've had more than our share of tea over the last few days with all the visitors.' She gave another small sigh. 'And no doubt we'll be drinking plenty more before this is all over.'

'The funeral is at eleven o'clock tomorrow, isn't it?' Kate checked, glad of the excuse to ask something that sounded reasonably relevant.

'It is,' Michael answered this time, nodding and looking directly at her. 'It would have been today, but we had to wait for an aunt to travel over from Edinburgh. She's arriving later this evening.'

Agnes O'Brien looked up at the clock on the mantelpiece, and then her eyes moved from it to scan the spotlessly clean kitchen and sitting-room that were all in one. She took in the whitewashed walls and the two comfortable chairs on either side of the fire and the small, two-seater wooden-framed sofa. 'Our family don't usually behave the way we did on Sunday afternoon...' she suddenly said, her attention turning back to Kate. 'But several things had come to a head just before you arrived.'

Michael straightened his back in the pine wooden chair, a quizzical look on his face. 'I thought I said I would explain this to Kate? There's no need for us to go into it now.'

'You weren't there, Michael,' his mother said, almost dismissively, 'and it might as well be told while the two of you are together.'

Kate felt her throat run dry. She had no idea how on earth a casual Sunday-afternoon visit to a new boyfriend's house had suddenly become such a serious issue.

'To a large extent I blame Helen for the atmosphere in the house on Sunday,' Agnes O'Brien went on. She glanced fleetingly at Michael, as though warning him not to interrupt. 'You see, she deliberately landed up at the house with her friend, knowing that Michael was bringing you home for a visit...' She paused, as though searching for the right words.

Kate swallowed hard, trying to get rid of the tight feeling in her throat. She stole a quick glance at Michael to see his hand come up to rub his chin in an agitated manner.

'Fiona McGlynn has always had an eye for Michael and Helen is forever trying to matchmake them.' She gave a little shrug of her shoulders. 'Fiona is a lovely girl, she's been coming around our house since she and Helen started school together. They've been best friends all these years. Her parents own the big farm half a mile up the road from us. In fact, Fiona's family are very fond of Michael too. I think they had always hoped that there might be a match there as well ... they felt that the families were similar being farmers and all that kind of thing.'

Kate nodded slowly, her thick dark plait bouncing lightly against the top of her spine. 'I see,' she said in a low voice, as the picture started to become clearer. 'So everyone was disappointed when Michael started seeing me, and obviously you weren't too happy when he brought me out to the house?'

'Well, to be honest, that's more or less the situation,' the older woman admitted.

'It's all nonsense, Kate,' Michael put in sharply, his hand coming across the table now to touch hers. 'I've never had the slightest interest in Fiona McGlynn, and everyone knew that.'

'Helen was sure it was only a matter of time,' Agnes said quietly. 'She thought you would eventually see that you and Fiona were well suited. And Sinéad and Patricia both like her as well.' She shrugged. 'They didn't mean any real harm . . .'

He sucked the air audibly in through his teeth. 'How on earth they should have thought that I was suddenly going to change my mind is beyond me.' He gave a bitter little laugh. 'In a year or two it will be *nineteen hundred and sixty* – we're not living in the Dark Ages any more where all the marriages were matches. And if I was to live until the year two thousand and sixty, I still wouldn't have any interest in Fiona McGlynn. I'm big and ugly enough to choose the kind of girl I want for myself – I'm not going be treated like an imbecile who has no control over his own life.'

'Nobody's saying anything like that,' his mother said quietly. She moved sideward in her chair now, as though readying herself to leave. 'In any case, you've made it quite clear that you won't be pushed into anything you don't want – be it choosing girlfriends or helping out on the farm instead of drifting up and down the Grand Canal.'

'Please don't start on about that again,' Michael moaned. 'This isn't fair at all.'

Kate held her breath.

'That, of course, was the other problem on Sunday,' Agnes O'Brien said, her voice getting lower and lower. She looked directly at Kate. 'As you probably realised, Michael's father and brother wanted him to be at home working the farm, especially since his father had had the last heart attack last Christmas.'

'For God's sake, Mother,' Michael said, rolling his eyes to the ceiling, 'I didn't realise we'd come out here to go over all this personal business . . . I thought it was to thank Kate for trying to help my father and to say we would like her to come to the meal after the funeral.'

'I was getting around to that,' Agnes told him, her voice sounding weary now. 'But first, I felt I needed to explain why there was such an awkward atmosphere at the house on Sunday . . . and I wanted Kate to realise that it was nothing personal to her.'

'I understand,' Kate said, flushing furiously. She wondered if Michael would ever have got around to telling her about any family rifts over his work or over anything else. He looked as though he was extremely reluctant to discuss or explain anything that just might prove uncomfortable for him.

'It was all just an unfortunate series of events . . .' Mrs O'Brien went on. She looked at Kate with dark-ringed eyes, and attempted a tight little smile. 'I hope you understand – it really was not personal at all.'

Chapter 14

On Wednesday morning Noelle left the house at the canal just after nine o'clock to catch the bus from Ballygrace up to Dublin. Her father and Sarah took her in on the horse and cart and waited with her outside the local pub where the coach drew in.

It was a mixed sort of morning, dry but with a threatening, cloudy sky and with a little nip in the air. She wore her belted cream raincoat over one of the flowery American dresses and a red lace-patterned cardigan that she had worked on during the damp spring evenings. She had a matching white one in her case, which would make a bit of a change with the three other summer dresses she had packed.

Noelle had bought a light suitcase from the thirty-odd pounds she had saved up together with a few new bits and pieces, like a pink cotton nightdress and dressing-gown and slippers and some underwear.

There were three or four other people waiting for the bus and a farmer who was putting a cage full of noisy chickens on board to be collected in Dublin.

'You have everything with you that you need?' her father checked, as the bus came into view.

Noelle nodded, scornfully thinking that he was a bit late in asking. Her mother had been the one to check that she had bus fares and a bit of money for essentials to keep her going until she got paid at the end of the month. Her father hadn't asked her a single question about the job or where she would be staying or anything like that. He had simply said 'it's up to you' when she had asked his opinion on whether or not she should take the job.

The journey was the usual winding and bumpy three-hour ride up to the city, with stops every few miles to pick up more passengers. The bus got busier the nearer it got to Dublin, and by the time they arrived, people were standing in the aisle and falling over the seated passengers every time they turned a sharp corner or came to a sudden halt.

The grey clouds were dispersing and the sky had turned a deep blue, heralding another warm and sunny day. Noelle began to feel quite excited as the bus pulled in at the station. She waved when she spotted her Auntie Delia waiting for her at one of the shelters, an anxious frown on her face.

'Thank God!' Delia said as her niece came carefully down the steps carrying her case. 'You caught the bus all right, and we should make it out to Ballsbridge in plenty of time.'

'Is it far?' Noelle asked as they walked out of the bus station.

'Not too bad,' Delia said, gripping Noelle's arm as they crossed a road. 'But it's too far to walk, especially with a case. We'll have to catch another bus around Grafton Street out to Ballsbridge, then, if I remember rightly, it's only a couple of minutes' walk.'

Noelle couldn't believe how busy O'Connell Street was, with both traffic and people. Delia insisted that they take turns carrying the case, and after starting out at a fairly brisk pace, they found themselves gradually slowing up due to the crowds and the awkwardness of getting through with the case.

Eventually, they came to a halt at a bus-stop outside Trinity College and after a few minutes a bus pulled up that took them on the short trip out to Ballsbridge.

'Have you been inside the doctor's house?' Noelle asked in a slightly anxious voice as they disembarked from the bus, and she found herself amongst very large buildings and heavy traffic.

'Several times,' Delia said, taking the case from her niece and setting it down by some long, black iron railings, keeping out of the way of other people until they got their bearings. 'I've even stayed there for a few days. When the doctor was away on holiday, she told Anna that she could invite a friend to stay to keep her company, so she asked me.' Delia took her bag from her shoulder now, and started rummaging inside for her compact and lipstick.

Noelle's face lit up at the news, and suddenly the busy road and the buildings seemed a little more exciting. 'Maybe,' she said, leaning casually against the railings, 'I'll be able to invite Sarah or Kate Flowers to stay with me. They'd love to come up to Dublin.'

'Hold your horses!' her aunt said, her eyebrows shooting up. 'Ye haven't even started in the job yet. I think you'd be better served going about your work business before you start making plans about anything else.' She tutted to herself then opened the powder compact. After quickly glancing in the cloudy circular mirror, she dabbed the small velvety square over her nose and cheeks and chin, thinking it wouldn't do to go into a doctor's house with a shiny face.

Noelle's face fell. 'I didn't mean that I wanted to invite people straight away,' she said in a wounded voice. 'I just meant it would be nice to have people I know come to see me sometime . . .'

Delia applied a quick coat of pink lipstick, pursed her lips together, then put her cosmetics back in her handbag. Then, she lifted the case again. 'You'll have me to visit when you have time off,' she said in a kinder voice, 'and then we'll see what happens.'

They walked along the main road for a short distance then turned onto a wider, sweeping residential road with trees flanking the pavements on either side of huge, red-brick houses.

'Is it one of these?' Noelle said in a low voice, suddenly reaching to take the case from her aunt. The houses were much bigger than she'd expected and she was beginning to feel completely out of her depth.

'About halfway up,' Delia said, her voice sounding slightly tense. She knew she would have to do all the talking and sorting things out with Dr Casey, and she was beginning to feel more than a touch nervous herself. In the past any dealings she'd had with the doctor had been through Anna Quinn, and all she'd had to do was nod and smile and agree with her friend. The thought of having to introduce her niece and maybe negotiate payment and time off was not something she relished.

'Is she nice?' Noelle said, her breath now coming in short little bursts. 'The doctor ... is she nice to talk to?'

'I wouldn't worry about her talkin' to you. She'll not be sitting to have long chats over cups of tea or anything like that. Don't forget – she's a *doctor*,' Delia said, 'so she's not like us.' Then, sensing her niece's anxiety, she tried to think of something to reassure her. 'She's a real lady – you can tell it the minute you see her. She's very genteel, like.'

'Is she very posh and uppity?' Noelle asked, her voice fearful.

Delia decided that a firm tack was needed here. 'Don't be getting yourself all worked up. Dr Casey is a very nice woman ...' She paused. 'So long as you know your place.'

The house was tall and built in the same red bricks as the others in the road, with pristine white paintwork on the windows. It was joined onto another identical house except that the neighbour's house had a scarlet door.

'Oh, Auntie Delia,' Noelle whispered as they walked up a set of high steps that led to the yellow front door, 'I'm fierce nervous!' She put the blue case down on the wide top step, then stood clutching the handle with both hands as though it might protect her.

'You'll be grand,' her aunt told her, running a reassuring hand over her niece's shoulder. 'Just mind what you're saying and listen to everything she tells you and you'll be just grand.' Before ringing the shiny brass doorbell, Delia patted her hand over her hair now, checking that the stiff waves were still held tidily in place with the copious amounts of hair lacquer that the hairdresser had sprayed on yesterday afternoon. Delia had explained to the woman she went to every fortnight that she needed it still to look perfect for a business appointment the following day, and then the hairdresser had given it an extra good going-over with the large tin of lacquer.

The bell sounded its musical chime and a few moments later stiletto heels could be heard clicking their way down the tiled hall floor. Delia Clarke clasped her hands together and lifted her chin high.

The door was opened wide and a small, thin woman with a plain face and hair cut in a severe blackish-brown bob welcomed them in. She wore a moss-green sweater with a row of neat, even pearls around her neck and a plain black skirt and shoes.

Noelle took a deep breath, lifted her case and stepped over the threshold and into her new life.

The first thing that hit Noelle was the distinct smell of lavender and beeswax, as she walked along the Victorian tiled floor, following her aunt and the doctor. There was a huge marble-topped, cream carved table with a matching mirror against one wall, and down at the bottom of the hall between a room and what looked like the kitchen door was a tall grandfather clock.

When they got halfway along the hallway, the doctor suddenly stopped. 'I take it you're Noelle Daly, the young lady who is going to help me out here?' She smiled and put her hand out and shook Noelle's and then Delia's hand, saying, 'It was good of you to bring Noelle out from the city. I hope we haven't taken up too much of your time.' She tucked a wing of her bobbed hair behind her ear.

'Not at all, Doctor,' Delia said, wondering why someone with plenty of money like a doctor wouldn't go and have their awful plain straight hair done into nice waves or curls at the hairdresser's. She was also thinking that a bit of lipstick or mascara mightn't go amiss either.

'I only have a short while before getting back to the surgery,' the doctor said in a voice that didn't sound like any Irish accent Noelle had ever heard before. In fact, it sounded more English than Irish. 'But,' she said, leading them into the drawing-room, 'I have enough time to show you around and go over the important details about your employment.'

Noelle followed slowly behind, her heart sinking a little as she took in the formality of the darkened room with its heavy draped green curtains and tasselled tie-backs and pelmets, and the pale green fitted carpet that was almost the same olive shade as Dr Casey's sweater. Greyish-white lace curtains hung at the windows, keeping out any little bit of sunlight that might have attempted to break through.

The doctor motioned to both women to sit down on the gold and cream sofa with a high back and carved mahogany legs, while she sat down on a matching chair at the opposite side of a low glass-topped coffee table. A plate decorated with old roses held a modest pile of sandwiches cut into tiny triangles, another held three little white iced cakes each with a cherry on top. Beside the bigger plates were three side plates, a white paper napkin folded in half on each, and three old-rose china cups and saucers.

Noelle glanced anxiously at her Auntie Delia, worrying about how she should approach the sandwiches and plates and serviettes.

'If you take your coat off now, Noelle,' Dr Casey said, standing up, 'you can help me to bring in the tea and milk and sugar.' She moved towards the drawing-room door. 'It will give you a chance to acquaint yourself with the kitchen and I'll show you where your bedroom is.'

Noelle stood up, taking off her cream coat as quickly as she could. Then, as she was folding it up to put on the arm of the chair, the belt swung out and the buckle caught one of the sandwiches, sending it flying off the rose-patterned plate and onto the spotless, pale green carpet. *'Jesus!'* she whispered, her eyes wide and shocked. She turned to look at the door and was overwhelmingly relieved to find that the doctor had gone out to the hall and hadn't witnessed her almost destroying the set table.

'Go on, you clumsy goat!' Delia hissed, shooing her out of the room. 'I'll pick it up and she'll be none the wiser.'

The kitchen wasn't as big or as fancy as Noelle had imagined, and she felt her confidence returning a little as she looked around the plain cream walls, which had a dresser on one side with white everyday china and a simple pine table and four chairs, which didn't look an awful lot different to the one she often sat at in the Flowers' house.

'I suppose you could say that this is the main part of the house,' Dr Casey said, as she filled the silver teapot with boiling water, then put the kettle back down on a small Baby Belling two-ring cooker. 'And it's obviously the place where you'll do most of your work.' She indicated a small narrow door. 'You'll find the milk and sugar in the pantry,' she said now. 'I filled them this morning in readiness – they're in the same rose-pattern as the china in the drawing-room.' She glanced up at the circular wooden clock on the wall. 'We must speed things up a little now, because I only have half an hour before I have to get back to the surgery.' Then her busy heels tapped across the stone-flagged kitchen floor and back out into the hallway.

Noelle rushed across to the pantry and opened the door. She paused for a moment, immediately taken aback by the tidy, but half-empty shelves, for she had expected to find an array of bread and meats and cheese – and all sorts of things that plain people like her own family would never have. Instead she saw half a small brown soda loaf, a single iced cake the same as the other three in the drawing-room, and a small plate with two tiny, grey-looking lamb chops. There was also a wicker basket with half a dozen potatoes, a straw basket of mushrooms, a couple of onions and a small cabbage.

Noelle carefully lifted the jug and sugar bowl, her eyes still checking out the cut-glass butter dish with the very small pat of butter and the tins of peas, butter beans and string beans and two tins of Carnation Milk.

All in all, Noelle thought as she followed the doctor back into the drawing-room, a very poor show for such a big, posh house.

The conversation over the tea and sandwiches was predictably stilted, but neither Delia nor Noelle could complain that the doctor wasn't nice to them. Although, Noelle thought ruefully, she had gone on at great length about how wonderful Anna Quinn had been as a housemaid, and had said that she knew that it was going to be hard for Noelle, being younger, to fill her shoes.

'Noelle's used to hard work at home,' Delia had said, smiling encouragingly at her niece, 'and I'm sure she'll pick up the run of the house in no time at all.' But then she had gone on to agree with Dr Casey just how lucky she had been to have someone so thorough and dependable as Anna Quinn, and wasn't she a great person sacrificing such a grand job to go back to look after her ailing, elderly father?

'A saint,' the doctor sighed, taking a sip from her rose-patterned china cup.

Noelle had bitten into her sandwich, and apart from discovering the unfamiliar flavour of cucumber with tinned salmon, she had been shocked to discover that the thinly cut pan bread had actually been *stale*. She managed to eat three small sandwiches – the bread hard on all of them – and by the time she'd finished the last one, she was beginning to enjoy the unusual cucumber taste mixed with the salmon.

Still, she thought, as she sipped at her tea as delicately as she could from the china cup, it would have to be a very poor day in the Daly household before anyone would have to eat hard bread. Her mother baked two big soda loaves every morning, and scones or apple tart every other day, and they often bought fresh pan bread at the weekends. Their food mightn't be fancy but there was no shortage of basic provisions in the house.

The little white-iced cherry cakes had been very nice although Delia had managed to show herself up by dropping cake crumbs all over the perfect carpet. She had got herself so flustered that she ended up spilling half her tea into the saucer. Noelle had immediately put down her own cup and bent to help her aunt pick up the crumbs. Dr Casey rushed off to the kitchen to get a brush and crumb-tray, and as soon as she went out of the drawing-room door Delia hissed, 'For Christ's sake, Noelle, help me to clear this up before she comes back.' She bent down now and started picking the larger crumbs up as quickly as she could.

In an effort to speed things up, Noelle made to get down on one knee but in her haste she lost her balance and almost toppled over her aunt. There was a silence and then they both went into peals of silent laughter.

'Jesus!' Delia hissed, pushing her niece off her and back on to the sofa. 'You nearly killed the pair of us.' She craned her neck now to see if the doctor was coming back. 'And you've crushed all the crumbs into the feckin' carpet and she'll think it was me!' She continued to anxiously scrabble around for more crumbs.

'She'll probably just be glad that it's me that's coming to work for her,' Noelle giggled, 'and not you!'

'She doesn't know what she's taken on,' Delia said, dramatically rolling her eyes to the ceiling. 'The blidey house could fall down with the likes of you in charge.'

'Is everything all right, ladies?' the doctor's formal tones called from the hall as she headed back in with her fancy little antique crumb-tray in one hand and brush in the other.

There was a small pause, then both voices called, 'We're grand . . . thanks, Doctor.'

Chapter 15

Noelle followed the doctor through the kitchen, and then they went out of the door next to the pantry, across a five-foot-square hallway with an outside door, and into a tiny bedroom that barely held the two of them standing in it.

'This is your private quarters,' Dr Casey told her, indicating the narrow single bed and the small grainy-oak wardrobe with a narrow mirrored panel running down the front, which stood to the side of the window. There was a bedside table squeezed in between the bed and the wall, which held a plain white china bowl and jug.

Noelle beheld the little room with definite pleasure. These arrangements were a big step up in the world for her because at home she shared a room and a double bed with Sarah, and had never slept a night on her own.

'You have an electric light switch for night time,' the doctor continued, flicking the brown switch up and down to demonstrate how it worked.

Noelle nodded, a little excited blush coming to her freckly cheeks.

'Your toilet arrangements are out here,' Bernadette Casey said, going back into the hall and opening the outside door. She pointed across the garden to a little wooden shed with two plant pots on either side of the door. 'There's a flush toilet out there which you have all to yourself. There's also a tin bath that you might like to use on occasions when you have the house to yourself. There's toilet paper and cleaning equipment there for you, too, and I think you'll find that Anna Quinn left a good-sized candle and holder for you as well.'

Noelle felt a surge of pleasure at the sound of the words *flush toilet*. At home they had a similar little shed at the bottom of the garden, but it was more of a makeshift affair than this nicely painted construction. The Dalys' toilet back in Ballygrace was dry – a bucket half filled with sawdust or turf-mould which had a wooden toilet seat arranged over two stout planks of wood. And their 'toilet paper' was the *Irish Independent* or the local newspaper cut up into tidy squares and hung on a rusting nail with a piece of string. It was the same with all their neighbours, the Flowers included.

'We'll sort out your uniform when I come in this evening,' the doctor said, going back through the kitchen and into the hallway. 'But I'll show you upstairs now, so you have an idea of the lay-out of the house, and where you will be coming and going to.'

As they passed the open drawing-room door, Noelle glanced in and saw her aunt perched anxiously on the edge of the sofa. She caught her eye and when Delia raised her eyebrows in question, Noelle held her thumb up in approval.

Their footsteps made not a sound as they made their way upstairs on the thick-piled blue carpet which was fitted the full width of each step and then continued all the way along the landing leading to the bedrooms.

Dr Casey strode along, her confident manner giving the impression of a taller, more formidable person. Noelle followed behind, suddenly feeling self-conscious of her own taller, more solid frame. She knew she wasn't fat by any manner of means, but she was definitely larger in every way than this elfin woman. The doctor – although small – appeared as though there was nothing she wasn't capable of, mentally or physically.

'This is my bedroom,' the doctor announced, opening the first door at the top of the stairs. It was a good-sized bedroom with two windows dressed with red velvet curtains and a fringed pelmet, but on the whole it was surprisingly plain, with subdued pink flowery wallpaper, a dark wardrobe that was only a larger version of the one in Noelle's little room, a dressing-table and a small chest of drawers. The small high double bed had plain white sheets and pillow-cases with a faded pink counterpane on top.

'I have my breakfast in bed every morning around eight o'clock,' the doctor informed her now. 'I usually have bread and butter with two slices of bacon and an egg and mushrooms during the working week.' She glanced at Noelle now, as though weighing her up. 'So you will have to give yourself plenty of time to get up and dressed and get the kettle and the frying pan going. I have to be up and out of the house for nine o'clock.'

'Grand, grand,' Noelle said, nodding her head profusely. There was nothing that had been mentioned that sounded too difficult, nor anything she wasn't used to doing at home. In fact, she was surprised that the doctor didn't want something fancier. But Noelle wasn't allowing herself to be too confident, as she guessed that the doctor would want something more substantial in the evening that would stretch any cooking skills she had to the very limit.

They moved back out into the carpeted landing and down to another door. 'This is my niece, Gabrielle's, room. She's at school in the Isle of Wight during term time, but she spends most of her time here when she's in Dublin.'

'Will she be here later today?' Noelle asked curiously.

'No,' Dr Casey told her, 'she's on holiday in France at the moment.'

'I see,' Noelle said, nodding her head. She must ask Delia about the niece, because she hadn't heard any mention of her before.

They went to the end door down the landing, which was the bathroom. 'One of your duties will be to clean and check this every single morning,' the woman said, pointing to the white porcelain sink and toilet bowl. She tapped her finger on a small cupboard by the side of the sink. 'There's bleach and disinfectant and such-like things there for your use. I cleaned it myself this morning, but you might just give it a more thorough going over this afternoon, and perhaps mop the floor.'

Noelle wasn't a bit surprised that the doctor was fussy about the toilet and sinks, and she would make sure they were spotless. Sure, didn't a doctor know everything there was to know about germs and diseases and the like? She wouldn't be much of a doctor if she wasn't fussy. 'Grand,' the new maid said, as though she were used to being in such a luxurious bathroom every day of her life, with hot and cold running water and thick towels on the radiator beside the bath.

There was only one room they hadn't been in, at the far end of the hall, which the doctor informed Noelle was her study. 'That only needs cleaning and polishing once a week,' she told her new housemaid, 'so we can leave that until we have more time.' She checked her tiny gold watch. 'I have to go in a few minutes, so that's all we can do for the moment.' Then, as they walked back downstairs, she said, 'I usually have my lunch at work and then I have a boiled egg and bread and butter when I come back in the evening. A bit of toast or a scone around nine o'clock does me for supper before bed.'

Noelle was surprised at the simplicity and frugality of the doctor's diet. Sure, they had a far bigger meal at home every evening of the week than that.

Delia was standing at the white marble fireplace. The empty grate was covered by a wooden fire-screen, lavishly decorated with an embroidered peacock. She was looking at the family photographs lined up on either side of a glass-domed clock which had a pendulum that went round in a circle. She scurried back to her perch on the corner of the sofa when she heard Noelle and her new employer coming back down the stairs.

'If it's of any help, I can give you a lift back into The Quays, Mrs Clarke,' Dr Casey said, walking into the drawing-room. 'It would save you the trouble of getting the bus.'

There was a little pause as Delia considered the offer.

'You can decide while I'm getting my keys and my jacket,' the doctor said, obviously not bothered one way or the other.

'You should go in the car,' Noelle urged her in a whisper. 'It's a nice fancy one.'

Delia's mind worked quickly. If she took the lift she would have the treat of sitting in the front seat of a car and she would have longer to spend around the shops in Henry Street. But it would also mean having to talk to the doctor all the way into the city and try to sound all highfalutin and intelligent.

Noelle had a point though, Delia reasoned to herself, she would be able to brag to everyone back home about a posh doctor giving her a lift in a fancy car. She would be able to dine out on the chat about it for a good while, and she could maybe take the chance of asking Dr Casey for advice about her husband's gout. She turned to her niece, lifting her handbag. 'D'you know . . . I think I will take the lift.'

When the car pulled out of the driveway taking her Auntie Delia – the only familiar person she really knew in the whole of Dublin – Noelle Daly suddenly felt very alone. After waving them off, she closed the heavy front door and walked down the hallway to the drawing-room, where they had all had their tea and sandwiches just a short while ago. She slowly walked across the room to the big bay window and stood for a few moments looking through the dull lace curtains.

Noelle watched the street outside, people coming and going, children on holiday from school playing in gardens or going for a walk out, and then she counted the cars going up and down the road. Altogether, she counted six in the fifteen silent minutes she stood peeping through the lace.

You could wait all day in Ballygrace Main Street before you would see six cars going past, she thought. And you could wait outside the Dalys' house at the canal all week and never see even *one* car go past.

She suddenly wondered how things were back at home – how Sarah was getting on without her and what she was doing. It was only this morning since she saw her . . . but it somehow seemed an awful lot longer.

She thought of her sister and her mother and everyone back at home, and then Noelle turned to wonder about Kate and how she would get on at Peter O'Brien's funeral. She thought about the two phones she had seen in this big Dublin house earlier on, and she wished there was a phone at home or at the Flowers' so she could ring up and ask about all the things that had happened in her absence. Not that she expected anything major to happen. It never did. It was more the small, inconsequential things that would mean nothing to anyone else – the things that had been the mainstay of her life, until she had moved today up to this big, busy city.

Then, Noelle was jolted out of her mounting homesickness when she spotted a fair-haired girl around her own age coming along the pavement towards Dr Casey's house. She slowed down as she reached the gate and, almost coming to a halt, she looked directly up at the window where Noelle was standing. Then, she actually stopped and leaned her hand on the gatepost, staring straight up at the house. She stood for a few moments, as though debating whether or not to come in, but then she seemed to make up her mind and suddenly went off at a stride and turned into the gate next door. Within seconds her blonde hair was lost behind the dense foliage and the bushy trees.

Curious, Noelle stepped forward to the right-hand side of the window and pulled the brocade curtains back far enough to let her peep out at the gap between the lace and the window-frame. She was rewarded by the sight of the girl's pony-tail bobbing along above the panelled fence that divided the two houses. She watched as the girl took out a key and let herself into the neighbouring house. The door closed behind her and then the heavy silence in Dr Casey's house descended all around Noelle Daly once again.

Chapter 16

❧

The church was packed out with mourners, just as Kate's mother had predicted. Big farmers always drew big crowds to their funerals, and Peter O'Brien was no exception. As the three Flowers cycled along the canal tow-path towards Tullamore, they could see people walking purposefully over the bridge and down the streets heading in the direction of the church. Turning down the small road to the church, they could see the crowds outside in the yard – and just by the church door, the shiny black funeral car.

'Bad oul' feckin' business,' Brendan said under his breath as they dismounted their bikes.

'Shush and don't be cursing outside the house of God,' Mary admonished. She looked at Kate and shook her head in despair at his tactlessness.

The three cycles were leaned against the church wall amongst numerous others, then Kate and her mother quickly took out their black lace mantillas from their handbags and carefully draped them over their heads. Both wore black outfits that were kept especially for sombre occasions like today, while Brendan looked well polished and handsome in his dark suit and black tie.

'Where do you want to sit?' Mary whispered to Kate as they walked towards the church door.

'Around the middle will be fine,' Kate whispered back, dipping her fingers into the holy water font. She certainly did not want to be anywhere near the O'Brien family and the main mourners. Under normal circumstances she would have gone up to the front and offered her condolences to the whole family, but given the tragic scene she had been part of out at their house on Sunday and the harsh truths Agnes O'Brien had spoken at the cottage yesterday, she knew that it wouldn't be expected. Kate reckoned that she would see how things looked after the Mass and then decide whether or not she and her mother would join the mourners for the meal as invited.

They paused for a few moments at the back of the church to look for a suitable pew and Mary turned to Brendan. 'Are you coming in with us?'

'I'll stand at the back,' Brendan replied, running a finger around the collar of the sparkling white shirt his mother had starched for him the night before. He cast a glance around the other men at the back of the church to see if there was anyone he knew. A man in his thirties leaning casually against the wall at the back corner caught his eye, and Brendan recognised him from the butcher's shop they bought the meat from for the boat.

Immediately Brendan made his way over to join him. This was exactly the type of company that he was looking for, with the chance of a bit of light-hearted banter and maybe a few pints in the pub afterwards. Brendan knew well by the cut of his head and his red face on a Monday morning that the butcher's lad would be looking for a drink the very same as himself. Especially with the hot weather and the cycle back out from Tullamore to be faced later in the day.

Funerals could be miserable enough unless you got in with the right company, Brendan reckoned. Different if it was a family member or a close neighbour, but when it was a man that you'd never met in your life, it was always better if you had somebody to liven things up a bit. There was no point in having a day off work if you couldn't knock a bit of enjoyment out of it.

'Well,' the fellow said as Brendan approached him. He gave a sidelong grin. 'How's it goin'?' His face became more serious, although his eyes were still sparkling with humour. 'I'd say the O'Briens have got a fierce land with the father just droppin' dead like that? No warning or nothing from what I hear.'

Brendan leaned his elbow up on the stone window-sill. 'I'd say they did, although I never met the man meself.'

The butcher's assistant nodded his head. 'Neither did I. Bad oul' business all the same . . .' He nodded to the front of the church. 'I didn't know Michael had three fine-lookin' sisters. I saw them all comin' in a few minutes ago. The smaller ones are a bit on the young side, but that eldest one is a fine specimen.' He leaned towards Brendan. 'Is she walkin' out with anyone, do you know?'

Brendan stretched up to his full height then craned his neck to look down to the pews in front of the altar. Disappointingly, he could only see the back of their black-covered heads 'I know hardly nothin' about them at all,' he said in a low voice. 'Mickey doesn't be talkin' about his family too much, and I'd say he's not the kind that would take too kindly to you messin' around with his sisters.'

The butcher lad nodded. 'Nice enough lad,' he said, pulling a face and giving a slow, meaningful wink, 'but fierce serious at times, isn't he? He can be deadly.'

'He can be good enough craic on the boat,' Brendan said, raising his eyebrows, 'good with the oul' guitar . . . but he can be mighty serious at times.' His mind flashed back to the heated conversation between him and his workmate outside Ballygrace church. And all over his sister who couldn't take an oul' joke. Brendan's brows knitted together. 'Ah, you're feckin' right there, Michael O'Brien can be a mighty serious man altogether.'

They stood in silence for a few minutes, observing the mourners as they came in. Then the lad leaned over and gave Brendan a light dig in the ribs. 'Who's the blondey one that just came in with the oul' lad?' He motioned towards an attractive girl helping what looked like her elderly father into one of the back pews.

Brendan narrowed his eyes to study the girl more closely. 'I haven't seen her around at all,' he whispered back. 'And she's not the kind you would forget in a hurry.'

'Indeed not,' the fellow replied. 'I've never seen her in the shop anyroads.' A sly look came on his face. He cast a glance around to make sure none of the men beside him were listening. He lowered his voice, speaking out of the side of his mouth. 'I wonder is she partial to a bit of steak now and again – or maybe even an oul' sausage? What would you say? Is there any likelihood of her comin' into the shop looking for a bit?'

Brendan grinned at him. This was exactly the type of craic that he enjoyed – the type of banter that Michael O'Brien disapproved of. 'Oh, you can never tell,' he whispered back. He glanced over at the girl who was now settled in the pew and reading through her prayer-book. 'She looks strait-laced enough, but that goes for nothing.' He leaned in closer now. 'Looks can be very deceivin'.

I've often found the strait-laced ones to be the best once you get them goin'.'

The butcher's shoulders heaved up and down in subdued laughter. 'I'd say you'd be well versed in those kind of matters.'

'Oh, begod, I've certainly had me times,' Brendan whispered, giving a bit of a laugh. 'I can't deny it – I've had me times.'

Mary and Kate sat very straight and still in their pew. Mary cast the odd surreptitious glance through the lace mantilla to see if there were any familiar faces, but apart from a few of the boatmen that she was acquainted with through Brendan, she spotted no-one she knew particularly well.

Kate looked very pious with her rosary beads entwined around her fingers, staring up at the altar. But prayers were far from her mind as she mulled over the events of the last few days. Truthfully, the actual funeral Mass wasn't upsetting her the way funerals of people she knew would have – although she was heart sorry for Michael and his family. She hadn't known Peter O'Brien at all. She'd only met him for those few uncomfortable hours.

No, it wasn't the funeral that was discomfiting her – it was the whole business of her and Michael O'Brien that was uppermost in her mind.

As the parish priest and his entourage of visiting priests came out and started the funeral Mass, Kate's thoughts flitted back and forth from the solemn religious service to her ill-fated romance with Michael. She couldn't work out where their friendship was going to go from now on. She knew that he would have to have a bit of time off work to sort out all the business at home with the farm and everything. And she also knew that, whatever happened, not one of the O'Brien family had been happy with Michael walking out with her.

In fact, she wasn't too sure what she thought of it all herself now. With everything that had happened recently, she felt he was back to being even more of a stranger than he had been when they first met. All the nonsense that Brendan had stirred up over Michael supposedly having another girl had been bad enough, but after the awful visit to his house and then Agnes O'Brien coming out to the cottage, she wasn't sure she knew him as well as she thought.

The picture of Michael O'Brien that she had first been impressed with had been the quiet boatman who carried his guitar around and had a nice easy-going nature. But that picture had been erased and she wasn't quite sure what she felt about this sombre, dark-suited man who had sat at the table in his home on Sunday with the rest of his very sombre-looking family.

As the Mass progressed from the offertory to Communion and then to the final prayers, Kate found herself dreading the walk to Tullamore Cemetery and then the cycle out to the family house for the funeral lunch. Apart from having to speak to the O'Brien family again, she could tell by the way the sun was glinting through the stained-glass holy windows that she would probably arrive at the house all hot and perspiring, and looking anything but her best.

'We'll be grand,' her mother told her as they stood to the side of the church yard watching and waiting as all the chief mourners filed out. The men came first carrying the coffin – headed by Michael and his brother Thomas – and then out came Agnes O'Brien and the girls. Mary leaned over to Kate. 'The mother and the daughters are all very good-looking like Michael, but if you look, there's hardly a tear out of them,' she whispered. 'I wonder if that's their nature, or if maybe they're still in shock?'

Kate gave a little shrug. 'I don't know,' she told her mother quietly. 'I wouldn't know what any of them would be thinking.' And as she watched Michael now, helping to push the coffin into the back of the big black hearse, she realised that she wouldn't have the slightest clue as to what he was thinking either.

'I'm sure they're all upset in their own way,' Mary said in a slightly distant voice. 'It's just that some people find it hard to show it . . .'

'He was Mrs O'Brien's husband and the girls' father,' Kate whispered back, 'so they're bound to be upset.'

Mary Flowers nodded vaguely. She was now going back over Kate's father's funeral where she had experienced a myriad feelings herself – sometimes changing from minute to minute. At times she had been relieved that the long years of living in a house with a man she didn't – couldn't – love as a husband were over. Then, almost as soon as she had felt it, she would find herself engulfed with guilt and fear. Guilt at feeling relief that a good, decent man was dead and then fear at what her future might hold without him. She had even felt excited in the dark of the nights following the funeral, thinking about the freedom and choices that might lie ahead for her now that she was a free girl again.

Except that she wasn't. She was neither a girl nor free.

By the time Seamus Flowers died, Mary could not be called a girl by any stretch of the imagination. She was a woman in mid-life – and her reflection in the mirror told her that she looked every last day of it.

And even if she hadn't been past her prime, she soon realised that the girlish dreams of meeting a boyfriend at a dance had long faded. In the years since her marriage she had grown into a well-respected wife and mother. She was regarded as a pleasant-faced, pleasant-natured woman who, now widowed, would be expected to devote the rest of her life to her son and daughter.

Oh, she would be allowed the odd outing at Christmas and the summer without any fault being found, and indeed there would be plenty of encouraging comments that she was entitled to enjoy a nice trip out now and again with her children by her side. And over the coming years that would no doubt extend to encompass grandchildren as well.

But that's all it would be. She would certainly not be expected to have any kind of an independent life that might just leave room for a man. And she couldn't allow herself to be seen looking for a man. Not if she wanted to keep her reputation.

Not under any circumstances.

'You go to the door first,' Mary Flowers urged as they leaned their bicycles against the wall of the farmhouse. She had kept up a good front for Kate in the church and on the bicycle ride out to the O'Briens' house, but now her nerves were defeating her. Nothing she had heard about the family gave her any cause to feel confident or genuinely welcome in this house.

'We'll just give ourselves a few minutes to catch our breath and tidy up,' Kate said quietly. She went to the saddle-bag at the back of her cycle and took out her small black handbag and a packet of paper hankies. She opened the tissues and handed a couple to her mother then she took the same for herself and proceeded to rub them across her hot, damp face. Next she took her compact from her handbag and after checking her reflection she dabbed the pad across her pink-flushed face to tone it down. She took her lipstick out of the bag and carefully outlined her lips, then she passed the compact and lipstick over to her mother. She then reached into the clutch bag for her small hairbrush and after loosening her thick curly hair from its pony-tail, she then started to brush her hair out.

'We'll be grand,' her mother repeated nervously, looking at herself in the mirror and trying not to see the crow's feet and the lines that were starting to appear around her mouth. 'We'll be grand . . . '

'Is my hair okay?' Kate asked now, trying to keep her voice steady and not un-nerve her poor mother any further.

'Beautiful,' Mary told her, reaching to touch one of the long, thick curls. 'You're very lucky, your hair is always beautiful.'

Just then the sound of the front door opening gave both women a jolt. Quickly, Kate pushed her brush back into her clutch bag while Mary stuffed the tissues into her own small beaded bag.

'Kate, Mrs Flowers,' Michael O'Brien said, coming towards them, 'I'm delighted that you both came . . . I looked out for you several times in the last while.' He put his hands out to Kate then clasped hers tightly.

Kate was taken aback by this open show of affection, and relaxed a little as she felt the warmth of his hands on hers. It reminded her of the long, sunny afternoons when they had walked together along the banks of the canal. 'I hope your family are all coping as well as they can under the circumstances.'

He closed his eyes for a second, and then he just nodded his head.

'We've been thinking about you and praying for you,' Mary said, her eyes full of concern. 'And your poor mother and all the family . . .'

He nodded his head. 'It was a terrible shock, the way it all happened.' He looked at Kate now, his eyes searching her face. 'Are you all right, Kate?' he asked.

'I'm grand, Michael,' she said in a soft voice. 'I suppose we're just feeling a little bit anxious about meeting everyone.'

'Don't be,' he said, squeezing her hand. 'There's nothing at all to be anxious about.' He turned to Mary now. 'You know my mother called out at the cottage yesterday?'

'Of course,' Mary said. 'It was very good of her . . . the poor woman. Taking the time to come out to the house with everything that she's going through.'

'How are you all coping?' Kate asked quietly, looking at him directly now.

Michael shrugged. 'I suppose we're managing in a fashion,' he said. 'There are so many things to sort out with the funeral and the farm and everything . . .'

'Indeed,' Mary Flowers said understandingly. 'I know all about it . . . when Kate's father died we had the same kind of thing.'

He gestured towards the back of the house. 'If we go into the kitchen,' he suggested, putting his hand under Kate's elbow to guide her along, 'you can have a cup of tea or a sherry or whatever you like, while you're waiting to have the meal served.'

'Is there many in the house, Michael?' Mary asked anxiously as she followed behind, picking her steps carefully with her heeled shoes on the rough stone path.

'There's a good few in,' he said in a low voice. 'The priests and the nuns and the headmaster and that kind are all eating in the parlour at the minute, and there's another group at the big table in the kitchen.'

'Oh, we'll be grand in the kitchen,' Mary said quickly, 'won't we, Kate?'

Kate's mind flashed back to the tea and sandwiches in the parlour on Sunday. 'Yes,' she agreed, suddenly feeling all awkward again. 'Yes, we'll be more than grand in the kitchen.'

The kitchen was hot and bustling with people. Several neighbours dressed in aprons were tending to pans of potatoes and vegetables on the large cream cooker; two other women were busy cutting slices of glistening brown meat from a large goose that had been cooked the night before, and transferring the cut meat to plates on the table. Around a dozen people were already seated at the huge kitchen table and progressing well with their heaped plates.

'Have you eaten yet, Michael?' one of the women asked, giving a curious glance at the two new arrivals. 'There was a place set in the parlour for you with the rest of the family.'

He hesitated for a moment, glancing around the room and then towards the door that led out to the hallway. 'I'll go inside in a minute, thanks,' he replied politely. He turned to Kate and Mary. 'Can I get you a cup of tea while you're waiting for the meal?'

'You go on in,' Mary urged. 'We'll be grand.'

Kate took a deep breath, just desperate for this whole ordeal to be over and done with. 'I'll sort cups of tea for us both,' she said decisively, putting her handbag down on the window-sill. 'You go and join your family and we'll see you later.'

She eased her way through the small groups, giving a smile to anyone who caught her eye, until she reached the table where an urn of tea was set up along with glasses of sherry and whiskey. Kate lifted two teacups, but when she realised that the milk jug was empty and she would have to go and ask someone to get her some more, she put them back down. Then – on a sudden impulse – she turned to the row of glasses and lifted two small but well-filled schooners of sherry instead. Before she could change her mind or stop to wonder if anyone was watching her, she strode back across the floor and handed her mother one of the glasses.

'Good girl!' Mary said, her eyes lighting up in delighted surprise. She glanced around her, checking that nobody was taking any notice of her, then she took a good-sized gulp of the sweet but strong red liquid. She hadn't liked to mention to Kate that she had been getting little panicky flutters in her chest since she had arrived at the farmhouse and she knew that the sherry would be the very thing to calm it down. She took a deep breath now, feeling the comforting warmth of the sherry as it worked its way down through the tight knot in her chest.

Kate took a small sip of her own sherry and struggled not to shudder at the unusually strong taste. She wouldn't normally go for alcohol as a rule – not that she'd tried that many things, but the taste of beer or whiskey did absolutely nothing for her, and the sherry wasn't a lot better. A cup of tea or milky coffee was more to her liking, but just holding the fancy little sherry glass gave her a feeling of purpose and she knew that the drink might help her mother to relax. 'Do you think Brendan will appear?' Kate now said in a low whisper,

Mary almost choked on her second mouthful. 'Not at all!' she said, her eyes wide with horror at the very thought. 'I told him he wouldn't be expected . . . that none of us would be expected if it hadn't been for the situation on Sunday.'

Kate nodded. 'Good,' she said quietly. 'All we need is him turning up with a skinful of beer on him. And the fella he'd linked up with in the church didn't look a whole lot better. I'd say the pair of them will be well jarred by now.'

'Ah, Kate ...' her mother said, touching her arm and smiling benignly, 'you shouldn't be so hard on poor Brendan. I know he can be a bit of a rake at times, but he's not the worst and he minds the pair of us well.'

Kate gave a little laugh of disbelief and shook her head, her black curls swirling around as she did so. 'Minds us well?' she repeated in an incredulous voice. 'He drives the pair of us flaming mad – that's what he does!'

Then, the door from the hallway opened and Agnes O'Brien came in, followed by two priests and then Michael and his brother.

'That's Michael's mother now,' Kate whispered, taking a sip of her drink.

Mary looked across at the severe-looking woman with her sombre black dress decorated with a nun-like crucifix, her hair tightly pulled back in a greying bun. They stopped at the top end of the room to have a few words with the people there and then after a short while they moved on to the next group.

Instinctively Mary knew that the widow would be across to talk to them soon and that behind all her grief and upset she'd be busy weighing up the kind of family that Kate Flowers came from. The little flutters suddenly came back into Mary's chest and she quickly lifted the glass to her mouth and gulped down the remainder of the sherry in one go.

'This is lovely, Kate, isn't it?' Mary Flowers said as she cut into her slice of goose. Her eyes were bright and sparkling from the two glasses of warming sherry and she was now more relaxed. Her ordeal with Michael's mother hadn't been half as bad as she'd dreaded; in fact the poor woman had been as pleasant as she could have been under the circumstances. She had thanked Mary for coming and said how grateful she was to Kate for trying to help her poor husband when he had collapsed.

Agnes O'Brien had then brought one of the neighbours over and said to let Mrs Flowers and Kate know when there was space at the table in the parlour. Mary and Kate had immediately started to protest, saying that they would be more than happy to eat in the kitchen, but Mrs O'Brien would not hear of it.

Then Michael had joined them and echoed his mother's sentiments that they eat in the more formal room. 'After all the lovely meals I've had out at your home,' he told the two women, 'it's the least we can do.'

'Thank you both for coming to Peter's funeral,' Mrs O'Brien had said, 'and thank you for all your kindness to Michael.'

After the effort that the grieving widow had put in to making them feel welcome, there was really nothing they could do or say that would not have appeared ungrateful or churlish. They would have to go into the parlour with all the other guests.

Kate smiled back at her mother in a manner more reassuring than she actually felt. As she picked at the very nice meal, she wondered just exactly what she was doing there. This whole thing with Michael – which had started off nice and easy and taking its own time – had suddenly grown into a situation she hadn't at all reckoned on. Last Sunday she had felt she was on some kind of trial with the whole O'Brien family – and it was one she had failed dramatically. Then, after the tragic business with Michael's father, she felt that she had been given an unexpected reprieve.

And now, as she looked around this sombre, grieving room, she no longer knew if she wanted them to accept her. And although she liked Michael better than any other lad she'd ever met, there were times when she felt she hardly knew him at all.

Chapter 17

❧

Noelle unpacked her few belongings and hung her dresses and blouses on wooden hangers in the narrow wardrobe. She put her two skirts and her underwear and stockings and winceyette pyjamas in the drawer at the bottom of the wardrobe. She hung her dressing-gown and light nightdress and raincoat on the brass hook behind the bedroom door. Then she put the bar of pink Camay soap and the bottle of Silvikrin shampoo in the small drawer of the table beside her bed, along with her brown mascara and peach-coloured lipstick. She had worn peach lipstick and brown mascara ever since she read in a magazine last summer that they were the shades most suited to redheads.

The last item in her case was the tin of Jacob's biscuits that Kate's mother had given her as a little going-away gift. Noelle had a sneaking feeling that they might have been a Christmas present that somebody had given Mary Flowers, but she was grateful for the biscuits none the less. It wasn't often that such a luxury was available for the family at home, and to have a whole, fancy tin to herself was a treat indeed.

That done, she stood up on her tiptoes to put the empty suitcase on top of the wardrobe and then she walked back to the door to stand and have a good look around her. She stared at the plain walls and the single bed with the wooden and brass crucifix above it, and then moved around to take in the picture on the wall opposite of a bunch of pink roses in a crackled-looking cream jug. The floor was plain varnished wood with a small rectangular rag rug that, although clean and well cared for, had obviously been made a long time ago.

It wasn't bad, she decided. All in all – the room wasn't bad. And, most importantly, it was her own.

Tonight or tomorrow, she decided, she would definitely sit down for half an hour and write to her mother and to Kate and Mary Flowers to let them know how she was getting on. And hopefully, she thought, Brendan might be around when the letter arrived. Maybe Kate might leave it out for him to read, and he would get the surprise of his life to hear that she was living in such luxury in Dublin. He might suddenly see her in a different light and maybe – just maybe – he would realise what he was missing.

Deciding to explore her new surroundings, Noelle went out into the garden, stepped onto the flower-lined path and then took a look around her. The garden at the side was as perfect as the front. She wondered if the doctor tended to the grass and flowers and shrubs herself or whether she had someone come in.

A cold shiver ran through her as it struck her that maybe the garden was part of her household duties! *Surely not?* She thought to herself. Dr Casey hadn't said anything about it, and anyway, she hadn't the foggiest notion about gardening. Then, before she had time to worry any more, she heard a voice calling, '*Excuse me!*' to her from the adjoining fence.

Noelle turned and looked to where the voice was coming from and she spotted a face peering over the fence from next door. Noelle immediately recognised her as the slim blonde-haired girl who she had seen go into the house earlier.

'Howya?' the girl said in a Dublin accent, giving a bright, confident smile. 'You must be the new one – the girl who's taking over from Anna Quinn?'

'That's right,' Noelle said, smiling back. She folded her arms upon her chest and walked over to the fence. 'I'm Noelle Daly from the canal at Ballygrace – near Tullamore.'

The girl raised her eyebrows and shook her head. 'I can't say I've ever heard tell of the places ... Whereabouts are they near?'

Noelle thought for a moment. 'Have you heard of Mullingar or Athlone?'

'Yeah, I'm sure I've heard of them,' the girl said, her head bobbing up and down now, 'but I wouldn't have the foggiest notion where they are.'

Noelle started to laugh. This girl's accent was lively and bubbly and suddenly underlined the fact that she was in an exciting new place where she might meet exciting new people. 'I don't really know myself,' she confessed. 'I think I've only been in Mullingar once and I've *never* been to Athlone!' She shrugged her shoulders. 'But seemingly, they're very near to where we live.'

'And what's brought you all the way up to Dublin?' the girl asked, folding her arms on top of the fence and leaning her head on them.

Noelle shrugged again. 'The woman who was here was leaving and she knew my auntie, so my Auntie Delia spoke up for me and I was told I could come up and start today.'

The girl raised her eyebrows as though thinking hard for a few seconds, and then she suddenly said, 'My name is Carmel, by the way – Carmel Foley.' Then she laughed. 'And I'm not as tall as I look.' She gestured down behind the fence. 'I'm standing up on an old chair, otherwise I'd have to peep through the hole in the fence like a peepin' Tom!'

'I kind of guessed you were standing on something,' Noelle said with a grin. She paused for a moment, suddenly feeling light and giddy, the way she did with Sarah and her friends at home. 'Are you allowed to come over here?' she heard herself suddenly say. 'What I mean is – would you like to come in for a cup of tea?'

Carmel's brow knitted together in thought. 'Is there anybody else in the house? Dr Casey's not around, is she?'

Noelle shook her head, already half-regretting her rash offer. 'No, she's gone off to her work in Dublin . . . I wouldn't be so free offering invites if she was around. I don't think she would approve.'

'I was just thinkin' that meself!' Carmel said, starting to giggle. 'I couldn't imagine herself sittin' down drinking tea between the two of us. She's yer typical old-fashioned, uppity doctor type – an' a real spinster, through an' through.' She thumbed back towards her own house. 'The man I'm workin' for – Ben Lavery, he's a solicitor, like – well, he's a grand boss. A real down-to-earth type an' a good laugh at times. I know from what Anna Quinn used to tell me that he's a lot more easy-going than the doctor.' Her cheeks suddenly flushed and she gave a coy little smile. 'He's a really grand boss . . . he gives me the run of the place when he's not around and lets me bring me friends over to keep me company if he's away for the weekend.'

'That sounds a grand set-up,' Noelle said, feeling a stab of jealousy. But then, she quickly reasoned, it was early days with her new employer, and all those little perks might come in time.

'Oh, I do me work, like,' Carmel informed her. 'I'm up early in the mornin' to get his breakfast ready for him and I do him a lovely meal in the evening, and I keep the place like a palace for him.' She fiddled with a strand of her blonde hair. 'I don't take advantage of the fact he's easy-going, like. I do a good week's work for a good week's wage – so it cuts both ways.'

Noelle wondered how much Carmel's boss was paying her. She herself had no idea what she was going to get from the doctor, but she knew from her Auntie Delia that it wouldn't be as much as Anna Quinn got because she was older. She pushed the thought out of her mind and turned to more pleasurable matters. 'Dr Casey said I could make tea anytime I wanted,' she told Carmel with a big smile, 'and I've got a nice tin of Jacob's biscuits I haven't opened yet.'

Carmel's face lit up. 'That would be grand . . . give me five minutes to lift the rugs I was beatin' back into the house, and then I'll be over to you.'

Noelle rushed back into the house now, all homesickness forgotten as she flew about the kitchen getting the kettle going on the small cooker, and quickly washing the china cups and saucers that had been left soaking in the sink. She pushed away any guilty thoughts at having a visitor behind her employer's back, because she knew that having a friend would make her life up in Dublin much nicer.

'You climbed across the fence? What about your skirt and stockings?' Noelle said with wide, incredulous eyes, as she let her new friend in through the back door.

'Oh, don't mind me – I take it very slow and careful,' Carmel told her, smoothing the back of her skirt down over her neat little bottom. 'I use the chair at Lavery's side, climb on top of the lavvie roof, then slide down.' She gave a grin. 'Mind you, it's a lot easier with trousers on.' She looked over her shoulder at her legs now. 'And I think I got a bleedin' ladder in me tights!'

They walked through the kitchen now and across the hall and into the drawing-room.

'Aren't you bothered that anyone might see you?' Noelle asked. 'Imagine if Dr Casey came out and saw you climbing down the roof of the toilet!' Then she went into a fit of giggles at the thought.

Carmel started laughing along with her. 'Wouldn't it be worse if some of them old nosy folks across the road saw me coming out of me own place and casually walking up the path to visit you? The first chance they got, they'd be on to the doctor and Mr Lavery, tellin' them that we were wasting time chatting and drinking tea all afternoon, when we should be doing our work.'

Noelle's face darkened. 'Would they do that?' she asked in a low voice. 'Would the neighbours report us?'

'There's two in particular who have nothin' else to do all day but peep out through their lace curtains, and it would give them the greatest of pleasure to inform Dr Casey or Mr Lavery that you and me were skiving off from our work.' Carmel gave one of her careless shrugs. 'That's why I jump over the fence – no point in givin' them ammunition to shoot us, is there?' She started laughing again. 'Mind you,' she said, pointing to the tray all set with the rose-decorated teacups and the tin of biscuits, 'they wouldn't be too far off the mark about us chatting and drinking tea in the afternoon, would they? Could you imagine Dr Casey coming home early and catching us drinking out of her fancy china?'

'Maybe it's a good job you jumped over the fence,' Noelle said, 'because I could be out of a job if Dr Casey found out.'

'Don't worry your head about it,' Carmel said. 'Nobody will find out.' She paused, her gaze sweeping the round of the room. 'Would you believe that I've never even been in this room before?' she said in her sing-song Dublin accent, reaching out for one of the fancy chocolate biscuits. She took a bite of the circular biscuit with the hole in the middle, then lay back in an over-relaxed, sprawling position in the armchair, looking around her. 'That Anna Quinn always kept me in the kitchen if I came over.' She pulled a little face. 'She was nice enough – but dead old-fashioned and strict about things.'

Noelle felt a surge of delight to hear something a bit more negative about her predecessor. 'I kind of got that feeling about her, from what my auntie and Dr Casey said, but then I suppose she's old enough to be my mother.'

'You're dead right there,' Carmel agreed. 'In fact, the way she dressed and did her hair, she was more like yer granny!' She pulled a face. 'Anna hardly ever sat down, she was always fussin' about with dusters and polishing or she was faffing about in the garden. She was dead proud of working here for the doctor, and she was that careful an' fussy that you'd think it was her own place.'

'I think it's a lovely room,' Noelle said, deliberately changing the subject. She had heard quite enough about Anna Quinn for today from both her aunt and Dr Casey. The more she heard of the work that the older woman did – especially with extra things like the garden – the more alarmed she felt. She had expected to find fewer things to do in a modern house like this than the work she did at home. 'Don't you think it's a lovely room?'

Carmel shrugged, not terribly impressed. 'It's a bit plain and boring . . . not half as nice as Mr Lavery's. He's got *really* beautiful things – lovely ornaments of white and blue ballerinas and gorgeous little statues that they brought back from Italy and places like that.' She waved her hand around the room as though indicating the filled-up shelves of ornaments. 'They were his wife's of course . . . she obviously had very good taste. She had lovely clothes as well –

some time when I have the house to meself, I'll show them to you. He still has them all in the wardrobes upstairs.'

Noelle straightened up in her chair, suddenly very interested. 'Was she old or young when she died?'

Carmel pursed her lips together in thought. 'Age-wise, I s'pose you'd say she was kind of in-between. Not that old and not that young. Maybe about thirty or thereabouts.'

'And d'you know what she looked like? Was she very good-looking? Have you seen any photographs of her or anything?' Noelle had recently read a book called *Rebecca*, which she'd got out of the library, and this little scenario about photographs and clothes suddenly reminded her of the dead wife in the story.

'Loads,' Carmel said, her eyes widening as she imparted the information. 'She was lovely, nice and slim and blonde hair a bit like me own.' She laughed. 'Not that I'm praisin' myself of course! But no doubts about it – she was a good-lookin' woman.'

Noelle suddenly felt very sensitive, wondering if the girl was having a little dig about her own pale red hair. Having been teased about it so much in school, she was always on the defensive when other people turned the conversation around to hair.

'There's only a wedding photograph on the wall that she's in,' Carmel went on, 'but Mr Lavery has photograph albums in his study and in his bedroom that I've seen.'

'Did he give you them to look at?' Noelle said curiously. She wondered if the doctor would ever show her personal things like that.

Carmel tossed her hair with her hand. 'Well . . . when he has a few jars at the weekend, he's more easy-goin' and talks about things, like.' She raised her eyebrows. 'You know yourself what these men are like, when they have a few pints or whiskeys in them.'

'Oh, men are the very devil,' Noelle said, nodding in agreement, but in truth she wasn't quite sure what Carmel was on about. She only knew that when her own father drank too much he withdrew even further into himself to the point that he said almost nothing. On the other hand, she knew quiet well what Brendan Flowers was like when he had had a few drinks and he was different again. It wasn't so much a case of talking openly with a drink in him, it was more a case of how friendly and often *over-friendly* he became. He was also inclined to be just *nicer* – more complimentary and mannerly – when he was a bit jarred, and Noelle had often wished he showed that side of himself more when he was sober. There were even times when he'd caught up with her and Sarah as they walked home after an evening out, where his talk about his widowed mother and his dead father became almost sentimental.

A picture of Brendan's handsome face floated into Noelle's mind just then, but she quickly pushed it away. She had allowed herself to think well of Brendan Flowers before, and she knew where that had got her.

'And did they not have any children?' Noelle asked now.

'Two boys,' Carmel said, examining her fingernails now. 'Ten and twelve years old. They're at boardin'-school most of the time, thanks be to Jaysus! They're a pair of terrors when they're home for the holidays. I have me hands full then, I can tell you.'

'That must be a big difference,' Noelle said, 'running after the children, when you've had it so nice and quiet.'

'Don't be talkin'!' Carmel said, nodding her head vigorously. 'It's me that knows all that.' She paused, then gave Noelle a slow, sideways look. 'But you'll know the difference yourself when the doctor's niece – *Miss* Gabrielle – comes home from her holidays. She's gone off somewhere foreign – to get away from her father and her stepmother. They hate the bleedin' sight of each other, them pair. That's why she lives with her auntie. When her father got married again she moved across Dublin to live here. She wasn't stupid – she knew she wouldn't get her own way with the new wife, the way she did before. This way she gets the best of both worlds dodgin' between them both.'

'Dr Casey mentioned her . . .' Noelle said, feeling another little pang of alarm now. 'What's she like?'

'What's she like?' Carmel repeated, rolling her eyes to the ceiling in despair. 'Lady bleedin' muck – that's what she's like! Did nobody tell you about her? She's only a year or two older than you and she'll talk to you as if you're somethin' the cat dragged in. That's the type of her. She'll have all her posh pals around an' all, demandin' afternoon tea and the likes. She used to have Anna Quinn runnin' around like a blue-arsed fly when she was home from school.' Carmel gave a snort. 'In my opinion it's a good feckin' kick up the arse she's needin', an' the afternoon tea pourin' over her head.'

'Will she be here all the time when she gets back from her holidays?' Noelle asked, her voice low and anxious now.

'Indeed she will.' Carmel got to her feet now. 'I'll have to be goin' or Ben – I mean Mr Lavery,' she quickly corrected herself, 'will be back home an' I'll have bugger all ready for him.' She picked one more biscuit to eat on her way out. 'I'm surprised they didn't tell you about Miss-bloody-Gabrielle! That's why there was all the rush about gettin' somebody new settled in before she came back from her holidays. Dr Casey could have managed all right on her own for a few weeks, for give her her due, she's not afraid to dirty her hands.' She took a bite of the chocolate biscuit. 'For all she's a doctor, she's not above weedin' the garden or hanging out a line of washing if she has to. Anna Quinn told me that herself.' She looked at the clock on the wall now – it was after half past four. 'Jaysus, I'd better get a move on.' She gestured to the messy coffee table now and the biscuit crumbs littering the pale green carpet. 'An' you'd better get a move on too, Noelle, or she'll be back before you know it.' She raised her eyebrows and looked down her nose in an imitation of the doctor, and then she grinned. 'You don't want to go getting on the wrong side of your boss on your first day, do you?'

'I don't want to go getting on the wrong side of her at all,' Noelle said, with a little anxious sigh.

She accompanied her new friend out into the garden and watched as she hoisted herself up onto the roof of the toilet, balanced on the shaky wooden fence and then hopped down on the other side. Noelle stood up on her tiptoes and looked over the top of the fence.

'See you tomorrow around the same time,' Carmel said, giving Noelle a wave. 'I'd better get on with the dinner before Ben Lavery gets in.' Then she disappeared in through the back gate of the house.

Noelle turned back towards the house now, more than a little rush in her step. There was plenty of work tidying and cleaning to keep her busy until Dr Casey came back, and plenty to think about since she had met Carmel Foley.

As she cleaned away any evidence of her entertaining in the

drawing-room, her mind flitted back over the conversation she'd had with Carmel and the way the girl had talked about her own boss. She certainly seemed to have landed nicely on her feet there, but then, Noelle supposed, Carmel was the type of girl who would land on her feet anywhere.

She went out into the hallway now to the cupboard under the stairs, where Dr Casey had shown her where the brushes and the cleaning things were, and she took out the Ewbank. Then, she came back into the drawing-room and proceeded to run the sweeper back and forth over the crumbs on the carpet.

After she had ensured that the drawing-room and the kitchen were spotless, Noelle quickly moved upstairs to the bathroom with the mop and bucket and spent ten minutes cleaning and scouring in there. She had just emptied the bucket down the sink and put it back under the stairs when she heard the drone of the car engine coming up in the driveway.

'Hello, Noelle,' Dr Casey said, coming into the house carrying her briefcase. 'Has everything gone well this afternoon?'

'Grand,' Noelle said, blushing a little and nodding her head. 'I did everything you asked . . .'

They walked down the hallway and Dr Casey stuck her head into the drawing-room as they passed.

'Lovely . . .' she said, smiling at the perfectly tidy room. They moved onto the kitchen, which equally met her satisfaction. 'I think we might put the kettle on now,' she said, switching on a ring of the Baby Belling.

'I had it boiled for you already,' Noelle said, rushing to lift the kettle up onto the cooker.

'Good girl,' her new employer said, sounding impressed. 'I like to see a young girl who can use her own initiative.' She paused for a moment. 'Did you get yourself settled into your own quarters?'

'Oh, I did,' Noelle reassured her. 'I emptied my case and tidied everything away.'

'Good, good,' the doctor said, looking thoughtful. She turned to Noelle. 'Did you find the afternoon very quiet compared to home?'

Noelle looked at her, not quite sure what to say. If she said *yes*, it might look as though she wasn't happy and maybe even homesick, and if she said *no* it might look as though she was a bit odd saying it wasn't quiet when she was totally on her own. She decided on a safe middle road. 'I suppose it was quiet all right,' she said, giving a little smile, 'but I was so busy that I hardly noticed it.' She nodded her head. 'It was grand . . .'

'That's what I like to hear,' Dr Casey said, 'a young woman who can fill her time well.' She paused. 'I was just thinking that if the weather continues to be nice, maybe I should show you where the gardening things are . . .'

'I meant to say,' Noelle rushed in, 'when I was out in the garden earlier, I met the girl from next door.'

The smile slid from Dr Casey's face and her eyebrows shot up. 'That young Carmel girl that works for Mr Lavery?'

'Yes . . .' Noelle nodded.

'And what did she have to say for herself?' the doctor enquired.

'She was very nice,' Noelle said quickly. 'Very friendly.'

The older woman's hand came up. 'Stop just there!' she said in a brusque manner. 'I should have warned you about that young lady before I left. I should have warned you to have nothing to do with her at all.'

Noelle's cheeks were now bright red and her mouth was in an 'O' of shock. She wondered if someone had told on her – had seen Carmel coming in through the back door and reported her.

'Under no circumstances should you have *anything* to do with that girl!' The doctor wagged her finger now, reminding Noelle of her strictest teachers in school. 'If she calls you when you're out in the garden, just ignore her. And if she persists, tell her you're not allowed to chat to anyone when you're on duty.' She halted, catching her breath, and then her voice dropped a little. 'Is that quite clear, Noelle?'

Noelle swallowed hard and then, in a little thin voice said, 'Yes, Dr Casey.'

'Good,' her employer said, 'because that young lady will take advantage wherever she can, and under no circumstances should you encourage her.'

'Yes, Dr Casey,' Noelle repeated, sounding chastened and shaky. *What if she found out that Carmel Foley had been in her house this very afternoon? And sitting drinking tea in her drawing-room?*

'Now,' the doctor said, moving out into the hall again in her quick, at times jerky manner. 'Let's get onto more important matters now – your uniforms. I have them hanging up in the wardrobe upstairs. Then,' she said as they mounted the stairs, 'we'l have our evening meal. I did tell you already that I usually have a boiled egg in the evenings, didn't I?'

'Yes, Dr Casey,' Noelle said, wondering how her days would pass without the cheery, bright company of her new, short-lived friendship.

Chapter 18

Kate had not expected to see Michael O'Brien the week following the funeral, and she had deliberately made no mention of him to Brendan. On the Sunday afternoon when her brother volunteered the information that Michael had taken the rest of the week off work after his father's burial, she had made no comment. She had busied herself, sorting out the cold remains of the Sunday roast for a meal the following day.

'I heard there's a bit of a dispute goin' on down at O'Briens' about the farm,' he said, sitting back in the armchair, full from the Sunday dinner. 'It's the same oul' shite that goes on with farmers and the family when something like that happens.'

Mary, sitting in the armchair opposite, gave an irritated little tut at his bad language but went back to the cushion cover she was mending and said nothing.

'Mickey could wind up having to leave the boats,' he mused, as he shook out the *Sunday Independent*. 'And that would be an awful pity, because he's just like myself – a sound worker, a grafter.'

'D'you think that might happen?' Mary said, sounding surprised.

'Easily enough,' Brendan told her. 'Anyway, there's talk about the boats stopping altogether in the not too distant future. We could all be out of a feckin' job then.'

Kate looked over at her mother and watched as Mary Flowers' face grew tight and pale. She knew her mother would be worried sick – she was always anxious about anything happening that could leave the two of them in a precarious position. And Kate herself hated the fact she was dependent on Brendan, but given her mother's recent health problems, she had no option but to stay at home and look after her.

'Don't be talking like that,' Mary said in a hushed voice. 'That would never happen . . . surely they'll still need the boats? How would they manage without them?'

'Don't they have the lorries and the trains now?' he said with a shrug. 'They're quicker and cheaper. The oul' boats will soon be a thing of the past.'

'But they could never carry all the things that the boats can carry,' Mary persisted, 'the coal and the turf and . . . and the beet for the sugar factory. And how would Guinness manage without them bringing the barrels of porter down?'

'Like I just explained,' Brendan said, raising his voice now, clearly getting irritated. 'They have their own lorries and every-thing. The oul' boats have as good as had their day. It's the way things go, times have to move on.' He suddenly folded the paper up and put it under his arm, and then he stood up – a clear signal that he was headed for a spell in the small shed at the bottom of the garden. 'The way things are lookin' it could be time for us all to move on. I may start lookin' around for something else myself.'

Mary's face was now drained of life and colour as she sat looking at her son, her sewing needle poised in the air whilst the cushion cover slowly descended into her lap. All sorts of thoughts whirled around in her mind. What on earth would they do if Brendan was out of work? How would they manage? The little bit of savings that Kate's father had left wouldn't last them too long.

'Surely they would give you plenty of advance notice?' Kate suddenly put in. She was always suspicious of Brendan's announce-ments, as they usually turned out to be nothing more than idle chat, and, she felt, they were often designed solely to put the wind up her mother. 'They can't just tell you that you have *no* job?'

'Ah, you wouldn't know what the feckers would do,' Brendan said, tucking the paper higher up under his arm. Then he started whistling 'Danny Boy' and casually sauntered through the kitchen and out of the front door.

'Jesus, Mary and Joseph!' Mary said in a faint voice, gesturing towards the chair that Brendan had just vacated. 'Kate – what are we going to do?' Her right hand flew to the comforting little hollow at the base of her neck. 'What will happen to us all if Brendan loses his job?'

'Don't pay any heed to that fellow,' Kate said, her eyes narrowed in thought. 'We would have surely heard if anything was going to happen – he's only codding you.' She shook her head. 'Do you not think he would have been more worried himself if he thought he was going to lose his job? He didn't sound to me like a man who was the slightest bit worried.' She turned back to her job at the table.

'I wouldn't be too sure,' Mary said, her voice sounding a little breathless. 'Maybe he's planning on moving to America after all—'

'*America?*' Kate repeated. She lifted her head, her brows furrowed in confusion. 'Brendan going to America?'

Mary slowly nodded her head, her hand still unconsciously stroking the base of her throat. 'I didn't say anything at the time . . . but I found American newspapers in his coat pocket the week before last.' Her voice was weak and fading away. 'I knew it the minute I saw them. I knew there was something in the air.'

Kate recognised the signs of her mother getting agitated and possibly working herself into a state. 'He could have picked them up anywhere,' she said in a low, soothing voice. 'There are plenty of folk around here who get papers sent over from America.'

'I'm not so sure,' Mary went on. 'He usually only reads the Irish papers. He must have something new in his mind to be reading American newspapers.'

'But did he say anything about actually *going* to America?' Kate persisted. 'I don't recall him ever showing the slightest interest in it before. He was always bragging about his great job on the canal and how he couldn't imagine how all these fellows could leave Ireland and head for England or America.'

'I would have said the very same meself up until now,' Mary whispered, 'but there was the section in the newspaper all about jobs, and he had even marked some of them.' She pursed her lips. 'I saw it with my own eyes . . .'

'What kind of jobs?' Kate asked, her whole demeanour suddenly serious.

'There was all different kinds,' Mary said, glancing over at the door in case Brendan came back in and caught them talking about him. 'But the ones that were marked were all bar jobs.' She took a deep breath. 'And they were in places like New York and Boston and there was a whole list of them marked for a funny place called Yonkers.'

'Why don't you ask him outright?' Kate said now. 'We need to know what's happening . . . if he has any plans to move away then we should be the first to know.'

There was a small pause.

'It might be innocent enough,' Mary said, picking her sewing back up again. *Busy hands,* her mother had always said, *make busy minds and leave no room for worrying.* 'You know what Brendan's like. There's no point in putting ideas into his head about emigrating to America . . . we'll just leave it and see what happens.'

The following Friday evening when Brendan came home from work, he informed Kate over dinner that Michael O'Brien was back on the boats.

'Seemingly, they've worked out some kind of a system back at the farm that'll let Mickey work on for a while longer,' he said. 'They've got some oul' lad helping them out that knows the run of the place well, and he'll give the brother a hand until Mickey is home at the weekends.'

'It sounds as though he's going to be very busy,' Kate said, handing the dish of potatoes to her mother.

Brendan leaned over and poked Kate in the ribs, knowing that it would annoy her intensely. 'Ah, but you needn't think your boyfriend has forgot you,' he said in a mocking tone. 'He said to tell you when he has five minutes to spare he'll drop out to see you.'

'Oh, Kate!' her mother said delightedly. 'Isn't that lovely? Michael says he's going to call out to see you again.'

Kate raised her eyebrows, her face serious. 'Lucky me . . .' she said airily, looking back at them both. 'But maybe I won't have five minutes to spare to see him.'

There was a stunned silence, then Brendan looked over at his mother and shook his head.

'Women,' he said, his voice coming out in a low sigh. 'You can't do right for doing wrong as far as they're concerned.'

'Kate,' her mother gasped. 'Poor Michael! How can you say such a thing? He's just lost his father . . .'

Brendan guffawed and pointed his knife in his sister's direction. 'Oul' hard-hearted Hannah there won't give a shite about that. When she gets her dander up, we may all look out. None of us are safe from that sharp tongue.'

'Shut up, you,' Kate told him in a low, hissing voice. She turned to her mother. 'I don't know if there's any point in us meeting up. After seeing him with his family, I'm not sure if we have that much in common.'

It was around six o'clock on the Saturday evening when Kate heard the drone of the motor car coming along the tow-path to the cottage. Her heart quickened as she recognised the engine noise and knew immediately it was Michael O'Brien.

It was strange to see him come in the car, because she had imagined this scene in her mind for the past week, where he would turn up at the house unannounced, and then – when she managed to get him on his own as he was leaving – she would have to explain the change in her feelings towards him.

She felt more than a little disconcerted when she saw him get out of the shiny black car, because she had pictured him arriving on his familiar black bicycle. The car somehow underlined the differences between them – or rather it underlined the differences between their families.

She glanced at herself in the shaving-mirror by the sink, then hurriedly pulled a brush through the long thick curls that she had shampooed earlier in the afternoon.

She had taken time for herself after she had washed and hung out to dry Brendan's work clothes and a few bits and pieces of her own and her mother's. She had then helped her mother scrubbing and cleaning around the kitchen while she waited on the pans of water heating on top of the range for her bath. She had carried first the tin bath and then the heavy pans of warm water into the privacy of the bedroom she shared with her mother. She had knelt in the tin bath and poured several large jugs of water over her hair as she shampooed and washed it.

After her bath, Kate had stood in the kitchen in her dressing-gown chatting to her mother and ironing the freshly dried clothes that had been brought in from the washing-line. All these simple routines had been the pattern of her days since fate had conspired to dictate that she stay at home to look after her mother.

Mary had sat at the kitchen table peeling the potatoes and vegetables for the evening meal, relaxed and enjoying dissecting Noelle Daly's latest letter. They had then discussed Brendan and his situation with the boats, and decided that he had definitely been exaggerating how bad things were the previous week. He had made no more mention of it, and the subject of emigrating to America had not crossed anyone's lips in the house. They had chatted about other local news and events, but Mary had studiously avoided the thorny subject of Michael O'Brien.

And now, as he stepped out of the car, Kate didn't know whether to be relieved or anxious that her mother was out. Mary had walked down to the Daly house, taking with her Noelle's letter describing all the latest goings-on in Dublin. Mary knew that Mrs Daly, and Sarah particularly, would want to hear any news, albeit second-hand through the Flowers. Noelle did keep regular contact with her mother and sister but they were always happy to hear any extra little snippets of news in between their own letters.

Brendan had gone fishing that morning with two lads from Ballygrace and hadn't returned as yet – so that left Kate to see to her visitor entirely on her own.

She walked to the door now, summoning up all the words she had practised saying to him in her head. All the things about how they weren't really suited, and how he would be much too busy with his work and the farm to have time to go dancing or for long walks by the canal in the evening.

And then she opened the door and Michael O'Brien was standing there. His clear blue eyes met hers and all the words and reasons she had ready deserted her.

His hand reached out to touch hers. 'Can I come in, Kate?' he said in his mannerly, gentle way.

And Kate silently turned and led him into the cottage, feeling exactly as she had done the first time she saw him, his handsome face and bright eyes touching something deep within her once again.

An hour later, after they had talked and listened to each other, and after Michael had kissed her several times with increasing intensity, Kate realised that her time with Michael O'Brien was far from over.

She now knew that it had only just begun.

Chapter 19

Kate took the letter from Mr O'Reilly, the postman. 'You're sure you won't come in for a cup of tea?' she checked. 'We had tea a short while ago and there's still some in the pot.'

'Ah sure, I'm fierce busy this morning,' he told her, pushing his stiff cap back on his head. 'You see, I went into Behans, and the old lady set about makin' me tea and she said there was a batch of scones ready to come out of the oven.' He shook his head. 'I had the second cup nearly finished by the time they were baked and she insisted on me eating two of the scones. Sure, they were that hot they nearly roasted the mouth off of me.'

'Well,' Kate said, trying not to laugh, 'you're more than welcome to another cup if you'd like one.'

He hesitated for a second, and then he pushed his sleeve up to check his watch. 'Ah, begod, no . . . I'd better leave it be for this morning.' He gestured further along down the canal bank. 'I have a parcel for the Flahertys on the bike and that'll add another few minutes on to my round. It looks like their luck's in – it has American stamps on it, from their son Declan in New York no doubt.' He gave a little sigh. 'No shortage of money out there, I'd say – there's probably a good few dollars in it, I'm thinking.'

'Good luck to them,' Kate said, smiling. 'And isn't it nice that he thinks of them?'

'Oh, indeed it is,' Mr O'Reilly said, bringing his cap back to a straight position on his head now. 'No more than yourself, Kate – lookin' after your mother inside there.' He lowered his voice and thumbed towards the cottage door. 'Is she keeping well these days? Is she back to her old self?'

'She's grand, Mr O'Reilly,' Kate told him. 'She's just grand.' Kate saw him out to the gate then went back into the house.

'Is that *another* letter from Noelle?' her mother asked, dusting her floury hands together. She then rubbed them down the front of her faded apron. 'The poor girl must be very lonesome to be writing to you so often.'

Kate opened the envelope and took out the two folded sheets of notepaper. She quickly scanned down one then handed it to her mother, then went onto the second. 'There can't be too much wrong with the job,' she remarked. 'From what she's written in the letter, she sounds happy enough.' She smiled at her mother. 'I think she was just writing back to let me know that she was delighted about myself and Michael going out together again . . .'

'Ah, sure, Kate,' her mother smiled, 'aren't we *all* delighted?' She gave her daughter a warm smile and then she went back to the letter. 'I see Noelle was out at her Auntie Delia's again on her day off, and she mentioned that she had another afternoon out at Stephen's Green with a girl that works in the house next door.' Mary looked over at Kate now, beaming at the good news. She loved receiving letters from people and particularly enjoyed all the small details that gave her a picture of what the other person was going about on a daily basis. 'Ah, we've no need to worry about Noelle by the sounds of it. And she's certainly getting to know the big city of Dublin, comin' and going on the buses and everything.'

'She mentioned at the end that she'll be home for a weekend before the summer's over.'

'It won't be while we're away, I hope,' her mother muttered, reading down the page. 'She says she's not too sure when it will be,' she answered herself, having just come to that part. 'But it will probably be towards the end of August.' She gave a little tut now. 'I'm sure it will be around that last fortnight sometime when we're away.'

'If she comes home while we're over in England,' Kate says, 'then we can always take the bus or the train up to Dublin when we come back, and meet up with her then. Wouldn't a day up in Dublin be lovely?'

'It would,' Mary agreed, but instead of her looking happy about Kate's suggestion, her face suddenly became more serious. 'She said she hoped that Michael doesn't miss you too much when we go over to your Auntie Rose's . . .' She looked up at Kate, the letter resting on her lap. 'Maybe you'd rather not go now . . .'

'Not at all. Sure, he'll manage just fine without me,' Kate said airily, 'just the same way that Brendan will manage without the two of us.'

'I wish Brendan would come with us,' Mary sighed, all the light-heartedness seeping out of her. 'He used to enjoy it when he came over to Stockport with us . . . and it's nice to have a man on the boat with ye to manage the tickets and everything . . .'

'We'll be grand,' Kate told her in a firm voice, recognising the note of anxiety creeping into her mother's tone. The fact was, Kate needed a break from her brother, and the last thing she wanted was to have the selfish Brendan dominating the trip over and then having her mother and her auntie waiting on him hand and foot.

Her Auntie Rose wasn't as easy-going or as soft as her mother – running a fruit and vegetable business meant she had to be able to stand her corner where the men at the markets were concerned. And she was no soft touch when it came to her English husband Graham and his drinking. Kate had often heard her giving out to him when he went to the pub on his way home from work and the like. But fit and all as Rose was, she would always soften for the fortnight when her nephew was over from Ireland, and would end up laughing about the state of Graham and Brendan when they came in jarred from the local Irish clubs. And always, on the last weekend of their holiday, the women would join in with the men and have a night dancing at the club. As far as Kate was concerned, it was always the low point of the holiday, as she would feel self-conscious and embarrassed when Brendan inevitably drank too much and carried on in his customary way with the ladies.

It would be a great relief, she now thought, to be away without him and she wasn't going to worry about him one little bit.

And though Kate would miss Michael, she wasn't too worried about that either. He had been very busy over his last few weekends off from the barge, and she had felt acutely aware when they'd gone to the pictures or to a dance that he'd made a supreme effort to get there just for her sake. And she had truly felt sorry for him lately when they were out because he looked so tired and weary. The terrible business with his father had taken it out of him and then with all the extra farm work heaped on him, the poor man couldn't possibly be anything else but exhausted.

In fact, Kate reasoned, although he said he would miss her badly, he would probably be secretly grateful to have one less pressure on him. It would give him a few weeks to catch up on everything, and not have to be running backwards and forwards to Ballygrace feeling guilty about neglecting her.

'I still think we would manage better if Brendan was to come with us . . .' Mary said, not convinced. She gestured anxiously with her hands. 'What about the Customs people? What will we do if they pull us over and search our bags and everything?'

'We don't need a man!' Kate stated forcefully. She reached over and took her mother's hand. 'We can manage the boat trip and the Customs and anything else that comes our way. We're not exactly a pair of amadáns, now are we?' She squeezed Mary's hand tightly. 'This summer we'll manage *everything* perfectly well on our own. Is that understood?'

'Oh, Kate!' Mary said, her eyes lighting up with confidence. 'The way you're talkin' I don't doubt for a minute that we will!'

The following Tuesday evening Brendan came cycling home from the barge to join his mother and sister for the annual Cemetery Mass. Like all the other towns and villages in Ireland, this was held in Ballygrace churchyard every summer. For weeks before, families washed and scrubbed the headstones, cut the grass and generally tidied up the small area that surrounded their own individual plots.

Kate and her mother had cycled out to the cemetery on several occasions and were now happy that Seamus Flowers' grave was every bit as respectable as all the others and better than most.

After dinner, Mary washed the dishes then, while Kate dried them, she went out into the garden to pick bunch of pink peonies and some white carnations.

Kate wiped over the kitchen table, checked everything was in its proper place and then went into her bedroom to get the large flowery jug to fill it with hot water for a freshen-up before she changed into one of her good summer dresses for the Mass.

Brendan had removed his shirt and was standing at the sink, bare-chested, all prepared to do his own ablutions. He face was creased in concentration as he studied Noelle Daly's latest letter.

'I don't think that's addressed to you,' Kate told him curtly as she poured the water from the kettle into her jug. 'I didn't see your name on the envelope.'

'I see she's got herself all nicely settled in Ballsbridge up in Dublin,' Brendan replied, completely ignoring Kate's little jibe about reading her mail. 'I'm surprised that that one could find her way up to Dublin, far less find her way around it.'

Kate gave an irritated sigh. 'I'm sure she's every bit as capable of finding her way around as the next one,' she said. 'And you're not exactly far-travelled yourself.' She suddenly thought of the American newspapers and wondered whether she should steer the conversation into calmer waters for her mother's sake.

'Further travelled than you'll ever be,' he said airily, folding the letter over and putting it back into the envelope. He threw it up onto the window-sill. 'I'm surprised that a so-called intelligent girl like Noelle Daly didn't try to make something better of herself than an oul' skivvy.' He turned the tap on and filled the basin with cold water. 'We were always hearing how brainy she was in school. You wouldn't think it to hear what she's doing.'

'She's not a skivvy, and she wouldn't thank you for calling her that,' Kate retorted sharply. 'She's keeping house for a doctor.' She fetched a clean towel from the long, low cupboard by the fireside.

'Same thing,' he said, unruffled by her attitude. He went over to get the remainder of the warm water from the kettle and poured it in the half-filled basin. 'Anyway, no doubt by the posh address in Ballsbridge, she'll come back home and be all highfalutin and too good for the rest of us. She'll think she's as good as them that she's workin' for, and no doubt end up the same as all the others that go off and forget all them back home.'

'What are you giving out about?' Kate snapped, shaking the towel out from its folds. 'I don't know why you should be so interested in what Noelle Daly or anyone else does. You're usually only interested in yourself.'

He wet the bar of soap in the basin and then rubbed the lather vigorously over his face. 'I'm not a bit interested in her,' he said, raising his voice through the soapy foam. 'I couldn't give a feck what she does.'

'Well . . . it certainly doesn't sound like it to me,' Kate said. 'And if you read the letter correctly you'd see that Noelle is planning a visit back home in the next few weeks.' She walked swiftly to her bedroom door and banged it closed behind her. Then, she smiled broadly to herself, knowing full well how annoyed Brendan would be at not having had the last word.

Chapter 20

❧

Kate sat back in the leather car seat, smiling to herself with pleasure at being in such a lovely car, but feeling a tinge of self-consciousness. It was hard getting used to something so different after years of only travelling on a bicycle or – on odd occasions – the local bus. Michael had driven down to the cottage to pick her up for a farewell night out at the pictures in Tullamore on the Thursday night before she left for England on the Friday.

'I thought I'd call a bit early since it's such a grand, sunny evening,' he told her, 'and I thought we'd take a drive up around Tyrrellspass and out the Kilbeggan road and into Tullamore.'

'Grand,' Kate had agreed. It was only six o'clock – the earliest he had arrived all summer due to the work on the farm and getting back from the barge. Today, he had got off the barge around three o'clock and cycled home, washed and changed, had his dinner and then come straight out in the car to Kate's.

She had been ready and waiting for him, no longer guilty at leaving her mother, who had a new lease of life about her with the good weather and the holiday to her sister's coming up. Kate had put on a nice white cotton dress with red and green flowers on it and a red cardigan, which was simple but very flattering with her tanned skin and black curly hair. 'It's good of your mother giving you the car,' Kate said as they drove past the road for Daingean and turned towards Croghan.

Michael shrugged. 'It's only on the odd occasion,' he said lightly. 'And anyway, most of the time myself and Thomas drive my mother and sisters around, so it's fair enough to expect me to use it now and again.' He paused, a frown clouding his face. 'My mother says you must come over to the house for Sunday dinner when you come back from England . . .'

A little chill ran through Kate in spite of the warm summer

evening. No matter how hard she tried, she couldn't feel comfortable at the thought of going back into the O'Briens' farmhouse. 'That was nice,' she said, giving him a bright little smile, but she couldn't bring herself to actually say she'd go. She would wait until she came back from Stockport and see if she felt more confident about it then.

'You know, my mother doesn't have a problem about us courting any more,' he told her. 'All that nonsense about Helen's friend has never been mentioned since the funeral . . . and Helen herself often asks for you.'

Kate stared straight ahead out of the car window, feeling her face flushing now. 'Good,' she murmured, not feeling in the slightest bit good about anything.

Then, suddenly realising that she felt uncomfortable, Michael changed the subject. 'I'd say your mother's looking forward to her holiday.'

'Oh, she is,' Kate agreed, smiling and looking at him now. 'She loves seeing my Auntie Rose and she loves going into Stockport town and Manchester. And if my Auntie Rose is working, she's happy helping out in the shop.' She touched his hand on the steering wheel. 'I did tell you that my Auntie Rose and her husband Graham have a fruit and vegetable shop, didn't I?'

'You did,' he said, smiling back. There was a little pause. 'And you, Kate – are you looking forward to going over to England or is it really just for your mother's sake? Do you feel you have to go to look after her?'

Kate took a few seconds before replying – not quite sure what he was asking her. 'Well, I've gone every summer since I was a little girl,' she explained, 'and so has Brendan. This is actually the first summer he's not come. My Auntie Rose and my mother are very close . . . and I do feel she needs me for the company travelling.'

'So, would you go if your mother wasn't so pushed?'

'Yes, I would,' she said, suddenly feeling quite definite about it. 'I really enjoy the holiday myself. I like the change, the difference. I like the feeling of being in a busy town.'

'You surprise me now,' Michael said. 'I would have thought you were more of a country girl . . .'

'Well, obviously I am,' she laughed. 'You can't get more country than living in such a quiet spot by the canal.'

'True . . .' he said, nodding his head and reaching forward to go down the gears as they were now climbing the hill to Tyrrellspass. 'But don't you find the English way of life very different – especially in the big towns?'

'It is different,' Kate said. 'But that's what I like about it.'

'It might be all right for a holiday,' he went on, 'but surely you couldn't imagine yourself actually *living* there? They have an entirely different approach to life compared to the Irish country way.' There was no disguising Michael's own disapproval of England and all it represented.

Kate looked at him, slightly taken aback by his attitude, which she took to be rather old-fashioned. 'I could live there,' she told him, 'maybe not for ever – but if I ever had to go and live over in somewhere like Manchester, I wouldn't mind it. In fact, I had planned to go over to stay with my aunt a few years ago to do my nursing qualification but my mother took ill and I couldn't leave her.'

'Nursing?' Michael repeated in a surprised tone. He turned to look at her now, his brow wrinkled. 'I've never heard you say anything about nursing or going out to work before . . . and I'm sure Brendan has never mentioned it.' He turned his attention back to the road.

'Sure, that fellow doesn't pay the slightest attention to anything anyone tells him,' Kate laughed. 'And anyway, I haven't mentioned it at home for a while as I know it makes Mammy feel guilty that I couldn't go.' She suddenly became serious 'She offered to pay for me to train here, but it would have taken most of her savings and I couldn't do that to her . . . And anyway, I would probably have to go and live in Dublin anyway.'

'You've really surprised me now, Kate,' he said in a low voice. 'I would never have imagined you being interested in such a different way of life. I thought you were more like your mother, content to be at home minding the house and that kind of thing . . .'

'Well,' she said, tapping his hand playfully, 'it just shows that you don't know me as well as you think!'

'I'm beginning to think that I'm going to have to work a lot harder to keep up with you,' he said, laughing along with her now. 'I didn't know you were such a girl about town . . . and maybe I should be a small bit worried about you going over there on your own?'

'What do you mean?' she asked.

'All those fancy Englishmen ... maybe they'll turn your head and you won't find me exciting enough when you come back.'

Kate looked at him now, not sure which way to go. They had never really discussed where either or them thought they were up to with their romance. It had just slowly sailed on in the right direction – a bit like the barge on the canal. 'Are you serious, Michael? You surely don't think that, do you?'

He laughed again, looking a bit more relaxed. 'I'm only codding you.' He turned the car onto the road for Tullamore. 'I think the best thing would be if I come over to England the next time you're going, then I can find out all about it for myself.'

Kate's heart skipped a beat. Things were definitely going in the right direction if he was talking about next year. 'You've never been over, have you?'

'No,' he said. 'I've never had the inclination before ... but if I went with you it would be very different.'

'Grand,' she said. 'If all is going well between us, we might take a trip over to Stockport next year.' Kate felt a glow of happiness run through her now with his last remark. Michael must obviously feel that things were going *very well* between them if he was suggesting they go to England together. She wondered now what Agnes O'Brien would have to say about it.

For all that Michael was saying that his mother had changed her mind about their romance, Kate still felt very unsure. Deep down she knew that she wasn't the type of girl his family had hoped for.

There was a big crowd at the cinema, so there was little chance for any kind of chat between them, other than deciding which kind of mineral or ice-cream Kate would like at the break. But Kate was quite content sitting in the flickering dark of the cinema with Michael O'Brien, his arm around her shoulders, pulling her close into him. She could feel the warmth of his skin through his shirt and when her head rested on his chest she could feel the thud of his heart beating – and she realised that she had never felt so content beside another human being.

As the film carried on around her, she thought how strange the next few weeks would be without seeing Michael or knowing that he was on the barge slowly making its way up or down the Grand Canal or back at the farm in Tullamore.

Later, as they said goodnight in the car outside the cottage, Michael leaned across to the passenger seat and gathered Kate up in his arms. 'I'm going to really miss you,' he told her in a gentle tone. 'It will feel funny knowing that you're not where you always are.'

'I'll miss you as well,' she said quietly, 'but it won't be for too long.'

He nodded his head slowly. 'When you come back . . . maybe we should talk about things – sort some things out.'

'What kind of things?' Kate asked.

'About us,' he said. 'You coming over to our house again soon . . . that sort of thing.'

Kate's stomach tightened at the thought.

'I think that we need to make it more obvious that we're a steady couple.'

Kate looked up at him, surprised but pleased. 'Is that what you feel?'

'Definitely . . . and I hope you do, too.' He paused, his brows knitting together in thought. 'Your mother and Brendan are grand about it all, aren't they?'

'Yes,' Kate confirmed. 'You know they both like you very much.' She gave a smile. 'Even though Brendan has a peculiar way of showing it at times.'

Michael laughed. 'Ah, he has his own ways, but he's not the worst.'

Kate decided to take the bull by the horns. 'I think it's your family who have the bigger problem,' she said, raising her eyebrows. 'I'm still not sure how I feel about going back.'

'It'll work out,' he told her, stroking her hair. He leaned forward and kissed her now. 'You know I love you, Kate, don't you?'

She felt a surge of joy at the words she'd just heard, the words she'd hoped to hear for the last few weeks. Those words confirmed that they could now start planning a future together. She looked up into his eyes and nodded, suddenly feel shy and awkward.

He looked deep into her eyes now and she knew he was waiting.

'And I love you too, Michael,' she whispered.

'I'm relieved you said that,' he told her, his eyes bright. 'Because it means we can start making plans – sorting things out for the future.'

They stayed wrapped together for a few minutes longer then Kate gently pulled herself out of his arms. 'I've got to go in and get things ready for the morning,' she said apologetically.

'Before you go,' he said, an urgent note in his voice, 'tell me that things will be the same when you come back – that you won't forget me.' His hand gripped hers tightly. 'That's the one big thing worrying me, Kate – that you might just find somebody more to your liking over in England.'

'There's no fear of that happening,' she reassured him. 'I'll be with my mother or helping down in the shop most of the time – and I'll be counting the days until I get back to Ireland.'

'Do you think we have everything we need, Kate?' Mary Flowers checked for the third time in an hour. She was sitting all fresh in her nightdress and dressing-gown, enjoying her last cup of tea of the day now that Kate had returned from the cinema. While Kate was out she had spent a large part of the evening preparing for, and then actually having, her bath for going on holiday. Kate had lifted the tin bath into the bedroom for her and had instructed her mother to fill it very carefully with slightly hotter than lukewarm water, from the kettle and pans on the range.

Having a bath was a big event for Mary, as her ablutions usually consisted of a good wash using a flannel and soap in the basin every morning and night.

'We have every single thing,' Kate said patiently, nodding over to their tickets and the brown envelope with English money. She had cycled over to the bank in Tullamore for the money the previous week, making sure they were prepared well in advance and hopefully giving her mother nothing to worry about. Their bags were all packed and had been checked and re-checked several times.

'And if we are short of anything,' Kate added firmly, 'then Auntie Rose will make sure we get what we need.' She took a sip of the tea she hadn't really wanted, but didn't want to disappoint her mother by refusing. What she really wanted to do now was to go into the bedroom and close the door and lie down in the silence and re-run the last scene of the evening where Michael O'Brien had told her that he loved her.

'True, true,' Mary said, sounding more soothed. She looked up at Kate. 'If you aren't too tired, I wonder if you'd put a few rollers in for me before we go to bed? It's just that the curls seem to hold longer if they're in all night.'

'I'll do it now,' Kate said, getting to her feet. Mulling over her private thoughts would have to wait until her mother was asleep later on.

'How was Michael?' Mary asked, watching Kate's pensive face as she walked across the room to the bedroom door.

'Grand,' Kate told her in a slightly distracted voice. 'He's been working hard, but he seems all right. He was in good enough form tonight.'

'And his mother and brother and sisters? Are they managing the farm between them without their poor father?'

'They seem to be . . . he didn't really say a whole lot about it.' She went into the bedroom now and returned a few moments later with the toilet bag that held the rollers and pins.

Mary couldn't contain herself any longer. 'Do you feel bad leaving him, Kate?' she asked. 'Are you wishin' we weren't going?'

'No, Mammy . . .' Kate said, giving a reassuring smile. She wanted her mother to enjoy this holiday very much, and she hoped that Mary hadn't been sitting here all evening fretting about whether her daughter was only going to please her. 'You know I always enjoy going over to Auntie Rose's, and I'm looking forward to it the very same as any other year.'

'Good . . . good,' Mary said. 'But I do understand if you're a bit worried about leaving him – I wouldn't expect you to feel otherwise.' She bit her lip, trying to reach out to her daughter with understanding but not wanting to pry or interfere too much. 'Do you know the extent of Michael's feelings for you?' She paused, picking her words carefully. 'What I mean is – do you think it's getting serious? Do you think you could end up gettin' married?'

Kate laughed, slightly embarrassed. 'I think you're getting a bit carried away,' she said. 'We're nowhere near that stage . . .'

Mary nodded her head slowly. 'I don't mean to be poking my nose in or anything . . .'

'Michael and me are grand, Mammy,' Kate said, 'and we're just taking things nice and easy.'

Chapter 21

❧❧❧

The boat-train from Holyhead pulled in at Manchester's Piccadilly Station around lunchtime. Kate took her canvas case and then her mother's holdall down from the rack, and then they made their way towards the train door.

As they walked along the platform, Kate noticed that her mother's breathing was getting a bit tighter and the furrows were deepening on her brow as she anxiously scanned the crowds waiting outside the ticket barrier.

'If they've not arrived yet, we'll just wait until they come,' Kate said in a calm, even voice, knowing that her mother was getting herself more worked up, desperate to catch a glimpse of her sister and brother-in-law who had arranged to come and pick them up. 'Don't be worrying, Mammy. We've managed all the way over to Manchester from Ireland, we're not going to get lost now.'

They handed their tickets in and then, a few minutes later, they heard a familiar voice calling out, 'Mary, Kate!' as Rose Hopkins came rushing towards them, her arms outstretched.

'Oh, thanks be to God and his Blessed Mother!' Mary gasped, sounding as though she might expire with relief on the spot.

'That flamin' Graham has disappeared, supposedly to go to the lavatory,' Rose Hopkins informed her older sister and niece, after she had given them a huge, emotional welcome. 'He should have been here for you – but he's like all the other men, he's never where you want him to be!'

'Now don't be givin' out about him!' Mary said good-naturedly, slipping her arm through her sister's.

Kate suddenly thought of Brendan, and knew he would be the exact same as Graham Hopkins if he were ever in a situation like this, waiting for people while there was a pub nearby. But, she thought privately, it was unfair to say that all men were the same. It was especially hard on decent men like Michael O'Brien who were dependable and always tried their best.

'It's good of Graham to come all the way into Manchester to pick us up in his delivery van,' Mary went on, pouring oil on the troubled waters. 'Isn't it good of him, Kate?'

'It's very good of him,' Kate hastily agreed, giving her aunt an encouraging smile.

Rose craned her neck for any sight of her husband. 'He's always the flamin' same – takes every opportunity when he's anywhere near a pub,' Rose rattled on. 'Oh, there's times when that bloody man drives me up the wall.' She grimaced at the thought of him.

'He'll be here shortly,' Mary soothed, patting her sister's arm. 'We've come this far, and another few minutes isn't going to make any difference, is it, Kate?'

'No, no,' Kate agreed, thinking how natural it was for her mother to slip into defending her brother-in-law now she didn't have Brendan around.

'Here, give me one of those bags,' Rose said, suddenly noticing her niece trying to manoeuvre between the other passengers with the two bags. She reached over and took the holdall from Kate.

'So you had no trouble getting over on your own?' Rose Hopkins asked as all three walked out of Piccadilly Station. 'You managed through Customs and everything?'

'No trouble at all!' Mary Flowers replied with a beaming smile. She gripped her sister's arm tightly. The last twenty-four hours had been full of unfamiliar people and places and very little sleep, and the sight of her sister's welcoming face had given her a boost of energy. 'Kate sorted everything out without the slightest bit of bother.'

'Isn't she a great girl?' Rose said in her Stockport mixed with County Clare accent, her eyes wide with admiration. 'And was the boat very busy?'

'It was packed,' Mary said. 'But give her her due, as soon as we'd boarded the boat, Kate went on ahead and got us a nice little corner where we could make ourselves comfortable.'

Something suddenly caught Rose's attention as the crowd moved through the station. 'Oh, here he comes at last,' she said with an exaggerated sigh, extricating her arm from her sister's to give a vigorous wave. 'No doubt managed to get himself lost in the nearest pub, on his way back from the Gents.'

Graham Hopkins came striding through the groups of passengers, tall and well built, his friendly face beaming at the sight of their visitors. 'Five minutes!' he said, shaking his head. 'I was here all this time wi' Rose waiting for you, and I just took five minutes to go to the Gents and here youse all are!'

Rose looked at Kate and rolled her eyes in disbelief. 'He'd tell you anything and expect you to swallow it hook, line and sinker,' she said in a whisper.

Graham came forward to take the holdall from his wife and Kate's case. He made a vague, clumsy gesture of a hug to both women as he leaned in close for the bags and instantly they got the whiff of fresh whiskey.

'It's good of ye both to come and meet us, Graham,' Mary said quickly, anxious in case her sister started on at him for sneaking off for a drink. She hated it when there was any friction between them in her presence. 'I know you have a lot more to do with your time than come driving all the way into Manchester for us.'

'No problem at all, Mary love,' he told them, pointing the holdall in the direction they should all head. 'It's always a pleasure to come and meet you, and Betty can manage the shop on her own for a couple of hours. It's usually dead enough at this time of the afternoon.' He moved off now at a quick pace towards the car park.

Hopkins' white fruit and veg van came to a halt in the busy street outside the shop bearing the same name, which stood beside the large house that was home to Graham and Rose. It was busier than any of the streets in Tullamore and it was far, far busier than the main street in Ballygrace. And that busyness was exactly what Kate and Mary both liked about these visits to Rose. They liked the difference between home and here. For the next few weeks they would enjoy the novelty of shops all within a few minutes' walk and they would enjoy travelling on the bus or the train into Manchester. They would relish all the differences. And then, by the time their holiday had come to an end, they would enjoy getting back to the peace and quiet of life by the canal in Ballygrace.

'I hope that it wasn't too uncomfortable for you sittin' on them potato sacks, love?' Graham asked as he helped Kate down the high step of the van. 'One of these days we'll get around to affordin' a proper car that's comfortable for everybody.'

'It was grand,' Kate fibbed, giving him a grateful smile. In actual fact, the cushion had kept slipping away from under her and she'd felt every bump on the road and the rough sacks snagging the back of her stockings. 'And anyway, all we have at home are our shaky old bikes, so we're not exactly used to luxury cars.'

The mention of cars made her think of the nice family car that Michael was now often driving, and she found herself wondering what he was doing back in Tullamore at that very moment.

'The shop looks very busy, Rose,' Mary remarked as they walked ahead of Kate and Graham. 'There's a grand crowd in it . . .' She suddenly halted now as she saw a policeman's helmet in amongst the crowd.

'Where's Betty?' Rose said in a rising voice, going over to look in the shop window. She cupped her hands around her eyes to get a better look. 'There's nobody behind the counter and a whole crowd of people in the middle of the shop . . .'

'I think,' Mary said, standing up on her tiptoes, 'that Betty's sittin' down on a chair and there's a policeman there in amongst them all—'

'Jesus! There's something wrong with Betty!' Rose said, pushing past her sister and rushing on into the shop.

'Graham!' Mary said in a strangled voice, whirling back round to her brother-in-law. 'There's something wrong with Betty!'

'Bloody hell!' Graham said, dumping the cases on the pavement. He threw his hands up in the air. 'You can't leave the flamin' place for five minutes but something happens!' And then he stomped off behind the two women, leaving Kate with the luggage.

Kate lifted the bags over to the side of the door and left them there and then went quickly in to join the others in the shop. She knew Betty well from all the summers she'd spent with her aunt in the shop, but she knew that her mother and aunt would be the ones that the elderly assistant would be more likely to respond to.

'What's the matter? What's goin' on?' Rose said, her gaze moving through the small crowd of people to the very young-looking policeman, and then the stricken figure of Betty sitting on the armchair that had been carried through from the back of the shop.

'Are you the proprietor, Madam?' the policeman said, holding his notebook and pencil, a nervous lump working its way up and down in his throat.

Rose nodded her head vigorously, then came to kneel by Betty's chair. 'What's happened, Betty love? Are you not well?'

The waxen-faced Betty looked up at her employer and then made a groaning noise.

'We think she's had some kind of a little turn, Mrs Hopkins,' a middle-aged customer put in. She lived in the houses opposite and came into the shop for her potatoes and vegetables on a daily basis. 'She was lyin' on the floor behind the counter when we came in, and she looked proper poorly. White as a sheet, and tryin' to catch her breath and not able to talk.' She gestured to the woman beside her. 'Edna here ran up the street and got the policeman to come and help us, and then these other nice people came in as well.'

'In my opinion, it's a doctor she needs,' an elderly man in a smart raincoat and hat announced. Everyone turned to look at him now and he suddenly became embarrassed. 'It could just be a faint . . . but on the other hand, it could be something more serious.' He gestured with his hands. 'Only a professional doctor can tell those things.'

'How are you feelin', Betty love?' Rose said, rubbing the elderly shop assistant's arm.

Betty took big gulps of air but said nothing. 'Are you all right?' Mary came around the other side now, and held Betty's other hand. 'It's me, Mary,' she told the older woman. She gave a tense smile to the assembled group. 'Sure, haven't me and Kate come all the way over from Ireland just to see you?' she added, hoping it might just cheer the old lady up.

Rose touched Betty's cheek now, and was surprised to find how cold it was. 'Are you going to say hello to your old friend Mary?' she said, her voice sounding more anxious now.

Betty moaned again and closed her eyes as though thoroughly exhausted.

'Are you all right, Betty love?' Graham Hopkins asked, although his eyes were flicking from the stricken shop assistant to the items he had painstakingly displayed on the shelves this morning and then back across to the till.

The policeman cleared his throat, attempting to take charge of the situation again. 'I think the gentleman might be right,' he said in a slightly squeaky voice. 'I think that maybe we should call a doctor . . .'

'David McGuire,' Graham suddenly announced. He pointed somewhere outside the shop. 'I saw his car outside his house when we were drivin' in.' He looked at the man in the hat. 'He's a good customer of ours, like. Lives in one of the big houses down in Fairley Road. He lives with a couple of other lads who are doctors in the hospital as well – we deliver all their fruit and veg to the house.' He gave a little shrug. 'These doctor fellas want to eat healthy like – so they're fond of their fruit and veg.'

Rose tutted impatiently at Graham's waffling on about unimportant details that he hoped would impress the man in the hat. 'But David McGuire's not a GP – he's a *hospital* doctor!' she said, her eyes wide with worry.

'All the better,' Graham said, making for the door. 'By the looks of poor old Betty, it's a hospital she's going to need.'

A short while later Graham came striding back into the shop followed by a tallish, well-built, tousle-haired man in his late twenties wearing a casual sweater and jeans, who did not look in the least like a doctor apart from the fact he was carrying a traditional doctor's leather bag. A silence descended on the assembled group and the policeman gestured to them to move back a bit to allow the doctor through to the patient.

Kate found her gaze drawn away from Betty and now focused on the young doctor. He wasn't at all what she'd expected. Then, when she heard him speaking, it wasn't what she expected to hear either. The Irish name *David McGuire* had led her to expect an Irish accent, but this man's accent was in fact Scottish.

'Mrs Green,' he said in a calm, clear, reassuring voice, 'it's Dr McGuire here and I'm just going to give you a little check-over. Take a few deep breaths and try to relax.'

Betty made a few vague noises that immediately made Rose and Mary close in on her again, stooping down to her mouth to hear, but what she said was unintelligible.

'If you wouldn't mind giving me a wee bit of space,' the doctor said, giving a slightly weary but polite smile now, and the two ladies quickly retreated a few paces. He opened the case and first produced a stethoscope. After a short while listening to Betty's heart, he then got out his blood pressure monitor and checked that too.

All the while Betty kept taking big, slow breaths.

Mary and Rose watched every move of the doctor's face muscles, trying to ascertain unsuccessfully what he was looking for. After a while, he got to his feet and looked at Graham. 'I think we need an ambulance here,' he said quietly. 'If you could phone one to come as quickly as possible . . . '

Graham dutifully rushed off to the phone in the back of the shop.

Betty gave a particularly agitated groan now, and the doctor took her hand and gently rubbed it, while saying in a kind, soothing voice, 'You'll be fine, Mrs Green, there's nothing to worry about. You'll be absolutely fine.' He looked around the assembled group. 'And I think if you could perhaps clear the shop, it might make things a little easier.'

The customers immediately started to move out of the shop – including the policeman who seemed relieved to hand over responsibility. He and two other men waited outside the door and the two women who found Betty told Rose that they'd call back later.

Soon, only Rose, Mary and Kate were left.

The doctor stood up now, and his gaze fell on Kate, who immediately reddened. He obviously thought she was a nosy customer, still hanging on to see if anything more dramatic might happen.

'I'm not a customer . . . I'm here on holiday . . . Rose is my aunt,' she heard herself explaining in an apologetic voice.

'Oh, right,' he said nodding, his eyes still holding hers. 'I wasn't questioning that you shouldn't be here.' His voice lowered. 'Sorry if I'm a bit vague – but I've been at the hospital for the last twenty-eight hours and I'd only just got home.'

Kate nodded her head, wishing the ground would open up and swallow her.

'They've been up all night themselves, they've just travelled over on the boat from Ireland,' Rose rushed on, in case he hadn't caught Kate's accent. 'We only got out of the van outside and we noticed the crowd and the policeman and we realised something had happened . . .' She leaned forward now and patted poor Betty's shoulder. 'They come over to see Betty as much as me,' she said in a loud voice in case the shop assistant's hearing had gone as well. 'They're very fond of her.'

Graham came rushing out from the back now, holding a brandy bottle. 'That's the ambulance on its way,' he announced. He held the bottle aloft. 'Would a small brandy maybe help her? Help to calm her down a bit like?'

Rose took a deep breath, thinking how typical it was of her husband to bring alcohol into it, but she said nothing. It wouldn't do to be arguing in front of a doctor.

David McGuire bent down to Betty. 'Would you take a little sip of brandy, Mrs Green?' he asked.

Betty managed a little nod of her head, and actually managed to whisper, 'Just a small one,' which sent Rose scuttling along to help Graham find a suitable glass. A few minutes later Rose came rushing back in to give the brandy to Betty, while Graham stood behind the shop counter, surveying everything and surreptitiously sipping from a small glass of his own.

'Which part of Ireland are you from?' David McGuire asked as Rose held the glass to Betty's mouth.

'The midlands,' Mary answered, with her big beaming smile. 'Tullamore . . . I don't suppose you've heard of it?'

'I have heard of it, although I've never been there,' he said, his dark head moving up and down. 'My mother's actually from Athlone, although she moved to Scotland over thirty years ago.'

'Indeed,' Mary said, delighted at the Irish connection. 'And what brought you all the way down to Stockport?'

'Work,' he said, lifting his bag and checking that he had fastened it properly.

Sirens could suddenly be heard in the distance and everyone moved quickly to have Betty organised and ready for the ambulance men.

Kate and Mary had finally got themselves settled into their bedroom in the house next door, and then they'd gone back and forth between the house and the shop until it was closing time. Due to the way things had turned out, Rose suggested that they have their dinner at the café down the road.

'We'll be here all night waiting on the meat to cook,' Rose had explained, 'so we might as well keep that until tomorrow and have the chip suppers this evening.' She looked anxiously at her sister and niece. 'If it's okay with you?'

'Okay?' Mary said, smiling broadly. 'Sure, it'll be a lovely treat for me and Kate. We don't often get the chance to have things from cafés. Sure, the only time really is when we're over here.'

'It doesn't open until six o'clock though,' Graham reminded his wife. 'So we'll have to give it another quarter of an hour.'

'I'll make us a cup of tea while we're waiting.' Rose went to get to her feet.

'Stay where you are,' Graham told her. 'You chat to Mary and Kate and I'll see to it.'

Rose's face was a picture of shock. It wasn't often that her husband offered to make tea.

He came out a short while later with a tray with filled glasses on it. 'I thought we could all do with this after what's happened. We can have tea later on.'

'Oh, Graham!' Mary said, her eyes lighting up at the unexpected treat.

'That's been some bloody afternoon,' Graham Hopkins stated as he handed small sherries around for all three women, without catching his wife's eye, and then turned to another brandy for himself.

'As you know, we don't normally drink in the house apart from Christmas,' Rose said, pulling a face behind her husband's back, 'but I suppose with the shock of Betty and everything . . .'

'Definitely,' Graham said, his mouth turning down at the corners.

'I wonder how long she'll be in hospital,' Mary said, sipping at her drink.

'Could be weeks, bein' her age and everythin',' Graham said. 'When it's the heart you just don't know.' He gave a shrug. 'You're on dodgy ground when it's the heart.'

'Her son's coming up from London tomorrow,' Rose said, trying to be more optimistic for her guests. She checked her watch. 'And her daughter should be there by now, she has only to come from Bolton.'

'It's landed us with a bit of a problem, though, hasn't it?' Graham said, shaking his head. He gestured with his finger over to Rose. 'We're going to have to get somebody else, otherwise you an' me will hardly see the light of day outside of the bleedin' shop.'

'We can help,' Kate quickly offered, 'can't we, Mammy?'

'But it's your holidays . . .' Rose said, looking daggers across the room at her husband.

'Of course we can,' Mary said, looking delighted at the thought. 'We'd be only too pleased. And anyway, Betty could be back on her feet again before the week's out.'

'Thanks and all that for the offer to help out,' Graham said, 'but in the long run, we'll have to get somebody else to replace Betty.' He shook his head vigorously. 'I got the shock of my life when I came into the shop and saw all those people and the policeman standin' in the middle of them.'

'So did I.' Rose sighed. 'I didn't know what to think at all, but I could tell that it wasn't good news.'

'For a terrible minute I thought the very worst had happened and we'd been robbed,' Graham went on, his eyes wide and bulging. He took a gulp of the brandy. 'I nearly had an effin' heart attack meself! I couldn't wait till the ambulance had come to check out the till.'

'Graham!' Rose gasped. 'What a terrible thing to say . . .' She looked over at Mary now, shaking her head in disbelief.

'Well . . .' he said, 'some of them thievin' gets could take the chance to rob the place when there's no-one takin' charge of things, like.'

'Well, nothing did happen,' Rose told him, 'apart from poor Betty almost dropping down dead in our shop.'

He shook his head now. 'No, Betty will have to go. We couldn't trust her to run things on her own after this. She's obviously past it. And I was just thinkin' – that fall a few weeks back when she was up the ladder. I'll bet a pound to a penny that she took one of her dizzy spells and fell off the ladder. I'll bet that was the start of it.' He sucked in air through his teeth. 'It's lucky the way it all happened today, or the shop could definitely have been robbed.'

'Graham!' Rose snapped. 'That's a terrible thing to say! It's poor Betty we're all bothered about and not the flamin' shop!'

'Easy said,' Graham shrugged, 'until there's no money in the till to pay the bills.' He shrugged again and held his hands out palm up. 'Easy said.'

Chapter 22

❧

Brendan Flowers had had a very good week so far. The weather had been perfect and each day on the barge had been almost a pleasure. After their stop-offs at the various towns, and loads being dropped off or loaded on, the boatmen could then take it easy as the boat ambled on to the next stop. When they found they had a few hours to themselves between stops, they stripped off their shirts and lay back on the top of the boat to enjoy the alternating hot sunshine and the cool shade from the overhanging trees and bushes.

On a couple of the trips they had brought down several loads from Guinness's brewery in Dublin to deliver to the country pubs, and Brendan and the other lads had enjoyed several pints of creamy porter from the barrels. Michael O'Brien would wave away any more than a single pint and Brendan was always glad to help him out.

On the Friday evening Brendan took his leave from the boat at Ballygrace and walked up to the nearest pub where he had conveniently left his bike. He had a good feed of potatoes and fish and peas and a couple more glasses of beer with some of his drinking cronies and then contentedly he set off on his bike, weaving along the tow-path back to the empty cottage.

He was looking forward to this weekend and then the following weekend when he would have a whole week off work to enjoy the empty cottage all to himself, before his mother and his briar of a sister came home. The very thought of it warmed his heart and brought a smile to his tanned face. The time on his own would be better than any holiday away with them. No women to be giving out or fussing over him, and, for once, he could be his own man and do exactly what he liked when he liked.

The first thing that hit him when he entered the strangely echoing cottage was the lack of warmth from the dead cooker, and then the absence of welcoming cooking smells. Then, as he wandered around the kitchen, dropping his workbag on the floor and his folded good suit over the back of the armchair, he suddenly realised that if he wanted anything, he would have to do it for himself.

This had never happened before.

There had always, always been someone in Brendan Flowers' life to do things for him.

Even when his mother had been ill in hospital, and not fit to do much for months after she came out, he still had Kate cooking and cleaning for him. But then, he reasoned, didn't he deserve it? Wasn't he the bread-winner in the house? Surely a decent meal on the table and a warm house and clean bed and clothes wasn't too much to ask in return?

He wondered now how he was going to boil a kettle to make a cup of tea for himself. He went over to the range and opened it, and there it was, all cleaned and set with papers and wood and turf. It only needed a match putting to it.

But was it worth the bother? He had only come home to have a quick wash and a cup of tea and then he would head out to the pub again for the night. By the time he waited for the fire to catch on and then the water to boil for both his wash and the tea, it wouldn't be worth the bother of going out at all.

Brendan sank down into the comforting armchair now, running his hands through his black hair. He suddenly felt tired and knew he could easily drop off asleep, but he knew there would be no Mammy there or irritated sister to wake him up before it was too late to go out. The way he felt now – after several days of lugging barrels in the hot sun and several wakeful nights in the barge cabin – he would probably sleep straight through until the early hours of the morning. And all for the want of a kettle of boiling water, because he knew well that a good strong mug of tea would have knocked the sleep off him. 'Oh, feck it!' he said aloud as he got to his feet. He might as well have a quick strip wash in the cold water to wake himself up and then put on one of the clean, starched shirts that Kate had ironed before leaving.

He would get himself organised and go out for the night. He was sure he'd heard there was a crowd going into a dance in Tullamore later on at night.

Who knows where it might lead? Who knows who he might meet?

And he could drink as much as he wanted without having to face his mother or sister. In fact, it was the perfect time to get as jarred as he liked.

Chapter 23

֍

Noelle walked backwards to the door and looked around Dr Casey's bathroom. She gave a small sigh of satisfaction at the shining taps and the door plate and knob that she'd just bruised her knuckles polishing with Brasso. She had made a particular effort this morning, determined that there would be not one single fault that the doctor could find with her housework. She wanted to have everything just perfect as she left for her first week back home.

As soon as Dr Casey had left for her surgery that morning, Noelle had opened all the kitchen windows while she washed up the breakfast dishes then moved, room by room, around the house, scrubbing, cleaning and polishing.

She had paid particular attention to dusting the shelves and window ledge in Miss Gabrielle's room, as she was due back home from her holiday on the same Sunday that Noelle was due back from Ballygrace.

Noelle didn't know how she felt about having the girl in the house. She had heard conflicting reports about her. Dr Casey and her Auntie Delia had nothing but praise for the girl, while Carmel from across the fence hadn't a single good word for her. Noelle supposed she'd just have to take her as she found her.

She took a break around eleven o'clock after finishing off the bathroom and she made herself a cup of tea and a ham sandwich, using the white soda bread she had baked last night. After a few days of living in the house, she had suggested that she could bake bread and scones a couple of times a week rather than wasting money on buying them from the local baker's. As soon as her employer had tasted the lovely bread, she had told her new maid to bake them whenever she had the time.

When she went outside to shake the mat from the front door,

Noelle felt the warmth of the morning sun and decided to make the most of it. She carried one of the dark-wood kitchen chairs outside the back door then she went back in for her sandwich and cup of tea. After her break she would do an hour's weeding out in the sun. On the few occasions that she'd tidied up outside, Dr Casey had been more than delighted, and Noelle wanted to keep on her good side as she had been promised a little bit extra in her wages for the extra chores.

She had been sitting enjoying the sun and wondering whether there might be any dances on back in Ballygrace at the weekend when she heard the familiar sound of Lavery's French windows opening. She could hear Carmel Foley's light footsteps as she came down the paving stones of the path and then the scraping of the chair as it was dragged over the stones until it was positioned on the opposite side of Dr Casey's wooden shed. A few seconds later she was leaning on the fence, her face smiling and over-red from yesterday's sun.

'Howya!' she greeted Noelle. 'Nothing like it, out sunning yerself at this time of the morning.'

'I was up bright and early this morning, and I've all the indoor work done already,' Noelle informed her, feeling very pleased with herself.

'Take it that the doc's in town?' Carmel's plucked eyebrows were raised in question.

'She'll be back for her lunch in a bit,' Noelle said, 'so I suppose I'd better get a move on and tidy the kitchen up again after my break.'

'You worry far too much about doing everything right,' Carmel told her. 'You should take it easy now and again. She won't appreciate you any more for killin' yerself, and there won't be any more in yer pay packet at the end of the month. And anyway, you'll be earnin' your money when you come back, when that Gabrielle has you runnin' around like a scalded cat.' Then, without feeling any need for an invitation, Carmel hoisted herself up on the fence and made her usual way down into the garden via the shed roof. 'I'll have a quick cup of tea with you,' she said, 'seeing as you're going to be gone for the next week or more.'

'You sit down here,' Noelle said, quickly getting up from the chair, 'and I'll get you a cup now. It's the bottom of the pot, so I'll add a bit of water to it in case it's too strong.'

'You're all right,' Carmel said, following her inside the house now. 'I got a bit too much sun yesterday and I don't want to get more on top of it. I looked like a bleedin' Belisha beacon last night and Ben Lavery was jeering at me!' She smiled and shook her blonde curly head, as though talking about a young lad who was on an equal footing with her rather than an older professional man. 'I don't want to give that fella any more excuses to be coddin' me.'

Noelle got one of the ordinary mugs down from the cupboard for her friend, an uneasy feeling building up inside her. She felt a bit guilty about being off-hand with Carmel, but she couldn't help feeling anxious about doing something that she had been explicitly told *not* to do. She had never used the good china cups or sat in the drawing-room since that first day she had arrived, and after the fright Dr Casey had given her about Carmel, she had been very wary about allowing the girl inside the house at all.

Most of the time, during work hours, she had been able to keep her to conversations over the garden fence, but on odd occasions – like when it had been raining – she'd had no option but to let her into the doctor's house, although she had kept her strictly to the kitchen.

She had told Carmel after that first day that the doctor had given her a list of 'dos and don'ts' and one of the 'don'ts' was that she wasn't allowed any visitors. Noelle made it sound very general about having any visitors, and didn't enlighten Carmel that the instruction had actually been very specific towards her.

'I'm gonna be busy all over the weekend now,' Carmel said, 'but it won't be killin' myself with housework. We're taking the boys into the city tomorrow to the pictures to see a Walt Disney film and then Ben says we're goin' for something to eat to save me cookin' for them.' She examined her pink-painted nails now – nails that would have no doubt horrified Noelle's plain employer.

As she watched Carmel, all confident and making herself very at home at Dr Casey's kitchen table, Noelle realised that she had a most uncomfortable feeling, a feeling she often got when Carmel talked so familiarly about her boss. No matter how she tried to join in with her friend's chatter about work, the whole set-up with Carmel and her boss just didn't seem right – an older man and a younger woman living most of the time in the house all on their own. And by the sounds of it, they didn't act a bit like employer and housekeeper.

Noelle wondered if there was more to their relationship than just work.

The second the thought passed through her mind, Noelle felt immediately guilty. She shouldn't see her friend's working situation in a bad light when she had no evidence whatsoever. It was just as likely that Carmel had been very lucky, that she had fallen on her feet.

'On Sunday we're goin' to the zoo,' Carmel continued, her eyes shining, 'or maybe for a drive out to Bray, dependin' on the weather.'

Noelle leaned her elbows on the table and rested her chin in her hands. 'You're lucky,' she said, trying to look pleased for her friend. 'Dr Casey's never taken me anywhere, and I have to make something for us every single evening.' She pulled a face. 'Although most of the time it's just bread and a boiled egg.'

'Bleedin' hell!' Carmel spluttered out laughing, her hand coming to cover her mouth to save spraying tea everywhere. She shook her head now. 'She's a mean oul' cow that doctor! All the money she must have an' you're both sittin' at this table every night eatin' mouldy old eggs!'

'It's not that bad,' Noelle said, suddenly feeling a bit defensive. 'And anyway, she has her dinner in the middle of the day in a restaurant in Dublin, so she doesn't need anything more.' The doctor always left Noelle a little chop or a couple of sausages for her to have with potatoes every day, which was as much as she would have got at home. And they often had eggs in the evening as well, so she didn't know what Carmel was laughing so vigorously at.

'You're lucky to be gettin' away from this place for a while,' Carmel said now, taking another sip of her tea. 'An' if I were you, I'd be lookin' for a new position.' She cocked her head to the side, thinking for a moment. 'I could always ask Ben if he knows anyone who's lookin' for a good, hardworkin' housekeeper . . .'

'No, no . . .' Noelle said quickly, suddenly picturing her Auntie Delia's face if she were to tell her that she was leaving her new job already. 'I'm not here long enough to be thinking of moving . . . sure, I've hardly settled in yet.'

Suddenly, a noise at the front door startled them, and Noelle got quickly to her feet, making out into the hallway.

'Hello, Noelle – my last two appointments were cancelled,' Dr Casey called down the hallway in an unusually cheery voice, 'so I thought I'd drive home and let you away a little bit earlier—' She stopped in her tracks, seeing the shocked look on her maid's face. 'Is there something wrong?'

Noelle, chalk-white now, turned her head towards the kitchen, where Carmel was sitting at Dr Casey's table staring back at them. She also looked slightly startled, but definitely not as worried as her friend.

A dark cloud came over the doctor's face. 'Oh no . . .' she said in a low, strangled voice. 'I thought I could trust you, Noelle . . . I really did.'

Chapter 24

❧

The first week in Stockport had gone very quickly, with days helping out in the fruit and vegetable shop and several evenings spent visiting Betty in hospital, sitting by her bed eating grapes and chocolates and chatting with the elderly shop assistant, who seemed much improved.

'I don't know why they're keepin' me in here,' she complained to Rose on one visit, 'because I'm feelin' perfectly well. I'm anxious to get back to me work and back to me normal life.'

Apart from saying that there seemed to be a problem with her heart, the doctors hadn't been too specific. They told her they needed to do more tests, so it was likely that she would be in for another while.

'Oh, you're in the best place for the time being, Betty love,' Graham stated. 'You don't want to be out and about and havin' another one of them bad turns. You need to let the doctors make the decisions now. Don't be worrying about anything.'

'That's all very well,' Betty grumbled, 'but they're not sayin' much. They in't sayin' much at all about anythin'.' She reached for a box of Black Magic from the top of the bedside locker.

'Graham's right,' Rose said, patting Betty's hand. 'You shouldn't be worrying, I'm sure everything will turn out fine.'

'What about the shop though?' Betty said, taking the cellophane wrapping from the chocolate box. 'That's what I'm worryin' about – I'm lettin' you all down.' She paused, looking from Rose to Graham. 'You were supposed to be havin' a few days off with your visitors here, like ... and now you're havin' to work all day and then be runnin' backwards and forwards at night to visit me.'

'Don't be worryin' about the shop, love,' Graham repeated. 'It's only bricks and mortar. The shop will still be there when we're all dead and gone.'

Rose took a sharp intake of breath, ready to kill him now for his tactlessness. She rolled her eyes in disbelief. Imagine talking about dying to a woman who'd just had a heart attack!

Graham's gaze moved to the other beds in the ward as he thought about the work situation. He had already been making enquiries about a woman who came into the shop, who had told him that she used to work in a fruit shop in Bramhall. She had recently moved to Davenport and he knew she was looking for a new position. She would know the ropes in the fruit and veg shop, she could also drive a van *and* she was a lot younger and looked a good deal fitter than Betty. She also, he had quietly noticed, had very good legs.

'But we're enjoying ourselves, Betty,' Mary Flowers said, patting Betty's other hand. 'Kate and I like helping out in the shop and we enjoy coming in to visit you here as well.' She smiled over at Kate. 'It passes the time for us, doesn't it, Kate?'

Kate smiled and nodded. 'Of course it does,' she agreed.

Although Kate by far preferred the other social outings she'd had, saying she had enjoyed the hospital visits wasn't entirely untrue. She had been fascinated by the big modern building and the nice bright wards as she watched the nurses coming and going, and she suddenly realised she felt envious, knowing in her heart that it was the job she had dearly wanted to do. But she had pushed it out of her mind, knowing that it was the wrong time for thoughts like that.

Betty suddenly brightened up. 'Oooooh! I didn't tell you about that young Dr McGuire, did I?'

'No,' Rose said, shaking her head, 'what about him?'

'Well,' she said, looking around them all and smiling broadly, 'he called in to see me this morning.' She gestured towards the corridor at the bottom of the ward. 'He was working in the ward opposite and he decided to look in and see if I was still here. Wasn't that proper nice of him?'

'Oh, it was!' Mary agreed, her eyes wide with delight.

'He's a decent bloke,' Graham said now. 'Nothing hoity-toity about him. No airs and graces. Just a decent, down-to-earth fella.'

'He was really nice, wasn't he, Kate?' her mother prompted now. 'And very good-lookin' for a doctor. Would you say he was good-lookin', Kate? You being a young girl and everything.'

Kate suddenly felt everyone's eyes turning towards her. 'He seemed very nice,' she said, giving a little careless shrug. 'But then,' she added, giving a mock-prim smile, 'I have a very good-looking boyfriend at home, so I'm hardly likely to be looking around at other lads.'

'Oh, Kate!' her mother said laughing. 'Sure, you know that nature breaks out in the eye of a cat!'

Kate shook her head, laughing along with her now. 'Where did you get that saying, Mother?'

Since the weather was unusually fine, they spent some of their free evenings strolling around Stockport town or around one of the nearby parks in Davenport, which was always a novelty for Kate and Mary. Although they had wild nature in abundance by the canal back in Ballygrace, they both enjoyed the lovely flowering trees and beautifully laid-out flower-beds.

They were also near the cricket club in Cale Green and Kate's mother loved watching the men all dressed in their white outfits on the smooth, meticulously cut green. On the occasions that Graham came with them, they would stop off at one of the nicer local pubs where the women would have a glass of cooling shandy and Graham a pint of beer. And on one particular evening, they had gone to watch Graham in an outdoor bowling match in the park in Davenport and had sat outside watching the players as they sipped their cold drinks.

It was relaxed and pleasant and different from their normal

routine. Mary had also paid her annual summer visit to the wool shop two doors down from Graham's shop and sat happily knitting away at a white lace-pattern cardigan while watching the television.

On the following Friday morning, just before half past eight, Kate was busy outside the shop sorting the boxes of fruit and vegetables onto the green-baize-covered display stand. Her hair was long and loose – she had washed it when she'd been in her aunt's lovely deep porcelain bath earlier that morning and had left it to dry into the glorious black curls that she often cursed for being so unruly. She stopped when she heard a familiar Scottish voice.

'How are you enjoying your holiday so far? I hope Graham's not keeping your nose to the grind-stone all the time.'

She turned around to the friendly, smiling face of Dr David McGuire. He was dressed very professionally in a white shirt and dark suit, and he had his leather bag in his hand. His brown hair had the same tousled look as the first time she'd seen him, and his collar was open, his tie loosened. She presumed that he was once again coming home from the night shift in the hospital.

'We're grand, thanks,' she said, smiling back. She tucked one side of her black curly hair behind her ear. 'I was awake early and it's a lovely morning, so I thought I'd give them a bit of a lift in the shop.'

'And how's the patient?' he asked, putting his bag down on the paving stones. 'I looked in at her in the hospital the other day . . .'

'Oh, she told us all about it,' Kate said, lifting up an errant Granny Smith apple that had rolled onto the ground. 'She was delighted; I think it did her more good than the medicine they're giving her.'

'What have you been doing with yourself?' he asked, putting his hands casually into his trouser pockets.

Kate shrugged. 'This and that . . . we've been busy enough.' There was a small silence and she unconsciously juggled the apple between both hands for something to do.

He leaned forward now and said in a low, conspiratorial voice, 'You're not too bored on your own with all the older people then?'

Kate grinned back at him. 'I'm used to it,' she said. 'I've been coming here for years.'

He nodded. 'I suppose there are worse places.'

'Indeed there are,' she said, giving a little sigh.

He lifted his bag. 'Well, I should be heading home now . . . it's funny how the sleep goes off you at the wrong time. But at least I'm not working tonight, so if I don't sleep much now, I can catch up tonight.'

'Is it hard keeping awake all night?' Kate asked, suddenly curious. Then her face reddened, thinking that what she had just said sounded a bit stupid. 'What I mean is . . . is it hard keeping awake and really alert when you have such a serious job to do? I mean, you're dealing with people's lives.'

'Some nights are tougher than others,' he said. 'It depends on what happens, and on how many hours I've worked. If there's no-one to cover for you in the morning, you can often work well into the afternoon, and then you're missing sleep for the next shift.' He shrugged. 'It's a vicious circle . . .'

Graham suddenly appeared at the door. 'Rose said there's a cup of tea for you through the back,' he said, then he looked at David McGuire. 'I'll drop over that order to the house later on.' Then, when the young doctor frowned, he explained, 'One of the other lads left the list yesterday.'

'That would be Simon,' he said. 'He's the main organiser in the house. I was probably fast asleep.'

'Ah well,' Graham said, nodding, 'you can't be working nights and up all day.' He held his thumb up. 'I'll drop it over later.' Then he disappeared back into the shop.

David McGuire walked a few steps away, a little frown on his face, and then he suddenly turned back. 'I don't suppose you play tennis, do you?'

'I haven't played anything like that for a while . . .' Kate said, not at all sure what he was getting at. She used to cycle to the tennis courts in Tullamore with the Daly girls when she was a bit younger and had always enjoyed it. Maybe he was just making general conversation about the kinds of sports they played in Ireland.

'There's a court about five minutes away,' he said. 'And I booked it for six o'clock this evening, but my friend has to work now . . . If you want we could go over and have a couple of games.'

Kate felt a little knot tighten in the pit of her stomach. The same knot she had felt when she first saw Michael O'Brien.

The young doctor looked up at the sky. 'It's supposed to be nice

for the weekend, and I haven't had much fresh air this last week.'
He nodded back towards the shop. 'And it might get you into
livelier company for a couple of hours.'

'You'll be much better than me,' she said, her face beginning to
flush.

'I'm not that good,' he said, shaking his head and laughing. 'But it
doesn't matter. It's only for a bit of fun and to get out when the
weather's nice. The other two fellows will be out of the house
tonight and I'll just be sitting in looking at the four walls.' He
nodded towards the shop, where Graham was now busying around.
'It doesn't sound as if you're going to doing anything more exciting
than me . . .'

Kate paused for a moment, Michael's last words flying back into
her mind. Then, suddenly, she surprised herself. 'Yes,' she said,
throwing the apple a little way up in the air and catching it, 'I
wouldn't mind having a go at the tennis. It would definitely make a
nice change.'

Chapter 25

꧁꧂

Noelle told her sister about the whole scenario with Carmel
and Dr Casey when they went for a walk up the tow-path
into Ballygrace on the Friday evening, having both
changed into fresh summery dresses to look their best in case they
met anyone. It was the only chance the girls got to talk without
being overheard, as their father was in one of his touchy moods,
criticising everyone and everything.

'You must have nearly died when the doctor walked in on you
and your one havin' a cup of tea,' Sarah said, her face a mixture of
amusement and horror. She was linking her older sister's arm now,
delighted to have her back home for the next week or so. She hadn't
realised quite how badly she would miss her when she was gone out
of the house. Everything seemed lighter and more bearable with
Noelle home to share things with.

'She wasn't as bad as she could have been,' Noelle said ruefully. 'I thought she was going to sack me on the spot . . . and I'm a bit wary of going back to her after what's happened.'

'Is this Carmel girl as bad as the doctor thinks?' Sarah asked, desperate to know everything about her sister's new life.

Noelle shrugged and reached out to snap off a piece of wild honeysuckle as they walked along. 'She's been grand with me,' she said, 'and chattin' to her has helped me to settle in – she's been good company in a strange place.'

'Is she nice looking?' Sarah quizzed.

'Oh, she is . . . dyed blonde hair and very up-to-the-minute clothes and pink varnished nails.'

'She sounds very glamorous altogether,' Sarah said, sounding surprised and half-jealous of her sister's new friend.

'She might well be glamorous with the good wages that her boss gives her.' Her eyes narrowed now. 'She's a good laugh and everything, but the only thing I don't like about her is the way she goes on about her boss – *Ben La-very*.' She made a poor imitation of Carmel's Dublin accent now. 'The way she talks, you'd think she had an eye for him – that they were the one age.' She shook her head. 'Sure, he must be forty if he's a day.'

'*Forty?*' Sarah said, pulling a face. 'And she has an eye for him?'

'Well, maybe not exactly an eye – but she's very familiar with him by the sounds of it.'

'Have you seen him?'

Noelle shook her head. 'Only from a distance, like, but I've never had any call to be talkin' to him as yet.'

As they turned the bend in the path now, a male figure came into view, pushing a bike towards them.

'It's Brendan Flowers!' Sarah hissed. 'He must be coming home for the weekend.'

Noelle felt her chest tighten, wondering how he would react to her after not seeing her for a while. 'Just act all casual,' she said to her sister in a low voice.

'Howya, girls?' Brendan said, taking his cap off and coming to a halt beside them. He looked them both up and down, and then gave them one of his beaming smiles, which told them he was in a good mood. 'Out enjoyin' the fine evenin', are ye?'

'We are,' Sarah said, tossing her red hair over her shoulder, 'thoroughly enjoyin' it.'

He turned his attention to Noelle. 'And how is Dublin treatin' you?' he said in a particularly civil tone. 'Have you settled in at the new job?'

'It's grand,' she said, inclining her head. 'The weeks have flown in.'

'And which part of Dublin is it you're in exactly?' Brendan said, feigning ignorance of her situation, as though he had never heard his mother or sister mentioning Noelle Daly's name, as if he had never picked up and read any of the letters that had arrived at the Flowers' cottage.

'Ballsbridge,' Noelle said, looking vaguely over the top of his head rather than meet his eyes. She wondered if he noticed the nice summery dress she was wearing or the fact she'd had a couple of inches off her hair which had thickened it up nicely.

Brendan looked back at Noelle Daly now, noticing everything about her. He noticed her light summer tan and how nicely the summer dress looked on her well-shaped figure, he noticed how good her shiny hair looked and her long eyelashes that were emphasised with brown mascara. And then he noticed her lips which looked somehow fuller than before.

'Are you home for long?' he asked, a strange feeling coming over him, a feeling of self-consciousness that made his tongue feel suddenly too big for his mouth.

'For the week,' she told him, flicking her hair back over her shoulder. Then she lifted her head and met his eyes with her own. 'Did you hear from Kate and your mother yet?'

'No,' he told her, 'I've been on the boat all week. But there could be an oul' postcard or a letter waiting for me back at the cottage.'

'So you're not having any holiday yourself this year?' Sarah asked. 'Did you not fancy going over to England with them?'

'Ah, sure I wasn't bothered about travelling this summer,' he said. 'And anyway, is there anywhere nicer than around here when the sun's shining?' He gestured towards the shimmering canal. 'Where would ye see the likes of that over in England?' Truthfully, Brendan had been beginning to regret staying at home – especially with the weekend coming up and all the clubs and pubs he could have been at in Stockport or Manchester – but he certainly wasn't about to admit that to the two girls.

'Ah, but a change is nice,' Sarah said, pushing the point further.

'I get plenty of change working on the canal,' he said, putting his cap back on his head. He grinned now. 'And I'm enjoyin' the peace and ease of the empty house without the women goin' on at me every five minutes. I have next week off work and I'm goin' to enjoy every last minute while they're away, going to bed when I want and getting up when I want and eatin' when I want. No naggin' or argy-bargyin' from either of them.'

'Go away with you!' Sarah told him. 'You love havin' them waiting on you hand and foot.'

'I'm well able to manage on my own,' he said, his belly full from the customary Friday fish and potatoes he'd eaten back in the hotel in Daingean when they'd stopped off earlier on. It made a change of scenery from his usual pub in Ballygrace and it kept him up to date with any happenings in the nearby town. 'By the way,' he suddenly remembered, 'did youse know, girls, that there's a dance on in Daingean Town Hall tomorrow night?'

'Tomorrow night?' Sarah said, raising her eyebrows and then looking over at Noelle.

'Good band playing too, by all accounts,' he informed them. He whistled a few notes now and gestured as though he was playing the tin whistle. 'Could be a grand night, and ye never know, youse might get lucky and get a few rounds of the floor wi' me or one of the other Ballygrace lads.'

Noelle looked at him again. 'We'll see,' she said, a slight coolness in her manner. 'It depends if there's anything else happening.'

'Well, there's no Station Masses or any Mission coming to the church that I'm aware of,' he said, laughing again. 'So I think the oul' dance in Daingean is about all that's on the go, unless you're headin' in as far as Tullamore.' He straightened his bike up now, suddenly thinking that they might think he was trying to persuade them to go to the dance. 'I'll be headin' off now, so enjoy yer walk, girls,' he said, giving them a wink. 'And don't be talkin' to any strange men.'

'Oh begod, we've had our share of strange men for this evening, talking to you, Brendan Flowers!' Sarah said.

The two girls went off giggling to themselves while Brendan continued homewards, wondering if he should have bothered mentioning that dance to them at all. He was sure there was a change in Noelle Daly already from having been up in Dublin this past while. Apart from the changes to her hair and the bit of make-up, she was definitely more confident in herself.

He didn't know why he'd told them about the feckin' dance at all. Sure, there was no shortage of good-looking girls between Ballygrace and Daingean, and there were plenty who would be delighted to dance with him. Sure, he'd even had married women almost throwing themselves at him. The Dalys could go to hell for all he cared. There were plenty more fish in the sea.

As he cycled his bike back to the house, he found himself going over and over the little scene he'd just had with the two sisters, trying to make sense of the annoyance he felt about Noelle's coolness in particular.

Slowly he came to the conclusion that for all he could pick and drop the women, the novelty of those dalliances had worn off. Recently, he'd found himself looking around for a different kind of relationship – for a different kind of girl, the kind of girl he might like to settle down with. But however hard he tried there was nobody that he was too pushed about seeing on a regular basis. After a while he got fed up with their silly chatter and sneaking around the back of the pub or down a quiet bit of the canal to lie on damp grass for a bit of a feel or a fumble. He wanted something steadier than that, something with a bit more dignity. It was all a question of looking in the right quarter for it.

And by the looks of it, he wouldn't be looking too close at anyone like Noelle Daly. She had made it obvious by heading up to Dublin that Ballygrace wasn't big enough to hold her, that none of the Ballygrace lads – including Brendan Flowers – were good enough for her.

Anyway, Noelle Daly had had her chance last year when she left him standing like an eedjit outside the pictures in Tullamore; she wouldn't get the chance to make an eedjit of him again.

Chapter 26

❧❧

'**S**o what would you normally be doing on a Friday night back in Ireland?' David McGuire asked as they walked along the street towards the tennis court. He had the two rackets in their carrying cases slung over his shoulders.

Kate's voice was light and amused. 'Definitely not going to play tennis . . .' She looked down at herself now – at the new jeans she had bought and left at her aunt's the previous summer and at the pristine white tennis shoes she had bought an hour after she'd agreed to meet David. A blue checked, short-sleeved shirt was the best top she could come up with that would pass for the sport, but she knew that the colour suited her and she'd bought a yard of deep blue ribbon to tie back her hair. 'If there was a dance on locally I'd probably go to that,' she said, more serious now. 'Or maybe the pictures . . . or that kind of thing.' She thought of the pictures and Michael on their last night now and felt a little stab of guilt. 'But there's often weekends I don't go out at all, especially in the winter.' She looked at him now. 'Do you like dancing or anything like that?'

'Yes, when I get the chance. Occasionally there are dances in one of the local hotels for the staff in the hospital, and sometimes we go into the halls in Manchester.'

Kate nodded. 'I've never been to any in Manchester, but Graham usually takes us to one of the Irish clubs on our last weekend.' She pulled a face. 'It's more my mother's idea of a good night out than mine. And Graham loves taking us all up on the dance floor.'

David laughed. 'I can just imagine Graham in his element, waltzing around with three lovely ladies!'

'Don't!' she warned him. 'You're not safe while those tennis rackets are within reach.'

Kate surprised David McGuire *and* herself by being perfectly competent on the tennis court and managing to almost equal his playing.

'I must be really tired out after all those night shifts or I would

148

have beaten you ten minutes ago,' he joked when he hit the last shot home.

'I have to say I'm feeling tired out myself,' she told him, flopping down in an exaggerated fashion on the wooden bench at the side of the court. 'I'll probably be as stiff as anything in the morning, having not played any sport for ages.'

'You're an excellent wee player,' he said as he sat down beside her.

Kate went to smile at the way he said *wee* in his Scottish accent, but decided against it, thinking that he just might take it the wrong way. She was so used to the constant battle of wits with Brendan at home that she had to remind herself that not everyone found that sort of thing acceptable.

'Seriously,' he continued, 'if that's how good you are *without* playing tennis regularly, you'd make a brilliant player with practice.'

'Thanks,' she said, delighted at the compliment. 'I used to love all those kinds of sports when I was younger.' She gave a small sigh, and reached to untie her hair from the tight ponytail she'd worn for the game. Her hair tumbled loose about her shoulders now, and she ran both her hands through it to separate the curls. 'I suppose you get out of the way of these enjoyable games when you have things to do at home and everything.'

David looked at her, suddenly struck with her beautiful dark hair and eyes – and felt even more intrigued than he had been when he first met her. 'Do you work when you're home in Ireland?' he asked, wanting to know more about her.

'No,' Kate said, 'I wish I did, but I've not been in the position to do that for a number of reasons.'

'What would you like to do?' he asked, his arm coming to rest on the back of the bench just behind her shoulders.

'Nursing,' she told him. 'It's what I've always wanted to do.'

'I'm sure you will then,' he said, nodding his head. 'You're still young and have plenty of time to start.'

'I'm twenty,' she said without waiting for him to ask. 'And how old are you?'

'Twenty-eight,' he replied. 'Nearly an old man compared to you.'

Kate laughed. 'That's exactly the age I guessed you were, although my mother thought you might be over thirty.'

'You were discussing me then?' he said, smiling and raising his eyebrows. 'And your mother thought I looked years older than I am?' He shook his head. 'I'll definitely have to do something about all those late nights.'

'Not exactly *discussing* you,' she giggled. 'But we couldn't help but talk about you the way Betty has been praising you in the hospital and then of course Graham tells us about every potato and cabbage that you buy in the shop . . .' She looked up into his face, her brown eyes dancing with laughter. 'There's not a single thing about you that we don't know by now.'

He shook his head and started to laugh along with her, then something suddenly halted him and his face became more serious.

'What?' Kate asked him. She sat up straight and properly on the wooden garden bench. 'What is it?'

Then – at eight o'clock in broad daylight and oblivious to the other tennis players – David McGuire leaned forward and kissed her full on the mouth, with a passion that completely swept her breath away.

It was a passion she had never felt when Michael O'Brien kissed her.

Chapter 27

ary Flowers was studying a particularly complicated part in her knitting pattern, which involved the use of a third, smaller needle. She had been at it for the last quarter of an hour, but every time she attempted the lacy parts with the two big holes, she got it completely muddled up. She sat it down on her lap again, sighing in exasperation.

Rose was sitting opposite, in a corner of the deep, comfortably squashy sofa, half-reading and half-watching the television, which was on low in the background. The television was still a great novelty to Mary and she was glued to it any time there was anything vaguely interesting on it. The rest of the time the picture was on with a low sound in case she missed something good.

Graham had gone off to the local pub for what he described as a 'swift half' with a few of his mates, leaving the women to relax in peace together. Betty had her daughter and a sister visiting this evening so they didn't feel under any pressure to go to the hospital, and were quite happy taking it easy at home.

'Do you think the boyfriend at home will mind Kate going out with another fella?' Rose asked, looking up from her magazine.

'I do think he'll mind,' Mary said, giving an anxious little nod of her head. 'From what I know of him, Michael O'Brien's a very serious type . . . He's a lovely lad and well brought up in the old-fashioned way.' She lifted one of her knitting needles now and very carefully scratched her head with it. 'Mind you, they've only gone for a game of tennis . . . it's not exactly a romantic night out to the pictures or anything like that.'

'True,' Rose said. She paused, then gave a slow smile. 'Although anywhere can seem exciting when you're with a good-looking fella. I'm sure playing tennis and having a bit of a run-around and a laugh is as good as anywhere else.'

'D'you think so?' Mary mused. 'I can't say I was ever anywhere very exciting with poor Seamus . . . but then he wasn't what you could call a very exciting man – dependable and hard-working, but never exciting.'

'Ah, but he was a very, very *nice* man,' Rose said, a softness coming into her eyes now as she remembered her brother-in-law. 'And he was very good-natured. I remember how good he was to me when I first came up to Ballygrace.' She paused. 'And he was very kind to you, Mary. I know he was older and everything, but he wasn't demanding in any way, and he couldn't do enough for you.'

'Every single word you said about Seamus is true,' Mary agreed. 'But isn't it terrible . . . ? I just remember every day with him being the very same. No real ups and no real downs – not the way you have it with Graham.'

Rose's features darkened. 'Don't mention that fella to me. He's that many ups and downs that he nearly has my hair gone white!'

'Ah, but Rose,' Mary laughed, 'you were only mad about him when you were first going out! I remember you telling me how scared you were to tell Mammy and Daddy that he was an Englishman, and d'you not remember how you were plannin' to elope with him if they wouldn't let you marry him?' She shook her head. 'You were really under his spell, weren't you?'

Rose let out a long low whistle. 'I must have been under something,' she told her sister wryly, 'I was certainly seeing him through rose-tinted specs, no doubt about it.'

'You've not had it bad, Rose,' Mary told her. She waved her hand around the room. 'You've a lovely big house, your own fruit and vegetable business ... When I think about it, I feel very proud of how you've done for yourself.'

Rose looked thoughtful. 'I suppose I could have done worse.'

'Most definitely,' Mary said firmly. 'You've done *very* well for yourself.'

'Apart from not havin' children of our own,' Rose added, her face tightening now. 'What a difference that would have made to us.'

'That wasn't poor Graham's fault,' Mary reminded her. 'You did fall pregnant twice ...'

'Three times,' Rose corrected her, her voice sounding a little wavery. 'I'm sure I was expecting that last time, even though it was only a week late. I felt the very same as I did on the other occasions ...'

Mary put her knitting down at the side of the chair, suddenly uncomfortable with the turn that the conversation had taken. 'Will I make us a cup of tea, Rose?' she offered.

Rose thought for a moment. 'Ah, to hell with it,' she said, getting up out of her own chair. She went over to the well-polished walnut cabinet in the corner and opened the pull-down part. She took out a bottle of port. 'What's good for the goose is good for the gander.' She took two short but wide glasses from the same compartment. 'It's Friday night, we deserve a little treat.'

'Oh, Rose,' Mary tittered, 'what would they say back in Clare if they saw you and me drinking at home? We never saw anybody drinkin' at home in Ireland apart from at funerals.'

Rose shrugged. 'Who gives a damn what they would think? Sure, there's none of them left at home now to be thinkin' anything, and all the older ones are dead.' She came over to the coffee table and opened the port and filled the glasses three-quarters of the way up.

'Will that be very strong?' Mary asked, not too sure at all where alcohol was concerned. The odd sherry at funerals and Christmas or a medicinal brandy were the limit of her experience.

Rose handed her sister one of the glasses. 'Drink it up,' she said, taking a gulp from her own glass. She pulled a face now, as though it didn't taste quite the way she had expected. 'It's a Friday night and you're on your holidays.' She wagged a finger at her sister. 'Kate and Graham are out enjoyin' themselves, aren't they? So are we not entitled to a little bit of pleasure?'

'Ah, well . . .' Mary said, taking a careful sip of the port. It was very nice, she thought, so she took a bigger one, then sat back in the armchair, enjoying the warm feeling as the red liquid moved down through her chest.

Rose sat down heavily in the chair opposite. 'Do you think it would have made a difference?' she asked.

'What?' Mary's brow rumpled in confusion.

'Us havin' a baby . . . if me and Graham had had a child.' Rose took another drink of the port.

Mary shrugged, feeling very uncomfortable. She'd been in this situation several times with her younger sister, and it always led down the same path. 'Don't be thinking about it, Rose,' she said, reaching across to touch her sister's knee. 'If it was meant for you, it would have happened.'

'Three little babies,' Rose said. 'I could have three grown children by now. They would have been sixteen, thirteen and nine. Can you imagine that, Mary? Can you imagine me and Graham with three children?'

'I can't answer that, Rose,' Mary replied. 'It's something that never happened.' She paused, her mind scrabbling around for the right words – or any words that might halt Rose's run down the road of regret. 'It's whatever God decides . . . the way he took Kate and Brendan's father away from us . . . these are things we don't know anything about. It's all God's will.'

Rose's face crumpled. 'I don't care what's God's will – I just *know* I would have been happier if we'd had children . . .' She took another drink and after swallowing it, she took a big deep breath. 'And that bloody Graham – you wouldn't know *what* he was thinking. He never says a word about the children . . . he never says a thing about not having any or the difference it would have made.' She shook her head. 'Are all men like that, Mary? Not speakin', not letting you know what's going on in their bloody heads? Was Seamus Flowers like that?'

Mary blinked her eyes a few times as though searching for inspiration. 'Ah, the poor man didn't think an awful lot, really. He wasn't like Graham – he was more kind of quiet in himself.'

'The thing that annoys me,' Rose went on, 'is that Graham has plenty to say for himself when it comes to the shop and money and things like that.' She nodded her head vigorously. 'Oh, yes, he has plenty of opinions about things like that because it makes him feel he's a big man. But when it comes to the really important things like losing his children, he hasn't a bloody thing to say for himself.'

Mary took a little sip from her port, wishing she could think of something to say that would help her sister, something that would make her feel even a tiny bit better.

'I think,' Mary said, 'that it's a case of us trying to be grateful for what we *do* have.' She leaned over and patted Rose's hand. 'You have a husband to look after you and a lovely house and a good business.' She paused, getting her words right. 'While I have very little money and things compared to you, and no husband – but I have got Brendan and Kate.' She held her hands out. 'We just have to be grateful to God for what we have . . .'

Rose thought hard for a few moments. 'Yes,' she eventually said, her voice calmer now, 'I suppose there's wisdom in what you're saying . . .'

Mary gave a little silent sigh of relief, thinking that at least she had found something to say that might take Rose's mind off her frustrations in life. At least, she thought to herself, it distracted herself from the usual anxieties that dogged her. Somehow, in the shop and in the house with her younger sister, she felt she had a place. She felt she could listen to and advise Rose and, in some way, even be a help. That in itself made Mary Flowers feel a whole lot better.

Rose looked up at the clock now. 'I wonder how Kate's getting on with the doctor?'

Mary bit her lip. 'We'll soon see,' she said, giving a little smile. 'We'll soon see.'

Chapter 28

G ood evening, ladies,' Graham said, bowing rather unsteadily at the waist. 'Did youse have a nice quiet night on yer own?' He spied the port bottle sitting out on the coffee table and the two empty glasses with the tell-tale wine-coloured dregs at the bottom. 'I see you looked after yourselves in my short absence, that's what I like to see.'

Rose sucked in her breath, feeling like giving him a good kick up the backside. Some 'short absence', she thought, and so much for the 'swift half' – by the cut of her husband he'd had more like a swift half-a-bloody-dozen. But then, she thought, that was Graham Hopkins, always ready to take advantage of any situation.

'Did you have a nice night?' Mary asked, her eyes bright from the port. 'Was there many in the pub?'

'Packed – usual Friday night,' Graham informed her, sitting down on the sofa beside his wife. He patted her legs in an affectionate manner, which immediately made Rose move her feet onto the floor. 'I didn't have much to drink or owt . . . I spent half the time watchin' a darts match.'

Rose gave a little grunt to signal her disbelief, which he either didn't hear or chose to ignore. He looked from one sister to the other now. 'Kate?' he said, raising his eyebrows and holding his hands palm-up in question.

'She's not back yet,' Mary said, trying to sound all casual and not a bit worried – the exact opposite to how she felt about the situation. She reached down to the side of the chair now to tackle her knitting again.

'She's not back yet? Well, I only hope they have lights switched on in the tennis court,' Graham said, giving a snort of laughter, 'else they'll be playing in the flamin' dark!' He looked at his watch. 'It's half past ten now . . . maybe the Parky locked them in the park and they'll have to stay there all night!'

'Don't be so blidey silly,' Rose snapped, looking daggers at her inebriated husband.

'I'm not bein' silly, Rose. He's a real nowty little get, the Parky,'

Graham persisted. 'I know him well enough – a right little "jobsworth", a little Hitler ... he'd lock them in just to prove a point, like.'

Mary looked over at her sister, her eyes dark with concern. 'What d'you think could have happened to them? D'you think they could be locked in that tennis park all night?'

A broad smile spread across Rose's face. 'Indeed and I do not!' she stated vehemently. 'Are you serious thinking that, Mary? A young good-looking girl out with a handsome doctor?' She rolled her eyes to the ceiling. 'Would you be rushin' home?'

Mary raised her eyebrows and went to say something, then she thought better of it. She spread the piece of knitting across her lap, trying to work out the holey bit of the pattern again, and wishing that Kate would come home soon.

'Here y'are, love,' Graham said, taking the cork out of the port bottle and coming over to his wife's glass.

Instinctively, Rose covered the top of her glass with her hand, and then she suddenly thought, What the hell? Why shouldn't I have another drink? She moved her hand and allowed him to pour her a generous measure.

Graham then moved over to do the same for Mary, who smiled and thanked him, not really taking in what he was doing as her thoughts were still firmly locked in the park and Kate and that very handsome young doctor. She put the knitting back down on the floor again and sat back to sip her drink.

Graham then filled a glass with port for himself, then did his usual little trick of taking two good gulps out of the glass, then quickly re-filling it again to the very top again before anybody noticed.

'Crikey! I nearly bloody forgot,' Graham said, suddenly clicking his fingers in the air. 'I was chatting to Lance Williams down at the pub tonight and he's invited us all to a charity party at his house tomorrow night.' He gestured towards his sister-in-law. 'I thought Mary might enjoy a different kind of a night out ... and Kate, if she's not out gallivantin' with Dr McGuire again.' He gave a little chuckle. 'Out hob-nobbin' with the professionals like.'

Both women studiously ignored Graham's little jibe.

'A *charity* party?' Rose repeated in a high, incredulous voice. 'What kind of party is that?'

'It's to raise funds for the cricket club to have the roof re-done. Lance thought it would make a change from the usual dances and charity games.' He nodded over at Mary. 'He's a great one for ideas is Lance.'

'So how will they make money on it?' Rose persisted.

'Well, we all pay a few shillings at the door,' Graham explained, 'and then you get a couple of glasses of beer or wine and a sandwich and they'll have some raffles as well. Lance said they've got some crackin' prizes.'

'What do you think?' Rose said, looking across at her sister.

Mary looked startled to be asked a question as she was only half-listening to the conversation. 'I don't mind, it's up to you and Graham . . .' she said cautiously, then she took another sip of her port.

'It'll be a bit of a change, like,' Graham said. He jabbed his finger in his wife's direction, the port getting him all animated now. 'And don't forget that Lance is one of our best customers. Any time there's a "do" on down the cricket club or in the pub, he always gets the veg and the tomatoes from us.' He took a drink from the port. 'You have to remember the old saying – if you scratch my back, I'll scratch yours.'

'True,' Rose said. 'He is a good customer, right enough . . . and it's nice of him to open his doors to everyone. He's a widower and I suppose organising these charity events gives him something to do.' Her face suddenly brightened. 'It might be a good night, Mary. Lance Williams has got a lovely big house – he has a housekeeper and everything – and he was just sayin' recently that he'd had it newly decorated.' She glanced around the sitting-room. 'It might give me some ideas for doing the house up.'

'Don't go getting any notions about decoratin' this place,' Graham warned her. 'I've enough on me plate in the shop what with poor old Betty not bein' able to work any more. I'm run off me bleedin' feet what with goin' to the market early and clearin' up in the evenings'

'That's not what Betty thinks,' Rose said. 'She reckons she'll be back as soon as she's on her feet again.'

'She can reckon all she bloody well likes,' Graham said, nodding his head vigorously, all sympathy for his old shop assistant rapidly dwindling. 'As far as I'm concerned, she's far too old to be workin' in a shop and as of now she's pensioned off!'

'Ah, Graham!' Mary said in a shocked voice. 'Don't be saying that about poor Betty. We'd miss her terrible, wouldn't we, Rose?'

'Poor Betty my arse,' Graham said, the port fuelling the firmness in his voice. 'Business is business, and Betty's not up to being part of our business any longer – and anyroads, I've taken a new lady on as of Monday morning.'

'You've what?' Rose said.

'That woman that used to work in Bramhall fruit and veg shop is startin' on Monday,' he said, gesturing out the window in the direction of the up-market village. 'It's all organised.'

Rose's eyes narrowed. 'You mean you've gone and taken on somebody else in place of Betty without consulting me?'

Mary shifted in her seat, suddenly feeling very uncomfortable to find herself in the middle of a marital disagreement. She wondered if she should make herself scarce. She picked one of the knitting needles up and let on she was checking the end of it to see it was the right size.

'I told you all about it,' Graham said. 'I told you last week that we'd need to get somebody else in the shop.' He gave a shrug. 'Her husband was in the pub tonight and he asked me if it was definite we were looking for somebody, as his missus had been offered another job down in Stockport working on a fruit and veg stall in the market.'

'I hope you said it was only temporary,' Rose told him. 'You can't go giving Betty's job away like that.'

'Listen,' he said, pointing out the door now, 'whose name is it above the shop door? Does it say Betty? Or does it say Graham Hopkins?'

'I'll tell you one thing,' Rose said now, 'that was a low-down, mean trick you've just pulled, Graham Hopkins.' She tutted loudly. 'You never cease to bloody amaze me . . .'

Chapter 29

A s the bell for last orders sounded Kate looked at her watch. It was nearly eleven o'clock. 'God!' she exclaimed. 'I didn't realise the time . . .' She reached for her cardigan, which was lying on the empty chair beside her. She knew she'd taken a chance going for a drink after their game of tennis, but she had only meant to stay for a short while – an hour at most. Somehow, that hour had turned into almost three. And they had spent all of that time talking to each other – about everything and anything.

David McGuire had knowledge and opinions on loads of subjects – politics, religion, even working conditions for married women. Kate couldn't remember the last time she'd had such an intense conversation with anyone, and in spite of all her misgivings, she didn't want their evening to end.

'Another drink?' David asked. Then he reached over and covered her hand with his. 'Please . . .' he said in a mock-beseeching voice. 'You've got to take pity on a poor junior doctor – I haven't had a night out like this for weeks.'

Kate took a deep breath. 'I should have been back home ages ago . . .' Even as she said it, she knew the words sounded weak and pathetic.

He stood up now, reaching for his wallet in his back pocket. 'You're on holiday, Kate, you're entitled to a night out with someone your own age.' He opened the black leather wallet and took out a pound note. 'Shandy again – or do you feel a bit more adventurous?'

Kate laughed now. 'I think I'm going to need a large whiskey to get the courage to face them back at the house.' She paused, raising her eyebrows. 'I *am* joking, a shandy will be just grand, thanks.'

He came back from the bar a few minutes later with two half-pint glasses. 'We'll definitely make this the last one, okay?'

'Thanks very much,' Kate said, taking the glass from him, knowing that she shouldn't be sitting here with him. 'I don't think we've any choice since we'll be thrown out soon anyway, and I don't think there's much more left for us to talk about. We've talked non-stop all night.'

'Ah, but there's plenty left for us to talk about,' he told her. 'I've a big long list of things I still want to know about you.'

Kate's face became serious. 'Now you know the most important bit about me,' she told him in a firm voice. 'You know I'm walking out with a fellow back home.'

'Oh *that* . . .' he said, clicking his fingers as though he'd forgotten all about it. 'An extremely minor detail.'

Kate put her glass down and leaned her elbows on the table. 'Come on, David,' she said quietly. 'I told you that straight away so you would know it *wasn't* a minor detail. I told you that the minute you—'

'The minute I kissed you?' he finished for her. He looked at her now – deep into her eyes – all kidding and joking gone. 'I couldn't help myself,' he said, reaching over to take her hand. He lifted it now to his lips. 'And I feel like doing exactly the same thing again—'

'Well don't!' Kate hissed, pulling her hand away. 'If you try anything like that, I'll walk straight out of here . . .'

'Oh, c'mon, Kate,' he said in his soft Scottish accent. 'Give me a wee bit of a break. I'm the same nice guy that asked you for a game of tennis, and now you're acting as if I've suddenly turned into a mass murderer or something.' He looked straight at her and Kate suddenly noticed how startlingly green his eyes were – like dark, shiny emeralds. 'All I've done is kiss you – surely that's not the worst thing that's ever happened to you?'

Kate felt herself blushing now and she felt a bit silly, like a very young teenager. 'Of course it's not,' she said, almost stammering now. 'In fact I enjoyed it, but—'

His whole face lit up. 'Well, I'm very glad to hear that you enjoyed it,' he said, cutting off any protestations. He moved his arms onto the small pub table now, the bare skin of their forearms touching. 'I've never met anyone like you, Kate Flowers, and I'm not willing to let you go very easily. I like everything about you – the way you look, the way you talk, your lovely bright brown eyes. I like your sense of humour and your cheery laugh and I like all the stories you've told me about your life back in Ireland.' His hand moved to cover hers now. 'As I've said, I've never met anyone like you before.'

Kate looked back at this handsome, entertaining young doctor and knew she should not be sitting in a pub in England with him or letting him hold her hand – and then she heard herself say, 'Well, David McGuire, I've never met anyone like you either, and there are a lot of things I like about you, too. I know from the way you've talked tonight that you're an excellent, dedicated doctor with a very down-to-earth manner that your patients must be grateful for.'

He smiled at her and gave her a mock little bow. 'Thank you for that accolade, Miss Flowers. I'm very flattered.'

Kate eased her hand away from his now. 'In a different place and a different time,' she told him, 'we might have got on very well together. It's a pity that things are the way they are – but that's life.'

He sat back in his chair, frowning to himself, and took a drink from his beer.

Kate lifted her own drink from the table to give her hands something to do, and to try to still the pounding in her chest. What on earth had happened to her tonight? she thought. How had she got herself into this dreadful situation? It seemed as though she had not only betrayed Michael's trust, but she had managed to hurt a complete stranger into the bargain.

Somehow, in the space of a few months, Kate had managed to meet *two* men who seemed very, very suitable for her. All the time before she had bemoaned the fact that she never met anyone who held any great interest for her, and all of a sudden, she had come across *two*.

Tonight, she silently decided – when she got back to her aunt's house – she had some very, very serious thinking to do.

'How much longer are you here in Stockport, Kate?' David asked now.

'I have just over another week,' she replied.

'And then you're back home to Ireland and your serious boyfriend?'

'I am,' Kate said, looking him straight in the eye.

He slowly nodded his head, but his eyes deliberately avoided her gaze. 'Well, I was just thinking,' he said, 'that there's no law against us being friends, is there? If we make a deal not to cross any lines, then there's no harm in us seeing each other the odd day or night, is there?' He put his hands flat on the table now. 'I don't think anybody would object to that – not if we're straight and honest.'

'I'll have to see,' Kate said, her mind working hard to take any implications of his suggestions. She tried to imagine explaining all this to her mother and her Auntie Rose.

Then the bell behind the bar sounded loudly, giving its message now that drinking and talking time had come to an end.

David drained his glass and reached for the tennis rackets. 'Shall we head off?' he asked her in a very even tone, a tone that told Kate he was willing to go along with whatever she decided.

A tone that meant it was all up to her.

Chapter 30

৯৩২

Brendan carefully dodged a puddle as he walked the bike up a particularly rough part of the tow-path that was littered with potholes. After all the effort he'd put in lighting the fire this evening to get a good wash, he definitely didn't want to get his decent suit splashed with muck and then arrive at the dance hall in Daingean looking like a tinker.

When he got to the reasonable part of the path he got back up on the bike and set off into Ballygrace. He had a couple of pints and had a bit of craic with some of the lads there, then around ten o'clock a few of them made their way into Daingean, laughing and joking as they weaved their way along.

They had another couple of pints in McCann's Hotel in the main street before walking the bikes down to the Town Hall, parking them against the side wall and then heading into the dance. Since the dance hall had a strict no-alcohol policy and only sold bottles of mineral or cups of tea, most of the lads – including Brendan – came with neat little noggins of whiskey tucked in their inside pockets.

The lights were dim and the band were already in full swing as the boys queued to pay their money, joking and laughing with the older women at the table, and then they grew more serious as they moved into the main part of the hall, the confident Brendan Flowers taking the lead. The hall was an unusual shape, with the entrance higher and then descending downwards step by step through rows of cinema-type seats.

'Good oul' crowd tonight,' Brendan said, pausing at the top of the stairs to survey the line-up of women bordering the perimeter of the hall and the swirling couples on the dance floor. 'And a good few that don't look like locals ... maybe even a few back home on holiday.' And then a familiar figure on the dance floor caught his eye and his attention was suddenly fixed as he watched Noelle Daly being led around the floor by a fellow he knew vaguely from Geishill. They were in the centre of the floor and the low light in the ceiling was shining directly on her hair, giving it a lovely golden glow.

As soon as the dance finished, the more confident fellows made their move before the next tune struck up. Brendan walked over to where the two Daly sisters were now sitting with a group of friends, and after saying the usual 'Goodnight to you' greeting, he strode past them to ask an attractive dark-haired Daingean girl up to dance. Then, he made a point of waltzing over to their side of the floor more often than he would have usually done, just to make sure they saw him laughing and chatting with someone else.

Just to make sure they didn't think he was in the slightest bit interested in either of them.

'Do you honestly not mind if Gerry walks me back a bit of the way?' Sarah asked her sister towards the end of the night. They'd both been well danced as usual and both had had several offers of being 'seen home' and had turned them all down apart from this recent offer of Sarah's. Gerry Dunne was an old school friend and a quiet lad she had always half-fancied. 'He's gone to get us a mineral at the bar.'

Noelle shrugged. 'Haven't we always had an agreement on that?' she said. 'We've always said we wouldn't stand in each other's way.'

'I know,' Sarah said, 'but we usually have Kate along with us ... and it doesn't look as if anyone has caught your eye tonight.'

'I'll be grand,' Noelle told her. She grinned. 'As long as you're within distance to hear me screaming if anybody jumps out from the bushes.'

Sarah's attention was suddenly taken by the appearance of Gerry Dunne who was holding two bottles of lemonade and gesturing her to come and sit at the back of the hall with him. 'Are you okay dancing with the other girls until I come back?' she checked.

'I'm grand,' Noelle repeated, a slight feeling of irritation sounding in her voice. 'Haven't I managed just fine without you all those weeks up in Dublin?' She gave Sarah a friendly little jostle. 'Now will you go before that Dunne fellow gets fed up and gives the bottle of mineral to somebody else?'

'That's grand so,' Sarah said delightedly, lifting her bag and cardigan and making off towards the back of the hall and her admirer.

A few moments later, as the band struck up 'The Rose of Tralee', Noelle felt a tap on her shoulder and she looked up to see Brendan Flowers smiling at her. She could tell by his lop-sided grin that he'd had more than a few jars in the pub – but it didn't bother her. In fact she felt more relaxed, because he was usually easier in himself with a drink in him.

'Well, Miss Daly, I wonder if you would deign to take to the floor with a humble neighbour?' he said, in a slightly mocking tone, which he always used when he felt unsure of himself.

Noelle gave him a big smile, knowing that it had taken a considerable effort for him to come and ask her to dance. Although he never actually let his guard down with her, she had observed him and had heard enough about his ways from Kate and her mother to more or less deduce how he would be feeling. 'I'd be delighted, Mr Flowers,' she said, stepping onto the polished wooden dance floor with him.

'Did you get your postcard from England yet?' Noelle asked for something to say.

'Not a feckin' word from any of them,' he laughed. 'I think they must be too busy out and about to even think of me. Sure, there's plenty to keep them occupied over there, and anyway, the post is fierce slow from England. You could easily wait a week for an oul' postcard to be delivered, and a fortnight isn't unheard of.'

'Are you not wishin' you'd gone with them at all?' she asked as they moved along, both slightly self-conscious and deliberately keeping a bit of a space between themselves.

'Ah, sure, I've enjoyed the week at home on my own,' he said. 'With the fine weather it makes a difference. I've put a few hours in up on the bog as well, so I could have the turf ready to come home in the next week or so.'

'And are you managing well enough for cooking and that sort of thing?' she asked.

'Grand,' he said, even though he had cursed the air blue in the cottage this morning when he let the bacon and sausages burn black in the pan. 'I have a good feed in the town most afternoons and that keeps me going.'

'So you're not missing the home-cooking or anything?'

'Oh, I'm independent enough,' he said. 'I'm not the kind of lad who's lost without a woman. It's not as if I'm handless around the house or anything like that. We're well used to looking after ourselves on the boat.'

Then, just as they were moving easily around the floor, passing another couple who looked to be rocking and swaying as opposed to dancing, a bit of a scuffle seemed to happen and the couple fell in against them, the girl's sharp stiletto heel ripping down the back of Noelle's leg.

'Christ almighty!' Noelle said, her hand immediately flying to check the searing pain in her calf. When she bent down both her hand and her leg were smeared with blood and, to top it all, her brand-new stockings were torn to shreds.

As Noelle went to examine the damage, Brendan's arm shot out to grab the fellow who had knocked into them. 'What the feck were you up to?' he said, gripping the lad's arm tightly. 'Banging into us like that?'

'It wasn't our feckin' fault!' the fellow retaliated in a slurred voice, struggling and starting to make vague boxing gestures. 'Somebody knocked into me . . . it was a feckin' accident.'

Brendan looked at him with venom, but decided to let it drop since the lad was obviously jarred and wouldn't be fit to defend himself. He swore under his breath and then shoved the lad away into his equally drunken partner.

'Are you all right?' Brendan asked Noelle anxiously. Then, his hand came around her shoulder to steady her.

'I'm grand . . .' she said in a shaky voice. 'I just need to sit down for a minute . . . I think I feel a bit sick.' Then, just as she reached the chairs over at the wall, a strange feeling came over her, making her stop dead in her tracks and slowly sink to the floor.

'Noelle!' Brendan said, moving quickly to catch her in his arms. To break her fall, he had to drop to his knees onto the floor beside her. Then, everything moved quickly and people came to help him and lift her up onto one of the chairs.

Brendan quickly peeled off his good suit jacket and without a thought rolled it up and very gently placed it under her head. 'Move back,' he told the group around them. 'Give her a bit of air.'

Then, as he looked down at the prone figure of Noelle Daly – at her pale face framed by her golden-red hair – a strange, unfamiliar feeling washed over him, a feeling of real concern, of protectiveness. It told him that in spite of the coolness that had been between them, he really cared for her.

'What's happened?' Sarah Daly gasped, pushing through the crowd that had gathered around her sister. 'Oh, my God!' she said, glancing at Noelle's chalk-white face. 'She's fainted!' She got to her knees now, oblivious to the dirty floor and not quite sure what to do to help her sister, because Brendan Flowers seemed to have taken charge of it all.

'She'll be all right,' Brendan told her in a concerned but quite calm voice. He was stroking Noelle's hair now and saying her name over and over again, trying to get through to her, trying to bring her round.

'Quick – give her a drink of this!' a girl said, pushing a bottle of lemonade in Brendan's hand.

'Hold on,' he said, pushing the bottle away. Brendan looked at Sarah now. 'I think she's coming round. If you give me a hand, we might be better if we get her to sit up.'

Between them and with the help of Gerry Dunne and some of the girls' friends, they got Noelle into an upright position and gradually she started to come around. She took a sip from the lemonade bottle as instructed by Brendan and then she leaned her head back and opened her eyes.

'Oh God!' she whispered, feeling all weak and shaky again. 'What's happened?'

Brendan put his arm around her. 'You're all right now, Noelle,' he said, stroking her cheek with his other hand. 'You're okay now . . . you'll be grand.'

She turned her head to look into Brendan Flowers' concerned eyes. 'Did I faint or something?'

'You did,' he said gently. 'You had a bit of an accident – a cut on your leg – and the shock of it must have made you pass out.'

Noelle moved now, trying to sit up properly, and then she bent down to have a look at her leg. The sight of the blood and the mess of her new stockings made her go all weak and woozy again and she groaned and lay back in Brendan's arms.

'Take it easy,' he said, gently drawing her in closer to him, his hand lightly stroking her forehead. 'Just take your time. We'll sit here for as long as you like . . . and we'll take it nice and easy until you feel back to yourself.'

Sarah sat down on the chair at the other side of her sister. 'Can I get you anything?' she said, rubbing her hand.

'Maybe you could get a cold, wet cloth,' Brendan suggested. 'It might cool her down and we could clean her leg and put a plaster on it to make sure it doesn't get infected.'

Sarah couldn't believe her ears. Was this sympathetic, caring person really the cocky, full-of-himself Brendan Flowers? What on earth had brought this big turnabout with him?

'I'll go out to the people in the kitchen and see if they have anything there,' Sarah told him, 'and I'll be back in a minute.'

Half an hour later Noelle had drunk a cup of strong tea and eaten a digestive and was almost back to her old self. She was much brighter and the peaches-and-cream colour of her complexion was gradually coming back. Every few minutes she kept apologising over and over to Brendan Flowers for all the trouble she'd caused.

'You'll be sorry now that you ever asked me to dance,' she said ruefully. She was sitting up straight and feeling very embarrassed about the ungainly situation he must have seen her in earlier.

'Not a bit of it,' Brendan said, patting her hand comfortingly. 'If I couldn't help our nearest neighbour out, I wouldn't be much of a man now, would I?'

'You've been very good,' she told him in a quiet voice. 'Nobody could have done more for me . . . and I've ruined the best part of your night out.' She gestured towards the couples dancing past them on the floor. 'Maybe you want to go on now . . . and enjoy the rest of the evening.'

'Indeed I don't,' he told her firmly. 'I'm not a bit bothered about the oul' dance – I'd much rather see that you were back on your feet and home safe and sound.'

She looked down at her leg, which had a gauze pad with Germolene and a fine white stretch bandage pinned over it. She had had to take both her stockings off and was relieved the dress she was wearing was a good long one – almost down to her ankles – and thankfully covered her bare white legs.

Noelle bit her lip, suddenly realising the situation she was in. 'God, I hope I can manage the bike . . . it's a fair old walk from here to Ballygrace.'

'Right,' he said, standing up. 'We'll set off now and it'll give you plenty of time to take it easy.'

'But that's not fair on you,' she protested. She looked across the dance floor to check where her sister was. 'Sarah will come back with me . . . she can see Gerry Dunne another night.'

Brendan suddenly looked wounded. 'Are you sayin' you don't want to travel home with me?' he said, his face darkening.

'Not at all,' she said. 'I just feel I've ruined your night and it's not fair for you to be saddled with me and walk a good bit of the way home. I'll only slow you up.'

'Noelle,' he said, taking both her hands in his, 'it's a pleasure to see you home. Apart from being a neighbour, you're a good friend of Kate's. Isn't that reason enough for me to be seeing you home? Wouldn't any decent fella living near you do the very same?'

Something in his eyes suddenly made Noelle realise that he was being deadly serious and that she would end up causing a real feud between them if she refused to let him see her home. And he was right anyway, she thought, what harm could it do?

'Grand,' she said, suddenly smiling at him.

Noelle took a few minutes to catch Sarah and explain what was happening.

'So you're leaving now?' her younger sister asked, looking very disappointed. 'Then I'd better get my bag and head home with you. I don't want you going home on your own with a bad leg.'

'It's grand now,' Noelle said, shaking her head. 'You stay on until the dance is finished and let Gerry Dunne bring you home. I'll be fine walking back with Brendan ... he's been really good tonight.'

Sarah's face darkened. 'But you know what Daddy will be like if he thinks we've gone off with lads on our own ...'

'This is different,' Noelle said in a low voice, not wanting any of the girls around to overhear. 'I'll explain to him what happened about my leg and say that I came home early on my own.'

Sarah touched her sister's arm. 'Don't let him see you with Brendan Flowers. You know he thinks he's nothing but an oul' rake.' She shook her head, looking really worried now. 'He'll be giving out to you for the next week if he thinks you've walked all the way home from Daingean with Brendan.'

Noelle nodded. 'If he does by any chance see him, I'll say we just met up on the way home.' She smiled and gave a careless little shrug. 'I don't give a feck what Daddy says; I've had it up to here with his moods. I'm nearly twenty years of age and I don't even live at home any more. If he starts on at me I'll just say I'm going straight back up to Dublin in the morning.'

'Try not to get into a row with him,' Sarah pleaded. 'For me and Mammy will be on the receivin' end of his bad humour for the next week.'

Noelle glanced over her shoulder to the back of the hall where Brendan was waiting for her, hands in his suit pockets, chatting and laughing with some of the Daingean lads that he knew from loading the barges. 'I'll make sure he doesn't see us,' she promised.

Chapter 31

As they approached the closed and darkened shop Kate felt a sudden chilly breeze around her legs and then the rising wind whipped at her hair, sending it tumbling around her face and neck.

They stopped for a moment at the wall between the shop and house, then, when a particularly strong breeze whipped Kate's hair against her cheek, David put the rackets down on the wall and leaned forward to smooth her hair back in place. For a brief moment he paused, as though he might kiss her again, and then he drew back.

Kate checked her watch. 'I'd better go in,' she said quietly, 'and face the music...'

He smiled at her. 'I'm sure Graham's not the sort to give you a lecture for being late.'

'True,' she said, nodding. 'I don't suppose anybody will say anything that bad to me.'

'It was only a game of tennis,' he reminded her. Then he touched his hand to her cheek very gently. 'I hope I'll see you again...'

Kate looked back at him and for a moment felt an inexplicable rush of tears which she furiously blinked back. 'Thanks again for a lovely evening...'

And then, without another word, David lifted the tennis rackets from the wall and strode away.

'We were just a bit worried,' Mary Flowers said, trying not to betray the anxiety she'd felt earlier on, before the two glasses of port had relaxed her a little. She looked across at her daughter who was now sitting in the corner of the settee beside her aunt. 'We thought something might have happened to you ... with you being gone so long.'

'I didn't notice the time at all with it still being so light,' Kate explained, thinking that it sounded a bit lame even to herself. 'We were playing tennis for hours and afterwards we were thirsty so we went into a nice pub for a drink, and I suppose we got chatting...'

'Oh, easily done,' Rose said, raising her eyebrows and smiling in a conspiratorial manner. 'Especially when you're in nice company.'

'What was he like?' her mother asked, feeling more at ease. 'Is he a nice lad? Is he well able to chat?'

Kate felt a hot blush coming to her cheeks. 'Oh, he's well able to chat all right. He's very nice and easy altogether. You wouldn't think he had such an important job, he's so down-to-earth and everything.'

'And is he a good tennis player?' Rose put in, a look of amusement in her eyes.

Kate shrugged her shoulders. 'Better than me anyway, although I didn't do as badly as I thought.' She gave a smile at the memory of the game. 'I gave him a run for his money at times.'

'And did he make any arrangements to see you again?' Rose asked, knowing that her sister would find it harder to quiz Kate.

Kate felt her throat suddenly dry. 'Well,' she said, clearing her throat, 'it's a bit difficult . . .' She looked at her mother and pursed her lips together.

'You mean Michael?' Mary prompted.

Kate nodded. 'I don't think it would be fair to go on a real date with David.' She rubbed her finger up and down the arm of the sofa. 'It wouldn't be fair on either of them.'

'What the eye doesn't see,' Graham suddenly said in a deep melodramatic voice, as though he were giving a Shakespearian oration, 'the heart doesn't grieve. You're a young girl and you should be out havin' a good time for yourself. Mark my words – you're a long time dead.'

'Hark at the agony aunt there,' Rose mocked. 'Don't pay any heed to him, he doesn't know the first thing about women.'

'Any chance of a cheese bap and a cup of tea, love?' Graham asked, his hand rubbing his dome-shaped stomach. 'I could do with something to settle me for the night.'

'What you mean is, you could do with something to soak up the beer,' Rose told him, rising from the sofa. 'I'll make us all a last cup of tea and a bap.'

'I'll come and give you a hand, Rose,' Mary offered, getting out of her own chair now.

Most nights, if she was at home, she'd be heading to bed at this time, but she never felt as tired when she was over here on holiday.

Graham turned his attention to Kate now. 'I was just telling yer mother and Rose about a bit of a "do" we've all been invited to tomorrow night.'

Kate raised her eyebrows, affecting an interest she didn't really feel. Most of the nights out with Graham were spent in the company of older people like himself, people that, if Kate was honest, she found very boring.

'It's a charity kind of do,' he went on, explaining the whole story in minute detail once again, telling it with the same animation and interest as though it was the first audience he'd had for it.

'It sounds very good,' Kate said, trying to sound even half-interested. She was well used to Graham's ramblings when he had a few drinks in him. 'And it'll be a nice night out for Auntie Rose and Mammy.'

'And *you*,' Graham said. 'It'll be a bit of a change for you. Same as tonight was a bit of a change for you – playin' tennis with that nice David McGuire.' He looked over his shoulder now, checking that the women weren't within earshot.

'Don't pay any heed to them pair,' he said, thumbing backwards. 'You do what you like – go with who you like. It's no good lookin' back in five or ten years and bein' full of regrets. You've only got the one life, that's my philosophy, and you've got to make the most of it.' He shrugged. 'Where's the harm in havin' a bit of a laugh with a nice fella when you're over here on holiday? It'll all be forgotten when you go back home and nobody any the wiser.' He prodded his finger on the table now to emphasise the point. 'Take yer Uncle Graham's advice and enjoy life while you're young because it all disappears very quick.' His eyes became wide and staring. 'Enjoy it while you *can*! Get out there into the world and do what you want to do now,' he said emphatically.

Kate looked back at her inebriated uncle, partly amused at his seriously spoken words and partly alarmed. And for some reason, the notion of her wanting to be a nurse came flying back into her mind. Probably, she thought, it was all to do with her conversation with David earlier that evening.

She heard a little grunting noise now and looked up to find Graham had nodded off and was lightly snoring. His home-spun philosophies and advice all drowned in sleep – but his drunken words somehow had hit a little nerve within her.

Suddenly, Kate wished she was back home in Ireland where everything was much simpler and more straightforward. She wished she was back in the familiarity of Michael's arms, or ready to go to bed in the safety of the small canal cottage where she had nothing greater to think of than what she would cook for dinner tomorrow or what she might wear to the next dance.

Here in Stockport, things were much more complicated. There were far more things on offer, and greater things to achieve. But for Kate to go chasing dreams about training to be a nurse would mean so many changes for everyone else. Who would look after her mother? Who would look after Brendan? And would Michael O'Brien be prepared to hang about and wait for her?

The thoughts suddenly crowded all the spaces in her head and made her feel very, very tired. Kate stood up now and walked out into the hallway and into the kitchen where the sisters were bustling about with cups and plates and teapots.

'Don't make anything for me, please,' Kate said, giving a yawn. 'I'm really tired, and I'm just going to go straight to bed.'

'It's all that tennis playing,' Rose said, smiling at her. 'All that running about.'

Her mother put the teapot down and came over to her. 'Are you all right, Kate?'

'I'm grand . . . just tired.' She gave a weary smile. 'A good night's sleep will sort me out for the morning.'

'Make sure you get a good rest,' her mother said, giving her a kiss on the forehead. 'You have another outing to look forward to tomorrow night.'

Kate went upstairs to her bedroom, grateful to have the room and the bed to herself, grateful to think her own complicated thoughts without any interruptions.

Chapter 32

A lthough the night was cooler than it had been for the last few weeks, there was a full, bright moon as Brendan and Noelle walked along the canal towards Ballygrace. She had managed to cycle a good bit of the way, but the particular bit they were now on was on the bumpy side, so they had dismounted and were walking along, chatting as they went.

'Do you ever wonder,' Brendan asked at one point, 'how many times you've walked along this path in your life?'

Noelle laughed. 'When I was at school I often used to think things like that . . . but I haven't tried to work it out for a long time.'

'Have you missed it?' he asked. 'Being up in Dublin ... have you not missed the canal and the countryside and everything?'

A picture of Dr Casey's cross face came into Noelle's mind, then a feeling of dread at the thought of returning there.

'Well,' Brendan urged, 'do you ever miss it?'

Noelle hesitated, wondering if she could trust him enough to be honest. Before her accident tonight, she would never have dreamed of confiding in him. 'Sometimes,' she said. 'Especially at night ...'

'And what is it you miss?' he said, sounding all interested.

'I suppose I miss Sarah the most ... and then the younger ones.' She didn't mention her father or mother. 'I think I just miss the easy way things are down here, and the fact that there's always somebody you can talk to.'

'And is there nobody up in Dublin?' he said, bringing his bike to a sudden halt.

'Well, I have my aunt and uncle of course ...' she said, coming to a stop now herself. She bent down to check that the bandage around her leg hadn't become loose, wondering if Brendan would think she was in a really dire situation. 'And I've made friends with the girl who works in the house next door,' she quickly added. 'Her name's Carmel Foley and she's a really good laugh. On one of my Saturday afternoons off, we went into Dublin to see a film together, and we often go out for a walk in the evenings.'

The bit about the cinema was true – although Noelle's employer had thought that she was meeting up with her aunt in the city – but the last piece of information was a gross exaggeration, as Noelle had actually been out walking with Carmel on only one evening. She had gone for a message to the shops for Dr Casey, and she had coincidentally met up with Carmel who was coming back from the park with Mr Lavery's two boys.

'It sounds as if you're busy enough,' Brendan said, raising his eyebrows, 'and you're obviously well settled if you're going out with friends and everything.'

'It's grand,' Noelle said, 'although I don't think I'll be doing it for ever. I don't think I would like to live in Dublin for the rest of my life.'

Brendan started to move the bike slowly onwards again. 'It's nice enough for a change,' he said. 'I often have to stay the night when

I'm up there on the barge, and the Dublin lads are all right once you get to know them.'

They walked along, chatting about the pros and cons of Dublin, and then at one point when they came upon a makeshift bench Brendan insisted that they sit down for five minutes to rest Noelle's leg.

'Honestly,' she told him, lifting her dress just high enough to check on the bandage, 'it's not as sore as it was. Once we get around the next corner I'll be able to cycle most of the way back home.'

'That bandage looks as though it's going to come off,' he said, bending over to look at it. 'You'd be better tightening it,' he advised her. 'It could catch on the oul' bike chain and you'd be in trouble then.'

'True enough,' she said, 'I hadn't thought of that.' She attempted to take the safety-pin out of the bandage now, but it was at the wrong angle for her to manage it properly.

'Here,' he said, moving from the bench to kneel in front of her, 'let me do that for you.'

'It'll be grand,' Noelle said, all embarrassed now and trying to pull her dress down.

'Noelle . . .' he said, looking up at her, a hurt look in his eyes. 'I'm not trying to touch you or do anything . . . I'm only trying to help. You got a really bad knock to your leg and I want to check you're all right.'

Suddenly, Noelle felt silly, and she realised that she was indeed being very ungracious and childish. Without another word, she lifted her skirt just above her knee and held the wounded leg out for Brendan to inspect.

'If you hold the safety-pin,' Brendan told her in an efficient manner, 'then I'll wrap this bandage tightly enough to make sure it doesn't catch on the bike.'

'You've been very good,' Noelle said a few minutes later, as they pushed the cycles along the tow-path, within sight of the Dalys' house.

'Ah well,' he said, smiling at her, 'Kate and my mother would never have forgiven me if I'd left you to limp home on your own.'

Noelle sighed now, shaking her head at the memory. 'God knows what kind of shoes that one was wearing, the heels were that high she could hardly walk in them. I saw her when we were coming out of the hall and she was tottering all over the place.'

'I think that might have been more to do with the beer she had drunk earlier than the shoes,' Brendan said. He halted now as they came up to the wall outside the Dalys' yard.

'I'll leave you now, you'll probably want to get straight into your bed and rest your leg.'

'I'm surprised they're still up . . .' she said, noticing a light at the back of the house.

'I'll say goodnight to you then—' Brendan's words were interrupted by the sound of shouting and a door banging.

'Jesus,' Noelle said, 'there's a bit of a row going on in there, I think . . .' She tutted and shook her head. 'It'll be my father again . . . he's the crankiest man God put breath into.'

Brendan looked towards the house and then back at Noelle. 'Do you want me to wait for a few minutes?' he said, his manner suddenly hesitant. Matt Daly had a reputation for being very cross and awkward and he'd often heard Kate and her mother saying that he gave the girls a tough time at home. He knew from Matt's abrupt and surly manner towards him that he himself wasn't exactly held in high esteem, and he knew that if Matt came out he would be none too pleased to see him talking to Noelle. Brendan couldn't work the man out at all. It wasn't as if drink was to blame – sure, the man hardly touched a drop. If it had been the drink it would have been a whole different matter – you could understand that. It was only natural that a man became a bit obstreperous now and again with a drink on him. But to be awkward and thick all the time for no good reason was beyond all comprehension.

They could hear more raised voices – this time Noelle's mother's voice was the loudest.

'Walk on!' Noelle said in a loud whisper, starting to push her bike again. 'I don't want to go in while they're arguin'.'

Brendan did as she asked without question, trying to move himself and the bike as noiselessly as possible. They didn't speak a word until the Dalys' house was some distance behind them and the Flowers' cottage had come into view.

'What will you do?' Brendan asked. 'You can't go back there now, sure, you'll only land yourself in the middle of it.'

'I'll give them time to settle down and go to bed and then I'll go in . . .' Suddenly her voice wavered. 'I hate it when they're like that . . . I can't even come home for a feckin' week's holiday without some kind of an argument going on.'

Brendan watched her now, and in the dim light of the moon he could see her shoulders starting to heave and shake and he knew that she was crying. This was a new phenomenon for him, as the women in his own life rarely showed any great emotion when he was around, apart from the usual irritation and annoyance when he riled them too much. On the whole, he thought to himself, life in the Flowers' household was fairly smooth and easy.

'Come on,' he told Noelle. 'We'll go into the house and I'll make you a cup of tea and you'll feel better.' His mind suddenly pictured the half-dead fire he had left before going out and he realised that they would be waiting a hell of a long time for the kettle to boil. Jaysus, he thought to himself, I'll have to buy them an oul' cooker of some sort – we can't be carrying on like this with no kettle.

He felt a fleeting pang of guilt for not realising the effort it entailed to have the house and the dinners and the fires and everything up and running every single day. He hadn't understood the half of the work involved until, on this rare occasion, he'd been left to fend for himself.

He was just about to explain about the tea and the fire and everything, when he remembered the bottles of beer he had left cooling in the sink, and the medicinal half-bottle of brandy that his mother kept in the cupboard.

Feck the tea, he decided. The situation required a stronger solution.

Brendan leaned the two bicycles against the side of the cottage and then he opened the front door. Noelle went over to one of the armchairs by the dead fire while Brendan quickly went around lighting the oil lamps.

As the room gradually lit up, Noelle glanced around her. 'I'm surprised at how tidy you've kept the place,' she told him, her voice steadier now. 'I always imagine that when lads are left to their own devices the place ends up like a pig-sty.'

'Ah, sure the women have me well trained,' Brendan said, relieved to hear her sounding a bit more like her old self. He went to the bottom part of the pine dresser and took out an almost full bottle of brandy and two glasses, then he carried them to the table and poured a good measure into each glass. He then lifted a bottle of lemonade from the side of the sink and filled the glasses to just over halfway up.

'You'd have had to stay the night if we wait for the kettle to boil,' he joked now, 'so rather than have your spotless reputation ruined, we'll have to make do with a drop of brandy and lemonade.'

Brendan was gratified to see her smiling at his little joke, and was pleased she hadn't taken offence. He crossed the floor now and handed her the glass. 'Try that and if you're not too keen you can have a glass of beer or I could make you a lemonade shandy.'

'I've never tried brandy before . . .' Noelle said, holding the glass to her nose and sniffing it. 'It smells nice and sweet.' She took a tiny little sip and then paused, letting the taste settle on her tongue. 'I think this might be better than beer . . . if my father smelled beer on my breath he would go mad.'

'The brandy is no harm, and it'll do you the world of good after the night you've had,' Brendan told her, taking a mouthful of his own drink.

Noelle lifted the glass to her mouth again, getting more used to the sweet, strong taste. 'I'm beginning to think I should never have come back home . . .' Her voice had the same wavery note back in it. Her head and shoulders drooped. 'I hate all that trouble at home, and I feel bad for the younger ones having to put up with it.' She paused. 'I think Sarah will leave soon, too. She mentioned something about going to work in the factory in Clara. Seemingly they have houses over there for the workers.' She shrugged. 'When my father is in one of his moods, anything is better than living at home . . . but I don't know how I'd feel coming back if Sarah wasn't there.'

'Now, don't go upsettin' yourself again,' he said, putting a hand on her shoulder. 'These things have a way of working themselves out. It'll all sort itself out in the long run.' Brendan was amazed to hear himself offering advice to somebody else – far less Noelle Daly. Never, in the whole of his life, had he been in the position where he felt comfortable enough to speak to a girl like this. He wondered now if the brandy was having a strange effect on him, but dismissed it as he had often drunk a half-bottle of spirits and it had never caused such a thing to happen before.

His hand was still resting nice and comfortable on her shoulder and he worried that she might take it the wrong way, given the way she was feeling, so he went over and sat in the armchair opposite her.

That was another queer thing, he thought to himself, because if it was any other girl – or indeed older woman – he would have had no qualms whatsoever about putting his hand on her shoulder or anywhere else.

'You've been very good, Brendan,' Noelle said, looking solemn and thoughtful. After a few moments she looked up at him, her face working with emotion. 'And d'you know ... while we have this chance on our own to talk, I just want to say that I'm fierce sorry for that time last year when I let you down...'

Brendan suddenly felt alarmed – a tightness came into his chest and a hot feeling spread all over him. This turn in the conversation wasn't something that he had expected to happen – and it wasn't something that he was at all sure he could handle. He usually avoided personal conversations at all cost.

'That was my father again,' she whispered. 'When he found out I was meeting you he went mad ... and he wouldn't let me go. He locked me into the bedroom, and there was no way I could let you know.' She shrugged. 'I couldn't even send Sarah up to the house to tell you, for you were already in Tullamore.' She looked up at him, her eyes moist with tears but full of sincerity.

'Sure ... don't be annoyin' yerself over that,' Brendan said, all bluff now as though it had never been an issue, as though there had never been a cold war between them because he had taken the perceived rejection so badly, as though he had never called Noelle all the terrible names under the sun. 'That's all water under the bridge, and anyway, as you say, I was already in Tullamore with the boat, so it was only a step or two up the town.'

'But you were fierce annoyed with me at the time...' she told him. 'Kate said that she and your mother both tried to explain to you what had happened.'

'Oh, don't mention that Kate to me,' he said, attempting to elevate the situation to an easier note. 'She's like a bag of cats at times. She's forever finding things to go on at me about. I don't be listenin' to half the things she says – it would nearly drive a fella mad if you listened to everything she had to say.'

Brendan suddenly felt much lighter and better in himself. Having heard with his own ears the situation that the poor girl was living under, he could fully understand why she had had no option but to let him down. He could also see why she might decide to get out of the house and go and work in Dublin.

Noelle looked into the ashes of the fire, the glass cupped between her hands. What a desperate situation to be in, she thought. All the usual nonsense going on at home, and then to have the terrible atmosphere to look forward to with Dr Casey when I go back up to Dublin. She took a gulp from the glass now.

They sat in companionable silence for a few minutes, then, sensing Noelle's despondency about the situation, Brendan suddenly moved from his own chair to sit on the arm of the chair beside her. 'It'll all work out,' he said, his arm coming around her now. Then, when her head moved to lie on his shoulder, he felt a warm glow spreading through him. Whether it was the brandy acting on him now or whether it was pleasure at Noelle Daly being so close to him he neither knew nor cared.

'I didn't tell you everything about Dublin,' she whispered now. 'To be honest, I don't really like it ... the doctor's a cold, uppity type, and I'm sure that Carmel Foley from next door is up to no good with her boss ...'

Brendan's heart soared, feeling happier to hear that she wasn't completely settled up in Dublin. That she didn't sound as though she was one of the ones that came back to Ballygrace all uppity themselves and looking down on the ones they'd left behind. He squeezed her arm in a comforting gesture.

'I'd far rather be back down here,' Noelle whispered, 'amongst my friends and beside the canal and everything.' She gave a little sniff and then burrowed her face into his shoulder. 'If things were okay at home there would be no problem ... I could get a decent job locally, maybe in Tullamore or somewhere like that.'

'Give it all time,' he told her, 'and everything will work out for the best.'

He drew her closer to him and before he knew he was doing it, he had kissed her gently on the forehead. When she moved sharply away from him he was mentally kicking himself – rejected once again. He went to stand up and go back to his own chair but was halted when he saw how she was looking at him – staring at him.

Then, before he could say a word, Noelle almost threw herself into his arms and she was kissing him – kissing him with as great a passion as he could have ever imagined any woman kissing him. As he kissed her back, Brendan felt as though a great fire had just been ignited within him.

'Oh, Brendan,' she whispered, when they broke off for a few moments to take a breath. 'I'm fierce happy that we're friends again . . .'

Brendan looked back at her, and for once in his life he found himself lost for words.

Chapter 33

After a fitful night's sleep where she awoke several times from dreams about Michael and David playing tennis together or, alternatively, rolling on the ground together fighting, Kate rose early on the Saturday morning. She had no appetite, so she had a cup of milky coffee with her aunt and then – after checking the grey sky – she dressed for the cool summer's day in blue and white check trousers and a deep blue sweater. Then she went down to help Rose and Graham in the shop.

She busied around, filling display baskets with fresh oranges and bananas, onions and cauliflowers, turnips and cabbages and leeks, and then she went outside to do the box display as she had done the previous morning.

This time, there was no warm summer sunshine to help her to linger, nor was there any sign of David McGuire. In a way she was relieved, because she was in two minds whether she wanted to see him again or not. The time she had spent with him last night had left her feeling very confused. This young Scottish doctor was so different from any other lad she had ever met, and he was definitely very different to Michael O'Brien.

David had strong views on women being encouraged to work after marriage if that's what they wanted, and about women being independent generally, which was quite unusual even in England and certainly in Ireland. Kate had felt quite strange listening to him, because he was echoing all her own unspoken hopes and dreams which she had quietly put to the side to concentrate on her new romance.

He had also touched on a raw nerve with regards to Michael. They had never fully discussed his views on these sorts of things, but Kate instinctively knew that Michael came down on the more traditional side.

Things had been cool all day between Rose and Graham, and Kate and her mother took the chance to take the bus to the market in Stockport and leave the couple to sort out their differences. 'It'll all blow over,' Mary laughed as they got off the bus in Mersey Square. 'It always does. Rose has him in the dog house for a while and when she thinks he's suffered enough, she lets him find his way back into her good books.'

'I suppose Graham has got a point about Betty,' Kate said, as they linked arms to run across the road. 'They wouldn't feel too confident leaving her in charge of the shop after what happened.'

'True,' Mary agreed. 'But I still feel sorry for her. I've never really had a proper job myself, but if I did have one, it would be in a shop like Rose's.' She looked up at Kate now. 'I think sorting out the stock and mixing with all the people every day keeps your mind active. I've quite enjoyed myself helping out there this week – it gives you a whole new outlook on life. Being stuck at home all day isn't good for anybody.'

Kate looked at her mother now, wondering if she was talking solely about herself or whether she was hinting to Kate that she should think of doing more with her life. But she kept her thoughts to herself because they both knew the reason that Kate had stayed at home.

Although it was dry, the weather was dull and blustery and could easily go either way, so the two women weren't taking any chances and had brought their light raincoats and umbrellas just in case. They both wore their light summer hats, which they knew was obligatory wear for women shopping in Stockport and which would afford them some protection should the sky decide to open up on top of them.

They walked along from Mersey Square to Great Underbank and then up the steep cobbled hill to the market.

'D'you know,' Mary said, as she panted her way up the hill, 'it's very warm in spite of it being dull and breezy. I always think the weather's that bit better over here. I think it's more sheltered with all the big buildings.'

'It's dustier though,' Kate mused, 'and there's always a smell of petrol or oil about the roads. There's not the fresh air or the same coolness that you get back in Ireland.'

'But aren't we lucky having the change, Kate? A bit of a change does you good. I always feel ten years younger when I go back home. The change of scenery and the shops and everything gives me a bit of a lift.'

'Definitely,' Kate said.

'And you getting the chance to have a game of tennis last night,' Mary babbled on, 'and then us going out to a party tonight. Isn't Stockport very exciting altogether? I'm not surprised that Rose loves living here.'

A picture of David McGuire flashed into Kate's mind and she could almost feel his lips on hers again. Perhaps things were a bit *too* exciting at the moment, she thought.

They spent the next couple of hours walking slowly around both the open-air street market and the stalls inside 'the Glass Umbrella' as the locals had nick-named the cast iron and glass indoor market.

Mary bought herself a nice black silk blouse with pink roses and small pearl buttons, which she said was a great bargain and would be perfect with her good black skirt for the charity party that night. Kate looked at each stall as she walked along, but didn't see anything that particularly caught her eye for herself, but she bought a beautiful red azalea plant for her aunt and a decorative china plant pot to put it in. When they made their way to the outdoor market again, Mary spotted a stall that sold hair tints and, after much deliberation, she bought a Midnight Black hair colour.

'Do you think you'd have a few minutes to put it in for me before we go out tonight?' Mary asked. 'It's just that I would hate to go into a house full of strangers with this grey showing in my hair . . .' Her voice dropped. 'Rose always looks after her hair so well. I feel ten years older than her instead of two whenever I catch sight of the grey ribs in mine.'

Kate looked at her and smiled. 'I think that's a bit of an exaggeration, but don't worry – I'll do it when we've had dinner tonight.'

'The darker shade will look well on me with the black blouse, won't it, Kate?' Mary said, already cheering up.

'It'll be grand,' Kate said, her voice slightly vague now as she caught herself wondering about David McGuire again.

They walked back down into the town centre and after a look around a few more shops Kate suggested that they went into a tea-room in Princess Street to give Mary's feet a rest and to escape the shower of rain that was just starting.

'I'm much better than I was this time last year,' Mary told her daughter as they drank lovely frothy coffee made from hot milk and ate scones and jam. 'I wouldn't have been fit for that walk, but thanks be to God and his Blessed Mother I feel as if I'm getting back to my old self.'

'Good,' Kate said warmly, 'and you're looking much better too. By the time we go home you'll hardly know yourself. You'll be flying in and out to Tullamore and Ballygrace on the bike.'

Mary laughed at the idea, and then there was a brief pause and she leaned forward and touched Kate's hand. 'What about that young doctor?' she asked, her eyes gentle and understanding. 'Is there anything for Michael to worry about there?'

Kate's face flushed. 'Nothing . . .' she said in an awkward, blustery fashion. 'Honestly – there's nothing going on. It was only a harmless game of tennis.'

'Kate,' her mother said now, 'I know I'm not a young one any more, but I really do understand how these things can happen. I couldn't say much last night with your Aunt Rose and Graham there, but I just want you to know that I'm not blaming you or criticising you or anything like that.'

'But nothing *did* happen, Mammy,' Kate said, sounding a little exasperated. 'And nothing will happen. I wouldn't do that to Michael.' She took her knife now and very carefully buttered the second half of her scone. 'I told David that I had somebody back home and that I wasn't interested in anything else.'

'So he was interested in you!' Mary said, almost a touch triumphantly.

Kate sighed and rolled her eyes to the café ceiling. 'He liked me . . . that was all.'

'Oh, Kate!' her mother said, all excited. '*Two* handsome, eligible men after you. You're very lucky, you know. Many a girl would give their eye-teeth to have even one of them after her.'

Kate looked at her mother, and then something in her melted a little and she smiled in spite of herself. 'I suppose I am lucky . . . but it's not an easy position to be in.'

Mary leaned her elbows on the table then glanced around to make sure no one was listening. 'Michael's never going to know,' she whispered. 'And if you don't take your chances in life now – while you're young – you might end up regretting it.'

'How can I regret meeting somebody as nice and dependable as Michael?' Kate said. 'He's the nicest lad I've ever known . . .'

'But Kate, you're very young,' her mother reminded her. 'And really . . . you've not travelled very far to meet anybody else . . .'

Kate's face darkened. 'Mammy, anyone would think you really didn't like Michael – and yet, the way you were going on about him back home, it was as if you nearly had us married off.' She sighed now, shaking her head. 'I don't know whether I'm coming or going with you. You're nearly as bad as Brendan – all for people one minute and all against them the next.'

Mary laughed and waved Kate's criticisms away, knowing full well that her daughter was correct in her summing up of her attitudes – but she couldn't help herself. Her own life was full of so many regrets and so many questions about what might have happened if she'd been brave enough to take a different path. But she knew that she had to walk a very fine line now between advising Kate and maybe encouraging her too much in a direction that would not be right for her. 'Now, don't be talking like that,' Mary said, 'you know fine well I think the world of Michael. I'm just sayin' that if you don't enjoy yourself while you're young, you mightn't get the chance to do it again. And don't forget,' she pointed out, 'this could be your last holiday on your own. After this summer, you could be engaged or even married.'

'Mammy!' Kate gasped. 'Where are you getting all the ridiculous ideas from? I've never said anything about getting engaged.'

'You don't have to, Kate,' her mother said, lifting her coffee mug.

'I can see it in Michael's eyes every time he looks at you. Do you think his mother came up to our house that time for nothing? He's obviously made his feelings about you plain to her, *and*, I'd say, the rest of the family.'

Kate shook her head. 'I think you're racing ahead of yourself,' she said. 'Miles and miles ahead of the rest of us.'

Mary turned now to look out of the tea-room window at the busy street full of people. 'Rose said there's a nice dress shop that's opened further along from here,' she said, changing the subject completely. 'She said they have lovely summer dresses and it's not at all dear. Why don't you have a look and see if there's anything you like, and I'll treat you?'

Kate looked at her then suddenly grinned. 'That's very good of you, but I hope you're not expecting me to pick a wedding dress.'

'Oh, Kate!' Mary said, laughing heartily. 'That'll be the day . . .' She shook her head. 'The way you're going on, the dress would be well out of fashion by then.'

Harmony appeared to have been restored between Rose and Graham, and they were both busy washing down the shelves in the shop window when Kate and Mary returned just after four o'clock.

'Looks as if ye've bought half of bloomin' Stockport when you were there!' Graham joked, gesturing to the carrier bags. He lifted a basket of onions out of the window and carried them to the shelves at the back of the shop, and then he went back for a basket of turnips.

'You didn't get too wet then?' Rose asked, putting her cloth down and coming to lean on the shop counter.

'We had a lovely time,' Kate said. 'We managed to dodge the rain for most of the time. We went to the market, stopped for a coffee and then had another hour around the main shops.'

'Lucky for some!' Rose said, throwing an eye over at Graham. 'Maybe I'll get time to do a bit of shopping with you next week, when Graham's new helper starts.' She turned her head to the side so he couldn't see her and winked at her sister and niece. 'If she's as competent and efficient as Graham says she is, then I'll hardly be needed here at all.' She looked back at her husband now. 'Isn't that right, Graham?'

'You're more than welcome to a day off, my love,' Graham said in a magnanimous manner, coming over to put his arm around her. 'There's nobody deserves it more.'

'Oh, isn't that lovely, Kate?' Mary said, all smiles at the touching scene.

'He won't be saying that when he sees all the bags I'll be bringing home!' Rose laughed, shrugging off Graham's overture. He went back to lifting stuff out of the window. 'Well,' she asked now, her eyes a little weary, 'did you get anything nice for yourselves?'

'I got a lovely blouse and Kate got a really nice dress from that shop you told us about. Apart from that, we just picked up a few odds and ends,' Mary said. She looked at Kate and then looked down at the bags on the floor.

Kate lifted the bag with the azalea in it. 'This is a little thing to say thanks to the both of you for having us.' She put the plant on the counter then bent down for the china plant holder and put that on the counter beside it.

'Oh, you shouldn't have!' Rose said, shaking her head. 'You had no right getting me anything . . . sure, the pair of you have been up at the crack of dawn helping us out in the shop – haven't they, Graham?'

'They've been a right pair of smashers,' Graham said, coming over to join them again. 'If you weren't livin' in Ireland, I'd have you workin' in this place like a shot.' He looked at the plant and the pot and then he wagged a warning finger at the two guests. 'You shouldn't have been buying stuff for us. You're meant to be over here on a holiday and treatin' yourselves – not treatin' us!' He suddenly grinned, his attention focused on Kate now. 'Oh, by the way, you missed Dr Dolittle this afternoon – he was in collecting the order for the house.'

Kate felt her throat tighten. She had been trying unsuccessfully not to think of David McGuire all day.

'Would you listen to him – *Dr Dolittle*!' Rose gasped, then tutted in exasperation. 'You wouldn't call him that to his face.'

'Course I would,' Graham sniggered. 'He's a crackin' lad – got a good sense of humour, not like some of them dour Scots.'

'And was he lookin' for Kate?' Mary asked, all interested.

'Well, he didn't exactly ask for her by name or anythin' like that,' Graham said, 'but I saw him havin' a nose around the back of the shop when he thought I was busy in the window. And he knows that I'll drop the order across to the house when we're quiet, like I usually do.' He stood up straight now, his hands on his hips. 'I reckon him comin' in were only an excuse to see if Kate was around.'

'Well, it's a compliment to Kate if he was,' his wife said, clearly irritated at him.

'Now, Rose,' Mary said, cutting across the uncomfortable conversation, 'how about if me and Kate go back to the house and start getting the dinner ready? It would save you time with us going out later.'

'Oh, you'll have to give yourselves time to get yer glad rags on,' Graham chipped in again. 'It'll be a posh do the night. You'll have to get the cement and the white flour out to look yer best!'

'Would you take that fella away with you?' Rose said. 'He's been driving me totally mad all day.'

'Come on, Graham,' Mary joked, lifting the bags now.

'Take no notice of her,' Graham said, thumbing in his wife's direction. 'She'd be lost without me – and who would do all the heavy liftin' and everything in this place?'

'I'm sure our wonderful new assistant will do everything and you won't be needin' me at all then,' Rose retorted, then she reached over the counter and touched her niece's arm. 'Do yourself a favour, Kate, don't ever get married!'

Chapter 34

As Noelle helped her mother to cook the breakfast on the Saturday morning, she thought how lucky she had been with her timing last night. She had stayed at the Flowers' cottage for a good hour and a half and then she and Brendan had walked back down to her own place, their voices growing softer and more cautious as they neared the house.

'Are you sure you'll be all right?' Brendan had said in a low voice, although he knew there was nothing he could really do to make things easier once she was inside the house.

'I'll be grand,' she said, 'and thanks again for looking after me tonight . . .'

'Are you sure about tomorrow night?' he asked her, a slight hesitancy in his voice.

'Yes,' she said, her eyes searching his now. 'I explained to you all about that last time . . . and I would never let that happen again.' She paused. 'Are *you* sure?'

He nodded. 'I wouldn't have asked you if I wasn't sure . . .' His voice went lower. 'What if your father stops you again?'

'He won't stop me,' she said, her chin jutting out defiantly. 'If he tries to stop me, then I'll just pack my bags and come and meet you in Tullamore anyway. If the worst comes to the worst, I'll stay the night at my friend's in Cappincur and I'll go straight back up to Dublin on the bus on Sunday.'

'I don't want you getting into a whole heap of trouble because of me, Noelle,' he told her. 'And it would be hardly worth all the aggravation if you're going to miss your week's holiday.'

'It won't happen,' she reassured him. 'And like we said, I want to see you during the week when we're both off and Daddy's out at work.'

Brendan smiled and drew her into his arms again and kissed her. 'We'll take it a day at a time,' he whispered. 'Starting with the pictures tomorrow night.'

Mercifully, it had all been in darkness and there wasn't a sound to be heard, and there hadn't been any sign of Sarah's bicycle outside the house, so Noelle was still home before her. She had planned to tell the truth about her leg if her father heard her coming in, but there had been no need. She slipped in the back door and through the kitchen and down the hallway to the bedroom the girls shared with their younger sister.

Quarter of an hour later, Sarah had returned, tiptoeing into the bedroom the same as her sister. Then, they had lain in the dark, whispering exchanges about what had happened to them after they parted.

'I can't believe it!' Sarah had giggled when Noelle had told her all about Brendan and how he had looked after her, and how they had gone back to the Flowers' cottage together. And then Noelle had told her about Brendan kissing her. 'Oh, my God . . . and are the pair of you going to meet up again?'

'Tomorrow night,' Noelle had whispered. 'And I'm going to need your help to make sure I get out . . .'

'Will we go up to the bog for an hour?' Sarah asked Noelle as they sat chatting over breakfast. 'It'll get us out the house and give us a bit of exercise.'

Noelle turned to look out of the window. The sky was a bit scattered with grey clouds but it was dry enough. She looked at her mother. 'Is Daddy up there now?'

Her mother nodded her head slowly. 'He is, thanks be to God – and it might straighten his face if he had a bit of help up there.'

Noelle felt uneasy about spending too much time with her father before going out tonight, just in case he asked her too many questions she couldn't answer. Then, before she had a chance to decide, Colm, her ten-year-old brother, turned to her.

'Can me and Donal come with you?' he asked, his eyes full of eagerness. The younger children loved having Noelle back home, and were happy to go anywhere she was going. 'We can help to foot the turf, we've helped Daddy the other evening and he told us to come up when we have no jobs to do down at the house.'

'If you're all going, then I want to come too,' Marie, the youngest girl, said now, her eyes wide and hopeful. 'It's not fair to leave me behind on my own.'

'Okay,' Noelle said, smiling at them now, as though she had never had any doubts about going. 'Go and get your old boots and trousers and we'll head up there when we've washed up.' She's right, Noelle thought, it isn't fair for me to try to dodge any awkwardness with Daddy, when they have to put up with his moods every single day. She had far too many memories of arguments between her parents, always caused by her father, and she knew just how the three younger ones felt. If she could do anything that might help to take their minds off the rows or to lighten the atmosphere at home then it was her duty to do it. She would have been grateful for the distraction from the anxiety of living with Matt Daly when she was a child.

'I'll tidy up,' her mother said, a rare smile breaking out on her face. 'You go on up to the bog now while the weather's reasonable.

I'll have the dinner ready for around two o'clock – so that'll give you a few hours to get a fair bit done.' She gestured to a cupboard at the side of the fire. 'Your old trousers and blouses are in the cupboard there, so you don't destroy anything decent.'

It took them nearly quarter of an hour to cycle to the bog, which was almost midway between Ballygrace and Daingean, and by the time they turned off the main road onto the dirt-track to push the bikes, the sun had come out, making it seem a more pleasurable prospect. The boys ran on ahead, their excitement fuelled by the bottle of lemonade and packet of biscuits that Sarah had put in a bag and tied on the back of her bicycle.

The Dalys' own plot of turf was a couple of minutes' walk in off the road on a bumpy, lumpy well-worn path between scraggy bushes, and they passed by several other plots with local people they knew working on them. Noelle and Sarah stopped to have a few words with a family they knew well from Daingean as Sarah had been in the same class in school in Tullamore as the daughter, Maggie.

'How's the leg, Noelle?' Maggie asked. 'I heard you got a bit of a knock at the dance last night and fainted and everything . . . and that Brendan Flowers was there on hand looking after you.'

'I didn't see you at the dance,' Noelle said, feeling a little pang of alarm. 'Were you there?'

Maggie shook her head. 'No, I was too stiff from the flamin' bog yesterday and I couldn't be bothered shifting myself to get bathed and cleaned up to come out again last night.' She sighed now and rolled her eyes. 'This feckin' turf would break yer back, but I suppose we'll all be grateful for it in the winter.'

'How did you get to hear about my leg?' Noelle said, her eyebrows raised in question. And more importantly, she thought to herself, who told you about Brendan Flowers?

'Ah, sure, word gets round easily,' Maggie laughed. 'You don't need to be at places to hear things. Anyway, did you make it home okay?'

Noelle pulled her trouser leg up to reveal the bandage. 'My leg's a lot better . . . I think it was the blood that made me faint. Feckin' stupid, wasn't it?'

'I'd be the very same,' Maggie mused. 'I hate the sight of blood.'

They chatted a few minutes longer about the dance and other snippets of local gossip and then, when the younger ones came back, calling them and waving them to come on, the girls shifted themselves to move towards the area of work.

They walked down the first open part of the bog – a huge square, sectioned off into the various families' plots, where the men would dig deep for huge pieces of turf with a slane – a small, elongated spade shaped specially for the job. The big pieces of turf would then be cut into smaller, lighter pieces between a foot and eighteen inches long, and these would then be painstakingly piled up into four or five criss-cross layers to enable the air to get into the structure and dry it out.

Noelle and Sarah followed the younger ones down an overgrown lane that took them out to an even bigger rectangular area where the brown turf had been dug out and was in varying states of cutting and drying.

Matt Daly was at the top of their plot – dressed in his old black waistcoat and collarless shirt with sleeves rolled up to his elbow – leaning on his slane and talking to two identically clad men who owned the plot next to his. All three men raised their arms in solemn greeting and then went back to their conversation.

'Did you see that the Mullens have the ass and cart along with them?' Sarah said in a low voice to Noelle. 'That means that they must have some of the turf all dried and ready to bring home.'

'Of course I noticed,' Noelle sighed. 'And no doubt Daddy's seen it, too. He'll be like a bull now that some of the others are bringin' the turf home before him.'

'Aw, pity about him,' Sarah said, shaking her head. 'He can't do feckin' everythin'. He's been out with the cattle morning and night, fixin' blidey oul' fences, and then at night he's up in the garden digging around the potatoes and the vegetables. Why the hell does he have to have everythin' done better and before everybody else?'

'Look at him watching us now . . .' Noelle hissed. 'We better get started.'

The girls looked around for a few moments, deciding where would be the best place to start. Sarah pointed to a corner where the turf had already been dug and cut and laid out in long rows. 'That looks the easiest bit to start on,' she said, getting the lemonade and the biscuits from the back of the bike. She then went over to put them under a thick bush, which would keep them cool if the sun came through the cloud and the chilly breeze.

'Right, c'mon, you three!' Noelle called to the younger ones who were running and skipping between the rows of turf, and then they all set to work on the back-breaking task.

'What d'you think?' Sarah said after about an hour. She straightened her back and wiped her hand across her sweating brow. 'Are we making any dent in it at all?'

Noelle straightened up and turned to look back at the rows and rows of little criss-cross heaps of turf that were now in place of the single lines. 'That's not bad at all,' she said, shielding her eyes against the sun, which had just made its first appearance of the day. 'Will we go on for another while and then stop for a break?'

Twenty minutes later the children were complaining of the heat and saying that the midges were biting at them, so the girls waved them over to the banked-up edge of the bog where there was shade from a group of young silver birches and yellow gorse bushes. They all flopped down, tired and sore, to devour the Rich Tea biscuits and take their turn to drink from the bottle of red lemonade.

'You'd better save a drop of that for Daddy,' Noelle warned Colm as he put the bottle to his mouth again. 'He'll get thick with us if we drink it all.' She checked the biscuits to make sure they had left two for him as they'd been told by their mother.

Just as they were ready to start back to work their father came striding through the heaps of turf towards them, his eye scanning the area that was still to be done. Noelle looked at Sarah with narrowed eyes, but neither of them said anything.

'I see you're making the best of the fine weather to get out in the fresh air for an hour,' he said, looking around at the bit they'd done. 'It'll all help I suppose. Every small bit is a bit less for me and your mother to do on our own.' Sarah held the lemonade bottle out and he took it from her and drained it in one go, handing her back the empty bottle

Noelle watched him, wondering how hard it would be for him to give them a civil word or even a grudging thanks. And it would be a rare day when he would joke and mess around with the lads as a lot of the other fathers did when they were up on the bog – any kind of pleasantness seemed to equate weakness in Matt Daly's books. He put the biscuits that Noelle gave him in his waistcoat pocket without a word and it dawned on her that he had never asked how long she was home for or when she was going back. But she knew well that he would have checked with her mother how much of her wages she'd handed over.

Peg Daly passed around the steaming enamel basin of potatoes that had been boiled in their scrubbed skins. The boys had picked them from their own garden earlier in the week and even though they ate them every single day, the novelty of them being home-grown never wore off.

Sarah had put several big knobs of butter on the top of the dish, which had slowly slid down and melted into the potatoes. Everybody at the table took two or three potatoes to start with, apart from Matt who took half a dozen. They each had a couple of slices of newly boiled bacon and a heap of home-grown new cabbage.

Peg glanced round at the full plates and then stifled a little sigh of satisfaction, telling herself that seven was no huge number to feed compared with the fifteen children her mother had reared on little or nothing. For all Matt Daly was an awkward, cantankerous man, he worked hard and if they went short on anything, it had been things like patience, peace and contentment. They had never, thanks be to God, gone short on food.

Matt Daly looked up at his pale-faced wife. 'Did you remember we're supposed to be going up to Martin's for a game of cards this evenin'?'

Noelle's ears pricked up at the mention of her parents going out to her uncle's house just outside Ballygrace. She glanced over at Sarah, who was concentrating on cutting the fat from the edge of her ham.'

'Are you girls in tonight?' their mother asked. 'Marie and the boys need to have their baths later on for Mass in the morning and it takes a while getting the kettles boiled and everything.' She glanced at the turf-streaked faces. 'You two will need a wash as well, and it'll take two good fills of the bath to do you all.'

Noelle shrugged and looked at Sarah, hoping she would remember what they had agreed.

'I'm not going anywhere, so I'll sort them out,' Sarah said. 'Oh, and Noelle, I forgot to say to you, that Brennan girl from Daingean who works in the butcher's said would you call out to her this evenin' with that book that she loaned you.'

'What book?' Noelle said, her brow creasing in what she hoped looked like a genuinely confused manner. 'I don't remember having borrowed a book from her.'

'It's some book about Dublin,' Sarah said, shrugging and cutting into a hot potato. 'She said she loaned you it before you went away, and she says she has a cousin calling over tonight and she needs it for her.'

Noelle nodded her head. 'I forgot all about it – I have it on top of the wardrobe. I suppose I'd better drop it over to her later on or she'll be complainin' about me.' She looked at her mother. 'I'll have my bath before the kids, but I'll help you with the dishes and do the bit of ironing for you first, while the water is back on boiling for the baths.'

Her father speared another potato from the basin with his fork, then he pointed it at Noelle. 'Don't be borrowin' stuff from anybody else if you can't remember to give it back. We don't need the likes of that Brennan one yappin' to everybody that goes into the shop about you holding on to her book.'

Noelle felt her throat tightening with anger at being spoken to like a child in front of the others, but she swallowed it back. It was worth putting up with it to get out to see Brendan tonight. 'I didn't ask her for the book, she gave it to me when she heard I was going to work in Dublin,' she said in a quiet, even tone. 'And I won't be borrowing anything else from her.'

'Well, make sure you don't,' her father said, annoyed that she'd had the nerve to answer him back. He turned to the two boys beside him. 'And don't any of you bring anything back to this house that doesn't belong to you. Forgetting to give something back is the exact same thing as stealing – and we don't need any thieves in this house. There's enough trick-acting going on without adding stealing to it.'

Noelle clamped her teeth down as hard on her tongue as she could without doing damage to herself, determined not to be drawn into any further debate with him. She just wanted to get through the next few hours until it was time to escape out of the house and, hopefully, into Brendan Flowers' arms again.

Chapter 35

≈∞≈

Graham gave a low whistle as his sister-in-law and niece came into the sitting-room wearing their new outfits. 'Very glamorous, ladies,' he said, 'very glamorous indeed!' He put his arm around Rose now, who was also dressed up in her best blue outfit and white stiletto heels, which made her look far more sophisticated than she usually did in her shop overall. She had her bobbed brown hair set in delicate waves which made her look younger and more relaxed.

Mary looked very different too. The dark tint that Kate had put in her hair had taken deeper than either of them expected, initially making Mary's face look very pale in comparison. But Rose had come up with a medium-tan foundation cream which brought a healthy glow to her sister's complexion and blended in perfectly with the new hair colour.

'That dress is lovely, Kate,' Rose said admiringly. 'I've never seen that deep mauve colour on you before, it really suits your dark hair and olive skin.'

'And the lady in the shop said how the broad belt shows off her tiny waist,' Mary said proudly. She laughed, tugging at her own skirt waistband. 'I wish my waist was that size, don't you, Rose? Do you remember when we had twenty-inch waists?'

'Many moons ago,' Rose said, 'when we were young and innocent and didn't realise how well we looked.'

'Now, now, ladies,' Graham said, coming over to put an arm around each of the two sisters. He hugged them close into him and Rose dug her elbow sharply in his side to make him step back. 'You both look very fetching and only half your ages,' he went on, undaunted by his wife's rebuff, 'and I'll be proud to escort you to the do tonight. But I'll have to keep a close eye on you, else you might be lured away by some of the other appreciative gentlemen.' He waved his hand over in Kate's direction now. 'We already have one of ye here who has caught the eye of a professional man—'

'Graham Hopkins,' Mary laughed, 'it's supposed to be Irishmen that have the gift of the gab!'

'Oh, oul' Casanova there would give them a run for their money any day,' Rose sighed. Then she laughed, rolling her eyes to the ceiling. 'He talks a good job anyway – God knows what they'd think once they got to know what he was really like. It was too late in my case by the time the rose-tinted glasses wore off.'

'Ah, Rose,' Graham said, putting his good navy blazer on now, 'you have the name of the most beautiful flower, but unfortunately your temperament can be pricklier than the worst of the thorns.'

Rose looked at her sister and pulled a face, then she went over to the sideboard and lifted her handbag. 'Are we all ready?'

'As ready as we'll ever be, my little rose petal,' Graham said, laughing at what he thought was the cleverness of his own joke.

'I'm glad it's only a five-minute walk with these stilettos on,' Rose said as they turned the corner and walked down the road to Lance Williams' house. 'And thank God it's brightened up a bit. It's nicer this evening than it's been all day.'

'Thanks be to God indeed,' Mary said, looking up at the patches of bright blue sky amidst the clouds. She looked at the buildings, which were very different to the ones in the previous streets. 'These are lovely big houses,' Mary said, 'far bigger than I imagined.' Her eyes were wide with interest as she took in the tall red-brick façade and the beautifully kept gardens.

'He has the biggest one on this road,' Graham said out of the side of his mouth, as though someone might be listening. 'He's definitely worth a bob or two, is Lance Williams. Has his own tool-hire business, like.'

Mary looked at Kate and pulled a little face that showed she was feeling apprehensive about the night. Kate moved close beside her as they walked along, and touched her hand to reassure her.

'Did I tell you that Dr Dolittle lives just off this road?' Graham said now, slowing down and looking back at Kate. He gestured towards a cul-de-sac on the opposite side of the road. 'The one at the top, in on the left,' he told her. 'Black-painted windows and door.' He gave a little sniff. 'You can tell by the looks of it that it's all lads that live in it. Very plain, like.'

'Every house needs a woman's touch to finish it off,' Mary said. 'It's the little ornaments and knick-knacks that make a house a home.'

'Maybe he'll ask you in to polish his brasses, Kate!' her aunt said, raising her eyebrows suggestively.

'I think he's quite capable of looking after himself,' Kate said, giving a little amused sigh and raising her own eyebrows in a more exaggerated fashion of her aunt's gesture, which made them all laugh.

The front door was wide open when they turned in the gateway of the white-painted, double-fronted house, and they could tell by the music and the babble of conversation that there was a nice crowd already at the house.

Graham hesitated at the door, craning his neck to see if he could see anyone inside. 'D'you think we should just walk in,' he asked Rose, running a finger inside his collar to loosen it, 'or d'you think we should ring the bell?'

Rose shrugged. 'Now, don't be askin' me – you're the one that knows him better . . .'

Graham rang the bell and waited, and a few moments later a slightly built man with a tidy greying moustache and beard came rushing down the hallway towards the door. There was no mistaking his English nationality in his summer attire of cream trousers with a short-sleeved linen shirt, striped wine and blue club tie, and cream straw hat with a red band.

'Ah, Graham and Mrs Hopkins and guests!' he said, giving them a beaming smile. He politely took his hat off, revealing a good head of dark hair with the odd fleck of grey. 'I'm so delighted you made it . . .' He shook hands with them all, tilting his head to the side to listen carefully to Mary and Kate's names. When they were all introduced, he waved his hand back down the hallway. 'The others are out in the garden, making the most of the lovely evening.'

As they followed him down the comfortably wide hallway, Rose and Mary had a good look at the walls, panelled halfway up in a light pine and the top half decorated with a discreet gold and white striped paper. White light fittings and a white half-moon-shaped wrought-iron table with a big crystal vase full of white chrysanthemums.

'Lovely!' Rose mouthed to Mary as they went along, through a big airy kitchen with yellow walls and plenty of white-painted cupboards and modern appliances.

Mary's left hand carried her neat little purse-style handbag while her right came up to flutter comfortingly in the hollow in her flushing neck – a sure sign she was beginning to feel anxious and out of her depth.

They walked out through the back door and into a big, open flower-bedecked garden, which had numerous groups of tables and chairs dotted at various intervals. There was a sandstone path running around the perimeter of the garden and a narrower path in the middle

'I'm sure we'll find you a nice place to sit,' Lance said, his grey-blue eyes scanning the area, 'and then I'll fetch you all a cold drink. Oh, there's a nice spot over by the apple trees,' he added, pointing over to the side of the garden. 'You'll still catch the sun there for another hour or so.' He turned to Graham. 'I've beer and lager and white and red wine or sherry for the ladies, if you wouldn't mind taking the order while I attend to the latest arrivals.'

'Lovely,' Rose said, catching Mary by her arm. She lowered her voice so their host couldn't hear her. 'We'll grab it quick before anybody else gets in first.' She set off at a trot across the perfectly cut lawn towards the table, quite forgetting that she was wearing stiletto heels. Then, as she turned back to speak to Kate, her heel disappeared into the grass and when she went to go forward she discovered that the shoe had firmly stayed behind, leaving her hobbling on one foot.

'Oh, to hell!' she gasped, feeling her stockinged foot on the cold, damp grass. She looked up at Kate and they both started to giggle, bringing curious glances from the other guests.

Mortified at the show they were all making of themselves, a blushing Mary rushed forward to assist her sister, and discovered that she was none too steady on the lawn herself, even though her sandal heels were not as spindly as Rose's. She bent down and yanked at the white stiletto and then put it down on the grass for her sister to hop into.

'I'm blidey well mortified!' Rose gave a nervous giggle and shoved the shoe back on. Then, both of them picking their steps very gingerly, they made their way over to the coveted table where Kate was sitting grinning at them.

'I see you've managed to liven things up a bit,' Kate laughed.

'I'm here for the night,' Rose said, sinking down on one of the chairs, 'and I'm not moving until it's time to go home.'

'Oh, Rose,' Mary said, sounding all breathless. 'It's a very fancy house altogether – what are we going to say if people talk to us?'

Chapter 36

❦

Noelle Daly was amazed. She had expected to feel all awkward and shy with Brendan Flowers. She had expected to feel embarrassed about him having heard her father shouting and bawling the previous night, and she had expected to feel stupid for telling him about how she didn't like her job in Dublin and how she'd only taken it to get away from home.

But she hadn't felt any of those things.

When she saw him waiting for her outside the picture house, dressed in his good suit, she had felt a rush of warmth all through her body. And when he smiled as she came up the road towards him, wheeling her bicycle, she had felt the same comfortable way they had felt in the Flowers' cottage the night before.

When she leaned against him in the cinema, she could smell the beer that he had drunk in the pub before she arrived and she knew instinctively that he had drunk it to give him the courage to take the chance on her standing him up again.

'Was everything all right last night?' Brendan whispered in the flickering dark of the picture house. 'Your oul' fella . . . ?'

'He was in bed, thank God, so it was all quiet.'

There was a pause. 'I was worried about you . . .' he told her. 'I waited outside for a while just in case.'

The same warm feeling ran through Noelle now. No one had ever said such a nice thing to her. No one had ever said they were worried about her, that they cared what happened to her or what she felt.

Then at one point he had asked in a very low voice, so that the people in the row behind couldn't hear, 'Does he know where you are tonight?'

Noelle held her breath for a second before replying, wondering if she could really, *really* trust him. 'I said I had to go to see a girl from Daingean.' She shrugged, feeling very childish, like a school-girl who wasn't allowed to make her own decisions. 'They were going out to play cards tonight anyway . . . so hopefully they won't miss me.'

When the film was over they walked down to the local chipper, and then they sat in one of the booths eating steaming hot chips covered in salt and vinegar, chatting and laughing about the film and silly things they remembered from years ago. Then they cycled out along the canal path from Tullamore all the way to Ballygrace.

A couple of times they stopped to catch their breath and walk the bikes slowly along, sometimes quietly chatting and at other times in companionable silence. And on one occasion as they passed the bridge at Cappincur, Brendan pushed his bike in front and reached back to take Noelle's hand and guide her over the potholes. Further on, they stopped altogether, parked the bikes and sat on a pile of logs – and this time Brendan did all the talking about his life. He talked about his father dying and his mother's illness, and his worry over Kate being stuck at home all the time with their mother until Michael O'Brien had come along and saved the day.

'I'm not pretendin' that me and Kate are the best of friends,' he admitted. 'There's times when she drives me totally mad, but she is my sister and I suppose I do have feelings for her.'

'Maybe it is hard to see people you live with as others see them,' Noelle mused. 'But everyone I know thinks that Kate is a lovely, kind girl. You only have to look at the way she looks after your mother.'

'I know, I know,' Brendan said. 'Maybe it's that we're too alike . . . maybe that's why we clash so much.'

'Sometimes me and Sarah argue as well,' Noelle said. 'I get the feeling that she thinks I've deserted her by going to work up in Dublin.' She shook her head. 'I wasn't planning on going to Dublin at all, it was just the way it worked out.'

They continued walking and talking or talking and cycling until they were back in Ballygrace and then back in sight of the cottage.

Two nights, Noelle thought. Two nights with only the light of the moon and Brendan Flowers alongside me. The happiest two nights of her life.

Chapter 37

❧❦❧

Mary Flowers was on to her third large glass of French white wine – the little shudder she had given at the first few mouthfuls now forgotten. It was the first proper wine Mary had ever drunk. Rose was on her third glass, too – although she was well acquainted with it compared to her stay-at-home sister. Kate had found her first glass pleasant enough, but was going warily with the second as she could feel the effects already. She could *see* the effects of it on her mother and aunt – and it was starting to make her feel slightly uncomfortable.

After their rather shaky start, the two sisters had settled into the atmosphere of the evening in the pleasant floral surroundings, enjoying the fancily cut triangle sandwiches and the vol-au-vents and sausage rolls that were being passed around. At first Kate had been relieved to see her mother gradually relax and lose the nervous expression that told Kate she was struggling with the very different social ambiance of the charity evening. But as she watched her mother now, the slightly guarded look was gone, replaced with a wide, child-like smile that made Kate feel uneasy.

When two women came to the table later to sell raffle tickets, Kate found herself blushing to the roots of her dark hair as she watched her mother fumbling and footering about in her bag, trying to find the right change for the tickets.

'You see, I've gone and mixed up my Irish and my English money,' Mary explained to the little group, opening her purse and searching painstakingly through her coins one at a time. She waved away Kate's help but after a few minutes she grew agitated at not being able to select the right coins and suddenly tipped her purse over onto the table, scattering coins in all directions and sending Rose into peals of embarrassingly loud laughter.

The two raffle-ticket sellers bent down to help and eventually the correct coins were located and her mother purchased a string of tickets. Feeling embarrassed by the whole debacle, Kate bought far more tickets than she had originally intended and she was so flustered she didn't even ask what the prizes were.

Things settled down for a while and then Rose left the table when Graham gestured to her to come and speak to some couple they had met the previous Christmas at the bowling club annual dinner.

Kate and her mother chatted quietly, picking at the plate of sandwiches on the table. When Kate said she was going to the bathroom, her mother suddenly looked anxious again, clutched at Kate's arm and asked her if she could wait until Rose came back.

After a while Rose returned with two fresh glasses of wine and Kate took the opportunity to go looking for the bathroom, carefully picking her way over the grass and into the back entrance of the house. Mary seemed more relaxed, and Rose soon engaged her in a big, convoluted story about the couple they had been chatting to, her voice dropping when she told her that the couple had just got married. 'Seemingly, it was her *third* time!'

'Third time for what?' Mary asked, her brow furrowed in confusion.

'For getting *married*!'

'She's been married *three* times?' Mary said, aghast.

'Shhhhh!' Rose warned, glancing around to see who might be listening to her indiscreet sister. 'She's a widow . . . twice over.'

'And she got married again after losing two?' Mary's eyes were wide and interested. She tried to look casual as she glanced at the people sitting at tables or milling around in the garden. 'And what one is she?'

'D'you see that fella over at the back door with greyish hair and a glass of beer in his hand? He's standing next to Graham.'

Mary moved this way and that in her seat trying to see who exactly Rose was referring to, but apart from the fact that there were several men with greying hair, other people kept moving around and it was difficult to pin-point anyone in particular.

'That's her!' Rose said now. 'The little one with the well-lacquered French roll and the pink flowery dress. She's just gone over to stand beside the husband and Graham.'

Mary twisted around in her chair and suddenly there was a clear space where she could see the small, thrice-married woman quite clearly. She was surprised to see that the focus of their conversation was a fairly non-descript woman she'd noticed earlier in the evening making a big issue of asking Lance Williams all about his climbing clematis plants. The woman had subtly commandeered the host's attention away from the other guests and then had been very vocal in her praise of his gardening skills, and full of admiration for the clever mixture of spring and summer flowering clematis that covered the back of Lance Williams' house and attached garage. Mary had watched her bending and stretching, all full of gestures and closely examining the trailing ends of the prolifically growing plant.

'Oh she's the one that was all over his clematis earlier on,' Mary whispered.

'All over his what?' Rose said, not as up on plants as her sister.

'His *clematis*,' Mary repeated, trying to keep her voice low. 'You know,' she said, gesturing towards the back of the house. 'She was examining all his trailing bits ... she was taking cuttings from them.'

Rose's eyes opened wide and then, unable to stop herself, she broke into a loud, raucous laugh. 'I'd say she'd be well used to examining men's trailing bits after gettin' married for the third time.'

Mary's hand flew to her mouth. 'I meant the plants!' she said, flushing furiously and looking around to see if anyone was listening.

'It's obviously her talent with the trailing ends that attracts the men,' Rose laughed, enjoying her little double entendres, 'for it's certainly not her good looks.' She gestured over towards the woman now. 'She's that dowdy and old-fashioned.'

Mary shook her head, a censorious look on her face. 'Sure, they could be sayin' that about me ... I'm hardly a fashion plate comin' straight from the country in Ireland.'

'Don't be so silly,' Rose said, waving away her sister's worries. 'You always look nice, and anyway – do you think I'd let you out if you didn't? D'you think I'd let you show me and Graham up?' She reached across the table and patted her sister's hand. 'You should have more confidence in yourself, Mary Flowers. You're a very good-looking woman – the best in our family. Sure, everybody used to say that back home.'

'Did they?' Mary asked, her voice still uncertain but her face brightening up at the rare compliment from her sister. This was the first time she'd ever heard anyone say she was particularly good-looking, far less the best looking one in the family.

'Of course they did,' Rose stated. 'Sure, all the lads in the village couldn't believe it when you went off and married Seamus Flowers.' She gave a little theatrical sigh. 'You only left them all heart-broken. They kept askin' the rest of us if it was true you'd married a much older fella with plenty of money. I think they all thought he was nearly a millionaire.'

Mary bit her lip. 'Sure, I suppose I thought that myself. All he had was an old family cottage, a couple of small fields and a dozen cattle – but it was a lot more than we had back at home in Clare.' She shook her head. 'Wasn't I very young and foolish, Rose? Rushin' in and marryin' the first man that asked me? Grabbing the first man that I knew would be able to provide for me . . .'

'You didn't do too badly at all,' Rose told her. 'Didn't you get your nice little cottage and didn't poor Seamus make sure you never went short of anything?' She took a big gulp of her wine now.

Mary nodded her head vigorously. 'Oh, I'm not complainin' . . . far from it. As you said, I had a good enough life with Seamus, and I got Brendan and Kate from it . . .'

'And you're free now to suit yourself,' Rose pointed out. She nodded over in her husband's direction now. 'Sure, you're miles better off than me – stuck with old grumpy-drawers over there. Look at him now, all hail-fellow-well-met with his bowling pals when he has a few drinks in him, the life and soul of the party.'

Mary looked over at her brother-in-law. 'Ah, Graham's not the worst.'

'And he's by no means the blidey best either,' Rose said ruefully, 'not by a long shot.' She gave a little exaggerated sigh, rolling her eyes to the sky. 'I can only live in hope . . . I keep the insurance policies well dusted.' She playfully dug her sister in the ribs. 'Wouldn't we be a gas pair to be two merry widows out on the town?'

'Rose Hopkins!' Mary gasped, but her eyes were dancing with laughter. 'God forgive you for sayin' such a terrible thing. I hope you're going to tell that at Confessions at the weekend?'

'Oh, I don't go that regular any more,' Rose told her sister in a very matter-of-fact manner, draining her wine glass. 'Every few weeks does me. I prefer to save it all up until I have something worthwhile to tell the priest.'

Mary flushed a little, half-shocked at her sister's admission about not receiving the Sacrament every week as she used to, but after all her trips across the water, she was getting used to people doing things differently in England. 'Oh, I'm the very same about trying to think of something to tell the priest. Since I got back to better health I go every Saturday, and half the time I have to exaggerate my sins or make them up. Sure, what could I get up to down at the canal that would amount to any great sin? The worst I do is say the odd swear word in my head when Brendan is gettin' on my nerves.'

'If you lived with Graham you wouldn't be able to keep the swear words inside your head,' Rose laughed. 'There would be that many you couldn't help yourself when they all came tumbling out!'

'God, you're a little devil, Rose!' Mary said and went into another torrent of wine-fuelled laughter.

Their giggling and general light-heartedness drew glances of amusement from the other guests and brought Graham, accompanied by Lance Williams and another man from the bowling club, to find out the cause of their merriment.

'What's ticklin' you pair?' Graham asked.

'Oh, Mary's just givin' me a few tips on trailing plants,' Rose said, winking at her sister.

Lance's face lit up. 'And are you a keen gardener, Mary?'

'I wouldn't say I'm very knowledgeable about them, but I do love flowers,' she told him, suddenly feeling all shy with the limelight on her.

'Flowers by name,' Graham said, taking a drink of his beer, 'and flower by nature. That's our Mary.'

'Is it true?' Lance asked, his eyebrows rising in surprise. 'Is your name really Flowers?'

Mary nodded her head. 'It is ... Mary Flowers.'

'And your husband's name?' he enquired.

'His name was Seamus Flowers ...'

'The Lord have mercy on his soul,' Rose chipped in, automatically blessing herself in the traditional Irish Catholic custom.

'My dear ... I do beg your pardon,' said Lance, coming to sit down on the chair that Kate had vacated. He took his white straw hat off again, clutching it to his chest. 'You're obviously in a similarly sad situation to myself ...'

Kate took the opportunity of freshening up in the peace and quiet of Lance Williams' lovely bathroom. She slowly brushed her dark curls out, powdered her face and then took out her lipstick and filled in her curving, generous lips. She thought how last summer – and all the other summers before – she would have enjoyed attending such a nice party.

She found the warm summer evening very pleasant in the garden, but she only had to glance around her to know that the gathering was more suited to her mother's age group than her own. There were only two younger people there – a married couple who ran the post office – and they seemed to know everyone else there and besides, being old-fashioned sorts, they fitted in very well with the older people.

Kate knew that there was nothing wrong with the night – lovely food and drink and surroundings – and she was well used to spending time in her mother's company. Then, as she looked at her reflection in the gilt-edged mirror above the sink, she knew that she was comparing it to the previous night she had spent with David McGuire. *Dr* David McGuire, she reminded herself.

She looked deep into her own eyes in the mirror, remembering the way he had suddenly kissed her full on the lips – harder and much more passionately than she had ever been kissed before. The memory brought a flush to her cheeks, quickly followed by a wave of burning guilt at betraying Michael – and for comparing his steady, comfortable courtship with the heady excitement she had felt when she'd been kissed by the more confident, impulsive young doctor.

Kate stopped dead in her tracks when she came out of the back door and into the garden and caught sight of her mother sitting alone at their table with Lance Williams. She was even more taken aback when she realised that Lance was holding her mother's hand. And as she looked at them, she realised that he was not only holding her hand but *stroking* it.

Kate's heart dropped like a brick.

She had never seen her mother in such an intimate position with a man before. She had sometimes seen her dancing with a neighbour or relative at weddings and the odd parish dance – all innocent, perfectly harmless stuff – but seeing her mother now in such an unfamiliar situation made her feel as if the world had suddenly turned upside down.

Kate dragged her eyes away from the scene, frantically looking around for her aunt and uncle. Eventually, she spotted them over in the corner with a group, all laughing and chatting and having a great time. Kate rushed over to them, making sure her gaze didn't stray back to the table where her mother was.

'Kate!' her aunt exclaimed. 'We wondered where you'd got to . . .' She took a drink from her filled-to-the-brim wineglass. 'I was looking around for you.'

'Did you see Mammy?' Kate said, her voice breathless. 'She's sitting at the table with that Lance man . . .' She gestured towards the table where the couple were now sitting on their own.

'Ah, isn't it lovely?' Rose said, looking at her niece, her eyes glassy from all the wine she'd drunk. 'Poor Lance's been through the very same as your mother . . .' She shook her head, her voice trailing off. 'They're able to understand each other.'

'But she's not used to drinking and she's not used to being on her own with *men* . . .' Kate persisted. 'We should go over and rescue her.'

'Sure, they're only cheering each other up,' Rose said, smiling benignly and shaking her head. 'A widower and a widow . . . that's all they are. Two poor souls.'

Kate looked over at the table again, and saw her mother take a hanky out of her handbag. Then, she watched mesmerised, as Lance Williams reached across and took the hanky from Mary's hand and proceeded to delicately dab at her eyes. 'Oh, my God!' she whispered, clutching at her aunt's arm. 'Do you think I should go over?'

'Indeed and I do not,' Rose said, patting Kate's hand. 'Let them at it . . . they're only swapping stories and getting to know each other. They've both had a hard time in life, what with losing their spouses—'

'But Mammy looks as if she's *crying*,' Kate said, her voice sounding almost anguished. She scanned the tables around them to see if anyone was watching. 'People can see her . . . they'll all be talking about her.' She took a deep shuddery breath. 'I don't know what to do – she'd never behave like that back at home.'

'Ah, Kate . . . Kate,' her aunt said in a placating, slurred voice.

'Sure, you're not back in Ireland now. It's different over here. People can do and say as they like and nobody will really bother that much.' She waved her hand around the garden. 'Sure, there's nobody payin' the slightest attention to your mother. They're all enjoying themselves, just chatting and looking at Lance's nice flowers . . .' She shook her head, her eyes struggling to focus on her niece. 'Your mother's not that old, you know – it's not as if she's got her feet in the grave yet.'

'There's nobody suggesting that she is old,' Kate said, hearing her own voice sounding strained and irritable now.

'And she used to be a fine-looking woman, you know,' Rose rambled on. 'The finest looking girl in the village. Of course our family were all good-lookin' in their own way, and you're a lucky girl to have taken after us.'

Kate sighed and rolled her eyes but Rose either ignored her niece's growing irritation or didn't even notice.

'Oh, your mother left many a broken heart behind her when she married Seamus Flowers . . .' She put her arm around Kate now, rubbing her shoulder in a comforting manner. 'Not that I'm saying your father wasn't a very nice man. Not at all – he was the finest. It's just that poor Mary was far too young and innocent to be getting married. She should have had a bit of time to enjoy herself when she was a girl.' Rose let out a giggle. 'But you know, Kate, it's never too late. She's not an old lady or anything like that. Now that you and Brendan are fully reared and on your own two feet, it's time she got out and enjoyed herself – and there's no harm in her chatting to a nice man like Lance . . . or any other nice man.' Her hand tightened on Kate's shoulder. 'Don't you agree now?'

Kate bit her lip hard to stop from saying something to her aunt that she might regret. They had never had a real disagreement before, and this was neither the time nor the place to have their first. If she looked at it calmly and logically it was simply a matter of extricating her mother from their host without drawing any undue attention to them.

Rose's hand was still patting Kate's shoulder in a comforting and conspiratorial manner. 'And don't forget, Kate, there was nobody sayin' anything to you when you went off with that young doctor fella the other night. There was nobody said a word to you, far less your poor mother. There was nobody sticking their nose in tellin' you that you'd no right to be going out with him when you had a boyfriend at home – was there now?'

Kate saw Lance Williams lift her mother's hand to his mouth and kiss it and she suddenly decided it was time for action. Rightly or wrongly she was going to break up their little tête-à-tête, which was providing entertainment for the rest of the company.

She carefully wriggled out of her aunt's grasp and was preparing to step across the grass to her mother, when a school-type hand bell rang loudly at the kitchen door to silence everyone.

'If we could have everyone's attention please!' an officious-looking man called. 'The raffle is about to be drawn.' He then gestured towards Lance to come and join them as they picked the winning tickets.

Kate saw her chance now and as soon her mother was alone she made a beeline for the table.

'Kate!' her mother said, all bright-eyed and delighted-looking. 'Have you got your raffle tickets all ready?' She lifted her own handbag now and started rummaging again to look for her own tickets.

'Never mind the blooming raffle tickets,' Kate said in a low voice. 'What on earth are you doing making a show of yourself with that man?'

The smile slid off Mary's face. 'What d'you mean? Who's been making a show of themselves?'

'*You!*' Kate hissed. 'How can you sit there all wide-eyed and innocent, as if you didn't notice that man was holding your hand and dabbing your eyes with a hanky in front of the whole place?'

Mary's mouth opened in an 'O' of shock. She was unable to believe that her daughter was speaking to her in such a manner and even more shocked to hear that people had been taking any notice of what she thought was her private conversation with their host.

The bell rang again and the first winning ticket was drawn out and then the number called. An elderly woman stepped forward to receive her prize – a beautiful azalea plant in a fancy basket, which had been donated by the flower shop a few doors down from Rose and Graham's shop. The next prize of a bottle of whiskey was handed out, then a bottle of brandy followed by a bottle of sherry, a small hamper with more bottles and cakes and a tin of luxury biscuits.

During the proceedings, Mary sat with a white, crestfallen face while Kate sat opposite, her own face tight and grim – both looking at their strings of yellow tickets, but neither taking in any of the details about the numbers or the prizes being called out.

Then, when the last prize number was called out, there was great whooping and cheering as the host himself turned out to be the lucky ticket-holder and winner of two tickets to a concert in Stockport Town Hall the following Wednesday night.

He smiled and bowed and when presented with the prize, held the tickets aloft in the air. Then, as the buzz of the raffle subsided, he spent a few minutes going round the tables, chatting to the other guests, but within a very short time he found his way back to the table to join Mary and Kate.

'How is that for coincidence?' he said to them both, sitting down in one of the garden chairs.

Seeing that her mother was all flustered and tongue-tied, Kate had no option but to respond to his statement. 'What was the coincidence?' she said, trying to keep her voice light.

'Winning the tickets for the jazz concert!' he said, beaming. 'I had just been telling your mother all about my record collection earlier on. We were discussing the kind of music we both liked, and I had been very effusive about jazz music, and your lovely mother here was saying that she knew very little about jazz.' He waved the tickets in the air. 'Someone must have been listening to our conversation, because we now have the opportunity to educate her.' He studied the tickets for a moment. 'You did say you were here until next weekend?'

Mary looked over at Kate, trying to read her face – but she was met with a blank wall of disapproval and disappointment. Then, when she turned back to Lance, he was looking at her expectantly, obviously waiting for an answer.

'Yes,' Mary said, in a voice that was almost a whisper. 'We're here until next weekend, but we're very busy . . .'

'Surely,' he said, reaching over to pat Mary's hand, 'you can spare one evening to come to the concert with me?' He smiled over at Kate. 'You must help me out here – help me persuade this lovely lady to join me.'

Kate lowered her gaze, wishing they could find an excuse to get out of this embarrassing situation.

'I'm not sure . . .' Mary said in a cracked, croaky tone that gave away her mounting anxiety.

Then, in the awkward silence that followed, Lance suddenly caught onto the fact that Kate's presence had brought about the total change in her mother. He looked across the table at the beautiful young Irish girl and saw the coldness in her eyes and instantly he understood the position. He withdrew his hand from Mary's and straightened his back.

'If there is the slightest problem regarding your mother accompanying me to the concert,' he told Kate in a crisp, very articulate voice, 'then I should be more than happy to offer *you* the spare ticket, so that you might accompany her instead.'

Kate looked back at him, stunned and speechless at his suggestion.

Lance kept his eyes and his voice steady. 'I have numerous well-connected friends who will undoubtedly vouch for me as a person who is trustworthy and honourable – but if you still feel that I'm not a suitable companion to accompany your mother to a concert for *one* evening . . .' His words hung in the air.

Kate became aware of a burning feeling working its way up from the pit of her stomach, a feeling that told her she had misjudged this situation very badly, and that she had also misjudged this elderly man who now sat beside her mother.

'I wasn't thinking . . . anything of the kind about you,' she said, her voice sounding contrite and apologetic, although she felt her Irish accent was suddenly very pronounced. 'And it's none of my business whether my mother goes to the concert with you or not.'

'Splendid!' Lance said, patting the silent Mary's hand again. 'I'm terribly sorry if I misunderstood your attitude.' He smiled benignly at Kate, but there was a determined glint in his pale blue eyes.

Kate lowered her head, breathing deeply to try to reduce the heat from her face and neck. She felt as though a spotlight had been placed over her head, showing her up to be churlish and silly. At the back of her mind she knew that her mother had been behaving out of character and she had definitely shown signs of having taken too much to drink – but Kate now knew that an obvious little mistake still didn't give her the right to treat her mother like a child.

'Maybe you would like to take one of your other friends to the concert,' Mary said to Lance now, her voice hesitant. 'Maybe you would prefer—'

'Not at all,' he said, shaking his head. 'You were the first person I thought of when I won the tickets – after our lovely conversation. And wouldn't it be a nice addition to your holiday? Something a little different.' He looked over at Kate, still smiling. 'However old and decrepit we get, we all need a little variety in our lives. We live with our own sad and lonely thoughts for most of the day, but we can't hide ourselves away *all* the time. I don't think the loved ones that we've lost would want that whatever age we are, do you?'

Kate found herself murmuring in agreement, and suddenly understanding the wisdom in his words. She reached over and patted her mother's hand.

Mary glanced up at her, an unsure look in her eyes. The whole idea of a man asking her out for the evening – especially to a *jazz* concert – was totally unfamiliar to her, and in some ways it was far easier to just agree with Kate and stay in the house knitting or watching Rose's television.

'Go to the concert,' Kate said, her voice back to being kind and sincere – the voice of the old understanding Kate from home. She'd have a word with her mother about the wine later, when things had cooled down a bit. 'It sounds a lovely idea and it's very nice of Lance to invite you.'

Later that night – after Rose and Graham and her mother had weaved a slightly unsteady path back to the house – Kate lay curled up in her bed, mulling over the unusual happenings of the night.

Graham had teased her again as they passed by David McGuire's house – which had been brightly lit up with the curtains wide open – and when she glanced back over her shoulder, she had seen figures moving around in the sitting-room.

One half of her had hoped he might come out of the house or come walking along the street towards her – but the other half knew that it was foolish to have anything more to do with him. Anyway, she knew that doctors – particularly handsome doctors – were notorious for breaking women's hearts, and she wasn't naïve enough to get caught up in a situation like that. She already realised how silly she had been, allowing David to kiss her. That, she decided, would remain a little dark secret in the depths of her heart that she would share with no one. Not even her old friend, Maura, or either of the Daly girls.

The way Michael had left things back in Ireland, her life was all but mapped out in front of her – a safe and predictable life – and Kate wasn't going to let anything spoil that now.

She lay in the dark of the bedroom, the flickering lights from the street playing through the slight gap in the curtain, thinking how complicated life had suddenly become. And thinking how reckless of her it was to have *allowed* complications. Kate decided she would rectify that when she got back to Ballygrace.

There would be no more complications like David McGuire.

Then, when she closed her eyes, a picture of Michael O'Brien's handsome face swam into the darkness behind her eyelids, and brought a warm and contented glow to her whole body, and she drifted off into a deep and dreamless sleep.

Chapter 38

Graham's new shop assistant arrived at ten to nine on Monday morning and Rose's hackles were raised immediately when she saw the dyed red hair, the tight sweater and skirt and the fancy white kitten-heeled shoes.

'How can she work all day in those flamin' shoes?' she demanded of her husband in a heated voice in the back-shop.

'She doesn't need to move around all the time,' Graham said, craning his neck to watch how Valerie Dobson got on with serving the small crowd that was in the shop. 'As long as she can walk up and down behind the counter and count out the right change – that'll do me.'

'And what about walking backwards and forwards to the display out at the front?' Rose demanded. 'And what about walking in and out of the back of the shop carrying sacks and boxes and climbing up the ladders – the same as poor old Betty had to do? How's she going to get up the ladder in that flamin' tight skirt?'

'Give her time,' Graham said under his breath. 'Give her time to settle in and we can sort out any little teething problems like shoes and skirts.'

'She's cheap lookin',' Rose stated. 'Even that overall she brought with her to wear over her clothes is too tight. She just doesn't look respectable.'

'Give the woman a break, Rose,' Graham sighed. 'She's only just arrived and she's tryin' her best.'

Rose folded her arms high up over her chest. 'The regular customers won't like her at all with that tinted hair and her tight jumper – they're used to bein' served by the likes of Betty.'

Graham gave her a sidelong look. 'An' what about you? Aren't they used to bein' served by you?'

'Of course – they're used to bein' served by me *and* Betty. That's the very point I'm makin'.'

'Well,' Graham reasoned, '*you're* not a bit like Betty, are you? You wouldn't want anyone sayin' you looked like an old lady, would you?'

Rose's cheeks reddened in irritation. 'You know exactly what I mean, Graham Hopkins. Don't try to be smart with me now—'

'An' you dye your hair as well, don't you?' Graham went on confidently, knowing that his argument was perfectly valid.

'Not as flamin' obviously as *that*!' Rose snapped, pointing out to the shop. 'That hair's not a natural colour, is it? It's bloody pillar-box red!'

Graham reached up for a box of greenish-yellow bananas, which he planned to put outside to ripen in the sun. 'As long as she does a fair day's work for a fair day's pay, that's all I'm interested in.' He lowered his voice. 'And I got her for ten bob a week cheaper than Betty.'

Rose raised her eyebrows in interest, but there was a sceptical look in her eyes. 'And how did you manage that?'

'I checked what the fella in Bramhall was payin' her and said I'd match that.'

Rose's mind worked quick. 'And will she be working all day Saturday like Betty?'

'Half-day,' Graham said decisively, swinging the box of bananas down. 'She says she has an elderly mother that she has to visit on Saturday afternoons.'

Rose stared at her husband, her narrowed eyes glinting with fury.

'You're nothing but a feckin' amadán, Graham Hopkins!' she told him. 'You might have saved ten bob taking her on, but she's going to be doing less hours than Betty – so it's not going to work out any flamin' different in the long run.'

Graham ran them to Salford Cathedral for Mass on Sunday for a bit of a change and a run out, and then, since it was a dry and warm day, they had a walk around the city centre to have a look at the nice old buildings. Being Sunday, there were no cafés or tearooms open so they bought ice-creams from a van and sauntered back to the car then headed for home. Rose had left a slow roast cooking, so it was all hands on deck getting the potatoes and vegetables ready. With the dinner being that bit later than normal, the evening ran away from them with the washing-up and tidying around.

Monday was taken up with Rose complaining about Valerie Dobson and her shoes, and on Tuesday, Rose suddenly decided to take the day off work to accompany her sister and niece into Manchester for a look around the shops.

'You can't just decide to take the day off like that!' Graham had protested when Rose announced her plan at eight o'clock on the Tuesday morning as they were both getting dressed in the bedroom.

'I need a day off,' Rose told him firmly, as she adjusted the straps on her white, lace-trimmed, sharkskin petticoat, 'and you've that Valerie there to help you out.'

'But it's only her second day—' Graham halted with his casual four-buttoned shirt poised in mid-air, ready to pull over his head.

'If she's as brilliant a shop assistant as you keep makin' out,' Rose snapped, 'then you won't even miss me.'

He pulled the shirt on now, thrusting his arms into the sleeves with some viciousness. 'But you bloody well know we have all the orders for the convent and the old folk's home and the two big bed and breakfasts on a Tuesday,' he argued. 'They've got to be done today, come hell or high water. Valerie won't know owt about those, and it'll take half the day for me to do them on my own. Why can't you take another day off?'

'Because I want *today* off,' she said, going over to the wardrobe to pick out one of her nice Sunday frocks. The walk around

Manchester after Mass had put her in the mood for a day out around the shops and she suddenly felt that she deserved it. Besides, she'd had very little time with her sister apart from the evenings and a Sunday, and she fancied a ladies' day out in the more refined shops in the city.

Graham ran his hands through his wavy hair, making it stick up like two horns at either side of his head. 'After all these years of workin' in the shop, you know bloody well that Tuesday is the worst day of the week to take off. You know them nuns are dead pernickety about the fruit and veg they get. You have to examine every bleedin' onion before you put it in the box.' He jabbed an accusing finger in his wife's direction, but she was too busy doing up the buttons on the back of her frock to notice. 'What about that cauliflower that old Sister Malachy brought back the other week, just because it had a speck of black on it? You were givin' out stink about her when she left the shop, callin' her for everything.'

'You'll manage,' Rose told him airily, 'you and Valerie . . .'

'Oh, Rose!' Mary gasped, when they had climbed upstairs on the swaying 92 bus and collapsed into a seat. 'I thought Graham was going to take a heart attack this morning, the way he was cursing and swearing and throwing the potato sacks around the place.'

'I hope he bloody well does have a heart attack!' Rose stated. 'And I hope she takes one an' all, tryin' to help him with the orders and serve the customers at the same time.'

Kate sat in the seat behind her mother and aunt and looked out of the window, trying not to laugh. There were times when Rose and Graham's arguments were like something out of a Laurel and Hardy film.

'He didn't even take any time to have his breakfast,' Mary said, shaking her head.

'It won't do him a bit of harm for once,' Rose said, searching in her handbag for her purse. 'And it might do his beer belly the world of good.' She made a little snorting noise. 'He's had it too easy for too long with me and poor Betty shouldering all the work. Let him see how he gets on with only Valerie to help him tottering around in her kitten heels.'

'I meant to tell you,' Mary suddenly remembered, 'she nearly broke her neck coming into the shop this morning!' Mary had popped into the shop before they left to get change of a five-pound note from the till. 'Graham had dropped a punnet of strawberries when he was setting up the stall at the front door and he must have missed a bit of the juice when he was mopping it all up. Valerie walked in all dignified and the next thing she went skiting across the floor. She just managed to save herself by grabbing onto one of the shelves.'

A delighted smile spread across Rose's face. 'An' was she wearin' the white shoes again?' she asked, having kept well away from the shop until it was time to leave for Manchester.

Mary nodded, a grave look on her face. She had been surprised that Valerie Dobson had turned up in those unsuitable shoes again after all the little digs that Rose had made about them the previous day. She was obviously a determined type who wouldn't listen to any advice.

'Ah, well,' Rose said, giving her sister a conspiratorial wink, 'she'll learn soon enough. Fashion and working in a busy greengrocer's shop don't go hand in hand.'

The bus conductor came up now and there was a minor battle as all three women insisted on paying each other's fares. Eventually, Rose reluctantly put her purse back in her handbag as Kate paid the fares on the strict agreement that her mother was allowed to pay for them on the way back.

On arriving in Manchester, Rose led them straight to the tearoom in John Lewis's department store where they sat chatting and admiring the other smartly dressed customers, while drinking tea and eating hot buttered crumpets and scones with jam and cream.

Every so often, Rose would look at her watch and then speculate about how far Graham would have got with the orders and which of their customers was likely to have come into the shop to be served by Valerie Dobson.

When Kate went to the Ladies', Rose leaned forward to her sister. 'I don't like to say too much with Kate being so young and everything, but I knew perfectly well what I was doing when I left Graham to himself this morning.'

'Oh, Rose!' Mary said, attempting to sound shocked, but knowing her sister was more than capable of manipulating the situation to suit her own ends.

'I woke early,' Rose explained, 'and I was just lying there thinking about the way he'd been so high-handed about letting poor Betty go – not even having the decency to discuss it with me or anythin', and I just thought to myself, You need a spoke puttin' right in your wheel, Mr Smart-arse.'

Mary shook her head. 'I have to say I felt very sorry about Betty leaving.'

'So,' Rose said, 'I was just thinking of all the things that needed to be done in the shop in the morning, and how much of it Graham leaves to me when he saunters off to the bank or the betting shop for hours at a time.' She dug Mary on the thigh, laughing as she did so. 'I wish I had a cine-camera I could have set up back in the shop to watch Lady-go-lightly steppin' around the cabbages and turnips in her spindly little heels, when Graham does his vanishing act.'

'Oh, you've a bad streak in you, Rose Hopkins!' Mary laughed.

'And I haven't even started . . .' Rose said, lifting the delicate china teacup and saucer. She started laughing so hard that she had to put them back down again as the tea had splashed out of the cup. 'I hope it starts bucketin' rain and they'll be runnin' around like a pair of blue-arsed flies, trying to bring in all the stuff from outside the shop.'

'Shhhh!' Mary told her, seeing Kate coming back through the women's section towards the tearoom. She paused to look at a rack of fine woollen sweaters. 'Oh, we're okay . . . she's stopped to look at something.'

Rose stretched her neck to see how far away her niece actually was. 'Changin' the subject,' she said in a low voice, her face serious now, 'your Kate didn't seem too impressed by you having a date with Lance Williams.'

'Well, it's not *exactly* a date . . .' Mary said, looking over at the plate of scones. 'It's only because he won the tickets or we wouldn't be going out at all.' She bit her lip. 'To tell you the truth, I'd do anything to get out of it now . . .'

'Why?' Rose demanded. 'What's wrong with Lance?'

'Oh, there's nothing wrong with him – nothing wrong at all . . . In fact he's a very nice man – a real gentleman. It's just, well, can you imagine *me* going out with a man?' She rolled her eyes to the ceiling. 'If our Brendan was here, he'd be on the floor laughing at the very idea. I'm a bit long in the tooth for going out on dates.'

'Rubbish!' Rose stated. 'You're only a few years older than me, and I certainly don't feel old.' She glanced over at the women's section again. 'Now, don't be paying the slightest bit of heed to what Kate or Brendan have to say. It's your life and you're perfectly entitled to go out with whoever you like – especially when you're over here. Who's to know?'

Mary nodded her head, but her solemn countenance showed she didn't feel at all reassured. 'What will I wear? That outfit I wore to the party was the only really good one I have. All the other things are day dresses like this one and they're not fancy enough.' She looked down dismally at the dull gold and yellow dress she was wearing, its narrow, unflattering belt now lost in the little rolls of fat around her waist. She sighed and reached out for a scone, in need of something sweet to soothe her nerves over the forthcoming date. 'I'd need something very swanky for a concert in a town hall.'

'You can borrow something of mine,' Rose told her. 'I've several things that would suit just fine. I have a lovely dress and bolero jacket I bought for a wedding at Easter. It would be perfect on you.'

'But you're a good size smaller than me, Rose,' Mary said. 'It would be all stretched over my spare tyres.' She patted her midriff and shook her head. 'I would look a real show in one of your outfits.'

'We'll see about that,' Rose said, raising her eyebrows in a mysterious manner.

Half an hour later, Rose led the way through the ladies' department and straight on to the underwear and lingerie department. 'A good, firm all-in-one corset is all that you need,' she told her sister. 'I've been thinking about it since I set eyes on you this holiday.'

'Do I look that bad?' Mary whispered, looking anxiously at Kate. 'Rose said that the cotton underwear I usually wear makes me look like a sack tied in the middle!'

Kate smiled in amusement. There were times when she felt her mother and aunt were more childish than any of the girls she had gone to school with. In fact, they were even worse than Noelle and Sarah Daly when they got going. 'You always look fine, Mammy,' she reassured her. 'But there's no harm in trying on a corset to see if you look any different.'

Rose marched across the floor to the sales lady and after chatting to her for a few minutes, they both came towards Mary.

'This nice lady will measure you up in the changing-room,' Rose informed her sister. 'And then they'll let you choose from an all-in-one with suspenders or a three-quarter corset with a separate bra.'

Mary's face flushed at the mention of the intimate garments and she opened her mouth to object, but Rose waved away any protests. She took Mary by the arm and propelled her towards the curtained changing-room. 'And don't go looking at the price tags and start complaining that they're far too dear,' she warned her in a low voice so that the assistant wouldn't hear. 'It's an early birthday present from me, so there's to be no arguments about it.'

Another assistant emerged from the behind the pay-desk and guided Kate and Rose over to a velvet-covered couch, then she gave them both a magazine, to keep them pleasantly occupied while Mary was being attended to.

'I hope it doesn't look as if I'm bossing your mother around or anything like that,' Rose said in her straightforward manner to Kate. 'But I noticed that she was wearing an old-fashioned brassiere that couldn't have been giving her any support, and it's the same with those white cotton knickers that she wears – she could do with something to pull in her stomach.' Then, seeing Kate's slightly embarrassed manner, she put her arm around her shoulder. 'I know it all sounds like a load of codswallop to a lovely, slim young thing like yourself – but when you get that little bit older, you have to make more effort.' She suddenly jumped to her feet. 'You see,' Rose said, her hands coming to rest on her bust, 'when you hit your forties, things start to slip and slide downwards.'

She made a sliding motion with her two hands down either side of her body and then pointed towards her feet, which sent Kate into a fit of silent laughter.

Rose put her hands on her hips and pretended to look stern. 'Well may you laugh, young lady,' she said, 'but I promise you that all the slipping and sliding will come to *you* one day!' She pointed towards the dressing-room. 'And I hope you're as lucky to have somebody like me, who's honest enough to tell you when you need a bit of help.'

A good ten minutes later, Mary emerged from the changing-room, her face red but smiling. 'Can you tell the difference?' she asked, giving them a little twirl. The gold and yellow dress she was wearing looked totally different on her now, with her waist clearly defined and the belt sitting just as it should.

'A difference?' Rose gasped. 'It takes at least a stone off you and a good five years.'

Mary looked at Kate, knowing that she would tell the truth. 'Well?' she said, touching an anxious hand to the back of her hair.

Kate stared at her mother, amazed at the difference. She did indeed look both younger and slimmer – in fact, the best she'd looked in years. 'Rose is right, you look fantastic in it.'

'How does it feel on?' Rose checked.

'As light as a feather,' Mary replied. She was slightly exaggerating the situation, but compared to some of the other garments the woman had hooked or zipped her into, it was very comfortable. And, more importantly, she herself was amazed at the difference. She now went in where she should and, even more amazingly, went *up* and *out* where she should.

Looking in the mirror now, Mary Flowers realised that she wasn't as old and decrepit as she thought she was. She looked almost as slim as Rose and she looked firm and toned – and that in itself, she thought, was nothing short of a miracle.

'Buy it,' Kate said, with a definite nod of confirmation, 'whatever it costs.'

'That,' Rose said, taking her purse out of her handbag, 'is my department.'

Chapter 39

❧

The door of the shop was still open when the three women returned, and the boxes and baskets still piled outside.

'Straight into the house,' Rose instructed when they got off at the bus stop across the road. 'Don't look anywhere near the shop or he'll have us in to tidy up and close the shop after him. He can finish the blidey day off as he started – on his own.'

They scurried across the road and into the house, with their various packages and bags, but Kate had barely closed the door when Graham's key was heard in the lock.

'You might at least have had the decency to answer me when I called you!' he spluttered, his face red with rage. 'Not very nice snubbing your own husband in the street. Not very nice at all.'

Rose whirled around, her face a picture of injured innocence. 'We never heard you calling anybody.' She looked at Mary and Kate. 'Did either of your hear him calling out?'

'Oh, that's right!' Graham said, his hands on his hips. 'You're bringin' your sister and your niece into it now! Makin' them tell lies for you.'

'No,' Mary said, her face draining of colour, 'we never heard you calling us, Graham – honest to God.' She put her John Lewis bag down on the sofa. 'You know we wouldn't ignore you ... '

Kate felt her throat tighten. She'd often heard Graham and Rose niggling at each other, but this was the first time she'd seen them having a full-scale row. 'We definitely didn't hear you,' she said in the same sort of tone she used when Brendan started. 'Why would my mother and I ignore you? Your row with Rose has nothing to do with us.'

'Well, I'm glad to hear it ...' Graham folded his arms across his chest, and turned his attention back to his wife. 'You don't know what you've done this time, Rose. You really landed me in it, goin' off like that.' He pointed his finger towards the wall that adjoined the shop. 'That place has been like bloody Bedlam all day. I've been run off my flamin' feet!'

Rose gave him a long, cool look – totally unruffled by his outburst. 'And what about the wonderful Valerie?'

'Don't talk to me about her!' he said, his eyes wide and staring. His finger now moved to the fireplace. 'She was as much bloody use to me as that china dog on the mantelpiece. Less, if it were possible! She didn't know a parsnip from a turnip and she didn't know how to use the weighin' scales or anythin'.'

'I thought she had all this great experience from the shop in Bramhall?'

'Oh, aye!' Graham said, making a loud snorting noise. 'Turns out all she ever did in the shop was stack the shelves and wash the bleedin' floor!'

223

'In those white shoes?' Rose said, looking all innocent.

'Never mind the bloody sarcasm,' Graham said, sinking down into the sofa. 'You've no idea the day I've had . . . no idea at all. I'd to tell that Valerie to go at three o'clock – I couldn't take any more of her askin' me to weigh this and weigh that for her – an' I couldn't let her near the till. Betty in her wheelchair would have been more use to me.' He gave a long, weary sigh. 'I'm bloody well knackered, I am. Got no proper lunch and no afternoon tea. I had to eat a bag of flamin' chips while I was workin' – and then all the bending and lifting after eatin' them gave me terrible indigestion.' He shook his head at the memory of it. 'If I don't have a heart attack after this, I never friggin' will.'

Rose looked over his head at Mary and Kate and winked. 'Ah well,' she said, 'it just shows you that the shop can't be run single-handed for long. I certainly feel like that on the days that you get stuck in the bank or wherever else you have to go and I'm left on my own.' She paused, letting her point sink in. 'And whatever you thought of Betty – good honest workers are hard to come by.' She waited to see if he was going to come back with another sharp retort and when he didn't, she leaned forward and ruffled his hair and said, 'Do you want a lift in with the boxes and things?'

There was a little pause as Graham considered the situation. 'Aye . . . all right,' he finally conceded, his tone still injured and defensive.

'Mary,' Rose said, her tone suddenly back to her efficient shopkeeper's, 'would you mind sticking those steak and kidney pies in the oven for us, and putting the potatoes on to boil? I left them in the pan all peeled this morning.'

'Grand,' Mary said, a smile of relief spreading on her face. She wasn't used to being in the middle of warring couples and it made her feel very uneasy. She also felt bad for Kate being subjected to Rose and Graham's differences, but she was more or less a grown woman now and couldn't be sheltered for ever from other people's lives. In fact, Mary thought, it made their own lives back in Ballygrace seem almost idyllic. From the distance of Stockport, even Brendan seemed like an easy-going fellow to have around the house.

'And would you mind opening the tin of processed peas that I left out, Kate?' Rose asked.

'Grand,' Kate said, 'and I'll set the table as well.' She glanced over at Graham. 'Do you want me to come down to the shop and help you when I've finished?'

'No, no,' Rose said, 'me and himself will manage it fine on our own.'

Graham paused at the front door, the shop keys looped around his fingers. 'I had to phone the convent this afternoon and say I was goin' to be late with the order . . . but thank God they were okay about it.' He gave a weary sigh. 'For once, that crabbit old nun was civil and understanding about it.'

'You did well managing on your own,' Rose told him. 'You did really well.' She came behind him now, patting him on the back the way an adult would pat a child who had just been through a terrible ordeal.

On Wednesday night at half past six, Mary stood in front of the wardrobe mirror scrutinising herself. The pale lilac dress and jacket that Rose had loaned her fitted her much better than she had imagined it would. As long as she kept the jacket on, she looked absolutely perfect. With the jacket off, the dress was a bit tight around the waist and the neckline plunged a little too low for Mary's comfort. The all-in-one girdle had made a massive difference, especially to her bust. It was so long since she'd bought a decent brassiere that she had forgotten how well-endowed she was in that department, especially when she was hoisted up in the right direction.

After her bath in the afternoon, Kate had put rollers in her tinted hair – which had washed out a bit to a nice warm brownish shade – and it had made a huge difference. The soft waves framed her face and flattered her blue eyes, and the light layer of foundation and powder, and the mascara and pinkish-mauve lipstick that matched her outfit gave her face a real lift. All in all, the reflection looking back from the mirror was the best Mary had seen in years.

It was a very different Mary Flowers: an elegant, attractive, slimmer and younger version of herself. And yet, although she looked so much better on the outside, inside she was less certain of herself than ever.

Every time she pictured herself walking to the door of Rose's house to greet Lance Williams her legs felt weak. And every time she thought of getting into his fancy car, she thought she might actually get sick.

She had eaten practically nothing of the chicken and potatoes that she and Kate had cooked, and both Graham and Rose had teased her saying she didn't need food, that she was living on love. She had blushed red and attempted to make some light-hearted comment back to them, but her stomach had churned at the thought of Lance coming to collect her at the door. She had also kept her eyes well averted from Kate's as she felt that deep down her daughter still didn't approve of her having agreed to go out with a man.

Lance appeared at the door on the dot of seven, dressed in a dark navy blazer with shiny gold buttons and a red tie and matching red hanky. The minute he pressed the doorbell, the nerve-ridden Mary was out and on the doorstep before he had a chance to come into the house to greet anyone else.

Not wishing to miss out on any of the excitement of the date, Rose and Graham followed the couple out into the street to wave them off in Lance's shiny blue car.

'Crackin' car you've got there, Lance,' Graham said, as Mary's escort held the passenger door wide open for her.

Mary went forward to climb into the car in as delicate a fashion as she could, hoping that Lance wouldn't realise that she had only ever been in half a dozen cars in her life.

'Have a lovely evening,' Rose called over Lance's shoulder, 'and don't do anything I wouldn't do!'

A flush of embarrassment washed over Mary at her sister's vaguely crude comment, and she was so flustered that she found herself *stepping* into the car, completely forgetting what Kate had advised her about sitting down first and gently twisting her body and legs until she was facing the front.

Eventually – after banging her head off the roof of the car and catching her leg on the gear-stick – Mary landed into the car in an ungracious heap with Rose's dress dangerously riding up towards the top of her stockings and her handbag on the floor.

'Are you all right?' Lance asked anxiously, leaning forward to retrieve the bag for her.

'Lovely, thank you . . .' Mary lied. Then, when he shut the car door, she closed her eyes and leaned back in the seat, taking huge deep breaths.

Graham stood with his hands on his hips, studying the car. 'I've never seen it close up to,' he said, following Lance around the back of the car to have a better look. 'Austin Cambridge,' he read aloud. 'No doubts about it, it's a really smart car.'

'Ah, it does the job,' Lance said modestly, coming around to the driver's side.

Graham shaded his eyes with his hands now to look in the back seat. 'Nice leather upholstery too, I see,' he called out loud. 'Definitely a crackin' bit of motor.'

Mary took a deep breath and clutched her handbag tightly with both hands.

Chapter 40

꿈꿈

The silence in the kitchen was deafening. It wasn't so much the words that had been spoken as the tone that was used to convey them.

'Now, Noelle, where did you say that you went on Saturday night at all?' Matt Daly repeated, putting his knife and fork down carefully on his half-finished plate. He leaned on his elbows, his chin resting on his big joined hands, staring straight at his eldest daughter.

Noelle's brain worked fast. 'I told you before I went,' she hedged, a defensive note automatically creeping into her voice. 'I went into Daingean to give a book back to Tess Brennan...'

'That's exactly what I thought you told your mother and me.' He paused, his eyes not flinching one inch from her face. 'And tell me now, where did you go when you left Daingean?'

Noelle realised immediately that she had been seen in Tullamore and that she would now have to adjust her story to fit that of any witnesses that had reported back to her father. 'Tess asked me if we would go for a ride into Tullamore on the bikes, since it was a nice evening.' She glanced over at her mother and sister, but both had their eyes cast down towards their plates as they continued to eat, trying to make out that everything was normal. 'We weren't that long . . . and I knew that Sarah was at home minding the children.'

Matt Daly's large head moved slowly towards Noelle's direction although the rest of his body seemed to stay still. 'It wasn't with the Brennan girl that you were seen.'

Noelle lowered her brow in confusion, almost convincing herself that she had indeed been cycling around Tullamore town with her old school friend. 'We met up with a few others . . .' She shook her head as though she couldn't quite recall the events of the evening, then she shrugged. 'I suppose we were talking to various ones . . .'

'And would Brendan Flowers have been one of the ones ye were talking to? And *you* in particular?' He gave a little sarcastic smile and shook his head, mimicking the way she had shaken her head.

Noelle's face drained of colour the minute Brendan's name was mentioned. 'Now that you say it . . . we did happen to meet him.' She swallowed hard. 'We just had a few minutes chatting to him—'

'In the picture-house?' her father said, his voice ominously even. 'From what I heard there was just the two of ye – and the Brennan girl nowhere to be seen.'

Noelle put her hands together now and looked down at her plate.

The breathing of the whole family could almost be heard in the silence.

Matt Daly loosened his joined hands now and then proceeded to crack his knuckles in a loud manner. 'It seems,' he said, pushing his half-eaten dinner away, 'that we have *two* problems here. We first have the problem about the Brennan girl – whether she was ever involved in the evening at all.' He leaned forward and stabbed a hard, prodding finger into Noelle's forearm. 'Whether *you* ever went anywhere near Daingean at all.' He halted, waiting for some reaction. 'And then we have the problem about Brendan Flowers.'

Again there was a silence.

Peg Daly gestured towards the younger ones to leave the table, her face pale and pinched. They did so quickly and with the minimum of noise, being well versed in the way to behave when their father was in one of his moods.

Sarah suddenly jerked her head up – her eyes moved towards Noelle and then slowly to the top of the table to look at her father.

She knew that he was building up to a scene and they might as well get it over and done with. 'He's not that bad . . .' she said.

Matt Daly's eyes narrowed and he turned his head just enough to have his second daughter in his view. 'And who asked for your opinion?' he said, through clenched teeth. 'I thought I was having a conversation with your sister.' He stared at her for a few more moments until he was sure of her submission, then he turned back to Noelle. 'Did you arrange to meet that blackguard Flowers?'

I am a grown woman, Noelle said inside her head. *I'm entitled to meet anyone I choose.*

She took a deep breath, deciding to take the bull by the horns for once. It was as well to get it all over with quickly, she reckoned, because whatever was going to happen would happen anyway. 'Yes,' she said, her heart beating rapidly now. 'He asked if I would like to go to the pictures with him . . . and I said I would. When I hurt my leg the other night he helped me and checked I got home okay – so I felt there was no harm going to the pictures with him.' She looked her father straight in the eye. 'I wasn't sure what your attitude would be, and I didn't want another row in the house. We have enough of those—'

In a split second Matt Daly was out of his chair, had reached across the table and grabbed Noelle roughly by the collar of her dress, pulling her face to only an inch from his. 'What did you just say?' he said in a low growl of a voice.

Noelle tried to pull at his hands and struggle away from him. 'Leave me go!' she said in a voice that was more of a cry. 'I'm a grown woman—'

'Matt! Let her go!' his wife echoed. 'For God's sake—'

'We're rearin' nothing but liars and whores in this house!' he roared, his free hand thumping down on the table, making all the dishes and cutlery rattle and crash around. 'And now she thinks she's going to be stepping out with that Flowers bastard!'

His hand flew up now and Noelle knew that he was going to strike her – as he had done many times in the past.

'No!' she screamed, shielding her head and face with her arms. 'I'll tell the doctor! I'll tell the doctor and she'll get the Guards on you!'

His hand halted in mid air and his other hand loosened its grip just a fraction. It was enough for Noelle to wrench herself free and tumble back across the table from him – and she kept on tumbling, over the chair and around the back of her father's chair before he could catch hold of her again, and out of the kitchen door and into the yard.

'Threaten me with the Guards, would you, you bitch?' she could hear him calling, and then the sound of the plates and the meal things banging and crashing around the kitchen amidst the screams from her mother and sister.

Without any thought or plan Noelle found herself running and running up the tow-path towards the Flowers' cottage. Towards Brendan Flowers and hopefully towards safety.

Chapter 41

'I hope you've enjoyed the evening so far?' Lance asked, his hand reaching across the small round table to squeeze Mary's hand.

'Grand,' she replied, an over-bright, slightly anxious smile on her face. She was afraid to look too closely at him and more afraid to look around her in case people were staring at them, thinking that they were a bit too long in the tooth to be holding hands and things like that. Thankfully, the lights were low and people were now up and moving to the bar and to the Ladies' and Gent's, so they were probably not as conspicuous as they might be.

'Now,' he said, standing up straight, 'what will you have to drink?'

Mary looked back at him blankly. Rose usually picked what she drank when they were out. She gave a little shrug. 'I don't really mind . . .'

'Sherry?' he suggested. 'Gin and tonic?'

The thought of the sweet sherry reminded her too much of the wine at the garden party last weekend, and the sickly way she had felt the next morning. It might be safer to try something else. 'A gin and tonic sounds grand,' she said. Then, she bent for her handbag. 'Let me pay for this.'

'Not at all,' her escort told her. 'You're my guest for the evening, and it's a privilege to buy you a drink.' He leaned back down towards her. 'It's a privilege to be out with such a lovely lady, and I'm enjoying every minute.'

A blush immediately stole over her face and neck. 'I'm enjoying myself too . . .' she said, her voice low and embarrassed.

He reached a hand out now and touched Mary's warm cheek, looking deep into her eyes as he did so.

As Lance left the table to walk across to the brightly lit bar, skirting the empty stage, Mary discreetly glanced around her at the other tables. A few were like their table, small, with chairs for two, but most were bigger with places for four or six. A self-conscious feeling came over her as she realised that she couldn't remember ever being out for the evening with a man on her own. Surely, she thought, she must have been out at some point on her own with her husband? But she couldn't honestly remember. Seamus and her had never really gone out as a couple. It wasn't the way it was done in Ballygrace with married couples. Men went to the pub with other men, and if they went out with their wives for a special occasion, it was always as part of a group.

Mary mused now as to why things were done that way, and she supposed it was because there wasn't the money to spare for nights sitting in pubs and, anyway, there were the children to look after. In any case, she thought, what would her and Seamus have found to talk about for a whole night on their own? She remembered feeling at a loss for conversation with him on numerous occasions, when they were just sitting across from each other at the fire. She always felt she had to put the radio on to fill the little silences when the children were in bed. The little gaps spoke volumes about the differences between them, the differences between Mary's unful-filled girlish hopes and dreams and Seamus Flowers' contentment with his small lot in life.

The early part of the evening was usually grand when she was busy with the children and cooking and cleaning up afterwards. Then she would carry on with her household chores, perhaps ironing while he was sitting reading the paper or doing something like chopping up kindling for the fire.

But there would always come that time of night when they were across the fire from each other, when they had little to say about a day that was only a repeat of all the others that already had gone. And then they would face another night of lying beside each other until nature took over in the form of sleep or with their rare and slightly awkward physical couplings.

But it hadn't been a bad marriage, Mary thought. No worse than many of her neighbours – and better than a lot. And she consoled herself by remembering that latterly the awkwardness and differences between her and Seamus had faded into a quiet, fairly contented way of life.

Then, trying to look relaxed and not bothered about sitting at a table on her own, Mary fixed her gaze on the elaborately patterned Town Hall ceiling and the pillars. Then, she looked back to the tables around her, and she noticed the couples that were there on their own and how confident they seemed about it. Her eyes settled on one of the larger tables and when she noticed two women looking back at her, she suddenly felt all flustered. She bent down and lifted her handbag up again, pretending she was looking for her hanky and wishing that Lance Williams would hurry back and stop her from feeling that she was sitting in a goldfish bowl.

Lance was a great talker, Mary thought. And as the evening wore on, she realised he was an even better listener. When he asked her all about where she lived in Ireland, he really listened to what she had to say. Then, he asked her more questions, interested questions – not prying, nosy questions – about Kate and Brendan and about living beside the canal.

The second part of the jazz concert had definitely been more enjoyable, and Mary had found herself relaxing and gently clapping her hands along with some of the songs she knew. On one occasion, she had caught Lance looking at her with a strange, thoughtful look on his face and she had felt self-conscious all over again. But it hadn't lasted. The very next song had got her clapping and enjoying herself again.

When the concert ended at ten o'clock, Lance suggested that since it was a nice night, they go for a drink to a pub that was just a short walk down from the Town Hall, close to where Lance had parked the car. They walked out with the rest of the crowd and into the busy pub, which was now full of other concert-goers.

All the tables were taken, but Lance managed to get them two high bar stools tucked away in the corner at the side of the bar, and as he helped her up onto the stool, Mary gave a silent prayer of thanks that no-one from Ballygrace was there to see her.

As they drove along the A6 road back up to Davenport, Lance told Mary all about his wife and her long illness. 'She was the love of my life,' he said in a hoarse, cracked voice. 'But over a period of four years, the woman I knew disappeared in front of my eyes.'

'Oh, I'm very sorry to hear that,' Mary said, instinctively touching his arm. A little part of her was surprised she did it, but the couple of drinks in the pub stopped her worrying. 'And your son?' She moved her hand back down to her lap to rest on her handbag.

'Lovely boy – well, *grown man* now, of course,' he said, giving a sad smile. 'Charles is down in London – works in banking in the City. He phones me every week and comes up every month or so, and occasionally I go down to him for the weekend.'

'Is he married?' Mary asked.

'No, no . . .' Lance said. 'He never will . . . he's not that kind.'

'Oh, you never know,' Mary said, nodding her head. 'He could surprise you.'

'And your son?' Lance said, turning the question around. 'What are his circumstances?'

Mary gave a great big sigh. 'Oh, the Lord only knows, and he's not telling. Brendan is what they would describe in Ireland as "a bit of a rake".'

'He sounds very interesting,' Lance hedged, playing safe in case the description was not a compliment.

'Oh, he has plenty of women,' Mary said, 'but they're never the right kind – or so he says.' A dark look came into her eyes. 'He's my own son and I love him dearly – but there are times when I'm not sure if I actually *like* him.' She paused. 'Does that sound terrible?'

Lance laughed now. 'I'm sure you don't really mean it as harshly as it sounds – but yes, I think I can relate to that. We would all like to keep control of our children and direct them towards the lives we want them to lead.' He turned off the main road now and up Bramhall Lane towards Davenport and the shop. 'A way of looking at things that helped me with Charles,' he went on, 'was to ask myself what *I* had wanted to do when I was his age – and what I would have asked of my parents.' He turned his head to look at Mary. 'And the resounding answer is always the same: let me live my own life.' He shrugged. 'I try very hard to do that with Charles. It's not a bit easy – but it's the only way that works I think.'

There was a little silence as Mary mulled over his words. 'I don't think I ever knew what I wanted when I was young,' she suddenly said. 'I think I've just followed along with whatever happened, did what seemed the best thing to do at the time...'

'That, my dear,' Lance said, 'is often the best way.'

'Well,' Mary mused, 'looking back I think I did what other people thought I should do. I could never make up my own mind. By the time I did, it was often too late – I'd asked for advice and not listened to what I really wanted.'

'And are you still like that?' Lance asked, his voice low and gentle. 'Or have you changed? Do you now know what you want?'

Mary looked down at her hands, clasped tightly over her handbag. 'I don't suppose it matters much now – at my age there's not that much to look for out of life.' She lifted her head up and looked out into the yellow streetlight darkness. 'The basics are enough. Your family and your health are the most important things, and thank God I have both of them for the moment.'

Lance drew the car up a little way from Rose and Graham's house, and they sat talking for a few minutes. At one point there was a silence and Mary looked up and caught Lance staring at her.

'What is it?' she asked, feeling all self-conscious.

'I was just thinking,' he said. 'I was just looking at you and thinking.'

Mary suddenly felt engulfed with embarrassment. She attempted to smile at him but it didn't quite work. Then, just to fill the silence, she asked, 'What were you thinking?'

'How lovely you are ... your face, your hair, your voice...'

'Get away with you!' she said, laughing lightly now. 'People always say that Offaly accents are very flat and boring compared to some of the nicer Irish accents. After all the years in Offaly I've probably got that terrible flat accent now.'

'Your voice and accent are beautiful,' he told her. 'Just like you.'

Mary shook her head, her eyes turned away and looking out of the side window now.

He took a deep breath. 'I wonder,' he said, his voice unsure, 'if you might like to come back to my house for a cup of tea?'

Mary turned away from the window to look at him. 'Tonight?' she asked in a whisper.

'Yes, tonight...' he said quickly. 'I was just thinking that you have only a few days left here, and you'll probably be spending most of that time with your sister and her husband.'

'It might look very bad,' she told him. 'The two of us being in the house on our own late at night...'

'Who's going to know?' Lance said. 'My neighbours don't pay any attention to what I do. And really – who's going to *care* that much if you come in for a harmless cup of tea? Rose and Graham? Your daughter?'

'Well, I don't think Kate would be very pleased... and Rose and Graham would only laugh and make jokes about it.'

'Half an hour?' he said, looking at his watch. He had a beseeching look on his face. 'I've enjoyed talking to you so much, and I just don't want the night to end.' He reached out now and took her hand, then he lifted it, turned it over and kissed the back of it. 'You have enjoyed yourself, haven't you, Mary?'

'Yes,' she said honestly. 'It's been one of the nicest nights I can ever remember.' She bit her tongue now, to stop herself from telling him that she'd never been on a proper date with a man before and she'd certainly never been anywhere so romantic, where she'd sat at a table for two with flowers and a candle on the table. And she had definitely enjoyed herself. How could she not? Sitting in a lovely place with lovely music with such a smart, distinguished-looking man. The sort of man she had never dreamed would ever look at her, far less want to spend hours in her company.

'Well, let's finish it off properly,' he said, gently letting go of her hand and turning the car engine on now. 'What do you say?'

She took a deep breath, thinking about all the things she had said earlier about never doing what she wanted at the time. 'Okay,' she said. 'I don't suppose that a half an hour will make any great difference.'

235

Chapter 42

B y the time Noelle arrived up at the Flowers' cottage – breathless and sweating – all the bravery she had mustered to run out of the house had drained away. She found herself on the doorstep, shaking and lost for words. And then, after building herself up to knock on the door, there had been no reply.

She rapped several times, all the while looking back over her shoulder, down along the canal tow-path, where she feared her father might just be coming towards her.

Then, just as she turned back to the gate – desperately wondering what to do next – Brendan appeared from the back of the house. He had either been working out the back in the turf-shed or maybe – more embarrassingly – Noelle thought, he might have been in the outside toilet.

'I thought I heard something . . .' he said, digging his hands into his trouser pockets. He stared at her tear-streaked face, a deep frown appearing on his brow.

'There's been a big row,' she blurted out before he had a chance to ask her anything. 'He found out about me goin' to the pictures with you at the weekend . . .'

'What happened?'

'He went mad,' she said, her voice low and trembling. 'He went to hit me and I ran out . . .' She looked back over her shoulder again. 'I was terrified he would follow me.'

Brendan nodded towards the house. 'Do you want to come in?'

She shrugged, not meeting his gaze. She didn't really know what she wanted. Or what Brendan Flowers would want of her.

She was sitting in the armchair by the fire, drinking a cup of tea, when the urgent knock came on the cottage door. 'Oh, my God!' she gasped, and her hand shook so much she had to put the cup down on the hearth.

Brendan was on his feet immediately. 'Stay where you are,' he told her. 'I'll get it.' He looked out of the window by the sink first, checking who it was. Noelle could tell by the way his shoulders eased that it wasn't her father.

Sarah stood on the doorstep of the cottage, holding Noelle's bag and coat. Her eyes were red and her hands were shaking just as her sister's shook.

She turned her head constantly to check if her father was anywhere in sight. 'He told me to pack all your stuff . . . and he said you've to go to Dublin and not to come back.'

Noelle put her head in her hands, suddenly feeling that it was much too big and heavy for her body. 'What am I going to do?' she whispered.

'I don't know,' Sarah said, going to her sister's side. 'Mammy said to tell you to keep away for a while . . . until he calms down. She said you'd be better off going back to Dublin, she says if you come back too soon *anything* could happen.'

Tears sprang into Noelle's eyes – the seriousness of her situation was just starting to sink in. She was an outcast from her family and had nowhere to go apart from back to Dublin.

'But I wasn't due back there until Friday,' she said, looking wildly from Sarah to Brendan. 'Where will I go until then?'

Brendan looked back at her blankly. Any spur-of-the-moment thoughts he had of offering for her to stay in the cottage for the couple of days were silenced in front of Sarah. He felt awkward about displaying any overt friendliness or sympathy to Noelle when her younger sister was present. Their romantic entanglement – or whatever it was between them – was in the very early stages, and he had no idea how it might pan out in the long run. And in any case, he knew it would be playing straight into Matt Daly's hands. God knows what sort of trouble he could bring upon Noelle and the rest of the Daly family if the tyrant found out that she had spent any time in the Flowers' cottage when there was no one else there. In fact, Brendan knew that Matt Daly was quite capable of appearing up at the house at any minute to confront him over the fact that he had been anywhere near his daughter.

'There's a boat going up to Dublin this evening,' Brendan suddenly remembered. 'I think Michael O'Brien and Jimmy Morris are on it, and they're both easy-going. Maybe we could sort something out there. It will be leaving Ballygrace around six o'clock this evening and it won't be up there until the morning. They moor in at Ticknevin for the night and then start off early again in the morning.'

'Are you sure they won't mind?' Noelle asked. 'I don't really know Michael that well, I've only met him a few times … and I don't know the other fellow at all.'

'Michael is the finest,' Brendan reassured her. 'And the other fella is grand, too. He's from out Banagher way.' He held his hands out. 'They wouldn't normally carry anybody up to Dublin on the boat, but if I explain the situation to them and offer to give a hand when they're loading the boat up again – I'm sure they'll do it as a favour to me.'

Noelle glanced anxiously over at Sarah, a nervous tic working in her cheek. 'What do you think? Would you get on a boat for the night with two lads you don't know?'

Sarah shrugged, awkward at being put on the spot. 'It depends …'

'Don't worry about that,' Brendan said. He paused for a minute. 'Sure, I could come up with you, just for the run. I could give the two lads a lift with the barrels and things.' He nodded now, having made a decision. 'I've nothing better to be doin' here and the craic with the lads on the boat can be mighty.'

'Are you sure?' she checked.

'Definitely.'

Noelle looked at her sister. 'I'll phone Dr Casey in the morning, and if she isn't back home yet, I could always stay up at Auntie Delia's for the night.' She gave a little watery smile. 'She knows full well what Daddy's like, so there shouldn't be any problems with her letting me stay.'

Brendan looked at his watch. 'We can head into Ballygrace any time you like,' he said to her. 'The boat's there for a while before it moves on.'

'But I've no bike,' Noelle said. 'And it'll take ages walking there.'

'You can take Kate's bike,' he offered. 'An' I'll bring it back for her later on.'

'When are Kate and your mother due back?' Sarah asked.

'Saturday, they're travellin' back overnight on the boat. They'll catch the coach down and be back in Ballygrace in the afternoon.'

'It'll be grand to see them back,' Sarah said, feeling relieved at the thought. It was always good to know she had a bolt-hole to escape to, when she needed it.

Feeling more relaxed without Sarah Daly watching his every move, Brendan loosened up a bit as they cycled along to the canal, Noelle's bag tied onto the back of his bigger bike. They were both tense and quiet until they had safely passed the turn in the road for the Dalys' house and then they had started chatting, in the same way they had talked over the previous weekend.

'How d'you feel about going back up to Dublin?' Brendan asked.

'Well, I suppose you could say I'm relieved in a way,' she told him, her red hair flying in the breeze behind her, 'but it's only because of the way things are back home. I'd never leave Ballygrace if my father was halfway like the thing.'

'Ah, sure it might all work out,' he said. 'Maybe when you're gone for a while he might think on about it. Cop himself on a bit, like.'

'My *father* cop himself on?' Noelle said, her voice full of scepticism. 'It would take a miracle for that to happen – a feckin' miracle!'

Brendan glanced across at her as they cycled along, surprised at the determination in her voice. He'd always thought of Noelle Daly as fairly easy-going, especially compared to Kate, and, like Kate, he couldn't recall hearing her use strong language before.

'No,' Noelle said in a bitter tone, shaking her head, 'that fella will never change – especially now that I've dared to cross him . . . not now that I've admitted to seeing you and making it worse by telling a lie.'

'I'm sorry for any part I have to play in the row,' Brendan said. 'I know that people like your father don't think too highly of me—'

'If people knew what my father was like at home, they wouldn't think very highly of *him*,' Noelle countered. 'And anyway, Sarah spoke up for you as well. She stuck her neck out saying how nice you were when we were in the middle of the row.'

'Did she?' he said, sounding surprised and quite pleased.

'She did, and don't forget that you and me got together because you'd been good enough to help me the night the girl nearly took the leg off me,' Noelle reminded him, 'and I told my father that as well.'

Brendan felt a small surge of pleasure at the thought of the Daly girls standing up for him. Strange to think that only a week or two ago they were at loggerheads and now the two sisters seemed to be his strongest advocates.

It wasn't quite as easy getting the two boatmen to agree to take Noelle as a passenger as Brendan had envisaged. He found himself offering to change weekends working and helping with the loading up in Dublin and the unloading all the way down, plus taking responsibility for most of the steering – effectively, giving an unpaid night and day's work in return for her being allowed to join them on board.

'Where will she sleep?' Michael O'Brien challenged. He was the one who could always be depended upon to do things by the book.

'She can have my bunk,' Brendan told him. 'I'll be up in the cabin for most of the night anyway.'

'It's a very awkward situation altogether,' Michael went on, glancing upwards to the bridge where Noelle stood with the two bikes and her bag. 'If the bosses were to hear about it . . .'

The congenial Jimmy Morris just nodded his head when either of his workmates were speaking, indicating that he would agree to whatever they decided.

'If there's anything said,' Brendan reassured Michael, 'I'll carry the can for it.' He lowered his voice further, although there was no way that Noelle could have heard them from that safe distance. 'The thing is, the girl is in deep, deep trouble. That madman of a father of hers could do anything when he gets riled.' He paused. 'And I do mean *anything*.' He held his hands out now, palms up. 'And what would we do, boys, if something disastrous was to happen and we all stood by watching?' He raised his eyebrows and shook his head.

There was an uncomfortable silence.

'What do you think now, Jimmy?' Michael asked.

'Ah, sure . . .' Jimmy shrugged.

'No,' Michael insisted. 'How do you feel about us taking that decision? Having the responsibility of another person on board?'

'Ah, c'mon now, Michael,' Brendan muscled in again. 'Haven't we often brought lads out from Tullamore to Daingean or Ballygrace or wherever locally? Didn't we bring Paddy O'Hare out just the other week when he had the bad knee and the hospital told him he wasn't to cycle back out to Daingean?'

'That was different,' Michael argued, standing his ground. 'That was another lad and it was during the day. And anyway, we all knew him.'

Brendan shrugged and looked up towards the cloudy sky. 'C'mon, lads,' he said, 'help me out now . . .'

Michael put his hands on his hips, shaking his head as he sucked his breath in through clenched teeth. 'The responsibility if anything happened . . . if anything went wrong—'

'It won't,' Brendan stated. 'The weather forecast is for it to stay mild . . . and we've never had anything go wrong on the boat.'

'Other boats have gone wrong,' Michael reminded him. 'And it's worse through the night. The forecast isn't always right – the weather could change or anything.'

'Look,' Brendan said, 'we'll bring the bikes, and if anything goes wrong we'll be off before anyone knows anything about it. How's that?'

Michael looked at Jimmy. 'What do you think? Will we risk it?'

'Aye . . . go on,' Jimmy agreed, smiling over at Brendan. He didn't care one way or the other whether the girl came on the boat and it was useful to be on Brendan Flowers' side – you never knew when a favour might be needed yourself. Plus, it would have fallen to Jimmy to take over most of the handling of the boat, so he wouldn't be losing out.

Brendan gave a sigh of relief. 'Grand!' he said, rubbing his hands together. 'An' if you want to get moving on, we could make it to Ticknevin for last orders and I'll stand you both a couple of pints.' He knew it was best to be out of Ballygrace as quickly as possible and avoid Daingean, too. There was little chance of anyone they might meet in Ticknevin reporting back to Matt Daly.

'Good man!' Jimmy said, delighted with the promise of the few drinks on top of a good night's sleep.

'I'm not too bothered about the drink,' Michael said, 'but after what you've said about her father, we might be as well to be moving on now.'

For the first hour on the boat, Noelle felt a mixture of relief and embarrassment. Although she couldn't hear their conversation, she was able to tell by the way the men had been moving and the tone of their voices that there had been some disagreement about her travelling with them.

When Brendan came back for her, he explained that they were willing to carry her up to Dublin, but that she would need to keep a low profile until they were well on their way.

Michael O'Brien had been polite and pleasant enough to her when she came on the boat and the other younger fellow had been very friendly. Brendan had taken control of it all, by bringing her down below to sit inside the boat and read the *Irish Independent* while the men worked on the deck up above. Every now and then he came down to check that she was all right, and then he showed her how to boil the kettle on the stove and make them all a cup of tea.

Noelle sat on the long wooden seat looking out of the windows as the barge passed by the fields and the bogs of the midlands. Her fingers played with strands of her hair – a childish habit she reverted to when she was anxious – but gradually she grew less tense. The humming noise of the engine and the motion of the boat as it slowly made its way along the canal seemed to somehow soothe her jangled nerves and, very gradually, she found herself relaxing and enjoying the journey.

Her attention was taken up by the tall rushes and the reeds and the different wild flowers that she had never seen from this close angle on the water. Noelle and Sarah and Kate often went for walks on sunny evenings along the canal, but actually viewing the plants from the water was a whole different experience. At one point she was thrilled to see a whole family of ducks – the drake and the mother and five babies – swimming along in a line at the edge of the canal.

For a few moments it reminded her of her own family, but she quickly pushed the thought out of her mind and busied herself with the boiling kettle and the teapot.

She called up to the men that she was making the tea and a short while later they came downstairs to join her. By the time it was all poured and the packet of chocolate digestives opened, the atmosphere between them all had lightened considerably.

Michael O'Brien was much more relaxed and chatted very pleasantly to her, telling her about a funeral he'd been to that morning in Tullamore. 'An old grand-uncle,' he explained. 'He brought my father up, so he was more like a grandfather.' He'd given a little shrug. 'Poor ould Sean wasn't in the best of health – he didn't even make my father's funeral. And I think that when my father died, it knocked him entirely – and he went downhill very quickly.' He sighed and turned his head to look out of the boat window. 'I'm sorry he didn't go first . . . because it must have been hard on him. It's certainly been very hard on the rest of the family – in fact, it's turned the whole house upside down.'

Then, as though he suddenly felt he was being too personal, or maybe too morbid, he abruptly changed the subject and started asking Noelle all about her job in Dublin.

'It's grand,' she told him, feeling slightly awkward, knowing that Brendan and Jimmy Morris were listening in to the conversation, too, but she carried on anyway. Brendan, she hoped, would know that she was making the job sound better than it was for the sake of chat. 'It's in a lovely part of Dublin, and the house is very nice and so is the doctor. A bit old-fashioned and uppity, but nice in her own way.' She had then gone on to describe the house and the surrounding area, and by the time she had finished telling him all about it, she found that she meant most of what she had said. Compared to life back at home with her father, her position in Dr Casey's house now seemed desirably peaceful and predictable. The situation with Carmel Foley she would sort out when she got back, because she couldn't afford to let anything like that jeopardise her job.

The conversation then changed to more general stuff about the canal and Jimmy told her all about an area they passed through outside Daingean called The Red Girls.

'That's a very unusual name,' Noelle said. 'Where does it come from?'

'Seemingly, there was a lock-keeper around here years ago, and he had five daughters,' he explained, 'and they all had lovely red hair.' He smiled at her. 'I should imagine their hair was something like your own.'

Noelle glowed at the compliment.

When the men had finished their tea, Michael and Jimmy went back up on the deck, leaving Noelle and Brendan on their own.

'How are you finding the trip so far?' he asked her in a low voice.

He was sitting on the long wooden bench opposite her, one leg crossed over the other and his arms leaning straight out along the back of the bench.

'Grand,' she told him. 'I'm enjoying it. The scenery is lovely . . .'

'Well, thank God for that,' he said, smiling at her. He gestured towards the window. 'There's something different to see all the time as you move along, and at this time of the year when it's warm and light until late, you see all the more.'

'It's very peaceful,' Noelle said, turning right around in the bench to look out. After a few minutes Brendan moved over to sit beside her and he put his arm around her and kissed the back of her head. Then, both his arms tightened around her and they sat together in companionable silence, looking out of the cabin window.

As the boat moved along the shimmery evening water, Noelle felt a glow steal over her like a warm, comforting blanket and she felt herself relax against his chest, feeling safer than she had felt in a long time.

After what seemed a long, long time, he gently touched the back of her neck. 'Are you all right?' he whispered into her hair.

She nodded, tears suddenly pricking at her eyes. She kept her gaze ahead, looking out at the green grass and the tall swaying reeds.

'You've had a tough enough time of it lately,' he said, 'no doubt about it. I knew Matt Daly was always an awkward man, but I'd no idea that he was leading you all such a life.'

Noelle took a deep breath, trying to stop herself from dissolving into a damp shower of tears. 'I don't know what's going to happen to me,' she whispered, 'but I feel one thing in my bones – I'll never come back to live in Ballygrace.'

'Don't be saying things like that,' Brendan told her. 'You don't know what lies around the corner.' He paused for a few moments. 'I don't know what lies around the corner for myself.'

'What do you mean?'

'The oul' boats – there are only a few of them left now, and this time next year there won't be one left on the canal.'

'What will you do?' Noelle asked, suddenly fearful of all the changes that were being thrust upon her. She had heard rumours about the boats being done away with for the last few years, but actually hearing it from one of the crew made it very real. It would totally change life as she knew it living close by the canal ... but then, she thought, she would probably never live beside the Grand Canal again.

'Ah, something will turn up ...' Brendan said, but there was an uncertain edge in his voice. 'You never know, I might travel a bit – maybe go to America or even Australia. It all depends.'

Noelle turned around now to look up at him. 'Depends on what?' she asked.

'Depends on what happens back home. I can't really just up and leave my mother and Kate.' His voice lowered. 'There are a number of factors to be taken into account. Michael O'Brien for one. You never know what could happen there ...'

'It's all very frightening,' Noelle said. 'Everything is changing too fast for me ...'

'That's life,' he told her, sounding strangely philosophical for the type of fellow that he was. He paused, then his arms grew slightly tighter. 'Would you say you would miss me if I went to some far-flung place like America or Australia?'

Noelle felt the tears again, and when she went to speak her voice wouldn't work. She closed her eyes tightly and simply nodded her head.

'Isn't it strange the way things work out?' he said to her. 'A few weeks ago, you and me were hardly lookin' at each other and now ... Well, if things had been different, you never know, we might have made a good match. I think underneath it all, we're quite similar ... we have the same ideas about life.'

Noelle wasn't too sure what he was getting at, all these deep thoughts about life and the way things work out, but she knew that he was saying that he liked her and that, under different circumstances, things might have worked out long-term between them.

She turned around again and looked up into his face. Even in the growing twilight she could see the serious look in his dark brown eyes. And deep in those dark eyes Noelle could see the same uncertainty and fear of the future that were mirrored in her own.

He looked back at her for a long moment and then he suddenly gathered her up into his arms and crushed his lips hard down on hers.

Chapter 43

❦

Kate looked at the clock and suddenly decided that she didn't want to be up when her mother came home. She didn't want to have to sit opposite her and pretend she was as excited and as interested as her Auntie Rose obviously was about this exciting new intrusion into her mother's life. She gave a little yawn. 'I think I'll head off to bed now.'

'Okay, love,' her aunt said. 'You're probably tired after all the work you've done in the shop today.'

Graham was fiddling about with the radiogram, trying to get a late-night sports station.

'You were a great help,' Graham put in. 'You're a beltin' little worker. I wish we had you here all the time. You were great weighin' and then shiftin' them five-pound bags of potatoes around. I wish we could get a full-time helper that was half as good.'

Rose threw her husband a gimlet eye as a reminder that *she* was the one who would decide on any future helpers in the shop. He studiously ignored her and went back to fiddling with the radio.

'I enjoyed it,' Kate said, and quite truthfully – she had. As a young girl, she had always enjoyed pottering about in her aunt and uncle's shop, and anyway, she was glad to be able to do something to repay Rose for her kindness and generosity to her and her mother.

'Take a long lie in the morning,' Rose advised her. 'You'll be home soon enough and back to the grindstone with washing in sinks and lighting fires and all the usual.'

Kate nodded. 'Tell my mother I hope she had a nice time and I'll see her in the morning.'

When Kate closed the sitting-room door behind her, Rose looked over at Graham, who, having found his station, was now sitting back in the armchair, his arms casually folded behind his head. 'It can't be easy for her, you know.'

'How d'you mean,' Graham said distractedly, half-listening to the summing-up of a cricket match.

'You know,' Rose said, raising her eyebrows and nodding

towards the hallway. 'Seeing her mother going out on a date after all these years. It must feel very strange.'

'She'll get over it,' Graham said. He gave a shrug. 'She's a down-to-earth girl, is Kate.'

'What do you think about Mary and Lance?' Rose asked now, drawing her feet up under her on the sofa. She glanced at the clock. 'It's nearly twelve o'clock – the pubs must be well closed by now.'

'Maybe they got after hours. There's one or two pubs around the Town Hall will give late hours if you know where to go.'

'Well, trust you to blidey well say something like that!' Rose gave an irritated little sigh. 'Do you honestly think Lance Williams is the type to go looking for after hours? I can't see it myself. He's too careful to put himself on the wrong side of the law.'

'You never know,' Graham grinned, 'he might have got so carried away with Mary's scintillating conversation that he never noticed the time.'

'Maybe he's got carried away with something else,' Rose said, smiling knowingly.

'D'you think so?' Graham turned around in his chair now, his attention suddenly grabbed by the turn in the conversation. 'D'you think your Mary would be interested like?'

Rose rolled her eyes, still smiling at the thought. 'You never know – they say that nature breaks out in the eye of a cat . . .'

Graham started to laugh now. 'I can't imagine it all the same – her and old Lance.'

'Why?' Rose asked. 'Don't you think Mary's attractive enough? People often say me and her look alike, and she's only a couple of years older than me.'

'No, no,' Graham said, 'I wasn't meanin' owt like that.' He gave a little sniff. 'Your Mary's a fine-looking woman and everything . . . it's just I couldn't imagine her in bed like.' He shook his head. 'I've never thought of her that way. With her being your sister and a widow and everything, I kind of thought of her a bit like a nun.'

Rose looked at her husband incredulously. 'A *nun*?' she repeated. 'You think our Mary's like a nun?'

'Well no . . . not exactly,' Graham backtracked. 'Not in the way you mean it . . . but you have to admit that she is very much on the religious side. A lot more than *you* are.'

'I go to Mass most Sundays,' Rose said defensively.

'Ah,' Graham said, wagging a finger at her, 'that's exactly the point I'm makin' – you go *most* Sundays, but Mary goes *every* Sunday. She goes whether she feels up to it or not. She goes unless she's completely bedridden, whereas you miss it at the drop of a hat – a headache or a hangover. Big difference there.'

'Forget about religion,' Rose told him with a wave of her hand. 'I'm more interested in your opinion of Mary as a woman.'

'Well,' Graham winked, 'I can't exactly give you my opinion of her as a *man*, can I?'

Rose rose up from the sofa now, grabbing one of the small cushions. Knowing what was coming, Graham's hands instantly came up to defend himself, as she hit him around the head with the cushion in one hand while the other came to tickle him in the ribs.

'Gerroff!' Graham shouted, laughing and pushing her away.

'Not until you say you're sorry and take me more seriously,' Rose laughed. She hit him a few more time and then she fell on top of him, laughing as he now grabbed both her hands in one of his large ones and started tickling her.

Eventually, tired from both the exertion and the laughing, Rose moved to sit on the side of her husband's armchair. He reached up and pulled her towards him, and gave her a big smacking kiss on the lips.

'Shall we go bed now?' he said with a glint in his eye. He moved his hand to grip her thigh suggestively.

Rose looked at him for a moment, deciding. 'Give it another five minutes to see if she comes in.' Then, after giving him a last playful swipe with the cushion, she lifted it and moved back to the safety of the sofa. 'Right,' she told him, her voice breathless from the nonsense. 'Go on with what you were saying about our Mary. I find it very interesting hearing outside opinions on things like that.' She drew her legs under her again and got into a comfortable position.

'Will you make me a cup of tea afterwards then?' Graham bartered, all thoughts of passion now draining away.

'I will of course,' Rose said, 'just as soon as our Mary gets in. Now, tell me what you *really* think of Mary – what a man like Lance would see in her.'

'Like I said – Mary's very nice,' Graham said, sounding mildly exasperated now. 'She's a good-enough looking woman.' He nodded now. 'In fact, she looked very well tonight in that nice rig-out of yours – very nice indeed. Much younger and slimmer.'

Rose looked down at her nails, checking on the state of her nail varnish after her day's work. 'That was the all-in-one girdle I bought her yesterday.'

'The all-in-one what?' Graham said, looking totally confused. 'What the hell's that when it's at home?'

'Never mind,' Rose said, 'it's just something to give her a bit of hold-in and push-up.'

Graham shook his head. 'Well, whatever it was, she looked the best I've seen her look in years.'

'So,' Rose said, 'do you think that Lance would try anything on with her? Do you think he's the type?'

'He's a man, isn't he?' Graham mused. He scratched his head. 'And he's been on his own for a year or more and his wife wasn't well for a good while before that.' He gave a shrug. 'Who knows? As you said yourself about nature and all that . . .'

'Well, if he has any notions like *that* about her,' Rose said, smiling, 'he won't get too far tonight in any case.'

'How d'you mean?'

'The blidey girdle!' Rose said, sounding really exasperated now. 'He'd need a flamin' large tin-opener to get her out of that.'

The thought of it now made her dissolve into hysterical giggles.

Kate lay in her bedroom, trying to concentrate on a *Woman's Own* magazine. Every now and then, she could hear the high-pitched giggles of her aunt and her intuition told her that her mother was part of the cause of the hilarity. She knew well that Rose didn't mean any harm, and fully expected the laughter to increase and continue when her mother eventually came home.

She turned on her side now, burying her head in the pillow. She couldn't wait to get back to Ireland, she thought again. Back to sanity and normality. Back to the familiar, comfy mother that she knew exactly where she was up to with.

Chapter 44

❧

Lance handed Mary a very large sherry schooner filled to the brim, then came to sit on the sofa beside her.

'Oh,' she said, taking it from him, 'I'm not too sure if I'll be able to manage all that. I've never seen a sherry glass so big.'

'Of course you will,' Lance said. 'Gloria had a glass of sherry every single night and it did her the world of good.'

Mary took a sip of the sherry, wondering which way he meant it, as poor Gloria was now dead and gone. She vaguely remembered him saying something about her heart, so presumably drinking too much sherry wasn't the cause of it. It was usually the liver that drink affected, she was almost sure of that.

'And have you a key for the house?' Lance queried.

Mary shook her head. 'They're not early-bedders, and they said they would leave the latch off for me anyway.'

Lance sat back in the sofa, whiskey glass in one hand and his arm stretched casually across the sofa behind his guest. Light jazz music, very like the music they had heard earlier in the evening, played on the radiogram in the background.

They sat sipping their drinks and chatting about trivial things like gardening and walking in the summer and what it was like living by a canal in Ireland. Then, Lance shifted forward in the sofa to look directly at her. 'Tell me, Mary,' he said, 'have you had any other men in your life since your poor husband died?'

Mary shook her head, keeping her gaze straight ahead. 'None at all,' she said in a quiet voice.

'Well,' he said, his voice full of sincerity, 'I think that while it's very commendable of you, you're far too young and beautiful a woman to be hiding yourself away from the enjoyable side of life.'

'But I am enjoying myself,' she said, giving him a small smile. 'I've had a lovely night tonight, I really have. In fact, I've had a lovely holiday – one of the best I've had for years.'

'And all the other nights?' he said, his grey-speckled eyebrows raised in question. 'What about all the other lonely nights back at home in Ireland?'

'Sure, I'm not a bit lonely,' Mary laughed. 'Don't I have Kate and Brendan to keep me company?'

He took a good mouthful of his whiskey. 'But my dear,' he said in a slightly hoarse voice, 'they don't keep you company the way a man would?'

'No, of course they don't,' Mary said, her face burning up now at his straightforward talk. She had known that going back to his house might lead to some kind of romantic gesture, but she hadn't reckoned on this sort of personal talk. It had taken Seamus all his time to talk about the practicalities in life and he would never, ever have discussed his feelings. 'But it's not so bad and I'm used to it after all these years.'

Lance reached out and put his glass down on the coffee-table and then, very gently, he took Mary's sherry schooner out of her hands. Then, he leaned forward and took her face in his surprisingly smooth hands. 'May I?' he asked. 'May I kiss you, Mary?'

Mary took a deep shuddering breath and suddenly she was back to being an inexperienced teenager again, back to the time before she married a man old enough to be her father. But this wasn't an older man who was touching her face now. He was around the same age as herself, and he was a smart, well-dressed, good-looking man – the type of man she read about in the romantic books she often got from the library in Tullamore. She looked back at him now. 'Yes, Lance,' she said, nodding her head.

He leaned forward now and kissed her gently on the lips. Then, when she didn't resist, his kisses became stronger and more intense. And then, before Mary Flowers had time to think about it, she was kissing him back.

One half of her wanted to flow along with the lovely warm feelings that were racing through her body, but there was a little warning voice at the back of her head telling her not to be so ridiculous. What did she think she was doing? A middle-aged woman acting like a silly love-struck teenager.

As though he had heard her speak her thoughts out loud, Lance's romantic overture came to a halt. He moved to an arm's distance. 'Mary,' he said, his expression suddenly serious, 'I've had the most wonderful time with you tonight . . . and I really don't want it to end.' He waved a hand around the beautifully furnished sitting-room. 'The house has suddenly come alive again with the presence of such a feminine woman.'

'I'm sure you enjoy it anyway,' Mary ventured. 'You keep it so lovely.'

'Well, I do have a bit of help. I have a very nice elderly lady who comes in to help on a Friday,' he told her. 'She started when Gloria was ill and I've kept her on. She gives the place a thorough going over for me and I just have to keep it ticking over during the week.'

Mary looked around at the gleaming dark wood sideboard and then at the display cabinet with all the little fancy things like gold coffee cups and saucers and china ornaments and a collection of plates with different coloured fairies on them.

'It's a beautiful house,' she said. 'It would be a pleasure for any woman to look after it.'

'Oh, admittedly, it is a lovely house,' he agreed, 'but it's also a *lonely* house. A very lonely house.' Then, he leaned forward and looked into Mary's eyes again. 'Meeting you has been the most wonderful episode in my life for a long time,' he shook his head, 'but how very, very unfortunate it is that you live in Ireland.'

Mary stared back at him, unable to believe that such a fine man would be truly interested in her. 'I've had the loveliest time, too . . . but I suppose all good things have to come to an end.'

'We still have a few days left before you go back,' he said, the tips of his fingers touching her face.

Mary closed her eyes.

Chapter 45

The boat crept along the canal and into Dublin early on Thursday morning as the mist was steadily rising up to meet the low grey sky. The fields and the buildings were silent and sleepy as they moved along, Brendan at the wheel with Noelle by his side – wearing an oilskin coat for warmth and her hair covered up by a thick scarf – leaning against the safety rail.

When they had come back from the pub in Ticknevin the

previous evening, all four had settled down for the night in the deckroom – the three men at one end and Noelle at the other. She had slept on and off until six in the morning, when she had suddenly become wide awake and had realised that the boat was moving again. When she'd looked around her, she had also become acutely aware that she was sleeping only feet away from two men who were relative strangers, and that there was no sign of Brendan.

After a while – when her eyes became accustomed to the darkness – she had grown restless and slightly anxious. She had worried about what lay ahead for her in Dublin and whether Kate would feel funny about her being in such a close, intimate situation with her boyfriend.

She had decided to shake herself and join Brendan on the deck.

He had been both surprised and pleased to see her, and while she held the tiller for a few minutes, he had got her a spare oilskin and scarf, and then he had found a couple of bottles of beer and they had leaned against the rail drinking and talking until the sky gradually lightened.

Just after seven o'clock, Brendan looked at Noelle. 'I'll give the lads a shout in a few minutes and then we'll get the breakfast cooked,' he said, pulling her closer to him and kissing her forehead. 'This will be the last time we'll have on our own, so I just want to check that you're going to be all right up in Dublin by yourself.'

'I'll be grand,' Noelle told him, nodding her head vigorously. 'Don't be worrying about me . . . you've done more than enough.' She looked up into his eyes. 'Whatever happens, I'll never forget what you've done for me – how kind and good you've been.'

'Ah, go on with ye!' Brendan said, all blustery and awkward. 'Sure, all I did was sort a lift on the boat for you, and it would have been a great pleasure for me being on it with you, if it hadn't been for the unfortunate circumstances.'

'I don't care about the circumstances,' she whispered, 'I've enjoyed every minute of it.'

Noelle insisted on frying up the breakfast for the men by way of thanks. She got the kettle boiled and made them all a mug of tea first and then she organised the frying pan and the sausages and rashers and eggs. She bustled about, more than impressed with the clean and tidy way they kept the small kitchen area.

As she chatted to him, Noelle began to see exactly what Kate saw in Michael O'Brien apart from his good looks. She hadn't been too sure of him the night before because she knew he was concerned about taking her on board the boat – and in the cold morning light she could understand that perfectly. He had a nice, easy manner with the other fellows and he took Brendan's codding around and banter well. But there was a serious side to him that she knew Kate would be attracted to, because she had that very streak in herself. Noelle looked over at Brendan now, watching him telling some silly old joke to the laughing, appreciative Jimmy, and she thought how strange it was that he and Kate had only their dark looks alike. Apart from that, they were quite different. And where they had both got their fiery temperaments from she had no idea, for their mother was the gentlest soul going and apparently their father had been an equally quiet man.

When she had washed and cleaned up the kitchen for them, Noelle decided that it was time she made a move towards her aunt's house. The Guinness lorries had arrived with the barrels that would be loaded on the boat and taken back to Tullamore – and Brendan and the others were now making moves to get started on their work.

'You should get a bus straight into Dublin further along the road there,' Brendan said, pointing across to the other side of the canal. 'We'll walk back to the bridge and cross over and I'll wait with you until the bus comes.'

'I'll be grand,' Noelle told him. 'You go on and help Michael and Jimmy. They were good agreeing to give me the lift up, so it's only fair that you should give them a hand now.'

'Sure, there's enough of them there to start off,' Brendan said, 'and it's going on for half eight now, so we shouldn't have long to wait until there's a bus.'

Ten minutes later Noelle was on the busy work-time bus heading into the city. She had pinned a brave smile on her face as she waved out to Brendan Flowers from the bus window, but silent tears had slid down her cheeks when he was out of sight.

She was now entirely on her own. No family or friends to fall back on – and no Brendan Flowers to run to for help.

She fingered the little piece of paper that Brendan had given her with the phone number of the canal depot office in Dublin, where she could leave a message for him if she ever hit any trouble. He had taken Noelle's address in Dublin too, and said that he might have the odd night or Sunday afternoon when the boat was held up for repairs in the city or if the weather was particularly bad. She had also promised him that she would write regularly to Kate and his mother so that they could keep him up to date on all her news.

They both agreed that writing directly to him would make too much of a thing of their friendship. Kate would have to know about Noelle's untimely departure from Ballygrace, and anyway Michael would tell her – but Noelle knew instinctively that Brendan wouldn't want his sister to know about how close their friendship had recently become.

Oddly enough, Noelle found she felt a bit funny about Kate finding out as well, although no doubt Sarah would tell her.

She gave a little sigh and the woman next to her gave her a strange look, so she quickly found her hanky and dried her face. Then, to take her mind off leaving Brendan and leaving Ballygrace for ever, she started planning exactly what she would tell her Auntie Delia when she arrived on her doorstep in about an hour's time.

Chapter 46

❧

Graham stood in front of the sitting-room mirror, combing a light touch of Brylcreem into his hair in preparation for his day's work. It wasn't one of his early-morning market days, so he took it a little bit easier. 'Well, ladies,' he said, moving slightly so he could see them in the mirror, 'have you decided what you'd like to do for the last night of your holiday?'

'That's if they're fit enough to go out after another day helping in the shop,' Rose said wryly. She took a bite of her toast and marmalade. 'And Mary's already been up bright and early and had the breakfast on for us all before we even moved.'

'Sure, I was wide awake anyway,' Mary told everyone. 'What else have I to do?'

'Oh, give over, Rose,' Graham said, turning around now and putting his little tortoiseshell comb in his shirt pocket. 'They've told us every day they've enjoyed helpin' out, haven't you, girls?'

'Of course we have,' Kate said now, knowing that her aunt wanted the reassurance. 'It wouldn't be the same having a holiday here if we didn't give a hand in the shop.'

'And you would never have met Dr Dolittle if you hadn't been outside sorting all them boxes out for me,' Graham said, winking over at Kate. He clapped his hands out loud now and rubbed them together, looking in Mary's direction. 'Ah, she's a dark horse, is your Kate. She's still never told us what was in the letter he gave me yesterday. *And* she's still keepin' us all in suspense, aren't you?' He pointed at Rose. 'If I had listened to your aunt there, we wouldn't have been kept in suspense because she'd have gone and steamed it open!'

Mary gave a little whooping kind of laugh, enjoying the banter. 'Pay no heed to that fella, Kate,' she said, 'you know perfectly well that Rose wouldn't interfere with anything private.'

Kate smiled and shook her head, determined not to be drawn into any discussion about David McGuire. 'Did you say you wanted some help in the shop this morning, Graham – or do you want to lift all those boxes on your own?'

Everyone laughed as she turned the tables back on her uncle.

'Oh, she's got the measure of you, Graham!' Rose chortled.

Graham turned to his wife and gave her a smug smile. 'I hope that woman you've got startin' this afternoon is as good as your Mary and Kate are.'

'You'll just have to wait and see,' Rose told him. 'If you'd been in the shop you might have had your say, but since you left me to it, I had to make the decision.'

'Well, I hope she's able to lift the boxes and the sacks,' Graham grumbled, 'because my back's been givin' me flamin' gip lately. I hope she's not got one foot in the grave like Betty.'

'Well, let's put it this way,' Rose told him, giving a mysterious little smile 'they'll be a damn sight better than Dilly-blidey-day-dreams and her white kitten heels was.'

Graham made a face at his wife but wisely decided to say nothing. A truce had been wordlessly declared on the matter of Valerie, and Rose had taken the initiative on finding a new assistant, since it was plain that Graham wasn't capable of doing so. It had also been decided by Rose that the new assistant would be more in the mould of the dependable Betty this time around. She had wasted no time over the last few days realising that when Mary and Kate went they would really be stuck. She had put a notice in the shop window and another one in the post office.

Yesterday and the day before she had had nearly a dozen people enquiring about the job, and when Graham was supposed to be at the bank and was really at the bookies, Rose had found the ideal candidate.

'Come ten o'clock this mornin',' Rose said, draining her cup of tea, 'all will be revealed.'

Graham had his hand on the doorknob, but couldn't resist one last jab at his wife. 'As a matter of interest, Rose,' he said, one hand on his hip, 'why did you tell her *ten* o'clock instead of bloody nine? We need more help first thing in the morning than at any other time of the day.'

'Rubbish,' Rose told him. 'When did you ever see a rush in the door at nine o'clock? Anyway, there are three or four of us here this morning, so I thought it would be easier for us to explain things when we've all the things set out.'

'Whatever you say, Adolf,' Graham said as a parting shot, closing the door behind him.

'He's going to get the shock of his life when the new assistant appears,' Rose said, giggling to herself.

Mary's brow wrinkled in confusion. 'Why, what's there to shock him?'

'Wait and see,' Rose said, putting her empty cup and saucer on top of her breakfast plate.

Kate knew the morning routine automatically now, and moved into it without having to check anything with Graham or Rose. She went back and forth from the sweet citrus and peat-smelling shop and into the fresh morning air, shifting oranges and apples and firm tomatoes – and trying not to think of the letter that was in her bedroom. The letter she had lain awake reading for hours last night. Trying not to think of the reply she would have to give David that afternoon.

Kate was just putting the finishing touches to a heaped basket of peaches when she heard a little cough behind her. She whirled around to face a tall, dark-haired, good-looking young man in his late twenties. He was dressed casually in jeans and a stripy sweater and was carrying a brown paper parcel.

'Is Mrs Hopkins in the shop yet?' he asked.

Kate put the peaches back in the cardboard box and dusted her hands together. 'She should be around here somewhere,' she said smiling at him. 'If you want to come in with me, I'll find her for you.'

There was a small queue at the counter and Graham was doing what he was good at, chatting and laughing with the customers and serving all at the same time. He threw an eye over at Kate and the fellow as they passed through and went towards the back of the shop in search of Rose.

She came through the back door that led out to the yard, where she had been stacking up wooden tomato boxes. When she caught sight of the young man, her face lightened up. She checked her watch. 'You're early, Frankie,' she told him. 'It's only half nine and I didn't expect you until ten.'

Kate looked at her aunt, her eyebrows raised in question, but Rose didn't catch her eye.

'Ah well,' he said, 'I was up and about and doing nothin' else anyway. I thought I might as well come in and get to know the ropes as quickly as possible.' He motioned to the brown parcel. 'I brought brown working overalls and a plain navy apron ... we didn't talk about what I should wear to work, and I thought I'd bring both just in case.'

'Good lad!' Rose said. 'I like your initiative – that's exactly what we need around the place.'

'I don't believe it, Mary,' Graham said, sinking back into the chair in the sitting-room. 'She's pulled a right fast one on me there ...'

Mary leaned forward to the coffe-table and poured her brother-in-law a cup of tea, then poured one for herself. This was part of the little daily routine that she had carved out for herself when on holiday: she would spend part of the day happily pottering around in Rose's nice big house, then, when she felt like company, she would wander down to the shop and give a hand. 'It'll all work out for the best,' she comforted him. 'A fit young man around the place will be a great help to you both.' She lifted the jug and poured milk into both their cups then added two sugars to Graham's and one to her own.

Graham shook his head. 'I don't know what's got into her, I don't,' he muttered. 'Droppin' me in it on Tuesday by goin' off into Manchester when I had all the orders to do, and now bringin' a lad in to work with us without sayin' a word to me.' He paused for a moment, thinking. 'Did *you* know?' he suddenly asked. 'Were you and Kate in on it?'

Mary started coughing, almost choking on her tea. She shook her head vigorously, not able to catch her breath for a few moments. 'No,' she eventually spluttered, 'I didn't know a thing about it – honest to God.' She took a drink from the tea and eventually the coughing subsided. 'How's he getting on anyway – the new lad?'

Graham's mouth turned down at both corners. 'He's doing all right so far – but he would then, wouldn't he? Trying to make a good impression, like.'

Just then Rose's heels could be heard tapping down the hallway. 'Oh, great, Mary,' she said, when she saw the teapot and biscuit tin out. 'I'm parched this morning.' She lifted the teapot and started pouring herself a cup.

'I'm just sayin' to Mary,' Graham said, 'that you pulled a right fast one on me this mornin' . . .'

'I wanted it to be a surprise,' Rose said, reaching for a Penguin biscuit. 'I thought you'd be delighted when you saw we'd got a lad – and a good one at that.' She shook her head. 'He's a real grafter, and no doubts about it.' Her eyes flickered in Graham's direction as she unwrapped her biscuit. 'I don't know what you're complainin' about – you can only benefit from it. He'll save your back that you're always complaining about.' She looked at Mary. 'He lifted *two* of those great big potato sacks. With his bad back, it takes Graham all his time to lift one of them.'

Graham's mouth tightened. 'I do no end of heavy work in that shop,' he said, sounding all wounded and defensive, 'and I've done it single-handedly for years. I'm up at the crack of dawn on market days and it's all them heavy sacks an' boxes that's done my flamin' back in.'

'Nobody's saying you haven't worked hard,' Rose said airily. 'We've all worked bloody hard in the shop, me and Betty included.'

She took a bit of her biscuit now. 'And anyway it was thinking about your back that made me take Frankie on. He's a good strong lad and you can tell by his easy-going nature that he'll get on just fine with the customers as well.'

'He seemed very nice when I was down in the shop earlier,' Mary chipped in.

'A fit young lad like that might bring in a few more young female customers as well,' Rose mused, knowing it would irritate her husband no end. 'Because we have to realise that it's mainly women that come into the shop. They don't want to be served by somebody like that Valerie who's more worried about her nail polish than she is about weighing up their mushrooms. Frankie is far more down to earth and he'll suit our kind of customers fine and dandy.'

'Well, let's just hope that he turns out to be as bloody wonderful as *you* seem to think he is,' Graham grumbled.

The hard-working Frankie joined them all for lunch at the house and was obviously so amiable and humorous that Graham had no option but to gracefully give in and laugh along with him. After they'd all finished their sausage-rolls with baked beans and fresh buttered rolls, Rose and Graham and Frankie headed back down into the shop while Mary and Kate cleared up.

'I'm going to go out for a half an hour when I've finished helping you,' Kate told her mother as they stood washing up at the sink.

'All right,' Mary said, a little too quickly. She had been expecting something like this ever since Graham had made the big palaver about giving her the note from the young doctor.

Kate turned now to look at her mother. 'I won't be long . . .'

Chapter 47

A s soon as she turned into the park, Kate could see David McGuire sitting on the bench by the tennis court, waiting for her. It was the very same bench that they had sat on last week when he had kissed her.

She really thought she had managed to put him out of her mind, but the moment she set eyes on him again, she knew she had made a big mistake coming to meet him. Her mouth suddenly went dry and her stomach tightened as though she had just been punched, leaving her with a feeling that was so intense that she stopped in her tracks. She was sorely tempted to turn on her heel and go very quickly back to the shop.

But there was no turning back because the young doctor had now seen her and was already on his feet and striding towards her. She swallowed hard to get her mouth and throat back to normal so that she was ready to say her little rehearsed speech, the speech that went along the lines of: I have a serious boyfriend at home, I am going home tomorrow and the little silly thing that happened between us meant nothing.

But all the words somehow melted in her throat when he stood there in front of her and then pulled her into his arms. Right in the middle of the park on an ordinary afternoon.

They stood like that for a few moments, then he bent his head and his lips slowly traced a path down the side of her neck until they reached the little hollow there and stopped.

The touch of his lips on her skin suddenly shot through her like an arrow. Kate felt herself falling towards him, but a small reproachful voice at the back of her head reminded her that not only should she not be with this man, but that they were in a public place.

She moved her head away from him and stepped back. His arms tightened around her again and then he reluctantly moved back at arm's length again. 'I wasn't sure if you would come,' he said in a low, slightly breathless voice that told her he wasn't as self-assured as he appeared. 'I know I shouldn't have sent the letter, but I couldn't think of you going back to Ireland without seeing you again. I had to at least give it a try . . .'

'If I had any sense,' Kate said, her voice surprisingly normal, 'I wouldn't have come anywhere near here or near you. I've already told you how things are back home.'

He reached his finger out now and pressed it gently to her lips, then, very easily – as though he had done it a hundred times before – he put his arm around her shoulder and guided her back to the bench, Kate all the time knowing that she should be travelling in the opposite direction. But since she had been stupid enough to come here in the first place, she thought, she might as well give him a few minutes.

They sat side by side in silence, he looking down at his joined hands, then he turned towards her, looking at her in a direct and steady way.

'Have you decided whether you'll come to the party at the hospital with me tonight?'

'I can't come,' Kate said quickly, suddenly remembering all the words she had planned to say to him after reading his letter inviting her to the party. 'And that's exactly what I've come to tell you.'

'But why not?' Although his words were serious, he was talking to her in an easy way, as though he had known her for a long time.

Her dark brown eyes met his straight on. 'You know perfectly well why not.'

'Is it your mother or your aunt?'

'It's got nothing to do with anybody else,' she said, 'I just don't think it's a good idea.'

'But we could just go as two platonic friends,' he told her, 'get you out with people your own age on your last night.'

Kate started to laugh. 'Platonic?' Her eyebrows were raised in disbelief. 'I don't think there's much chance of that. Not with the way you were just a few minutes ago. There wasn't much platonic about that.'

He made the sign of the cross on his chest. 'Honest to God,' he said, looking up at her almost the way a little boy would, 'promise I'll spend the evening sitting and talking to you – nothing more.'

'No,' Kate said, shaking her head. 'As I've already said, I don't think it's a good idea . . .'

'But I thought we got on well,' he argued, 'I thought we were friends.'

'We do get on,' Kate told him, 'but the problem is we get on *too* well.' She stood up now. 'I'm sorry, David, but I'm not going to the party with you and I'm not going to stay here with you now.' She lowered her eyelids. 'It's only making it harder—'

'Harder for *who*?' he asked, his face serious now.

Kate shrugged, wishing she hadn't said quite so much.

'It won't make it harder for me.' His voice was low, almost a whisper. 'If I could see you tonight it would make things *fantastic* for me. I'd feel as if I'd got to know you that wee bit better – I'd feel as if I'd got something that would keep me going for a long, long time. Something I might never get again.' He looked at her now with sadness in his eyes and shook his head. 'It wouldn't make it harder for me.'

Kate stared at him very hard now – as though she were trying to take a photograph of him that would stay imprinted in her mind. 'If I were to go to the party with you tonight, David, it would make it very, very hard for me.' And this time it was she who silenced him with her finger to his lips. 'And it's quite hard enough for me already.'

Then, she leaned forward and kissed him lightly on the lips and walked very quickly away without looking back.

Chapter 48

Dr Casey made no reference to the awkward circumstances under which she and Noelle had parted before the holidays. She was pleasant and smiling, enquiring as to how Noelle's family were back in Offaly and saying she hoped she had had a nice rest before coming back.

'It was grand,' Noelle lied, 'everything was just grand, thanks.' There was no option but to pretend. How could somebody like Bernadette Casey even begin to understand the life they all led with their father back home?

After she had unpacked her few belongings, Noelle joined her employer for an afternoon cup of tea and a slice of fruit cake in the kitchen, and politely answered all the questions that were asked of her without giving too much away.

'Now, Noelle,' the doctor said as they cleared away the side plates and cups, 'we have a different regime for this evening. Gabrielle will be brought to the house by her father and his wife, so we'll have a more substantial evening meal than we usually have.' She went to the pantry and brought out a brown paper package with the local butcher's stamp on it. 'I have five nice pork chops that you can do in the oven,' she went on, 'with a head of cauliflower and some tinned garden peas. We'll have both boiled potatoes and a few roast potatoes as well, and a dish of gravy.' She looked at Noelle, her eyes narrowing. 'Do you think you'll be able to manage that?'

'Grand, Dr Casey,' Noelle assured her.

The older woman looked at her watch. 'They won't be here until around six, so if you start the meal between half past four and a quarter to five, that should give you plenty of time to lay the table in the dining-room as well.'

'Grand,' Noelle repeated.

Dr Casey's pointed finger came to rest on her chin as she thought it all through. 'You can put out wineglasses as well,' she said, 'the ones on the tray at the side, and a small dish of apple sauce. There's a jar in the pantry.' Then, her eyebrows rose as she thought of another point. 'You only need set *four* places at the dining-table ... I'm sure you'll feel much more comfortable eating yours in the kitchen as usual.'

Noelle felt her face flushing, feeling as though her employer was suggesting that she had wanted to join the family gathering. 'Of course,' she said, 'that suits me grand.'

When the tea things were washed and put away, Noelle went around the house dusting and straightening things, making sure the bathroom and the bedrooms upstairs were perfect. She paid particular attention to the spare bedroom, which would be occupied later that afternoon by Gabrielle, the doctor's niece.

Dr Casey called to Noelle at one point to come downstairs and sort out a bunch of newly blooming mixed roses to put in her niece's bedroom. As the young maid carefully cut the stems and arranged the flowers in a cut-glass vase, the doctor came back with a fancy little painted dish and a blue and gold striped paper bag of pot-pourri that she had brought back from the gift shop in a stately home she had visited, when she was on holiday in London.

'Oh, it smells absolutely lovely,' Noelle commented as she breathed in the Old English Roses perfume from the dried flowers. Then, she lifted up the striped packet that contained the remainder of the scented rose petals and examined the label, amazed that such a thing existed and yet she'd never even heard of it. It struck her that in the short time she'd been up in Dublin, she had discovered that there were other ways of doing things than the ways she'd learned back home.

The doctor reached up into a kitchen cupboard now and brought out two more small dishes. 'You might as well finish off the pot-pourri now that it's open,' she told her. 'Put one dish on the window-sill in the bathroom and one on the coffee-table in the sitting-room.' She smiled at Noelle now and handed her a smaller cranberry-coloured glass dish with a frilled edge. 'Fill that and put it in your own bedroom.'

'Oh, thanks, Dr Casey,' Noelle said, her face glowing with delight. It wasn't just the little gift so much as the fact that it signified that her employer had obviously forgiven her for the incident with Carmel Foley.

There wasn't much to be done inside the house as it had all been done before the holidays, and, since it was a cool but dry day, Noelle and the doctor had set about tidying up the garden.

'We have a few hours before we have to start on the meal,' the older woman had said, 'so maybe you wouldn't mind mowing the lawns and I'll get stuck in with the weeding and the pruning.'

'It's a lovely afternoon,' Noelle replied, 'so it'll be nice to be out in the sun for a bit.' She would have been happy and grateful to do anything she was asked, as she now realised that this was the only solid, dependable place she could call home for the foreseeable future.

As she pushed the small but heavy lawn-mower up and down the back garden, Noelle pondered over the situation back home, wondering how her mother and Sarah and the young ones were. Then, just as she moved onto the more pleasurable thoughts of Brendan Flowers, she suddenly heard a knocking coming from her neighbour's house. She looked up towards the bedroom window where Carmel Foley stood jumping up and down and waving to attract her attention. Noelle gave a small, careful wave back and then gestured towards the front of the house and shook her head.

When they had cleared all the garden tools away, Noelle peeled the potatoes and put the boiling ones in a pan of salted, cold water until they were needed, and she put the ones that were to be roasted in the oven with two or three lumps of lard. After that, she washed the cauliflower and cut it up, taking care to remove any bruised bits, and put that in cold, salted water as well.

Dr Casey came back into the kitchen checking all was going well. 'Now, Noelle, when the meal is nearly ready and the table set, give yourself a few minutes to wash and freshen up,' she advised. 'Put on your black dress and white apron and cap, please, as I think it would look better when my niece and the guests arrive.' She paused for a moment, rubbing her hands together to remove the dried compost from the garden before washing them. 'And I think it would be best if you address her as Miss Gabrielle, right from the very start.'

'Whatever you think,' Noelle agreed.

Bernadette Casey's eyes narrowed a little. 'I don't want us to run into any difficulties . . . get off on the wrong footing. You see, Anna Quinn was a very different person from you. Different entirely. She has known Gabrielle since she was a small child, so they were understandably that little bit familiar with each other.' She went over to the sink now and turned the tap on to wash her hands with the bar of carbolic soap. 'But it's a very different circumstance with someone younger, and it wouldn't be right for you and Gabrielle to be over-friendly; and I want that known from the outset.' The doctor looked her straight in the eye now, awaiting her reaction.

Noelle flushed red. 'I wasn't thinking of being over-friendly . . .'

'Of course you weren't,' the older woman continued, looking up at the kitchen clock now. 'But I just wanted us to be very clear so that we don't run into any problems. Gabrielle will be here most of the time from now until she starts university in October. She's following in the family tradition by going into medicine, so she'll be studying very hard.'

Noelle nodded her head. 'If it's all right with you,' she said in a quiet, almost meek voice, 'I'll go and get washed and changed and be ready for Miss Gabrielle arriving.'

'Good girl,' Dr Casey said, her head nodding in approval. 'I thought it was best to catch any small difficulties in advance, especially since we had the misunderstanding about the hired help next door.' Her eyes were now cold and distant. 'That is one young woman who certainly doesn't know her place, who has been very badly mishandled by her employers.' She shook her head. 'Mark my words,' she said darkly, 'no good will come of that situation at all.'

Chapter 49

The grey and misty morning of Kate and Mary's arrival back in Ireland underscored the end of summer, the end of the truly warm weather, the end of their time away from their daily routine.

And the end of their lives as they knew it.

Brendan was waiting for his mother and sister when the Dublin coach pulled up in Ballygrace Main Street, a welcoming smile on his face. The smile was partly due to the several pints of beer he had drunk in the local pub while waiting for them, and in part to the great relief he felt on their return.

He had managed very well on his own for most of the time, but there was no doubting the fact that the novelty of the bachelor life had worn off after the first week. Time had hung very heavily on his hands and there were only so many hedges to cut, fences to mend and turf to clamp into a tidy pile for the winter to fill the hours. And in order to get through the day-to-day tedium inside the house, Brendan had approached the household chores in the same methodical way they did on the boat, but the routine had quickly fallen by the wayside.

Facing a sink full of dirty mugs and plates and having the effort of lighting fires to boil the water was tedious and trying in the extreme, and it had awakened in him an appreciation of the work involved in running the house the way his mother and Kate did.

But he couldn't let them know that of course – and anyway, women had their own way of doing things.

'Brendan!' Mary Flowers exclaimed when she followed Brendan in the door and saw the small gas stove in the corner of the kitchen. Her hands flew to cover her mouth and tears sprang into her eyes. 'Oh, my God . . . When did you buy this? It must have cost you a fortune . . .'

'Never mind the cost,' Brendan blustered, looking all embarrassed and awkward but in reality delighted with her reaction.

Kate came in after them, having had a bit of trouble extricating her holdall from the back of the bike. Her nose wrinkled as she came through the door at the musty smell and she threw a glance at the bin by the door, which needed emptying, and the pile of greasy dishes that had obviously been left from the last few meals that her brother had eaten.

On hearing her footsteps, Mary turned now to look behind her. 'Oh, Kate – look what Brendan's bought for us,' she said, gesturing towards the gleaming white oven in the corner. 'An oven – a *real* gas oven . . .' Her face suddenly seemed to crumple and she almost staggered her way across the floor to collapse into the armchair, her hanky now clutched to her eyes.

'Are you all right, Mammy?' Kate asked anxiously, going over to kneel by her chair.

'I can't believe it . . .' Mary sobbed. 'It's one of my dreams come true . . . I always wanted a cooker that you could use day or night – summer or winter.' She dabbed at her eyes. 'It's a dream come true, so it is.'

Kate patted her mother's back in a comforting gesture. 'If it's one of your dreams come true,' she said in a light, cheery tone, 'then it's happy you should be,' she told her. She looked up at Brendan who was leaning against the sink, his arms folded across his chest. 'That was very decent of you,' she told him. 'Very decent indeed.'

It was on the tip of her tongue to ask him what had brought on this great gesture of generosity – to provoke him into admitting that he'd found the going hard on his own without it – but she bit it back. What was the point in spoiling her mother's pleasure and creating bad feeling on their first day back? She gave her mother's shoulder a final pat. 'Have you used it yet?' she asked, standing up. 'Is it a lot easier than the fire?'

'It's mighty,' Brendan declared, his chest puffed out with pride at his purchase, 'mighty altogether.'

'I'm looking forward to our first cup of tea boiled on it,' she said, smiling at him.

'And I'm the very man to make you your first cup.' He lifted the kettle from the top of the cooker and went over to fill it. 'I'll have it all ready by the time you have your coats and bags put away.' He took his jacket off, and put it on the back of one of the kitchen chairs, then he rolled his shirtsleeves up to his elbows. 'And I suppose you'd like me to fry you a few oul' rashers and an egg on it, with a bit of fried soda bread? I went to the shops this mornin' to make sure I had them in all nice and fresh for the pair of ye, with all the travellin' and everything...' He nodded over in Kate's direction.

'That's good of you,' she said, smiling at him, knowing that he needed the acknowledgement for his efforts.

'Aw, will you go on with you?' he said, waving away her praise as though he had never been looking for it.

'Oh, Brendan...' Mary said, getting up to her feet to throw her arms about him. 'It's lovely to be back home and all the better now that we have the new cooker.'

Although embarrassed at the show of affection, Brendan made a small gesture of putting his arms around his mother for a few seconds, which was enough to gratify her.

Mary stood back, her eyes shining with emotion as she took in her tall, handsome son and the lovely new cooker. Her gaze shifted along to the grimy pile of plates and mugs and cutlery. She shook her head and smiled indulgently at him. 'Did you miss us looking after you? Was it hard managin' on your own?'

'Not a bit of it,' Brendan said airily, lifting the frying pan onto the cooker with a little swinging motion that gave away his good mood. He cut a piece of white dripping from the dish and put it into the middle of it to melt. 'Don't forget I'm well used to doin' for myself on the boat. I don't need to depend on anybody.' He lifted the grease-paper-wrapped packet of bacon from the shelf beside the cooker and started to peel off individual rashers and put them straight into the pan.

'Go on with you!' Mary said, giving him a light-hearted slap on the behind. 'Every man needs a woman behind him – don't they, Kate? They need lookin' after properly, don't they?'

'Oh, I think Brendan is well able to look after himself,' Kate replied, feeling they'd given Brendan more than enough praise and attention. 'I'll shift these things out of the way now before we sit down to eat.' She went over to the door and lifted the bags and took them into her and her mother's bedroom, pausing for a moment to take in the smallness of the room and, if she was honest, the whole of the house. She had had a room to herself in Rose's house, a room twice this size, and this year, in particular, she had grown used to every inch of the solitary space.

Kate wondered if she could become as accustomed to the close proximity of her mother and brother again, as she did every summer after the holiday – because she knew this year that a change had taken place within her. She had matured into a fully fledged woman and now felt she needed the space that could accommodate that.

She put her own bag on her single bed and the other bag on her mother's. Then she went quietly back across the floor and pulled the door to, not completely closed but enough to give her privacy and to shut out the rest of the small house for a few minutes.

She sat down on the edge of her bed, her face resting in her cupped hands, and with very mixed feelings pondered her return to Ballygrace.

And her return to Michael O'Brien.

Chapter 50

❧

Noelle looked in the narrow wardrobe mirror and checked that her maid's little white band was sitting straight on her pale red hair. She fiddled about with it for a few more moments then she flattened down her apron with her hands and went out to start her chores.

'Very smart,' Dr Casey said when she came into the kitchen a few minutes later. She had changed into a fine grey-wool twin-set with a single long rope of pearls and a dark grey skirt and matching shoes. She was struggling with the catch on the good gold watch she wore on special occasions, and eventually had to elicit Noelle's help to fasten it properly.

'Thank you, Noelle,' she said, when the watch was sorted out. 'And always remember that appearances count for everything.' She swept a hand down over her outfit. 'I could easily have worn those older clothes I did the gardening in, but changing into something a little more elegant like this means that I'm taking the occasion seriously. Clothes maketh the man *and* the woman. People judge you on your appearance – it tells them who you are. I've always told my niece that, and now, I'm giving you the same advice.'

Noelle nodded her head, trying not to look bored. The doctor had told her this on a number of occasions – each time as though it was the first time. She wondered if she was deliberately repeating herself because she felt that her point wasn't being taken seriously. Given the fact that she wore her uniform most of the time, people would have no illusions about Noelle's station in life. The black dress and the frilly white apron and cap told them all they needed to know. She was obviously a member of the serving classes – a maid through and through.

Gabrielle Casey arrived just after six o'clock. When the black car arrived in the driveway, she was first out of it and came rushing ahead of the others like an excited eight-year-old child, as opposed to the nineteen-year-old woman she actually was.

Noelle had been watching and waiting by the dining-room window, and as soon as she saw the car turn in the driveway, she moved quickly. 'That's your guests arriving now, Dr Casey,' she said, looking into the drawing-room where her employer was sitting reading the *Irish Times*.

'You go on and open the door for them,' the older woman said, taking off her glasses and laying them down on the coffee-table with the folded newspaper.

Noelle opened the front door wide, and then lifted the heavy iron door stopper to secure it in place. Then, with one hand resting on the inside door knob, she stood with a straight back as she'd been instructed to do, and with just a trace of a nervous smile on her lips.

She watched now as the tall, slim girl with short hair and a surprisingly boyish-looking face came bounding up the steps and into the house – completely ignoring the fact that there was a person standing holding the door open for her.

'Aunt Bernie!' Gabrielle called in a high-pitched voice, and then when her aunt appeared at the drawing-room door she rushed forward and threw her arms around her. 'Why on earth did you let *them* pick me up at the airport?' she demanded.

'Calm down, Gabrielle, calm down, dear!' the doctor said, untangling herself from her niece's embrace. She craned her neck to check if her brother and his wife were on their way into the house, and when there was no sign of them, she ushered the whining girl into the drawing-room.

As Noelle stood ramrod straight like a sentry guard, continuing to hold the door open for the other guests, she could still hear the girl's muted complaints. And, peeping out through the gap in the hinges at the front door, she could see Gabrielle's father and the woman in the front of the car having a heated discussion. Noelle's throat tightened at the thought of a big row breaking out in the doctor's house.

'Why didn't you come for me?' Gabrielle's complaints went on. 'I had to sit in the back of the car while *she* sat in the front.'

'I had no say in the matter,' Dr Casey said, keeping her voice low to bring down the heated temperature. 'It wasn't my place to decide who would pick you up. Your father is the one for those decisions.'

'Well, I haven't spoken a word in the car,' Noelle could hear Gabrielle saying. 'He knew I didn't want *her* there to meet me. I wanted it to be a proper *family* occasion – I didn't want any outsiders there.'

'She's not an outsider, Gabrielle,' the doctor said firmly. 'She's your father's wife. Now calm yourself down, and behave in the manner you've been brought up to behave in.'

The car doors slammed now and the couple came walking up to the front door. The man was tallish, with glasses and a grave-looking face, and he had his arm wrapped protectively around a small, blonde, busty woman who looked equally serious.

'Good evening,' he said, nodding fleetingly at Noelle. The woman glanced at her and after attempting a smile she mouthed a vague greeting and they walked on down the hall.

Dr Casey appeared at the drawing-room doorway and took them in, and then the door closed after them.

Noelle waited in the kitchen until she was called. She went back and forth to the oven, alternately turning it down in case the chops and the roast potatoes became too dry and turning it back up again in case they became too cold. The boiled potatoes and cauliflower were perfectly cooked, but she kept them just at simmering point. The garden peas were in a separate pan, swimming around in their lukewarm green juice, awaiting the sudden boiling they would get as soon as they were required.

Finally, the drawing-room door opened and the doctor and her entourage made their way into the dining-room. Noelle immediately swung into action, draining the potatoes and cauliflower and decanting them into two white, bone-handled serving dishes.

Dr Casey's heels tapped their way down the hallway and came to a halt at the kitchen door. 'All ready?' she asked, a slight frown on her face.

'Grand,' Noelle said. 'I'll bring the serving dishes in now.'

The doctor and her three guests sat in total silence as Noelle brought in the hot dishes, one by one. The silence so unnerved her. that by the third dish, her knees were shaking so much she was praying that nobody noticed.

'Thank you, Noelle,' Dr Casey said, when she came with the gravy boat and the small dish of apple sauce. She smiled warmly at her helper. 'Now, go and sit down and have your own meal.'

Chapter 51

L ater that evening, after they had settled back into the cottage, Brendan looked up from the *Independent*. 'By the way,' he said to his sister, 'Mickey O'Brien says to tell you that he'll call in on ye some time tomorrow.' He made a little amused, snorting sound. 'I'd say he must have missed you . . .'

Kate looked back at him, trying not to show how gratified she was with the information. Already, she found, she was comparing the busy daily routine she had had for the last two weeks in Stockport with the rural isolation of the cottage and the long hours spent only with her mother and Brendan. She knew that she would eventually settle into her familiar life back home as she did every summer, but somehow she felt that this time it was going to be harder. Michael O'Brien's presence in her life was the one thing that would fill all those little gaps. 'And is Michael well enough? Busy working away on the boat and the farm?'

'Ah, yeah,' Brendan said, absent-mindedly scratching his curly dark hair. 'Some oul' grand-uncle of his died while ye were away, so he had to have a few hours off to go to the funeral.'

'There's always some poor cratur goes when you're away on holiday,' Mary mused, looking over her spectacles as she sat sewing new elastic into her white waist underskirt. It had driven her mad, slipping down on her every few minutes, as they travelled back on the boat. 'Every year it happens when I go away to England. I never know who'll be gone when I get back. Another poor soul gone from this earth and we didn't even know it.'

Brendan looked at his mother and rolled his eyes in amazement. 'Sure, you don't even know the oul' fella that died! And anyway, people are dyin' all the feckin' time. It stands to reason that some oul' shagger will cop off while you're away.'

'Nice to see you're as sympathetic as ever, Brendan,' Kate said, giving him a sidelong look.

'Honest, that's me,' Brendan said, winking over at her, knowing full well that it would only annoy her further. 'I'm only sayin' out loud what most people think and are too hypocritical to say.'

'Did you see anything of Noelle and Sarah while we were away?' Mary asked. 'Noelle had the week off from the doctor's place in Dublin while we were away, didn't she, Kate?'

'She did,' Kate agreed, her head stuck in a magazine.

Brendan looked back at his mother from the armchair opposite – newspaper resting in his lap – stunned for the moment into silence. What the hell was he to tell them? His mind raced around for a few moments, trying to find the most inconsequential incident to relate, that would satisfy his mother's longing for news while she was away.

'I was at an oul' dance in Daingean the other week,' he began, 'and I saw the pair of them there . . .'

Kate tore her gaze away from her magazine to look up at him with narrowed eyes, waiting on the usual derogatory remarks that he always levelled at her friends.

Brendan cleared his throat. 'Now that you mention it,' he said in a peculiar croaky voice, 'Noelle had a bit of a fall at the dance. Some big-footed heifer nearly tore the leg off her with a sharp spiky heel. Her leg was bleeding fairly bad.'

'Mother of God!' Mary said, dropping her sewing into her lap. She took her glasses off now to see him more clearly. 'And was she all right?'

'She got a sore one, right enough,' Brendan said, warming now to his story. 'And lucky I came upon her, because just as she got to the side of the dance floor, she went down in a dead faint. I managed to catch her and get her over to the chairs until she came around.' He shook his head. 'She got a right bad one.'

'Was she all right when she came out of the faint?' Kate asked, her brows deep in concern. 'Was she able to get home?'

'Well,' he said, 'she wasn't too grand at all . . .' Suddenly, as he related the story, Brendan found himself coming over all self-conscious. 'Anyway,' he said, in an over-loud voice, 'I wasn't in the humour for dancin' meself, and as I left the hall, I saw her with the leg still bleeding and everything, and what could I do but offer to walk back along the canal line with her?' He shook his head. 'The poor girl wasn't herself at all, at all . . .'

Kate watched her brother closely, detecting a complete turn-around in his attitude towards her friend. 'And have you seen her since? Is the leg all right now?' she asked him.

Brendan shrugged, still not sure what information he should keep to himself and what he should divulge. Usually, he told very little, but he suddenly realised that he was in an awkward spot here – Sarah would no doubt be happy to tell Kate every last little detail, and then there was the matter of the lift in the boat. 'Ah . . . I saw her up and down the town a few times and she seemed well enough.' Then, feeling Kate's dark, watchful eyes on him, he suddenly realised he needed to come clean now or he would be found out later by his own workmates. Mickey O'Brien would no doubt fill Kate in on any details she asked about, and it would make him look as if he'd been hiding something. 'Now that you ask, I don't like to be one that's talkin' about his neighbours – but there was a bit of an uproar down there in Dalys' one evenin' and Noelle was turfed out by the oul' lad.'

'Her father threw her out of the house?' Kate repeated, checking that she'd got it right.

Brendan nodded. 'Out on her ear ... bag and baggage, like.' He lifted the newspaper back up now, hoping they would leave him alone.

'And where did she go?' Mary asked, sitting up straighter in her chair, all eyes and ears about the story he was relating.

'Back to Dublin,' Brendan informed them, a note of irritation creeping in now. Women were the damn limit, wanting to know every little detail. 'That was after she called up here – or to be more exact, after she *ran* up here to escape from him.' He shook his head. 'That Matt Daly is nothin' short of a pure madman.'

'He's more *bad* than mad,' Kate stated. She looked over at her mother and shook her head sadly. 'Poor Noelle, she would have been mortified having to come up here and none of us around apart from Brendan.'

Brendan swallowed, his throat suddenly feeling dry. 'Ah well,' he said, 'lucky enough, the oul' boat was heading back up to Dublin, so I managed to get her onto it and away from the place nice and quick ...'

Mary's eyes widened. 'She went up on the boat to Dublin with the lads? And was Michael on it?'

He rustled the newspaper loudly now and cleared his throat. 'He was ... and young Jimmy.' There was a little pause. 'I went up with them myself ... I felt it wasn't fair landing them with a passenger they didn't know.'

'Ah, Brendan!' his mother said, admiration shining out of her eyes. 'Aren't you the decent fella, doin' all that for poor Noelle?'

Brendan shrugged, feeling the heat rise to his face as he thought back to that night. 'Now,' he said abruptly, lifting the paper up in front of his face, 'ye have all the information that ye're going to get. Can't the pair of ye leave a man in peace for a while to read the paper?'

Kate stared at her brother, seeing the side of his reddened face behind the newspaper. There was definitely something about the situation that didn't quite add up. 'You sound as though you were quite the gentleman there with Noelle,' she said. 'She'll be wondering what came over you . . .'

Brendan started straight ahead at the black-and-white print and said nothing.

Chapter 52

~∞~

It was almost five o'clock when Kate heard the familiar purring of the car engine coming down the tow-path. Her heart quickened and she ran out of the cottage to meet him.

'You're back, I see,' Michael greeted her, his warm smile telling her all she needed to know. He came forward to the gate and took her into his arms, then, in an uncharacteristically bold way, he pressed his lips to hers. 'I'm delighted to see you,' he said after a moment.

Kate looked up at him. 'Good,' she said, smiling back at him. 'And I'm delighted to see you as well.' She took his hand and brought him into the cottage with her.

Mary Flowers was standing at the sink, washing out a few bits and pieces to hang out on the line. Brendan, tired of all the questions and talking from the women, had taken himself off to the pub. 'Ah, Michael!' Mary said, going to dry her hands before greeting him properly. 'I'm sorry about your bad news while we were away. Was it a grand-uncle right enough?'

He nodded his head. 'Uncle Sean, my mother's uncle. Ah, he was well up in years – going on for eighty-three.'

'Ah, still and all,' Mary said, 'his family will miss him. Was he a married man?'

'Never married,' Michael said, sitting down at the kitchen table. 'He was a quiet kind of man – very self-contained.'

'A farmer like your own people?'

'Yes,' Michael said. 'He had a small bit of a farm.' He shrugged. 'It kept him going, right up until the last.' His eyes flickered over towards Kate who, as usual, was letting her mother do the small talk.

They chatted on for a while longer, then, when Mary went into the bedroom looking for something, Michael turned to Kate. 'Will we have a walk out?' he said in a low voice. Then he paused, looking out at the early autumn sky. 'Or maybe we could take a drive? Would you like to take a drive out to somewhere like Charleville Castle? We could park the car and have a bit of a walk.'

'That would be lovely – something a bit different,' Kate agreed, feeling even more delighted than she looked with his suggestion. One of the little reservations she had had about Michael was the fact that he was fairly predictable. Sunday afternoons were usually a walk down by the canal. A drive out to somewhere further afield was a nice change. 'Would you like a cup of tea before we go?'

'No,' he replied. He looked towards the bedroom door, his eyes intense and serious. 'I'd rather we headed out now ... there's something I want to talk to you about.'

Kate's heart dropped. 'Is there something wrong?' she asked in a low voice. Surely there wasn't going to be another obstacle in the way? Before she'd gone on holiday, he'd been spending more and more time on the farm – and less and less time with her. But then, hadn't he looked delighted to see her ... and the kiss he'd given her? Maybe she'd imagined that it was more passionate and spontaneous than usual. Maybe it had been a kiss born of embarrassment – and of a wish not to hurt her too badly when he let her down.

A cold chill ran through her. How could she go back to the routine, mundane life she had had before she met him? Then, a picture of David McGuire suddenly flashed into her mind, almost leaving her breathless.

She didn't want *that*.

It was all too frightening and new. She wanted the safety and the familiarity of somebody from Ireland – better still, somebody local. Somebody who would understand her ways – somebody who wouldn't challenge her. Somebody who would fill most of the little gaps in her. Maybe not all the gaps, but enough.

She wanted Michael O'Brien.

She went into the bedroom to get her cardigan. 'We're going out for a drive,' she told her mother.

Mary looked up from the bed, where she had been sitting glancing at one of Kate's magazines – giving the young couple a bit of time on their own. 'Lovely,' she said. 'Ye might as well, the good weather will be coming to an end shortly.' She gave a little sigh. 'The summer is always the shortest season.'

Kate took her cardigan from the hanger in the wardrobe and her straw hat, then she went out to join Michael – and to hear whatever he had to say.

Kate suddenly realised as they walked along the narrow path inside the gates of Charleville Woods that autumn was on its way. In the few weeks that she had been gone, the red berries of the hawthorn tree were now in evidence and the blackberries had sprouted from little hard green knots to full-blooded purple pillows. And when a cooler breeze came, she smelt the honeysuckle that was entwined around the trunk of the trees, and was left in no doubt as to the passage of time.

She carried the straw hat in both hands in front of her, feeling slightly foolish for having brought it as the evening was only middling, and the sun well hidden behind the clouds.

'Kate,' Michael started as they walked along, his hands behind his back, 'do you mind me asking . . . did you give any thought to you and me when you were over in England?'

Kate looked quickly at him. 'In what way?'

'How things are going between us . . . whether you feel we are really suited or not?' His voice was low and steady, giving nothing away.

She turned her gaze straight ahead again, and she could feel the colour rushing to her cheeks. 'I think I'm happy enough,' she said, 'I think we get on well.' Was she making an awful fool of herself, she thought, telling him that she liked him when he was maybe going to say that it was best if they parted?

He caught her by the arm now and drew her to a halt. 'Do you think we get on well enough to get married?'

'*Married?*' Kate gasped, the breath whipped away from her. Whatever she had imagined he was going to say, this was definitely not it. 'But how can we?'

He nodded his head, and there was a glint of a smile in his eyes, which seemed afraid to move to his mouth. 'If you agree,' he went on, his hands now gently gripping her on both arms just above the elbows, 'we have a house and a small farm and everything to start off with.'

'*How?*' Kate repeated.

'My Uncle Sean,' he explained. 'He left the farm to me.' His Adam's apple moved up and down, indicating to Kate that he wasn't as calm as he was trying to appear. 'Well, he left it between me and my brother, but the family have had a discussion on it and they've agreed that I can have it now – if I want it.'

There was a little silence, and it suddenly struck Kate that she hadn't really responded properly to his proposal – not in the way she would have imagined herself responding to an offer of marriage. This was, she realised, because he had asked her in a strange kind of way. There had been nothing romantic about the proposal, nothing passionate about it. There had been nothing said about *love*.

These were the things that Kate needed – the things that were essential to her.

Then, a picture of David McGuire flashed into her mind, and she instinctively knew that he would have approached the situation in an entirely different way.

There would have been no talk of practicalities like houses and farms – his feelings would have come first. And although she had been taken aback by the young doctor's directness, she had been undeniably flattered by the openness of his attraction for her.

In the very short time they had known each other, David had left her in no doubt as to his feelings. Surely, she could expect that openness from her future husband.

'Kate?' Michael said now, aware that her thoughts had drifted off.

She looked him in the eye. 'How do you feel about us getting married, Michael? Is it what you really want?' She couldn't stop herself, she had to know properly. 'Are you sure of your feelings for me?'

His eyes opened wide with surprise and he suddenly started to laugh. 'Am I sure of my feelings for you? Kate ... Kate,' he said, pulling her into his arms. 'I've never been more sure of anything in my life.' He kissed the top of her black curly hair, over and over again. 'I should have said that first – I've probably gone about it all a bit ham-fisted.' His voice dropped now. 'I've loved you since the first minute I clapped eyes on you ... Your lovely dark hair and dark brown eyes, your beautiful smile. I've loved everything about you ... and I just hope you feel the same about me.'

Kate's heart lifted. This was what she was waiting for. *This* was how she had imagined it all happening. She may have had to almost force the romantic side out of him, but he had eventually said all that she wanted to hear. 'And I love you, too,' she whispered into his chest.

'So?' he said, moving back to look at her. 'Will you marry me, Kate Flowers?'

'Yes,' she said, nodding her head and grinning back at him. 'Yes, Michael O'Brien – I'd be delighted to marry you!'

Chapter 53

The alarm clock went off, startling Noelle out of the deep sleep she desperately needed. She sat bolt upright, staring into the dim morning light of her little bedroom, trying to work out where exactly she was. Slowly, the familiar outline of the bedside table and the little wardrobe came into focus and she felt herself relax. She lay back in the bed, cuddling the blankets cosily around her and mulling over the rambling dream she had just wakened out of – a mixture of her father rowing with everyone at home coupled with something to do with the barge and the barrels of Guinness being loaded on.

It was the fourth bed she'd slept in over four different nights – at home in Ballygrace, the bunk on the boat, a night at her Auntie Delia's and then last night at Dr Casey's – and she hadn't had a decent night's sleep in any of them.

Some of her wakefulness had been caused by all the disruption at home and the anxiety of returning to Dublin – and some of it had been caused by pleasurable reminiscences about the hours she had spent with Brendan Flowers. She had lain in bed every night, running over the images in her mind of their long walk back from the dance hall, of his arm around her when they watched the dawn come up on the barge and the kind look in his eyes which she had never seen before. And then, when she had run all those scenes over in her mind, she would play back the wonderful feeling she had had when he kissed her on those few nights they had spent together.

She was just contemplating moving when the church clock in the distance struck the quarter-to-eight reminder for eight o'clock Mass and immediately Noelle threw the bedclothes back. Dr Casey was expecting two trays with bacon and sausage and perfectly fried eggs to be brought up to her and her niece by quarter past nine, along with the Sunday papers, which would be delivered by then. They would eat breakfast in bed and then they would wash and dress and walk out for ten o'clock Mass while Noelle stayed at home and cleared up. She would cook lunch for them for two o'clock, clear up after that and then have a few hours to herself in the afternoon before making supper. Most Sundays she would go across Dublin to her aunt's, but she felt she had done enough visiting this weekend and would leave it until next week. Today, she planned to stay in the house, reading or having a rest. She still felt tired from the lost sleep over the last few days and anyway, her period was due and she felt a bit sluggish and achy.

She took her dressing-gown from the hook behind the door, slipped her feet into her slippers and went into the kitchen to put the kettle on for a quick wash. She then padded out of the back door – mindful not to bang any doors or make any sound that would waken those sleeping – and made her way down the garden path to the outside toilet.

A few minutes later she came hurrying back in to lift the lukewarm kettle off the ring and take it into the bedroom. She filled the china bowl and then lathered up the scented bar of soap and started to wash her hands and face and under her arms.

Within minutes she was dressed in a jumper and skirt and on the bicycle heading to the church in Donnybrook. The eight o'clock warning bell was just chiming as she leaned the bike up against the church wall with all the others, and scurried to join the other last-minute worshippers.

She found a pew near the back with only four people in it, so she slid in just as the priest and his helpers came onto the altar. The main part of the Mass up until Communion flew past with very little of the ritual sinking in, as Noelle's mind was back in Ballygrace, where she knew her mother and father would be attending to their own religious duties in the local church. A figure came up close behind her in the queue for Communion, and it was only when she went back to her wooden pew and the figure followed her in that she glanced back and realised it was Carmel Foley.

'You've surely been hiding yourself since you came back,' Carmel said the minute the priest left the altar at the end of Mass.

Noelle sighed and rolled her eyes. 'It's not my decision, it's Dr Casey ...' She was trying to pick her words very carefully as she didn't want to offend the girl. 'She wasn't happy to find you in the house that day, and she's told me that I haven't to mix my social life and my working life.'

'Pity about her!' Carmel said in a voice that was too loud for church, as several accusing eyes looked over towards them. 'I suppose she'd like to keep you locked up in the house with no contact from the outside world?'

Noelle gave an embarrassed shrug, and moved back to let a group of elderly women out past them. 'The thing is, I daren't cross her ... I'm in an awkward spot at the moment.'

Carmel's eyebrows shot up in interest. 'In what way?'

Noelle threw an eye to the people standing close by her, all taking short steps in the slow queue for the big heavy open doors. 'I'll tell you when we get outside ...'

They walked round to collect their bikes and then as they walked along pushing them, Noelle gave her friend an edited version of the situation at home.

'Jesus!' Carmel exclaimed, bringing her bike to a halt. 'The old fucker threw you out?'

Noelle's face flushed at the girl's language. 'He doesn't like Brendan ...'

'Obviously,' Carmel said, 'but to throw you out with nowhere to go.' She paused and then gave a small sly smile. 'And you said that this Brendan was up at the house on his own?'

Noelle nodded. 'His mother and sister – who's one of my best friends – were over in England.'

'And is he a good-looking fella?'

'Very good-looking,' Noelle said, smiling as she pictured Brendan's dark handsome face. 'And once you get to know him, he's a really nice lad. He's a lot softer than he lets on. I wouldn't have gone to the pictures and met up with him if he wasn't.'

'But your father doesn't like him at all?'

Noelle shook her head. 'I knew he didn't like him, but I didn't think he would react as hard as he did.'

'And you know that night you went up to Dublin on the barge with Brendan?' Carmel asked now. 'Well, did he not ask you to stay the night with him in the cottage, like? Could you not have stayed and then got the coach up the next day?'

Noelle's brow moved into a deep furrow. 'But there would only have been the two of us there . . .' she said, confused about the point of Carmel's question. 'Kate and his mother weren't there.'

'Exactly,' Carmel said in a low, knowing voice. 'That was yer chance if you really like him. The two of ye could have spent the night together and really got to know each other.' She shrugged. 'Men are men after all, and maybe he would have made some kind of a statement after it – maybe you wouldn't have had to come back to Dublin to skivvy after that cross Dr Casey. If you give fellas what they want, they come runnin' back looking for more.'

Light suddenly dawned. The bicycles came to a halt.

'Oh, no,' Noelle said, making no attempt to disguise the shock in her voice. 'How could I have stayed the night with Brendan? If anyone found out, my reputation would be gone for ever.'

'Who would have known?' Carmel persisted. 'Only yourself and him.'

Noelle started pushing her bike again so that Carmel had to almost run to keep up. '*I* would have known!' she stated through gritted teeth. 'And I think a lot more of myself than *that* . . .'

'There's no need to take it like that,' Carmel said, sounding slightly wounded, as though she hadn't really meant it. 'I was only thinking of you and the situation you're in now, with no place to call home except for the doctor's house.' Her voice became more indignant. 'I wasn't suggestin' that you actually *do* anythin' with him, like . . . more like, kind of lead him on. Just enough to make him really interested.'

Noelle gave the girl a really long, hard look. 'I don't think we have the same outlook on lads, Carmel. If I have to do things like that to keep a lad, then he's not the kind of lad I want.' She moved the bike on again, pushing it harder and quicker this time.

'Oh, well,' Carmel said, panting a little with the exertion of keeping up, 'as I said already, I wasn't talkin' about anything that serious, and it's not as though *you* have that much experience with lads yourself now, is it?'

Noelle shook her head in exasperation and let out a low, weary sigh. 'I've got to get back to the house,' she said now. 'I'm already running late as it is.'

'Please yourself,' Carmel retorted, her face tight with annoyance. She suddenly threw her leg over the bike and got up on the seat. 'I'm in a hurry myself,' she said, moving off onto the road. 'I'll see you when I see you.'

Noelle stood for a few minutes watching the blonde girl as she pedalled up the slight incline without glancing back. She had a strange feeling in the pit of her stomach – similar to the feeling she had had the evening she left Ballygrace. That's another one, she thought. Another one I won't be seeing too often.

Chapter 54

❧

Noelle cursed Carmel Foley under her breath when she got into the house and saw the time – she was a good quarter of an hour late for starting the breakfast. She quickly put the kettle on to boil and threw six sausages into the frying pan with a lump of lard, then she ran into her bedroom to change into her black working dress with an old stripy apron on top to keep her clean while she cooked.

She made a cup of tea for herself and drank it standing by the cooker as she added rashers of bacon, then three circles each of white and black pudding. When they were ready she put them on two plates and put them under the grill to keep warm while she very carefully fried two eggs. One of the yolks burst as she was turning it, so she pushed it to the side of the pan for herself and cracked another egg in to make sure her employer and Gabrielle each got a perfect egg with the yolk intact.

As the eggs were cooking Noelle went into her bedroom and

quickly replaced the stripy apron with her white starched pinny and mob-cap for serving the breakfast. Then she came back into the kitchen and added the eggs to the hot plates. She put one of the plates on a tray with two slices of brown bread and a cup of tea and very cautiously carried it out into the hallway and up the stairs to Dr Casey's room.

The older woman was already awake and sitting up in bed reading when the knock came on the door. 'Good morning, Noelle,' she greeted the maid, straightening down the bedclothes for the tray to lie flat. 'Has the paper not arrived yet?'

Noelle flushed. She'd completely forgotten about it. 'I'll just bring it up to you now,' she said, keeping her fingers crossed that it had arrived.

She made her second slow journey upstairs with *The Irish Times* under her arm and Gabrielle's tray. She dropped the paper on a chair in the hall before knocking on the young girl's door. She stood waiting for a few seconds, but there was no reply. She waited and then knocked again, a little louder, but there was still no sound.

Noelle opened the door with one hand then stepped into the bedroom. 'Miss Gabrielle?' she said in a tone that she hoped was loud enough to wake the girl. 'I've brought your breakfast tray up for you.'

There was a grunting noise from the bed, which Noelle could not decipher.

'Miss Gabrielle?' Noelle repeated. 'I have your breakfast here.'

The top of the bedclothes was suddenly thrown back. 'Are you deaf or something?' the girl said in a cross, snappy voice. 'I said leave it bloody there!' Then, she pulled the covers back over her head, obviously waiting until Noelle left the room.

Out in the hallway again, the maid took the newspaper up from the armchair and went back to Dr Casey's room to deliver it.

'Thank you, Noelle,' the doctor said, putting her knife and fork down, 'and the breakfast is lovely. You're an excellent cook for such a young girl.' She hesitated for a moment, then her eyes moved towards the window. 'Don't mind Gabrielle's moods in the morning – you'll get used to her. Unfortunately, she's not at her best until she's been up for a while.'

Noelle moved her head up and down although her employer wasn't actually looking at her. 'I see,' she said. But as she closed the door she thought that she didn't see it at all – and she was quite sure she wouldn't get used to it. The girl was nothing but a spoiled brat.

Noelle went back downstairs, her stomach churning with annoyance at the way she had just been spoken to – especially by someone of her own age. She had gone into the bedroom feeling envious of the girl, wishing that some day she might find herself in such a lovely house being pampered and spoiled as Gabrielle was. But quite obviously Gabrielle didn't see her treatment as anything special or out of the ordinary. And she saw Noelle as nothing more than a skivvy.

The nice breakfast helped in some way towards making her feel a bit better, although the egg – with its hard yolk and over-cooked frilly brown edging – annoyed her. In some childish way it made Noelle feel that a less-than-perfectly fried egg wasn't good enough for the doctor or her niece, but it was okay for her to have it – as if her own taste didn't count.

If she'd been back home, she would have given it to one of the dogs without batting an eyelid, and got a fresh egg from the bowl in the pantry. But this wasn't home and Dr Casey counted the eggs out carefully and would have enquired as to where the missing one had gone.

She poured herself a second cup of tea and sat drinking it and eating a piece of buttered bread while staring out of the kitchen window. Then, when she heard movement in the landing upstairs, she finished her breakfast off quickly and started moving around the sink to make sure she looked busy when they finally came downstairs.

When the front door closed behind the two Caseys a while later, Noelle breathed a little sigh of relief. She threw the cloth she was wiping the table with into the sink and pulled off the elasticated mob-cap and went into the drawing-room where her boss had left the Sunday newspaper.

She kicked off her shoes and then stretched out on the sofa to read the paper in peace for the next half an hour.

Chapter 55

꧁꧂

'**A** winter wedding!' Mary exclaimed, hugging Kate for the third time. 'I don't believe it – can you believe it, Brendan?'

'Ah well,' he said, shaking his head and smiling, 'I suppose it could be worse. Better the devil ye know and all that.' He stood up to shake hands with his future brother-in-law and to give a kind of awkward kiss and hug to his sister. 'You've got yourself a good man there,' he told her, his face suddenly becoming serious. 'No doubts about it.'

'Thanks,' Kate said, smiling warmly at him and then turning to look at Michael who was standing by the kitchen table with the same delighted look on his face that had been there since she had accepted his proposal in Charleville Woods just an hour or two ago.

Mary rushed over to the cupboard in the corner and took out a brandy bottle, which she then handed to Brendan to open. 'Get the glasses, Kate,' she called. 'We have to do something to mark the occasion.'

'Have we any lemonade?' Kate checked, dreading the thought of drinking the spirit on its own or even diluted with water.

'There's a bottle of red lemonade under the sink,' Mary told her, 'and there's a bottle of beer if Michael would prefer that to the brandy.'

'Mickey and me will share the beer,' Brendan said, making the decision for the both of them, 'and we'll have a small drop of brandy as well.' He clapped his future brother-in-law on the back. 'Isn't that the best idea now?'

'Whatever you say yourself,' Michael agreed.

The four brandy glasses and the bottle of lemonade were found. Two glasses were poured halfway up for the men and the women's around a third of the way up, to allow for a good topping-up with lemonade.

There was a little awkward moment when they all stood with the glasses in their hands, then Brendan suddenly took charge. He lifted his glass high in the air with an uncustomary flourish. 'To Michael and Kate!'

'To Michael and Kate!' Mary repeated in a high, emotional voice. While she was almost overcome with joy at the announcement, a dark little fear was clutching at the back of her mind.

After they had all toasted the happy couple and then the future for all of them, they sat around the kitchen table chatting.

'I was hoping and praying this might happen,' Mary told them all, a little pink circle now growing on her cheeks from both the excitement of the occasion and the effects of the brandy and lemonade. 'I knew the pair of ye were well-suited from the first minute that Michael O'Brien walked into this house.'

Brendan drained his brandy glass. 'Ah well,' he said, shaking his head and affecting sadness, 'I never knew the harm I was bringin' on the family the day I brought this fella into the house – I never dreamed of the hardship it would cause us all.'

'Will you go away!' Mary said, giving Brendan a dig in the ribs with her elbow. 'We're delighted, Michael and Kate, we really are.' She took a little sip of her drink. 'And I suppose you'll be startin' to make all sorts of plans, won't ye? February will come around very quickly – sure, it's only a couple of months away. Once we get Christmas over, we'll hardly feel it.'

'We actually have another little bit of news,' Michael said, leaning across the table and touching Kate's hand for a few seconds. His touch was light – he wasn't a man given to public gestures – but it was enough to signify his feelings for her. 'We have a house and a bit of a farm all sorted out for us—'

'A house?' Mary said, trying to keep her usual smile pinned on her face, trying not to show the fear that the words had brought to her heart. All the things that secretly haunted her in the dead of night were now being brought to the surface.

'My Uncle Sean,' Michael explained, 'God bless his soul . . .'

The others automatically chimed in: 'God bless his soul.'

'He left the house and the farm between me and my brother,' Michael went on, 'and the family have agreed that I can have it.' He looked over at Kate. 'It needs a bit of work doing on it, but nothing too bad.'

Kate looked back at him, wondering if he had discussed getting married and living in the house with his family. Had he discussed asking her to marry him *before* he had actually asked her? Surely he wouldn't have done that. She could now half-imagine the grim-faced Mrs O'Brien and Michael's equally grim-faced brother and sisters all sitting around the table in the austere parlour, giving their opinions on whether Michael and she were a good match. The thought of it made her blood run cold.

'And is there much of a farm?' Brendan asked, all interested.

'A few acres and a few head of cattle,' Michael replied, shrugging his shoulders. 'Not that big, but big enough not to let it go outside of the family.'

'You're going to be pushed now between the boats and the two farms,' Brendan told him, 'not to mention fixing up the oul' house.'

Kate looked at her mother and instantly recognised the small pained smile that covered up her mounting anxiety. She could have kicked herself for not discussing her mother's situation with Michael privately, before talking out in the open about where they would live.

Michael nodded his head thoughtfully. 'True enough,' he said, glancing at the silent Kate again. 'But you know as well as I do that the boats will have to go shortly. There's few enough of them on the canal now and the boatmen are getting fewer too.'

'One of these days,' Brendan prophesied, 'the boss-men will come down from Dublin and make it all official – then we'll all be scattered to the wind lookin' for work.' He threw a friendly punch at Michael. 'Of course, there's some of us will be in a better position than others. There won't be any fear of you havin' to travel to Dublin or even England lookin' for work.'

Mary's face registered shock at the turn in the conversation, and all pretences of keeping a smile up became too much. 'Now, lads,' she said, her eyes blinking furiously as she got up from the table, 'how about a bite to eat? Will ye have a bit of cold ham and some nice fresh tomatoes?' She made towards the front door, still talking out loud as much to herself as to the rest in the house. 'I have the tomatoes outside on the window-ledge to help them ripen in the sun.'

Kate stood up and followed her out, leaving the two boatmen chatting, oblivious to the small bombs they had just dropped in Mary Flowers' life.

'Are you all right, Mammy?' Kate asked, coming around to the front of the cottage.

'I'm grand, Kate,' her mother replied in a high, forced voice. She kept her back to Kate, going down the row of a dozen or more tomatoes, squeezing each one to check which ones would be the most easily digested.

'We haven't made any definite plans,' Kate said, putting her hand on her mother's shoulder. 'I haven't even seen the house yet...'

'It sounds just lovely,' Mary said, putting a few of the tomatoes in her cardigan pockets and lifting the rest.

'We only got as far as talking about getting married after he asked me,' she explained. 'We had no discussion whatsoever about me moving to the house or anything like that.' She paused. 'You needn't be worrying about anything. From the sounds of it, if it's a typical farmhouse there should be plenty of room for you in it as well...'

'Sure, I'll be grand, Kate, don't I have my own place here?' Mary said, giving a brave smile that didn't go anywhere near her eyes. 'A pair of newlyweds won't be wantin' me around. And anyway,' she gestured with her thumb towards the house, 'how many times have we heard Brendan sayin' that he's going? He could still be here in twenty years' time, knowing him.'

Kate nodded slowly. 'We'll chat about it again later.' Then, on impulse she moved forward and put her arms around her mother's neck, causing two of the tomatoes to spill out of the cardigan pocket and roll onto the little path surrounding the cottage. 'Don't be worrying about a thing – you know you'll always be looked after,' she said with emotion.

'I'll be grand, Kate,' Mary reassured her. 'You get on with making your wedding plans.' She gave a small, forced laugh. 'And as you say, for all we know, that fella could be here in twenty years' time.'

Kate hadn't said anything of the sort, her mother was only echoing the words she herself had said only minutes ago, the words she was holding onto for comfort.

They both bent down to pick up the straying tomatoes, bumping heads together in the process.

'Stand still,' Kate said, 'and I'll get them.'

Mary laughed as Kate bent down to lift the tomatoes and put

them back in her mother's cardigan pockets. 'Between all the comings and goings of the last few weeks in Stockport,' she said, 'and now with all the news here, we won't know if we're on our head or our heels.'

Later on, after they'd eaten and listened to the radio for a while, Kate walked Michael back out to the car.

'Is everything all right, Kate?' he asked, an anxious note in his voice. 'It's just that you seem to have got quieter as the evening has gone on ... You're not having second thoughts, are you?'

'Not at all,' Kate said quickly. She hesitated. 'It's just that I feel a bit awkward about a couple of things ...'

'What?' he said. He turned now and opened the car door. 'Get in for a few minutes and we'll chat it over – whatever it is that's bothering you.'

As she slid into the black leather seat, Kate told herself that there was no point in holding things back, not if they were going to be married soon. They'd have to talk about everything then, wouldn't they?

She folded her arms over her chest and stared straight ahead out of the windscreen. 'I was just thinking,' she began, 'that it sounds as though you discussed everything with your family – about the house and the farm – before coming to propose to me ...'

Michael's eyes opened wide with amazement. 'Where did you get that idea from?'

She turned to look at him now. 'You said that you'd discussed your uncle's house ... you said it was left between you and your brother, and he said it was all right for you to have it.' Her eyebrows lifted in question. 'You must have talked about it with him.'

He gave a small sigh, then he reached over and drew her close into his arms. 'I said *nothing* to Thomas or any of the family about any plans I had of proposing to you ...'

He suddenly started to laugh – a real shaking kind of laugh that made Kate shake too.

She looked at him in alarm. Michael was rarely up or down – he was a very even, steady kind of man. This fit of laughing wasn't a bit like him at all. 'What on earth's wrong with you?' she gasped. 'What's so funny?'

'You!' he said, shaking his head. He eventually stopped laughing and then he gave her a huge bear-hug and planted a kiss on her forehead. 'You've no idea how terrified I was asking you to marry me, have you?'

Kate looked back at him in silent amazement. The thought had never entered her head.

'Why would I tell anyone before I asked you?' he went on, incredulous at the thought. 'I'd have looked a right eedjit if you'd turned me down, wouldn't I?'

'I wasn't sure...' she said, blushing at her mistake. 'I thought you might have said to your brother.'

Michael shook his head again. 'I had a talk to Thomas about my uncle's farm and the house, and he said he had no interest in moving out of our own house for the foreseeable future.' He gave a little shrug. 'I said that I was interested in it, and that we could come to an arrangement over it and he agreed.'

'But surely,' Kate persisted, 'he must have wondered what you would want the house for?'

'He probably did,' Michael agreed, 'but he never said anything. Thomas is like that – he's very quiet. He'll leave it up to me to tell him anything when the time comes.' He paused now. 'Is it all right with you if I tell them all back at the house tonight?'

Kate found herself holding her breath at the thought of Agnes O'Brien's reaction – or Michael's sisters' reaction.

Ignorant as to her fears, Michael gestured towards the cottage. 'Since your mother and Brendan know ... I think maybe I should let them know back home as well.'

She suddenly realised how churlish and cowardly she was being. If they were to be married, she couldn't keep a constant distance from his family – not when he was so good with her mother and so tolerant of Brendan. 'Fair enough,' she said, mustering up a smile. 'Tell them as soon as you like.'

His face lit up. 'That's grand.'

'Michael,' Kate suddenly said, 'while we're getting things sorted between us ... out into the open.'

He looked at her closely. 'Go on,' he said, a slight hesitancy in his voice, as though he was wary of what she was going to say next.

'After we get married ... will you want me to be at home all the time?' She paused, suddenly feeling self-conscious and awkward.

'You know I had notions of nursing – I mentioned it to you a while back . . .'

He nodded his head slowly, his face serious. 'It depends on the rest of our plans,' he said quietly. He rubbed his chin with his forefinger. 'For a start, there's the transport to think of – how would you get in and out to the hospital?'

'Maybe I could learn to drive,' she suggested.

'But we couldn't afford our own car just yet,' he told her incredulously. 'We'll have to borrow the family car to let me come and go between the farms.' He paused. 'And then there would be the money for your training . . .'

'My mother would be giving me something when I get married,' Kate said now. She watched as Michael continued to nod his head as though he understood, but she noticed that his face had grown a little darker.

'Have you given any thought about us having a family?' he ventured. 'Because that would take care of any plans you have for nursing – even if we could afford it.'

Kate looked at him now, realising that he had already given the matter careful thought. All the points he had raised were very reasonable. And of course he was right. Maybe she should have thought it all out herself before bringing the discussion up. 'I'd love children,' she said honestly, 'and I would rather be at home with a child than going out to work.' She gave a little wry, almost embarrassed smile. 'I suppose everything has happened so quickly that I didn't have time to think it all through . . .'

'Sure, there's no harm in that,' he said, a relieved smile breaking out on his face. 'I'm glad we can talk these things out.'

Mary had gone to bed and Kate was sitting reading by the fire when Brendan came in from the pub later that night. Kate gave him a few minutes to sort himself out while she made him a cup of tea.

'Brendan, we need to have a chat about my mother,' she said in a low voice, looking back towards the bedroom door.

Brendan's brow came down. 'What about her?' he asked, taking a noisy slurp of his tea.

'We need to make sure that we take her interests into account as well,' she explained. 'What'll happen if I get married and go to live at the farm near Tullamore and you have to go away looking for work?'

Brendan gave a shrug and looked into the dying embers of the fire with eyes slightly glazed from one too many pints of beer. 'Time enough to be worryin' about things like that—'

'*You* might think that,' Kate pointed out, 'and I might think it, too, but she's worrying already.' She gave him a long, steady look. 'How would you feel if she came to live with me and Michael?'

Brendan's head shot up. 'Has she said she wants to live with ye?'

'I've mentioned it to her,' Kate said evenly, 'but we haven't really discussed it seriously.'

Brendan's chin jutted out in thought. 'I suppose we'll have to think about it right enough.' He took another gulp of the tea. 'I suppose she's gettin' up in years and we can't be leaving her on her own.'

'Exactly,' Kate said. She picked her words carefully now. 'I know there's nothing definite about the boats yet, and Michael said it could be into next spring before they make any decisions.'

'It could easy be next spring,' Brendan said. 'And we'll just keep going until they tell us different.' He gave a shrug. 'They could put us up to Dublin for a while before laying us off completely. Ah, ye never know what those bastards could do.'

'It's not going to affect Michael as much,' Kate said now, 'because he'll go when they close the canal down this end of the country. He says he won't go to Dublin . . .'

'It's all right for the likes of the O'Briens with their big farm of land,' Brendan said, a defensive note creeping into his tone now. 'But the likes of me will have to go lookin' for work where I can find it.'

'Well, as you say, it's not something we need to worry about too much for the minute.'

'A day at a time,' Brendan said philosophically. 'Sure, I'm only goin' back to work tomorrow after the break off. God knows what might await me.' He gave a little sigh. 'I'll be glad to get back on the boats and get the last bit of the summer weather – it's nice to have a few days off, but you get fierce bored indoors all the time.'

Kate stood up now. 'If I get the right time, is it okay by you if I ask my mother about coming to live with me and Michael?'

There was a pause as Brendan thought about how lonesome he'd been in the cottage when his mother and Kate had been away, How pointless it had seemed being entirely on his own. Then he thought of Noelle Daly and the way he had felt when they had spent those few hours together. 'Give it a bit of time and see how it all works out,' he said quietly. 'We don't want to go makin' any quick decisions right now.'

Kate stifled an irritated sigh. She might have known – she'd wasted her time waiting up for him. That was Brendan all over. Putting things on the long finger – making no decisions until they were thrust on him. Well, she'd given him his chance to have his say. Tomorrow she'd talk to her mother about it. She had to – she knew her mother so well she could almost read her mind. Kate knew that her mother would be lying in bed worrying about everything. She had to know that they weren't just going to go their own way without giving a thought to her.

With or without Brendan's consent, Kate would approach the subject as soon as she felt it was the right time.

Mary lay in bed, catching snatches of conversation between her son and her daughter. She was fully aware of the situation she was now in, the one she had dreaded for so many years. And how foolish of her to be so upset, she thought – hadn't she known it was coming? Then, as she heard Brendan's notion of her 'getting up in years', her heart sank to its lowest depth. Was that really what people thought of her?

She pulled the bedclothes tight up to her chin, cuddling them around her for comfort.

Only a week ago she had felt useful and needed. She knew she had been a help to Rose and Graham in the house and in the shop – she knew she had something to give. And after meeting Lance Williams she had suddenly felt young and carefree, almost an attractive woman again – a woman in the prime of her life.

But as she listened to Kate's concerned tones and Brendan's evasive comments, the only thing that Mary Flowers felt at that precise moment was a burden.

Chapter 56

When Kate walked into the hallway in the O'Briens' farmhouse the following Tuesday evening, she was sharply reminded of the first time she had set foot in the house – the day Michael's father had dropped dead.

'Come in, Kate, you're very welcome,' Agnes O'Brien said, her voice soft and low. They walked down the austere hallway and into the parlour, where Michael's brother and sisters were all sitting around as before. But this time, they were all smiling and saying 'hello' and looking as if they were genuinely welcoming her. When she had reciprocated their greetings, she sat down and a quick glance told her that the table was set almost identically to the previous visit, with sandwiches, cake and tea. But this time there were also two bottles of wine, a bottle of sherry and a bottle of lemonade in the centre of the table.

Michael and Thomas sorted out a glass of sherry for their mother and glasses of wine for those old enough to drink alcohol and lemonade for the youngest girl. When everyone was seated and attentive, Michael stood up.

'Unlike our last sad gathering in this house,' he said, 'on this occasion, we have something good to celebrate. He reached over and took Kate's hand in his. 'As you all know, Kate has kindly agreed to be my wife, and I wanted her to be here with us all today, to share in the good wishes you all gave me.' He paused for a moment, looking around the group expectantly.

Thomas, on cue, now stood up, holding his glass aloft. 'To Michael and Kate – wishing you all the best for your married life together.' The rest of the O'Brien family echoed his words and held their glasses up in a toast.

Kate smiled around the group and thanked them. Then they all sat together eating the sandwiches and cake and talking around the wedding in circles. The only definite detail was the fact that the wedding would be around February – to let the first Christmas without the head of the household go by. It would be quiet on the farms by then too.

'A *small* wedding,' Michael emphasised. 'Kate and I have discussed it, and with it being so close to our family loss, we feel a bigger "do" wouldn't be at all appropriate.' He squeezed Kate's hand again. 'And anyway, Kate has very few family around, so we're happy to keep the occasion small and quiet.'

When they left the farmhouse an hour or so later, Kate heaved a sigh of relief, glad that it had gone so well and even gladder that it was over.

'That went very well,' Michael said, as they sat in the car heading back for Ballygrace. 'I'm sure they think of you as part of the family already.'

'That's nice,' Kate said, smiling back at him. She couldn't deny that there had been a definite improvement – but she wasn't going to pretend to herself that the O'Brien family liked her. Or that they thought she was a good match for Michael – she knew in her heart of hearts that it wasn't the case.

Chapter 57

Two letters arrived in the post the following Thursday morning, along with grey skies and the coolest breeze they'd felt in a long time.

'Ye have *two* writing to you this morning,' Mr O'Reilly, the postman, told Mary. 'One from Dublin and one from England.' He handed the letters over now, watching her with great interest as she scanned the handwriting on the front.

'Ah, that'll be my sister,' she said, 'and the other from Kate's friend.' She tucked them into her apron pocket, then she folded her arms. 'Will you have a cup of tea with us this morning, Kevin?'

'Ah sure, I might as well,' he said, taking his cap off. 'The oul' bag is fairly light this morning, so I'm in no great hurry.'

Mary turned back into the kitchen. 'I think it's that bit cooler this morning, what do you think?'

'Oh, it is,' he agreed, following her in. 'Howya, Kate?' he said, nodding over to where Kate was tidying up the fireplace after filling the grate with turf.

'Grand, Mr O'Reilly,' she said, brushing the turf dust onto the small shovel and throwing what she had gathered onto the flickering fire.

He lifted the postbag up over his head now and hung it on the back of one of the kitchen chairs, then sat down. 'We're well into autumn now, I can tell ye,' he said, nodding his greying head vigorously. 'There's a good strong breeze out there this morning, and the oul' leaves are comin' down thick and fast. Ah, ye can always depend on it. We'll soon have to watch ourselves on the bikes. The leaves can be fierce slippy.'

After giving Kate her letter, Mary poured him a cup of tea and then thickly buttered two slices of soda bread for him.

'Well,' he asked, taking a drink of the tea, 'have youse any news?' Usually, he was the bearer of all the news in the town – especially in the bad weather when people might be confined to their houses for days at a time.

Mary glanced over at Kate and when she saw her warning look, she said, 'No news at all, Kevin . . . all quiet down this end of the canal.'

'And thanks be to God for that,' he said, taking a bite from the soda bread. 'And all quiet up the town as well this long time – not a ha'p'orth of news anywhere.' He nodded his head. 'Ah well, I suppose no news is better than bad news.'

After Mary had seen the postman off, she came back into Kate. 'You didn't want me to say anything about the engagement yet?'

'Not yet,' Kate said, resting her opened letter in her lap. 'Not until we've bought the ring at the weekend.' She and Michael had planned to take a drive up to the jeweller's shops in Dublin on Saturday. 'I thought I'd tell my friend Maura and Sarah then.'

'It's just the other day you said not to say anything until you told the O'Briens,' Mary said, her manner slightly wounded. 'I thought it would be all right to talk about it to people now, since you've been over to the house.' She gave a little sigh. 'I suppose I'll just have to put it out of my mind now until you say so.' She glanced out of the window at the blustery morning. 'I probably won't be going too far until we go to Mass on Sunday, so it'll hold until then.'

Kate looked at her mother now, suddenly realising that she was being a small bit selfish. She had given her mother wonderful news then almost immediately had pulled the rug from under her feet, telling her that she would be moving away. Now, she was taking the good out of the occasion by being secretive.

Kate stood up and went over to her mother. 'I'm sorry if it seems as though I'm being awkward, Mammy – I don't mean to be.' She put her arms around her mother and squeezed her tightly. 'I think I'm just a bit overwhelmed with it all myself...'

Mary looked up at her. 'You're not havin' second thoughts about Michael?'

'No, no,' Kate said. 'It's not like that ... I definitely want to marry him.' She loosened her arms now. 'It's just all a bit sudden – big changes very quickly.' She went over and sat down at the table now, her elbows on the table and her chin resting on her hands. 'I didn't even know about the old uncle or the farm ... and I don't have the faintest notion where it is. It sounds as though it's in a very quiet bit altogether.'

Mary nodded her head. 'Aren't ye going over to have a look at it on Sunday?'

'We are,' Kate said. 'If we're to be married, it doesn't look as though there will be any choice but to go there.' She looked around the kitchen. 'I don't really want to leave the cottage here at all, but in all honesty, there's no room for the two of us.'

Mary glanced around the room now, as though it might suddenly grow a few yards here or there that might just accommodate them as she herself would have liked. 'No,' she sighed, 'I don't suppose there is. It's a tight enough squeeze as it is.' She paused. 'But if Brendan goes, I could always take his room and give ye both mine...'

Kate raised her eyes to the ceiling. 'We're only codding ourselves. That wouldn't work either, Mammy,' she said quietly. 'Michael needs to be close to the two farms. He's going to be hard pushed going from one to the other as it is. He's promised Thomas that when he finishes on the canal he'll work the big farm full time with him. They've come to some arrangement over him working there, to pay for Thomas's share in the uncle's farm.'

Mary nodded. 'It's understandable,' she said in a small voice. 'It's very understandable.'

'When the time comes,' Kate suggested, 'maybe you could spend the weekdays with me over at the farm, and come back here at the weekends when Brendan is about. What do you think of that?'

'Oh, I wouldn't like to be on top of ye both, and you only newly married.'

'But you'd be company for me,' Kate argued. 'When Michael's on the boats I'll be all on my own. What am I going to do with myself all day stuck out in the middle of nowhere in a farm?'

The older woman looked thoughtful now. 'We'll see,' she said, brightening up a little. 'That might not be a bad idea. We could keep ourselves busy enough with the animals and I could maybe help you in the garden and that kind of thing.' She paused for a moment. 'You wouldn't think of going into nursing then? It's something you always had a notion to do . . .'

'It is,' Kate agreed, 'and I've thought of it often.' She looked down at her hands. 'It would probably be very complicated now, and I don't think Michael is too keen on the idea. He's more old-fashioned about these things and would prefer to have me at home.' She gave a little embarrassed smile. 'I think he's hoping we'll start a family as soon as we're married . . .'

'Oh, Kate!' her mother said, joining her hands together in delight. 'The thought of it all . . . you married and with a little baby. Wouldn't it be wonderful?'

'Well,' Kate said, lifting up her letter again, 'it's all a long way down the road yet – and we don't want to be tempting fate with plans.'

'No, indeed,' Mary said. 'We'll just have to put our faith in God and his blessed mother.'

Then, deliberately changing the subject, Kate slid her letter across the table to her mother. 'Have a little read at this and tell me what you think . . .'

Mary suddenly patted her apron pocket and laughed. 'Sure, I haven't even opened my own yet from Rose. I was that busy chatting that I nearly forgot all about it.' She lifted her reading glasses now and slowly read down Noelle's letter, ooh-ing and aah-ing as she went along. When she came to the end, she put the letter on the table and took her glasses off.

'What do you think?' Kate asked, her eyebrows raised.

'I'd be worried about that girl if she was my daughter,' Mary stated. 'I'd be very worried indeed. That doctor's niece sounds like a spoiled little oul' brat to me and the doctor doesn't sound a whole lot better.'

Kate nodded her head. 'I feel she's having a hard time of it. It might be a lovely part of Dublin and a nice big house, but it doesn't sound as if it's an easy job she's gone to.'

'And when you think of all Noelle's gone through with the father . . .' Mary said in a hushed voice as though Matt Daly might burst through the door at any minute and catch them talking about him.

'Well,' Kate said, 'the only good thing is that she says the job will give her somewhere to live in the meantime, and give her the chance to save up a bit of money until she gets a better job.'

They talked over poor Noelle Daly's situation for a while, then Mary suddenly smiled. 'Did you notice the one good thing she mentioned in the letter, Kate? I could hardly believe my eyes as I was reading it.'

Kate's eyes widened now, knowing exactly what her mother was referring to. '*Brendan*,' she said in a surprised tone. 'According to what she says, he turned out to be the good Samaritan while we were away. He only told us half the story.' She put her head to the side. 'Mind you, Michael said he was real nice to her that night when they took her on the boat up to Dublin. He said Brendan was falling over himself to help her and doing everything on the boat to thank the men for bringing her up.'

'It just shows you that he's not half as bad as he'd like us to believe,' Mary said, a little note of pride in her voice. 'The way he used to go on about the two Daly girls, you'd think he couldn't stick them, and yet the minute he was needed, he was there to help out. He's a decent oul' skin under all his bluster, you know.'

'We must tell him about the letter when he comes off the boat tomorrow,' Kate said, folding it up and putting it back into the envelope.

'D'you know something, Kate?' her mother said now, nodding towards the letter. 'I wouldn't be the slightest bit surprised if Brendan had a notion of Noelle Daly . . .'

'Get away!' Kate scoffed. 'I wouldn't think so – not with the way he's gone on about her and Sarah this long time. He's never had a good word for either of them.'

'Don't be too sure,' Mary said. 'Aren't love and hate two sides of the one coin?' She turned to her own letter now, full of the anticipation of more news.

Kate stood up. 'I'll hang those towels out on the line now while it's still dry.'

Mary nodded, her concentration intent on sliding a knife under the sealed part of the envelope to open it without damaging the letter inside. She was surprised to see another smaller, sealed envelope inside beside the letter from her sister. She took both out and placed them on the table. Then, as she began to read down Rose's letter, her face suddenly reddened and, checking that Kate wasn't looking, she quickly retrieved the other, smaller, envelope and slipped it back into her pocket.

She quickly finished reading Rose's letter, which had small inconsequential pieces of news and a whole paragraph full of praise for Frankie, their new shop assistant. Seemingly, he was ten times better than poor Betty – able to do everything and anything in the shop – and all the customers had taken to him in a big way. The only fly in the ointment was that Graham had taken to him too. Seeing how capable and trustworthy his new helper was, he was quite happy to leave Frankie and Rose in charge while he went off about his usual banking and betting-shop business.

Rose had finished off saying that Lance Williams had called into the shop on the very afternoon that they had left for Ireland, and had asked her advice as to whether it would be all right if he was to write to Mary. Rose said she had taken it upon herself to say go ahead, and within an hour he was back round with the letter already written.

There was also a reference in the letter to the young 'Dr Dolittle', who apparently had asked Graham to pass on his kind regards to Kate. Mary had paused for a moment when she read that, wondering if there was any point in raising the subject with her daughter. She quickly decided it was wiser to say nothing. Kate obviously found the subject uncomfortable, and there was no point in spoiling her excitement over the forthcoming wedding by reminding her of the small holiday indiscretion.

When she came to the end of Rose's chatty letter, Mary looked down at the small sealed envelope with her name written in neat, efficient handwriting. She turned it over and over in her hands, scanning the envelope as if she might have missed something – or as if the blank paper might give some clue as to the contents within.

Then, the door opened and Kate came back in, and Mary hurriedly stuffed the letter deep into the depths of her apron pocket. She would read it later when she was entirely alone.

Chapter 58

❧

October had come around very slowly in Dublin. At least it had been slow in coming for Noelle Daly. Each day in September had been a trial, with Gabrielle Casey being her only human contact for most of the day – any brief conversations she had with Carmel Foley were few and far between.

Since the girl had arrived, Noelle's relatively easy-going work-load had increased until she was constantly on the go. And the thing she found the most difficult was the unpredictability of what had once been a very predictable routine.

Whereas before, she had her own and Dr Casey's breakfast over and done with, and everything in the kitchen cleared up by half past nine, she now found herself starting all over again with Miss Gabrielle. And no two days were the same. Some mornings she would decide she wanted only a bowl of Cornflakes as she was rushing off to meet her friends, and the very next she could wander in at half past ten looking for a full Irish breakfast.

Any time that Noelle hinted that she was busy washing bed sheets or cleaning or gardening, the girl would give her a withering look and say something along the lines of, 'Well, I'd be grateful if you'd do it as soon as you are ready . . . but I really don't think my aunt would expect you to keep me waiting for my breakfast.' And then she would flounce off, and make Noelle come looking for her when the food was all ready.

And it wasn't just extra cooking that was causing the problem. It could be a blouse that needed to be washed and dried and ironed within a few hours, or a skirt that needed a button sewing on while Gabrielle stood tutting and sighing, waiting on her to do it immediately.

And then there were the friends she brought back to the house in the afternoon after swimming or tennis or her horse-riding. They would come bounding in the door, laughing and chatting and throwing their things on the kitchen table or the drawing-room floor and calling for Noelle to make tea or coffee and supply sandwiches or biscuits.

There were days when Noelle thought that her maid's uniform made her invisible – because the girl would rush past her without a glance or keep her eyes studiously fixed on the book she was reading as Noelle lifted cups and plates and generally tidied around her.

The worst thing about it was that it was causing friction between herself and Dr Casey, who was querying the mid-week shopping money that Noelle had always managed very carefully.

'I know that there are three of us now, Noelle,' Dr Casey had said on several occasions, 'but we seem to be getting through a lot more food than we ever did with Anna Quinn.'

Noelle found she had to stand her ground. 'Miss Gabrielle likes to have a variety of things,' she explained, 'and I often find myself running to the shops for bacon and sausages and far more chocolate biscuits than we ever used before.'

'Well ... we don't want to stint on the girl's breakfast or little treats that she's used to,' Dr Casey said, looking disgruntled. She'd glanced down at the shopping receipt that Noelle had handed her. 'But at the same time ... we don't want to be throwing money away on nonsense.'

'Maybe you'd like to speak to Miss Gabrielle,' Noelle dared to suggest. 'It might be better coming from you.'

Dr Casey had given a huge sigh. She knew quite well how her niece would react to being told she was eating beyond the household budget and she wasn't in the mood to tackle the girl's histrionics. 'I've far too much on my plate, Noelle,' she said, 'to be dealing with things I pay *you* to do.' She'd thrown the receipt on the table. 'Just do your best to manage things more carefully, without causing ructions with Gabrielle. She's only here for a few more weeks and then she'll be off to university.' She'd then walked a few steps towards the hall before halting again. 'This is the place my niece calls home and I don't want her feeling that she can't treat it as such.'

'That's grand, Dr Casey,' Noelle had said in as steady and even a voice as she could muster. 'And I'll continue to do my very best.'

The weeks passed and eventually Noelle found herself standing at the door with Dr Casey waving Miss Gabrielle off. Her father had insisted on coming to collect her and her luggage to deposit her in the students' lodgings and Noelle had noticed that he had come alone, which seemed to have added a lightness to his daughter's mood.

'She said she won't come home for the first few weekends,' the doctor said with a little catch in her voice as the car drove on up the road. 'The house won't feel the same without her.'

'No, it won't,' Noelle had agreed. She had then gone into her little bedroom on the pretext of looking for a hanky and had bounced up and down on the hard mattress with the greatest of glee.

One morning, towards the end of October, as Dr Casey was sifting through a handful of letters that had just arrived, she paused for a moment to pass a handwritten letter across the breakfast table to Noelle.

Noelle looked closely as the unfamiliar handwriting then examined the Tullamore postmark. She looked up at the clock and decided she would wait the five minutes until her employer had gone before opening it. She continued to drink her tea and eat the two slices of brown bread and butter she had most mornings.

'I've just been thinking, Noelle,' Dr Casey said, touching her finger to the postmark. 'You might like a Saturday off soon to pay a weekend visit home or maybe visit your relatives in Dublin.'

Noelle looked up with some surprise. 'That would be lovely . . .' She would not be going home, because there was no indication from either her mother's or Sarah's letters that Matt Daly would have a welcome for her. But she might go and visit her Auntie Delia.

The doctor studied her for a moment. 'I've noticed you've been looking a bit pale recently . . . are you feeling all right?' She stood up now and drained the last of her cup of coffee.

'I'm grand, thanks,' Noelle had automatically replied.

'Well, a little break might not do you any harm.' She put her cup down on the table now and lifted her brown working handbag. 'And if it's of any help to you, I have a little bit extra in your wages this month.' She paused for a moment, a slight awkwardness descending on her. 'I realise that you had more to deal with than normal when Gabrielle was here towards the end of the summer . . . and I just wanted to give a little recognition for that.' Then, she actually smiled. 'And I notice that the household accounts are looking more like they used to without Gabrielle.' She raised her eyebrows, still smiling. 'I suppose all our little pleasures in life come with a price.'

When the doctor had closed the front door behind her, Noelle lost no time in opening the envelope. 'Oh, my God!' she cried out loud when she saw who her letter was from. '*Brendan Flowers!*'

Then, with one hand covering her mouth in disbelief, she read down both sides of the small sheet of blue notepaper.

Dear Noelle,

I have a few days next weekend when I'll be up with the boat in Dublin. There's some repairs needing to be done and I said I'll stay on it while it's in the dock. It's the very same place that we came into with you that morning, which is handy enough for the town.

If you have time during the day we might have a walk around the city and if you can get an evening off we might go to the pictures or to a dance.

I'm putting the address of the canal workshop on the back of this and you could maybe drop me a line there and let me know how you are fixed. If you are too busy don't worry, as it was only an idea.

I have seen your father several times since you left, but he has never lifted his head or broke breath to me. You might like to see a friendly face in Dublin and hear any bits of news when we meet up. Don't mention anything about this to my mother or Kate as you know what they're like.

Yours sincerely,

Brendan Flowers

Noelle sat staring at the letter, unable to believe her luck. *For once,* she thought, *God is on my side!* She couldn't have planned this if she'd tried. She checked the dates and worked out that she could meet Brendan on the Friday night and they could have all day on the Saturday to tour around Dublin as he had suggested.

She took the letter into the bedroom with her and lay down on the bed, hugging it to herself. This was the best thing that had ever happened to her. She had thought of Brendan constantly when she'd come back over the summer, and remembered vividly the sweet hours they'd spent together. But over the weeks and months the memories had gradually faded away until she began to think she had imagined the closeness she had felt with him.

But now, it all came rushing back to her in a huge wave of excitement and happiness.

Chapter 59

❦

Noelle sat back in the cinema seat, and a warm glow descended on her as she felt Brendan's arm tighten around her shoulders again. She felt so snug and secure in the darkness of the velvet-covered seats that she could have easily drifted off into a contented sleep – except that she was much too excited and aware of every tiny little movement that Brendan made to consider anything like going to sleep. And the way she felt now, she might never sleep again.

Looking back to the barge trip, she had thought that the anxiety and fear over her father had been the main reason that had kept her awake, but she now knew that a large part of it had been that she hadn't wanted to miss a minute of being on her own with Brendan. She had felt so lucky having the chance to spend all that time with him, and she knew it was only because of the dramatic circumstances of her departure from Ballygrace.

But the thing that made her feel so wonderful now was that he had no reason to spend time with her. He didn't feel obliged to help her out as he had done on that night. He had no reason whatsoever to contact her or to suggest spending a weekend with her in Dublin if he hadn't wanted to.

And the longer they spent together, the plainer it was becoming to Noelle that Brendan Flowers *liked* her. And not just liked her – he had made it obvious this evening that he actually *fancied* her.

They had met up as arranged at six o'clock under the clock at Clery's shop on O'Connell Street, Noelle carrying a small package with the bare necessities for an overnight stay – a change of underwear, a nightdress and a toothrush. She hadn't been in touch with her aunt about staying, but the family never went anywhere and it was just a matter of squeezing into one of the beds with the younger children.

After looking her up and down, the first thing Brendan had said was, 'You're lookin' fierce well, Noelle.' A little frown had come on his face. 'Have you lost a bit of weight since I last saw you?'

Noelle had smoothed down the front of her empire-line, sleeveless green dress. 'I suppose I have lost a fair bit ... it's probably all the running up and down the stairs in the doctor's house.'

'Well, it suits you,' he said, smiling warmly at her. 'But don't go losin' any more now ... you look just grand as you are. I wouldn't like you lookin' all bony and skinny.'

They had walked slowly along O'Connell Street for a while, looking in all the shop windows, and then Brendan had suggested that they check out what was on at the pictures and what time they needed to be there.

The only decent film that was on was one that started at eight o'clock, so he had suggested that they go to a nearby café for something to eat beforehand. Noelle had tried to pay towards the fish and chips, but he had waved away any suggestions.

'Wasn't it me that asked you to meet up?' he'd demanded. 'And anyway, what kind of a fella do you take me for?' He had raised his eyebrows in admonishment. 'Askin' a girl out and then lettin' her pay! Have you ever heard the likes?'

When they came out of the cinema, Brendan looked at his watch. 'It's a quarter to ten,' he said. 'Would you have time for a drink?'

Noelle nodded. She had time for anything that Brendan suggested.

They found a lively pub just off O'Connell Street, and Noelle sat looking around her and enjoying the great atmosphere as Brendan queued at the busy bar for a pint of Guinness for himself and a glass of port for Noelle. He waited so long to be served that he ended up buying them two drinks each to save queuing again so quickly. They sat back in their chair, swapping stories about their respective workplaces, and then later, as she was coming back in from the Ladies', Noelle slipped over to the reasonably quiet bar and bought them another round.

'You're a fierce awful woman, going and doing that!' Brendan said, when she came back and placed the drinks in front of them. But she could tell by the slightly embarrassed look on his face that he was actually delighted and flattered that she'd done it.

'It's my pleasure, Mr Flowers,' Noelle giggled, beginning to feel the effects of the port.

By the time they came out onto the street, they were both in the best of form, having had a great night. They walked along O'Connell Street, Brendan's arm around her waist and hers around his.

'Oh, Dublin is a mighty place,' Brendan said, drawing her closer to him. 'If some of the lads at the pub could see us now with all the lovely bright lights and the people around, they'd wonder why they stay so close to home.'

'Talking of home,' Noelle said, 'I'll have to be lookin' for a bus soon to get out to my Auntie Delia's.'

'Ah, no!' Brendan said, steering her over to a narrow cobblestoned alley at the side of the shops, where there were few lights. They walked a few yards down the lane in companionable silence, then Brendan suddenly brought them to a halt. He put both hands gently on Noelle's waist and turned her around until her back was flat against the wall, then he took her handbag and her overnight package from her and laid them on the ground.

'What are you doing?' Noelle giggled, looking up into his eyes.

'I'm doing what I've been waiting to do all night,' he said in a low voice. Then, his head bent towards her and his lips touched her bare neck.

Noelle felt a dart of absolute pleasure as he touched her skin and instinctively she tightened her arms around his neck drawing him tight into her. Then, his lips were on hers kissing her deeply and in a way she had never been kissed before, and without the benefit of any previous experience, she found she was responding with the same ardour.

When someone passed close to the opening to the narrow street, Brendan guided her along the wall and further into the darkness, leaving her possessions unheeded where they had first been dropped. And there, where they couldn't be easily observed, he moved his passions further by adding tentative caresses along her shoulders and back while he kissed her face and hair and throat.

'Why,' he murmured into the fragrance of her newly washed, pale red hair, 'did you and me waste all this time? Only living down the canal from each other and we could have been enjoyin' ourselves instead of hardly talkin' . . .'

'It was my fault,' Noelle whispered, 'because of my father. But he's not here now – and he won't be interferin' in my life ever again.'

And later, when she offered no protestations, their coupling moved onto a more serious level and Brendan's hands sought and held her heavy breasts. As things progressed and she became aware of the hardness of his groin pressing with great passion into hers, she suddenly knew that she wanted to have Brendan Flowers in the same way he wanted her.

Then, there was a little scuffle in the alleyway and they both jumped apart, Noelle's heart pounding and her hands covering her face.

'What the feck was that?' Brendan uttered, stepping out to the opposite wall to look down into the narrow lane. There was silence for a few seconds, then they both relaxed into laughter as the shiny green eyes of a black cat came out of the darkness.

Brendan came back towards her now, taking her into the welcoming circle of his arms. 'I have an idea,' he said in a low voice. 'Why don't you come back to the boat along with me tonight?'

Noelle looked back at him, her heart still beating rapidly. 'What do you mean?' she said in a breathless voice.

'The same as we did before . . .' His lips brushed hers again now. 'We can make a cup of tea and sit and chat . . .' He kissed her again. 'We can have a bit of comfort and privacy.'

Noelle lowered her gaze. 'Wouldn't it look very bad? Just the two of us on our own.'

'To who?'

'To anyone who might see us . . .'

'Sure, there won't be a soul around,' he reassured her. 'There won't be a person within miles of us . . .' Brendan's description of that particular point of the canal was wildly exaggerated, and they both knew it – Noelle having seen it for herself.

She turned her head to the side now, so that she couldn't look into his appealing eyes – looked to the sensible side of her to lead the way. 'I'm a bit afraid . . .' she whispered, 'of what might happen.'

'No-elle,' he said, touching a tender hand to her cheek and down under her chin, 'there's not a thing in the world to be afraid of. Isn't it only yourself and meself involved? There's not a thing going to happen if neither of us wants it to . . .'

'I think that's what I'm most afraid of.' Her whisper was so low he could hardly hear it.

They slept very little on Noelle's second night on the boat, and they did not spend it up at the steering-wheel as they had on that first occasion. From the minute they arrived onto the boat, there was no pretence as to why Noelle had come back with him instead of going to her aunt's.

The reason was plain and simple – she now realised that she loved Brendan Flowers, that she had probably loved him since she was a young girl going to school.

And given the dire circumstances of her life at present, she decided that there was little point in depriving herself of the most beautiful thing that had ever happened to her. And if it was all to end on the stroke of midnight tonight – just like Cinderella – she wasn't going to let herself regret a moment of it.

The thing that had given her the final push was that Noelle also knew by now that Brendan had deep feelings for her, the kind of feelings that were required for her to take this momentous step. To have come all the way up to Dublin for no other reason than just to see her was blatant proof. He mightn't be able to put his feelings into words, but telling her that he had plotted and planned for weeks to be the one to bring the boat up so he could see her was words enough.

Brendan got the stove going with his boatman's expertise, which gave them heat and boiling water for tea, and a makeshift double bed was made by throwing the long cushions from the benches on the floor as a mattress, with an open sleeping-bag and an old eiderdown on top.

With the hanging lamps lit, the glow from the fire and the stirrings of the bushes and trees outside, Noelle felt she was in a safe little cocoon with Brendan there to look after her. Her knight in shining armour. That's how she had thought of him since the night he had rescued her in the dance hall and the night he had stowed her away to safety on the barge. She had told him that as they walked back from the bus stop along the canal-line to the barge.

'Me?' he said incredulously. 'A feckin' knight in shining armour? Don't let the lads in the pub hear you sayin' that! My reputation could be ruined for ever.' His laughs could be heard all the way across the water to the houses beyond.

While Brendan was up on the outside deck checking that the boat was secure for the night, Noelle quickly undressed and put on her nightdress and slid under the eiderdown. When he came back down below and saw her, he took off his outer clothes and shoes and socks and lay down beside her, still modestly dressed in his suit trousers and shirt.

As they lay together on the makeshift bed, a slight awkwardness grew between them – a shyness that Noelle had never seen on Brendan before. She knew perfectly well that he had had women before and, if the rumours were to be believed, plenty of them. He was a fine-looking man, lean and fit with broad shoulders. What girl wouldn't have their head turned by attention from him? And yet Noelle knew that well-hidden by all his bluster and over-emphasised manliness lay a sensitive soul.

How else could he be with Mary Flowers for a mother and Kate for a sister?

He lay on one elbow for a while, just looking at her. 'You're sure about this . . . aren't you?'

She nodded. 'If the time comes that I'm not sure, I'll tell you . . .' Her arms reached up to wrap around his neck and pull him towards her. Then, there were no more words as they fell into each other as naturally as if they had done so a hundred times before.

Within minutes Noelle Daly found herself brave enough to pull away from Brendan's hot and ardent kisses to unbutton his shirt and then watch with a mixture of fear and excitement as he unbuttoned his trousers and stood up to take them off. Modesty prevented him from stripping off completely, and he came back under the quilt to her still wearing his underpants.

Noelle knew nothing about sexual encounters on a practical basis or from her own experience, but she was a willing learner in his arms. She had sneaked a look at some of Dr Casey's medical books and had a good idea as to what lay under the white cotton. Recently, and especially since the boat trip up to Dublin, she had lain awake at night wondering what it would be like to have a man make love to her. And now, as Brendan's eager hands moved down along the curves of her generous breasts and over her stomach, she knew she didn't want to wonder any longer. When his hands reached the bottom of her cotton nightdress, she moved to help him to take it up and off over her head. And when she lay back, she found her own shaking hands almost moving of their own accord towards the waistband of his undergarments where she suddenly felt the hard reality of all the pictures she had seen in the books.

His work-rough hands came to cover hers. 'Are you sure?' he checked again.

'I'm more than sure,' she whispered back. She paused for a moment, then her hand came up to gently move a stray black curl back from his forehead. 'I love you, Brendan . . . and I want to feel every bit of you inside me, loving me.'

They did not move from the downstairs part of the boat until mid-day on the Saturday, when they escaped into the fresh air for a short walk to the nearest shop to find the makings of a lunch. Noelle cooked them up chops and fried potatoes and onions and opened tins of creamed rice and pears. They washed it down with glasses of beer and then they sat on top of the boat wrapped in their coats, talking and watching the world go by.

'You're not thinking of going to your auntie's tonight, are you?'

Noelle looked back at him. 'Do you think I should?'

He smiled and raised his eyebrows. 'Indeed and I don't,' he said. 'There's only one place I think you should go tonight, and it's back down those little stairs.'

An anxious shadow crossed Noelle's face. 'There's only one problem,' she explained. 'I never brought a proper change of clothes.' She looked down at the green dress she had worn again today and suddenly thought of the extra money Dr Casey had given her. 'I have a few pounds on me, and I could catch the bus into Dublin and pick something up.'

Brendan looked at his watch. 'Have we a half an hour before we go?'

Noelle nodded her head. 'Why?'

He smiled, took her by the hand and led her back downstairs to the warmth and comfort of their little nest.

Chapter 60

❦

After a full week of wind and rain, there were a few calm, cold February days, which led up to the snowy crispness of Kate Flowers' wedding day. Being both sensitive and sensible, she chose a silvery blue suit with a matching hat trimmed with a small white veil, instead of the traditional white dress and trailing veil that many girls of her age would have been swayed towards. Apart from the weather, she felt that it was too close to Michael's father's death to have a full-blown wedding celebration.

Rose was planning to make the trip over on her own for the wedding, leaving the shop in the capable hands of Graham and the dependable Frankie. Graham would take her to Holyhead for the overnight boat and then she would catch the coach to Ballygrace in the morning and Michael would drive her down to the cottage in his family car.

Rose had written to Mary after Christmas, making arrangements and saying that after the wedding was over they would take the train from Tullamore to Galway and have a few days in a bed and breakfast. She had suggested that they might even catch a bus out to County Clare and visit some of the relatives they hadn't seen in a long time.

'I think Rose is being a bit adventurous suggesting we go touring around in *February*,' Mary said to Kate when she read the letter. 'Although I suppose if the weather's not too bad, Galway would be lovely for a few days.'

'Well, Michael and me will be touring around Donegal in February for our *honeymoon*,' Kate reminded her, giving a little wry smile.

'Ah, but Kate,' her mother said, coming over to throw her arms around her, 'it doesn't matter what the weather is like when it's your honeymoon – especially two young lovebirds like yourself and Michael. You'll be too busy enjoying yourselves to worry about it.'

'I think,' Kate had said, lightly shrugging off her mother's embrace, 'that it's time to change the subject . . .' She lifted some of the dishes from the table and went over to the sink.

The smile slid from Mary's face. 'Sure, I was only codding . . . you're not worrying about the honeymoon, are you, Kate?'

'Not a bit,' Kate said breezily, lifting the boiled kettle up from the cooker and pouring the hot water into the basin. They didn't know themselves this winter with the new cooker Brendan had bought, and Mary was particularly delighted to have it with Rose coming over as it made things a whole lot easier.

'That's grand.' Mary reached across the table to put the top on the glass butter dish. 'You know if there's anything you're not sure about – anything that's worrying you – you can always ask me . . .'

'*Mammy!*' Kate said in a high voice, the voice she usually reserved for Brendan when he annoyed her.

'Okay, okay . . .' Mary said, regretting her offer. She got up from the table and went across to the fire to fiddle about with the basket of turf. 'I wasn't going to talk about the real personal bits, I was only saying . . .' Mary wondered if Kate would become easier about things like this when she was married and settled. Since last summer she had been acutely aware of Kate's tetchiness when the subject came around to anything like this, and she knew exactly where it had stemmed from – her little encounter with Lance Williams.

'Well, don't!' Kate bit back. 'Don't say any more about it.' She'd turned back to the sink, instantly annoyed at herself for being so snappy, because she knew her mother had touched a raw nerve.

She was of course nervous about her wedding night, but the thought of discussing it with her *mother* totally gave her the creeps. It reminded her of the excruciatingly embarrassing night back in Stockport, when she'd seen her mother all giddy and silly with Graham's friend – and she was only grateful that it had happened hundreds of miles away in a different country.

The memory of that night still haunted Kate, and she occasionally caught herself observing her mother – going quietly about her household business or pottering about in the garden – and wondered what was going through her mind.

It had unsettled Kate in many ways – reminding her that her mother had once been a young married woman who, having had two children when she was around Kate's age, had obviously had considerable experience in the physical side of life.

Having spent most of her grown life viewing her mother as an unequivocally single, totally contained person, it was most uncomfortable to think of her in any other way.

When Kate's mind had flitted back to her mother's offer of advice, she realised that she didn't have *anyone* she could discuss it with. Neither she nor her friends had ever really discussed anything like that. Of course they'd talked about boys they liked, and they'd speculated and giggled over the physical act that married couples got up to. But as far as she knew, none of her friends had any real experience whatsoever to go on.

Even her oldest friend, Maura, from Tullamore – who was engaged to a fellow she was mad about and getting married in the summer – had kept very quiet on the subject. And although Sarah and Noelle Daly were giggly and chatty types about lads, they had been brought up very strictly and would have been too terrified of their father to put a wrong foot in that direction.

Sarah had moved out of the house after Christmas and was now living and working in a factory at Clara, coming home for the odd weekend visit, and as far as Kate was aware, she was now going out with a lad from Tullamore.

And given the contents of the regular letters they had received, poor Noelle was unlikely to meet up with any lads in Dublin. It didn't sound as though she got the chance to go to any dances or social occasions – in fact, her social life sounded distinctly quieter than anything back in Ballygrace. The doctor sounded as though she had more than a watchful eye for anything like that. Whatever limited experience with lads that Kate had, she reckoned that Noelle had even less.

The physical side of her marriage, Kate had concluded, was an unknown area that she would have to venture into fairly naïve and unprepared. She was lucky that Michael O'Brien was such a gentleman, and his ways bordering on the old-fashioned. He wouldn't expect too much from her – and in all probability was every bit as inexperienced as herself.

They would just have to learn together.

And it was at times like this, when Kate had these thoughts about her forthcoming physical life, that little flashbacks to the summer would creep into her mind. Pictures of David McGuire's handsome, slightly mocking, smiling face, beckoning her towards a part of herself she hardly knew, a part of herself she was scared of. Pictures of them kissing each other with such a natural, burning intensity, an intensity that she had never felt with Michael.

And behind all her worry was the fact that she might *never* feel such intensity with Michael O'Brien.

Before and after Christmas Michael and his brother had spent as much time as they could spare from the farms on doing up the old uncle's house. They did all the basic work of cleaning and painting and decorating that they could do themselves, and brought in a plumber to update and replace the ancient pipes and fix a new inside bathroom and toilet. They had window-frames replaced and had a carpenter make up a few new kitchen cupboards.

By the middle of January, Kate and her mother were walking around the shops in Tullamore, choosing curtains and bedding for the new marital home. As a wedding present, Mary had given Kate quite a substantial sum from the money that the bank in Tullamore had carefully guarded since Seamus Flowers' passing away.

'That old farmhouse is going to be a palace by the time ye're finished,' Mary stated, and a little glow of pride warmed her heart every time Kate showed her something else she'd bought for her bottom drawer.

One Sunday afternoon, Michael came in the car and picked up both Kate and her mother and drove them out to the house to see the finished product. They walked from room to room and then upstairs until they came to a halt outside the bedroom that was opposite Michael and Kate's room.

Kate swung the door open wide. 'This is your room, Mammy...'

'Oh, Kate!' Mary had exclaimed as she walked in, and immediately her eyes filled up with tears at the sight of the lovely big double bed with the satin flowery eiderdown and matching pillowcases, and the lovely big window with swept-back floral curtains and a deep fringed pelmet. 'It's like a hotel room,' she gulped, 'and twice the size of the one me and you are sharing...'

And there had been more work done in wedding preparation out at the cottage by the canal. Brendan had been unusually cooperative about giving up his room for his aunt, and there had been ferocious activity getting the room painted and brightened up for her. After Christmas they had spent the weeks giving the house a very early spring clean as well as whitewashing the outside of the cottage when they had an unexpected few days of dry weather.

All the wedding preparations had helped keep Mary's mind occupied and away from thoughts of Lance Williams. He still wrote regularly via Rose, and Mary found herself looking forward to the letters with greater and greater anticipation. She spent hours poring over his beautifully written notes when she was on her own, and spent an equal length of time composing her own letters back to him, with the help of a dictionary as her spelling wasn't great.

They both wrote about their gardens and the little jobs they had been doing over the winter around them, and Mary of course had told him in great detail about the wedding preparations. All in all the communication with Lance had given Mary a new lease of life, but it caused her some unease and sadness that she couldn't share her enjoyment of the friendship with Kate. She hadn't even broached the subject of Lance Williams with Brendan, because if Kate – who was normally so kind and understanding – had reacted so badly, she knew that her son's response would be even worse.

Rose had arrived a few days before the wedding with a suitcase in one hand and a bag containing wedding gifts in the other – but the greatest gifts she brought, as far as Mary was concerned, were her company and advice.

'Get the wedding over and done with,' Rose had told her, 'and when you're living on your own, you'll be free to write to whoever the hell you want to.'

'But I'll be staying some of the time up at Kate's house,' Mary reminded her.

'You can still pick up your own mail when you're home,' Rose said. Her eyes had suddenly narrowed. 'I'm surprised at you, Mary, letting Kate dictate to you like this. You're not a child – and you're not an old woman either. You're entitled to have a bit of a life, you can't stay buried away down by the canal for ever.' She had looked Mary straight in the eye. 'One day you'll turn around and realise that you gave your own life away – and Kate and Brendan will be the first ones to say they never asked you.'

Mary had said nothing as a cold fear had engulfed her at her sister's words – in her heart of hearts, she knew it was the truth.

The wedding morning went ahead without any mishaps, the crisp, light flakes of snow adding to the drama of the occasion without causing any great harm. A hackney carriage with white ribbons carefully carried the Flowers group along the frosty canal tow-path to the church where Michael O'Brien and his family were waiting, along with other relatives, neighbours and friends. Rose was the only member of the family who had travelled any distance, because they had kept the wedding small, given the time of the year and the O'Briens' recent bereavement.

One of the smaller hotels in Tullamore was chosen as it had an ideal sized room, which had been nicely decorated with floral wreaths and colourful table displays.

There was a long main table at the top of the room for the bridal party – the wedding couple; Maura, Kate's oldest friend and chief bridesmaid; Tom O'Brien, the best man; the two mothers and Brendan Flowers. The other smaller tables were placed to the side and the middle of the room.

The hotel provided the traditional wedding lunch of a thick vegetable soup, followed by turkey and ham or roast beef with dishes of floury mashed potatoes, roast potatoes and tureens of mixed vegetables. There was a choice of trifle or apple pie and custard for dessert, and later on in the afternoon, the larger tier of the two-tier wedding-cake was cut and distributed to the guests with cups of tea or coffee.

Michael and his brother said a few appropriate, rather self-conscious words and when the meal was all cleared away a three-piece band played pleasant, suitable traditional music.

By the time darkness had fallen on the wedding day and the little bit of snow had melted, Kate Flowers – now Mrs O'Brien – and her new husband were well on their way to the Dublin hotel room where they would spend the first night of their married life.

Mary and Rose had gone back to the cottage in a hackney carriage, and they would spend the rest of the night drinking tea and talking over Mary's friendship with Lance Williams, then read and analyse every word of his letters. They would also re-examine the expensive box of crystal wineglasses that Lance had sent Kate and Michael as a wedding gift. The sisters would spend the Sunday quietly at home – only venturing out for Mass – and then on Monday they would catch the train for their little holiday down in Galway. Rose had booked and paid for the holiday, knowing the huge, yawning gap that would be left in her sister's life now that her only daughter – and the light of her life – had departed for a married life of her own.

Brendan Flowers had gone as far as Ballygrace village in the hackney carriage and repaired off into the local pub. He had done his bit at the wedding – kept the side up – and mixed well with Michael O'Brien's dry family, and had danced the legs off all his sisters and even his tight-faced mother.

He had done and said all the right things and, as he had promised his mother, he hadn't drunk too much either. He was entitled now to go and have a few drinks in the pub and have a bit of harmless oul' craic with the local lads. Later on in the night, no doubt some of them would probably head off on bicycles or in cars looking for a bit of a dance. And that would be when Brendan would head for home.

Since his weekend in Dublin with Noelle Daly – and the odd nights they'd snatched since then – Brendan had lost all interest in dancing or in other women. The only one that held any interest for him was stuck up in Dublin, and their relationship had to be kept a deadly secret from her madman of a father.

What the future held for them, neither of them knew.

Chapter 61

❦

The winter had passed and the May blossoms were being blown from the trees when Kate O'Brien discovered that she was pregnant. She had suspected as much for the last few weeks but had kept quiet about it until she saw the doctor in Tullamore, late on a Friday afternoon. She had come out of the surgery and whispered her good news to her delighted mother, who had uttered her usual words, 'Oh, Kate!' Then, after the two women had gone their separate ways, she had pedalled her bike as quickly as she could back out to the farmhouse that was now her home.

Within an hour of her return, the fires in the sitting-room and the dining-room were re-kindled and the range was well heated up. The air in the kitchen smelled of white fish basking in parsley sauce and onions and chunks of potatoes that were crisping in a dish alongside thick strips of parsnips. Boiled potatoes simmered on the stove, waiting to be drained and mashed. A freshly baked coconut cake – Michael's favourite – that she had mixed this morning and left ready for the oven stood cooling on the sideboard.

Kate had set the dark-wood dining-table with a white lace cloth and then lifted the two silver candlesticks from either side of the mantelpiece and placed them in the middle, beside a white jug filled with long sprigs of the honeysuckle that grew on the side of the house. She lifted a bottle of white wine from the cupboard and stood it beside the flowers. Neither she nor Michael were great drinkers of wine – or any other alcohol – but this special occasion called for something more celebratory than their usual cup of tea or glass of milk. They would probably have only a glass each and put the cork back in the bottle to use when they had visitors.

Michael was due in from the boat in the next half-hour or so and they would settle into their weekend routine, making the most of their three nights together before he was back out on the boat – the boat that had been predicted to be long gone off the water but was still there, chugging up and down to Dublin. And could go on chugging for the foreseeable future, taking Michael and Brendan along with it.

Kate hoped that the baby coming would give Michael the final push he needed to leave the boats, before the boats left him.

She wanted him home every night the way a husband should be. She wanted him sleeping beside her in their bed. And she wanted him making love to her as any young couple should want. The physical side of their marriage – which Kate had worried so much about – had gradually become as easy and relaxed as all the other areas. After their honeymoon night – their first uncomfortable and slightly awkward encounter – each time they made love became more natural and more enjoyable. Michael was more spontaneous and confident, and after the first few weeks their lovemaking had moved towards the more romantic realms that Kate had hoped and prayed for.

Michael was a considerate lover and surprised her by checking that she was as satisfied with that side of their marriage as she was. Kate had assured him that she was. She loved the closeness between them – the feeling of his hands on her skin and his warm hard body pressed up close to hers at night. She loved the feeling of safety that it gave her, and the certainty that life with him brought.

If Kate had been asked to hold her hand up and say that she had not been happy with her new life, she would have been lying. Apart from him being away during the week, marriage with Michael O'Brien had worked out better than she could ever have imagined.

Since their wedding, the weeks had fallen into a routine, with her mother coming over on a Monday afternoon and staying with her in the bigger house until Friday, when they would both cycle into Tullamore and do their bits of shopping, then go home and cook for the men in their lives. But just recently, their routine had been interrupted when one of the weeks Mary had had a heavy cold and Kate had locked up the farmhouse and gone out to stay with her at the cottage. Then, after going back to their usual arrangement for a couple of weeks, Mary had suddenly announced that she was quite content to have a few nights at the beginning of the week on her own, and had only stayed the last two nights out at Kate's.

Kate had checked that there was nothing wrong with her mother, but Mary had assured her she was fine.

'I feel I need a few days to catch up on things at home,' she'd explained to Kate. 'The garden needs a good bit of work and now that the days are longer I could spend the evenings there as well. When Brendan is at home I'm busy cooking and baking and I don't get as much time to do a bit of knitting or writing letters or any of the things I used to do when you were both home.'

'Are you sure you won't be lonely in the house at night?' Kate had said anxiously.

'Not at all,' Mary had said. 'I've plenty to keep me occupied, and anyway, I know I can always come over to you if I feel lonely.' Then, she had looked at Kate, a thought just occurring to her. 'You're not lonely or frightened out here on your own, are you, Kate?'

'Not at all,' Kate had said.

In truth, while she wasn't afraid as such, she didn't actually enjoy being in the house all night on her own. Her mother being there had certainly helped in the early weeks, and Kate supposed that gradually – by spending the odd night or two on her own – she would eventually get used to the solitude. And now, with the baby due at the end of the year, hopefully Michael would leave the boats and be home every night.

When he returned home that evening, Kate sat Michael down at the table and told him their news. For a few moments he seemed speechless, then he pulled her down to sit on his knee and he hugged her tightly. 'I missed something in my speech at the wedding.'

'What?' Kate said, surprised that he hadn't reacted to her news immediately. Why on earth was he going on about his wedding speech?

'I should have thanked Brendan,' he went on. 'I'll owe Brendan Flowers a debt of gratitude until the day I die.'

'What on earth do you owe that fella?' she demanded.

He traced a finger down her cheek. 'He introduced me to the best thing that ever happened to me in my life.' Then, his hand moved to her stomach. 'Maybe now I should say, he introduced me to the *two* best things in my life.'

Kate looked back at him tenderly, and for once was lost for words.

Chapter 62

❦

The last year had been one of discovery for Mary Flowers, and as she cycled along the tow-path to the cottage in Ballygrace, she pondered over the exciting news that Kate had just told her. A baby! The most wonderful news that Kate could have given her. Their whole lives would undoubtedly change with this addition to their family.

Another change to add to all the others.

On reaching the cottage, she dismounted the bike and went inside. There were two envelopes on the floor, underneath the letter-box. She scrutinised the hand-writing and felt the usual little jump of excitement as she recognised that the one in the small blue envelope was from Lance Williams. The other was a printed brown envelope from the bank, which she would deal with much later in the day when she had caught up on her household business.

Without waiting to take off her coat, Mary dragged a kitchen chair out and sat down to read Lance's letter. It contained all the usual day-to-day news about his tool-hire business and a blow-by-blow account of his gardening activities and any events held in the cricket club. Then, he had moved onto the more personal business, once again imploring Mary to come back to Stockport for a visit as soon as possible. A much longer visit this time. And a visit on her own – where she could go where she liked and do what she liked, without feeling that she had to answer to anyone. Without feeling she had to answer to Kate, as she had done on the previous holiday.

Brendan, of course, wouldn't care what she did. As far as he was concerned, she would just be going to the same old places and doing the same old things that they had always done on holiday at Rose and Graham's. He wouldn't for one minute imagine that his mother might want to spend time with a man her own age, enjoying all the things that older couples did – and Mary certainly wasn't going to enlighten him.

In any case, he was much too busy coming and going to Dublin these days. He'd obviously got in with some girl up there, because Mary couldn't think of any other reason that would take him up so regularly. She'd gently probed and hinted, asking if he was going to dance halls in Dublin, and trying to get out of him what was the big attraction, but Brendan Flowers wasn't giving anything away.

Kate hadn't made any mention of a summer holiday in Stockport this year – and Mary hadn't expected her to. No doubt she would probably want to spend any holidays Michael had off going for car trips here and there.

With Kate so newly married – and especially now that she was expecting – Mary couldn't expect her to make the trip across on the boat just to keep her mother company. And it wouldn't be fair to ask her because no doubt Kate would go through the queasy early-morning stage that most women did, and the last thing she would need was a long journey on a bumpy boat. Which left Mary facing a big decision.

Was she up to making the journey over on her own? The thought of it filled her with fear and anxiety. She had always vowed that she would never travel on her own, and she had never, ever expected to want to do it. She had imagined that by the time Brendan and Kate were adults, she would be an old lady, content to stay at home by the fire with her radio and her books, her main excursion of the week to Sunday Mass. But it hadn't turned out like that at all.

At forty-five years old, Mary, in many ways, felt the same as she'd always felt. In fact, in some ways she felt younger. That last holiday had given her the biggest lift she'd had in years. Whether it was because she had just passed the final stages in her recovery from her previous ill-health, or whether the sheer enjoyment of the holiday and the busy days she'd had in the shop had taken her mind off her anxieties, she didn't know. But *something* had happened that now made her seriously question the future she had been slowly drifting towards.

The seeds of it had certainly been sown that night at Lance's house – and in all probability by the dowdy widow with the tight bun, who was out there living a life for herself, and catching herself a third husband as she went along.

Mary read down Lance's letter to the part where he outlined all the summer activities that were coming up, activities he wanted her to join him in. A night of outdoor jazz at a stately house in Cheshire, a wedding he had been invited to in Manchester and the bowling club summer outing to Blackpool. She would never have such lovely events at home – if only she had the courage to make the journey over there all on her own.

Mary closed her eyes, clutching the letter tightly to her chest.

Chapter 63

Noelle looked at the small 'Holy Family' calendar pinned on the kitchen wall. It was now June, and Noelle saw that Gabrielle finished her first year in university the following week. She gave a little weary sigh at the thought. In all the time she'd been in the house with Dr Casey, she had never warmed to the doctor's niece.

Almost a year had flown around since Noelle Daly had seen her family. She had met up with Sarah on a couple of occasions, and she had nearly met up with her mother and the younger ones – until her father had got wind of their plans and put a stop to it.

Mrs Daly and Sarah had planned to catch the coach up to Dublin on the eighth of December – a Holiday of Obligation from school – and Noelle was going to meet up with them. She'd saved a few pounds from her wages, and intended to treat them all to lunch in a café, then buy a few bits and pieces for the younger ones for Christmas presents. But it had all come to nothing.

Instead of meeting her family, she ended up staying in Dublin for Christmas at Dr Casey's and had spent Christmas Day over in Gabrielle Casey's father's house. She and the nice young maid who worked there had thankfully sat at the kitchen table eating their own Christmas dinner, away from the stuffy family atmosphere, and away from Gabrielle's black moods.

It was Noelle's first Christmas away from home and she sorely missed her mother and sister and the younger ones – but she didn't miss the atmosphere that her father would no doubt manage to create. She didn't miss that one little bit, and there were times when she felt selfish about being so relieved to be away from home and all the trouble with her father.

She had bought presents for her mother and the children but, as far as she knew, the Christmas parcel she had sent them had never reached the house. Whether it had got lost in the post or whether it had been handed to her father and then destroyed and dumped was anybody's guess. She could have made a fuss with the post office in Ballygrace or checked with Mr O'Reilly the postman, but she had a sinking feeling in her heart that they would tell her it had indeed been delivered – straight into Matt Daly's hands.

Noelle wouldn't take a risk on that happening. It would only give rise to gossip with the nosy postmistress and her customers and further fuel the rumours that were undoubtedly going around Ballygrace about her long absence from home. No doubt a few wrong conclusions had already been jumped to, but Noelle could live with that. She certainly wasn't pregnant – as was often the case in these kind of circumstances – and she'd done nothing *that* terrible that had warranted her being barred from her own house.

All she'd done was go to the pictures in Tullamore with Brendan Flowers.

And if her father hadn't caused all the hullabaloo about it, their friendship mightn't have gone any further. But he had put two and two together and come up with a dozen, and that had sparked all the trouble off.

Now, looking back on it, Noelle didn't really regret a thing. In a funny sort of way, she reckoned that it had all been meant to happen. If her father hadn't run her out of the house that afternoon, then she would never have ended up in the boat with Brendan that night, and she might never have got to know him the way she did now.

Since their first weekend on the boat, they had taken every opportunity to meet up, and Brendan had even found a bed and breakfast around the bus station where they could stay, without any questions being asked. And after the first weekend, Brendan had come prepared for their romantic weekends with contraceptives that he'd got from some unnamed source in one of the pubs.

'There's no point in taking any chances,' he'd said, his face red with embarrassment.

Noelle had pressed her fingers to her lips. 'But isn't it a sin to use them?' she'd gasped. 'Isn't it illegal?'

Brendan had shrugged. 'If I let anythin' happen to you, Noelle, especially with the way things are at home, there would be a bigger sin committed.' Then, he had put his arms around her and stroked her hair. 'I don't want anything to go wrong between us – I don't want us forced into situations we're not ready for . . .'

A little warning bell had gone off at the back of Noelle's mind. She looked up at him with tear-filled eyes. 'You mean you don't want to get too involved with me?'

He shook his head. 'Too involved with you?' he repeated incredulously. 'How could I be more involved? I just mean that I don't want us getting into any sort of trouble while you're still at that doctor's place.' He paused. 'If we were in a different situation it wouldn't be so bad . . .'

The sound of the words *us* and *we* had filled Noelle's heart with joy, and gone some way to assuaging the guilt she felt for the path her life had taken recently. She'd been brought up strictly, and until her nights with Brendan had always adhered to the Catholic Church's teaching. She had never planned to be in the kind of situation she now found herself in – and she wasn't to blame for her being thrown out of her home. But whatever the rights and wrongs of it all, she wasn't going to give up the only bit of happiness she'd ever really had in her life.

She got on with her daily routine at work, giving her best to the job and trying not to tell her employer too many details about her weekends. Noelle had simply told the doctor that she sometimes stayed with her aunt, and since she knew the girl had no other company, she was happy to let her off for a Friday or Saturday night. Noelle reckoned that after the business over Carmel Foley, the doctor preferred her to keep her friendships well away from her work, and would rather give her a night off to spend with her relatives in town than have her consorting with any of the neighbours' workers.

Brendan had always come and gone from home as he wished, without answering to anyone, so there was no problem there. Mary Flowers was easily fobbed off and Kate wouldn't bother her head questioning him anyway. Both he and Noelle had decided that under no circumstances did they want Matt Daly to hear about them, so they had decided that it was best to trust no one around Ballygrace with their secret.

Every so often Brendan broached the subject of having to find a new job it the boats were taken off the canals, but Noelle was grateful that it hadn't happened yet – because *where* he would find a job would throw up a whole new set of problems.

Seeing each other as often as they could was difficult enough already.

Chapter 64

❧

Kate met Michael at the farmhouse gate one Friday evening in August and walked up through the garden alongside him – he pushing his bike and she walking slowly beside him as they chatted.

The garden had been a neglected wilderness up until Mary and Kate had started tackling it around Easter. They had spent mornings and afternoons and evenings – in between the cleaning and washing and baking – cutting back dead wood and pulling out clumps of weeds, sowing grass seed in the bare patches of lawn and planting rose bushes and small seedlings that were now, several months later, a blaze of colour.

Kate was elated at the news he'd just told her. 'So it's definitely official?' she checked.

Michael nodded his head. 'I finish on the boats at the end of August, then I'll be home full time after that.' He gave a sidelong grin. 'Well, at least I'll be home at *night* full time after that.'

Kate put her hand on his shoulder, her face suddenly serious. 'I don't care how long you spend out on the farms as long as you're at home with me at night.'

He gave a soft, easy laugh. 'I'll remind you of that, when you start giving out to me for spending too much time over at Thomas's place.' Then, his face grew more serious. 'I'll be delighted to be sleeping beside you every night, Kate, and I'll be delighted to be at home more ... but there's a bit of me that will miss the oul' boats and the lads. I've been on them a long time now. There's something about the way of life – the water and everything – ah, I can't really explain it.'

'I think I know what you're trying to say,' Kate said, smiling understandingly. 'Brendan is the very same about it – he might moan about working weekends now and again, and complain when he's had a rough trip with bad weather, but I know he's dreading the day they take the boats off the canal.'

'Ah, he'll find something else,' he said. 'For all his messin' around he's a good worker.'

Michael leaned his bike in its usual place under the kitchen window, and they went into the house through the back door. There was no great surprise as to the meal – always fish on a Friday, as decreed by the Catholic Church – but Kate did her best to vary the type of fish they had. Tonight, she had two good-sized salmon steaks, which were now in a dish swimming in a buttery sauce. The fish had been bought in Tullamore on Thursday morning, and kept cool at the back of the pantry until today. She had stayed out at her mother's cottage the night before, and on her way home had bought a fresh turnip and garden peas from the general shop in Ballygrace. Her mother had given her carrots and small potatoes from the garden, reminding Kate that by this time next year, they would have the vegetable garden going out at the farmhouse.

'It'll be *you* that will be giving *me* the vegetables then,' Mary had laughed, 'instead of the other way around.'

Kate had shaken her head. 'I can't imagine us ever getting that bit of the garden ready to sow vegetables, the state that it's in. Michael's old uncle couldn't have touched it in years.'

'Ah, but you said the very same thing about the flower-beds around the house and the lawn,' Mary had reminded her, 'and look at the difference in them only a few months later. That vegetable patch isn't half as bad as it looks. I'd say the old lad was using it up until the last year or two. We'll get Michael and Brendan to pull the bigger weeds out of it, and give it a good digging over for us, and once we get a few barrows of manure into it, it'll be grand. We'll have it all ready for planting in the spring.'

'D'you think so?' Kate had looked sceptical.

'I know so,' Mary had confidently replied. 'By the time the baby's crawling around next summer, you'll have all your own potatoes and carrots ready to pick in the garden.'

Kate planned to spend the rest of the summer – while she was still reasonably trim and able to bend – getting the garden into good shape. It would keep her occupied while Michael was out cutting and baling hay and doing all the heavy farm work that autumn

331

demanded. Also, it would fill the gap that her mother going away would undoubtedly leave.

'Any news over at your mother's?' Michael asked, taking off his working jacket to come and sit at the table.

'She's decided to go,' Kate said, raising her eyebrows and shrugging. 'Heading over next Tuesday morning.'

'You sound surprised,' he said.

'Maybe I shouldn't be,' Kate said, lifting a dish-towel and going over to check the fish in the oven, 'but I am actually surprised at her. Only last year she was a nervous wreck going over with me, and now she feels she's fit enough to make the trip on her own.' Holding the towel in both hands, she took the cream enamel dish out of the oven, and placed it on the top. Then, she lifted the lid off, stood back a little to let the steam rise out of it, and then peered in. All looked as it should, so she put the lid back on to keep it hot while she drained the boiled potatoes.

'I think it's great altogether,' Michael said, lifting the salt-cellar and giving it a shake to see if it needed re-filling. It was one of the many little helpful tasks that endeared him to Kate. 'Not that I've any great notion about ever going over to England myself – it holds no interest for me at all. But for somebody in your mother's position, with her sister over there and the shop an' all, it sounds like a very good idea to me.'

'Maybe . . .' Kate said, sounding doubtful. 'But I can't help but worry about her managing the boat and the train and everything. It was always me who had to mind the tickets and do any talking to the boat and train guards.' Kate drained the potatoes at the sink and then came over to the table to mash them. She lifted first the butter dish to put a few knobs of butter into the white, floury potatoes and then she poured a small amount of milk on top, then she began to mash them vigorously in the pot

'She'll be grand,' Michael said reassuringly. 'She's been back and forward on the boat and train enough times to know the ropes by now.' He put his head to the side. 'I see a big change in your mother since I first knew her – she's a lot more confident in herself. I can't really explain it, but there's a lightness about her that wasn't there before. Oh, she was always cheery and good-natured, but there something else there now that I can't quite put my finger on . . .'

Chapter 65

'It's as well you're going at the beginning of the week,' Brendan said, as he tucked into his Sunday dinner, 'for they're givin' fierce bad weather towards the end of the week. You wouldn't want to be out there on a boat in the middle of the Irish Sea if the weather gets too rough.'

Mary's heart leapt into her throat. This was the very sort of news she did not want to hear. 'Oh, don't be sayin' that!' she gasped, dropping her knife and fork onto her plate. 'You'll make me too terrified to go.' She looked out of the window now, as though expecting to see signs of the bad weather already, but the sky was still blue and the sun shining.

He gave her a grin and shook his head. 'You'll be grand,' he told her. 'The weather is to be fine up until Thursday, and anyway, I think it was off the west coast that they said would be the worst hit.' He leaned across the table and patted his mother's arm. 'You'll be grand . . . those big boats are built to stand up to anything. Sure, we're more likely to feel it on the oul' barge than you are, especially if we hit the river at the wrong time.' He shrugged his shoulders. 'Sure, you've nothing at all to worry about – you'll be well over and long settled in England before it hits here.'

'I hope so . . .' Mary said, not sounding too sure at all. 'Will you be all right?' she checked for the fourth time that day. 'You'll go over to Kate's for your dinner on the Sundays, won't you?'

'Now, don't go starting on that caper again,' Brendan said, shaking his head in exasperation. His mother would tie up every spare minute for him, if he let her. 'Didn't I manage just fine last year when ye were both away? What kind of a fool d'you think I am?' He nodded over to the small cooker he'd brought the previous year. 'I have the means there to cook anything I want, and there's places in Ballygrace and Daingean and Tullamore that'll serve me a good feed, so you can rest your mind on that one. And if it makes ye both happy, I'll go out to Kate and Michael's for my dinner on the Sunday. There – does that please you?'

'That's grand, so.' Mary gave him a grateful little smile, then she lifted her knife and fork again and began to pick at the chicken and potatoes and carrots on her plate. 'I wouldn't worry so much if you had a nice girl to look after you—'

'Enough now!' Brendan stated, his brows coming down very seriously, but there was a little humorous glint in his eye. 'Haven't I enough to put up with, with the pair of ye always going on at me? What would I need another woman in my life for?'

'But you're a good-lookin' lad,' Mary persisted, 'and you should be settled down by now with a lovely girl to look after you. I worry about you—'

'Well, don't be worryin',' he told her, 'you've no need to be worryin' at all.' He speared two pieces of carrot now on his fork. 'For all you know, I could have a girl tucked away somewhere.'

'I knew it!' Mary exclaimed. 'I was only sayin' it to Kate the other day. I said I wouldn't be at all surprised if Brendan had met up with some girl at the dancing in Dublin.'

'Who said anything about dancing in Dublin?' he said in a low, suddenly serious tone.

'Well,' Mary said, picking her words carefully, 'you seem to be spending a fair amount of time up there recently. You've been gone two weekend nights in the last month.'

'Checkin' up on me, are you?' he said accusingly. 'What d'you think I am? A complete amadán? A grown man having to answer to his mother now?'

'Ah, go away with you,' Mary said in the light manner that usually worked with him. 'It's only natural that any mother would be anxious to see her only son settled, and delighted if there was any signs of it.' She paused. 'You're not as big a devil as you let on, Brendan, you've settled down a lot recently. If you keep goin' the way you are, you'll make some girl a fine husband one day.'

'That'll do you now,' he replied. 'More than enough said.'

Armed with a list of Kate's travel instructions, Mary made her way over to England on the overnight boat the following Tuesday. As Brendan had predicted, the weather was calm and perfect for the journey, but she kept a constant watch on the sky as though her watchfulness might just waylay any plans it had for changing.

She travelled up on the coach to the bus station in Dublin then got a bus out to the boat as instructed, and was surprised both at the ease of the first part of the journey and at herself for managing it so easily. She refused Kate's suggestion of booking a berth, saying she would rather be out in the middle of the boat where she could see all that was happening. Also, she would be handy for the bar for a little nightcap to help her sleep, she thought, if she could get the courage to actually walk up to it.

As it turned out, in the queue to get on the boat, she met up with a lovely family who were heading over to Bolton – a young married couple with three children under five, and a grandmother called Josie, just a year or two older than herself. They found a good-sized area with cushioned benches where the children could stretch out and sleep, and comfortable chairs for the adults, and insisted that Mary joined them.

She was over the moon, as it meant she had company for the whole of the journey, and the man in the group – who she quickly found out were all from Wexford – was more than happy to troop up and down to the bar for drinks for all the adults. This cheered Mary up enormously as she knew that a bit of a drink – purely for medicinal purposes – would help her relax.

When they had finished their first drink, Mary insisted that he take money from her to buy them all another, and after that, she sat back and enjoyed the company and the mollifying glasses of sherry.

The two older women were enjoying their chat about their respective families so much that the boat was out of the port and on the sea before Mary even noticed, and by the time she thought to check her watch again, it was after midnight. A group of musicians had gathered at the side of the room, and as the boat moved further out into the dark, deep night waters Mary Flowers congratulated herself on having the bravery to set out on the journey all by herself.

Things started to quieten down around three o'clock in the morning, and the passengers found relatively comfortable spots in chairs or squeezed up on the benches beside the already sleeping children. Mary slept very little on the boat, but then – even with Kate and Brendan by her side – she never did. Every time the boat gave a little shudder, or when she heard the bottles in the bar giving their protesting jangling sound as the boat lurched, her previously calmed nerves were stretched again.

As the night neared its end and the black of the sky started to

335

break up, Mary Flowers drifted off to sleep, only to be woken up a few hours later by the excited screeches of the children and the clamour of feet passing her by in search of early morning cups of tea.

Mary joined the Wexford family for a breakfast of meat-paste and tinned salmon sandwiches, that they had made the previous day, and several comforting cups of tea, and before long the boat was on its final leg of the journey into the port at Holyhead.

Another few hours on the train with her new-found friends saw them swapping addresses and promising to keep in touch, and then Mary was in Manchester and walking out of the train station to where Lance Williams waited for her in his newly valeted car.

Chapter 66

The blustery weather that the radio station and Brendan had predicted crept into County Offaly in the early hours of Thursday. Kate woke early to the sound of a banging door on one of the farm outbuildings. She got out of bed and padded barefoot across the floor and out into the shadowy hallway, to look out of the window and check that it was indeed the decrepit door, normally held in place by a couple of stone blocks. Somehow, it had managed to loosen itself away from the blocks and was making a brave attempt to free itself entirely.

Although the banging noise was irritating, the heavy rain and the dark sky made her decide to ignore it. She would temporarily sort something out with it in the morning. She padded back to her bedroom, thinking that it was lucky her mother wasn't there. Mary would have come scurrying into Kate's room at the first sound of any threatening noise, and straight into the bed beside her if there was the slightest hint of thunder or lightning. Mary was of the old superstitious school of thought with things like that, and would go around closing all the curtains with her rosary clutched in her hand.

Kate went back to bed and slept fitfully, waking every hour or two until it was daylight, and when she looked out of the window again, she was relieved that the wind seemed to have eased.

Around mid-morning Kate went out into the yard to check on the banging door, and she managed to push it in hard and secure it again with the large bricks, adding a third one for good measure. Then, feeling the large drops of rain starting again, she scurried back indoors. She busied herself for the afternoon and evening, making soup from a large ham bone and a variety of vegetables – scraping her knuckles in the process as she grated carrots to thicken the mix – and then she settled down to knitting the matinée jacket she was working on for the baby.

She went back and forth into the kitchen every so often, checking on the soup that was simmering away on the hob, her thoughts flitting from Michael on the boat with Brendan, to her mother over in Stockport. She was half-relieved that her mother had gone and half-worried about her being over there on her own. But Kate knew deep down that she hadn't really any right to question her mother's actions as she was only trying to be independent, trying to take a bit more responsibility for her own life.

She only hoped that her mother wasn't going out and about drinking, the way she had the night of the garden party – or, even worse, making a fool of herself with a man again. Although Mary hadn't put a foot wrong since coming home last year, there was still something that told Kate her mother had never been quite the same since then.

The rain continued into the night, and as Kate went around closing curtains and blinds and locking the outside doors, she heard the door in the yard making a bit of a noise again – nothing like the banging during the night, but it was definitely rattling. She decided to go out again and see if she could secure it further, but when she opened the back door to the yard, she realised that the wind had really picked up. She threw a coat over her head and made a dash out into the wind and rain and across the yard. She had just reached the outhouses when the wind suddenly whipped the coat from her head and sent it tumbling across the yard. She looked back at it, and decided she'd probably get even wetter chasing after it.

She turned back towards the door, her long hair flying over her wet face now, making it difficult to see properly. She pushed the bricks in hard against the door again and lifted a fourth one on top. Then, as she saw a streak of lightning cross the dark sky, she decided that whether it held or not, the door would just have to do. She ran across the yard, picking up her coat she went, and was just securing the back door when she heard the low rumble of thunder.

When she got back into the shelter of the kitchen, Kate went over to the range and took one of the towels that was hanging on the bar, pressing it to her face.

'Thank God my mother's not at home tonight to hear this,' she murmured aloud to herself, 'and thank God it wasn't tonight she crossed the sea.' Then, a picture of Michael came into her mind and she thought of him and Brendan out on the boat. Hopefully, they'd have made their journey down to the Shannon River, turned the boat safely and would be starting on their way back up the canal by now. They'd probably moor the boat in for the night early, and if the wind got up really bad, they might take themselves off to a bed and breakfast for the night.

Kate gave a wry little smile, knowing that Brendan was always delighted to pull in at one of the towns and have the night there. He would know people in the pubs from bringing the barrels of beer who would give the lads a great welcome and a few free pints. The weather certainly wouldn't spoil Brendan's enjoyment, she thought to herself as she went upstairs to her and Michael's bedroom for a hairbrush to comb out the wet tangles in her hair.

Chapter 67

❧

Brendan came downstairs into the cabin of the boat, cursing aloud. 'Feckin' rain!' he called out to Jimmy Morris. 'I've just slipped on me arse on the feckin' deck, and I'm blidey soaked!' The rain was lashing down in sheets now, forming windswept pools of water on the top deck. 'I should have put the oilskins on earlier.'

Jimmy was at the cooker, making a bit of a supper of fried soda bread with rashers of bacon. He made suitably sympathetic noises and tried not to laugh at Brendan's description of his mishap, while steadying himself by hanging onto the edge of the cooker. 'Ah, ye'll be grand,' he called, grateful that his workmate had gone down to the other end to change out of his wet trousers and couldn't see his amusement.

'It's gettin' worse,' Brendan said. 'We could be held up this side of the feckin' Shannon all night, if we don't get down there soon.'

'What does Michael think?' Jimmy asked.

Brendan threw the damp trousers onto the bench and stepped into the oilskin ones, steadying himself with a hand on the bench against the rocking boat. 'He said we'll keep going and see how it goes. We haven't a big load to collect at the maltings at Banagher, and if we can get in and out of it quick enough, we should be grand.' The run to collect the malt at Banagher was a regular one for Guinness and saved the boat returning back up to Dublin empty.

'And what d'you think yourself?' Jimmy said, holding the frying pan with one hand as he turned the bacon slices over.

Brendan fastened the buckle on his belt now, staggering slightly. 'I'm inclined to agree with him. We don't want to get stuck down that end of the country for the feckin' weekend. If we can get the boat turned and headed back this way, we should get home for the weekend in reasonable time.' Brendan hoped that if all went to the usual schedule then he'd get up to Dublin to meet up with Noelle Daly. Pity about her father and the family living so close, because it would have been dead handy bringing Noelle down to the cottage when his mother was gone. They could have had the place completely to themselves.

There was a sudden thud on the side of the barge, indicating that it had hit the bank or maybe even another vessel, immediately causing the boat to lurch over at an angle. Downstairs, cupboards flew open, and pots and pans, newspapers and ledgers and tins of beans and other miscellaneous items came showering out, skidding noisily onto the wet floor.

'Feckin' hell!' Brendan shouted. 'We better get up there and see what it's hit.'

Michael O'Brien was at the back of the boat, struggling with the tiller. 'We're going to have to leave it, lads,' he yelled, when they went towards him, bodies angled against the gusts. 'That was a bad one there – landed the boat in on the bank. It must be getting up to gale-force winds by now. If we make Shannon Harbour, that'll be good enough going. I don't think we'll make Banagher tonight . . . I think we'd be mad.'

The two deck-hands looked at each other from under their wide-brimmed hats, and Brendan shrugged. 'You're the captain,' he called, his voice obviously resigned. 'If you're not inclined to push on . . .' He moved his feet now to steady himself on the heaving deck.

'*Safety!*' Michael called back. 'The boat could go over in this wind if we were out in open waters – it's not worth the risk.'

'But we could be stranded out here for ages,' Brendan argued, the wind whipping his voice away and making him shout louder. 'The radio is givin' worse weather for the whole of the weekend . . . if we don't make a go of it now, we could be stuck on the canal for days.'

Michael shrugged. 'We can see what it's like when we hit Shannon Harbour . . .'

'Do you want me to take the tiller for a bit?' Brendan offered. 'You could go down and get a cup of tea and a bite to eat.'

Michael looked from Brendan to Jimmy, then he nodded, his face weary from the effort of steering the boat. 'See if you can make a better fist of it for a while – it's the worst I've handled in a long time.'

By the time the boat had blustered its way against the rising wind and rain into Shannon Harbour, Brendan had conceded to Michael's misgivings about the weather. The dramatic flashes of lightning across the racing black sky, and the increasing rumbles of thunder quickened his decision. That, and the bad fall that Jimmy had when he came up on deck at one point and was thrown across the boat into the barrels of beer.

That's what I feckin' well get, Jimmy thought ruefully as he nursed his badly bruised elbow, for sneering and laughing at the big fella's fall earlier on.

'We may look for a bed and breakfast for the night, lads,'

340

Brendan announced as they moored into the dock at Shannon-bridge. 'There's nothin' else for it.'

Between the three of them, they spent longer than usual making sure the boat was secure and tight against the bank. The way things were with the wind and lashing rain, they could come back in the morning and find the boat in splinters from continual banging against the rough stone wall – and then they would be in serious trouble.

'Watch your feet when we get on the bank,' Michael reminded them as they prepared to disembark. 'It's full of oul' slippery red clay here when it's raining. One of the lads took a bad tumble on the boat last year when he carried it on his boots onto the deck.'

'We've had enough tumbles this evenin' already,' Brendan laughed, 'and that's without a drink – haven't we, Jimmy lad?'

'Ah, sure at least we'll get a few oul' pints and a dry bed,' Jimmy commiserated as they walked up the road, all three still dressed in oilskins from head to foot, their decent dry clothes in rainproof bags and their bodies at an angle against the driving rain.

'I'd rather have had it in Banagher,' Brendan shouted back. He made a fist and shook it up to the sky. 'Feckin' oul' weather. Ye can give everything else your best shot, but it's the one shaggin' thing that'll beat you.'

Michael nodded in agreement, weary from the trip down and his mind half on Kate, who would be enduring this spectacular feat of weather entirely on her own. Hopefully, the house and the surrounding trees would hold up to it. Himself and Thomas had done their best to secure the house and the outbuildings for the winter, but the ferocity of this weather couldn't have been anticipated.

Maybe, he mused as they tramped along the road, this bad journey was meant to happen. Because it had definitely confirmed his decision to get off the boats. He'd been looking forward to getting home tomorrow evening, every bit as much as Brendan, if not more. As he'd told Kate at the weekend, he'd be sorry to leave the boats and the canals – but the time had come. His life and his responsibilities had changed. It was a different kettle of fish altogether now that the baby was on the way. And he'd known when he married Kate that it was going to be a case of give and take – he couldn't put himself first any longer. Besides, it wouldn't be fair. Kate had willingly put aside any ambitions she had for a career in nursing when she agreed to marry him. She had made no huge deal of it, but she had let him know that she'd had other options. Whilst he couldn't imagine a woman going out to work when she was married and with a family, he'd had to acknowledge that some women did – and that Kate Flowers may well have been one of them. But she'd bowed to his wishes, she'd let him know that she'd chosen him above any other kind of life.

And he now had to make the same choice.

Chapter 68

❧

Dr Casey had gone to Evening Devotions, as she sometimes did. She left it entirely up to Noelle whether she wanted to accompany her or not – sometimes her maid did, and other nights she didn't.

Tonight, Noelle had decided against it. Apart from the horrible wet, windy night that had suddenly blown in, she had all the signs of her period coming on, and felt an hour lying on the bed with a hot-water bottle and a book would be more in her line.

She had been reading for about ten minutes when a sound came at the back door. She put her book down, unsure as to what the noise actually was. There were branches and bits of trees being blown around the garden, and she wondered if something had just hit the door. Then, a loud, almost frantic rapping on the door left her in no doubt. Startled, she dropped the book and ran in her stockinged feet to the door.

'Who is it?' she called, trying to sound sure and assertive. If it had been during the day, she might have opened it without a thought – but a dark, windy night was very different.

'Carmel . . .' an unfamiliar, strained voice called back. Then, 'It's me, Noelle, it's Carmel,' came in her calmer, usual tone.

Noelle took a deep breath – trying to think of a firm, inoffensive reply that she could shout through the locked door.

'Please . . .' Carmel called. 'I'm going away and I just wanted to have a few words before I left . . .'

'I know you won't understand,' Carmel said, her voice cracking with emotions as she sat on the bed beside Noelle. 'I know you'll think I've been stupid, but I really did think that I loved him.'

'Don't go upsetting yourself again,' Noelle soothed, patting the girl's hand. I don't think you've been stupid at all.' This last bit was a lie, because although Noelle had always had her suspicions about Carmel Foley's relationship with her employer, she had never been really sure. Part of her couldn't imagine any girl of her age – particularly a very pretty girl like Carmel – bothering with a man old enough to be her father. The thought of it gave her the creeps.

'I shouldn't have slept with him,' Carmel said, 'that was my big mistake.' She sniffled into her hanky. 'I had him where I wanted him until then . . . buying me presents, taking me away to a hotel with him and the boys. I could have asked him for nearly *anything* and I'd have got it . . .' She looked up at Noelle with big watery eyes. 'I thought we might have even got married. You hear of plenty of girls marrying their bosses. I didn't care that he was older, and I thought we liked the same things.' She dabbed her eyes now. 'I'd even got him listenin' to Elvis Presley and Pat Boone . . . and he'd got me to listen to some of his classical music. I thought we were going great together . . .'

'So, what happened?' Noelle asked, eager to hurry the story up before Dr Casey's return from church, but intrigued and tantalised at the same time by what she was hearing.

'It was his birthday two weeks ago,' Carmel explained, 'and he asked me to go away for the night with him – just the two of us.'

'And what age was he?' Noelle couldn't help herself – suddenly hungry for all the gory details. 'And where did ye go?'

'Forty-five,' Carmel sniffed, as if it was of no consequence that he was more than double her age. 'He took me to a hotel down the country – Athlone, I think it was.'

'And,' Noelle ventured, 'is that where it happened?' She couldn't believe that Carmel would actually have had sex with that boring, older man.

Carmel nodded. 'And he's never been the same to me ever since . . . it was as if *that* was all he wanted.' She rubbed her eyes again, very hard – almost angrily – with her hanky.

'And was it only that once it happened?' Noelle checked.

Carmel shook her head. 'Four or five times over that weekend – he was at it all the flamin' time ... couldn't leave me alone.' She took a big shuddering breath. 'And I didn't even enjoy it a bit. I don't know what all the hullabaloo about sex is. In fact, it was really sore. He took that long every flamin' time, I was red raw down below. I still am.' Her eyes widened. 'I didn't know that it took so long for men to ... you know ... to be satisfied. One time he went on for well over half a bleedin' hour!'

Noelle gave a little shrug now, and could instantly feel her face starting to burn. Nothing that Carmel had just described sounded a bit like the way things were with her and Brendan. After their first time together it had always been great, and Brendan was often so desperate for her that the problem was having to take it slower. And she felt as keen on it as Brendan – the minute she saw him she wanted to take his clothes off. But then, she wasn't going to tell Carmel or anyone else that. 'Maybe it was his age ... forty-five is fairly old.'

'I don't know what it bleedin' was,' Carmel uttered, 'but I'll tell you one thing, Noelle – if you take my advice, you won't go rushin' into sex with any lad. It's not anything like it's cracked up to be.' She shook her head adamantly. 'No wonder women don't talk about it much – it's because it's so bleedin' sore and so bleedin' boring.'

'So you didn't enjoy the hotel or anything?' Noelle quizzed, sneaking a look at her watch. They had about another quarter of an hour before the doctor returned.

'I didn't see that much of it,' Carmel moaned. 'I think he was trying to keep me up in the bedroom in case anybody saw us. He was terrified of being seen for some reason – I even heard him sayin' at the reception that I was his bloody *niece*.'

'And did you say anything to him about it?'

'What could I say?' Carmel shrugged. 'We went down for meals to the restaurant and then out for runs in the car.' She rolled her eyes dramatically then shook her head. 'That was another thing – you should have heard what he wanted me to do to him in the car out at a lake in the middle of bleedin' nowhere! That's what finished it for me – that's one of the reasons that I'm leavin'.'

Noelle's eyes widened. 'What?'

Carmel pressed the hanky to her lips and lifted her eyes to the ceiling. 'I can't say it . . . it's too revoltin' . . . and anyway, you'd be absolutely shocked.' She halted now, closing her eyes in anguish. 'I can't tell you how glad I am to be away from him, Noelle. And me thinkin' all that time that he was a lovely man – a real posh gentleman – when he was only after one thing.'

'He sounds terrible,' Noelle whispered, her mind working furiously as to what Ben Lavery might have suggested that was so disgusting. She would have to ask Brendan if he had any idea.

'Anyway,' Carmel said, giving a huge sniff, 'since that weekend things have been really awkward . . . and I was just thinkin' of getting myself another job, when he told me this afternoon that he doesn't need me any more. He said his mother has offered to come up from Tipperary and stay for a couple of months, and that she'd have her own ideas about the way things should be run in the house . . .' She shook her head. 'I'd swear he only lost interest in me after we went to bed together. I can't think of anything else . . .'

Noelle stood up now to give Carmel the hint. She couldn't take the risk of Dr Casey finding out that she'd been in the house. 'Maybe it's just as well; in the long run you might be glad you went.' She paused. 'Just think what would happen if you became pregnant . . .'

'Thanks be to God and his blessed mother that *that* didn't happen.' Carmel stood up, too, slightly shivering and her arms crossed over her chest. 'I've decided that when I get back home, I'm goin' to train as a hairdresser. It's something I always wanted to do . . .' A little smile crept on her face – the first time she'd smiled that evening. 'And at least I'm not going away empty-handed.'

'How do you mean?' Noelle said, her brow furrowing.

'He gave me fifty pounds on top of me wages – he said it was a kind of bonus to help me to get back on me feet.'

'Fifty pounds?' Noelle repeated in an incredulous voice. 'That was good of him at least . . .'

Carmel walked towards the bedroom door now. 'Anyway, I know we've not seen much of each other recently with that oul' cow of a doctor, but I wanted to say goodbye to you . . .'

'I'm glad you did,' Noelle said, suddenly feeling very sad. There would be nobody her own age around the place now, apart from the awful Gabrielle, who didn't count. 'I would have worried where you'd disappeared to, and there's nobody around here that I could have asked.'

They stood at the back door for a couple of minutes, watching the rain battering down. 'D'you think you'll stay here much longer?' Carmel suddenly asked.

Noelle shrugged. 'God only knows . . . I've nowhere else to go at the minute.'

'You don't want to go wastin' your life on that old witch and her niece. You want to get yourself out there and meet a nice fella and get married.'

Noelle looked back at her and suddenly heard herself saying, 'I'm still seeing that lad I told you about.'

Carmel's eyes grew large. 'You've surely kept that quiet.'

'And I'm going to keep it quiet for a bit longer,' she said, smiling, 'because it's the only thing that's kept me going.'

A flash of lightning cut across the sky.

'Jesus, Mary and Joseph!' Carmel screeched. 'We better get inside before we're struck down!' She dug into her cardigan pocket now and took out a scrap of paper. 'That's me ma's address in Ballymun. You're good at writin' letters, so I thought we could keep in touch.' She gave a little smile. 'When I get me trainin', you can come over and get your hair done for nothin'.'

'Thanks,' Noelle said, taking the paper from her. 'I'll write to you next week, I promise.'

Then a particularly loud clap of thunder sounded and the two girls flew off in opposite directions.

Chapter 69

❦

'I think the table looks very nice now,' Lance said, stepping back to survey their handiwork.

'Lovely . . .' Mary agreed, as she looked at the round table with the pink tablecloth and matching pink napkins, and the silver cutlery. It was the first time she'd ever set a formal table in her life, and her hands had been shaking when she started out, but as usual

Lance had helped and guided her. There was nothing he wasn't able to do, or so it seemed to her.

Mary looked up at the clock now. 'They'll be here in about ten minutes.'

Lance came round the table towards her and gathered her up in his arms. 'Oh, Mary,' he said, 'how is it that the most ordinary thing turns into something special when I'm with you?'

Mary laughed, embarrassed now. 'Sure, I've enjoyed myself every bit as much as you.' She waved her hand in the direction of the table. 'It's all a great novelty ... I never do anything like this back in Ireland.'

The smile disappeared from his eyes. 'But surely,' he said, his voice hesitant, 'it's not just a *novelty* – something short-lived to fill your holiday? At least, I hope it's not just that ... I've counted the days since last summer.'

Mary felt her chest tighten. How was it that she always said the wrong thing? She was no good at all with words, she thought. 'No, no,' she said, stroking his arm. 'I didn't mean that. What I meant is that every day with you is excitin' and different ... it's all grand. Even walking out to the butcher's shop for the steaks this afternoon was lovely.' She took a deep breath. 'I've never enjoyed myself so much in my life, Lance – you make me feel like a young girl again.'

'You *are* a young girl, Mary,' he said softly, stooping to kiss her on the lips. 'And you make me feel like a young man.'

On the day she arrived in Manchester, Lance had suggested that they invite Rose and Graham around for a meal to his house on the Thursday night. Mary had got up this morning and sorted the breakfast out, and she'd busied herself doing her usual bits of tidying around the house for Rose, then she'd gone down into the shop to see if they needed a hand.

After only a few minutes of watching the energetic Frankie striding up and down the shop floor and climbing up and down the ladder in the back-shop, she knew she wasn't needed at all.

'Go on,' Rose had urged, 'Get yourself over to Lance's house and give him a hand getting the dinner ready for us. I've never had a man cook me a meal before, and we don't want us all to get poisoned.'

'No flamin' fear of that,' Graham had interrupted. 'It's a well-known fact that men make the best chefs in the world. And anyway, old Lance must know a thing or two about cookin' – he's been looking after himself for the last few years.'

'An' what would you know about cooking?' Rose had demanded. 'You couldn't even boil a bloomin' egg!'

Mary had walked around to Lance's house and they'd chatted about what was needed for the meal that night, and what time it should all be cooked. Then, they went out to the shops for the meat and vegetables that Lance needed and for the ingredients for the lemon meringue pie that Mary would make and put in the oven to cook while she was getting bathed and ready for the night.

As Mary lay back in the bath, fragranced with Rose's lemon-scented bath cubes, she found herself pondering over all the little gaps that were in her life before, and she hadn't even known it. Every minute of the last two days had been filled with something – whether it was chatting to Rose or going up and down to the shop or spending time with Lance. She was so busy she hardly had the time to ask herself if she was anxious or worried about anything. In fact, she had been so busy that she hadn't even found the time to pop down to the wool shop to buy the pattern and materials for the baby outfit she had planned to knit for Kate. And to think that knitting by the fire at night had been one of the highlights of her quiet life before.

Without telling her, Lance had taken a fortnight's holiday from his work, so they could spend as much time with each other as possible. When he first told her in the car on the way back from the station, Mary had felt her chest tighten. It sounded like a huge responsibility, as though she would be accountable for filling that big long stretch of time.

What on earth would they do with all those hours together? What would they find to say to each other? But the last couple of days had given her all the answers. They would simply just *be* together – taking things as they came. Like today, when they had done very ordinary things together in Lance's house, sitting chatting over cups of tea, walking around the garden dead-heading the roses, walking up to the butcher's shop. And all of that fitted in around the busy backdrop of Rose's house and shop.

One of the things that Mary found she really enjoyed was spending time with people her own age. She hadn't realised that being at home all the time with Kate and Brendan had made her feel and act like an old woman at times. She could now see that she had become used to sitting on the edge of their lives, and not living her own.

It had become all the clearer to her when she started to spend time at the farmhouse with Kate, where she just replicated the routines she had back in the cottage – the washing and cleaning and sorting out the garden. Oh, it was grand for Kate, because she could look forward to Michael coming back at the weekends, and now they had their first baby to look forward to too. It was wonderful for Kate and it was the way things should be. When Mary came back to the cottage at the weekends, she then got stuck into the cooking and cleaning again for Brendan, until Monday came around again. Eventually, Mary knew, Brendan would sort himself out with a new job, and it could be in Dublin or it could be in America. It could be anywhere. But one thing was clear, when he did sort himself out, Mary wouldn't enter into the picture.

It was time for Brendan to lead his own life as Kate was now doing, and she couldn't and *wouldn't* expect him to feel responsible for her. For all he was an awkward devil at times – and the clashes between him and Kate drove her mad – he was a decent fellow underneath it all. And he had kept the three of them afloat since he'd left school. He'd taken on the role of the bread-winner and he'd done it well. It was time for him now to have his own life, and one way or another that had to happen.

In a lot of ways, Kate moving out to the farmhouse had been a good thing. It had given Mary a change of routine and a change of scenery, and it had made her realise that she was perfectly capable of filling time on her own. The solitary afternoons spent tending to her flowers and vegetables and the quiet nights sitting by the fire, reading or knitting, all had their place. When they were part of a week that was busy with comings and goings, they were a comforting, welcoming respite.

But Mary now realised that it couldn't be her *whole* life. She couldn't just slip into old age, stealing bits from her son and daughter's lives, pretending that it was her own life. She knew that she needed more – and as she went about the routine in Rose's house and the shop, she discovered that she had a role here and a place in amongst people her own age that she would never have back home. Rose made her feel more confident and lively and she laughed more in a day here than she did in a week at home.

And then there was Lance – a whole new dimension to her life that was still unfolding and still surprising her. A lovely man with lovely manners, who she now knew had very strong feelings for her. And the more she got to know him, the stronger her feelings were growing for him, both emotionally and – embarrassing and worrying in a way for her – physically.

How could they not?

How could any woman's head not be turned by his smart appearance and his attentiveness – not to mention his lovely house and car, and his beautifully tended garden? If she'd been asked to paint a picture of the perfect man, this would have been it. Truthfully, she might have preferred him to be Irish rather than English – but you couldn't hold that against him. There was a little bit ingrained in her that the best men were always of her own stock.

But the fact was, Mary mused, she had never met a man like Lance Williams in Ireland, nor was she ever likely to. He was completely different to any man she'd ever met. Where their friendship would lead now was anybody's guess, but Mary decided that she wasn't going to worry tonight – or tomorrow night. She would start worrying when a problem came up. She would face it then. Tonight was another special night that she would look back on and remember during the long, dark winter nights back home.

She reached to the corner of the bath now to check the time on her watch and decided she had better get moving if she was to be back at Lance's house again for six o'clock.

When he opened the door to her, Lance stared at Mary for so long that her cheeks flushed red. 'What's the matter?' she asked anxiously, patting the back of her hair in case the light wind had made it stick up.

'Oh, I'm sorry . . .' he said, suddenly realising that he was keeping her on the doorstep. He opened the door wide and ushered her in. 'I couldn't help it,' he said when they were both inside. He looked at her now, starting with the softly curled hair that Kate had coloured for her on Sunday, all the way down to her feet. 'Oh, Mary . . . you look so, so lovely . . .'

Mary blushed even harder, but was secretly delighted that her efforts hadn't gone unnoticed. She was wearing a new peach-coloured dress that she'd bought in Tullamore the week before in the summer sales. It was one that had a cross-over front – not too low – and tied at the side with half-length fluttery sleeves. It came just to her knees, and showed off her nicely shaped legs, which looked a little longer than usual in her high-heeled white sandals. And, with Rose's encouragement, she had experimented with a bit of mascara and a peach-coloured lipstick to match the dress, which, she had to agree, definitely lit up her whole face.

When she had finished dressing and putting on her bit of make-up, Mary had also dabbed some eau de toilette on her wrists, behind her ears and down her cleavage. And, as Lance drew her into his arms now – breathing in the feminine combination of the lemon bath cubes she had bathed in, and the sprinkling of perfume – she knew his compliments were genuine. And as his lips touched hers, she felt a now-familiar stirring of desire deep in the pit of her stomach, and she tightened her arms around his neck.

A short time later they were into the swing of cooking the meal together – Lance on the grilling of the steaks and making the onion gravy, while Mary took charge of the vegetables and the potatoes. They stood at either side of the cooker, sometimes chatting, and at other times just slicing and chopping vegetables in companionable silence.

When the preparations were well underway, Lance poured them each a glass of light, sparkling wine, then touched their glasses together in a toast.

'To us,' he said, 'and many more happy evenings like this.'

'D'you know something, Lance?' Mary said, as they stood back, surveying the carefully cooked oven-ready dishes. 'We haven't eaten a bit yet, and I feel as if I've thoroughly enjoyed myself already! If I had to go home now, I'd feel as if I'd had a great time.'

'And me,' Lance told her, 'and this is your holiday only starting.'

Rose and Graham arrived a little while after the allotted time, Graham carrying four bottles of beer and a bottle of sherry.

There was a little glint in Rose's eye as she came into the sitting-room. 'We didn't want to come too early in case we interrupted anything . . .'

Mary waited until Lance's back was turned and she made a face and held a little warning fist up to her sister, which only made Rose laugh all the more.

Well after midnight, Rose and Graham got up from the dining-table to head home – both slightly unsteady on their feet.

'Oh, I shouldn't have had that last sherry,' Rose said, lifting up her handbag. 'I know I'm going to regret it in the morning.'

'I did tell you that when you were makin' me pour it out for you,' Graham retorted, winking over at Lance and Mary. 'Thanks, Lance, that was a crackin' meal – no two ways about it.'

Mary got up to go now too, but Rose put out a warning hand. 'There's no need for you to rush back, Mary,' she said, a sweet smile on her face. 'You can stay and give Lance a hand with the washing-up – can't she, Lance?'

Lance looked slightly flustered. 'I wouldn't want to keep her back . . . I can easily manage on my own.'

'Not at all, mate,' Graham said, putting on his jacket. 'You've done enough with all that cookin' – let Mary get on with the dishes now.' He gave Rose a playful slap on the rear end. 'The best chefs in the world are men – but they never do the washing-up. Did you not know that that's what they have women for?'

There was a slight air of tension as Lance and Mary walked back into the sitting-room, A feeling of awkwardness between them as they gathered up the plates and cutlery and Lance put the crumpled pink linen napkins in the washing-basket. It grew and grew until there was a deafening silence between them as Mary washed the dishes and plates and knives and forks and Lance methodically dried them.

Then, as the last knife went tidily into the top drawer beside all the others, Lance suddenly threw the tea-towel down on the worktop and pulled Mary into his arms. His kisses – fuelled by the wine and brandy he'd drunk – were slightly rougher and harder than the way he'd kissed her before. But Mary didn't mind in the least as she kissed him back with equal enthusiasm.

Then, he took her by the hand and led her through the kitchen and out into the hallway and upstairs into his large, airy bedroom with the blue regency striped curtains and the deep blue shiny satin bed-spread with the matching padded pillowslips.

'Mary,' he said, as they sat down on top of the bed together, 'I want you to know that I bought a brand-new bed especially for you coming over. I wasn't sure if you'd ever see it, or if we'd get this far together ... but I thought that in the wonderful event that we did, we wouldn't have any ghosts between us.' He ran his hands over the satin cover. 'And all the bedding is brand new as well ... I put it on the bed for the first time this morning.'

'Oh, Lance ...' Mary said, running her own hands over the soft, luxurious fabric. 'I'm just a bit scared ... I'm not sure I'll be able to ... it's been years and years.'

His hand sought hers now. 'I feel exactly the same,' he whispered. 'But I'm sure we can learn again together ...'

Chapter 70

The pub was very quiet – a few of the locals sitting up at the bar and one or two other tables. The three boatmen sat at a table beside the warming turf fire. They had a deck of cards divided between them, and were just about to go into their fourth game of the evening.

'Do you think it has eased any?' Michael O'Brien said, craning his neck to look above the stained-glass window towards the plain glass at the top.

'I doubt it,' Brendan said, shaking his head. 'We may content ourselves to have the night here, and see what tomorrow brings.' He examined his cards for a bit longer, then suddenly threw a jack of diamonds down on the table and then grinned up at the youngest boatman. 'Now, Jimmy boy, see if you can better that!'

While Brendan and Jimmy continued with their usual bit of banter, Michael glanced back at the window again, his face thoughtful. He was unable to settle for some reason, and the two pints of beer he'd drunk so far hadn't relaxed him at all.

He kept thinking of Kate at home on her own on a night like this, wishing even Mary had been with her for company. He knew his mother-in-law would have been terrified of the thunder and lightning, but at least they would have been company for each other.

Maybe, he thought, leaving the boats and the canals would turn out to be the best thing he ever did. Kate would be relieved to have him home, he knew, and his mother and Tom would be delighted, too.

Every time Michael spoke to Tom lately, he was full of the great plans he had to expand the farm at home, and reclaim some of the fields that Uncle Sean had set to neighbouring farmers. Tom had suggested that they might go into sheep-rearing as well as the cattle – a plan he'd always been suggesting to his father, but they'd never got around to it.

'I think we might have enough on our hands with the cattle, for the time being,' Michael had said only the week before. 'I've to think of Kate and the baby over the winter. Maybe next year, when things are more settled.'

'We could take somebody else on,' Tom had suggested. 'You said that Kate's brother could be looking for work when the boats finish – would he be any good on a farm? I know the two of ye get on well.'

Michael was surprised. He'd never thought of them taking anyone from outside the family into the farm. But then, he supposed, Brendan was family now, in a roundabout way. 'It might be worth thinking about,' he said cautiously. 'Let's see what next year brings . . .'

Tom had looked back at him and suddenly smiled. 'It could bring another wedding . . .'

Michael's brow had deepened in confusion. 'You?' he asked, and when Tom nodded he could hardly hide his shock.

'A girl that works in the bank in Tullamore,' Tom had gone on to tell him, amidst much clearing of his throat and flushing of his face.

When Michael had told Kate the news, she had expressed delight and then her face had suddenly grown serious. 'Where will they live?' she asked.

Michael shrugged. 'Oh, Tom will work something out.'

'Will he move the girl into the big farmhouse along with your mother?' Kate had checked.

Michael had shrugged again. 'I've really no idea—'

'You might have to think of something,' Kate had said quietly, 'because by rights, Tom has a share in this house.'

Around ten o'clock, Michael took a walk outside to the Gents', and was sure that the wind had calmed down a bit from earlier. It was still raining heavily, but it definitely wasn't quite as blustery. Then, as he looked up at the dark night sky, another flash of lightning streaked across it to be followed a few moments later with a clap of thunder. He shook his head and uttered a curse under his breath and then walked quickly back into the pub.

There were three steaming glasses of hot golden liquid now in the middle of the table.

'Whiskey?' Michael said, looking from one boatman to the other.

'To warm ye up and to calm ye down!' Brendan said, giving him a sidelong grin. 'You're like a feckin' oul' mother hen goin' in and out, and looking out of the window. Will ye settle down, for Christ's sake, Michael, and just enjoy the oul' night?' He rapped his knuckles on the table beside Michael's face-down hand of cards. 'We have a serious game goin' on here, and you're only giving it half your attention.' Brendan lifted one of the glasses and plonked it down in front of his workmate. 'Now, drink that up and relax yourself, man. We're going nowhere tonight, and we might as well accept it.'

Michael lifted the glass and took a slug of the sweet hot toddy. Maybe he did need to relax, but he couldn't shake off the feeling he had about Kate and her being alone in that big old house all by herself.

By eleven o'clock, Michael was refusing any more drink and telling Brendan that it could sit on the table until the morning for all he cared. 'I know when I've had enough,' he told his brother-in-law, 'and I've had *more* than enough tonight.'

'Aw, go on,' Brendan said, checking through the punts and the coins in his hand. 'You'll have one more pint before the bar closes—'

'I've had enough,' Michael stated emphatically. 'I shouldn't have drunk that last pint nor the whiskey before it, so don't waste your money, because you'll have to drink it yourself or have it poured away.' Then he glanced back at the dark window, and seeing that the rain wasn't pouring down in the absolute sheets it had been earlier, he stood up. 'If it's not as bad outside,' he announced, 'I'm going to take a walk back to the boat.'

'Are ye mad?' Brendan said, screwing up his face in disbelief. 'It'll be muck up to the eyeballs down there and the deck will be feckin' swimming . . .'

Michael pushed his chair in against the table, undeterred. 'I just want to give it a bit of a check-over . . . see if there was any damage or anything like that. I won't be long.'

'You're a feckin' eedjit goin' out into that oul' wind and rain,' Brendan told him. 'Isn't he, Jimmy?'

Jimmy grinned from one to the other and shrugged his shoulders, preferring not to fall on either side. Like all quiet men, he had his own thoughts, and he was wisely keeping them to himself.

The minute the fresh air hit him, Michael O'Brien knew that he shouldn't have had the last few drinks. Why he had let Brendan coax him into them, he didn't know. His mind had been so far away at times during the night that he had been lifting glasses and swallowing down the drinks without monitoring what had passed his lips.

But he could feel it now. The slightly lighter rain was hitting off his face and body as it had when they left the boat, but it wasn't bothering him in the same manner. In fact, he found as he walked along he was actually smiling to himself. Smiling as he thought of his beautiful dark-haired wife and the beautiful baby they were due to have in a few months' time.

He was thanking God that he'd had the courage to go against his mother and the rest of the family when he'd asked her to marry him. Already, he knew, they were discovering all the good qualities that he'd seen in Kate when they first met. It had taken them some time, but his mother had told him only recently that she was sorry for the way they'd treated her in the beginning. Sorry that they had judged her wrongly. And his sisters had been the same. They mightn't have said it in so many words, but their actions when they were over at the house or when Kate visited them spoke volumes. They were all growing to like her and when the baby came, he was sure it would settle things down completely.

He walked towards the boat, musing to himself about Kate and the baby and Tom's suggestion that Brendan might come to work on the farm with them. Brendan wasn't a bad oul' stick at the end of the day. And he had improved recently – he was showing a more thoughtful and intelligent side this last six months than Michael had ever imagined he was capable of.

Michael wondered now if Brendan's change in attitude had anything to do with the regular trips that he had been making up to Dublin. He knew from the lads around the docks up there that there was a girl involved, and if his instincts were anything to go by, it sounded very like the girl they had brought up on the barge that night last year – Noelle Daly. A few times he had thought to mention it to Kate, because he knew they were friends, but he didn't want to go saying anything in case he was wrong. If there *was* something going on, Michael reasoned, then at some stage either Brendan or Noelle would surely come out and say it.

There was a bit of a lull in the rain as Michael walked towards the darkest part of the canal where the boat was moored, but there was still enough falling for the surface of the huge puddles to give the impression of bubbling, simmering water. He picked his steps carefully across the grass, mindful of the bare patches that left the red slippery clay exposed to the rain.

When he got down onto the actual tow-path, he slowed down to get a good view of the abandoned boat. He wondered if the knock the boat had got earlier had done much damage to the outside. He walked up and down the tow-path for a few minutes, trying to estimate where exactly it might have hit the wall – but with the shadowy dark and the constant drizzle it was impossible to see anything properly.

He stopped now to look down onto the deck, where he could see the deep pools of rain that had gathered on the tarpaulin and were still dripping their wet way onto the wooden floor and down the stairs and into the living quarters. Michael wondered now if there was much damage downstairs and whether it was likely to slow the whole operation up in the morning. He glanced upwards – the blackish-grey sky was quietening down now, and by morning all traces of the storm could quite easily be gone. He gave a little sigh. They would have some job clearing up after this night.

He stared at the slightly moving wet boat and on a sudden impulse decided to go on board and check it out for himself. He leaned forward to catch the end of the boat and steady it, when suddenly the red clay on the sole of his boots made his foothold slip from under him. Then – in the same clumsy moment – the boat jerked treacherously out of his grasp, propelling him head first into the black yawning gap before coming back to close in on him.

Down and down he tumbled – between the murky darkness of the boat and the wall – and into a watery oblivion.

Brendan Flowers and Jimmy Morris had given Michael a good hour or more after leaving the pub before reluctantly going out to look for him – Brendan cursing under his breath about having to go out in the feckin' oul' wind that had picked up again, and the rumbling rainy sky. As the two boatmen neared the rocking boat, there had been neither sight nor sound of their third workmate.

'What do you think?' Brendan called into the wind, shielding his eyes against the heavy rain to look towards the tiller.

Jimmy wiped his wet face with the back of his hand and shrugged. 'I can't see anythin' – maybe he's down below ... He could have fallen asleep or anything. He's not used to the amount of drink he took tonight.'

They looked at each other for a few seconds without speaking, then Brendan reached for the edge of the boat – just as Michael O'Brien had done a short time ago – and while Jimmy held it fast for him, he jumped on. Then, when he felt he had got his balance again, he started to move across the darkened rain-soaked deck.

'Are you all right there, Michael?' he called hopefully, shielding his eyes against the darting rain, checking the tarpaulin-covered loads as he went. 'Michael?' Brendan called again, looking towards the tiller. A sudden fear clutched at his stomach as he realised the deck was completely empty.

He made his way across the slippery wood and down the steps to look into the darkened cabin – but like the deck above it was devoid of any life.

He slowly came back up the stairs, the taste of fear now bitter in his mouth.

'Michael!' he roared, again and again, turning around and looking at the empty deck of the boat – as though he might just conjure up the missing boatman. He skidded down it again, looking at the sides where the tarpaulins were rolled up, checking to see if he'd fallen.

Jimmy came scrambling onto the deck now, his face white and panic-stricken. He looked around him as his workmate had done, then he threw his hands up in the air. 'Has he gone over?' he called in a broken voice. 'Has Michael gone over?'

The two deckhands silently moved from one side of the boat to the other – gripping the edges and leaning over, vainly crying out their workmate's name.

A short time later, the people from the pub and the surrounding houses came to join them – and the Guards were then sent for. But all the efforts of the boatmen and the extra helping hands yielded no success. There was no sign of Michael O'Brien.

Eventually, the relentless rain and wind drove them all back to the warmth and safety of the pub, where Brendan Flowers and Jimmy Morris sat at opposite sides of the fire – waiting, waiting for the morning light to break. Waiting for the weather to ease.

Waiting and hoping – and silently praying.

There was no conversation or banter between them, no card games. Just anxious glances and unspoken fears.

In the morning both men would stand on the deck of the boat, and watch in shocked silence and guilt as Michael O'Brien's body was removed from the now calm dark waters that had claimed him.

Chapter 71

Michael O'Brien was buried in the cemetery in Tullamore where his father had been buried only the year before. His funeral was one of the biggest that the area had ever seen, with people spilling out from the church and into the yard and streets beyond – all shocked and shaken that such a steady, careful man could have met his death in such an unpredictable, frightful way.

Kate had followed behind the hearse, her dark hair and face shrouded in a thick black veil, supported by her mother and her brother, her aunt and uncle, and the remaining O'Brien family. She had slept and eaten very little since Michael's death and she was being closely monitored by both her doctor and her family.

Agnes O'Brien had hardly spoken since she had heard the news that terrible Friday morning, and when she did, it was to ask why God would punish her in such a cruel way by taking the two men she needed and loved.

Michael's brother and sisters had been similarly silent, each asking themselves why they had, for all those months, put such a wall between Michael and themselves because he had chosen Kate Flowers. It now seemed so stupid and futile.

And Brendan Flowers' face still had the same ghostly white pallor that had gripped him the night that he knew Michael O'Brien had disappeared. If anything, it had got worse. Both his body and his mind were at constant war with himself, and he could see no end to it.

Deep in the back of his mind he blamed himself for the extra drinks he had bought Michael that night, the drinks that could well have caused his footing to be unsteady as he attempted to climb on the boat. And no matter how many times Kate and his mother and Jimmy told him that all the evidence pointed to the stormy night being to blame, he somehow couldn't allow himself to be let off the hook.

He hadn't let a drop of alcohol touch his own lips since that night, and he doubted if he ever would again.

Three months after Michael was buried, Kate went into labour several weeks early. She had slept little since the funeral and wakened every hour or two when she did – often reaching across to his empty side of the bed, freshly shocked each time to find he wasn't there.

Her days had drifted by, the darkness and bleakness of the season echoing the feelings in her heart. She got up each morning and went about the daily routine with her mother close by, checking and watching and trying to anticipate everything that Kate was going to do, in order to do it first.

'How did you do it?' Kate had asked her mother on numerous occasions. 'How did you cope after Daddy died?'

And each time Mary had to think hard. 'I don't remember,' she had told Kate in a wavery voice. 'I honestly can't remember much about it. I suppose I just had to cope, I had you and Brendan to think about.' She had taken Kate's hand on each occasion. 'It'll get easier when the baby comes . . .'

Then, when Kate had gone upstairs or out into the garden, Mary had tortured herself asking, How can I tell her? How can I tell her how different it was from her and Michael? How can I tell her that my heart is more broken not seeing Lance Williams than it ever was by her father dying?

On that particular night Kate woke up feeling that something wasn't right. She got out of bed and was making her way downstairs when she suddenly felt the rush of warm water flowing out of her and down her legs. As she went back upstairs to wash and dry herself, the first of the contractions started.

As arranged, Mary used the phone Kate had recently installed in the house and phoned for Tom O'Brien. Within twenty minutes he was out at the farmhouse and they were on their way into Tullamore hospital.

Mary held Kate's hand tightly as the car bumped along the rough farmhouse track and onto the main road, and said decades of the Rosary in her head, asking the Holy Virgin to give her sad and bereaved daughter a quick and easy delivery.

Knowing the circumstances, the hospital gave Kate a room off the general maternity ward, for which she was very grateful. The last thing she needed was cheerful new mothers enquiring as to when her husband would be in to visit her and the baby.

The labour had been painful and drawn-out – nearly fifteen hours – and as the drugs the doctors and midwife administered did their work, she alternately called and cried for Michael O'Brien, her beloved dead husband and the father of her baby.

Finally, as the afternoon light turned towards evening, Elizabeth Mary O'Brien made her way into the world. The midwife and Mary gave little whoops of delight as the baby was lifted up and put to rest on her weary mother's breast. Kate looked down at the small dark head and as the child instinctively curved towards her, she felt a little melting of the ice-block that had been her heart for those long dark weeks.

Chapter 72

❧❧❧

Kate stared out of the kitchen window at the crimson and yellow roses, and remembered her and Michael planting them last summer. She moved a little to the left and looked out at the vegetable plot she and her mother had spent so many hours clearing in preparation for this spring. She thought of all the plans they had had for planting onions and cabbages and lettuces, all the plans that had come to nothing.

The garden had suddenly come way down the list of priorities that Kate now found herself dealing with. Top of that list had been Elizabeth. After the first few days of feeling full of emotional gratitude, and then the planning of the christening, the hard work of being a widowed mother had settled in with a vengeance.

Elizabeth had been a colicky baby, and it was not until the spring that she had finally begun to sleep the whole night through. The breast-feeding had also taken it out of Kate, but thankfully now Elizabeth was on some solid food and seemed to have settled down.

Mary came into the kitchen carrying her grand-daughter, talking and laughing to the child as she always did. 'You're lookin' very thoughtful, Kate,' she said, a little frown coming on her face.

'I've been thinking about the house and the situation with Tom O'Brien.'

Mary came to sit at the kitchen table with Elizabeth perched on her knee. 'Well?' she said, an anxious note in her voice.

'I think after we come back from Stockport that I should move out . . . come to some arrangement with him – and let him and his wife have it.'

Mary reached across the table for the child's rattle and gave it a little shake and then handed it to her. 'From what you've told me, Kate, they're not putting you out or anything . . . I think they're concerned about you being stuck out here on your own with the child.'

Kate nodded, her face still wearing the pale and pinched look it had since last October. 'I know that . . .' She gave a weary little sigh.

'I can't expect you to be here all the time, and I know that you worry about Brendan being up at the house so much on his own.'

'Oh, he's grand,' Mary said, waving away Kate's concerns. 'Brendan is big and ugly enough to look out for himself.' She gave a little smile. 'At least, that's what he's always tellin' me.' She looked at Kate now. 'Would you consider coming back to live at the cottage? We could put what money we have together and build on . . .'

Kate bit her lip, thinking. 'I don't think I could bear to be so near the canal again . . . I'd always be thinking about Michael.' Then after a small silence she said, 'My nerves would be on edge when Elizabeth started walking in case anything happened to her.'

'Are you still having the dreams about it?' Mary said in a gentle voice.

Kate inclined her head. 'They're not as bad . . . and I'm not getting them every night now.'

'The holiday will do you and the baby good,' Mary told her. 'It'll be a change of scenery for us all.'

'I'm delighted that Brendan is going to come with us for the first week,' Kate said. 'Whatever has made him change his mind?'

'I think,' Mary said, 'that he's anxious about us going over on the boat with Elizabeth on our own.' She gave a little shrug. 'I can't be sure . . . you know he wouldn't come straight out and say something like that.'

'Well, it's good of him if that's why he's coming,' Kate mused, 'and I don't think it'll do him any harm. He always gets on well with Graham, and I'm sure he'll enjoy a bit of craic with Frankie in the shop.'

'It might take him out of himself,' her mother agreed. 'He's very quiet these days and although he's started going back to the pub occasionally, he doesn't touch the drink.'

'Well, it won't do him any harm,' Kate said quietly. 'There was a time when he was drinking too much.'

'Oh, I'm not complaining,' Mary said quickly. 'I'd just like to see him a bit lighter in himself . . .'

'And what about you, Mammy?' Kate suddenly asked. 'Have you heard any more from that Lance fellow?'

A red tinge worked its way up Mary's throat towards her face at the mention of his name. She had broached the subject of their friendship on a few occasions with Kate recently, and although her daughter seemed more comfortable with it, Mary still felt like an awkward teenager. 'Well,' she blustered, 'he still writes to me every now and then . . .'

Kate nodded her head. 'No doubt you'll see him when we get over there?'

'Ah sure, we'll wait and see . . .'

The baby knocked the rattle onto the floor now and Mary used the welcome diversion to cut the conversation short.

How, she asked herself, could she be such a coward? Why couldn't she tell the truth?

Why couldn't she tell Kate that Lance Williams had written two weeks ago and asked her to marry him?

Chapter 73

R ose and Graham did everything they could to keep things light and easy for Kate and her daughter. They even left Frankie in complete charge on the half-day Wednesday and they bundled everyone in the back of the van and drove to the train station in Manchester and caught a train out to Blackpool for the day.

'She's looking a bit better,' Rose whispered to Mary as they all walked down the promenade – Kate pushing Elizabeth in her go-chair, and Brendan and Graham following behind.

Kate stopped at a Punch and Judy show and lifted Elizabeth out of the chair and high up in her arms to let her watch, while the others stood a few feet behind her.

'She has more to distract her over here,' Mary whispered back, 'and I think she's improved in herself, because she's had a bit of a rest.' She thumbed back towards the men. 'They've been great, you know, both Graham and Brendan – and they've been fantastic with Elizabeth, bringing her up and down to the shop and showing her to all the customers.

Rose looked at her niece now, the flowing black curly hair, the lovely slim figure. 'D'you think she'd ever look at another man?' she asked in a low voice.

Mary shrugged. 'God only knows ... Kate's not the kind that you could ask anything like that...'

'She's a lovely young girl, and it would be terrible to see her on her own.' She put her arm through Mary's now. 'I would hate to see her going the same way you did for all those years.'

There was a little silence where Mary just nodded her head.

'Pity about that Dolittle fella,' Rose said now. 'He fell for her in a big way – any time he saw me and Graham he would always ask for her, and you could see it in his face when we mentioned that she'd got married.' The sea breeze caught her hair now, and she lifted her hands to flatten it down again. 'He moved away last year. There's a young couple in the house now with two kids – they did it up lovely. You wouldn't know it was the same place.'

'Where did he go?' Mary asked.

Rose gave a little shrug. 'I haven't the faintest ... he could have gone back to Scotland for all I know, workin' in one of the big hospitals in Glasgow or Edinburgh. Graham's never seen him since he moved away.'

They stood watching the show for a little bit longer, then Rose tugged Mary's cardigan sleeve. 'Have you said anythin' to her or Brendan about Lance yet?'

Mary's eyes grew wide. She shook her head. 'No ... not at all.'

'You'll have to say something soon,' Rose told her. 'It's not fair on Lance.' She indicated towards the two men. 'He would have enjoyed the day out with us all.'

Shortly afterwards they moved on to a shop that sold postcards and souvenirs and Brendan bought a colourful whirling windmill for Elizabeth, which she promptly stuck in her mouth and attempted to chew, making them all roar with laughter.

Mary lifted some postcards from a stand. 'Shall we send one to Noelle up in Dublin?'

Brendan's whole body stiffened at the mention of her name.

'Oh, that's a good idea,' Kate said, smiling at the suggestion. 'She's been so good, she never forgets to write to us regularly.'

'And that was a lovely wreath she sent...' Mary's voice faltered now, realising she'd put her foot in it – mentioning the funeral – when they were supposed to be having a cheerful day out.

'Is that one of those nice red-haired Daly girls?' Rose put in, rescuing the situation.

Kate nodded her head. 'It is, the girls that lived down along the canal from us.'

'Oh, I still miss poor Noelle,' Mary said, giving a sigh. 'She was the loveliest girl – and that oul' devil of a father of hers deserves to be reported for the life he's given them girls and their mother, the poor oul' cratur.'

'D'you think she'll ever come back home?' Rose asked.

'Not while the oul' fella's still alive,' Mary said. 'And anyway, she'll probably be well settled up in Dublin after all this time.'

Brendan walked out of the shop now and over to the promenade wall. He leaned his elbows on the wall and stared out across the blue sea. He'd have to do something soon, he thought. This was getting ridiculous. He couldn't keep silent about Noelle for much longer – it wasn't fair on her to deny their feelings and it wasn't fair on Kate and his mother. And the whole feckin' situation, he suddenly thought, wasn't fair on him either.

When they arrived back home around eight o'clock, Mary and Rose made a quick supper of scrambled eggs and toast, then later on Graham and Brendan walked down to the pub for the last hour. Kate went off to bath Elizabeth while the women did their usual clearing up.

When Kate had got Elizabeth settled and off to sleep, she came back into the sitting-room to join her mother and her aunt.

Rose went over to the cupboard and lifted out the sherry bottle and poured three good-sized glasses. Then she came over and handed one to her sister and one to her niece. 'It'll help us all to sleep tonight after all that sea air,' she said, before they had a chance to protest.

She waited and watched until Kate's glass had gone below the halfway mark, and then she threw the rest of her own sherry back in one mouthful and put the glass down on the table with a little thud. 'Right!' she said. 'I think it's time we women had a serious talk while the men are out.'

Mary, who had just taken a mouthful of her sherry, started to choke. She had an awful feeling that Rose was going to say something that she shouldn't.

'Kate, darlin',' Rose said, reaching over and taking her niece's hand, 'your mother has something to tell you, but knowing your mother as I do she's never going to get around to it, so I'm going to help her out.'

'Rose . . .' Mary spluttered, dabbing a tissue to her mouth.

'Your mother has received a proposal of marriage from a very nice man,' Rose stated. 'And she's kept the poor man hanging on for weeks for an answer, because she's terrified to tell you and Brendan.'

Kate's face drained. She looked across at her mother. 'Is this true?' she whispered, clearly shocked. She swallowed hard on the lump that had formed in her throat. 'Is it Lance?'

Mary's eyes darted across to her sister who was nodding her head and making eyes at her, and she remembered all the things that both Rose and Lance had told her, and how they said she should handle this occasion when it eventually arose. 'Yes, Kate,' she said in a low, shaky voice. 'It is Lance – and he has asked me to marry him.'

'Your mother has devoted herself to you and Brendan all these years,' Rose interrupted, 'and it's time she had a life of her own. She's not an old woman you know, Kate . . .'

Kate lifted her glass and took a careful sip of the dark, sweet sherry, shocked at the news and taken aback by her aunt's firm attitude over it all. Quite obviously, her mother had been so terrified to say anything that Rose had now taken the situation in hand. 'I don't know what to say . . . I don't think I've ever been so surprised in my life.'

'Well,' Rose said, going over to get the sherry bottle to refill her and Mary's glasses, 'I've another suggestion while you're at it . . . and this time it's to do with *you*.'

Kate looked up at her with startled eyes. 'To do with a man?' she said in a horrified tone. The old fiery, indignant Kate that used to spar with Brendan so often came flooding back. 'Because if this is some kind of suggestion to do with men,' she pointed towards the door, 'then I'm going to walk straight out of this house and never come back.'

'Hold your horses,' Rose told her, putting the sherry bottle down on the coffee table. 'As if I would suggest anything of the kind . . . so soon after what's happened. What do you take me for?'

Kate sat motionless, while her mother sat nervously screwing the paper tissue up into little tiny pieces.

'It's to do with you and Elizabeth and your situation back in Ireland.' Rose refilled Mary's glass and then her own. 'I want you to give some serious thought to this suggestion.' She sat back into the sofa now. 'Why don't you all consider moving over here? You've always wanted to do nursing, Kate, so why don't you move in here with me and Graham and we can all help you with Elizabeth while you're at the hospital doing your training?'

Kate looked at her aunt, trying to take in her suggestion.

'Just think of it this way,' Rose went on. 'If your mother and Lance were to get married, they'd only be livin' across the road and round the corner there.' She indicated towards the window. 'Sure, you were in it yourself the summer before last and you know how close it is. Your mother could come over here every day and look after Elizabeth when Lance is at work and you're at the hospital. They could be up and down to the shop; the child would love the company and seeing other children coming and going.'

'But we can't pack up and leave Ireland just like that . . .' Kate said, looking across at her mother. 'You're very quiet – what do you think?'

'I haven't thought it through in any way . . .' she hedged, terrified of saying the wrong thing. 'But you know I won't leave you and Elizabeth on your own, whatever happens. I'll stay on in Ireland until she's old enough to go to school if need be . . . Lance would understand.'

'But what about the O'Briens? They might have something to say about me taking Elizabeth away.'

'You can do the same as everybody else,' Rose said softly, 'bring her back to Ireland every summer. I'm sure your mother would want to go back home every now and again as well, wouldn't you, Mary?'

Mary nodded. 'Of course I would . . . and maybe if you come to an arrangement with Michael's family, you could use the bit of money they give you to eventually get a nice little place of your own over here. There are some lovely houses around.' She paused. 'If me and Lance were to get . . .' The words stuck in her throat, but she swallowed and tried valiantly again. 'As I say, if me and Lance were to get married – I could give you most of the money I have in the bank to help you out.'

Kate's brow deepened. 'You can't do that,' she said, her voice becoming a little brittle. 'You'd need to have something of your own.' She couldn't believe she was actually sitting here talking to her mother about her getting *married*. Her whole world seemed to have turned completely upside down.

'Lance has everything, Kate,' Mary said quietly. 'He said I don't need to bring anything to the house, except myself.'

'Kate,' Rose interrupted now, 'you should really consider what we've just said to you. It all makes perfect sense. It would be the best thing for your mother and the best thing for you and Elizabeth.'

Kate felt as though a steel band had tightened around her head. It was all too much to take in. She suddenly stood up. 'I don't mean to be funny with either of you, but I'm going to have to go to bed.' She gave them both a weak little smile. 'I'll sleep on the situation and we can talk about it in the morning.' She walked towards the door and then she suddenly halted and looked back at her mother. 'Congratulations, by the way. Lance is a very nice man and he's lucky to have you.'

When Kate closed the door behind her, Mary promptly burst into tears.

'Now,' Rose said, patting her sister's shoulder, 'that wasn't so bad after all, was it?'

'Oh, Rose,' Mary sobbed, 'I can't believe she took it so well . . . but now we're going to have to tell Brendan, and he'll be worse.'

'Don't worry too much about telling him,' Rose said, giving a little satisfied smile. She looked at her watch. 'I should think by this time Graham has already told him and introduced him to Lance Williams.'

369

Chapter 74

❧❧❧

Brendan caught the boat back to Dublin on the following Friday night, still elated from the events of the week. Who would believe that his mother was all sorted out now and the worry of her completely taken out of his hands? And not only that, the old fella was miles better than anyone he could ever have imagined his mother meeting up with at home. He was well set up in a lovely big house – car and everything. Who would believe it?

And Kate – his heart always sank when he thought of her and Elizabeth all on their own – seriously considering the options that Rose and his mother had presented to her. He hoped with all his heart that she would decide to move over to Stockport and get a new life for herself and Elizabeth. Every time he visited them both in that big farmhouse, he came home struggling to shake off the feeling that he was partly to blame for their predicament.

He arrived home in the middle of the Saturday afternoon, walking from where the coach dropped him off in Ballygrace out to the canal and up along to the cottage. In the old days, he would have stopped off at the pub for a few pints, but those days were gone. He had never touched a drop of whiskey or beer since the night Michael O'Brien had gone missing.

He slowed up at the bend in the road where he could see down towards the Dalys' cottage, and stood for a few moments, thinking, then he continued his journey home. On reaching the cottage he threw his bag down and took himself off to bed for a few hours, because he needed a good, clear head for the situation he had to deal with that night.

He rose around six o'clock and then took another hour boiling water to half-fill the tin bath, and then he gave his whole lean, hard body a brisk, thorough scrub.

He dressed in the black suit and white shirt that he'd bought for Michael O'Brien's funeral, but this time he wore it with a navy and white patterned tie instead of the black one. Then he brushed his dark hair until the unruly curls were lying as flat as he could get with the aid of a bit of Brylcreem. He gave his good black low shoes a quick rub of polish and then shone them vigorously.

Then, satisfied that he looked his best, he set off on his grim journey down to Matt Daly's door.

Why he hadn't done this a long time ago, Brendan suddenly couldn't understand. He was mad to have let it slide so long – but maybe that was only in the looking back. Up until now, there hadn't seemed to be any way out of it. Now, it all seemed as clear as day.

His mother had opened the floodgates for all sorts of possibilities, and he wasn't going to miss his chance too.

He gave three loud knocks on the cottage door and waited. After a few moments, Peg Daly cautiously opened the door, her face draining when she saw who it was.

'Could I have a quick word with Mr Daly, please?' he said, as pleasantly as he could

'He's not here . . .' she replied in a low voice. 'He was out in the yard a few minutes ago.'

Brendan heard a noise behind him and turned around to see Matt Daly advancing towards him with a rake in his hand.

'Who let you in and around my house?' the older man demanded.

Brendan straightened himself up to his full height. 'I've come on a bit of business . . .'

'Oh, have ye now? And what kind of business would that be?' He came to stand directly in front of his visitor, the rake held like a spear tightly in his hand.

'It's about Noelle,' Brendan said, his voice not wavering. 'I've come to ask for her hand in marriage.'

Matt Daly's face blanched at his words. 'You?' he said. He turned his head to spit on the ground. 'You have the nerve to walk into my yard and ask me that?'

'I do,' Brendan said. 'I'm giving you the courtesy of askin' you because she's your daughter.'

'Well,' he said, indicating to the field beyond, 'you might as well go on out there and ask the oul' cattle, because you'll get as much good out of asking them as you'll get out of asking me.' He moved his face to within an inch of Brendan's now – so close that Brendan could feel his hot breath and smell the bacon and cabbage he'd eaten earlier. 'No flesh and blood of mine will ever be linked up to the likes of *you*.' He gave a low, bitter laugh. 'You'll get no hand in marriage from anything that belongs to me – not even the hand that belongs to the whore of a daughter I have up in Dublin.'

'Don't use that word when you're talkin' about her,' Brendan warned.

'Oh . . .' Matt Daly's eyes narrowed. 'And do you suppose you're going to do anything about it?' He spat on the ground again. 'To my mind, she's been nothing but a whore since the day she took up with you.'

Brendan stepped back now. 'You're an older man,' he said, 'and only because of that will I keep myself in check . . .' He turned now and started to walk back to the gate when suddenly he heard a noise and when he whirled around, the rake caught him on the shoulder and the side of the face.

Brendan stood for a moment, framed in disbelief, and then – before he gave himself time to think about it – he ran back and grabbed Matt Daly by the throat and pinned him up against the side of the house.

'Don't ever, *ever* use that word again when you're talking about Noelle,' he said in a low, threatening voice. His adversary looked back at him now, with stunned, terrified eyes. 'I came here in peace and in courtesy,' Brendan went on, 'which is more than you've ever given me or your family.' He moved his face closer now – until their noses were almost touching. 'Now, I'm going to tell you this once – and once only – so listen carefully. If you ever lay a finger on Noelle again – or if I hear of you laying a finger on any of the rest of your family – I'm going to drag you down to the Guards.' His voice lowered further. 'And if they don't do something to sort you out, I'm going to give you the biggest beating you ever got in your life. Mark my words, if you put a hand on any of them, and I get to hear about it, you'll be a sorry man.'

Matt Daly made a choking noise, and he struggled to make free – but found himself gripped all the harder.

'Do you understand me?' Brendan hissed now. 'Have I made myself clear?'

Slowly, Matt Daly nodded his head.

Brendan stared him straight in the eye for a few moments, then he gradually loosened his grip. 'Now, whether you like it or not, I'm bringing Noelle back here,' he told her father. 'Being the decent girl that she is, I'll marry her first, and then we'll be living up in the cottage.' His eyes narrowed. 'If you *ever* say a wrong word to her or about her, you'll have me to answer to . . .'

Matt Daly ran his fingers around the inside of his shirt. 'The mammy will be delighted to have her back,' he croaked in a hoarse voice, 'and so will the childer . . .' He cleared his throat. 'It was all a bit of a misunderstandin' anyway . . . the way families make something out of nothing. It'll all be forgotten . . . We must all forgive and forget.'

Brendan let his breath out in a low, disbelieving whistle and just caught himself from returning the older man's comment with a scathing remark. But he held his tongue, deciding that there was no point in undoing all the good work that had just been done.

Besides, he had another job to do up in Dublin in the morning.

Chapter 75

A fter giving Dr Casey her breakfast tray, Noelle came back downstairs and lifted Gabrielle's tray with the bacon and sausage and black and white pudding, and her fried egg done just perfectly, and went back upstairs.

She took a deep breath before giving a brisk knock on the door, then she went in. 'Good morning, Miss Gabrielle,' she said, walking across the room to lay the tray down on the bedside table.

Gabrielle grunted, then, as Noelle drew the heavy curtains back, she pulled herself into a sitting position. 'Did Auntie Bernadette tell you about the tennis group?' She pushed her hair back with her hands.

'Yes,' Noelle replied in a flat voice. 'Tea and cold drinks and cheese and biscuits at six o'clock.'

'And did she ask you about the iced tea and coffee?' Gabrielle said, motioning Noelle to lift the tray across from the table and onto her lap. 'Some of the girls have just come back from America and I want to surprise them – show them that we're every bit as cosmopolitan as they are.'

'Yes,' Noelle replied. 'We practised it the other night.'

'Good.' Gabrielle managed something that looked vaguely like a smile. She lifted her knife and fork and prodded the centre of the fried egg to check it was done just the way she liked it. 'There's no point in us having a spanking new fridge that makes ice cubes and not using it . . .' Her eyes flitted back to Noelle. 'I want you to wear the new apron and cap when they come tonight – I want a good impression made.'

'That's grand,' Noelle said quickly – almost snappily.

The doctor's niece turned her attention back to her plate. 'If I think of anything else I want you to do, I'll let you know.'

Noelle went back downstairs to have her own breakfast, swallowing back all the feelings of annoyance that Gabrielle Casey always managed to provoke in her. The girl had only been back from her long summer holiday in France less than a week, and already Noelle's nerves were in strands. She found something new to complain about every time they had any discussions, and Noelle knew there was no point in saying anything to Dr Casey, no point at all.

When the problem actually arose, she would give the impression of listening very carefully, and would often join in with a few criticisms of her niece herself, but by the time the difficulty was mentioned to Gabrielle, it would suddenly all be turned back on Noelle.

On the worst occasion last Christmas when Gabrielle humiliated the maid by shouting at her in front of a group for giving her the wrong drink, she was made to apologise by her aunt, but then she hadn't spoken directly to Noelle for the rest of her university holidays.

And when she left, Dr Casey had given Noelle a big long lecture on being more attentive when she was serving people, and it would save all the dramatics that poor over-worked university students were apt to indulge in.

Noelle had long since learned to keep her mouth shut – and on far touchier subjects than Gabrielle Casey. She had learned never to comment on Dr Casey's personal life too, especially since it now involved her next-door neighbour, Ben Lavery.

374

Their relationship had started after the female doctor was invited over to his house last New Year for a drinks party. The invite had come personally from Ben Lavery's mother, who, it turned out, had been instrumental in ridding him of Carmel Foley. The small, bird-like woman had appeared at the door just after Christmas, with a hand-written invitation requesting Dr Casey's presence at the small, exclusive 'do'. Noelle remembered the occasion well, because it was the first time that the doctor had gone to the hairdresser's and come back with a deep, rich colour in her hair.

Since then, Ben Lavery had been a regular visitor to the house – and, if Noelle wasn't mistaken, had been an *overnight* visitor on several occasions when Noelle was off meeting Brendan. The sudden change in the doctor's choice of nightwear and underwear from serviceable cotton to fancy lace had confirmed Noelle's suspicions.

After the first few times that the solicitor and the doctor had been out for meals together, the doctor came in one night and sat Noelle down and quizzed her.

'Now, Noelle,' she had said, 'I would like you to tell me everything that you know about the situation between Mr Lavery and Carmel Foley. I don't want you to leave a single thing out – every detail that you ever remember her telling you.'

Noelle had been silent for a few moments, trying to decide whether or not to reveal the awful things that Carmel had told her.

'Now don't forget,' Dr Casey had said, 'an employee's duty is towards her employer. This information is very important to me, and I need to know the truth.' Her eyes had narrowed into hard little slits. 'And if I find out that you've not been honest, I'll have no option but to dismiss you there and then.'

Fear had prompted Noelle to spill everything that she knew. And anyway, she had thought, what does it matter now? Carmel Foley had been gone a long time.

After she had finished the story about the weekend that Carmel and her boss had spent in the hotel, Dr Casey had pressed the back of her hand to her mouth and closed her eyes. Then, she had composed herself again and sat up straight. 'Is that all?' she'd asked.

Noelle had nodded her head. 'That's all that she told me anyway.' She hadn't mentioned anything about the awful thing that Ben

Lavery had tried to make Carmel do, and after talking to Brendan about it, Noelle now had a very good idea of what he had suggested.

Just thinking about it – with a horrible older man like Mr Lavery – had given her the creeps.

'There was never any question of a child being involved then?'

Noelle had looked blank. 'What child?'

'That awful girl – that *Carmel*,' the doctor had said, clearly irritated now, 'she never said anything to you about her being pregnant or anything like that?'

'No, Dr Casey ... she never said anything like that to me,' Noelle had said in a low voice. 'I'm quite sure that when she left here she wasn't expecting a baby ...'

Bernadette Casey's face had suddenly brightened up. 'Good,' she'd said, getting to her feet as though her business was now conducted and finished. 'A girl like that couldn't have kept quiet about it if there had been a baby on the way. She would have had to tell somebody of her own kind.' She had walked towards the drawing-room door then suddenly turned back. 'Take that as a lesson, Noelle,' she had said, raising her eyebrows. 'Young girls like you and Carmel Foley should learn their place in life and make sure you stick to it. As I explained to you when you first met Gabrielle, mixing the classes together in any kind of social situation just does not work.'

Whatever went on between the doctor and her neighbour after the conversation, Noelle never found out. But it certainly hadn't put Dr Casey off, as they were going out now every weekend and people regarded them as a couple. The doctor had her hair washed and set every week and had a colour put in it regularly. She was also more feminine in her choice of clothes. But she hadn't changed in all respects; she was still as penny-pinching as ever when it came to household expenditure, and made her employee account for every item that was bought.

'That's how the rich are rich,' Brendan had told her once. 'Some of them would live on fresh air if they could get away with it.'

Noelle sat picking at her breakfast, wishing the minutes away until Dr Casey and Gabrielle were up and dressed and gone to Mass. It was the only time she felt truly relaxed, when they had both gone out.

She was just clearing her half-eaten plate into the bin – carefully concealing the leftovers at the bottom in case Dr Casey told her off for wasting good food – when the confident rap came on the front door.

As she walked quickly out to answer it, she could see the tall, dark figure of a man outlined in the stained-glass panel who looked very like their next-door neighbour. Ben Lavery and her boss must have made an arrangement to go to Mass together this morning, she thought. They were becoming more and more open about their relationship and Noelle wouldn't be a bit surprised if they ended up getting engaged soon – even married.

She opened the door and stood back to welcome him in, and then, when she looked up, her knees went weak. 'Brendan!' she said, her face turning pale. She looked back into the hallway. 'You can't come in . . . I'll be in trouble if they see you.'

'Forget them,' Brendan told her briskly. 'Get your coat and your bags, you're leavin' this dump right now.' Then, he stepped forward and took her into his arms and kissed her tenderly on the lips. 'I'll explain it all to you later, but you're leaving here now and in a few weeks we're going to be married.'

Noelle stared at him with wide, shocked eyes. 'But how? We've talked about it before and there was no way out until you leave the boats . . .'

'Things have changed,' he said, smiling at her. He raised his eyebrows, his brown eyes twinkling. 'And for once in our lives, they've changed in the right direction.' The tone in his voice was certain and confident, and as she looked at him, Noelle suddenly felt inspired by his words.

'Oh, Brendan . . .' she said, moving closer to put her head on his chest for a few moments. Then, hearing a noise upstairs, she suddenly pulled back. 'I can't tell her now . . . it's too soon.'

Brendan's eyebrows shot up – he hadn't got up at the crack of dawn to get a lift up to Dublin to walk away without her. 'Soon, my arse,' he said. 'Go on in, and tell her right now. She can send any money that she owes on to you later.' He looked at his watch, then pointed down the street. 'I'll walk back to the corner and I'll catch you there in five minutes.'

'What will I tell her?' Noelle said. 'She'll go mad at me just walkin' out . . .'

Very gently, he took her face in his hands. 'Tell her that we're getting married and you have to go straight home to organise the wedding.'

'My father—'

'Never mind your father,' he said now, 'that's all fixed – and we have our own house and everything. I even have a new job fixed up at the O'Briens' farm if I want it.'

'Oh my God!' Noelle said, her brain trying to take in all the wonderful news he had just told her.

'Go on,' he said, tapping her gently on the backside. 'Get in there now – and make sure you take the greatest of pleasure in telling her your news.'

Chapter 76

⚮

Kate O'Brien walked quickly along the hospital corridor, checking the time on her little nurse's watch. It was quarter past eight in the morning, and she was just coming off a ten-hour nightshift. As she secured the button on the collar of her navy-blue cape, she wondered if there would be any news about Noelle when she got back to her aunt's house. The baby was a week overdue, and her mother and Lance had been on the phone to Ireland every other day, checking if the new grandchild had arrived yet.

She went through the swing door at the end of the corridor, then walked briskly down the stairs. She was surprisingly wide awake considering the long night she'd had, and planned to stay up for a few hours when she got back to her aunt's to dress Elizabeth and give her breakfast.

As she walked out of the coolness of the hospital and into the morning sunshine, she thought that she might stay up for a couple of hours extra and walk across to the park with her mother and the baby. She would have a few hours' sleep before getting up for her afternoon appointment at four o'clock with the estate agent. A little thrill of excitement ran through Kate at the thought of the lovely three-bedroomed Victorian house she'd just bought out in Davenport. A beautiful bright house with lovely big rooms and a nice-sized garden. A manageable, mature garden that would require very little work. Not like the wilderness she and her mother and Michael had tackled back in Offaly.

Kate pushed back a little pang at the memory of her old life – the life that she and the patient, kind Michael had barely even begun together. All their dreams and plans had come to an abrupt, tragic end on that stormy night two long years ago.

And now, Kate had been forced to move on and plan for different dreams and a very different life. Thanks to her Auntie Rose, things had fallen quickly and easily into place. Everything she had suggested had been both practical and hugely supportive for Kate and Elizabeth.

Kate had enrolled in the local hospital last October and was now nearing the end of her first year in training as a State Registered Nurse. She had always had a yearning for the career, but hadn't realised the huge gap that it would fill in her own life. She absolutely loved it, and planned to continue her training and maybe specialise in something like midwifery.

Mary and her lovely husband Lance looked after their grandchild when Kate was working, and Rose and Graham were always delighted to take turns at babysitting when they got the chance.

Next week, Kate and her mother and Elizabeth would be taking a two-week trip back to Ballygrace – the opposite of the trips they had made every summer for years. This time they would stay in their old home-cottage by the canal, visiting old friends and neighbours and helping Noelle with the new baby.

It would be a bit of a squeeze this year, with Mary and Kate and Elizabeth in Brendan's old room, but they would manage. It would be worth any small discomforts. Next year everything would be a whole lot easier – the extension would be built and Lance would bring them all over in his car.

Brendan had given up the canals now, too. His boat had finished the last journey back in Easter, and anyway, he had lost all feel for the canal since its dark waters had claimed Michael O'Brien. He had got himself a foreman's position at the factory in town, having decided against the labouring job at the O'Briens' farm. He'd had enough of late nights on the barges and wanted a more normal job with regular hours. He wanted to spend his nights and weekends at home from now on, with his wife and their new baby.

Kate planned to spend a few nights up at the O'Briens' house, giving Michael's family the chance to get to know his little daughter, and attending her husband's two-year anniversary Mass. And even though she still felt a little uncomfortable with the girls, she owed his mother that at least.

Agnes O'Brien had been very fair with Kate. The business of Uncle Sean's house had been amicably agreed and Tom O'Brien had now moved in there pending his forthcoming marriage. They had given Kate a good-sized lump sum, which, along with the life insurance, more than covered the cost of the house she had just bought.

All things considered, things had worked out well – as well as could be expected under the circumstances and much better than Kate would have imagined.

And now, two years on, Kate was moving forward in other directions.

She had made friends with some of the other trainee nurses and she had recently started going to the pictures with them every other week. The other social outings to pubs or dances she had given a miss, as she wasn't ready to move into mixed company and the complications that it would entail.

The following Friday night, she and a group of her friends were invited to a party in the doctors' mess, and after a lot of coaxing and interfering from her mother and Rose, Kate had eventually agreed – albeit reluctantly – to go.

Mary and Rose had fussed around her, dragging her off to buy an outfit from a new ladies' shop that had opened a few doors down from the fruit and vegetable shop. The shop assistant had studied Kate's tall, slim figure and glossy dark hair, and had picked out a beautiful, but simple, black lace dress with short sleeves and a red satin ribbon with a bow under the bust. Her mother and aunt had gone into raptures about how lovely her high black sandals and little beaded evening bag would look with the dress.

The group of nurses had arranged to meet up at one of the pubs outside the hospital, and the others all expressed surprise and admiration at Kate's flattering outfit, as they had never seen her looking any way glamorous before. Her evenings at the pictures had been casual affairs, suitable for the practical slacks and sweaters she wore for playing with Elizabeth, and for all the messy jobs that her little daughter managed to create.

When they arrived at the party, Kate had initially felt very quiet and self-conscious, but the lively atmosphere, the music and a couple of glasses of wine had helped to relax her.

Towards the middle of the night, as she went in search of the Ladies' to freshen her make-up, she felt a touch on her arm, and turned to find herself face to face with David McGuire.

'Kate!' he gasped, clearly shocked. 'What on earth are you doing here?'

'I'm nursing now ... I came with the other girls,' she told him, her cheeks flaming red and her throat suddenly tight.

Without a word, he took her hand and guided her towards a quiet corner of the room, and ten minutes later Kate lifted her coat and bag and they walked out together into the cool night air.

'I'm so sorry,' he told her, after he'd listened to her story about Michael and the tragic boat accident. 'I heard nothing about it – I've been down in London for the last two years, and I've only just come back.' He explained that he was now based in the main hospital in Manchester. He still kept friends with the fellows he had shared the house with in Davenport, and had come with one of them to the party that evening.

'I thought about you constantly after you went back to Ireland that summer,' he told her in his Scottish, forthright way, 'and I've often thought about you since...' He paused for a moment, considering his words. 'I've met plenty of other girls during those two years, but I've never met anyone like you.' He gave a little shrug. 'I can't believe you're here – I'd given up all hope of ever seeing you again.'

Later, as they stood outside Rose and Graham's house, Kate told him all about Elizabeth and she could see the shock registering in his handsome face at the fact that since he had last seen her she had not only been widowed, but was now bringing up a child on her own. 'You've really been through the mill, haven't you?' he had said, gently touching her cheek.

'Elizabeth and I are managing very well,' Kate told him, with a touch of pride in her voice. 'I have my job now, and I'm very lucky that I have my mother and Rose and Graham to help me – and I've made some very good friends.' She had then gone on to tell him all about her mother's new husband and the house she had bought close to them.

'You're an amazing woman,' he said, stunned by all her news.

'In the beginning, after Michael died, I was only surviving,' Kate told him honestly, 'but now, there are days when I feel I'm really enjoying things again – especially when I'm with Elizabeth.' She paused. 'Moving over here is not the life I had planned or the life I had dreamed about, but it's working. So far it works for us all.'

Kate had seen him on two occasions since the party, and was going to a dance with him on Saturday night, before leaving for her fortnight's holiday in Ireland the following day.

'You always seem to be going someplace else when I see you,' he had said the previous weekend, as they sat outside her house in his car having enjoyed a meal out together. Her mother and Lance were inside, babysitting Elizabeth for her. 'At least I know you're coming back this time.'

And then he had kissed her. The first kiss they'd had since meeting up again.

And as Kate felt his lips on hers, she was shocked to feel the same overwhelming passion that she'd felt that evening sitting on the bench at the tennis court. And then, she felt the pangs of guilt return at the thought of the loving, patient Michael who had never quite managed to stir her in the same way.

But she had loved Michael nonetheless – and had grown to love him more deeply each day of their short-lived marriage.

'I never in my wildest dreams imagined that this would ever happen again,' David said to her in a low, hesitant voice. 'I've been pinching myself ever since we met up at the party.' He paused. 'I've never met any girl since – not one – who came close to making me feel the way that you do. You know how much I care for you, don't you?'

Kate looked back at him now, her face dark and serious. 'Things have changed,' she told him in a quiet voice. 'And *I've* changed ... all the things that have happened in the last few years.' She glanced up at the bedroom window where Elizabeth lay sleeping. 'I have huge responsibilities that I didn't have then ...'

He had pressed a finger to her lips. 'Kate, Kate . . .' he said. 'I'm not putting any pressure on you. Let's just see where this goes . . . What do you say?' His hand sought hers now and he squeezed it tightly.

Kate looked up at his handsome, smiling face, and she felt a little spark ignite inside her – a little spark of hope.

Maybe, she thought, just maybe, this was the start of a different kind of dream.

THE HUNTER AND THE HUNTED

Further Titles by Cynthia S Roberts from Severn House

THE SAVAGE SHORE
THE STORMS OF FATE

THE HUNTER
AND THE HUNTED

Cynthia S Roberts

This first world edition published in Great Britain 1994 by
SEVERN HOUSE PUBLISHERS LTD of
9–15 High Street, Sutton, Surrey SM1 1DF.
First published in the USA 1994 by
SEVERN HOUSE PUBLISHERS INC., of
425 Park Avenue, New York, NY 10022.

British Library Cataloguing in Publication Data
Roberts, Cynthia S.
 Hunter and the Hunted
 I. Title
 823.914 [F]

 ISBN 0-7278-4601-9

Typeset by Hewer Text Composition Services, Edinburgh.
Printed and bound in Great Britain by
Redwood Books, Trowbridge, Wiltshire.

To Beryl and Ray Farrow
whose friendship burns bright
from our college years,
this book is affectionately dedicated.

Chapter One

It was a cruel moon. A hunter's moon. Its light as palely frosted as the grass. The cruelty lay in that it made all things vulnerable; the hunter with the hunted. They were victims, both.

The hunter was no more than a shadow, nebulous, soft-moving as the clouds that dappled furrow and hedgerow. He seemed at one with the landscape. Yet, moving or stilled, there was an intentness which set him apart. Like those night creatures he sought, his senses were pricked alert by fear and excitement. He was aware of a pulsing in his veins; a raw quickening of breath. A bloodlust that filled his nostrils as powerfully as the smells of rank earth and his own warm sweat. Familiar. Cloying.

The track lay before him now, silvered by frost and moonlight. He had but to cross it and gain the shelter of the copse beyond, then gather his snares and whatever warm flesh lay trapped within them. He slipped from the darkness of the blackthorn hedge and stood for a moment silhouetted starkly against the moon . . . Then they were upon him in a clatter of hooves and fierce wild cries, bloodcurdling, savage enough to drown even his own. He was aware only of terror that numbed thought and reason and killed all else, even the pain that burst within him. Dragged, trampled, torn asunder, he did not question why they came, or from whence. There was the salt taste of blood and tears, warm and viscous, then a coldness that he knew to be death. He wanted to cry out, but could not.

Dear God, he thought, was it like this for them . . . for those I hunted?

He was aware of a great languor; a great sorrow. He was no longer afraid.

*   *   *

1

The lone horseman making for St Samson village was unaware of the keen cold air whipping the exposed flesh of his face and stinging tears to his eyes. His thoughts lay elsewhere. The minor discomforts of life were natural to him, and of no account against the bleakness that overwhelmed him. It was true, Luke Farrow thought, that he was but one among many, their lives changed inexorably by the ending of the Napoleonic wars. God knows, it would be futile to wish such blood-letting prolonged, such savagery and mutilation. Yet, soldiering was all that he knew. There were those who would count him fortunate; change places all too eagerly. He was young, barely two and twenty, mercifully sound in wind and limb, and unencumbered by wife and family. The future was his to order as he chose.

The scream of some terrified creature startled him, causing his mare to rear in alarm, then halt, trembling. Something caught in the teeth of a trap perhaps? Human, or animal? He could not know. Yet the anguish in it chilled his blood, rendered him momentarily useless. He felt the prickle of fear at his nape as he urged his mount forward.

He rode with purpose now, made reckless by haste, the horse's metal shoes ringing clear as a tocsin upon the frosted stones of the highway. As he crossed the hump-backed bridge that forded the icy stream, he saw before him the jostling, heaving mass of horses and riders; a surging of hide and flesh, hooves and harness. He cried out harshly but saw nothing save the pallid faces, grotesque in the moonlight, white masks, distorted, unrecognisable. Then, violently, and with no word spoken, they were away. A cloud briefly obscured the moon, casting sudden darkness, and Farrow hesitated, confused. As it cleared, he impetuously reined in to follow, only to be halted by the filthy bundle of rags barring his pathway . . .

Some game they were playing, then? Some obscene ritual? The blundering of young men in their cups, and seeking distraction? From the glimpse he had caught of them they had been well dressed, no cloddish provincials, their mounts high bred. Luke Farrow dismounted and tentatively set out a hessian boot to prod the bundle, only to recoil in horror as he met living flesh. It had moved to his touch and, in a second, he was crouched beside it, supporting the bloodied wreckage of bone and sinew, cradling the dying remnants of a man. He sought despairingly to bring comfort, but could find none.

The unknown man had died in his arms, and Farrow could not regret it, for his injuries had been past enduring. Survival would have been crueller than death, of that he was certain. He could be certain of little else, save that the dead man was a labourer, or pauper even, for he was strong muscled for a man of middle years, hands hard-calloused by toil, and rough as his clothing. From the net and rough sacking he carried, a poacher about his night-work of snaring some creature for the pot. A venture that would have earned him a place upon the treadmill for his pains, a cell in a house of correction or, at worst, deportation or a place upon the gallows. Luke, fearful for those remaining of the murdered man's family, awkwardly lifted the lifeless flesh and carried it, with effort, to the grass verge at the roadside. Then he recovered the net and sacking and, wrapping them about a loose stone, hurled them deep into the ferny depths of a small copse near by. His hands were smeared now with blood, dark and sticky, and he wiped them viciously upon the frozen grass, feeling the gorge rise burning in his throat, the sour taste of vomit. He scrambled down the river bank, breaking the thin membrane of ice with his boot heel, plunging his hands into the freezing water beneath, grateful for the pain that engulfed him and drove out all other feeling. Yet he could not drive out the fury that obsessed him, his bitterness for those who had used a fellow man so savagely and with as little heed as if he were a stone or clod of earth. Inanimate. Unfeeling. A thing of no consequence. Luke Farrow mounted his horse and urged it towards the village. His hands upon the reins were so painful that he could have cried aloud, wept with that cruel return of feeling. Yet there was one, newly dead, who would know neither pain nor pleasure, only an emptiness deep as the grave itself.

Luke Farrow sighed. He had seen much of death, and learnt to accept its finality. Yet this was of a callousness that sickened him. A death performed for pleasure. The merciless feral bloodlust of the pack. He did not glance towards the victim as he rode away. The bloodiness and poverty, the grizzled hair, the tortured features were clear in his mind. He could not expunge them. Less clear was what he hoped to do; to learn. He could recall no features of the man's attackers. They were anonymous. Strangers all. He could not hope to identify them. Their voices had been silent, their savagery unwitnessed. All that he could dredge from memory was the moonlight upon pale masks of faces and the sudden glow of light upon a palomino mare, swift, elusive as its rider, then the dull gleam of silver. A saddle? Harness? Holster? Gun? Some brooch or emblem even? He sought, in vain, to recollect. It had been a glimpse, no more than that.

Luke Farrow had meant to ride through St Samson village, for it held nothing to claim him. It was the poorest hamlet, scarce worthy of the mention; a huddle of barren holdings, and set upon a savage shore. As savage, perhaps, as the murderers it sheltered. But there were those who would lie restlessly awake, awaiting one who would not return. They must be told, and the dead man decently buried. He was deserving of that, for pity's sake, and his own. Those who mourned him would believe him ridden down by some heedless coachman or drunken horseman. It was kinder so. Luke saw the crouched outline of an inn ahead, a lantern swinging high from the archway. He turned his mare towards it, her shoes clattering forlornly across the moonswept cobbles of the yard.

In the small limestone cottage within sound of the sea, Nerissa Pritchard lay wakeful, awaiting her father's return. Always, in his absence, she felt the same heaviness of spirit, a quickening of fear. She would not rest, she knew, until she heard the familiar click of the garden gate and the soft shuffling of his boots upon the pathway.

4

There would be the sounds of movement below, blurred, indistinguishable, then he would settle himself in the box-bed beside the fire, and sleep soundly until cock-crow, when his day's labours began. With his coming she would know again that old feeling of comfort and security that had been the essence of childhood. But she was no longer a child. She was sixteen years old and, since her mother's death of an aggravated fever, there had been little enough comfort, and less security. It grieved her that, with her mother's death, her father's joy in living seemed to have died too, and she was powerless to help him.

Nerissa crept from her bed to the casement, her bare feet moving soundlessly across the cold boards. Moonlight glowed without, pale and wintry, the garden an unknown place, mysteriously transformed by light. For a moment it seemed alien, menacing even, and she shivered involuntarily, filled with a coldness that had nothing to do with the frosted air.

It was naught but foolishness, she told herself. She would take her shawl from the chair and go below to warm herself at the fireside and await her father's return. She would brew him a hot spiced negus, to give welcome and thaw his blood. He would be near-frozen. Yes, that is what she must do, occupy her hands and thoughts, try not to dwell upon what might follow, should he be taken before the justices. She busied herself remorselessly at cleaning, tidying, tending to the fire, but always her mind stayed restless as her movements, her fears impossible to still. The negus cooled and congealed upon the hearth, the candles spilled their wax, the fire glowed brightly, then began to fade.

Daylight came. Nerissa sat sleepless in her chair, listening, waiting. At daybreak she dressed and washed herself in water from the yard, then drew on her hooded cloak and Sunday boots and went to search for him. The sound of the sea was loud to her ears, the wrenching of tide upon pebbles, its rhythmic suck and swell. The sharpness of iodine and salt stung in her nostrils. The wind from the sea blew cold upon her skin.

She turned, and saw them coming. A small, hesitant

company, awkward, bewildered, the landlord of the inn shuffling uneasily at their head.

"'Tis bad news we bring, mistress," he blurted clumsily.

"My father is injured? Hurt?"

"We had best come within."

She nodded.

"Yes. You had best enter." Her voice was as numbed and lifeless as her face, as drained of emotion. "He is hurt?" she demanded again.

"He is dead!" the innkeeper blurted. "I fear he is dead, ma'am." He cleared his throat painfully, florid face ugly with concern. "It is this gentleman here who found him, brought news. An accident it was. Some carriage upon the road, or some rider else." His explanation faltered and died.

Nerissa glanced towards Luke Farrow, her murmured acknowledgement inaudible, and he knew that she did not see him, indeed was unaware of all save her own hurt. He saw in his mind's eye that grotesque corpse at the roadside, and was filled with pity, disgust, for those who had wrought such violence. She was a pretty thing, he thought compassionately, so slight and fair, yet with a grave dignity beyond her years. She was scarcely more than child, a child with the promise of beauty that would bring her more sorrow than joy.

"My father, sir?" Her question was for the innkeeper, her eyes darkly troubled. "Where is . . . ?" She hesitated. "Where does he lie now?"

"At my inn, ma'am, the Pilgrim's Rest. You need have no fear. I will see to all . . . take responsibility," he added gruffly.

"No, I thank you kindly, sir, but I would have him here, at home. It is fitting that he be with his own. He would wish it."

The innkeeper fidgeted, glancing helplessly towards Luke Farrow, who gave a barely perceptible nod of the head.

"Then it shall be as you ask."

She watched them go, head held high, face set and tearless, a small forlorn figure further diminished by grief.

"What will become of her, landlord?" Luke Farrow asked quietly.

"God alone knows, sir! The poorhouse, like as not. 'Tis a small village, and work is hard to find."

"That house . . . is it her own? She will not be dispossessed?" he asked sharply.

"The cottage is tied, sir. Her father, Tom Pritchard, was a labourer upon a hilltop farm. His tenancy dies with him. It will be taken by another, and soon." He shook his head ruefully. "That is the way of things, in death as in all else. We are soon forgot. The pity is that such blows fall upon the frailest, those grieving and least able to withstand them."

"Indeed."

They gazed at each other in silence until the landlord said with shy awkwardness, "It was kind of you to bring warning, sir, to take such duty upon yourself. There are many who would have passed by, not concerned themselves. Life has become too cheap."

Luke said soberly, "I would pay for the funeral, if it can be done secretly, without giving offence."

"That would be a kindness, sir . . . for he would be buried in a pauper's grave else, uncoffined, and without winding sheet. He was a good man, deserving of better."

Luke nodded. "Then it is agreed," adding briskly, "I shall settle my account with you at the inn, and all else."

No, not all else, he thought wryly, not the murder of Tom Pritchard, for murder it had surely been. Yet to take his suspicions to the justices would avail him nothing, and serve only to add deeper despair to Nerissa Pritchard's grief. He had done what he was able. It was little enough in all conscience and woefully inadequate. Yet there was nothing to be gained by lingering here. The horsemen would be long gone, and all soon forgotten. He had neither proof nor reason for remaining. He settled his bill with the landlord, giving him instruction that the coffin be closed and firmly nailed before its journey to Pritchard's cottage. It was a poor enough resting place – no more than two arid rooms, scarce more than a hovel, more fitted for beasts of the field than human habitation. He saddled and mounted his mare and rode on. Yet what rode with him was not the memory of Tom Pritchard's tortured flesh, but the face of his daughter, wide eyed and tearless in grief. Well, he was free now, with nothing to hold him here. The future was of his own making. Why then this regret that there would be none awaiting his coming? None to grieve for him, as for Tom Pritchard, at his journey's ending?

The weathered grey stones of the manor house, set high on an eminence above St Samson village, had a quiet dignity. It was that rare dignity that comes only with age, an accidental softening and meliowing of that which is already beautiful. It seemed to have sprung from the soil like the boulders and stones in the ploughed fields surrounding it, and those rocks upon the seashore, honed smooth by the ceaseless ebb and flow of the tide. To those who dwelt in St Samson, the fishermen and labourers upon the land, the house seemed as remote and distant as the far-off hills; as fixed and unalterable. It simply existed, and they were aware of it, but its graciousness was as far removed from their own stark lives as the sun and the planets. Yet those within St Samson Court, seen or unseen, had as remorseless an influence upon their prosperity as the tide and the weather. The de Granvilles *were* St Samson; they owned, farmed, governed and ruled it. Like God Himself, they might as easily break as create, elevate or humble those who served them. If they lacked His charity and wisdom, then they were unaware of it. They were aware only that they had been born and chosen to rule, and had done so since their Norman forebears had claimed these lands for their own. They were entitled by blood and breeding, and none, then or now, had power or means to dispute it.

Sir Peter de Granville was not best pleased. It showed in his rigid bearing as he sat, grim faced, surveying the documents upon the library table before him. Any who might have doubted his Norman ancestry had but to study him to find confirmation. It was there in his bones and features; their etiolated gauntness common to his forebears, and sculpted in stone upon many a

8

Norman knight's tomb. If this lent him a certain elegance it also made him appear authoritarian and severe, which his present scowling ill-humour did nothing to dispel.

The cause of his displeasure were the demands for payment which lay scattered before him: invoices from tailors, saddlers, cordwainers, hatters and assorted creditors too numerous to name. It seemed that no gambling wager was too bizarre, no frivolity too obscure to have benefited from his son's reckless indulgence. It came to a pretty pass when tradesmen had the temerity to present their bills before the year was out, and in such an importunate manner. It was impertinent. Insulting even. Yet he could not deny that they had the right to be concerned. Not at Richard's extravagance and dissolute ways, which were none of their affair, but at his stupid attempts to dun them. The boy was immature. A rake and a spendthrift, without purpose or common decency. His mother had spoiled him outrageously, indulging him in every idle whim. That was the crux of it! Well, there would come a reckoning, and soon! He would no longer meekly stand surety for him, support his indolence! The boy must earn his keep; pay his creditors, or, by God, he would learn the reason why! De Granville would have summoned the young jackanapes there and then, given him a harsh dressing down, and demanded explanation. Even as he rose and reached towards the bell-pull upon the wall, the sound of horses' hooves upon the stones of the carriageway diverted him and he strode impatiently to the library window. Through the mullioned casement he caught a glimpse of his son and the noisy gaggle of young gentlemen, extravagantly attired, and dismounted now, surging around him.

"Milksops! Macaronis all!" he muttered in disgust. "Conceited young popinjays! Frills and furbelows, and not an ounce of sense between them!"

The library, his holy of holies, seemed to offer him neither solace nor refuge from the braying hilarity without. Yet, was he not being unduly harsh and critical, he wondered? They were, after all, young blades, carefree, over-indulged perhaps, but merely seeking adventure. It

9

was a natural "kicking over the traces", no more, as he himself had done. There was no real harm in them. No viciousness. He selected a cigar from the wooden box upon his desk, rolling it reflectively between thumb and fingers, savouring the texture of it, its colour and smell. He carefully lit it, then drew in its comforting taste and aroma. He looked about him with approval, enjoying the symmetrical rows of vellum bound books, the familiar atlases and spheres, the brass astrolobe, the navigational instruments, the paintings and etchings. The pungent odour of cigar smoke mingled with the mustier odours of leather and ink, paper and old parchment. A man's room. A bastion. Masculine and impregnable. He exhaled leisurely, then drew open a drawer, and swept the offending papers within.

None could deny that Richard de Granville was a handsome and exquisite young gentleman, and most fashionably attired in the manner of the *haut ton*. His doeskin inexpressibles were admirably close-tailored, his hessian boots elegant, and his roll-collared jacket, of dark blue velvet, quilted and cut in the latest mode. His three companions were no less sartorially stylish, yet they lacked the inbred arrogance, that superiority of mien, that set him apart. He was, now, the focus of a joshing, admiring coterie of his peers, their minds firmly set upon enjoyment or devilry.

His mother, Louisa, glancing indulgently through the leaded casement of the drawing room, thought with pardonable satisfaction that Richard was quite the most elegant of that high-spirited gathering. He undoubtedly cut a most eloquent figure. He was a natural leader; one to inspire and excite others. Her son was infinitely superior in every aspect . . . but such excellence was never an unalloyed blessing. As she had cause to know, it too often aroused envy and malice from others with sons less generously endowed by nature.

The groom had brought a horse from the stables, and with easy grace Richard de Granville had swung himself into the saddle. He glanced carelessly towards the house and, seeing her, raised his silk hat in greeting and made her a mocking bow, which she returned with a wave of her hand and an elaborate curtsey, unable to suppress affectionate laughter. He was handsome, she thought fondly, and had been from infancy. A captivating, engaging child, with his cloud of disordered curls, arresting blue eyes and engaging manner. He charmed all who met him, and none could stay vexed with him for long, for he had infinite power to seduce a smile or coax away hurt.

She watched him ride ahead of the others and out through the griffin-topped pillars of the court, then she returned to her discarded tapestry. With each new stitch a memory of his laughing and heedless ways grew in her mind, as bright as the threads she worked.

Richard de Granville and his companions had little purpose in mind save to fill the immediate tedium of their lives at St Samson. That it was no more than a desert, a cultural wasteland, they were agreed. It was merely an enforced halting place between the periodic forays to London and those fashionable watering places they enjoyed, and the civilised society denied to them. Here they were at ease only in each other's company; gaming, riding hard, hunting, frequenting the local taverns and the known gin-dens beyond, hell-raising, and oftimes whoring as they chose. It was a way of life familiar to the squirearchy and lesser aristocracy; indeed, an initiation rite. A rite of passage.

Sir David Hanford had urged on his horse and drawn abreast of de Granville's mount to demand languidly, "Well, sir? And did you sleep well after our sport of the night? No nightmares or phantoms, I trust?"

"None." De Granville's tone was indifferent. "I am not averse to exercise when the mood takes me, Hanford, and cannot resist an honest wager."

"And the paying of it?" Hanford's dark, saturnine face was wryly amused.

"Here!" De Granville impatiently thrust a hand into the pocket of his coat and produced a pouch of coins. "Take what is owed to you." As Hanford hesitated, he

11

said, "Take it, I say!" adding dryly, "One does not renege upon debts to gentlemen, only the lower orders. They are fair game."

They had slowed their pace, and Matthew Siberry, the son of the physician at Holly Grove, reined in his gelding beside them before blurting nervously, "I dared not tell you at the Court . . . could not make mention . . . but the man is dead."

"Dead?" For a moment de Granville was visibly shaken. "You are certain of this?"

"Certain. That rider who came upon us, you recall? He took news to the inn."

"And?"

"He summoned my father. Paid for his services."

"For what they were worth!" Hanford interjected, mouth wry.

Siberry flushed, but made no reply.

"The man was dead when your father arrived?" de Granville asked sharply. "There is no doubt about it?"

"None."

"Then there is naught to connect us with him. Naught to worry us." De Granville was coolly dismissive, in control of himself once more. He turned abruptly in his saddle to demand irritably of the lone rider behind them, "What ails you, Hardwicke? Has your mare cast a shoe? Or are you mooning after some field whore or harlot?"

Hardwicke reluctantly reined his mare towards them, biting at his underlip, eyes troubled. His skin, usually pale beneath its sprinkling of freckles and thatch of red hair, was cruelly flushed. Yet his voice was firm.

"We should not have done it," he said. "It was murder."

There was a painful silence.

"Murder? Hell and damnation, Hardwicke! Are you mad? Have you taken leave of the few senses you possess?" De Granville's voice was scathing, flaying raw. "Pull yourself together, man!"

Hardwicke paused, irresolute, then persisted steadfastly, "I shall confess to your father the justice, Hanford, tell him all."

"By God, you will not!" De Granville had dismounted in a fury and all but torn him from the saddle, raging, "You are as much involved in this as the rest! Would you court the gibbet and the hangman's noose?" His fierce grip was upon Hardwicke's neckerchief, wrenching, drawing tight. "Would you hang us all?"

Hardwicke trembled, but could not reply, and de Granville abruptly released him, thrusting him contemptuously aside. The flush that had disfigured Hardwicke's face had drained away, leaving him colourless, resistance spent.

"Speak one word of this," de Granville's voice was calm now, seemingly emotionless, "and it is you who will die, my friend. Be assured of it."

Hanford, distressed and trying vainly to ease the tension, said coaxingly, "Come, Hardwicke! Let us not fall out. It is not worth the aggravation and strife. We are friends of long standing. Worthy of better."

"He was naught but a common thief. A poacher," Siberry reminded him uneasily, "and of no account."

When Hardwicke remained unmoved, de Granville put an arm to his shoulders, pleading, voice penitent. "Believe me, Hardwicke, I sought only to protect my own property . . . my woods, my game, as any red-blooded man would. He would have fared no better at the hands of a gamekeeper, or the justices. I meant only to teach him a lesson, to mend his manners. Say you forgive me. Understand."

Hardwicke pulled away and murmured agreement, but did not raise his head. Then, silently, he remounted his horse and rode beside them. "Here . . ." Hanford said, thrusting the pouch of coins with clumsy awkwardness towards him. "Take this money, this wager, and give it to his kin . . . as payment, if you are so minded."

De Granville countered quickly, "You had best give it to me. I shall send a keeper or bailiff to offer it. It will be more fitting, and leave us uninvolved. It might arouse suspicion, else. Hardwicke, you are agreed?"

Hardwicke nodded, sick with shame at his own weakness, yet unable to force a stand. No, it would *not* leave them uninvolved. A man was dead, and they were culpable. He had played a part in that bloodshed. Murder . . . for murder it was. He must find excuse to see the dead man's kin, make reparation. It would not absolve him, nor lessen the act. Yet it was all that he could do.

De Granville's drawling tones drifted back to him, languid, deliberately provocative. "I said that I have it in mind to sell my mare, my palomino," he challenged. "It is too distinctive, too conspicuous. Well, what of it, Hardwicke? Will you make me fair offer? Secure yourself some good bloodstock for once?"

"No," said Hardwicke. "I am a poor judge of horseflesh and blood, de Granville. They seldom run true."

Chapter Two

Luke Farrow and the kindly innkeeper, Joe Protheroe, had not been deceived by Nerissa's quiet self-possession at news of her father's death. Each knew that it was not only stubborn pride that sustained her, but numbness of shock, a merciful deadening of feeling. Respite would be brief, and when feeling returned it would be crueller and more intense, and none could stem the anguish of it.

When they had quitted the cottage with those who awaited them without, Nerissa had returned to the chair beside the hearth. The fire had guttered and died to spent ashes, but the coldness of the room was less chilling than the coldness within her. She felt a sense of desolation greater than any she had ever known; a certainty that she was forsaken in flesh and spirit. Wholly alone. She would have welcomed the ease of grief, but could not weep nor cry aloud. The tears were locked within her, raw, deep buried, a painful hardness at her breastbone. A tightness that would not dissolve.

Almost without volition she arose and unlatched the door, then walked without. Her movements were stilted and unnatural, like those of an automaton, and she seemed as empty of thought and purpose. She found herself crossing the wasted drifts of sand and maram grass, those windswept dunes that bordered the shore. Her boots sank into the fine-blown sand and there was the familiar sound of the sea in her ears and the freshness of salt-laden wind upon her cheeks. Cold. Whipping her eyes with pained tears. She stumbled across the barrier of shifting pebbles, their restless grinding echoing the far-off suck of the tide beyond. Above her the circling seabirds wheeled and screamed, plaintive, desolate, their harsh

15

cries a sadness bleak as her own. She sank upon the wet sand and cried with them, in anger and rage and grief, that she was bereft. She wept for things ended and past, for a future unknown, and for those who had given her life, and loving, and who were no more. Then she arose, her tears spent, and walked slowly back to the empty house.

Nerissa knew that she must quit Scarweather Cottage, and soon, to make a new life. She would entrust the few hens and the contrary old rooster to those who came after, and they might make use of the few sticks of furniture, or burn them for kindling if they chose. Of one thing she was certain. She would not go meekly to some far-off poorhouse, deliver herself into the slavery of pauperdom. As long as there was strength in her arms and breath within her she would fight to stay independent and free. Her father had instilled into her the values of industry and self-reliance, the virtue of being beholden to none. Yet, to whom had *he* been beholden at the end? Who had removed the netting and sack he carried, to protect all that rightly belonged to him, his family, and good name? She could not think her father thief nor villain, as the law would judge. He had done what was forced upon him, and not for monetary gain, but simply to survive. Was it the innkeeper, Joe Protheroe, who had removed the evidence of her father's intent? Or, perhaps that stranger who had blundered upon him in death, and from pity remained and sought aid? She had treated him less kindly than he deserved, and was shamed by it. She hoped that he would understand and forgive. Who was he? The innkeeper had made mention, but it had slipped her mind with all else, so awkward had been her sorrow. She could not now recall his features. She remembered naught save that he was a gentleman in voice and bearing, and young, with a kindness and compassion that she had found hard to bear, for none but she had a right to grieving.

She would stay until the funeral upon the morrow, to see her father interred, then pack her belongings and be gone. She would walk the five miles to Holly Grove to the autumn hiring fair, and set herself up for bidding. She could clean and sew, cook and launder, and labour upon the land as determinedly as any other. She had health and strength enough, and was not lacking in wits. For an anguished moment she recalled that she was lacking in those who loved her without limits or restraint because she was of their own flesh. Those who loved her simply because she existed. Nerissa made a mash to feed the hens, then began to scour the house from top to bottom, clearing away all traces of those who had made it a home and refuge. But she could not expunge the past. It lay within her, living and inviolate, and would be with her always. The tears were raw upon her cheeks as she fell into sleep.

At St Samson Court the death upon the highway of a careless farm labourer gave less cause for speculation than the effect of the weather upon the hunting scene. Sir Peter de Granville had listened abstractedly to Jenkins, his bailiff, unable to hide his mounting impatience.

"The fellow worked for one of my tenant farmers, you say?"

"Indeed, sir . . . for John Manley over at Long Acre."

"Then have Manley deal with it," he ordered curtly. "It is no affair of mine. I cannot concern myself with such day-to-day trivia, Jenkins, these . . . irrelevances," adding testily, "that is why I pay you, and others! God knows, man, I cannot be expected to wet nurse my tenantry!"

Jenkins said stiffly, "You asked to be kept informed, sir, of those labouring upon the estate. Births and deaths and suchlike. You recollect?"

"Yes, yes, man!" he agreed. "At my wife's behest, that she might send help where needed, show proper interest, charity . . ." He broke off abruptly to ask, "There is family remaining? Dependants?"

"A young woman, a daughter, I am led to believe, of some sixteen or seventeen years."

"Then I had best inform the Poor Law Guardians. She will be unfitted to remain alone."

The bailiff shuffled, face reddening, to suggest, "Perhaps, if she might remain at the cottage awhile, sir?"

"It would serve no useful purpose!"

17

"Until her future is made clear, sir?" Jenkins persisted stolidly.

"Damn it, Jenkins! Have I not made myself plain? Her future *is* clear. These people know that their cottages are tied . . . that they may be dispossessed, through injury or a death. They accept our wages, our shelter, our bounty . . . They must accept all else, without whining or complaint. We cannot carry them all, from the cradle to the grave, else it would end in bankruptcy!" As Jenkins lingered uncomfortably, eyes downcast, Sir Peter demanded abrasively, "Well? Is there something more to discuss?"

"The funeral of the dead man, sir . . . Pritchard. Would you have me attend?"

"Attend, Jenkins?"

"As tribute from the estate, sir . . . Pritchard was a good worker. An honest man, and well respected." He paused, blurting awkwardly, "These folk set store by such things, their dignity and standing."

Sir Peter nodded. "Yes, yes, Jenkins! Do as you think fit," he agreed dismissively.

Really, he reflected, half exasperated, half amused, he would never understand these people. They were an unknown species. They inhabited a different sphere. "Dignity and standing", Jenkins had said. It was palpable nonsense! What dignity? What standing? They should be employed in honest toil, not crudely aping their betters, pretending to a distinction and refinement of feeling they could not hope to possess. The whole episode had irritated and unnerved him. He reached for the Canary wine, poured it and drank it at a draught. People should be contented to remain in that rank and station to which the Good Lord had seen fit to commend them, else there was no virtue in the order of things. There was a predetermined hierarchy in nature, as in all else. God knows, he had trials and responsibilities enough! Yet he accepted the vicissitudes of life equably, finding grace in his service to others. He would dwell no more upon it.

Upon Tom Pritchard's funeral morn, Nerissa arose at daybreak and fed the hens and rooster, weeping and railing at herself the while for such foolishness. Joe Protheroe had promised to send a sweeping boy from the yard of the Pilgrim's Rest to feed them and secure them against foxes at night, until such time as the new tenant of Scarweather Cottage came. She knew that he was a man of his word. They would not be neglected. Yet the feeling remained, the sense of guilt and self-reproach at deserting them. The rooster was a cantankerous creature, bellicose, and not averse to delivering a sly peck. A preening, ungrateful bird without affection. He had nothing to redeem him. Yet, perversely, Nerissa knew that she would miss him most of all. He had studied her suspiciously, head cocked, all aggression and beady eyes, and she had found brief solace in laughter that trembled too closely upon despair as she took her leave. She was, she thought, bidding farewell to a childhood that was over. A life outgrown.

From the cobbled yard she heard the sound of a lone rider hurrying by, taking the bridle way beyond, in a fierce clattering of hooves and urgent cries. Someone abroad early and not of a mind to linger. She knew no fear, only surprise, as she stooped to retrieve the kidskin pouch hurled to the pathway. Within were five gold sovereigns, bright and new minted. A fortune. More money than she had seen in all of her life. Nerissa gazed about her in bewilderment, anxious now and uncomprehending. Of the rider there was neither sight nor sound, nor of any other. Trembling and with legs painfully unsteady, she hurried within the house.

Tom Pritchard's coffin lay upon twin wooden stools before the fire of turf and kindling, two candles still burning low upon it and all but spent. Their charred wicks guttered in their melted wax, their spilt grease a frozen waterfall. Yet no colder, or more spent, than she. All night she had kept lone vigil beside her dead father and had felt no fear, knowing that there was naught to harm her. Yet, now, she felt oppressed by some nameless menace, vulnerable and truly alone. She could not doubt that the money had been thrown deliberately. But why? To what purpose? And by whom? None in the village could have afforded such reckless generosity, nor striven

19

so hard to remain unknown. A debt owed? A favour repaid? She could not believe it to be so. Her father had not been a wicked man, but gentle and kindly to all, a man to put one's trust in. Recompense, then, for his death? But that presupposed that it was not by accident, but by savage design. Who would have cause, or need, to kill him, since he owned nothing of value save his own life? Nerissa sank awkardly to her knees upon the bare boards beside the coffin, and prayed. Her words were clumsy and uncertain and brought her no peace of mind. She fetched a bucket of icy water from the well in the yard and washed herself painstakingly before the remnants of the fire, then tied her working clothing and small clothes into a crocheted shawl and dressed herself in her Sunday best, and drew on her good woollen stockings and boots. Then she wrapped the coins within a kerchief and thrust it deep into the bundle, together with the silver and few coppers remaining in the cracked jug upon the dresser. Then she sat quietly to await the coming of the funeral cart. It grieved her that she had no mourning clothes, only the dress of sprigged red cotton and the blue straw bonnet with the flowers at the brim.

" 'Twill be cheerful for you, Papa," she heard herself murmur foolishly, "it was ever your favourite, and 'tis all I own."

The words came to her clearly, as if they had been spoken aloud, as so often and tenderly in the past. "Handsome is as handsome does, my maid. And you are handsome in all you do, and all you are."

There was the rumble of cartwheels upon the stony track, the creak of the gate and the shuffling of boots upon the pathway. Nerissa snuffed out the candles between thumb and fingers and rested her cheek against the coldness of the coffin lid, then picked up her bundle and pulled open the door. Joe Protheroe took her arm firmly in his own fierce grip and led her, unspeaking, without. There were no other mourners before the cart, none save she and the innkeeper and the unknown man who tended the horse. Joe Protheroe's brawny face was polished red with cold, his plump cheeks smooth-glowing as apples as he stared fixedly ahead. He looked wretchedly ill-at-ease in his high starched collar, and she knew by his awkward gait that his boots were burdensome and new. A full mile and a half they walked in silence, with only the harsh creaking of the cartwheels, the clopping of hooves and the sound of the horse's laboured breathing to break the silence. That, and the plodding steps of the four hired pall-bearers who, sombre faced, followed the hearse. Nerissa held her bundle closer, hugging it jealously, for it was all of the past remaining now. If she stumbled upon some cart rut or stone upon the way, Joe Protheroe's hard-muscled grip was swift and calming. She thanked God silently for the innkeeper's gentle presence, the quiet reassurance of living flesh. She would not think of that empty husk within the confining box, devoid of all warmth and feeling. He was no one she knew. She would set her mind to past happiness, rekindling his humour and love, his warm protectiveness. She tried to picture his strong-boned features. Familiar. Loved. Yet, shadowy and unreal, they eluded her. She would be bereft of all now, even memory of him. She felt panic rise within her, a violence of loss, and stumbled awkwardly. Joe Protheroe, feeling her sudden trembling, steadied her with a kindly word and she nodded, head held high, eyes so blurred with tears that the fields and hedgerows shimmered as through a mist, a shroud as soft and all-enveloping as Tom Pritchard's own.

The tears did not fall, but stayed unshed, blurring all save feeling, making it bearable. She was dimly aware of the silent groups of cottagers at the roadside, gathered to offer their last respects to one who had no more need of them. Yet it was a kindness, she knew, and freely given, and her father had set store by such ancient custom; the ritual of death and grieving. It troubled her that she must make no sign of their presence, no acknowledgement, but walk blindly before the coffin as tradition decreed. The wayside mourners were no more than huddled shapes, hunched as bleakly and darkly as crows. Black. Anonymous. Yet, at the crossroads, where the cart halted, and those awaiting fell to their knees to recite the Lord's Prayer, Nerissa saw that the aged and the

21

feeble, and the young women with infants at their skirts or babes clasped protectively within their arms, felt real grief. It was an outpouring of love and pity; a kindness that wrenched her with such pain that she all but cried aloud.

At the Norman church of rough grey stone the cart halted, the coffin was lifted down with heavy awkwardness and a cloth of black mourning crêpe fastened upon it. The small Welsh cob that drew the cart had a purple plume upon his harness that danced as he tossed his head and pawed the grass. So alien a thing those purple feathers seemed; so bizarre and pitiful a decoration at life's ending. Was this all that life was, then? A heat and violence of feeling, then silence, and a rendering to dust? A return to that earth from which we had sprung? No! There had to be more than that, else 'twas not worth a corpse's candle.

There were few lasting memories of the funeral service within the church, or without at the graveside, for Nerissa felt detached and cruelly set apart. It was as if she watched from some far-off place, a pageant strange to her, and barely understood. Sounds, shapes, colours merged; swift as the patterns in a child's kaleidoscope and as awkward to recall. The spattering of copper coins upon the gravedigger's shining spade as he sought alms at the church door. Glowing candles seen through a haze of tears in prisms of rainbow light. Earnest faces, known and unknown. Voices joyously uplifted in hymns; subdued and reverent in prayer. The void that was filled. The void that could never be filled. The dry, sonorous voice intoning its certainty. The sure promise of life to come. And here, upon earth? The promise only of loneliness, and the rage, bewilderment and hurt of one forsaken and bereft. A travelling alone.

Nerissa had stood at the lych-gate and thanked those who were known to her: the clergyman and grave-digger, the pall bearers, the farmer at Long Acre, and those of his labourers who could be spared from toil, the fishermen and cottage folk, the tradesmen and artisans. Her eyes had been dry and her face set stiff with the effort such courtesy demanded, and Joe Protheroe, concerned at her paleness and fatigue, had been deeply troubled. There had been those present whose names or faces had been unknown to her, but she had greeted them with the same dignity, taking their hands within her own and speaking her gratitude. There had been one stranger whom the rector and others had greeted deferentially, and with whom Joe Protheroe had exchanged a few murmured words. Nerissa knew nothing of him, save that by his bearing and the elegance of his clothing he was undoubtedly a gentleman, and one well connected. Yet when he faced her and made his condolences, he seemed lacking in assurance, painfully ill-at-ease. He had flushed and stammered, skin as sorely reddened as his thatch of bright hair, so that she felt that it was she who offered the consolation of words, and he the bereaved. For a moment he had lingered uncertainly, then abruptly turned upon his heel. Whomsoever he was, Nerissa reflected, and whatever his past connection with Tom Pritchard, there was no denying that he was grieved by her father's death. Shy, inarticulate he might be, but she had surprised the beginnings of tears in his eyes, sorrow and regret as deep as her own.

Nerissa had taken up her bundle and turned to Joe Protheroe, putting a hand to his shoulder, trying to speak the words of gratitude and affection owed to him.

"You have been a good friend to me, Mr Protheroe," she said quietly, "I shall not forget you, nor the kindness you showed."

His bluff, rubicund face glowed with embarrassment and he shuffled uneasily, to declare, " 'Twas no more than was deserved. Neighbourliness." He cleared his throat. "I know that you would rather be gone. Memories and all such . . . 'tis the natural way of things. But should things not go right, you understand, there will be home for you at the Pilgrim's Rest. Aye, and honest welcome, and with work should you need it. There. I have said it, and will not speak of it again."

"And I shall keep it in memory, as kindly as I shall keep you."

Nerissa, much moved, reached up and set a kiss to his weathered cheek, and he blinked rapidly, unable to hide his astonishment and pleasure.

"I shall repay you the funeral costs." Nerissa's voice was low. As he made objection, she urged, "No, I beg you, hear me out. It is a debt my father would wish repaid. It is owed to you."

"No." He shook his head helplessly, bound by his promise to Luke Farrow, powerless to explain. "Think no more upon it, my lass. 'Tis over and done."

"No. I would not rest easy else."

He nodded. "Then we shall speak of it when next we meet. In kinder times, God willing."

"Yes, God willing." ·

He hesitated, broad face creased in concern, to say, "You are sure that you will not let me deliver you to the hirings at Holly Grove? 'Tis five miles and more, and . . . 'tis not a day for thinking overmuch, brooding upon things, the funeral and all." He broke off, shamed by his clumsiness, to blurt contritely, "It would be no distance by cart, my dear, and less with company . . . even such poor company as mine."

"I could wish for no better," Nerissa's denial was sincere, "but it is kinder that I find my way alone, else I would grieve our parting the more. You understand?"

"Aye. I understand. 'Tis the first day of the rest of your life. A new start. A new adventure . . . but have a care, my lass." His voice was rough with affection as he sought for words. "You have been loved and sheltered the while, made trusting by innocence. It is not always wise." He shook his head, declaring, "I will say no more, save that it is best to be on one's guard. Take nothing and no one at face value." He smiled wryly. "But you have endured preaching enough for one day, and I had best save my breath to cool my porridge! I'll wager that there is not one upon God's good earth who has learnt best from the experience of another. We must each make our own mistakes, our own way."

"I shall take care," she promised gently.

"Aye, happen," he said. "Happen . . ." Then, "You will send word by some carrier or pedlar upon the way? Give news of yourself, if you are able?"

"Yes. I will send word."

24

He thrust a hand into the deep pocket of his coat and, grinning sheepishly, produced an ill-wrapped parcel. " 'Tis nothing of account," he murmured, "no more than a few victuals to succour you upon the way. A slice of cold pie, some bread and cheese, and such. I would not have you go hungry, for you will be wanting your strength."

Nerissa took it from his outstretched hand, thanking him and setting it carefully within her bundle. Then, to his acute embarrassment and pleasure, she hugged him impulsively, eyes bright with unshed tears, confessing with honesty, "I have neither kith nor kin remaining now, yet I count myself blessed, truly blessed, to have so gentle a friend."

"Then I pray that you will find many such friends upon your way," he said, "and will always count me as one who cares, in good times and bad." He sniffed hard, then shuffled his boots, asking curtly, to mask his unease, "You have money enough for a night's lodging? For bed and board at some lodging house or drover's inn? Until you have found some workplace?"

"Yes. I thank you. I have money enough for that. A little carefully saved from . . ." she faltered painfully, "from earlier times."

He nodded, saying with awkwardness, "Then I had best be returning. I bid you Godspeed and a safe journey, my maid."

He watched her leave. She turned back once to wave to him, face pale and composed under her pretty bonnet-brim, head held firm. She was so brave and pretty a thing, he thought, so bright and trusting, that it near broke his heart to think upon what she might face. He could scarce restrain himself from crying out to her or running to seize her arm, begging her to stay. The inn was a poor enough place, God knows, but it could offer fare and shelter, protection and work of the roughest kind; more comfort than she would find upon the roads. Yet he knew that it would prove a brief respite before a greater danger, all the more insidious for being unknown.

He had not needed telling by Luke Farrow that Tom

Pritchard had been cold-bloodedly murdered. His mutilated body bore witness enough. The why and the wherefore of it remained obscure. Yet the savagery was indisputable. Whom had he offended, and how? And would the offence he had committed, and the resentment of it, put his daughter's life as brutally in danger? For her own sake, Nerissa Pritchard was best settled beyond St Samson. There had been violence and bloodshed enough. Joe Protheroe turned ruefully towards the Pilgrim's Rest, dispirited and saddened by Nerissa's leaving. He wondered uneasily why young Jeremy Hardwicke had been at the graveside, and so strangely troubled and withdrawn. He had always thought of him as a kindly lad, without guile or vindictiveness, although too easily led. Hardwicke was unwise in the company he kept, de Granville and his like, for he lacked their edge of cruelty, that selfish arrogance that would not be checked and must lead to disaster. Protheroe had too often suffered their boorishness at the Pilgrim's Rest, where their cloddish behaviour and crude taunts had offended many. Such self-styled "gentlemen" were no better than louts, for all their fine clothing and dandified airs. Surely it was inconceivable that they could have any involvement in Tom Pritchard's murder? And, if they had, then who would dare to lay complaint or hope to bring them to justice? The death of a poor farm labourer, and poacher, was of less account than the animals he snared. Save to Nerissa, his daughter. Joe Protheroe prayed most fervently that she would remain in ignorance of the murder. Should she ever suspect, and bring accusation, then she would find neither justice nor safety in St Samson. Nor would she escape vengeance, even should she journey to the ends of the earth.

Chapter Three

The journey to Holly Grove was not strange to Nerissa, for the spring and autumn hiring fairs were eagerly attended by those in the surrounding hamlets and the coastal villages and countryside beyond. She had travelled the road from infancy, in the earliest days clasped in her mother's arms upon an open farm waggon, then carried upon her father's broad shoulders. When she was capable of walking the few miles, she had trudged stolidly beside the others, adjusting her pace to their longer, more practised strides, fearful always lest she lag behind and be denied the glorious adventure beckoning. The fairs were an age-old tradition, and none in living memory could hazard when they had begun. They were ostensibly a meeting place for those wishing to sell their skills. The shepherds and herdsmen, the farm labourers and drovers, the thatchers, hedgers and ditchers, the carpenters and craftsmen, the ostlers and grooms, the milkmaids and scullery maids, those eager or desperate to bond themselves into the service or apprenticeship of others. Yet they were more than that. They were a place of enchantment, beyond the harsh confines of day-to-day living. A place for display and courting, for drinking and dancing, and squandering one's hard-earned pence in wilful extravagance. A place to buy dreams and memories to last longer than the tawdry trinkets upon a pedlar's tray. A place to be carefree.

Nerissa had travelled there, always, in hope and a fever of excitement, and arrayed, like all others, in her Sunday best. There had always been a bright cotton skirt of her mother's stitching, a hand-knitted shawl, gossamer fine, or a fresh scarlet ribbon to braid into her hair. She had stepped out jauntily in her high-polished boots, treasuring the admiring glances, the frivolity, the sheer good humour and exuberance of the crowd. It was a jostling, bustling, colourful scene, for all its practical purpose; more vital, perhaps, for its brevity. It was, Tom Pritchard had once declared, "a gauzy, ramshackle thing, of no more substance than a butterfly's wing, and as quick passing". Yet he had said it less with censure than regret, and had never willingly foregone a hiring. Never, until now.

Nerissa quickened her pace. Now, he too was gone, and the hiring fair no longer a joyous outing to be shared and mulled over at leisure, but a means of escape. A place to pledge her strength and future and to relinquish the past. She had walked but three miles and her feet were rubbed painfully sore by her stout leather boots and woollen stockings. Yet the deeper, more lasting pain lay within, disabling, too raw to be acknowledged.

She settled herself upon the grass of the wayside beside a shallow brook, its clear water lagged with waterweed and the skeletons of leaves. She cupped her hands in its icy coldness and drank gratefully, then dried them, first upon a tussock of coarse grass then upon the hem of her cloak. Her fingers tingled with life as she unknotted the shawl of her bundle and took out the ill-wrapped parcel, that food which Joe Protheroe had provided. She had no desire for eating, no appetite. Yet she would force herself to it, for it had been a thoughtfulness on his part, and given from kindness. She could not spurn it, else it would be rejecting the only real friendship that she had been shown. She opened the wrapping of Bristol brown paper and took up a hunk of ryebread and strong cheese. Beneath, stitched into a purse of waxed cotton, were four half-crowns and an enamelled pin. A likeness, in emerald green, of a four-leaved clover, worn fragile by age and use. A talisman, cherished, and tenderly given. Nerissa wept then, as she had wept upon the shore. Then she washed away all traces of tears in the clear running fastness of the brook and retied her bundle. The four-leaved clover she pinned firm into the ribbon band of her bonnet. It would lend her strength and resolution. Give memory of kindness past and a promise of hope. One day she would return,

God willing, to St Samson village, her fortune made. She would deliver the pin into Joe Protheroe's hands, and to his alone, with a gift of her own choosing. She took up her bundle and started upon the stony track. Her feet no longer hurt and there was new found confidence in her step, a sense of purpose. She was no longer fleeing a past, but striding towards a future. The hirings fair at Holly Grove was once more a place of promise.

Luke Farrow's journeying had taken him less distance than he might have wished. His discovery of the murder at St Samson had left him ill-disposed to linger thereabouts and he had no desire to become involved. He had done what little he was able to see the victim decently buried, and that was an end to the affair. Yet, insidiously, and against his will, memory persisted to bedevil him, and too often remembrance of the child, Nerissa Pritchard, her quiet dignity laying his pity raw.

Some fifteen miles inland from St Samson, at a country tavern where he sought food and refreshment, he had chanced upon an old acquaintance. Major Francis Miles Crawshay was a fellow officer in his former regiment, the 77th Foot, newly settled in the area, and at a loss as how best to occupy his time. He had as yet made few acquaintances and lacked diversion and stimulus. There is a natural bonding between those with shared hardship and history, and Crawshay's delight upon encountering his friend had been flattering and unfeigned. The outcome was that he would not countenance Farrow's stay at "so turgid and ill-kempt a den, for it would be the surest purgatory", and Farrow would clearly die of some rancid humour or else starve! It had taken little persuasion to effect Luke's swift removal to Knatchfield Grange, a manor house some three miles distant, an altogether more salubrious and relaxed an ambience. He could not regret it, and Crawshay, upon learning that he had no immediate plans, was at pains to amuse him, and therefore prolong his stay.

Crawshay's wife, Arabella, whom Luke had known and liked from his days in the regiment, was no less insistent upon his remaining as their guest. Her welcome had been as spontaneous as it was cordial as she had declared impulsively, "I beg that you will stay with us for as long as ever you are able without collapsing from vexation and boredom, Captain Farrow." Her clear, intelligent eyes were amused as she confessed, "I will own that your coming is most providential, an answer to a heart-felt prayer." As Luke glanced at her questioningly, she continued irrepressibly, "Were it not for your chance visit, the diversion it affords, I would undoubtedly have ended in Bedlam, or, at the very least murdered Francis."

"Then I am only grateful that such mayhem is avoided, ma'am," Luke responded, straight faced.

"His behaviour of late has been quite intolerable," she confided serenely, "enough to try the patience of a very saint and martyr, much less a submissive wife trying to bring a little order and discipline to a new household."

"Nonsense, my dear!" Crawshay's denial was absurdly softened by the look of indulgent affection which he gave her. "I have been a very pillar of patience and rectitude. As for wifely submission – I vow that I have yet to catch glimpse of it! Believe me, Farrow, it is as rare as hens' teeth, and as much a fiction!"

Arabella's delighted laughter so disarmed the two men that soon they were chuckling with her, and it was in this mood of companionable good humour that Luke accepted refreshment, before Arabella insisted upon accompanying him to view his room.

Arabella, Luke decided, following her obediently up the elegantly curving staircase, was altogether a most admirable young gentlewoman; charming and assured. Moreover, she was as sunny natured as she was beautiful. Crawshay was indubitably a fortunate man. What Luke found most appealing was that she lacked all affectation and simpering archness. She was agreeably direct in manner. In her dealings with those in Crawshay's regiment, she had shown rare tact and generosity of spirit, and was much respected for it. More than that, she was liked by all.

Arabella, preceding him into the newly furnished bed-chamber, made apology that the fire was not yet lighted nor hot water to hand, promising that she would have it rectified upon the instant.

"And I shall see that there are some well-chosen books brought, some sweetmeats and night-time refreshment, and a hip-bath and warmed towels for your use."

His protestations that the room was charming and lacking for nothing for his comfort were gently but firmly brushed aside as she crossed the room and threw wide the casement.

"You see, Captain Farrow . . ."

"Luke."

"Luke," she conceded smiling. "There is a delightful view of the gardens and park beyond, with a glimpse of the lake and gazebo. You will find it quiet and relaxing, I feel sure," adding wickedly, "yet not too quiet, I hope, for Francis swears that the statues we have inherited are all past guests, died of boredom and become petrified."

"Then I will endeavour to stay lively and amusing, and not add to their number," he promised.

"It is enough that you provide Francis company and diversion," she said fervently. "He is the dearest of men, but too easily exasperated by country living, its slowness of pace. I fear that he will find it hard to adapt to the more leisured pursuits of the squirearchy. He is a man who thrives best upon challenge, excitement, the constant stimulus of change."

"That is true of many whose lives are spent in soldiering, Arabella."

"Perhaps – although I do not see the same restlessness in you."

"Then it may be that I keep it deeper hidden," he said with an attempt at lightness. "I am altogether more devious, and lack a wise and perceptive wife such as you."

She would not be diverted, persisting, "You will not rejoin the regiment, Luke?"

"No. I am done with soldiering."

She nodded her understanding, confessing, "That is Francis's burden, and mine."

"Soldiering?"

"That it is all of his life. He could conceive of no other.

Accept no other. It is all he needs. The comradeship. The authority. The risks . . ."

"He has need of you, Arabella."

She shook her head, saying honestly and without rancour, "I do not deceive myself that I am all of his life, or even the important part of it, Luke. I offer him calm and loving. A respite from conflict."

He did not know how best to answer her.

"I have made it my mission to offer him a tranquil place . . . somewhere to soothe the rawness, the hurts of living, and dying."

"And is it enough?" His voice was low, scarce audible.

"It is enough."

"Then he is a fortunate man," Luke said with conviction.

Despite Arabella's regrets that Knatchfield Grange remained, in her own words, "in a state of unpardonable squalor", to Luke it afforded an oasis of tranquillity and order. Arabella had recently inherited the property from a great-uncle upon the distaff side, and with it all his bachelor's furnishings, books and a fine collection of Chinese porcelain. There had been a Spartan austerity in the old gentleman's surroundings, a cold reserve matching his own.

The library, panelled study, Great Hall and three bedchambers which were uncompromisingly masculine, Arabella prudently left unaltered. They provided Francis a welcome retreat, well-worn, faded, and with that comfortable shabbiness which comes only of age and usage. Elsewhere she wrought gentle transformation, with crystal and silver, cherished rugs and draperies, and those small personal bibelots and *objets d'art* lovingly collected. Bowls of pot-pourri subtly scented the rooms; candles glowed from elegant wall-sconces and candelabra; flowers and berried foliage blossomed again within. Arabella unobtrusively, and with natural artistry, had accomplished what she had set out to do. She had created for Francis a home, "somewhere to soothe the rawness and the hurts of living, and dying." Luke, whose own future was undecided, was only grateful that, for a short while at least, he was privileged to share it.

It was, Luke thought, a cheerful and well-run household, with the servants attentive and hard-working, yet plainly content. The atmosphere, both above and below stairs, was cordial and relaxed, yet with Arabella undoubtedly firmly in control as mistress. It was plain that the servants and household staff respected her, and Francis was clearly besotted by his handsome and efficient wife.

At dinner they were a relaxed and congenial small company, in perfect accord. The three had lingered pleasurably at table, for the meal had proved delectable, with excellent wines, and conversation as full-bodied and freely flowing. The two men had reminisced, wallowed in nostalgia and occasionally invented so outrageously that Arabella, overcome with laughter, had begged them to desist. There could seldom have been a more convivial reunion, or so sartorially elegant a trio. They perfectly complemented the graciousness of their setting: the pristine napery, the soft glow of silver and cut crystal by candlelight, the gleaming epergnes spilling bon-bons and sweetmeats, fruit and flowers.

Before Arabella rose to take her leave of the gentlemen and abandon them to their cigars and port, she had asked Luke how he had fared upon the way, and what quirk of fate had lodged him at the tavern where Francis had unexpectedly chanced upon him.

He had hesitated at first, then told of his gruesome discovery of Tom Pritchard's body at St Samson.

She had been distressed by the cruelty and senselessness of the crime, demanding, "You believe that he was killed by those whom you glimpsed riding away, Luke? Those so-called gentlemen?"

"Yes. I fear it to be so."

"In heaven's name, why? What motive could there be?" She was plainly bewildered. "It makes no sense. If, as you say, he was a poor man, a farm labourer, then they were not highwaymen or common thieves, out for gain."

Luke and Francis Crawshay exchanged glances before her husband said quietly, "Men do not always hunt and

33

kill with reason, Arabella. It is not always to destroy an enemy, or protect their own, nor even for glory or gain. Sometimes viciousness is born into them, bred in the bone. One savage animal can whip up a blood lust, infect a pack. It is the law of the jungle."

Arabella shuddered her disgust, protesting shocked and set faced, "Luke does not speak of animals, but men, Francis! Human beings, not savages, brutes."

"I fear that is *exactly* what they are, my dear."

"No! They are less than animals, Crawshay," Luke interjected with cold anger, "for they do not kill from instinct or purely to survive. Their killing is cold-blooded, cerebral even. A planned execution."

"Then I would wish them the same ending, the same fate!" Arabella exclaimed vehemently, rising abruptly to take her leave. She was visibly distressed and Crawshay made a tentative step towards her, but she shook her head, rejecting his concern, seeking to gain control of herself.

"Tomorrow you shall both accompany me to the fair at Holly Grove," she said with forced lightness. "The servants are agog with news of it. It will prove diversion and adventure."

"I do not think, my love, that it is a fitting place for a gentlewoman," Crawshay ventured doubtfully. "There will be drunkenness and rough horseplay, no doubt, and worse villainy . . ." He broke off awkwardly, colouring under her scrutiny.

"Then I shall be glad of your company and Luke's to offer me firm protection. Otherwise, I shall go alone."

Crawshay said vexedly, "Confound it, Arabella! You know that we will take you, if you are so obstinately set upon it! I would not allow you to travel unescorted. I would forbid it!"

Arabella had briefly stiffened, about to make sharp response, but swallowed her resentment, to say with deceptive meekness, "Then it is agreed, my dear, for you know how bitterly it would grieve me to go against your wishes."

Crawshay murmured inaudibly and tugged at the lace of his sleeve.

Arabella, poise and equanimity restored, glanced towards Luke. Her eyes were challengingly bright and a dimple appeared at the corner of her mouth as she fought to conquer a smile.

"Then I will bid you gentlemen goodnight, and leave you to your port," she said demurely, "and to setting the world to right. I cannot doubt that you have the wit, energy and tenacity of purpose to do whatever is required."

"And the deviousness and charm?" Luke hazarded, innocently straightfaced.

"I see that we are in perfect accord, Captain Farrow, sir." Arabella dropped him a mocking curtsey, eyes amused, and was gone with a careless rustling of silk skirts and a flurry of ringleted curls.

"Arabella is a charming and spirited companion, Crawshay, and a woman of rare good humour and intelligence," Luke praised warmly, adding awkwardly, "I regret that I spoke of the murder. It was foolishly insensitive. I would not willingly cause her grief."

In the flickering candle glow Crawshay's eyes were hooded, mouth wry, and his voice, when he spoke, was altered and subdued. "No more would I, Farrow," he agreed. "No more would I."

Nerissa knew that it would be best to do as Joe Protheroe had advised and find board and lodging for the night. She would find it strange to awaken in some unknown room and bed, for she had never before ventured overnight beyond Scarweather Cottage. The hirings would not begin until the morrow, but there would be plenty of folk converging upon Holly Grove in search of work, and clean rooms in the inns and small taverns hard to come by. The drovers, hardened by the rigours of weather and life upon the roads, would as like as not settle for the open fields or the shelter of a pig sty or cowshed. Their womenfolk might sleep rough beside them, or seek the comfort of some farmer's loft or barn, for the autumn nights were treacherous, and ice and cold winds had come early.

Nerissa, scuffling her boots through the drifted leaves at the wayside, saw a wooden stile abutting the grass verge of the byway beyond and halted, resting her bundle upon her hip. She would climb into the field and seek the shelter of a hedge, then take some coppers and small silver from her hoard. It would be wiser to do it unseen, for ahead there would be vagrants and footpads and, likely, pickpockets too, drawn by the lure of the fair and the innocence of the unwary. Perhaps it would be wiser to put Joe Protheroe's half-crowns with her pouch of gold coins and pin it within her petticoat or bodice, for she might sleep the sounder then, knowing it to be safe, inviolate.

Yet could she remain inviolate? The risks for a lone woman, and one unprotected, upon the highway, were clear to her. Despite Joe Protheroe's halting attempts to warn her, and his fears for her innocence, she was country bred, and knew what life and birth and death were about. She would be prudent in her dealings with others, not put herself foolishly in danger. She would travel, if she were able, in the company of other women, and not confide to any that she carried money upon her, lest it lead to envy and violence. Should she be set upon by a footpad, or some vagrant bent upon lust or savagery, she would not submit meekly, but give honest account of herself, make savage return. She had sound lungs and strength and spirit enough to protect herself.

Nerissa, despite her attempts to convince herself and bolster her confidence, glanced about her uneasily. Then, knowing herself to be unobserved, she pinned the pouch of coins firmly beneath the waistband of her cambric petticoat and took up her bundle.

When she returned to the byway a fresh, cold breeze had sprung up, ruffling the sere brown leaves upon the grass and stirring the topmost branches of the trees. She felt the cold sting of it upon her face, lifting the strings of her bonnet. A country wind, redolent of earth and bruised grass, and of all things living. She would not think upon that newly turned plot. She would not weep for a colder, rougher wind and flung spray, and blown spume, and the wild cries of seabirds – nor for the stiffening of salt upon her skin, raw as tears. What was it that Joe Protheroe had said? She tried desperately to recall the words. "Today is

the first day of the rest of your life, a time for adventure."
The truth was that she had no heart for adventuring or
change. She would have been content to spend her life
at Scarweather Cottage, within sound and sight of the
sea, and with those who loved her. Nerissa steadied her
bundle, and walked on.

She had known when she was within distance of Holly
Grove by the walkers plodding determinedly ahead, and
those converging from the adjoining tracks and byways.
Men, women and infants and babes in arms, mingled or
set apart, all were intent upon the same goal, the same
destination. Ill-shod or stoutly booted, ragged or neatly
clothed, defiant or dispirited, it made no matter. Each
strove to be first. The women seemed to be the more
footsore and weary, the children at their heels silenced
by fatigue or grizzling uselessly, too bewildered to cry
aloud. Nerissa had hurried forward as a child, a girl
of some three years of age, had stumbled upon the
uneven track and fallen awkwardly. The infant's palms
were scraped and bloodied, her anguished cries as much
from despair as pain, for her mother was trudging ahead, a
babe asleep within the tattered shawl pinned tightly about
her. She had turned at her daughter's cry, but Nerissa was
already beside the child, cradling her close, soothing and
quietening her. She had searched within her bundle for a
salve, spreading it gently upon the broken skin, binding it
with a clean white kerchief, then kissing away the smudged
traces of tears.

"There," she said, smiling, "you are a wounded soldier,
and brave, and the very next place where we may halt in
comfort, you shall share in my food."

The child's gaze was turned upon her mother, wide
eyed, anxious in its pleading, although she uttered no
word.

"That is a kindness," the young woman said, adjusting
the shawl about the sleeping babe, "and I will not refuse
it, for Sian has not eaten since early morn, when I begged
a crust at a farmhouse and some buttermilk for the babe,"
admitting with painful honesty, "what little pride I felt for
myself is long gone, and for Sian and Aled I have none.

37

I would work every hour God gave, beg, steal if need be, to see them fed . . . I have lost all sense of shame."

"The shame would lie in not loving them," Nerissa said quietly, "not in loving them too much."

The young woman's eyes filled with tears and she opened them wide, blinking rapidly, chin held high to stop them spilling. "I am Ruth Sayce." She offered Nerissa her free hand.

"And I am Nerissa Pritchard." She clasped Ruth's hand firmly, feeling its cold fleshlessness within her own.

"You are travelling alone, Nerissa?"

"Yes. My father has lately died. I go to Holly Grove to seek work at the hirings. And you?"

"Yes, we are alone now. My husband, Will, he was a master thatcher over Cornford way. A fall it was, an accident that did for him – and us."

"You had no friends and family thereabouts?"

"No, for he came seeking work from Talog, in Carmarthenshire, 'twould be a better life, he thought. And so it was, for he was a good worker, and honest too. Without an idle bone in his body. I miss him sorely. More than I can say."

"And where do you go now, Ruth?"

"I return to Talog as best I can, for the Poor Law Guardians will no longer support us. We are not native to the place, to Cornford. They took us by cart to the parish boundaries and bade me find my own way and not return."

"And will you?"

"Return? No . . . for fear we will be set apart in the poorhouse, or in separate towns, and I might never see nor reclaim them. It is the law."

"It is a long road to Carmarthen," Nerissa began, troubled, "and will take you weeks of hard walking, and in harsh weather."

"It would be harsher were I to remain." Ruth's voice was low, but filled with certainty.

"Will you put yourself for hiring at Holly Grove?"

"No. None would take me with a child and a babe in arms." Her tone held no rancour. "There are many such as you, young and able bodied, without encumbrances. A room and board would serve you well enough. But who would choose to give us place and shelter? Sian is too young to tend to the babe. No. I *shall* go to the hirings fair, but for remembrance's sake, for Will had a mind to take us there. 'Twas all arranged. He would have stood with the thatchers, do you see? In his best moleskins and with a favour of straw upon his hatband, to show his craft before others, as the shepherds wear tufts of sheep fleece and suchlike." Ruth's thin dark face was vivid with pleasure. "Oh, 'tis a rare, fine place for enjoyment and laughter, the hirings fair, and it would be a grief to Will were we to pass it by unseen. I will go, for that much is owed him."

They had come to a grassy bank at the roadside and Nerissa, holding fast to Sian's cloth-bound hand, ventured, "Shall we halt here awhile? Time is not pressing, and I'll own I am hungry."

They had seated themselves companionably upon the strand and Ruth had settled the sleeping Aled upon the grass beside her, well wrapped in his woollen shawl. He had not awakened but lay there, a small, swathed chrysalis in a checked cocoon.

The bread and cheese remaining and the cold pie were generously divided, with Nerissa claiming that she could not eat more than a morsel, for she had already eaten, and too well. Ruth too had eaten almost as frugally, restraining herself out of politeness, not wishing to offend. Sian had eaten not voraciously nor with greediness, but with joy, savouring each precious mouthful, intent upon making it last. They had watched her secretly, their warmth of pleasure as real as her own.

"Will you not thank Nerissa kindly for feeding us?" Ruth prompted.

Sian, shy and hesitant, had scrambled to her feet, then hung back for a moment, only to throw her bandaged hands about Nerissa in an impulsive embrace, putting a damp kiss to her cheek.

"I did not hear the words," Ruth rebuked gently.

"A kiss serves better," Nerissa said, smiling and brushing the crumbs from her red cotton dress.

She rose and took up her bundle, and Sian ran, without prompting, and slipped her hand into Nerissa's then looked up, eyes shining, to ask, "Will you come with us to Holly Grove Fair?"

"I will indeed," said Nerissa.

"Will it be a long road after, to Carmarthen town, Mama?" Sian's voice was anxious.

"The shorter for friendship," Ruth Sayce said, picking up the sleeping babe and settling him close.

Chapter Four

By mid afternoon the small market town of Holly Grove was abustle with human and animal life, for the autumn hirings were but part of the noisy activity and fevered gaiety that the fair commanded. Today was merely a rehearsal for the excitement of the morrow, but the din and clamour were no less frenzied. The stall-holders and cheapjacks were busily erecting trestles and setting out their wares, the sideshows were being assembled, the stages set. A cacophony of sounds pierced the air: nailing, banging, sawing amid a growing confusion of movement and shouted commands. Fire-eaters, jugglers, dwarfs, freaks and grotesques rubbed shoulders with bare-knuckled fighters; caged animals vied with clowns. Vegetables lay heaped beside cheap trinkets and colourful cottons. Fortune-tellers and mystics set up their booths alongside wood-carvers and lace-makers. Sweetmeats were enticingly displayed. And beyond, where the pens and barriers for the animals were being dragged into place, the scraping and grating was all but drowned by the shouts of the herdsmen and drovers, the bellowing of cattle and the mutinous cries of the sheep and, more strident yet, the squawking and hissing of geese.

For those with no pence to squander but a surfeit of time, it made rare amusement, and Nerissa, Ruth and Sian strolled, entranced, amidst the colourful splendours, although the babe, Aled, remained stoically unimpressed. Nerissa, despite Ruth's strictures, spent a halfpenny upon some sweetmeats for the children which were received with rapture and as rapturously disposed. Sian had earned too a little painted monkey upon a stick, as befitted a "brave and wounded soldier", and would not be parted from it. Her sheer, untarnished happiness infected the others, lifting their spirits. Her joy in the moment briefly dispelled the shadows of the past, the uncertainty of what lay ahead. They were a relaxed and carefree company, and for one small child it was a glowing, golden day that would never lose savour nor be forgotten. Nerissa was glad that such innocent happiness existed. Whatever the future held, memory of it would brighten many a winter darkness and rekindle warmth and hope.

While Ruth and the children were absorbed in the wonders of the fair, Nerissa, with a murmured excuse, slipped away to the small inn which she had glimpsed beyond the village green. It seemed clean and well ordered, and she would willingly have squandered a few of her pence upon a comfortable bed for the night. The landlord, a jovial red-faced fellow, with so many folds of flesh that it was hard to distinguish his neck from his chins, was cheerfully expansive and eager to please. Yes, there was a suitable bed-chamber remaining, he declared, and one only, for there were many attending the hirings. He could have rented his entire inn ten times over, to gentlefolk and cottagers alike, so fierce was the demand.

"I will not boast, ma'am, for it is not in my nature," he declared, tongue in cheek, "but I'll wager there is no better room in all of Holly Grove, no, nor linen as fresh starched and laundered, nor terms so reasonable. 'Tis a sacrifice to hire it so cheaply, and that is a fact that none can dispute."

"And the charge, sir?"

"Three pence for the night, ma'am, and a hearty breakfast thrown in, with victuals enough to please a starving drover, let alone a charming young lady of quality like yourself."

Such blatant flattery amused Nerissa, who knew that it was all too clear that she came of common stock. She found herself smiling involuntarily, then laughing aloud, and the landlord and his potman were swift to join in the merriment.

"Well, ma'am?" The landlord wiped his brawny hands upon his leather apron. "You had best inspect the room

42

to see if it will serve, else, I'll warrant, it will not long remain empty. If you will follow me . . ."

Nerissa hesitated, then blurted impulsively, "Begging your indulgence, sir. I would sooner have place in some dry loft or coachhouse. 'Twill be clean, I know, and straw will suffice for a bed. There is another woman and two young children, one no more than a babe in arms."

He listened in silence, face impassive.

"I would pay you well, sir," she pleaded anxiously, face hot with shame, adding hurriedly, "and give two pence extra for our breakfasts and milk for the child. And I would pay you *now*, sir, so that you will be sure of our money, and know that we are neither vagrants nor fly-by-nights."

"You are here for the hirings?" he demanded gruffly.

"Yes, sir, I am, but my friend, she is returning to Carmarthenshire, upon the roads, because of the Poor Laws. I would see her comfortably settled for at least one night." Nerissa's upturned face under her bonnet brim was gently appealing, and the landlord was not a wholly insensitive man. He turned his gaze enquiringly upon the potman, whose lips twitched irresistibly before he glanced pointedly away.

"Well . . ." The landlord's bluff face was irresolute then broke into a beatific smile as he made his surrender. "Well," he repeated, trying to force harshness into his voice, "since you are prepared to pay in advance and will be of no real burden to man or beast. Then, yes, you may have the stable loft."

The potman's smile was wider than Nerissa's own as she all but embraced the landlord in her gratitude.

Her face was warm with delight as she declared, "You will not regret it, sir, I swear. We will see to it that all is swept clean, left tidy upon our leaving. You will scarce know that it has been in use."

" 'Tis the horses who must bear the inconvenience, not I," the landlord said with dry humour. "You had best make your peace with them," adding, "I dare say that the heat from the stables will keep you warm enough."

"And the smell!" testified the potman, wry faced

43

Nerissa carefully counted out the small coins from the pocket of her dress, giving the landlord the amount agreed and setting it upon a marble-topped table.

He cleared his throat abrasively then thrust a penny of it back towards her, under cover of his hand. He shook his head in brisk warning as she made to offer him her thanks.

"You shall have bread and cheese for supper, with a tankard of best ale," he said with rough good humour, "and the same victuals as those within the inn, and there will be milk for the babe when morning comes. You may be served here with the other guests, if it pleases you better."

Nerissa said, voice low, "What pleases me is your kindness, sir, that you treat all with dignity and under-standing, whatever their estate, and I thank you for that."

The landlord's bucolic face was raw with pleasure, as, " 'Tis naught," he protested, "naught of account."

"It is the mark of a true gentleman, sir, and of every account." Nerissa smiled at him, then, curtseying serenely, took her leave.

The landlord turned sharply to surprise an expression of simpering foolishness upon his potman's face, quickly banished as whistling nonchalantly he set about replacing the pewter tankards upon their hooks.

"It is a rare treat to be in the employment of a true gentleman," he said to no one in particular.

The landlord scowled, about to make angry reply, then almost against his will, broke into laughter. "Aye," he said, humour restored, " 'tis the first time I have been accused of putting virtue above pence, and I will hazard I have small chance of hearing it again."

"As much chance as a field whore," ventured the potman slyly as their vigorous laughter filled the inn.

It was comfortable and dry within the stable loft with thickly spread straw for a bedding, and the innkeeper had been as good as his word. They ate their fill of bread and strong farmhouse cheese, washed down with mulled ale, sizzling from the thrust of a red-hot poker, and it warmed and cheered them beyond measure.

The babe, Aled, lay as replete with rusks and good whole milk, not buttermilk, and slept soundly with cheeks aglow and lips softly parted, his small fists ecstatically curled beneath the shawl which served as his blanket.

Sian, sated with warmth and victuals, had tried valiantly to stay awake, to listen to the murmured conversation and prolong the excitement and the glory of the day. Yet, despite her efforts, her eyelids drooped heavily then finally closed, lashes dark upon her cheeks.

Watching her, Ruth smiled, pushing a frond of hair from the child's forehead with gentle fingers, her touch protective. Her mild, brown eyes, so like her daughter's, were soft with gratitude as she said with quiet sincerity, "It has been a good day, Nerissa. A day I had not thought to enjoy at its beginning, for I'll own my spirits were low, and the children bewildered and fretful with hunger. It was all I could do to trudge on, keep myself walking."

"Yet you did," Nerissa reminded gently.

"Not from hope," Ruth confessed with honesty, "but because there was no turning back. I do not know, even now, how or when we will reach Carmarthenshire and what awaits us. Yet the people are my own, friends and family, and will not see us starve, of that I am certain. For Will's sake, and my own. 'Twill give me peace of mind, for should I fall sick, or die as he did, then they will have found shelter and belonging."

Nerissa said with conviction, "You will reach Carmarthenshire safely, and soon, of that I am certain, for you have courage and spirit enough to survive whatever comes," admitting ruefully, "Of my own future I am less sure, but wherever it takes me, I will come to Talog to search you out, believe it. When my fortune is made."

Ruth took Nerissa's hand within her roughened grasp, vowing with shy affection, "There will be the warmest welcome, you may depend, for none upon the way or since Will's death has treated us so kindly, nor cared so much. As to your fortune, whether rich or pauper-poor, it will make no matter, for you may share whatever we own, as you have shared with me and mine, you have my oath upon it." Her eyes were bright with tears, but she would not let them fall, pride and spirit forbidding such weakness. To hide her emotion she turned away, settling herself abruptly into the hay beside the sleeping children, murmuring, "We had best take whatever rest we may, for it will be a long day tomorrow."

"Yes, but we shall both find ourselves a step nearer a home and safety, God willing."

"Yes, God willing."

It was more prayer than conviction, and Nerissa, burrowing herself into the piled hay of the stable-loft, felt the treacherous prick of tears at her eyes and a loneliness of loss returning, the self-doubt, desolation.

Long after Ruth, exhausted by sorrow and her journeying upon the roads, had fallen into sleep and forgetfulness, Nerissa stayed painfully awake. For her, there was no such solace. Her mind stayed active, reliving the past, filled with fears for the future. The rhythmic breathing of Ruth and the children and the unfamiliar sounds and cries of the night creatures without added to her feelings of isolation and strangeness. From the stable beneath, the heat of the horses and the musky odours of their sweat and ordure rose thickly to her nostrils with the acrid ammonia tang of equine urine. The smells of leather, liniment and dried hay fused with the sounds of the sleeping animals as they stirred restlessly, coughing, snickering, endlessly fidgeting.

Through the solitary high window of the loft Nerissa glimpsed the moon, frosted, cold, a silvery paleness. On such a night . . . a hunter's moon . . . her life was altered for ever. In her grief and bewilderment she had all but forgotten that tomorrow, upon the day of the hirings, she would be seventeen years old. It brought no comfort. It was but one more day to live through, like any other, with none living to remember or mark it. Suddenly, illogically, she was filled with resolve, angered by her own weakness, her passive acceptance that life was a burden; that it was cruel and unjust. Life owed her nothing. She must succeed or fail of her own volition. She would not so easily be defeated. No. She would mark her own birthday, and share it with others. She would make it a celebration for Ruth and Sian and for Aled too. A day to remember. Smiling and resolute she at last fell asleep.

Before morning came and Sian shook her into wakefulness, she had put the coins for their festivities carefully into the pocket of her dress and repinned her pouch to her petticoats.

They crossed the cobbled yard to the inn, and ate a splendid breakfast, waited upon by the kindly potman, who spared no effort to see their needs handsomely met. He had accompanied them to the door of the inn, affable, dark jowled, all warm indulgence at Sian's excitement and growing impatience to be gone.

"Oh, but it is a rare old pleasure to see life through the eyes of a child," he said to Ruth, gently stroking the babe's soft cheek. Aled had stared at him solemn eyed and curious, then smiled and clapped a dimpled hand to the outstretched finger. "Aye, and 'tis a pity that such innocence of heart does not outlast childhood," he reflected, "else it would be a warmer world, and the kinder for it." He slipped a calloused hand into his leather breeches and put a small silver coin into Sian's hand, saying, "There, my dear, you must buy whatever takes your fancy at the fair. You will be the equal of any and beholden to none."

"She will be beholden to you, sir, as am I, for your kindness, for I know such money is hard earned, your labour long."

" 'Tis longer than childhood," he reminded gravely, "yet shorter than our remembrance of it, and of happiness shared. You are blessed, ma'am. Richly blessed."

Ruth reached up impulsively to kiss his cheek. "She shall spend every last halfpenny of it upon enjoyment," she promised gently, "and I shall not chide nor harass her."

He nodded, saying regretfully, "It will buy too little of worth."

"It will buy a day's happiness, sir, and there has been too little of late . . . I thank you again. May God bless you, as you deserve."

"Then I fear I shall be long in the waiting," he teased good humouredly, "but I wish you a joyous day at the fair." He turned to Nerissa. "And for you, mistress, an honest and kindly hiring."

Then he clasped his arms about his shoulders, as if suddenly made aware of the cold, and, shaking his head, walked slowly within.

At Knatchfield Grange, breakfast proved a leisurely affair. Luke, who had eaten too often of late in cramped taverns and inferior inns where the food was oleaginous and uninspired, found the Crawshay ménage admirably civilised. The conversation was stimulating and the array of dishes upon the serving board seductively varied. He served himself prodigally from the silver chafing dishes, relishing the informality as much as the succulent contents. Kidneys, bacon, kedgeree, sausages, eggs coddled and poached, plus cold cuts in abundance, tempted the eye and appetite. The savoury aroma of the cooked food was too tantalising to resist and the flavours as richly delectable. Luke, to his declared shame, and to Arabella's delight, made a hearty trencherman's meal, and Francis, well used to such epicurean pleasures, did not deny himself. Arabella had conducted herself more abstemiously, but indulged herself in two cups of steaming chocolate instead of the more conventional beverages, claiming that she must fortify herself for the excursion to Holly Grove.

Francis's insistent rumbling of complaint had been cut short with a brisk, "Stir yourself, you laggard! I have ordered the carriage. It will be ready and waiting in half an hour." As he continued to protest, she exclaimed in mock vexation, "You are forever making complaint of nothing to do, Francis! Stir yourself! Take action, else you will surely take root!"

"I am not a vegetable, some parsnip, Arabella!" he grumbled half-heartedly.

"Then prove it!" she said airily. "For I have seen parsnips with more animation, I swear."

He grunted, unimpressed.

"Besides," she coaxed with a swift change of tactics,

48

"Luke is our guest and has shown a liking for the fair, an urge to go. Will you deny him?"

"Damn it, Arabella!" Francis blustered, outfaced. "I have said that I will go! Promised. Take telling, will you not?"

Arabella, aware that the mutiny was quelled, smiled serenely.

"That is not to say," Francis persisted, "that I shall enjoy it for a moment! I shall be bored to distraction, no doubt!"

"You may go in any mood you choose, my love," Arabella blandly dismissed his petulance, "but you are such a handsome, impressive and altogether superior gentleman that I would naturally wish you to give honest account of yourself . . . to appear as charming to others as you are to me."

Francis grimaced expressively at Luke who was grinning foolishly, then erupted into laughter, declaring, "Arabella, you are the most cunning, devious and obstinate little vixen that God ever put breath into!"

"And you love me dearly," prompted Arabella.

"And I love you dearly."

They had looked at each other steadily for a long moment, amusement changing to shared affection, then a gravity which Luke, as onlooker, found oddly disturbing, as though all had subtly and inexorably changed.

"I had best go and put on my travelling clothes," Arabella said lightly, adding irrepressibly, "and I shall dress most sedately, and go easy with the powdered haresfoot, and abjure all rouge and cold cream, lest I am taken for some actress or sideshow freak."

Her pretty mouth was upturned in laughter, yet there was no amusement in her eyes or in the penetrating gaze which Francis kept fixedly upon her. Luke, aware of the tension but not the reason for it, thought in concern, surely Francis would not be so foolish, so crass, as to risk all upon some tawdry affair? Some stupid philandering with an actress or the like? It was inconceivable!

To lift the awkwardness, he said quickly, "There is no fear of that, Arabella. You will be the most elegant and

49

beautiful gentlewoman there, you will have no rival."
Then, cursing himself for his clumsiness, he tried to
redeem himself by teasing, "And will you have your
fortune told by some gypsy woman?"

"No. I will not do that, Luke."

In answer to his puzzled look, she said gently and without rancour, "There are some things best left unknown and
unseen. Even to acknowledge them lends them credence.
The power to corrupt or destroy that which remains. It is
sometimes easier to face an enemy unknown."

Blindly Arabella turned to leave, and Luke, deeply
perturbed, would have followed her and taken her arm
to comfort her, but Francis placed a restraining hand upon
his shoulder, saying, voice harsh, "No, Luke. Leave her
be. I can give you no explanation, make no apology. I
ask only that you forget what you have heard, consider it
unspoken, for Arabella's sake and my own."

There was such raw entreaty in his eyes that Luke
nodded instinctively, venturing, "If you would have me
leave, Francis, ride on, I mean, you have but to say the
word."

"No. I would have you stay!" Francis's denial was
emphatic. "I have need of a friend. A friend from the
old days, from the regiment. One who recalls the past." He
turned aside and poured two full measures of Canary wine
from the gadrooned wine table near the window, handing
one to Luke and saying, "It is early, I know, but humour
me," continuing with a wry smile, "to Holly Grove Fair,
Luke. To an outing we may enjoy and long remember."

It was less a toast than a challenge, Luke thought
uneasily. Was the woman to be at the fair, then? Or
was Crawshay in deeper trouble? Some problem with the
regiment? Money? Unlikely surely . . . What then?

"I had best make myself presentable for Arabella's
sake."

Francis's tone was purposely brisk. He drained his glass
then set it upon the table, studying it reflectively as if
he might somehow find imprinted upon it the words he
sought. Finally he looked up declaring, "You have always
been an honest man, Luke, one to be trusted."

Luke listened in silence.

"I have need of a friend," he repeated, "one upon whom I can rely, trust . . . You understand?"

"Then I hope you will put such trust in me." The words were calmly, unemotionally spoken, but Francis could not doubt their sincerity.

There was a tense silence which seemed to stretch interminably before Crawshay came to a decision, conceding, "Yes. There are things to confess, discuss . . ." The nervousness which had earlier plagued him was replaced now with relief, a return of his old ebullience and pride. He was once more a man in command.

"It is a matter which I could discuss with no other, Luke," he confessed, "a matter of . . ."

Even as he spoke there were the sounds of the carriage drawing up without and Arabella's footsteps hurrying across the hall, voice raised in some murmured enquiry to a postillion or coachman, and his deeper answering tones. Francis shook his head warningly as she recrossed the hall and paused briefly with her gloved hand upon the knob of the door.

"Later!" he adjured urgently. "Later! It cannot be spoken before Arabella."

Arabella, pushing open the door and hearing her name, looked from one to the other questioningly.

"I declare, Francis," she said, amused, "you are like two small boys caught at some mischief. The very picture of guilt and defiance. Confess it! You have been supping Madeira when you should have been climbing into your finery! Really, I despair of you both! You are quite incorrigible!"

"I confess we have fortified ourselves against the onslaught, my love." Francis was all shamed repentance. "But we shall go as we are, warts and all, lest our glory outshine you."

Luke, appreciating how modishly Arabella was dressed in her gown of rose-petal silk with perfectly matched slippers and an exquisitely pleated bonnet and pelisse of a deeper, richer hue, declared extravagantly, "But surely, Francis, *nothing* could hope to outshine her? Nothing

51

upon earth, nor yet in heaven! Arabella is incomparable
. . . unsurpassable!"

Arabella, amused, swept him a majestic curtsey, applaud-
ing amid laughter. "Oh, gallant, Captain Farrow! Exceedingly gallant, sir! You may lend me your arm and escort
me to the carriage." She cast a mischievous glance at her
husband. "You, Francis, may ride postillion!"

"Be damned if I will!" he declared robustly.

Chapter Five

Nerissa, Ruth and the children were soon absorbed into the hustle and bustle of the fair with its infectious gaiety. There was an aura of romance about it, far removed from the grim realities of everyday living. For a few brief hours those present could forget their harsh labours and the drabness and poverty that were their common lot. Here, all was colourful, exotic, rare. A new country to be explored. A place of music and dancing and sights to linger in the memory. A place of magic. Sian, wide eyed, and with the potman's silver coin burning a hole in her pocket, was determined to miss nothing, sample all. Even Aled jiggled and crowed in his mother's arms, beating wild time to the fiddlers and concertina players, viewing with the same fascination the fire-eaters and pedlars, the tumblers and jugglers and the clumsy cavortings of the chained bear. It had grieved Nerissa to see the poor creature so cruelly muzzled and forced to perform, for his antics were slow and ponderous. She fancied that she glimpsed in his brown eyes a great sadness; the sadness of one stripped of all dignity, the slave and prisoner of another's whim. She could not bear to watch a proud animal so degraded, and hurried the children away with a murmured excuse, first dropping a coin into the owner's cup. It was payment, she thought dispiritedly, not for amusement given but for suffering endured. She could but hope that it would serve to see the bear well fed and his owner kept sweet in temper. There was little in life that the captive might otherwise hope to enjoy.

Despite her misgivings, Nerissa could not long remain downcast, for the sheer delight of the children was a joy to be shared. Ruth had decided, upon their leaving the inn, that she would remain at the fair for an hour or two and no more, whatever the children's pleadings, for they must be well upon their way in daylight, or they would not find safe shelter before nightfall. She would stay to see Nerissa hired, she insisted, for she would not travel easy, else. If she knew beyond doubt that Nerissa was suited, her future arranged, then it would bring her the courage and endurance to face her own testing upon the roads. So it was agreed.

There was, they discovered, a platform set aside for those offering themselves for the hiring; a place to be publicly displayed on view. If Nerissa felt it to be little removed from the parading and haggling for the livestock on show, then she did not speak of it to Ruth. The bidding would begin, she was curtly informed, within half an hour, and, as like as not, would continue over most of the day. Those at first rejected might well find themselves hired by others "less choosy" by the end of the session . . . even at late evening, when the inns and taverns disgorged their loiterers. Some would then come searching for labourers or scullions for their hilltop farms or impoverished holdings, and would be content to take the dregs and leavings of others. Although, Nerissa was coldly reminded, she might then expect no more by way of payment than her scant board and keep. Nerissa thought that it was the awful humiliation of being publicly judged and found wanting that would most demoralise her, and she determined that she would parade herself for no more than half an hour before climbing down and seeing Ruth and the children set safely upon their way. It would be anguish enough to know herself rejected, without her friend being witness to her shame. Meanwhile, she would busy herself in exploring the fair with the others, for it might well prove the last freedom and enjoyment she would experience in many a long month. She would always in future be at the beck and call of another, a stranger, perhaps in some isolated and far distant place. She might never again sample the delights of Holly Grove Fair. All that was certain was that today she was seventeen, and in the warm, all-forgiving company of friends. She must live for the moment, demanding nothing, regretting nothing.

Sian's bandaged hand crept shyly into Nerissa's, and she looked down, smiling, as the child drew her towards the striped canvas booth of the Punch and Judy show. Outside it, a small white dog with one black ear and a matching patch spilling over its eye was balancing daintily upon its hind legs. A beribboned ruffle encircled its neck, its thin forepaws raking the air as it pirouetted endlessly. Nerissa was convinced that it actually revelled in the excitement it created, its antics growing ever wilder and more outlandish with the rising applause. Should interest briefly flag or be directed to some other, its staccato barks of censure quickly recaptured the defaulters. Soon a small vociferous crowd had gathered for the performance, and at Sian's silent pleading Nerissa had found them a place, with room enough beside them upon the grass for Ruth and the babe. The acrobatic dog, as proof of its versatility, ran among the audience with a velvet pouch upon a stick, clamped firmly within its teeth. The fee demanded by the Punch and Judy man was a halfpenny from each, and he had no need to bluster nor make appeal for it. The dog, Toby, would not be cheated. It sat, staring fixedly, until each coin was delivered. Mute and steadfast, eyes unblinking, it waited and waited. The audience, less patient, stirred restlessly, then it turned angrily upon its tormentors, haranguing them until all dues were paid. Honour, and the dog, Toby, satisfied, the play began.

The age-old spectacle was unchanged and unchanging, yet to every generation uniquely new. The audience sat entranced through murder and mayhem, tragedy and farce. The actors were the cruellest caricatures, with none living save the ubiquitous dog. Even the voices were grossly distorted, lacking discernible gender or speech. None listening could make sense of things. What did it represent? Domestic infidelity? Good versus Evil? Every man's violent journeying through life? It made no great matter. The audience were the actors. They shrieked and exhorted the hollow puppets upon the stage, warning, deriding, mentally delivering every last blow and curse. They arrogantly defied authority, humbled the strong. They vanquished their fears. Triumphed. Forgot themselves.

Nerissa, glancing covertly at the rapt faces, saw in them the release of old angers and frustration, the purging of fear. For a moment they inhabited another world, a world of make-believe, where death, poverty and authority held no dominion. Where every man was his own master, subservient to none.

Beside her, Ruth's face was radiant with pleasure, Aled's engrossed, and Sian was unaware of anything save the intensity of the drama being enacted before her. Nerissa felt a great love and sympathy for them, a sense of belonging; yet beyond that, an overwhelming compassion for those unknown to her within the crowd. She surrendered herself to their joyous good humour, their shared laughter and humanity, and all else was in that moment forgot.

The Crawshays' travelling coach, with its splendidly matched chestnut horses and bewigged, liveried postillions, was a most impressive sight. The cottagers of Holly Grove, with those gathered for the fair, had seldom seen so elegant an equipage. Handsomely crested and elliptically sprung, its slender wheels made light of the ruts and pot-holes scarring the highway. It moved, it seemed, as gracefully and effortlessly as the horses themselves, and was a vision to gladden the most jaundiced eye and lift the spirits. Those walking the dusty highways and tracks to Holly Grove Fair stood entranced to witness its passing, hats doffed, open-mouthed in their admiration. It was a spectacle to rival the hirings fair itself, and as much a cause for celebration. The lives of those riding within, the *haut ton*, were too far removed from those of common folk to arouse envious resentment. It was a shared pleasure that such beauty existed, whether God-given or man-made. There was pride, too, that folk of real quality, like Major Crawshay and his wife, lately inheritors of Knatchfield Grange, should think the fair worthy of their patronage. It was an accolade, a public sign of approval upon their worth and upon the village itself. Such distinguished visitors would be treated with the courtesy their presence deserved, yet always with restraint and dignity. They would not be made halfpenny peep-shows, like those at the fair. It would not be fitting were they the object of cheap stares and prurient curiosity.

Arabella was blissfully unaware of the stir her visit occasioned, and of the protocol demanded. It would have surprised her to learn that the hierarchy and behaviour of the lower orders was no less rigidly prescribed than her own. Indeed, it was only those as secure in the upper echelons as she who could occasionally afford to relax the rules and behave with spontaneity towards others. In a gentlewoman of breeding, such lapses were excusable. They betokened originality of mind, a spirit of generosity. Francis and Luke knew that Arabella possessed both virtues in full measure and that, whatever occurred, it would be impossible to curb them, or indeed to curb Arabella herself. Their day at the fair promised to be vastly unpredictable.

It was in this enlightened spirit of adventure that they descended from the coach at the local inn, abutting the village green. With the ostler and grooms uncoupling the horses and the coachman and postillions banished within to await upon their returning, the elegant trio crossed the cobbled yard. Arabella judiciously raised the hem of her silken skirt to avoid the detritus of straw and horse-droppings as a pinch-nosed sweeping boy cleared her pathway with a broom. The bystanders were enchanted. So pretty and gay was she, and engaging in manner, with her lacy petticoats swirling above the dainty slippers. Sweet-scented and fresh as a rose, they thought, and as delicately formed and coloured. It was a rare joy to see such fragrant loveliness in bloom. Francis had delved into the pocket of his immaculate doeskin inexpressibles and rewarded the sweeping lad with a sixpence, a return so generous that the poor creature could scarce summon the wits to make proper thanks. Yet Arabella had smiled at him with such warm approval that his foolishness had not mattered. He could not regret the painful stiffness of his fingers upon the handle of the broom, his tattered clothing or the wretchedness of the work he did. No more was he aware of the coldness of his bare feet upon the cobbles of the yard. A silver sixpence was rare treasure to him; bounty beyond imagining. Yet it was Arabella's smile he valued the more. Long after his six pence were spent, and the giver forgotten, memory of her would return, as spring returns to banish winter.

At the archway to the inn-yard, the sweeping lad saw the two fine gentlemen pause and bow to the lady, each offering a supportive arm. Their swift laughter and conversation floated back, a murmured gentleness. The sweeping boy set aside his broom, sighed, then walked to the open door of the inn. He would buy himself some hot toddy or mulled ale, he thought, in a tankard sizzling from the landlord's poker. There would be money enough remaining to victual him for a week upon fresh bread and cheese with raw onion and ale, were he so minded. He could feel the saliva at the corners of his mouth, juices already flowing and, as strongly, the gnawing hunger at his ribs. He turned abruptly from the threshold of the inn and retraced his steps across the grimy cobbles of the yard then walked out through the arch. He would join the revellers at the fair, for his pence were as good as any other's. He would eat and drink his fill and see the wonders so long denied him. Opportunity might never come again and he had no fear of deprivation, for it was a longtime companion, too familiar to fear. He walked, barefooted and eager, into the surging throng. A man of substance. Assured. Expectant. As rich as any gentleman.

Arabella was enthralled by everything that the fair had to offer, and her indulgent companions spared nothing in their efforts to amuse her. Her childlike enthusiasm was so infectious that soon they were as carefree and absorbed as she, and as determined to forgo nothing. If their easy elegance set them sartorially apart from the rest of the merrymakers, then their enjoyment did not. So cheerful and relaxed were they, and so courteously high-spirited, that none could resent them nor feel constraint. They were made welcome and accepted. Indeed, the two gentlemen's prowess at the clay-pipe shooting gallery brought unstinting support from the onlookers, and so many fairings for Arabella that she was forced to jettison them surreptitiously upon the way. The sideshows and booths provided the keenest diversion, with some advertised "Rarities of Nature", so obviously contrived and false that it had all but provoked a riot. Money had been hastily refunded, although Francis waved his aside, declaring that he had been vastly entertained, as much by the sheer impudence of the deception as by the ensuing fracas. Arabella, who had waited without, declared that the pair had but themselves to blame.

"A monkey woman," she castigated severely, scarcely merited the attention of two supposedly intelligent gentlemen, they were too credulous by half, adding, "It was plainly a fraud! You have no one to blame but yourselves!"

"Indeed, my love," Francis acknowledged, unruffled, "for the poor soul was stitched so crudely into the monkey-skin that the very seams were splitting."

"As readily as our sides," Luke agreed shamelessly, unable to control his merriment. "Really, Arabella, it was the drollest deception. One could not but be amused at the sheer effrontery of it!"

"The effrontery was yours!" Arabella responded tartly.

"How so?" Luke was puzzled.

"In seeking to exploit some . . . grotesque; some poor freak of nature!"

"Nonsense, my dear!" Francis said equably. "It was plainly a spoof, a money-making ruse. None but an imbecile would hold it to be otherwise."

There was silence as he reflected upon what was implied, and Arabella stared at him frostily.

"God damn it, Arabella!" he exploded. "Take telling! Monkey-women are as rare as hens' teeth, and as like to display themselves for pence at Holly Grove!" Adding in exasperation, "I have no yearning for any woman's company but yours!"

"Then I am flattered, sir," Arabella's mouth dimpled and broke into a wide smile, "that I am spared the expense of hiring a monkey-skin to render me hirsute."

"And the inconvenience . . ." reminded Luke wickedly.

"And the inconvenience," agreed Arabella, "for it would be vastly uncomfortable, I declare."

"I have no predilection for hairy women," Francis confessed.

"But I, sir, have a predilection for these delectable peppermint humbugs upon the sweetbread stall," Arabella confided, taking his arm.

"Then you may have as many as you choose . . . a bushel at least," Francis offered magnanimously.

"A paper cone will suffice," Arabella conceded, "for I fully intend to sample every *bonne bouche* offered, upon every stall."

"You will undoubtedly grow fat as a hog, my love!"

"Then you may display me and recoup your investment," declared Arabella irrepressibly.

Their spontaneous laughter and sheer good spirits turned many a glance towards them, and Luke was grateful that all was well between husband and wife. They were clearly in accord and, moreover, undeniably in love with each other. Whatever troubled Francis Crawshay, then it was not some infatuation with another, a clandestine affair. For the moment Luke could surrender himself to the pleasures of the day and the company of friends without guilt or hindrance.

The Punch and Judy show had ended and Sian, to her transparent delight, had been allowed to stroke the dog, Toby, and feed him one of her few sweetmeats remaining. He had eaten daintily, chewing with teeth as narrowly pointed as his tapering jaw, almond eyes bright with intelligence. The child had been reluctant to leave him and had to be coaxed away after a firm promise from the Punch and Judy man that he would buy the dog some titbit from the halfpenny spared to him from the potman's sixpence.

60

"Is it enough, sir?"

"Lord love you, Miss. He will dine like a prince."

Sian was assured. "And will you tell him it is from Sian Sayce?"

"I will indeed," he promised gravely, "and set it upon his pillow, that he may dream of you kindly."

"And will he know how to say his prayers, sir?"

Sian's dark eyes were watchful, anxiously intent, as she awaited answer. Nerissa and Ruth stood by as anxiously, hoping that he would neither betray amusement nor openly mock the child, for she was plainly in earnest.

The Punch and Judy man regarded her as solemnly and unwaveringly as she gazed at him, saying by way of answer, "Toby! Come here, sir!" When the dog ran immediately to obey his summons, he snapped a thumb and forefinger loudly in the air. The dog rose high upon its hind legs, paws thrust close, clawing the air as if it were indeed praying.

"You see, my dear?" The Punch and Judy man's voice was quietly reassuring. "Toby is a good, sensible dog, and as obedient and loved as you."

His shrewd eyes, set deep into their pouches, met Ruth's glance with understanding as she signalled her gratitude. He was, Nerissa thought, a pale, raw-boned creature, with his hollowed cheeks and long, pinched nose. Indeed, the likeness between him and the dog, Toby, was quite remarkable, as was the intuitive understanding between the pair. They looked, thought, even responded as one.

"You will be travelling far, ma'am?" he asked Ruth.

"We make for Carmarthenshire, sir, walking the roads. My husband, Will, was a master thatcher, over to Cornford way."

He nodded, blurting quickly, "You have seen the display of thatching, then?"

"No." Her voice was low, reserved, for she had need of no reminder.

" 'Tis worth the visit," he insisted, "I beg you will go!"

Nerissa, puzzled by his persistence, asked, "Where is the display, sir? I'll own we have visited the wood-carvers, the clog-makers, the blacksmiths and farriers, the wool-spinners and weavers, and other such crafts and trades, yet I saw no sign of it."

"No, and you would not, Miss. It is no sideshow, you understand, but thatching properly done." He gestured towards the end of the green. "I know, for it is my own small cottage being roofed, and at a fairer price than I could otherwise have hoped, it being a demonstration of skills, meant to bring custom and all."

"And the thatcher, sir?" Ruth's voice was uncertain.

"There were three, ma'am, two having served their apprenticeships and keen to set up on their own accounts. They worked under a master thatcher, Hugh Gravelle by name."

Ruth stood motionless, face drained of all colour.

"You have heard of him, ma'am?"

"Yes." Her response was hesitant, scarce audible. "Hugh is . . . or was . . . an old friend from childhood days. I have not set eyes on him this many a year. I doubt he would remember . . . wish to acknowledge me . . ." She broke off, confused, only to ask awkwardly, "He is settled here, in Holly Grove? Has wife and family, perhaps?"

The Punch and Judy man shook his head, eyes gently compassionate, "No, for his wife died in childbirth some three years ago, and the babe stillborn," adding quietly, "I think, ma'am, that he would welcome sight of a familiar face and a word of friendship. He is a good man, kindly and honest, but locked within himself. Shyness and pride set him apart from others, for he is awkward with words, too much alone."

"Yes. It was always so," Ruth confessed regretfully. "Hugh Gravelle was courteous to all, a gentle giant of a man . . . yet painfully ill at ease before others. A man hard to know."

"But worth the effort, ma'am," the Punch and Judy man ventured shrewdly.

"Yes. Perhaps."

"His work upon my cottage is ended," he continued quietly, "as is his life here at Holly Grove. He is of a mind to return to his roots . . . to Carmarthenshire. His house in the village is already sold to one of his thatchers and he has bought a small waggon and cob to transport his tools and those few chattels remaining. He leaves at eleven o'clock."

"Then you must beg a place upon the waggon, Ruth!" Nerissa cried out impulsively. "Now! Without delay! He would not refuse you, I am sure. It would offer protection for you and the children, for, you say, he is a kindly man."

Ruth was biting indecisively at her lower lip, face strained, although she spoke no word, simply clasping the babe more protectively to her, rocking him for comfort.

"Think well upon it, my dear! Make no hasty judgement," the Punch and Judy man advised gently. "There is much at stake. Do not let false pride nor dignity sway you. They are poor companions, and hunger a worse, especially to those too helpless to fend for themselves." His pitying glance was upon the babe in her arms, then turned reflectively upon Sian.

Sian, alarmed by her mother's silence and pallor, took Ruth's free hand, squeezing it fiercely in her own small fist. Her dark eyes were anxious, her whole body rigid with bewilderment.

She looked so painfully vulnerable that Nerissa exclaimed with false brightness, "I declare, Sian, I had quite forgot! I wanted to buy a pig's bladder upon a stick to amuse Aled, and a pretty trinket each, from the pedlar's tray, for your mama and you. As keepsakes. To mark our parting. Will you not take this sixpence and spend it for me? I vow I can scarce walk a step further."

Sian glanced at her mother uncertainly, fearing some protest or outright refusal, but Ruth simply nodded acceptance. Yet, with sixpence safely in hand, Sian hesitated, seemingly reluctant to leave, and saying in answer to her mother's murmured reproach, "But I cannot go without taking leave of Toby, Mama. I am his friend."

The Punch and Judy man's smile was indulgent, his eyes preternaturally bright, as he confirmed quietly, "You are right, my dear; it would vex him sorely were you to leave with never a word. Come, Toby, my lad! Offer your paw!

63

Say goodbye and Godspeed to the gentlest friend you ever knew."

Toby sat before Sian, paw dutifully extended, and suffered it to be shaken amidst delighted exclamations from all about them. Then the dog, of its own volition, rose upon its hind legs and licked Sian's face. Its roughened tongue was warmly abrasive, its affection as ecstatic as her own wild cries. Then, laughing and crying with pleasure, the child was gone. The Punch and Judy man called Toby to him, fondling the dog's ears, settling the ribboned ruff to order at its neck. He looked up.

"I wish you safe journey home," he said gravely, "and a loving welcome at its ending. Yes, I sincerely wish you that."

They watched him return to his tent, the dog at his heels. Immediately he was lost in his task, coaxing, chiding, willing the fickle crowd to attention, with Toby pirouetting and posturing as if his very life depended upon it. A true thespian.

Their shared laughter was warmly spontaneous until Ruth's gaiety died away as she took Nerissa's arm to say soberly, "With Sian away, I must tell you of Hugh Gravelle . . . make explanation."

As Nerissa made to demur, Ruth cried vehemently, "No! I beg of you, hear me out! It is owed to you." She hesitated, before confessing painfully, "We were to be wed, do you see? Promised."

"What happened to prevent it, Ruth?"

"Will Sayce happened," Ruth said simply. "After Will's coming, there could be no other for me. Oh, but he was a handsome lad, Nerissa!" Her face was alight with joyous recollection. "Strong he was, and proud . . . like no one I had ever known. Full of teasing and laughter, with never a care in the world."

"So you married him, Ruth?"

"No. Not then." Her voice was low. "Not then, for he upped and left Talog without warning, wanting his freedom to adventure, as young men do. I could not bear the emptiness after," she confessed quietly, "it was as if all joy and feeling had died with his leaving; as if I had died too."

"What did you do?"

"I left all to follow him. I had neither dignity nor pride, no purpose save to find him. I would have gone anywhere on earth, done anything, just to be near him. It was a kind of madness; a fever of the spirit. I can no more explain it, nor beg understanding, for I cannot understand it myself."

"And when you found him?"

"We were wed. Yet I would have stayed, Nerissa, believe it, whatever the ending. Even were I an outcast from all, and left deserted. I did not plead nor beg, weep nor threaten. I asked nothing, wanted nothing, save to be with him."

"Then perhaps in giving him such freedom you allowed him to surrender it willingly. You gave him the choice."

Ruth replied with stark honesty, "My own choice was already made. I would not, even now, change things, not for an hour or a moment, save to have spared Hugh Gravelle hurt. When others turned aside, he never reviled nor forsook me. He treated me always with gentleness, understanding all, forgiving all, for that is his way. He is an honest man, Nerissa," she declared impassionedly, "That is why I can ask no favours of him. How would it be were I to return to Talog with Hugh beside me? He would be the butt of every man's derision and scorn, thought to be weak and spiritless. I cannot inflict it! He is not deserving of that."

"And are Sian and Aled deserving of what *they* must endure, should you fail to ask his help?" Nerissa knew, even as she spoke the words, the grief she was causing, yet was forced to it. "You must ask him for the children's sake, if not your own. They are as innocent in this as he."

"I cannot!" Ruth's denial was wrung from her. "Do not ask it!"

"Hugh Gravelle is as much a victim as Sian and the babe," Nerissa persisted remorselessly, "yet *he* has choice when they have none. He is a man, and may choose his own way. You have but to ask him, Ruth! Do so, I beg of you, else you will always regret it."

"I do not know how I will be received." Ruth's eyes were

filled with anguished tears. "Perhaps none will succour us nor welcome us in, for I rejected them once and they felt it bitterly. Why should they not now reject me? I vow, Nerissa, I will not see Hugh Gravelle so cruelly humbled again, adjudged weak before all."

"From what you have told me, he has strength and courage enough to survive, as he has survived all else."

Nerissa broke off, following Ruth's tearful gaze. Sian was pushing her way triumphantly through the surging crowd, a pig's bladder inflated and held aloft upon a stick, face radiant with achievement. She could not wave, for her free hand was clasped tight to her chest, cradling the small treats and fairings which Nerissa had bidden her choose.

"Mama! Nerissa!" The child's voice was pitched high, to carry above the hubbub. "Look! See what I have brought you!" She could scarce get out the words in her excitement, blurting ecstatically, "Oh! 'Tis the best day ever!"

Ruth pushed the struggling Aled into Nerissa's arms and ran to greet her daughter, kneeling in the grass beside her, hugging her close.

Sian wriggled anxious release, fearful lest the gifts fall, or the babe's fairing drift skywards, to be lost for ever. Then, suddenly stilled, she demanded tensely, "Why are you crying, Mama? Did you think me lost?"

"No, my love. I knew you must find your way." Above the child's head her gaze met Nerissa's. "I was crying from pleasure."

"Because of the presents?"

Ruth nodded. "And because of a friend whom I have not seen this long time, a kind friend who will welcome and help us."

"As kind as Nerissa?"

"God willing," Ruth said. "God willing."

Chapter Six

Arabella was intrigued by the demonstration of skills at the fair, many so strange and esoteric that she had been unaware of their existence. Most fascinating of all, in her eyes, was the task of the master shoe-makers. She watched in admiration as they skilfully fashioned shoes for those oxen to be herded by the drovers to the great market at Smithfield upon the morrow. The sturdy shoes were made in two parts, to protect the beasts' cloven hooves, for the journey to London was long and the roads treacherous. Arabella, whose curiosity seemed insatiable, had learned that expert ox-fellers would control the animals for the fitting of the shoes, men who pitted their strength and will against those of the oxen. Too often, she was told, such men were the losers. Gorings and tramplings were commonplace, and death from infected wounds a constant hazard. Repelled, yet unwillingly fascinated, she was loath to leave with questions unanswered. Francis and Luke, at first indulgent, grew increasingly restless, and it was agreed that they would inspect the horseflesh for sale and return to collect Arabella when her enthusiasm was sufficiently blunted.

Francis was of a mind to purchase some reliable mounts, he confided to Luke, since both Arabella and he were fond of riding. He was already well supplied with carriage horses, for, in addition to those already in his possession, he had inherited the old gentleman's excellent stable. They had inspected some fine bloodstock and were all but decided upon a mount for Arabella, a spirited but well-schooled grey, when there was a sudden commotion among the dealers and onlookers at the edge of the ground, a flurry of heightening excitement. Francis and

Luke, curious as to the reason, pressed forward with the rest of the crowd.

"Dear Heaven, Luke!" Francis was all surprised admiration. "I'll own I never expected to find anything of such quality here! Have you ever laid eyes upon such a fine gelding?"

"I have . . . and I'll swear on oath that it is the very same!"

Francis, puzzled by the anger in Luke's voice, demanded, "But where? How?"

"At Tom Pritchard's murder!"

"Are you sure of it?" He was frankly incredulous. "You could not be mistaken?"

"I am not mistaken. It was this same palomino I saw."

Luke's voice was so harsh with certainty that Francis was all but convinced. "There could scarcely be another of such colour and breeding." he conceded, troubled, "but you laid no complaint, Luke? Without proof, or independent witness."

"I know. I can offer neither. It is but my word, and mine alone . . . but I swear, Francis, that it is the horse I saw, and its rider the leader and instigator of all."

"Yet you caught the merest glimpse of him, upon your own admission, and could never hope to identify him, nor bring him to account," Francis reminded sharply. "It is best forgotten, Luke. Pritchard is dead. You can no longer help him, are no longer involved!" Then, seeing Luke's closed and mutinous expression, he exclaimed fiercely, "No, God damn it, Luke, you *are* involved, and so am I by implication. We cannot let it rest!"

Luke's expression was wryly amused as he declared, "I would welcome you as ally, Francis, but you were right. Pritchard's battle is ended, and with it mine. Besides," he finished lamely, "I shall soon be away from here and all will be forgotten. There is nothing to be gained by pursuing the matter."

"Is there not?" Francis asked mildly.

"No." The answer was firm. "We had best be about our business, choosing horseflesh."

Francis, every inch a military gentleman, and clearly

one of importance and of means, strode to where the palomino was displayed and made a thorough examination of the gelding. His murmured conversation with Luke was inaudible, but the dealer was left in no doubt of his expertise. Sensing a sale, his manner became ingratiating, unctuous even. Francis grew increasingly remote.

"You are the owner?" he enquired disinterestedly.

"No, sir. The sale is in my hands . . . I work on behalf of a client. A gentleman like yourself."

"Indeed." Francis's voice was coldly dismissive. "This horse has known provenance? It is not of dubious ownership? Taken to pay off some debt? Stolen, even?"

The dealer's face, burned leathery by wind and weather, grew mottled with vexation, but he strove to be courteous, insisting loudly, "I assure you, sir, that all is above board, legal."

"Then why does the vendor not wish to reveal his name?"

"A matter of . . . family privacy, sir, delicacy . . ."

"Delicacy be damned!" Francis exclaimed scathingly. "I shall require the owner's name. I will deal openly, or not at all! Let that be understood!"

The small crowd of onlookers, delighted by the altercation, had fallen silent, the better to concentrate. It was plain that the gentleman viewing the horse would not yield an inch, and the dealer was growing restive, fearful of losing the sale. Cupidity overcame caution as he licked his lips and blurted, "If we might compromise, sir? If I could produce a gentleman who would vouch for his ownership, his integrity, without actually revealing the vendor's name? Someone of unblemished reputation?"

Francis regarded him superciliously, not attempting to hide his amusement as he drawled, "Any man who must depend upon another to defend his good name and integrity must be singularly lacking in both. I bid you good-day, sir."

He turned abruptly on his heel, and the dealer, in a lather of humiliation and despair, would have rushed after him to redress his failure. Even as he made to hand the gelding to a groom and call out to delay Francis, a thin, whey-faced man forced his way to Francis's side, saying hoarsely, " 'Tis no great secret, sir . . . the gelding's ownership. The horse is as well known hereabouts as its master, but, I'll wager, 'tis better respected, for it cannot choose the company it keeps."

"You know the owner?"

"Know *of* him, sir? The gelding is Richard de Granville's. I do not wonder that he would wish to be rid of it. It is too well known at every tavern and whorehouse, every gaming den. Wherever there is violence or devilry, de Granville is there at the heart of it. He is a villain, sir, and all know it, yet can prove nothing. He is protected by his family, his name."

Francis nodded his understanding and, delving into the pocket of his breeches, gave his astonished informant a half-crown, brushing aside his thanks with a murmured, "No. It is I who am beholden to you." Then he turned to Luke, saying casually, "I have a yearning to own that palomino, Luke. It will be my pleasure to bargain and beat de Granville's hireling down. It will add spice to the acquisition."

The bargaining had been brisk and relentless, with the dealer growing evermore florid and perspiring as he ceded ground. Francis, serenely unruffled, emerged the clear victor, to the delight of the partisan crowd. The dealer's discomfiture troubled them not a whit, and to add to his chagrin they actually applauded the new owner wholeheartedly, and he returned them an equally wholehearted and flamboyant bow.

"Well?" Luke's laughter was unfeigned. "And are you satisfied with your purchase? That you achieved all that you set out to do?"

Francis said obliquely, "No. Not *all*, Luke . . . but we have made a beginning. I have a fine horse, and you have de Granville's name. A fair day's work. But satisfied? That will depend upon the use to which we both put them. Agreed?"

"Agreed," said Luke, smiling despite himself.

"Then we had best rescue Arabella," Francis suggested

equably, "else she will be volunteering herself as an ox-feller, or worse."

"Life with Arabella will never prove dull!" Luke ventured.

"No, it has never been that."

For a fleeting moment Francis's face grew wary, his whole body tense. Then he visibly relaxed and, taking Luke's elbow, squired him through the restless, milling crowd.

Ruth and Nerissa came upon Hugh Gravelle tying his few possessions upon a ramshackle cart before the neatly thatched cottage of the Punch and Judy man. The Welsh cob harnessed to the cart was no less decrepit; a shaggy, pot-bellied creature with a patchy hide. Yet it looked sturdy enough and bright of eye, and Sian rushed forward with exclamations of delight to throw her arms around it in fierce embrace. At Ruth's anxious cry of warning, Hugh Gravelle turned abruptly, then stood motionless, face stricken. Nerissa, watching him, could have wept for his vulnerability; that nakedness of disbelief and hurt which could not be hidden. Yet, somehow, he had composed himself and come forward uncertainly, a huge, shambling bear of a fellow, to ask hesitantly, "Ruth? I am not mistaken?"

"No, Hugh. You are not mistaken." Ruth's voice was painfully subdued.

He had grasped her hands in his great roughened fists, to exclaim, "Oh, but 'tis a rare treat to see you! A rare treat." His broad, ingenuous face was wreathed in smiles. "And the babe and little girl! Oh, I am in a fair lather of excitement."

Ruth, shamed to awkwardness, had withdrawn her hands from his fierce grip and, sensing her reserve, he fell silent.

Ruth had made hurried introduction between Nerissa and Hugh Gravelle, and Sian had peeped shyly at him, still fondling the cob's damp nose, to blurt, "Will you take us to Carmarthen, sir? 'Tis a long walk and we are tired."

Ruth, humiliated, and vexed almost beyond endurance,

grasped the child's arm and shook her roughly so that Sian cried out in alarm and the babe, frightened, began to wail in sympathy. Shamed to repentance, Ruth wept too, while Nerissa looked on, helpless to comfort or explain. It was Hugh Gravelle who had knelt unselfconsciously beside Ruth and the children, gathering them into his brawny arms as if it were the most natural thing in all the world, and soothing and quietening them.

"Well, it was a rare old taking, and no mistake," he said calmly when their weeping was done. "Were the cob to take fright and bolt, or be washed away by tears, it would see us in a pretty fix. You had best be climbing aboard."

Ruth barely hesitated before climbing on to the bare board at the front of the cart beside the driver's perch, Aled bound tightly to her. Sian slipped a hand confidently into Gravelle's calloused palm, confiding, "Mama said you were a kind friend, like Nerissa, and would see us safely home."

"Aye . . . happen," he said quietly. His eyes were upon Ruth's as he swung the child easily on to the wooden board beside her. "A kind friend," he repeated, " 'tis a good enough beginning."

Ruth flushed, then steadily held his gaze. "I have always remembered you as a good man, Hugh Gravelle," she said with honesty. "A man to trust."

"I hope that I shall always be that," he said, "in good times and bad."

"I have no money," she confessed, voice low that Sian might not hear, "we must depend on your charity," adding remorsefully, "I have no right to ask it of you, after all that was once between us. Yet I do so for the children's sake. I have neither shame nor pride remaining!"

" 'Tis the past that binds us," he reminded gently, "and there is no call for pride nor shame, for you have done nothing save love another, and that, and your care of his children, is to your credit!"

She tried to answer, but could not, for her throat was constricted with tears. She shook her head helplessly.

"As for charity," he continued gruffly, "it is a cold old word, with echoes of the poorhouse and all. Yet the parson said, of a Sunday, that it rightly means 'loving' . . . giving with a generous heart. That is all I do for you, my dear, and I do it proudly."

"Then I accept it with as generous a heart, Hugh Gravelle," she murmured quietly. "Yet I do not know if others . . .?" She broke off despairingly.

"Sufficient unto the day," he said.

He put his hands to the reins to set the cart in motion, but Ruth cried out distraught, "No! Stop, I beg you! Nerissa, Hugh! Oh, in my selfishness I had forgot Nerissa. I must stay, for she is to put herself up for the hiring."

Ruth would have climbed down from the cart, but Nerissa would not hear of it, and despite all Ruth's anguished entreaties would not be moved.

"You must leave now, while it is daylight and the roads clear," she insisted, "else you will not make shelter before nightfall."

So, at last, and not without tears and reproaches, Ruth let herself be persuaded. She had embraced Nerissa tenderly, begging that she send word to Talog of how she fared, as soon as ever she was able. Sian had wept and clung to Nerissa affectionately, who had found it hard to disengage herself from the child's grasp or to keep her tears from flowing. There was a hard knot of grief at her breastbone, and Hugh Gravelle, sensing her distress, promised quietly, "I shall see that they come to no harm. Believe it. And there will be shelter and home for them at their journey's end. May your own be as richly blessed as mine, my dear, and the company as dear to you."

As the cob was stirred into reluctant life and the cartwheels creaked into movement, a shout from the highway startled them. The Punch and Judy man ran breathlessly beside the cart, with Toby at his heels, and thrust a sacking bundle into Sian's hands, crying, "A small keepsake, my maid, from one who loves you and seeks remembrance." His cadaverous face was drawn with the effort of hurrying, breath raw, as he was forced to halt, a hand pressed hard to his ribs.

Sian cradled the puppy to her, as tenderly as Ruth held her sleeping son. It wriggled a protest, warm and restive;

73

a perfect replica of the dog, Toby, even to the beribboned scarlet ruff.

"There are mouths enough to feed." Ruth's rebuke was sharp, made awkward by her dependence upon others. She felt shame at the grief upon Sian's young face and her cry of desolation. The child had suffered too much, she thought bleakly. It was unfair to strike at her from her own misery and fear for the future.

"There is room for another." Hugh Gravelle's calm voice was warm with compassion. "Let the child be. 'Tis comfort she is seeking, a sense of belonging." His huge, rough-grained hand left the reins to enfold Ruth's comfortingly. "It is what we all seek, Ruth, in childhood or manhood."

Sian was studying them apprehensively, face taut, whole body rigid with tension as she hugged the puppy jealously to her.

"Mr Gravelle . . . Hugh . . . says you may keep the pup." Ruth pretended indifference, but the sheer naked joy upon Sian's young face so pierced her with remorse that she chided with unnecessary harshness, "Well? Have you nothing to say? No word of thanks? Where are your manners?"

As Sian blurted awkward gratitude, Hugh Gravelle said, "'Tis naught to make a song and dance about for he must earn his keep."

"How, sir?"

"He will learn to protect you. Be always companion and friend, as you must be to him . . . 'tis a bonding. You must feed and care for him, then he will cleave to you, and no other."

Sian's face was clenched tight with the effort of understanding. "Then . . . we are bonded to you? Mama, and Aled, and me?"

Hugh Gravelle flicked the reins and stared straight ahead. "Happen," he said gruffly. "Aye, happen."

Nerissa had waved to the occupants of the poor makeshift cart until it was out of sight. With Ruth's leaving, she felt a sense of loss, a desolation as great as any she had known. She chided herself that she should feel nothing but the keenest pleasure that the young widow and her family were in safe hands, their future assured. Yet her own circumstances were so bleak, the future so empty of promise, that she could not dispel her sense of foreboding. Even as she felt the pricking of tears at her eyelids, the dog Toby's cold nose nuzzled into her curled fist, and the warm rasp of his tongue offered vicarious consolation. Torn between laughter and tears, Nerissa bent low to fondle him, burying her face against him. She looked up to see the Punch and Judy man regarding her gravely.

"It was kind of you to offer Sian the pup," she declared. "It will be friend and comforter."

"It will find a good home with Hugh Gravelle . . . I would not have given it else." He paused to stroke Toby's ears, saying reflectively, "Have no fear for your friend. He is an honest man, and no stray or outcast will be turned from his door. That is his way. He knows no other."

She nodded.

"I had thought to keep the pup," he confided, "to train it, like Toby here." The dog looked up sharply at mention of its name. "But Toby, well, he is special . . . like no other. We have grown together. 'Tis a relationship without need for words, and to put another in his stead would not be fair to either. I could not berate a dog for what he is and what he is not. No, my Toby and I will grow old together, and when one or the other fails, that will be an end to it." His lean face was full of concern as he asked, "And what of you, my dear? Have you hopes of the hirings?"

"Yes, sir. That is my hope."

"And have you none here to protect you or vouch for you?"

"No, sir. My father has but lately died, my mother these three years and more."

"I know many of the farmers and tradesmen here-abouts," he ventured hesitantly, "I know of their ways . . . their faults and kindnesses." He bit anxiously upon his lip, wondering how best to phrase it, before admitting, "There are those best avoided, those who arc not always what they seem. It is hard sometimes to recognise them for what they are."

"Sir?" Nerissa looked at him anxiously.

"If you will not take it amiss; think harshly of me . . ." He faltered awkwardly before continuing, "I would watch the hiring, if you will allow . . . see that you take no harm. I would advise you and stand briefly in your father's stead." He coloured painfully under Nerissa's scrutiny, blurting, "I beg you will not think me rude, nor presumptuous, but I see that you have been gently bred . . . are innocent of life."

Nerissa said, with honesty, "I would think you caring, sir, and take it as a kindness."

"I will carry no great weight," he warned. "It will impress no one, for all know I am a Punch and Judy man, living from hand to mouth, and upon the charity of others."

"You are an artist, sir, a performer," Nerissa reminded with sincerity, "that makes you special, and set apart. There will be none at the fair who could take your place. None of your worth. I would count myself honoured with your friendship."

"Then it is agreed?"

"It is agreed."

They walked companionably across the green, with Toby dancing excitedly ahead of them. It pleased the dog that there was such rapport between its master and this new friend, such easy accord. Toby was so abristle with self-importance that he could not prevent himself from giving sharp barks, sudden yelps of pure pleasure. If such excesses occasionally drew the Punch and Judy man's rebuke, they also drew amusement and laughter from others, and he could not long be cross with the dog, for it was so absurdly good natured.

Nerissa heard only the sudden wild cry of warning, then the thunder of hooves as the horsemen bore down upon them. She acted from instinct, hurling herself to the grass and somehow throwing the Punch and Judy man clear of the flailing hooves. It was over in a split second. There had been no time for terror or flight, yet now, shaken and dazed by the savagery of it, she felt herself trembling violently. The Punch and Judy man, too, was pallid and shocked, but as he rose unsteadily to his feet, he let out such a cry of despair that Nerissa felt her flesh grow cold and her blood congeal within her.

"Toby!" The cry was torn from him. "Dear God! They have done for Toby!"

In a second he was beside the senseless dog, cradling it feverishly in his arms, weeping uncontrollably. The dog lay unresponsive and lifeless within his arms and Nerissa thought that her heart would break with pity for his wretchedness of grief, and her own. She ran to him blindly and put an arm about his shoulders, the words of comfort she would have spoken locked hard in her throat . . . The Punch and Judy man was unaware of her, as of all else, rocking the dog rhythmically within his arms as if he would force into it his own warm life and heartbeat. Now there were others milling around, anguished, indignant, shocked or undeniably curious, but all railing about the four young horsemen who had callously terrorised the field, then ridden on unhindered.

Nerissa's concern was all for her companion and the rawness of his grief. It seemed to her that nothing else mattered. Not the hirings, nor the fair, nor even the childish posturings of those who had wrought such tragedy. The Punch and Judy man's loud cry set her trembling again, but it was less a cry of anguish than disbelief, for the dog had trembled, as if beset by some rigor, then briefly opened wide its eyes . . . Should Toby recover momentarily only to die, Nerissa thought foolishly, then she could not bear the cruelty of it, and no more could its master bear the hurt. But Toby was not so easily defeated. That savage kick which had rendered him unconscious might have felled a lesser spirit, but Toby, at first confused and unsteady upon his legs, had reacted as always to the plaudits of the crowd. His aim was to please, and please he did by making valiant recovery. Dazed, aching, painfully stiff in movement, he had persevered. The cheers and excitement of the onlookers were the most generous he had ever known and, to the Punch and Judy man's surprise, the coins spontaneously tossed to the dog exceeded the homage. Nerissa helped the Punch and Judy man gather up the money, refusing his kindly offer of a share in the bounty, and insisting that Toby had earned every last farthing. She had hugged the old man impulsively and made much of Toby, her tears and laughter flowing freely beneath the dog's ardent tongue.

"You had best take Toby home," Nerissa said tentatively, "for you will not wish to stay for the hirings."

"Indeed I will!" The Punch and Judy man's denial was emphatic. "And Toby too." He hesitated, confiding, "I will not let him perform yet awhile, although he has spirit and courage enough . . . No, we will stay quietly beside you and lend support, if you will have us, as you supported Toby and me."

"I was less than useless," Nerissa admitted remorsefully, "I was too grieved to help, for I feared Toby dead."

"As I, my dear . . . and had it been so, then I fear I could not easily have borne the loss. He is more than a working partner to me. My Toby is friend and companion."

Toby, hearing his name and the gentle affection in the old man's tone, cocked his head enquiringly, eyes alert, small stub of a tail twitching. His whole rump wriggled ecstatically as, to please and humour them the more, he rose up on his hind legs and attempted to pirouette. He looked, Nerissa thought, amused, like nothing so much as a jaunty pirate dancing a jig, eye shaded by a blackened patch. His whole attitude was as theatrically flamboyant and devil-may-care. Spurred by her laughter, he spun the faster, ears flying above the clownish ruff. When he finally ended, dizzy but triumphant, it was to lurch beside them with a decidedly nautical roll.

"A true virtuoso," the Punch and Judy man approved.

"Indeed!" agreed Nerissa as, replete with laughter and relief, the three made their way to the hirings.

Arabella, awaiting the return of Francis and Luke from the viewing of the bloodstock, was in a quandary. The crowds grew thicker now and more pressing, and she felt less at ease. She clutched her reticule more tightly, although it

78

contained little of real worth save a few half-sovereigns and some lesser coins. Francis had warned her to be alert for pickpockets or common thieves, and had adjured her, most sternly, that for safety's sake she must remain precisely where he had left her. Perhaps it was wiser so, for if she ventured too far afield she might easily miss them in that surging mass and remain adrift and isolated. She had been foolishly headstrong to linger without escort, spurning their persuasion to leave the shoemaker's stall. It had been a self-indulgence to travel without a servant or lady's maid, and now she repented her stubbornness. What should she do? She did not relish the prospect of launching herself into that heaving, restless crowd, perhaps missing the two men altogether. Yet she had seen all that was to be seen at the master shoemaker's stall, and earlier fascination gave way to boredom. She halted indecisively then made up her mind to visit the stall beyond, where flocks of geese were being shod for their trek to London upon the morrow. It was a bizarre spectacle, and the scene of great jostling and hilarity, for the geese were venomous and hissing, and ill-inclined to be co-operative. From where she stood Arabella could see those birds already shod waddling grotesquely in their strange contraptions. Their gait was comical as they tried to balance absurdly upon their inch-high spikes, miniature stilts that constantly defeated them.

Even as she crossed to view them more closely, the four horsemen, careless of the crowd, urged on their mounts. Their arrogant cries and sneering laughter drove a pathway before them as men, women and children leapt clear of the flailing, clattering hooves. All save one who, blind to the danger, or less agile than the rest, was caught a glancing blow by a horse's hooves. He fell awkwardly, clutching at the reins, only to be thrown off balance by the savage lash of the rider's whip. Arabella screamed so violently that the horseman turned sharply in the saddle and, arrogantly heedless of the damage he had wrought, made her a mocking bow.

Shaking with cold fury, she would have torn him physically from his mount, but in a split second he was gone with his noisy companions, and none had made attempt to halt them.

Sickness rose burning in her throat, as much from anger at their insolence as from fear for the injured man. Yet, defying her shock, Arabella pushed her way boldly through the crowd to tend the injured man.

The sweeping lad from the inn had been numbed by the blow to his head and, dazed and stunned, had awakened to find himself lying upon the grass, his precious cone of sweetmeats spilled all about. He put a tentative hand to his face, feeling the sting where the whiplash had split the flesh and the warm oozing of blood. He would have wept for his spoiled bounty, his humiliation and the unfairness of it. The breaking of a dream. Arabella, the purest vision in rose-petal silk, was ministering to him, and to him alone, speaking to him gently before all, soothing the cut upon his face with her own handkerchief. He could scarce believe his good fortune. Arabella had called for the assistance of others and they had helped him to his feet, commiserating, calling revenge upon his assailant, treating him with respect as if he were someone of consequence.

Arabella, glancing anxiously about her for Francis and Luke, had seen them in the far distance and raised a hand and they had hurried apprehensively towards her, fearing that it was she who had been injured.

Arabella loosened the string of her reticule and took out some coins. She bade one of those assisting the sweeping boy to return with him to the inn and see that he was rested and supplied with victuals and ale, inviting generously, "And you, sir, may provide the same fare and refreshment for yourself." She had thrust half a crown into the astonished good Samaritan's grasp, and into the sweeping boy's grimy palm a gold half-sovereign. It was ludicrously excessive, she knew, and Francis would rightly rebuke her for such extravagance were he to find out. Yet she could not regret it. Remembrance of the utter despair upon the sweeping lad's face as he beheld his spilled treasure wrenched at her heart. A halfpenny, a penny at most, had been lost and yet to him it had been the end of all. The utmost disaster. She had knowledge of how he felt; that enormity of loss. Arabella took quiet leave of the sweeping lad and with a smile that did not quite reach her eyes, made her way towards Francis and Luke.

Chapter Seven

The four riders who had cut a swathe through the fair-ground at Holly Grove were well pleased with themselves. They had attracted the attention they deserved; made their presence felt. Their boorishness they excused as high-spirited larking. It was, after all, a perquisite of leisured and wealthy young gentlemen, and none would dare to lay complaint against them. Such excitement would merely add spice to the affair, for it was well known that the common herd led lives of quite excruciating boredom. Indeed, they were scarcely less bovine than the cattle they tended, and with less diversions and expectations. At least none now would be unaware of their presence.

They had dismounted now, and left their mounts in the care of the ostler at the inn, walking with an easy arrogance that set them apart. They saw themselves as fine young blades; reckless, stylish, admired and envied by all.

Arabella viewed them differently, and made no bones about it. When Francis and Luke had reassured themselves that she had taken no harm, she could barely speak coherently in her vexation.

"They were no better than ignorant young oafs!" she raged impotently at Francis. "Louts! Lunatics! Indeed, had they been so afflicted, then their crassness might have even been excused. They were no more than idiots in the guise of gentlemen! Not worthy of notice!"

"Why, then, do you let them disturb you, my love?" Francis asked mildly, to soothe her wrath, but Arabella was past placating.

"Have I not told you what they did to the sweeping boy?" she stormed. "How they deliberately rode him down? Cut his face with a whiplash? I tell you, Francis, they were animals, brutes . . . No, worse! No animal would so mindlessly treat another of its own kind."

"Perhaps they did not consider him to be one of their own kind," Luke suggested grimly. "From all you say, Arabella, they are as conceited and boorish as they are empty headed." He added pleadingly, "But do not distress yourself further, I beg, else they will have achieved their object, to cause the greatest disruption and hurt."

Francis nodded agreement, demanding, "The sweeping boy was not gravely hurt, you say, Arabella?"

"No." She flushed guiltily, confessing, "I gave him a few small coins and sent him to the inn for refreshment and rest, and put him in the care of another."

"Indeed? An admirable solution." Francis raised an eyebrow expressively at Luke. "And those few small coins, my love? Do you recall how few, and how small?" he enquired, tongue in cheek.

"A half-crown, I believe."

"Dear life, Arabella! No wonder the poor creature recovered so quickly!" Francis exclaimed. "They will be queuing six deep and hiring out horses . . . hoping to make a fortune."

"And I," announced Luke, "will certainly volunteer! I do not doubt, Arabella, that the victim will already have eaten and drunk himself insensible at your expense!"

"Then he may still claim more intelligence and better manners than his assailants," Arabella gave opinion, adding tartly, "although my present companions are not noticeably overburdened with either . . ."

Francis, delighted that she had recovered composure enough to make light of things, chuckled appreciatively, and Luke's amusement was cheerfully unfeigned.

"By the by, my love, I have purchased the most handsome palomino – a gelding," Francis volunteered. "Is it not a fine specimen, Luke?"

"As fine as any I have seen," Luke agreed whole-heartedly.

"There is a grey I would have you see, Arabella!" Francis enthused. "A fine filly . . . spirited, high-bred, yet intelligent and reliable . . . A rare beauty!"

83

"Indeed?" Arabella's lips curved into a smile. "I fancy, Francis, that is precisely how I would have you describe me!"

"He is an excellent judge of women and horseflesh," Luke ventured, straight faced.

"In that order?" demanded Arabella, impressed.

"In that order," Luke conceded.

Arabella obligingly linked arms with the two gentlemen and graciously allowed them to escort her to view her rival, the grey.

Richard de Granville felt agreeably restored to humour after their stimulating canter across the crowded green. Like all else which briefly amused him, it was not without an element of risk. Some dolt might have easily blundered into a horse's path, despite their shouts of warning. Any small injury incurred might be miraculously healed by payment; not so a death. A coroner's inquest would have inevitably proved tedious and time consuming. Besides, it would have set him at greater odds with his father, who held the purse strings and who kept them, and his lips, rigidly drawn tight in his son and heir's presence . . . This simple conceit so amused Richard de Granville that he could not help but chuckle as he eased his way determinedly through the throng.

To those of the fairgoers who did not recognise him, he appeared to be a handsome, good-natured youth bent upon harmless diversion with his fellows. Certainly he was stylish to the point of dandyism, yet nonetheless an arresting figure with a natural arrogance and grace of movement that attracted the eye. If there was a certain weakness about the chin and mouth, then it was not immediately apparent, for his complexion was excellent and his eyes of a disarming blueness under the carefully disordered curls. Indeed, he and his well-dressed companions made a remarkably handsome and spirited sight, each one a perfect foil for the others. Where de Granville was flaxen haired and blue eyed, his friend Sir David Hanford was raven haired with a darkly saturnine face, and the third of the quartet, Jeremy Hardwicke, possessed that palely translucent skin which is peculiar to those with intensely red hair, while Matthew Siberry was the least colourful, the least impressive. The abiding impression he gave was one of brownness; brown eyes, brown skin, brown hair. Yet, if lacking the fire and drama of his companions, his very anonymity served to throw de Granville and the others into bolder relief, to actually enhance them. Siberry was wholly content to let it be so.

De Granville's earlier abrasiveness had been occasioned by Jeremy Hardwicke's ill-judged mention of Tom Pritchard's death, a subject certain to cause acrimony between them.

"It seems that the landlord of the Pilgrim's Rest is spreading false rumour," he began tentatively as they rode.

"Rumour? What rumour?" de Granville asked curtly.

"That the poacher spoke a few words . . . to the stranger who came upon him . . . after we . . ." He faltered and broke off.

"Poppycock, Hardwicke! Stuff and nonsense!" Sir David Hanford's denial was briskly contemptuous. "There has been no word of it to my father, the justice, else I would have heard of it! Where did you hear such claptrap?"

"It is all about," Hardwicke persisted stubbornly, skin fiery as his hair, "the inns and gaming houses . . . everywhere."

"You, Siberry?" de Granville demanded angrily. "Have you heard rumour of this from your father? He attended the dead man. You swore that Pritchard had not spoken," he accused. "Well, answer, man!"

Siberry's hesitation was fractional, yet enough to alarm the others. "I have heard rumour," he admitted uneasily, "but it is no more than that . . . idle gossip and speculation."

"And your father?" de Granville insisted. "What does he say?"

"He has made no mention of it of late."

He was aware of their cold silence, the disbelief.

"Why should he?" he blurted. "The man was dead! It

85

was plainly accepted as an accident. Why should he pursue it further?"

"Why did you not question him?" de Granville demanded implacably.

"It would have served to make him suspicious! What interest could the death of a common poacher have for me? Or for any of us? Besides," he said miserably, "he would not discuss such cases, nor things divulged in confidence."

"You are a damnable fool, Siberry!" de Granville exploded disgustedly, then turned his anger towards Hardwicke, demanding tersely, "That money I owed you, Hardwicke? What did you do with it?"

"I left it at the dead man's cottage," he mumbled, "to pay his debts."

"Then more fool you!" Hanford exclaimed.

"Were you seen? Recognised?" de Granville interrupted harshly.

"No."

"You are sure of it?"

"Sure."

He nodded, satisfied.

"There is a daughter, a young girl," Hardwicke said uneasily. "I spoke to her at Pritchard's funeral."

"Dear God in heaven!" de Granville exclaimed. "Are you mad, Hardwicke? Whatever possessed you, man?"

"I wished to make amends . . . to offer my condolences," he admitted stiffly, dropping his gaze under de Granville's remorseless stare.

"Condolences, he says!" De Granville's contempt was a whiplash. "You are a fool, Hardwicke! Worse, a dangerous fool! The next funeral might well prove your own!"

"God in heaven, de Granville!" he exploded irritably. "It is you who is mad! I barely acknowledged the girl, scarce spoke two words . . . I doubt she would even recognise me! What harm was in it? Tell me that!"

"If you cannot see the harm in it, then you are a bigger damn fool than I thought, or wilfully blind!" de Granville accused with cold venom. "You may place no value on your own worthless neck, but I will not suffer you to hazard mine. By God, I will not!"

"Nothing will come of it . . ." Hardwicke mumbled, looking anxiously to Hanford and Siberry for support, but finding none. They remained silent, faces closed and hostile, setting him apart.

"You would see us all finished, hanged!" De Granville's scorn was lacerating as he urged his mount away, whipping it savagely. The others followed, Hardwicke alone hanging back, not knowing whether to turn his horse and leave them. He halted, shamed and indecisive.

"For God's sake, Hardwicke!" de Granville shouted back. "Join us!"

It was a command arrogantly given.

When he drew abreast of them, Hardwicke murmured in stiff-faced apology, "I meant no real harm."

"Then it is to be hoped that none is forthcoming." De Granville's handsome face relaxed into a smile as he put an arm to Hardwicke's shoulder, saying coaxingly, "Come, forget what has occurred . . . what has been said. It is not worth a candle, much less the breaking of a friendship. We must not fall out. It is too high a price to pay."

Hardwicke nodded.

They were at the approaches to the fair now, their way slowed by the crowds spilling restlessly along the highway, chattering, absorbed, heedless of the riders' warning cries. To his outspoken annoyance, de Granville was forced to dismount and lead his horse, thrusting his way impatiently, his aggravation rising with every step. "This is a damnable inconvenience!" he fumed. "I will stand no more of it!" Yet he was powerless to halt the surging tide of human flesh, the flow of bodies, and was swept, protesting, with them, clutching the reins, fearful for his mount's safety and his own. His companions were no better prepared and were quickly isolated, as impotent to resist the sheer force of the influx as he. The drifted music, laughter and gaiety from the fair excited the crowd, luring them onward, but de Granville and his companions were barely aware of anything save their own fierce embarrassment and rage. They had been made to look foolish, deliberately humbled. It was an experience new to them and one they did not enjoy.

When they had finally broken free of the mob and were reunited at the edge of the green, de Granville exclaimed peevishly, "They are useless rabble, all! Mindless. Witless. No better than cattle." He plucked at a disordered cuff. "Well?" he demanded challengingly. "Shall we show them who are the real masters? Make them scramble for their useless hides?"

There was a swift clamour of agreement from the rest.

"A guinea says that I shall reach the far field before any other!" The wager was Hanford's. "And another that I shall do so unscathed!"

The four had briskly remounted and with fierce concentration set themselves out to exacting revenge. The risk to life and limb proved added incentive, and one which lent spice to the game, for game it assuredly was. They squabbled and yelled like infants, noisy, fractious, belligerently intent upon winning. The havoc they created and the injury caused were of as little account to them as the money to be earned. The game and the winning were all. They were individual and yet united, set against each other and the rest of the world. The faces about them were a confused blur, all save one, the face of an unknown gentlewoman. Beautiful. Unexpected. Made arresting by anguish and a rage of hurt. Richard de Granville, momentarily startled, had made her a mocking bow. Yet her arrogance had matched and exceeded his own. She had lost him the wager. Yet, perversely, he did not care, his only aim to find her again and learn more of her.

Hardwicke, who against all the odds emerged as victor, had been unnerved by the warmth of de Granville's congratulations, his outspoken praise. The old amity was safely restored. Siberry was equally cordial, and Hanford and the others handed over their guineas promptly and without complaint.

They had delivered their lathered mounts into the hands of the ostler at the inn with instructions to rub the horses down and see them watered and fed and made ready within the hour. They had returned in rare good humour to the fair, bent upon pleasure, their old animosity and abrasiveness quite forgot.

Hardwicke, glancing up from conversation, had been painfully startled, face grown ashen and cruelly drawn.

"What ails you, man?" Hanford demanded jokingly. "Have you seen some creditor? Or fancied some field whore to relieve you of your winnings, and all else?"

Hardwicke blurted numbly, "I have seen the girl . . . Tom Pritchard's daughter."

"Where, man? Where?" Hanford insisted.

"The girl in a red dress . . . holding her bonnet. There, you see her? She is standing in line for the hirings." He looked about him, awkwardly confused, before saying urgently, "I had best be away, lest she recognises me."

"No!" De Granville's abrupt denial halted him. "No," he repeated less forcibly. "It is best that you remain, that we all remain."

Hardwicke stared at him, uncomprehending.

"Our game is not yet ended." De Granville's voice was languid, but his eyes bright with malicious amusement at Hardwicke's discomfiture. "We had sport with the poacher," he reminded. "We might yet have finer and more public sport. I have mind to bid for a skivvy, a doxy, perhaps . . . Five guineas says that I succeed! Hanford?"

"It is an expensive wager," Hanford prevaricated.

"And so are our skins."

"I do not see . . ." Hardwicke began.

He was interrupted savagely by de Granville, who declared scathingly, "You see nothing, Hardwicke, else we should not need this . . . absurd charade! If Pritchard lived and named his attackers, then surely his daughter would know? She would certainly be told . . . It is money well spent. Hanford? You are with me in this?"

"Yes, I am with you," Hanford said carelessly.

"Siberry?"

"Yes. I agree."

"Hardwicke?"

Hardwicke nodded, bitterly ashamed, yet unable to free himself. "And after?" he demanded. "What after? The girl has done nothing."

"Take a grip on yourself, Hardwicke!" de Granville warned contemptuously. "You may rest assured that I shall make full use of my purchase . . . She will not be bored. You have my word . . . What is the expression, Hanford? For the moment it eludes me . . . Ah, yes, now I recall it." His mouth twisted wryly. "We shall have 'All the fun of the fair'!"

Nerissa, to whom the seasonal ritual of the hirings was a mystery, was grateful for the Punch and Judy man's presence and his firm assurance that he would stand by her. She felt ill equipped for the bargaining and shamefully conscious of her own inadequacy. Those with special skills, like the shepherds, blacksmiths and thatchers, were instantly recognisable by the favours displayed upon their hats or pinned upon their clothing. Some, like the drovers, were distinguishable by the very clothing they wore; the familiar uniform of their kind. Rough coats of tweed or Cambrian frieze were common to all, as were the stout boots and leggings, often greased well with mutton fat to keep out the rigours of the weather. Those of lesser merit made do with leg coverings of thick Bristol brown paper. The smock-clad shepherds, with their blackthorn crooks topped with carved ram's horn, were as easy to single out, and bidding for their services was brisk and genial. The Punch and Judy man explained that there would be cattle and sheep, ducks and geese driven to London from Michaelmas through to Christmastide, and the master drovers would be choosing their teams. As often as not, the men were already known to them, and a swift handshake would be enough to close the bargain, with a leisurely jug of ale at some tavern to seal it. Often women accompanied the drovers, to offer their services as scullery maids or at garden-weeding upon the way. They served too to milk the cows and to earn a few coppers by selling it, or by guarding the beasts or sheep in the fields at night. It was not, Nerissa thought dispiritedly, the work she had envisaged for herself, although she might well be forced to accept it, and life upon the roads.

"I have so little to offer," she said despairingly to the

Punch and Judy man. "I have no special skills, nothing to distinguish me . . . How will I fare among so many?"

"You will fare well enough," he consoled briskly, "for you are strong and healthy, and willing to work . . . Besides, you are young enough to adapt and learn and are clean-looking and comely."

Nerissa, although pleased by his kindliness, was not reassured.

"The menfolk may bargain freely," he admitted, "their strength is their protection, but women . . . they are more vulnerable and open to risk of abuse." He hesitated before stating firmly, "You had best pay a fee to one who will help you find a place."

"I do not understand."

"'Tis simple enough. You must hire some other, better qualified, to sing your praises."

"I do not think, sir," she began timorously, but the Punch and Judy man brushed her doubts aside.

"Wait here. I will arrange it," he instructed.

Nerissa watched him hurry to a wooden platform set prominently on display, with Toby following furiously at his heels. He had gestured in her direction then begun heated negotiations with a brawny, thickset fellow with a ruddy complexion and grainy jaw, who glanced towards her speculatively. His appraisal was cursory, dismissive even, as if he had yet to be convinced. Then, with a brief word and a nod, he had pocketed the silver which the Punch and Judy man offered, and the bargain was struck with a handshake.

Nerissa, standing in line with the rest of the women and young girls for hiring, felt a sick rush of shame. They were no better than the sheep and cattle for buying, she thought in anguish, and as coldly and dispassionately judged. Their physical flaws and deficiencies were put upon public view to be recorded and criticised by all. They would be as openly rejected. Age, weakness, and the urgency of their need for work and shelter would determine their value before others. It was demeaning. Inhuman. She wanted no part of it. Yet she was already a part of it, she reminded herself starkly, and must learn

91

to parade herself with the rest. She was destitute, a pauper now, and pride was a poor companion. Despite her inner resentment, she greeted the Punch and Judy man's return with genuine warmth, for she knew that it was from honest care that he acted. She could not belittle his kindness, nor spurn the one good friend remaining.

"You must let me pay the fee," she begged. "I would feel happier so, for I have money enough remaining."

But he would not hear of it, declaring firmly, "There are no debts, my dear, between friends. 'Tis privilege to help you, as you so readily helped Toby and me. What money you own is best kept for a rainy day, though I pray that there will not be too many!"

Those in the line beside her had grown sullen and morose, fearing that in purchasing a cryer for herself she had set them at disadvantage. They made their resentment plain, in nudges and spiteful jibes, and Nerissa, who knew that their jealousy sprang from fear alone, felt as grieved and threatened as they.

"Take no more notice, my dear," the Punch and Judy man said, troubled by her hurt. "There is not one among them who would not do likewise. Believe it. It would serve no purpose were you to remain here, save to make you as defeated and resentful as they, and as suspicious of the good fortune of others . . . Mount the platform, I beg you."

Reluctantly Nerissa did as he bade, to a fierce staccato bark of delight from Toby, who danced frenziedly about her skirts, drawing a smile from her and the amused attention of the crowd.

"Your name, miss?" the unknown cryer demanded. "'Tis best that we strike now, while the iron is hot . . . Your name?"

"Nerissa Pritchard."

"Your age?"

"Seventeen years, sir. Seventeen this very day."

"And your work? Quickly!" he demanded urgently. "We have little time."

"Anything, sir," she blurted, "I will turn my hand

to anything . . . cooking, sewing, cleaning, work upon the land."

He nodded, hissing sharply under his breath, "Stand tall, mind! Smile and walk about! Look at ease. Scowling and a sullen manner will bring you nothing. Your aim is to please."

Nerissa, aflame with shame and humiliation, did as he bade, trying to fix her gaze upon the Punch and Judy man's encouraging smile and upon the dog, Toby, that she might not see others in the crowd regarding her with contempt or pity. Did the cryer call but once for the money already paid, she wondered, or must she return again and again if rejected? She did not know how she could survive the ignominy of it, or bear continual rejection.

The cryer took up a huge brass handbell, clanging it so deafeningly that the crowd first halted, then crept in open curiosity to the platform's edge. His florid face was mottled with the effort it had cost him, skin blotched, eyes seeming to bulge from his head. His voice, although hoarse in timbre, was defiantly arresting, as clamorous as the bell.

"Those of you come for the hirings," he bellowed, "Nerissa Pritchard is seeking work. She will turn her hand to anything, and is not averse to working upon the land."

There was a tense murmured exchange between de Granville and Hanford before Richard de Granville's languid voice, rich with amusement, demanded, "She will turn her hand to anything, you say? And will even oblige upon the land? A lady, then, of prodigious talents and virtuosity." His sneering contempt brought awkward silence from the crowd but sycophantic laughter from his cronies, all save Jeremy Hardwicke, whose embarrassment was as painful as Nerissa's own.

"I should welcome a private trial of this . . . lady's services," he continued drawling, derisively, "but does one pay, sir, by the hour or the night?"

The cryer was for once in his life robbed of speech, glancing about him distractedly, anxious not to offend the speaker yet to keep the sympathy of the crowd.

"Have you gone mad, de Granville? Taken leave of your senses?" Hardwicke accused irately, face unbecomingly flushed. "I will stand no more of this! Your aim was to question the girl, not to degrade and insult her publicly . . . Enough is enough!"

He was so incensed that he would have struck de Granville a blow to his face had not Hanford grimly stayed his hand, muttering, "Be quiet, you fool! Would you wreck all by your stupid squeamishness? It is all arranged . . . the girl will refuse de Granville's offer, that much is plain."

"And then?"

"And then I shall make offer of my own, kindly, and with open generosity . . . I shall claim that my mother is in dire need of a serving maid, and none here will question it."

"But if she will not accept? What then?" he persisted stubbornly.

Sir David Hanford's saturnine features grew alive with malicious humour as he drawled, "It is a rare cachet to enter the household of a titled gentlewoman, Hardwicke, and to gain her *protection.*" His emphasis upon the word "protection" was deliberately provoking. "The creature cannot refuse!"

"Then you had best bid now, and swiftly," Hardwicke ordered fiercely, "else I swear that I will confess all, here and now!"

"Damn you for a fool, Hardwicke!" Hanford exclaimed vexedly, but he dared not refuse, taking de Granville's arm and whispering urgently.

De Granville, with a scornful glance at Hardwicke, shouted insolently to the cryer, "Display her more exactingly, sir! Put her through her paces! I would not buy a brood mare sight unseen, or with so little revealed . . . I would examine her more closely . . . more intimately . . . I would not otherwise buy a pig in a poke, much less a woman!"

There was uproar in the crowd, with angry muttering and protestation, but Nerissa, cut to the quick by such malevolence, held her head high, and continued her measured walking across the platform, never altering pace. Shamed and mortified and with cheeks flaming, she looked towards Hardwicke and, recognising him, made silent appeal.

He awkwardly dropped his gaze, as painfully humiliated as she, and, turning abruptly, walked swiftly away.

It was then that Nerissa, eyes blurred with tears, stumbled and all but fell. In a moment, de Granville was on the platform behind her, taking her arm, pretending assistance, his touch as offensive as he. Nerissa, glimpsing the smile of lascivious satisfaction upon his face, struck out at him, trying to wrench herself free . . . The cryer, angered now, began to rail at him, spurred by the resentment of the crowd . . . but it was another who came to her aid.

The Punch and Judy man, enraged beyond all caution, swung de Granville a blow that all but dislocated his spine, and sent him crashing to the boards. He was an old man, and lent strength by fury, but de Granville was stronger and in a moment had sprung up and would have killed his aggressor in a cold rage at losing face, being held to ridicule . . . In a flash, Toby was upon him, nipping, dodging, sinking his teeth into de Granville's heel, keeping his hold through curses and blows until a vicious kick sent him flying into the crowd, yelping pathetically . . . There was uproar and confusion everywhere, as Nerissa helped the dazed Punch and Judy man to his feet and kissed him publicly and proudly before all.

Her eyes anxiously searching the crowd for sight of Toby settled upon a face she knew. That gentleman who had found her father's body and come to pay his condolences, express his regrets. He cut a fine figure, dark haired, upright and dressed in most elegant clothes. She had forgotten how handsome and assured he was, yet how kindly and courteous his manner. He smiled widely now, eyes bright with delighted approval, and raised his high silk hat before making an impeccable bow. Instinctively, unselfconsciously, she curtsied in return, as Toby's wet nose pressed cold and consoling into her curled fist. Nerissa walked down from the platform with Toby and his master at her side. She spared no glance for de Granville or his fellows. She had been insulted and humiliated before all, and none had offered for her. Yet, strangely, it had been her tormentor and not she who had been demeaned. She retied her bonnet strings and linked her arm through the Punch and Judy man's. Victory or defeat? She was surprised at how little it mattered.

Chapter Eight

To Arabella's excited approval, Francis had bought the grey. It was a fine, high-spirited creature, and she had loved it at first sight. Luke, too, had been admiring of the mare's quality and temperament, and the bargaining and transaction were swiftly done. The trio had been returning to their carriage at the inn when the clanging of the cryer's bell and his raucous demands for attention diverted them, and they lingered at the edge of the crowd.

Luke at once recognised Nerissa as Tom Pritchard's daughter, and his pity for her and concern at seeing her so publicly and humiliatingly auctioned for hiring shocked him. With de Granville's insolence, shock and distress had given way to rising anger. So incensed was he that he would willingly have leapt upon the platform and publicly thrashed him. Indeed, he had tensed himself to do so when the Punch and Judy man and his dog had pre-empted him. The ensuing fracas, Luke was forced to admit, had been a splendid diversion for the crowd. More, it had set them firmly upon Nerissa's side and brought to her assailant the very disgrace and humiliation he had sought to inflict upon her . . . Luke fancied that the wounds inflicted by that stubbornly courageous little cur would heal sooner than the blow to the young man's pride, for he was puffed with self-importance; a conceited, cowardly little coxcomb who well deserved to be humbled.

"Why, Luke!" Arabella teased delightedly. "You did not tell me that the girl was a beauty . . . so delicately made and pretty a thing. Do you not think so?"

"I saw her only in grief . . . mourning," Luke murmured as Francis enthused admiringly.

"Well, she had courage and dignity beyond her years

and shows rare spirit! I'll wager that mannerless young boor regrets his impudence . . ." He glanced at Luke quizzically. "The owner of my palomino, would you think? Young de Granville?"

"It was certainly the wretch who rode the sweeping boy down," Arabella interrupted indignantly, "I could not mistake him. He is such an arrogant, self-seeking little toad. I am only glad that I witnessed his come-uppance."

"My dear Arabella," protested Francis, amused at her vehemence, "such belligerence is unbecoming from a lady of charm and refinement. One well schooled in the polite arts."

"Fiddlesticks!" Arabella exclaimed inelegantly, pretty face flushed. "Were the creature a gentleman, then I would treat him as such. He is no better than a lout, a vulgar oaf, for all his fine feathers."

"Then his wings have been well and truly clipped, my love," Francis said, laughing indulgently.

"But what will become of the girl, Francis? Will she be returned to the hirings?" Arabella asked, troubled. "I do not think that it would be fitting. She has suffered enough. What if he should torment her more . . . or wreak spiteful revenge upon her later?"

"He will not do that, my love."

Even as he spoke, de Granville, smarting with rage and humiliation, gripped Nerissa's wrist. His face was contorted with hatred, voice coldly venomous as he threatened, "Do not think that this is an end to it! I will not be made small by a drab, a common whore!"

Nerissa tried desperately to wrench herself free from his grip, but it was vice-like, as unyielding as he. Despite her terror, she stood up to him bravely.

"No, sir." Her voice, although fearful, stayed firm. "It is not I who have made you small . . . that is your own doing."

De Granville angrily tightened his hold upon her wrist, gripping so fiercely that she cried aloud. His engorged face was pressed close to hers, his lips flecked with spittle, and although she recoiled, there was no escaping his malevolence.

98

"Damn you!" He could scarce speak for fury. "Would you try to teach me my manners? You are a slut, in the presence of a gentleman."

"Where, sir?" Nerissa looked scathingly around her, gaze settling accusingly upon his two shamefaced friends. They shuffled awkwardly, loath to interfere. "I'll own that I see ruffles and lace aplenty, yet little of virtue beneath," adding disparagingly, "there is more of quality and breeding in the dog, Toby."

De Granville, hearing the appreciative laughter of the crowd, and enraged beyond caution, dealt her a blow to the face with his open palm that sent her reeling.

In a moment Luke Farrow had gripped him by the neckerchief and was first tightening his grasp then crashing a fist into de Granville's face. Again and again the blows descended, and pandemonium broke loose, with Hanford and Matthew Siberry seeking to extricate their friend, and Francis and the Punch and Judy man as determinedly restraining them. The urging of the onlookers and the shrill barking from Toby all served to add to the chaos. Blows rained indiscriminately as the mêlée strengthened and widened. It was, Arabella thought, viewing the disorder with the keenest enjoyment, as if all hell itself had broken loose. It was a spectacle as thrilling and diverting as any at the fair, and she would not have missed it, not for love nor money. She somehow managed to extricate herself from the turmoil and pushed her way purposefully to Nerissa's side.

Nerissa, appalled by the savagery she had unwittingly unleashed, was both shocked and repentant, confessing tearfully, "I should not have spoken as I did . . . brought such violence to others! It is my pride and stupidity to blame."

"Nonsense!" Arabella said briskly. "It was what the dunderhead deserved! You have nothing to reproach yourself with . . . Besides," she added equably, "can you not see how fiercely they are enjoying themselves? They will remember this excitement when all else is forgot."

Nerissa sniffed, gulped, then wiped away her tears and gave a watery smile.

"I have need of a lady's maid," Arabella said unexpectedly, "more than that, one who will serve as companion and friend in my husband's absences . . . Are you . . . free for the hiring, Nerissa Pritchard?"

"I am, ma'am." Nerissa's astonishment was matched only by her joy and she was aware that she was smiling inanely, unable for the moment to utter another word.

"Then we must agree a figure . . . suitable payment," Arabella decreed, suggesting a sum beyond Nerissa's most preposterous imaginings.

"Well?" she demanded. "Is that satisfactory to you? You may bargain, or reject it if you so wish."

"No, ma'am. It is satisfactory," Nerissa said primly, although it was plain to both that she would have accepted, even without benefit of fee. She hesitated before admitting, with painful honesty, "I have never worked in a great household, ma'am. I have none to vouchsafe for me, as to my honesty and such."

Arabella said, smiling, "You are your own best advocate, my dear child . . . Besides, I have the evidence of my own eyes. That will serve me well enough. I have seen that you are lacking in neither courage nor spirit and will not easily be set down nor intimidated by others . . . You are honest and loyal, and that will amply suffice."

Nerissa had glanced up to see de Granville, face bloodied, being led away, seething and coldly resentful, by his friends. They were bitterly and painfully cowed, their gazes discreetly lowered that they might not see the contempt upon the faces of the onlookers. But de Granville stared at her openly, expression so malign and hostile that she felt herself shiver involuntarily. His eyes had rested briefly upon Arabella and he had made her a mocking bow, which she disdainfully ignored. Francis and Luke, battered and disgracefully dishevelled, had come to stand beside them, trying in vain to render themselves presentable.

Arabella said, "This is Nerissa Pritchard, Francis. I have the good fortune to have acquired her services as a lady's maid."

"Indeed, my dear?" Francis tried to suppress a smile.

"Then it is to be hoped that her presence will occasion less of a furore in the household than at the fair," adding kindly to Nerissa, "I'll own I have seldom done battle in a better cause, Miss Pritchard, nor enjoyed a rout more!"

Nerissa smiled at him, shyly acknowledging his half-bow with a modest inclination of her head, as Arabella chided her husband indulgently.

"Really! You are quite incorrigible, Francis! But I concede that you fought handsomely," adding, tongue in cheek, "you were almost as distinguished as the dog!"

"Damning with faint praise!" Francis pretended outrage, claiming, "I'll vow, Arabella, that he held the advantage. With four stout legs and sharper teeth, I might well have excelled him."

To shared laughter, she observed charitably, "You taught that odious, posturing little bantam, de Granville, his manners. That is achievement enough!" Arabella, glancing towards Luke, saw that he was studying Nerissa covertly, eyes cautiously appraising, and confessed lightly, "I am almost as remiss in my own manners! But mine may be more easily mended. I believe, Nerissa, that you have already made acquaintance with Captain Luke Farrow? He is a dear friend and our guest at Knatchfield Grange."

Luke took Nerissa's hand in his as if it were the most natural thing in the world to greet a household servant so, and said with real warmth, "It is my pleasure to renew our acquaintanceship, Miss Pritchard, for our last meeting was under the cruellest of circumstances . . . I might hope that the future is kinder, ma'am."

Despite his dishevellment and bruising, Nerissa thought him the most handsome and distinguished of gentlemen. His brown eyes were kindly under the mass of wayward dark curls, disordered now from the affray, and his features were cleanly sculpted, jawline reassuringly firm. In her grief at her father's death she had been aware only of his patient sympathy. He had been no more than a fellow human being, respecting her need to mourn. Now she saw him as a man; virile, disturbing and far removed from her social sphere.

101

"You were courageous, Miss Pritchard." He had not let fall her hand. "You were brave, ma'am, and dignified and all were impressed."

"I thank you for that, sir." Nerissa's voice was low as she withdrew her hand, saying awkwardly to Arabella, "If I might make my farewells to the Punch and Judy man, ma'am? He is owed that . . . for he has been a true friend to me."

As Arabella gave ready approval, Luke offered quietly, "If you will allow me to walk with you, Miss Pritchard?" adding gently, "There have been anguish and disturbance enough . . . and my presence will offer some small protection. We cannot be sure that your assailant has left the fair. He has impudence and conceit enough to return."

"Then I shall be grateful for your company, sir," she admitted with honesty.

Arabella and Francis watched them leave, then Arabella took her husband's proffered arm, to return with him to the inn, demanding anxiously, "What can have vexed de Granville so, Francis? I cannot think that Nerissa was already acquainted with him. He was a stranger. Yet there was cruelty in his baiting, some open savagery. He sought to degrade and humiliate her . . . Why? It makes no sense! I cannot fathom it."

"Then do not try," Francis advised consolingly. "It is all ended now and best forgotten, for the girl's sake."

"But if he seeks her out, Francis? Means to take revenge?"

"He will not do so, Arabella . . . She is under our protection," he reassured, "he would not dare to harass her openly, else we would have recourse to the justices . . . He may be a young villain but he is no fool . . . He will not risk his own hide, be assured of it!"

Arabella seemed satisfied for she made no further complaint, but Francis was not as sanguine as he claimed. He was grateful that neither Arabella nor Nerissa was aware that Luke believed de Granville a murderer, the man responsible for Tom Pritchard's violent death. Now he, too, was satisfied that Luke was not mistaken. Arabella had spoken from innocence, yet more perceptively than she knew. Nerissa was still at risk from de Granville and those spineless popinjays who tended him . . . that much was clear. The whys and wherefores of it remained a mystery, but of one thing Francis Crawshay was certain, Richard de Granville was not to be trusted. Neither he nor Luke could afford to relax their guard.

Luke, walking beside Nerissa in her search for the Punch and Judy man, felt equally ill at ease. He could not make sense of de Granville's open display of hostility towards Nerissa, although he did not doubt his deviousness and cunning, nor his guilt of Tom Pritchard's death. Surely, he reasoned, de Granville and his cronies would have been better served by courting Nerissa's confidence and respect, rather than in deliberately antagonising her. What had they hoped to gain? What learn? Perhaps she was open reminder of the man they had murdered and they aimed to drive her away, too shamed and fearful to remain . . . She might have leapt eagerly at the first hiring offered to her. Yet they had reckoned without the girl's stubbornness; her strength of spirit and will. Luke felt a rush of admiration for the slight, fair-haired girl beside him, a tender protectiveness that was new to him . . .

With a cry of delighted recognition, Nerissa had glimpsed the Punch and Judy man pushing his way through the crowd, with Toby capering proudly at his heels, and called out to him. She hurried impulsively towards them, with Luke keeping her firmly in sight and keeping as careful a watch upon those milling about her. The story of her hiring excitedly blurted, the Punch and Judy man's delight was plain, his congratulations unstinting. To Luke's amusement, Nerissa had embraced the old man impetuously, then half suffocated Toby with hugs and kisses until he had somehow managed to wriggle exhaustedly free. Yet, despite their show of embarrassment, there was no mistaking the extreme satisfaction of dog and master, for both appeared to be grinning quite absurdly. Luke felt himself grinning as expansively, so ridiculously alike were the pair in features and manner.

"You will not forget us?" the Punch and Judy man asked. "You will visit us, perhaps, when you are able?"

"I will come," she promised, exclaiming vexedly, "but whom shall I ask for, sir? We have not even exchanged our names . . . I am Nerissa; Nerissa Pritchard."

"The Punch and Judy man will serve well enough to find me, and Toby here, with me, for we are never apart." He grimaced wryly before relenting, and confessing defiantly. "My name, since you would have it, is Goliath. Goliath Jones." He awaited the usual derisive laughter or some sign of suppressed amusement, but none came.

"It is a fine name, sir," Luke said with gravity. "That of an honest champion of his people, as you proved yourself today."

Nerissa glanced at Luke with gratitude.

"I fear, sir, that even a giant among men, such as he, was defeated at the end," the Punch and Judy man reminded with dry humour, "and I am scarce a giant."

"A giant in spirit, as Toby here," Luke assured him, smiling. "And you were not defeated, but victorious. It took courage to stand alone."

The Punch and Judy man coloured and blinked rapidly to hide his confusion. It was a generous tribute and generously made, and he would long treasure it.

"Nerissa will be safe in your hands and in the service of your friends, sir," he said, adding awkwardly, "I would have taken her to my cottage else. She would not have been set upon the roads nor gone to any who might have harmed her." Goliath Jones held out his hand in friendship and Luke Farrow took it firmly in his own. Then Toby and his master turned and were lost in the crowd.

Richard de Granville and his two companions were a sorry sight. They looked, the ostler at the inn thought, as dejected as whipped curs, and every bit as cowed and resentful. Their reversal of fortune caused him the richest amusement, but he was careful to hide it for fear of retribution. The three putative gentlemen were apt to take out their displeasure upon menials such as he, and a sly kick or whiplash were common currency. He had saddled their horses and brought them instantly, and the stable lad with him. They had received neither thanks nor recompense, the three gentlemen surly and sour faced, riding out across the cobbles with never a word spoken. It had not escaped the ostler that de Granville, the young ringleader, was the most severely chastened, for he was usually cocky and full of his own self-importance. He was also the most battered and dishevelled, which could not have improved his temper, for he was a regular little coxcomb, a fop and dandy. His fine frills had been torn and blood-spattered, his elegant doeskins streaked with dirt and as wrinkled as a paper concertina. That must have pleased him as little as his split lip and the rapidly closing eye, purple as a windfall plum.

"They were in a rare old taking," the stable lad ventured disconsolately, "not so much as a brass farthing nor a thank-you between them."

"Think yourself lucky!" the ostler said tartly. "They might have paid you in blows and curses."

"Gentlemen should not behave so," the lad grumbled.

"Gentlemen behave as they please. That is the difference between them and us! Now be about your business, else it will be the back of my hand you will be feeling! 'Tis not your place to criticise your betters. Your place is in the stable, my lad. Do not forget it!" The ostler's seamed walnut face broke into an unwilling smile as he watched the boy scurrying across the cobbles and dodging the puddles and scattered horse droppings. "And take a besom to that muck!" he called sharply after him. "The sweeping lad has had an accident."

The ostler retraced his steps across the stable yard, leathery face pensive. No "accident", he reminded himself, but violence knowingly done. The sweeping boy had told him so, yet what would it serve him to make accusation? His "betters", he had called them to the stable lad, "the quality". Yet quality lay within, 'twas not mere surface frills and furbelows. Those so-called gentlemen could scarcely be called men, and gentleness was bred out of them. They were of no more account than those horse droppings upon the yard, muck, stinking excrement . . .

105

At least such muck was useful upon the land and might serve to feed and nourish, to promote life. De Granville and his ilk were intent only upon destroying it. He shook his head regretfully and returned to the stable. There was much to be said, he reflected, for being in the company of animals. They had needs, but few pretensions. Their vices might be tutored or bred out, and they did not aspire to what they were not. Above all, they were dumb. Soon, good humour restored, he was tending his charges and whistling cheerfully.

The three young gentlemen who had ridden from the inn yard were altogether less cheerful in aspect. In fact, they were disgruntled and morose. Their defeat had been shamefully public and their ruined clothing and bruised and bloodied features did nothing to raise their spirits. Their return to their respective homes in such a state would demand explanation and the inns and taverns would be awash with idle gossip and speculation. It was one thing to be labelled young rakes and hell-raisers, quite another to be soundly thrashed in public view.

Of them all, de Granville was the most resentful, and he knew that although they would not accuse him openly, Hanford and Siberry felt him to be entirely to blame. Richard de Granville did not know which part of the affair humiliated him the more: the fact that they had been put to rout by a common showman and his dog, or that they had been set upon by others of their own class. Gentlemen. Worse, his discomfiture had been witnessed by the unknown gentlewoman whom he had earlier seen and tried so manfully to impress . . . Her indifference, contempt even, had been more lacerating than the dog's savagery, although God knows the ripped flesh gave hurt enough . . . As like as not, the wretched cur was verminous and rabid! He had a mind to inform the justices and have the creature put down. Or, better still, he would take a gun to it, shoot it out of hand. To lay complaint against the owner and the dog itself would only bruit the affair about more openly and increase the ridicule.

106

"Damn it, Hanford!" he exclaimed testily as they rode. "I will not let the matter drop! I have to learn what Pritchard's daughter knows of the affair . . . the murder."

Hanford's lean face grew stubborn, lips briefly compressed. "Then I hope that you will do it more circumspectly," he exclaimed coldly, "and not involve me. This whole charade has been humiliating, a fiasco! It will attract the very attention you sought to deny! God knows what my father will say!" he exploded angrily. "As justice of the peace it will soon enough come to his ears. He can scarcely ignore it."

"No more can we ignore the girl's part in this!" de Granville refuted heatedly. "If she even suspects our involvement, then we shall never be safe!"

Matthew Siberry, bruised and aching from the beating he had received, said fiercely, "Hell and damnation, de Granville! Have you not caused trouble enough with your confounded interference? You have baited the girl so openly that she can hardly do other than suspect! You have acted like a fool in this! A clod and a numbskull!"

"To vilify me will serve no purpose," de Granville declared sulkily.

"Will it not?" Siberry asked viciously. "It will turn my anger to where it is deserved! That is purpose enough."

They rode on in silence until Siberry expostulated, "And do not dare to ask me to pump my father further about what he knows! I will have no part of it! That is final! Finished!"

"You *are* part of it!" de Granville reminded coldly. "And it is not finished. Can you not get that through your thick skull? We are all at risk. If one weakens, then we all fall!"

"De Granville is right," Hanford intervened quietly. "We are all involved; all culpable. To argue among ourselves is futile. It will achieve nothing, save to put us in jeopardy . . . I have no fancy to wear the hangman's noose."

His words had sobered the other two, given them pause to reflect, and their animosity was turned elsewhere as de

107

Granville declared, "Pritchard's daughter is easily dealt with . . . The immediate danger lies with Hardwicke," adding contemptuously, "he is a weakling. Shallow and with no real stomach for a fight . . . else he would not have fled so cravenly!"

Hanford and Siberry did not deny it, although Siberry said, in an effort to be fair minded, "We do not know what urged him away . . . fear of being recognised perhaps, and setting us in greater danger." He trailed off uncomfortably, as little convinced as his hearers.

Hanford, clearly troubled, said firmly, "I will seek him out, without delay . . . I shall speak to him forcefully, remind him of what is involved, what is at risk. He will not renege upon us, of that I am sure. It is better to make appeal than to threaten him into submission. He will make a better friend than enemy!"

Neither de Granville nor Siberry sought to dissuade him, although Siberry muttered rebelliously, "You cannot provide him the backbone he lacks, Hanford!"

"I can but try!"

At the boundary of Holly Grove, Siberry announced curtly, "I shall leave you both here and make tracks for home. God alone knows what explanation I shall give or what my father will make of my injuries!"

"At least he will be qualified to treat them," Hanford reminded dryly. "My own treatment will scarcely bring relief. My father's invective will flay me raw! The beating I took will be as nothing . . ." He paused before suggesting, "Would it not be wiser, de Granville, were you to ride beside Siberry, seek help for the bites inflicted? Such wounds too often become corrupted." As de Granville hesitated he persisted, more lightly, "You might venture that you were set upon by a savage cur, and that Siberry rode heroically to your rescue . . . It is as near to the truth as dammit and will set Siberry in good odour, at least!"

So, amidst admiring laughter at Hanford's powers of invention and deviousness, it was agreed.

Hanford rode back to St Samson alone, determined to avoid his father, the justice, if he could, and to bathe and change into fresh clothing before riding out to find

108

Hardwicke. He could not risk a confrontation between Hardwicke and de Granville, for de Granville was swift tempered and abrasive and might cause more acrimony than ease. Hardwicke had behaved irrationally, certainly, but he would respond more readily to persuasion than a goad. As for Pritchard's daughter, for the moment she was best left alone; she posed no real threat. It would be easy enough to make social acquaintance of those who now employed her and offer abject apology if need be for de Granville's actions, and feasible explanation for his own. He was urbane enough, and practised enough, to charm, and his father's prestige and influence in the social hierarchy would not go unobserved.

So it was that having entered Lanelay Court unseen by any save the servants, he bathed and dressed himself fastidiously, and rode out to Hardwicke's house. His presence announced, he was greeted most amiably by Mrs Hardwicke, who remarked on his injuries with shocked dismay and a surfeit of ready sympathy. He would willingly have dispensed with the formalities and banal exchanges required, but knew that he could not. He was obliged to suffer the explanation of a fall from his horse, and the attendant cautions and commiseration, before he was allowed to come to the point of his visit.

"Is Jeremy here, ma'am?" he enquired. "I should be grateful to have word with him. We became regrettably separated at the fair, without time to make arrangement."

"Oh, my dear . . ." Her face, a paler echo of her son's under its faded red hair, was gently concerned. "Did he not tell you? I was sure that you knew . . . It was remiss of him! I shall take him to task most severely."

"Ma'am?" He tried to keep the irritation from his tone.

"He has left on an extended visit to his uncle at Rogerstone Manor . . . I do not know when he will return. He has a mind to stay for the shooting and hunting upon the estate. It was a swift decision, impetuously made but long promised. He has seemed listless and nervous of late, and I welcome the opportunity for change." She

109

looked up suddenly to see Hanford set faced and evidently disturbed. "Oh, my dear," she said contritely, "I fear that your injuries . . . your fall from the horse, distress you. You are clearly in pain, and I babbling so uselessly . . . Will you not rest awhile, take some refreshment?"

"No, ma'am, I thank you. I had best return home."

She nodded her understanding and accompanied him to the pillared *porte-cochère*, where a groom already stood waiting with his horse. As he set foot to the stirrup then swung himself into the saddle, she remarked conversationally, "I do not doubt that your father is concerned at your recklessness, David. Your spirit of adventure. I say the same of Jeremy. Yet it is a young man's folly, no more, and as natural as breathing. He would not have it curbed!"

"No, ma'am," Hanford said wryly. "He would not have it curbed."

Chapter Nine

Nerissa, riding to Knatchfield Grange in the open carriage through the autumn landscape, could scarce believe her good fortune. It had been a birthday gift more splendid than any she might have imagined, to be chosen so unexpectedly at the hirings, and by a gentlewoman of Mrs Crawshay's worth. The savagery of her father's death still grieved and hurt her and would long do so, yet now she could not believe herself to be entirely forsaken. Even the ignominy suffered at de Granville's hands, his sneers and insults, were made bearable by the knowledge that they had brought her to Arabella's notice and sealed her future.

The stiff autumn breeze whipped colour into Nerissa's cheeks and set her fair hair flying under her bonnet ribbons. Luke, seeing her blue eyes so bright with curiosity, her lips gently parted as she gazed about her, thought her enchantingly young and unspoilt. She was, he thought, childlike in her rapture. There was an innocence about her which he found absurdly touching, a dignity of self-possession. She had none of the affectations and artifice of the salon gentlewomen. Her enjoyment was unfeigned. He had taken her cloth bundle unprompted upon his knees and regarded it now soberly, reflecting on how poor a thing it was. Yet she had carried it with pride, for it was all of the past she possessed . . . So little to show for a lifetime of grief and harsh living, he thought compassionately, recalling Tom Pritchard's broken flesh . . . He watched her hand creep involuntarily to touch the cheap brooch of green enamel pinned upon her bonnet. It was as if she sought some sign, a talisman; an assurance that all would not be snatched away as violently and

111

greedily as before . . . None, he thought regretfully, could make her such promise.

Yet Arabella had given her refuge and safety. A new life. A new beginning. Strangely, unreasonably, he felt the deepest regret that he would not see her newfound joy in living. She must surely grow in confidence and blossom in Arabella's care. He felt a rush of tenderness for Arabella, who had not hesitated to offer the child not only practical kindness, but hope.

For Nerissa, too, he felt a new tenderness of feeling; disturbing in its intensity. It was no more, he assured himself, than the sympathy of a parent for a child, or the familial bond between siblings. He would soon be away from Knatchfield Grange as planned, his mind set upon the adventuring he sought. He wanted no encumbrances. By chance he had happened upon Tom Pritchard's savage murder, been drawn unwillingly in its wake. He had done the little he was able for the dead man and had now been privileged to see Pritchard's daughter settled . . . He owed her nothing. Yet it pleased him that she had not been left destitute, to trudge the roads alone, or forced into the poorhouse and pauperdom. It would have grieved him more had de Granville's henchmen and bully boys secured her for the hiring. She would, as like as not, have been brutalised and degraded, or met Tom Pritchard's ending. He felt a thrust of anguish almost too savage to be borne, then the hot blood flooding his face. When he glanced up, self-consciously, Arabella was watching him, eyes warm with concern. She reached out a gloved hand to rest briefly upon his, and nodded. No word was spoken between them, yet sympathy belied the need. Luke was aware that she knew his thoughts and emotions as certainly as if he had spoken them aloud.

When they reached Knatchfield Grange, the autumn daylight was already fading and Nerissa, whose excitement had neither lessened nor abated upon the way, had a vivid picture of wooded hills and pastures, the colourful richness of autumn leaves, ochre ferns, and the shadowy blue-mauve hills beyond. She had never before been driven in a carriage, only upon the meanest farm waggon to her labour upon the land . . . She thought that she would never forget the sounds and sights about her. She would savour and remember, too, the mingling odours of bruised grass and herbs, of leather, and the rich animal smell of the horses, their clattering hooves and jangling harness, their ordure and lathered sweat.

Yet, when they rounded the carriageway to the drive and Knatchfield lay before them, greyly symmetrical and austerely elegant in the late autumn light, her throat ached with the beauty of it. Then Francis's firm hand was at her elbow as she followed Arabella down the steps of the carriage.

"This is Knatchfield, Nerissa," Francis said. "Our home, and yours. You will be happy here, and safe."

She would have answered him, but could not, her throat was too constricted with happiness, her eyes heavy with tears . . . Luke, seeing her emotion and mindful of the rigours of the day, put her bundle gently into her hands, that she might find comfort in its familiar closeness. Then Arabella drew her companionably within.

Arabella had called immediately for her housekeeper, Mrs Pratt, a gaunt, desiccated woman in black bombazine, all bony angles and fleshlessness. She was impeccably neat, from her silver-grey hair in the lace-edged house bonnet to the sensibly buckled shoes peeping from under the immaculate skirt hem. Nerissa, who was overawed by such pristine perfection, could well have believed that Mrs Pratt's pleated collar and cuffs, and indeed the very objects upon her silver chatelaine, were measured precisely for conformity. What is more, they would not have dared to deviate, even by one quarter of an inch, for fear of retribution. In such an exemplary presence, Nerissa felt her own dishevelment more keenly, and, as depressing, her lack of experience as a lady's maid. She could never hope to aspire to such excellence. No, not even were she to practise hour by hour without ceasing until she reached Mrs Pratt's position and advanced age. She glanced up, to see Mrs Pratt's gaze upon her, yet there was no coldness, no censure. The housekeeper's boot-button eyes were bright with curiosity, yet kindly, her lips amused.

113

"If you will take Miss Pritchard, my new lady's maid and companion, to the kitchen, Mrs Pratt, and ask Cook to provide refreshment," Arabella gave instruction, "it will give time for a room to be prepared."

"Indeed, ma'am. I shall attend to it at once."

"Then return, if you please, Mrs Pratt," Arabella ordered, "that we may arrange details of what is to be provided by way of suitable indoor clothing and shoes, and more serviceable outdoor wear. You may engage the services of a dressmaker and give immediate instruction to the cordwainer and draper at Knatchfield village."

"Yes, ma'am."

With a brisk nod to Nerissa and a half-curtsey to her mistress, the housekeeper regally swept without, with Nerissa in mute attendance. Mrs Pratt's spine, Nerissa thought impressed, was no less rigid than those iron keys at her waist. She could expect neither warmth nor understanding from such a paragon. Mrs Pratt, as if to confound her fears, paused before the kitchen door, turned, then put a hand to Nerissa's elbow, smiling broadly.

"Come, my dear," she said with open amusement. "Do not look so terrified. You have a face wry enough to curdle milk! We have all been young and inexperienced . . . as awkwardly uncertain as you . . . We are ordinary folk, and servants all, whatever our rank or fine uniform. Do not confuse what we wear with what we are."

"No, ma'am," Nerissa responded shyly.

"There is no disgrace in serving others," she adjured briskly, "only in work grudgingly done, attention grudgingly given . . . There are four rules to follow, if you would be happy here."

"Yes, ma'am."

"Firstly, work always to your best ability. Secondly, do not attempt to ape your betters. Thirdly, live equably with those about you. Fourthly, remember always who and what you are . . . a person in your own right, neither owned by others nor subservient to them, even those you serve . . . If you are sure of your own worth, you will behave always with that dignity owed to yourself and others."

114

"Yes, ma'am. I shall try." Nerissa's voice was so small and unconfident that the housekeeper could not hide a swift smile.

"There, my dear, my sermon is done!" she said, adding expansively, "And I would not expect perfection at once, for it has taken me forty years and more to recognise the truth in it."

"Yes, ma'am."

Mrs Pratt hesitated, lips pursed, wondering how best to word it before advising kindly, "You will not call me 'ma'am', Miss Pritchard, for that is a courtesy owed to your mistress alone, or to those gentlewomen of her rank and station. For me, 'Mrs Pratt' will serve. It is a courtesy title, you understand? I have neither husband nor child, for I was never wed."

"I thank you, Mrs Pratt, for making explanation," Nerissa said, voice subdued, "and I beg you will set me to proper rights, correct me whenever I am wrong. There is so much to learn, and all is so new and strange to me."

Mrs Pratt nodded her understanding, agreeing, "Yes, there is much to learn." She paused. "There is one thing to realise before all others." At Nerissa's enquiring glance, she confided, "Your position here sets you at a disadvantage."

"How so, ma'am? . . . Mrs Pratt?" she corrected herself quickly.

"You are neither fish nor fowl nor good red herring! As companion to Mrs Crawshay and lady's maid, you will rank higher than the household servants, yet you can never aspire to being a gentlewoman nor to being accepted in their company . . . Like a housekeeper, or major domo, you must remain forever invisible, trapped between heaven and earth!" Her intelligent, deep-set eyes disappeared momentarily into their pouches as she smiled, only to re-emerge dancing with laughter as she confessed, "Indeed, my dear, upon occasion I have wondered whether I have descended into very hell itself, so great is the chaos below stairs!" adding good-humouredly, "Yet, at least it is always warm, the company congenial and the victuals better than any poor sinner has a right to expect! Perhaps it is true that the devil looks after his own!"

"And housekeepers and ladies' maids, Mrs Pratt?" Nerissa ventured timorously.

"We may hope so, Miss Pritchard. And we shall soon enough know." Her hand closed briskly upon the door knob. "It is time for your own baptism of fire!"

Despite her misgiving, it had proved less of an ordeal than Nerissa had feared, for the cook, Mrs Cobner, who was as generously fleshed as the housekeeper was lean and austere, had been immediately welcoming. There were few other present, save for the scullions and kitchen maids, and those swiftly rebuked for their curiosity and scolded good-naturedly to their tasks. They seemed to bear the cook no ill-will, and indeed it would have been hard for any to take offence, so jovial was she, and so comfortably fashioned. Had Nerissa been asked to describe her, she would have likened her to a well-rounded cottage loaf, well floured and with head and body plumply fused. She was all circles; face, torso, eyes, ears and mouth were symmetrically rounded. Even her stout arms and legs were no more than circles teased out, her fingers pale miniatures that might have been shaped casually from dough, the whole dusted then baked to crispness.

The glowing fire of kindling and turf was no less welcoming than the cook herself. It threw out a massive heat, pervasive and all-embracing. Nerissa found the mingled savoury aromas from the roast chickens crisping upon the spit, and the iron cauldron of soup suspended from a pot-crane, almost too tantalising to be borne. She was not long denied satisfaction, for a place was hurriedly set for her at the vast scrubbed table before the fire, and a bowl of steaming ham and leek soup brought, and with it a platter of floury potatoes and bread, crusty and still warm . . . Divested of her bonnet and cloak, Nerissa sat down to enjoy the feast provided, for feast it assuredly was. Never in all her life had she tasted a dish more flavoursome or delectable, and she was aware that in spite of her efforts to eat daintily and with restraint, she made a good stout trencherman's meal. Indeed, to her consternation and embarrassment, she found herself actually salivating until the soup cooled enough for spooning, and as she sipped it her eyes watered, her nose reddened and her skin grew increasingly flushed and hot. Yet she could not desist until every last drop was savoured, and despite Mrs Cobner's insistent pleas that she take another helping, she could manage not a morsel more. Warmly replete, Nerissa had thanked the cook with such fervour and sincerity that the good woman had been quite taken aback at such extravagant praise, claiming that to her shame little of worth had been prepared and available.

"It is the best meal I have eaten in all of my life, Mrs Cobner," she repeated with conviction.

The cook's plump face, florid from the fire, had grown warmer yet, and wreathed in self-deprecating smiles as she murmured protest. "Why, 'tis no more than a modest bite," she declared, "scarce fit to feed a robin! You shall dine with us later, and dine handsomely, my dear, and taste the full range of my cooking."

She had busied herself at stirring and seasoning, as much to hide her transparent pleasure as from culinary need. Nerissa had found herself a future friend and ally, although she was as yet unaware of it.

With Mrs Cobner occupied in supervising the kitchen maids, Nerissa had opportunity to look about her openly. The kitchen was a vast, lofty cavern of a room, larger, certainly, than the whole of her former home, Scarweather Cottage. Yet, strangely, for all its size, it lacked the remoteness she might have expected. There was nothing barren nor impersonal about it, rather it possessed a curious intimacy, as warming as the glowing fire at its heart. Everywhere there was movement and action, with maids and scullions toing and froing ceaselessly, their chopping, grinding, beating and mixing a constant background cacophony. There was the added clatter of pots and pans, the scraping of boot-soles across the stone-flagged floor, the carrying of water from the yard,

the babble of conversation, the shouted commands . . .
It was a scene of the greatest vitality and clamour, all
seemingly haphazard, yet sternly disciplined, for nothing
and no one escaped Mrs Cobner's omniscient gaze. Her
censure or praise were as readily given.

Yet it was the kitchen itself which commanded Nerissa's
attention. Stone walled and high raftered it had the lofty
spaciousness of a church, a likeness enhanced by the
scrubbed grey flags of the floor. It seemed to Nerissa
that this was a kitchen designed for giants. Everything was
massively carved, moulded or wrought. The rafters might
have served a man-of-war, the dressers and pot-boards
would have dwarfed an ordinary room. The table might
comfortably have seated a regiment and the wooden
settles aside the fire were as high-backed and capacious
as church pews. Even the hooded straw chairs beside
the hearth were as deep and solitary as caves, inviting
shelter.

Yet it was the cleanliness which impressed Nerissa most,
for all the utensils and platters, whether for use or display,
sparkled and shone. From the shelves, pewter chargers
and tankards gleamed, while upon the walls burnished
copper covers and domes glowed brighter than the dancing
flames of the fire. Brass glittered, earthenware shone.
Vast tureens, platters, crocks and sauceboats jostled
colourfully, cheek by jowl with the muted elegance of
silver for the dining room. Even the massive cauldron
upon its chain, the spring jacks and the iron pots gleamed
blue-black and iridescent as a jackdaw's wing.

The sights, smells and sounds were so vivid and over-
powering that Nerissa was scarce able to distinguish or
separate them. The dried herbs suspended from the rafters
were pungently aromatic, their brittle leaves a reminder of
summers past. The pearly hams, nacreous within, crusted
and darkly smoked without, hung sculpted as carvings
against the blackened beams, and as much a part of the
furnishings.

Mrs Cobner, seeing Nerissa's delight and open-mouthed
admiration of her kingdom, was inclined to be gracious.
Her formal catechism of Mrs Crawshay's new lady's

maid and companion was indulgently made, and Nerissa's responses received good naturedly. News of the violent death of Tom Pritchard and the knowledge that Nerissa was orphaned and alone aroused Henrietta Cobner's maternal sympathy, for she was a sensitive soul, tender and easily stirred to tears. Nerissa's timid confession that she had no experience as a lady's maid was met not with the pained superiority expected, but airy dismissal of such an irrelevance.

"Indeed, my dear," the cook affirmed stoutly, "it is of no account, for we must all begin at the beginning. I have made my own way by trial and error . . . yes, and with many a burnt offering and shed tear."

"But if Mrs Crawshay should require some service and I too ignorant to know?"

"Then Mrs Pratt will set you straight!" Mrs Cobner assured. "There is little of social etiquette unbeknown to her, for she has served a lifetime, and in some of the highest households in the land, with none to fault her."

"But if Mrs Crawshay should find me wanting . . . dismiss me?" Nerissa persisted, distressed.

"She will not," Mrs Cobner declared firmly, "for she is generous and fair minded. You are an honest girl without airs and graces or stupid affectations, else you would not have admitted your doubts. Do not be afraid to ask for help. It will be willingly given, for we are one family here, below stairs."

Her broad, homely face was shiny from the heat, grey hair wispily escaping her mob-cap, but there was no denying her kindness. She blinked rapidly as Nerissa impulsively bent and kissed her fleshy cheek, rising flustered from her chair as Mrs Pratt returned.

The glance exchanged between the two elder women was one of comfortable conspiracy, the understanding of friends. Nerissa Pritchard had yet to prove herself. She must gain acceptance from Hillier, the major domo, whose word below stairs was sacred writ; unalterable law. They were a tight-knit, insular community, fiercely loyal to the family they served and to their own kind.

Glancing surreptitiously at the frail figure beside her,

119

Selina Pratt was grieved that the child had seen so much of the grief and harshness of life so soon. Mrs Crawshay had told her a little of the girl's history and asked her to ease her way unobtrusively among the other servants, and to guide her gently at her tasks. All would be new and strange to her, she declared, and she would be in need of friends. Mrs Crawshay, or Miss Arabella as Selina Pratt thought of her, for she had known her mistress from birth and served her mother before her, was impulsive and generous hearted. Yet it had shocked and scandalised the housekeeper that she had so blatantly flouted convention by choosing a maid from the hirings! Worse, she had actually brought the girl home in the carriage, as if she were quality. Mrs Pratt, who was a stickler for etiquette and observing the mores of society, comforted herself with the knowledge that her mistress could afford such indulgences. She had married into the landed gentry, certainly, but her own pedigree was illustrious enough to make her a law unto herself, like her aristocratic forebears. Their eccentricities were excusable, indeed encouraged, for it was a mark of their difference; their very superiority. In any event, the child walking beside her was clearly well mannered, neat and presentable. Her gratitude would make her not only industrious, but stubbornly loyal to those she served. Selina Pratt had no qualms about her own role in Nerissa Pritchard's transformation into the archetypal lady's maid. She would coach her meticulously in all that was required. Of her value as companion to Mrs Crawshay she was more doubtful, for she would be expected to amuse and divert her and to accompany her upon excursions and on formal visits into polite society. She could soon enough be initiated into the social graces and those duties expected of her, for a companion was no more than a necessary appendage; an accessory, like a parasol, required to blend unobtrusively, and then forgot.

"Can you sew, Miss Pritchard?" she demanded brusquely.

"Why, yes, ma'am . . . Mrs Pratt," she amended, flustered.

"Coarse household mending? Or can you embroider and sew a fine seam?"

"I have learnt fine stitching . . . sewing delicate things, pin-tucked nightgowns, bodices with drawn threadwork, and such." At Mrs Pratt's look of profound astonishment she confessed, smiling, "Not for myself . . . for I had no call for such finery, but for the quality, the local gentry. My mother was, in earlier days, a dressmaker and seamstress."

"Indeed?" Mrs Pratt was plainly gratified by such an unexpected turn of events. "Then it will be to your great advantage . . . for it will be quite in order for you to work upon some fine embroidery or tapestry when Mrs Crawshay is similarly engaged, or when visiting. It is an acceptable occupation." She hesitated before pronouncing regretfully, "I fear though, Miss Pritchard, that you will be set at a greater disadvantage . . ."

Nerissa looked at her for enlightenment, spirits depressed.

"A lady's companion," Selina Pratt explained, "is less servant than friend. A gentlewoman in reduced circumstances, perhaps, or a poor but presentable relation. Someone well versed in the polite arts, you understand?"

Nerissa nodded dispiritedly as the housekeeper continued, "The daughter of a parson, perhaps, or of a schoolmaster, fallen into poverty through illness or one suddenly bereaved." Then, remembering Nerissa's own circumstances, she demanded quickly, "Can you read, and write a fair hand? Figure, perhaps?"

"No, ma'am." The admission was low, shamefacedly made. "I was never taught . . . Oh, but I feel the lack of it!" she exclaimed with feeling. "For there is so much I would hope to learn." She paused, scarlet faced with mortification, to blurt, "Should Mrs Crawshay think the less of me, or think I have failed or misled her, then I shall go at once, leave upon the instant. I would not remain here upon her charity alone. She is deserving of better."

"I do not think she would look for better." Selina Pratt's sharp-boned face was briefly softened as she offered, with a crispness that belied her true feelings, "I will teach you to read and write, if you will apply yourself to the task

121

wholeheartedly. There will be time enough from your duties, and you may study in your room at night, if you are so minded."

Nerissa, pleased and grateful, had tried to murmur her thanks but knew them to be stilted and inadequate. The words seemed to die in the thickness of her throat and hot tears of shame and regret stung at her eyelids.

"I . . . thank you, ma'am," she blurted, at length. "I truly thank you."

Mrs Pratt, seeing Nerissa's exhaustion and the cruel toll the past days had taken on her, would have hugged the child to her for comfort, but did not, for training and dignity forbade it. She contented herself with warning, "It will not be easy, I cannot pretend it. It will need all your powers of concentration." Her voice softened. "I know, for I, too, was determined to better myself, to learn to read and write . . . to advance myself and my knowledge."

"How did you do so, Mrs Pratt? Who taught you?"

"Miss Arabella's . . ." she corrected herself swiftly, "Mrs Crawshay's childhood governess. It was at her mother's instigation, through her kindness, that I was permitted to take lessons in my own time. I paid for those lessons from my own wages, for I would have it no other way. Like you, I was fiercely determined, too young and proud to accept charity."

"But I will not be," Nerissa said quietly, "for I have learnt of late that charity is but another name for caring, the friendship of others. To spurn it would be ungenerous and wrong." She promised with shy dignity, "I shall do as you have done, Mrs Pratt, if you will allow. I shall keep your memory and offer your kindness to some other in need."

"Yes," Selina Pratt agreed briskly. "That will do very well, I think. That way it will not be ended. There will always be a new opportunity, a new beginning . . . such as you have today." She opened the door to Nerissa's bed chamber and ushered her within.

Long after Mrs Pratt had exhausted her advice and instruction and left, Nerissa sat in the wooden rocking chair near the window, surveying her small kingdom. Her fatigue and inertia had left her and she felt only a calmness of relief, a sense of belonging. The room was upon an attic landing, but was light and prettily furnished and had the snug cosiness of a nest. There was a minute chimneypiece with kindling alight and cheerfully crackling upon the hearth. It gave off a warmth of comfort and the sweet pungency of woodsmoke and scented applewood; an evocative fragrance . . . There was a tiny pine washstand with porcelain ewer and bowl and a matching flower-patterned bucket with a chamber pot peeping discreetly from under the end of the bed. There was a closet for hanging her clothes, a miniature chest of drawers which might do duty as a desk, a handsome brass-framed bed with a coverlet of quilted patchwork and curtains of blue-sprigged cotton at the lead-paned lattice. Nerissa was enchanted, for everything had been thoughtfully chosen and provided, from the washball of lye and tallow to the facecloth of rough flannel and a fresh linen towel. Upon the chest of drawers lay an ebony hand-glass, a horn comb and a bowl of pot-pourri, aromatic and sweetly perfumed, a joy to the senses. Nerissa had never known such luxury nor such an all-pervading sense of quietness and peace, and she could have wept with gratitude for the deliverance it offered.

Yet she did not weep, but set about untying her bundle and carefully setting her few clothes and treasures in place. A cobweb-fine shawl that her mother had crocheted, a pottery fairing of a spotted dog, absurdly like Toby, and a pebble from the seashore, rubbed smooth without by the lapping of the tide but holding within jagged crystals of pink-mauve amethyst. Perfect. Unexpected. As filled with enduring beauty as the bright promise of the days ahead.

Nerissa unselfconsciously knelt beside the brass-framed bed and thanked God most devoutly that it should be so. Her prayers were direct and childishly spoken, an echo of past teachings and simple belief. She knew that here she was safe with those she trusted. She had to believe that those she had loved had found a deeper sanctuary, a lasting protection, and were reunited in spirit as they

123

had once been in flesh, else all was a lie and not worth a corpse's candle.

She washed herself in cold water at the washstand bowl, combed her hair, then changed into the only other dress she possessed, a high-necked gown of dark blue cotton, which she had stitched herself. At its neck she pinned Joe Protheroe's brooch, the enamelled likeness of a four-leafed clover, then, with heart beating fiercely, she closed the door upon the white-washed room with its bare stripped floorboards and descended the stairs.

The silence that greeted her as she hesitantly pushed open the kitchen door was coldly unnerving, the sea of faces a pale, anonymous blur. Then, seeing her confusion and shyness, Selina Pratt stepped forward to welcome her, with the major domo resplendent in liveried uniform of claret and gold. There was a shout of delighted laughter and a brave singing and clapping of hands, and all, from the youngest scullion to the major domo himself, were showering her with good wishes and greetings.

"A happy birthday, my dear." Mrs Cobner's plumply creased face was alive with vicarious pleasure as she took a spill from the fireside and lighted the single candle upon the rich fruit cake, so secretly pressed into service. Nerissa caught only the barest glimpse of the festive table before the candle flame blurred into coloured light, vivid as a rainbow. She felt no need to hide her tears nor to halt their dropping. If surprise and pleasure robbed her of sensible speech and those few wits remaining, then none resented it. Words may be left unspoken in the warm company of friends.

Chapter Ten

Upon the morrow Nerissa was awakened at daybreak by one of the serving girls bringing hot water from below, as Mrs Pratt had promised. The girl was a plain raw-boned child of some twelve or thirteen years who, Nerissa recalled, had remained timidly silent and aloof during the evening's celebrations. Lank hair escaped her mob-cap, the face beneath shiny and reddened, and her large hands were painfully chapped. So awkwardly shy was she and so clumsy in movement that Nerissa feared she must stumble and scald herself in her efforts to become invisible. Yet she did not interfere nor try to help her for she was aware of the child's excruciating nervousness, her wretchedness lest she offend.

"What is your name, my dear?" Nerissa asked when, to the relief of both, the jug upon the washstand had been painstakingly filled, the pitcher safely emptied.

The girl studied her shoes. She did not raise her head. "Bella, Miss. I am called Bella." The name had been muttered reluctantly, yet there was defiance in her tone.

Nerissa, sensitive to the cruelty of so ungainly a creature being so extravagantly christened and the hurts it must so often have caused, said quietly, "It is a good name. Honest and distinctive, and one not easily shortened or forgot. A name to be proud of."

The girl looked up, face anxious, suspicious of mockery.

"Proud because someone loved you enough, had joy enough in your birth to give you so honest and open a welcome . . . A declaration before all . . . Bella," she repeated approvingly, "yes. It is a good name, and one chosen from affection and pride." She added gently, "I do

125

not doubt that your mother still has that same pride in you, Bella, the same joy."

"I do not rightly know, miss," she confessed, flushing. Then in answer to Nerissa's puzzlement, "I was a pauper born, do you see? I have no knowledge of her, no remembrance. She died after birthing me."

Nerissa said quickly, to mask her sympathy, "Then you must bear your name proudly, for her sake and your own."

"Yes, miss." Bella's plain, earnest face glowed with newfound pleasure at discovery of her own importance. "Yes, miss," she repeated more confidently. Then, with a shyly apologetic smile, she clutched the empty pitcher protectively to her, sidled to the door and fled.

Nerissa, gazing after her, thought with an ache of pity that whatever the deprivation of the past, here Bella too had found safe haven. She would grow in security, and with it she would find that confidence and belief in herself that she now so painfully lacked. In time she might even develop and blossom to fit her name. She was not sorry that she had lied to save the child's feelings. It was unlikely that Bella's name was her mother's choice. A pauper would scarcely have been consulted, the child's name randomly given. The name perhaps of some public benefactor, or an attempt to bribe some favour from officialdom. It made no matter. To earn the belief of others, one must first have belief in oneself. The seed had been sown. Time and patience would help it first germinate then grow. Nerissa knew that a start had been made. For the moment it was enough.

Nerissa divested herself of her voluminous cambric nightgown, folding it carefully upon the bed, then standing naked she washed herself scrupulously from head to toe at the washstand. Hot water was a rare luxury, for every last drop had to be heated painstakingly upon an open fire. Yet here it was copiously provided and delivered. She could scarce credit the wicked indulgence of it and the sensuous satisfaction it brought. Mrs Pratt had suggested that as an upper servant she might consider buying a hip-bath for her personal use, the water to be well softened with herbs and oatmeal. Yet she had not openly agreed, for fear that it was no more than a jest, a joke played upon all credulous newcomers by the household staff.

The major domo, Mr Hillier, whom she had liked instantly despite his air of reserve and gravity, had confided that as a raw household lad he had been sent to the housekeeper for "an extra large helping of elbow grease and enough soft soap to spread it". He had innocently obliged. He related the story at table, and the scullions and kitchen maids had been convulsed with appreciative laughter and disbelief. Yet there had been no malice in their amusement, Nerissa recalled. It was so genuine and spontaneous that none could take offence nor resist joining in. Their laughter was with the major domo, not against him, for his fallibility made him at one with them; naive, trusting, prey to the erratic dictates of others. He was, Nerissa thought, a shrewd and intelligent man to identify himself so closely with them. In confessing to his earlier ignorance and openly denigrating himself, he had won their ready sympathy, yet had not sacrificed their respect. In future, he could chide and correct them without provoking resentment or rancour.

Mrs Pratt had declared provocatively that the major domo, she and Nerissa were always at a disadvantage, "neither fish, nor fowl, nor good red herring". Set halfway between heaven and hell, and at ease in neither. Nerissa, meticulously lathering herself with the washball of lye and tallow, would not have agreed. She was blissfully placed in her own small kingdom, here upon earth. With no inkling of sacrilege, she was quite decided that the kingdom of heaven could offer no more enticing rewards than those she already enjoyed. Hell itself could offer no greater temptation. She was wholly content.

When, cleansed, combed and carefully dressed, she made her way downstairs to the kitchen, it was with real pleasure at the prospect of a new and exciting day. She was not required to attend upon Mrs Crawshay, Mrs Pratt had given assurance. Her duties would begin in earnest upon the morrow. Today there would be a visit from the village seamstress, with measurements to be taken and suitable housegowns to be chosen and ordered. Mrs Crawshay's instructions were explicit, her preferences already made plain. In addition, the under-coachman had received orders to transport Mrs Pratt and Nerissa to Knatchfield village, where a visit to the cordwainer, the hosier and the bonnet maker would be arranged. Finally, they must make a call at the draper's shop, where those "delicate feminine necessities" might be discreetly purchased.

Nerissa, her mind upon the promised excursion, had all but blundered into Captain Farrow who, to her acute embarrassment, had been forced to steady her lest she stumble down the stairs. Luke had smiled reassuringly and made some polite and innocuous remark, yet so great was her embarrassment and confusion that she had been barely able to utter a coherent word. Anguished and with face flaming she had hurried upon her way. She had behaved like a dolt, she told herself. He would think her tongue tied and feeble witted. She should have made proper apology, behaved to him with the dignity owed.

Yet pained as she was by her gracelessness, she could not regret the meeting. He had been so respectful, gallant even, as if he were greeting not a servant but someone of gentle birth. It was no more than conventional good manners, she felt sure, natural courtesy, but try as she might, she could not forget the warmth of his smile nor the unexpected strength of his fingers pressed hard to her sleeve. It had evoked sensations new to her; a quickening of emotions too strange and shaming to define. It was best forgotten. Yet memory of his handsome, good-humoured face intruded, to rob her of confidence and peace of mind. He was, indubitably, a most handsome and personable gentleman, and dressed in his immaculate riding habit, as sartorially elegant as any ever seen. He would, she felt certain, ride effortlessly and skilfully. A man always at ease with himself and others. A man fully in control. He was as far removed from her in birth and breeding as it was possible to be, and would give her no more thought. It was only his accidental discovery of her father's death which had given him cause to remember her at the fair and to come to her defence. It was no more than Goliath Jones and Toby had done from friendship and pity. Yet the thought of Captain Farrow's pity filled her with a depth of despair, and it was not humiliation alone which so depressed her.

Luke Farrow had turned at the curve of the balustrade to watch her descending. The secret smile he had surprised before Nerissa was aware of him had moved him strangely. She was so pretty and delicate a thing, and yet with such fortitude and strength of spirit. He was stirred to a protectiveness disturbing to him, as he had been at the simple cottage after her father's death and then at Holly Grove fair. His physical defence of her, he assured himself, was an instinctive thing. It was the natural reaction to the savagery of the brute. He had wanted to teach that surly young jackanapes, de Granville, the manners he lacked. Why, even Francis, who had never before seen the girl, had answered with the same anger, the same impetuous urge for revenge . . . Any innocent victim would have provoked the same response. Besides, memory of Tom Pritchard's violent death and de Granville's involvement had raked his fury raw. Yes. That was the real crux of it.

Yet even as he tried to convince himself, the doubts crept in to harry and bedevil him. What of Arabella? She had no suspicion of de Granville's role as murderer, yet she had publicly rebuked him by taking the girl into her service, humiliating him more painfully than the thrashing he and his bully-boys had received. Luke paused uncertainly, hand upon the knob of the breakfast-room door. He was a fool, he told himself irritably, to become so involved in an affair which no longer concerned him. It was over. Ended. A raking-over of dead ashes would help no one. It would not resurrect the dead man, and only add to his daughter's anguish.

It was high time that he left Knatchfield Grange; made plans for the future. Here life was agreeable, sybaritic even, and the company of Arabella and Francis a constant delight. He had rarely felt so relaxed or pampered and might all too soon grow accustomed to such ease of living and be reluctant to move on as he must. Despite Francis's urging that he remain until his future was settled and Arabella's insistent pleas, he would tell them this very day of his decision to leave. When he and Francis were out riding would offer good opportunity. He would not be persuaded or swayed. There was nothing to hold him here, since his active role in the regiment was ended although his loyalty remained. He had taken his fill of soldiering. Unlike Francis and his own father, the regiment would not claim him for life. He wanted travel and adventure certainly, but of his own choosing and upon his own terms. He had time and money enough to satisfy his aspirations. Now was the time, before the edges of youth and ambition were blurred, or responsibility to others called a halt to his wanderings. The colonies then? Australia, even; a wide and uncharted land offering opportunity and wealth to any astute enough and pioneering enough to take it?

Or India, perhaps, where his parents were garrisoned? They would welcome sight of him, he knew, and he might stay for as long as ever he chose. Yet they would not try to dissuade him unfairly, should he wish to move on. Their peripatetic life had given them the taste for journeying and a spirit of independence and adventure despite the discipline imposed . . . Yes, Northern India might offer the stimulus and diversion he sought and give him pause to assess the future without hindrance. Thus decided, Luke confidently pushed open the door of the breakfast-room and went within to join Francis and Arabella at their early breakfast.

Arabella, who was to have joined them at their riding, had laughingly declared herself to be "quite prostrated" by the sheer excitement of their day at the fair. Despite Luke's good-natured bantering and Francis's sly innuendoes and tongue-in-cheek lecture on the perils of indolence, she would not be provoked. She had made a hearty breakfast then announced that she had duties enough to occupy her within Knatchfield Grange. If Francis and Luke were bent upon exhausting themselves and her patience, they were better removed.

"You may take my new grey, Luke," she offered good

130

naturedly, "else Francis, upon his palomino, will be reckless and quite insufferable in his conceit! He is in need of a firm challenge from a rider with skills to equal his own."

"Then I will endeavour to keep him on a tight rein," Luke promised, straight faced, "and see that he does not get above himself!"

She nodded approval, saying firmly, "You are both in sore need of exercise. It will do you good. You have breakfasted so well that it will be a miracle if the poor creatures can carry your weight! Indeed, Luke is becoming quite portly and you, Francis, are odiously stout."

Since the two gentlemen were handsomely spare in flesh and admirably military in bearing, neither was offended, although they good-humouredly pretended outrage to humour her.

"You say the palomino was de Granville's horse, Francis?" she asked, puzzled. "What would persuade him to sell, to part with it?"

Francis exchanged a startled glance with Luke before saying evenly, "Who knows, my love? Perhaps his creditors are pressing. Young men such as he are prone to extravagance . . . gaming debts, perhaps, or tailors' bills."

She was not convinced, pressing, "But it is so perfect a creature . . . high bred and distinctive. It makes no sense. De Granville is such an arrogant, conceited little coxcomb that he would want a mount as showy and flaunting as he."

"And I, my dear?" Francis asked mildly. "Am I too dull and soberly respectable for such a paragon? Too stout, perhaps?"

Arabella, in denying it, shared laughter with Francis and Luke before growing serious and venturing, "It would not surprise me had he treated the horse with the indifference he shows to others . . . with cruelty even, to break its spirit. He would think it a challenge to set his mark upon it."

"Then it is as well that it is delivered from his hands," Francis reminded quietly, to ease her distress. "It will have a good home and kindness here."

"Yes . . ." Arabella hesitated before blurting vehemently, "and Nerissa Pritchard, too. I am glad of that.

She would have been as much at risk from his malice and spleen. It would have pleased him to further humiliate her, to degrade her even."

Neither Francis nor Luke spoke and she continued impassionately, "I cannot even now think of her as wholly safe . . . de Granville is a malevolent creature and one who will bear rancour. He will demand his pound of flesh."

"Nonsense, my dear," Francis was alarmed by her agitation, "de Granville is a boor, certainly, but he would not dare to pursue her here. Why should he? She is nothing to him . . . Had she not been at the hirings he would have turned his scorn and bigotry upon another. Any victim would do to feed his intolerance . . . No. He will not show his face here nor trouble her further. Believe it."

"You are sure, Francis?"

"I am sure. He has taken beating enough. Should he persist, then he would answer first to me and then to the law. He would not risk further humiliation."

Arabella, satisfied, settled a kiss upon her husband's cheek, cautioning, "You will ride sensibly, Francis? Take no risks?"

Francis raised his eyebrows and glanced expressively at Luke, who was grinning absurdly. "I shall be discretion itself, my love," he promised, "and never venture above a trot. As for Luke, he shall lead the grey and not mount at all."

"Sarcasm," reminded Arabella as she swept regally out, "is the lowest form of wit. You will entertain each other admirably, since you are of like mind."

Their appreciative laughter followed her into the hall.

The early morning air was crisp and bracing with that frosty clarity which is peculiar to late autumn. The mountains and hills beyond seemed unusually close and sharply defined; a splashed redness of ferns, their contours sketched boldly in charcoal against a clean blue sky. Francis and Luke had set the horses first to a canter and then to a fierce gallop across the hills, relishing the freedom and wildness of the landscape, its healing solitude. They had spoken little, every nerve and effort upon their task, straining for mastery over their mounts, each other, and ultimately over themselves. They had ridden skilfully and with heady enjoyment, drawn close in companionship. Their faces were stung to iciness by the wind, flesh glowing, the pounding of hooves upon the turf rhythmic and powerful as their quickening heartbeats . . . When they reached the summit of the highest hill Francis reined in the palomino and dismounted, stroking its trembling crest and neck, soothing it to quietness. Luke swung himself from the saddle and came to stand beside him, praising the grey, setting her to ease, yet unable to still his restless exhilaration. The panorama which lay outspread below them was breathtaking in its breadth and majesty. Range upon range of hills and valleys, touched now by the colours of autumn, the small copses far below, a blurred softness of gold, crimson and brown, set against the bleached paleness of faded grasses and grey outcrops of stone. The far-off hills were misted by distance to the colour of woodsmoke touched with dark, clear purple, heather and lavender. The hills before them were riven by clefts and gullies, silvered now with waterfalls and foaming white cataracts; the surging of water and the sighing of the wind as gentle as the muted sounds of the horses, their snickering and soft breaths. Francis said, "I shall grow to love this place. There is such beauty here and quietness. A solace for the spirit."

Luke, recognising a sadness in his tone, said quietly, "Yes. It is a place for all seasons, all moods. A place to put into perspective the rest of the world, its demands and ills."

Francis stared before him and made no immediate answer. Then, as if nerving himself to make confession, he turned abruptly to face Luke, knuckles gripping white upon the rein.

"There is something I must tell you, Luke. Something kept hidden. I would have you know." He spoke haltingly and with effort. "There is none other I can turn to, to seek advice."

Luke, alarmed by Francis's agitation, pledged quietly, "Then you have but to tell me what so disturbs you."

"It is not easy." Francis fidgeted with the reins before staring once more into the distance. "I do not know where, or how, to begin."

"The regiment?" Luke prompted gently. "Does it concern the regiment?"

"Yes . . . indirectly as all else. I must make a decision, Luke, and God knows, I cannot think clearly. My brain seems numbed. I see no easy solution. I could not believe myself so useless or lacking in courage," he exclaimed despairingly.

"You have never lacked for courage," Luke said with honesty, adding firmly, "I have fought beside you and under your command . . . None could doubt your commitment, you care for those you lead."

Francis put a hand to Luke's shoulder in gratitude, then let it drop to his side, confessing awkwardly, "That is the nub of it, Luke. I do not know if I can return to the regiment. It has been my life. My whole existence. I have known no other. Could conceive of no other. Yet I would cause no harm."

"Harm? Speak plainly, Francis! I swear I do not understand. How could you do the regiment harm? Is there some secret you know? Some disloyalty by those in command?"

"No."

"Embezzlement then? Some crime that will implicate another and demand a court martial? A cashiering, even?"

"No," Francis repeated tonelessly. "It concerns no other."

"Why, then, are you unable to return to take command? What prevents you?"

Francis regarded him in silence, face taut with painful indecision, before blurting, "I do not know how long I shall survive."

"In battle, you mean?" Luke demanded stupidly.

"No. There is some disease of the nervous system . . . Some damage, perhaps, to the brain. A tumour, it is believed."

"Dear God!" Luke stared at him, appalled. "You are sure of this? You cannot be mistaken?"

134

"No. I have taken advice, consulted physicians both here and in London. The prognosis is the same."

As Luke made to murmur awkward sympathy, Francis halted him, chiding with much of his old spirit, "It is not death I fear, Luke, for I have faced it too often in the past . . ."

"What then?"

"What every fighting man . . . or every other, fears. A crippling dependence upon others."

"But Arabella would not count it so," Luke protested fiercely. "She loves you devotedly, Francis." Then, "Dear heaven!" he exclaimed in anguish. "Surely you have told her, Francis? Confided all? You have not kept her in ignorance? It would be too cruel!"

"No . . . I have kept nothing from her," Francis admitted, heavily, "she is already aware."

"Then . . . ?"

"Then the dilemma remains," Francis said wretchedly. "I am still without answer . . . Arabella will take no part in the decision. She will support me in whatever I choose."

"And you choose?" Luke asked gently.

"I would choose to die in battle," Francis confessed.

"Then your way is clear. The decision made."

"No. I do not know if I have the right." In answer to Luke's questioning look, he continued reluctantly, "I do not know if I have the right to set the lives of others in danger. On my own account, I have no reservations, no doubts. I am sure."

"But their lives *will* be in danger!" Luke reminded harshly. "They will be risking them, clearly, in battle . . . and with full knowledge and understanding."

Francis shook his head, saying stolidly, "Yes . . . but do you not understand, Luke? I can confide in no one save you . . . I would not have their pity; their knowledge that I am unfit to lead or command. What if I should fail them . . . my mind confused by sickness? Or lead them into disaster?" The torment he suffered was in his face and his voice, cruelly inescapable.

"There is no certainty that it will be so," Luke persisted, "there is no proof."

"None save the physicians' word and what has already occurred." At Luke's startled glance, he asked without emotion, "Did you not hear Arabella's plea that I ride carefully, take no risks?"

"Yes, but I had thought it a jest and humorously made."

"No jest," Francis said quietly. "There have been instances . . . warning signs. They come infrequently, but more often of late, for the disease is slow but progressive. There have been lapses of memory, confusion even. My limbs are sometimes awkward and slow to respond. My sight blurs and defeats me . . . at reading and all else."

"But cannot it be treated? Reversed even? Surely there is some known treatment, some antidote, however severe?"

"There is nothing." It was spoken without anger or self-pity. "That is why I would have your dispassionate advice, for I know you are honest and would speak only the truth, for the sakes of others as well as my own."

As Luke hesitated, plainly distressed, Francis continued quietly, "I know that the decision must ultimately be my own. I must take personal responsibility . . . too much is at stake to burden or destroy any other."

"What would you have me do?"

"I would have you stay, if you will, until I have made my decision. I have no right to ask it of you. No right to unfairly afflict you."

"You have the right of friendship." Luke's voice was firm. "I will stay for as long as ever you have need."

Francis, clearly moved, took Luke's hand, grasping it gratefully and saying, voice low, "I thank you, for Arabella's sake as well as my own. While my mind is so bedevilled, I am painfully distracted and the poorest of company. You will be friend and comforter to us both." He took up the reins, murmuring, "Shall we not ride on a while? I am loath to return until my mind is cleared of all that bewilders it."

"Yes," Luke agreed compassionately. "Let us ride on." He put a boot to the stirrup before asking anxiously, "You have told Arabella, then? That you intended to explain all to me? I ask because I must know how to treat her, you understand?" His voice faltered and died away. "Oh, hell and damnation, Francis!" he exclaimed impassionedly. "What can I say? What do? I am less than useless! I can find no proper words!"

Francis said wryly, "No more can I. Yet your staying speaks words enough." Then he added lightly, to hide his feelings, "We are soldiers both and know that one firm action is worth a thousand words . . . Come, I will race you to that mountain ridge yonder and show you how a real horseman rides!"

Luke was away as swiftly and with as ferocious a rivalry as his friend, neither willing to concede an inch and determined upon victory. They had arrived at the ridge with barely a hair's breadth between them, breathless, exhausted, yet filled with a wildness of exhilaration that set them laughing companionably, so that for a moment, Luke could almost believe his grief forgot.

Yet in their ride to Knatchfield Grange, the wind seemed colder and more penetrating, and the country-side, for all its beauty and solitude, a more hostile place. Lonely and filled with desolation. Yet he knew that the desolation came from within. What had been bewildering and puzzling suddenly became clear to him, yet it brought him no solution, no peace of mind. He remembered with sadness Arabella's words before their visit to Holly Grove fair.

"And will you have your fortune told by a gypsy woman?" he had teased affectionately.

"No. I will not do that, Luke."

Now that he knew their full meaning, her words of explanation had a courage and poignancy he had not before understood.

"There are things best left unknown and unseen . . . Even to acknowledge them lends them credence. The power to corrupt or destroy that which remains. It is sometimes easier to face an enemy unknown."

Luke stirred the grey into a violence of action, but the grief remained, cold and deep hidden. It would not go away.

Chapter Eleven

At St Samson Court, Richard de Granville's return had not only been remarked by his father but angrily seized upon as proof of his fecklessness and dissolute ways.

"Well, sir?" Sir Peter demanded icily as he intercepted him in the hall. "And what is your excuse this time for so blatantly defying custom and convention? What myth or fancy tale am I expected to swallow?"

Seething with resentment, Richard de Granville murmured something inaudible, gaze upon his riding boots.

"Speak up, sir! Do not mumble like a nervous governess!" Sir Peter ordered irritably. "And have the courtesy to look me in the face when you address me!"

Richard de Granville glanced up mutinously, but made no response.

"Good God, sir! Look at the condition of your face! And your clothes . . . You are not fit to be seen in decent company! You are a scarecrow. A disgrace. You disgust me!" As his son remained obdurately silent, Sir Peter exclaimed in exasperation, "Well, explain yourself! Or at least have the grace and good manners to make proper apology!"

"I apologise, sir . . ." Richard de Granville's jaw was stubbornly set, the words grudgingly said, yet he dared not show open insolence, for fear of reprisal.

He was, Sir Peter thought with distaste, for all his handsome arrogance no more than a fop, a dandiprat. He would lie, squirm, incriminate others rather than admit his own inadequacy or behave like a man! The crux of it was that Louisa had spoilt him absurdly, indulging his every whim. The boy had no sense of the value and order of things. No sense of responsibility or family pride. He was a moral bankrupt.

"Well, sir?" he demanded, incensed. "Have you no explanation for your injuries, your . . . disreputable state? Were you set upon by footpads? Highwaymen? Thrown from your horse? The innocent victim of some violent and unprovoked attack? The prey of some madman? Answer me!"

"No, sir . . . I was at Holly Grove fair, with Hanford and the others . . . Siberry was set upon, unprovoked, by some oafs hellbent upon trouble. Some idle clods who took exception to the fact that we were gentlemen."

"Indeed?" Sir Peter's lean, aristocratic face was expressionless, but his tone cutting as he observed, "Then they were sadly mistaken, were they not? It is not the province of a gentleman to descend to the level of clods and inferiors, but to set them example! You are a fool, Richard, and a greater one if you believe me so naively credulous! Do me the justice of crediting me with a little of the intelligence you so plainly lack!" As his son made to protest, he exclaimed curtly, "No. Do not antagonise me further! Get clear of my sight! When you are fitted to be seen in decent company, you will return to the library and give full account of yourself. You are indolent, sir! A disgrace to your name and station in society. You have no interest in the estate, no idea of the responsibilities it involves . . . but you will soon enough learn, else I will see that you are taught, and with a vengeance!"

"I will return, sir, as soon as ever I am able." Richard de Granville's bow was stiff, manner tight lipped.

"And I shall await our meeting with every whit as little pleasure as you," Sir Peter promised frigidly. "Meanwhile, you might occupy your mind in finding plausible explanation for your bootmaker's bill. It is ludicrously excessive, sir! He might have outfitted an entire regiment of cavalry for less . . . And there is the small matter of the palomino horse, which I lately purchased for you at your mother's urging. Where is it now? It is certainly not in the stables, for I have made enquiry of the head groom."

"It is sold, sir," Richard de Granville admitted, wry-faced.

"Sold? Upon whose authority?"

"My own. It was mine to dispose of, an outright gift."

"Was it, by God!" Sir Peter could not control his fury. "Then forgive me that I was not made aware of it! It was for your use, certainly, that you might ride fittingly and in appropriate style, not be disgraced before your fellows . . . It seems that you set as little value upon appearances as upon morals and behaviour."

"That is unfair," he countered stiffly.

Sir Peter brushed his objection aside, saying abrasively, "Perhaps I should have said no value upon appearances, save for your own vulgar frippery. You are a dandy, sir, an affected coxcomb, with no thought in your head save for gaming and idle pleasure . . . You made me look a fool, sir, and before my own groom!"

"Then I am sorry for that, sir."

Sir Peter looked at him sharply for some show of insolence, but finding him guileless said tartly, "It is high time that you gave up this aimlessness. You are no longer a callow boy but a grown man and must take responsibility for yourself and others. You had best be thinking of choosing a wife, one with a background and fortune equalling your own. We shall discuss it and make suitable arrangement." He turned upon his heel, expecting no answer.

"Suitable arrangement!" Richard de Granville fumed impotently. Suitable for whom? He would be wasted upon some lumpen brood-mare of a girl, charmless and with less appeal than a common doxy. That or some simpering ninny, vacuous of mind and spared of flesh. Oh, it was monstrous! Quite insupportable! He returned to his bed-chamber and his dressing room in the vilest of humours. His father's high-handed autocracy rankled bitterly and he knew that should he rebel, he could not expect his mother's support. He would have small choice in the matter! It would be a business arrangement, no more than that. It would be ordered as objectively and exactingly, and to the best advantage of the families concerned. Moreover, it would be as legally and morally binding, and as impossible to break. His thoughts turned to the gentlewoman whom he had seen at the fair. A woman of beauty and fiery spirit,

140

an arrogance matching his own. Then he recalled how she had seen him beaten and humiliated, the butt of everyone's scornful laughter and her own disdain . . .

He sought blindly for some scapegoat, someone upon whom to lay the blame for his own shortcomings. It was Jeremy Hardwicke's squeamishness that was at fault, his cringing weakness and remorse. The poacher was dead, and best forgotten. He had got no more than his villainy deserved. Pritchard was thief and destroyer, and a man was entitled to protect his own property, his own inheritance . . . He was permitted by law. And if the law was cumbersome and ineffectual, then he must take punishment into his own hands; act boldly, or be thought less of a man . . . As for Pritchard's daughter, then she was deserving of the same treatment that he had received. Her insolence and arrogance were astounding! She was no better than a common menial, yet she had challenged him publicly, made him a laughing stock before all. It would have pleased him to have seen Hanford's plan work, to have watched her humbled and degraded, to have taken her by force. He would soon enough have broken her spirit.

Richard de Granville stripped off his soiled and torn outer clothing and tugged at the bell-pull to summon his valet. A steaming hip-bath would soon enough ease his aches and pains, and fresh clothing would restore his confidence, which had been as bruised and bloodied as he . . . He caught sight of himself in the looking glass upon the shaving stand and felt a fury out of all proportion to the damage inflicted. He was a fright; a wretched caricature! He could not bear to see himself so ridiculously flawed, made pitiable in others' eyes. Someone would pay, and pay handsomely for it! When his ordeal with his father was safely over, his castigation ended, he would seek Jeremy Hardwicke out. He would vent his spleen upon him. He would put the very fear of God into him for his treachery. He would pay. Come hell and high water, Hardwicke would assuredly pay!

The proposed discussion with his father had, as Richard feared, turned out to be part catechism, part harangue, and

141

he did not acquit himself well. In fact, he barely acquitted himself at all, so voluble was Sir Peter's displeasure. His arbitrary disposal of the palomino caused considerable rancour, and the surfeit of pressing demands from his bootmaker, tailor and saddler did little to improve his father's temper. It was a chastened, aggrieved but stubbornly unrepentant young man who finally quitted Sir Peter's library. He was seething inwardly at the rank injustice of it, yet knew better than to show open defiance. His future pathway was charted for him. He must follow it slavishly. Should he deviate from it, then he must bear the consequences. His duties with the estate and tenantry were enumerated and would, he felt certain, be as dull and onerous as they sounded. In addition, he was reminded tartly, his ludicrous extravagances must be curbed. He would sell no more bloodstock from the stables. Should he default on any of his commitments, then he must make his way alone. Not a penny piece would he receive from the de Granville estates until he proved himself amenable to discipline and work. He had consented grudgingly to the new regime because he had no choice but to obey. His garbled explanation that he had sold the palomino because it was fractious and bad tempered, the product of ill-breeding and bad blood, was treated with the contempt it deserved.

"I fear, sir, that the same criticism might be made of you!" Sir Peter exclaimed sourly. "Would that I had the same recourse!" He had dismissed his son peremptorily.

Richard de Granville, smarting from the tongue-lashing received, was none the less sanguine about his future expectations. His mother would not see him made a pauper, but would indulge him in his extravagances secretly . . . Not extravagances, he corrected himself firmly, but the barest necessities for one of his position and wealth. He could scarcely be expected to dress himself like a ploughboy and live upon a paltry allowance, as his father well knew. Besides, if he were forced into wedlock, and his father seemed set upon it, then he must go courting elegantly, or not at all. His father would not cavil at such expense, but consider it money well spent. A sprat to catch a mackerel! All considered, Richard de Granville decided with satisfaction, he might yet emerge the victor. In marrying an heiress, he would have free access to her fortune; inherit it as irrevocably as he inherited her. His father would have no power over him then. He would not be dependent upon his whim and charity for the meanest farthing! To add to his triumph, his father could not disinherit him, since the estate was legally entailed. His own heirs would be desperately awaited; his every word law. As for taking a wife, it was no more than a social necessity. It would not alter his friendships or way of living, simply allow him to add freedom to style. His gaming, his drinking and even his whoring would not be at risk. Such diversions were normal coinage in society and accepted as such if discreetly done. His friends would remain friends, and life, if altered, would be altered only for the better.

Richard de Granville felt infinitely more optimistic and relaxed. He would leave word for his mother that he would be dining elsewhere and ride out to meet Hanford and Siberry, and Jeremy Hardwicke, too. It paid to be magnanimous. He could well afford to be seen to forgive him his treachery. Hardwicke was a weakling certainly, but with charm and persuasion he might be converted to see the error of his ways.

Richard de Granville had the groom saddle his horse and rode out to David Hanford's house, Lanelay Court. His newfound cheerfulness was shaken but not altogether dispelled by the news that Jeremy Hardwicke had fled to Rogerstone Court.

"It is best to leave him be," Hanford said decisively. "It will serve no purpose to harass or unsettle him, de Granville. A few weeks of hunting and shooting will set him to rights, put things into saner perspective."

"But if he should weaken, Hanford, confess all?"

"He will not! Depend upon it. There is too much at stake. Besides, he is said to be nervous, badly in need of country air, relaxation and proper rest. Who in his right mind would believe him? We are three ranged firmly against him, and will remain so . . . Nothing could shake our claim of innocence. Others would sooner believe that

143

Hardwicke is sick in mind. That having killed the man, by his own admission, he repents it and tries to lessen the blame . . . incriminating others unfairly."

"Yes, perhaps."

"When the time is right, I shall ride out to reason with him," Hanford promised. "At the moment he is too nervously plagued with guilt to be convinced." He hesitated before demanding insistently, "You will not harass him, de Granville? I would have your promise. He is unpredictable . . . not in his right mind. It would not do to unsettle him."

"You have my word upon it," de Granville assured him, adding handsomely, "you are the consummate diplomat, Hanford. I bow to your superior skills at persuasion."

"And at deviousness and deceit, de Granville?" he prompted slyly.

"Now there, sir, I might fairly claim equal advantage."

Laughing companionably, and with Hardwicke's perfidy all but forgotten, they rode to Siberry's house.

They ate a substantial meal at an inn near by, then, agreeably wined and dined, whiled away a few hours at a gaming house. The company was congenial and Siberry had won handsomely at cards, and they had been spared the company of the riff-raff from the fair, who frequented the cheaper, less salubrious taverns. None of their own class or acquaintance would have knowledge of their humiliating beating at Holly Grove, and they might more easily pretend that their battle had been no more than high-spirited larking, their injuries creditably won. They parted equably in a glow of good humour and alcoholic indulgence, each going his separate way. They had made promise to meet upon the morrow, as usual, and to ride out to a favourite drinking house together. The promise had been lightheartedly made. It might, de Granville consoled himself, be as lightheartedly broken. On the morrow he would ride out, alone and unseen, to convince Hardwicke to return home. He would feel safer were he nearer at hand and carefully watched. He cared little for Hardwicke's neck, but valued his own. When the hangman's noose threatened, he trusted no one's hand, save his own.

Nerissa's first day at Knatchfield Grange proved full and exciting, even if it lacked the intensity of her public ordeal and rescue at Holly Grove fair. So much had happened, and so quickly and inexplicably, that parts of it still held the strange unreality of a dream. Yet her present was real, and she thanked God for it. She thanked Him as humbly for those, oftimes as stricken and impoverished as she, who had offered her friendship. The ties, if brief, were strengthened by need and caring, would not be loosed in absence.

She thought with regret of her parting from Ruth, and of Sian and the babe, Aled, and prayed that they, too, might find such happiness and security as *she* now enjoyed. Hugh Gravelle was a fine and honest man and would offer her his loving protection, she felt certain, and love the children as dearly as if they were his own kin. He would shield Ruth from the malice and destructive cruelties of others, their envy and petty spite. Yet would it be enough? Her love for her husband, Will Sayce, had on her own admission been a fierce and consuming affair; a passion that had forced her to risk all. She had abandoned home, family and all else to follow him, and would have trailed him to the ends of the earth. Neither contempt nor rejection would have stayed her, and ostracism by those who loved or despised her was counted a small price to pay . . . Will Sayce's early death had not loosened his bonds upon her, but drawn them the tighter. Ruth would remember him always in that first wild torment of youthful loving, and time and living itself would not dim the fierceness of it. Rather, it would serve to brighten and enhance. Hugh Gravelle might, by his very kindness and compassion, triumph over living flesh, prove himself the better man. Yet he could not subdue a memory . . .

Unbidden, Nerissa's thoughts turned towards Captain Farrow and his kindness towards her, his unvarying sympathy. He was, she thought with gratitude, a gentle, warm-hearted man, as solid and dependable as Hugh Gravelle. He was a man to trust. Yet there the resemblance began and ended. She might have aspired some day to being loved and wedded by such a man as Hugh

Gravelle, an honest thatcher, or to a lesser craftsman or labourer upon the land. She was of the same working stock. Captain Farrow was a gentleman born and bred, his life and future decided. He would wed someone of his own world and social class, someone as elegantly beautiful and accomplished as Mrs Crawshay. A true gentlewoman, equipped to converse with him intelligently and well versed in the polite arts. A woman at home in the drawing room, not the scullery . . . One perfect in features and immaculately coiffed and gowned who could be presented to others with pride and do him full justice. A woman soft skinned and sweet scented. Someone assured and gently spoken who might stir him to desire and warmth of passion.

Nerissa, for all her pleasures in her newfound ease of living, felt suddenly cold and uncertain. Now, as Mrs Pratt claimed, she would be torn between two worlds and never at ease in either. She must face the reality that she was here on sufferance, employed from pity alone and not for what she was able to offer. She had neither background nor qualification for the work demanded of her. Yet she would work devotedly to repay Mrs Crawshay's trust and to improve herself. She would watch others and learn to copy their manners and ways of speech. She would apply herself to reading and writing lessons until she was fluent at both, word perfect even. She would make herself into the very model of what a lady's companion should be. Yet, however hard she tried, and whatever her accomplishments or success, Nerissa knew beyond all doubt that she could never be a gentlewoman. She would be counterfeit. A pale imitation only. A man like Hugh Gravelle would be ill at ease in her company and embarrassed by her airs and graces, believing her to be affectedly aping her betters. No more could she enter Captain Farrow's world. He would recognise the artifice and deplore it. He would seek the reality and not the fake, the substance rather than the shadow.

Nerissa straightened her shoulders and resolutely put all such thoughts aside as she carefully smoothed her red cotton dress into order. Bella had been sent to tell her that

146

the dressmaker, Mrs Pinchin, awaited her in the sewing room. Nerissa was grateful that her mother had insisted upon teaching her fine stitching, and that what she wore, both seen and unseen, was so exactingly executed and finished. Moreover, it had been sewn by her own hand. It was true that her dress was simple cotton, but none could fault it for skill in workmanship. Whatever came, she would be proud to don the self-effacing uniform of a servant. It would give her purpose a recognisable place in the hierarchy. Yesterday she had neither home nor future. Captain Farrow had rescued her and Mrs Crawshay given her life hope and meaning. She would not, even now, consider what might have befallen her at the hands of Richard de Granville and his bully boys. She was neither naive nor foolishly innocent. Her work upon the farms had shown her the realities of life; the bloodiness of birth and of death. The animal savagery that devolved as surely upon human flesh. Nature, too often bloody in tooth and claw. In those like Richard de Granville, it would be a viciousness of lust. A loveless violation. In others, a loving fusion; a tender giving of self. Nerissa firmly closed her mind to such a strangely disturbing prospect, and the shameful feelings it aroused. Then with a quick rap upon the sewing room door, she took a steadying breath, turned the handle and went within.

Mrs Pinchin, to Nerissa's relief, had proved to be the antithesis of her name. She was neither pinched, austere nor bony chested. Rather she was as gently grey as a pouter pigeon, and as soft fleshed and plump breasted. Her good humour shone as brightly as the neat parade of pins upon her bodice and her welcoming smile.

Her delighted exclamations at the neatness and fineness of Nerissa's stitching were spontaneous and genuine and served to set them both to ease. With measurements briskly taken and recorded, and patterns and cloth selected from those which Mrs Crawshay had approved, their business was cordially and efficiently transacted. There were to be five dresses made in all: three plain, serviceable "everyday" ones in suitably restrained style and colouring, and two for more formal visiting, or carriage outings, as

147

Mrs Crawshay's companion. In addition, there would be a thick hooded pelisse of cosy wool for outdoor wear in inclement weather, and a finer, more elegant one for special occasions. To Nerissa, who had never owned more than two dresses of cheapest cotton, even the "plain serviceable" dresses were a luxury beyond imagining, for they were of the most elegant styling and superior fabrics. In addition, they were to be hand pin-tucked by Mrs Pinchin's seamstress, with collars and cuffs of crisp Honiton lace. As for the two gowns of silk, Nerissa could scarce believe her good fortune, for she had never envisaged such rare elegance and luxury. They were more the accoutrements of a gentlewoman like Mrs Crawshay, their colours of softest blue and pale rose pink so delicate that she feared she might be too nervous ever to wear them. Or, if she did, that she would be forced to walk and sit as stiffly as any automaton, for fear of inadvertently creasing or spoiling them.

"Oh, my dear Miss Pritchard," Mrs Pinchin enthused extravagantly, "I declare that these pastel shades will do you the greatest justice! They will bring out the colour in your lips and cheeks quite delightfully. They will heighten the fairness of your hair and enhance the blueness of your eyes. Yes. You will be every inch the great lady." Adding with pardonable satisfaction, "You will not disgrace us, I think."

To the dressmaker's delighted confusion, Nerissa had hugged her warmly, despite the armoury of pins at the good woman's bodice, saying with affectionate honesty, "I am what I am, ma'am, and do not deceive myself that a silk gown will make me a lady . . . even one stitched by your expert hand, Mrs Pinchin, cannot work miracles! Fine feathers do not *always* make fine birds!" she concluded ruefully.

" 'Tis true that it is what lies within that counts," Mrs Pinchin agreed equably, "and none can alter that, for it is born and bred within, and cannot be snipped and stitched to order," she conceded. At Nerissa's wide smile she smiled in response, saying firmly, "You are honest and good hearted, my dear. That much is plain, for you have pride in your parentage and do not pretend to be that which you are not. Mrs Crawshay is a lady of the greatest sensibility, a good judge of character and not easily deceived. If she has chosen you to be her companion, then it is because she realises your worth. Believe it! She would not willingly inflict boredom and regret upon herself from misplaced charity. Her care must be for her own future, as well as yours. It would be crueller were you to be engaged through some passing whim, a gesture of pity, then rejected with as little thought."

"Yes," admitted Nerissa soberly. "It would grieve me the more."

Mrs Pinchin hesitated before putting a plump, bethimbled hand to Nerissa's sleeve and adjuring sternly, "And you, my dear, must believe in your own worth, too. 'Tis not false pride but good common sense to do so."

She gathered up her samples and sewing things and settled them firmly into a capacious hessian bag, glancing about her myopically lest something be forgot. Then she fastened her scissors upon the crowded chatelaine at her waist and carefully replaced her silver thimble in the case chained beside it, and smoothed all to order.

"Well, then?" She glanced up, apple-cheeked face wreathed in smiles. "I shall return on Friday, God willing, to fit the garments upon you, and make whatever alterations need to be made, though I declare without vanity that they will be few and minor, for I pride myself upon work well done." She pursed her lips, admitting wryly, "I know well enough that my younger seamstresses sometimes think me hard and unfeeling, an exacting taskmaster . . . Too often it ends in frustration and tears, for they must unpick and restitch until their hands are pricked raw. Yet 'tis kinder in the end, as many have admitted at the last, for then none can fault them. They will take pride in their work and themselves and others will share in it. There is but one way, and that is the right way!" She took up her cloak from the chair where she had laid it aside and fastened it securely beneath her plump chins, saying, with a disarming smile, "But I know from your own handiwork, my dear, that I am preaching to the converted. Your stitching is as fine as

149

any I have seen. I do not doubt that your mother would feel proud of you. 'Tis a rare compliment to her teaching and to her hopes for you." She nodded approvingly as she reached for her hessian bag, clutching it to her securely.

Nerissa asked teasingly, "Then should I ever feel need, you will consider employing me as apprentice seamstress perhaps? Find place for me in your workroom?"

"Willingly!" Mrs Pinchin promised, amused. "Upon my own recommendation, and there is no better!" She turned at the door of the sewing room to say quietly, but with conviction, "There will never be need. Depend upon it. 'Tis likely that one day you will be employing me!" Her eyes, warm with laughter, disappeared briefly into folds of flesh, only to reappear shining more brightly as she confessed, "I would hazard my scissors and best silver thimble upon it! My chatelaine, even, and all I possess." Then, with a smile and a delighted chuckle, she was away, surprisingly light upon her delicate feet.

Nerissa's visit to Knatchfield village in the open carriage, with Mrs Pratt seated majestically opposite in black bombazine and a black straw bonnet, was an event to treasure. Yet it had also been the cause of some awkwardness and concern to her upon the way, for she was not yet sure of her position at Knatchfield Grange, nor of how she was expected to respond to others. As the carriage quitted the Grange for the highway through the lion-topped pillars, they glimpsed Major Crawshay and Captain Farrow returning together from their morning ride. Mrs Pratt had made a formal greeting and nodded courteously, and Nerissa had made smiling acknowledgement. Yet to her shame and chagrin neither had made any but the briefest most curt response. Indeed, both gentlemen seemed too distracted to be even aware of her presence, their interest elsewhere. Had she been remiss, she wondered disconsolately, in greeting them openly? Perhaps they were offended, considering it gross familiarity. She was, after all, no more than a servant, and as such rendered invisible. She would have asked Mrs Pratt, but could not for hot shame tightened her throat, and her artless pleasure in the outing seemed diminished. No doubt Mrs Pratt deserved acknowledgement by virtue of long service and the position she held, and she, Nerissa, merited none. It was a lesson in manners hard earned, and one not easily forgotten. She would not repeat it. She turned her attention to the landscape without, seeing it blurred and strangely distorted, as if glimpsed through water, and tried to concentrate upon the prancing horses, their tossing manes, the rhythmic jangling of hoof and harness and the coachman's handsome livery.

Mrs Pratt, who was not an unobservant woman and knew of Nerissa's sad bereavement, said with gentleness as she leaned forward to set a gloved hand upon Nerissa's arm, "It is all strange and new to you, my dear. Give it time."

Nerissa nodded, unable to speak. The treacherous tears threatened to overflow now, quickened by sympathy, and Mrs Pratt glanced discreetly away as she strove for composure.

"We shall soon be at the village," Mrs Pratt announced with a return to briskness, "and our business quickly concluded. Then we shall purchase some notebooks, a slate and chalks and whatever is needed for our writing lessons. I have an old nursery primer of Mrs Crawshay's, and some schoolroom textbooks which will serve to teach you reading, and a few cherished books of my own . . . so you need have no fear that our purchases will arouse undue curiosity."

It was, Nerissa realised, a kind way of assuring her that none would learn that she could neither read nor write and was ill equipped to serve as a lady's companion.

"I thank you, Mrs Pratt," she said with genuine humility. "I thank you most kindly, and shall work hard at my lessons to repay your belief in me."

"Now! Have you money enough to make these purchases?" the housekeeper demanded crisply. "Or shall I . . . finance you and take return from your wages? No! Do not make heated reply, nor feel embarrassment. 'Tis no more than a business arrangement, an accommodation between friends . . . and I trust we are that?"

151

"Yes, ma'am . . . Mrs Pratt," she corrected herself quickly. "But I have money enough saved, and to spare, for whatever might be needed."

At Mrs Pratt's look of enquiry, she confessed, "It was given to me by friends . . . generously and without condition, save that I was to use it to ease my future."

"Then it will be money well spent!" approved the housekeeper firmly. "It will buy you security and confidence, but more, it will enrich your living. You will never regret it, nor the effort and discipline it demands. I know, for I am proof."

Before Nerissa could make reply, the coachman had called out a sharp warning and reined in the horses. The occupants of the carriage had been jolted into fraught silence as the vehicle clattered to a noisy halt, grinding and bumping perilously upon the rough cobblestones.

"Remember, my dear," Mrs Pratt cautioned as they descended the carriage steps with the groom's assistance, "our custom and favour will be jealously sought. We must remain civil and courteous always, but dignified. Aloof even. It is Major and Mrs Crawshay we represent. It would not do to appear over familiar. It would be to our disadvantage. You understand?"

"Yes, Mrs Pratt," Nerissa confirmed as she obediently followed the housekeeper towards the haberdasher's shop which was to receive their first visit.

She tried desperately to walk with that same purposeful authority which the housekeeper showed, and to emulate her dignified poise of manner. It was, she decided, a most difficult task, and acquired, she feared, only after years of hard practice. Yet she could not long be downcast, for the expedition held promise of such excitement and novelty. Smiling self-consciously, she entered the haberdasher's as he came forward, bowing unctuously, to greet them. Nerissa beamed benificently upon his two frozen-faced assistants hovering nervously over their merchandise, and saw them relax visibly into smiles. Mrs Pratt, she thought with pardonable satisfaction as they quitted the shop, could surely find no fault with her performance. She had disported herself as to the manner born. The rest of their purchases had been as agreeably made, and the bonnet-maker, cordwainer and all others as charmingly attentive and eager to please. In high good humour and with the attendant groom all but invisible beneath a surfeit of parcels, Mrs Pratt and Nerissa made their way to the waiting carriage.

Nerissa, filled with exhilaration at her purchases and the success of her outing, stepped unthinkingly on to the cobbled highway, deaf to the coachman's fierce cry of warning. The curricle which bore down upon her was erratically driven, the twin horses whipped to dangerous speed. They ran wildly to escape the cut of leather upon their hides, desperate to flee the whiplash. Had not the coachman leapt from his perch and hurled her aside, Nerissa would undoubtedly have been dragged beneath the wheels of the carriage, or beneath the horses' flailing hooves.

"Dear God!" the groom exclaimed, outraged. "The man is a lunatic! A bedlamite! He has as little thought for others as for those wretched creatures he drives!"

Nerissa, who had been hurled bodily to the cobbles, found herself shaking with shock and confusion as the coachman helped her to her feet. Mrs Pratt was every whit as white faced and trembling as she, and visibly distressed, as she hurried to her side, demanding anxiously, "Are you all right, my dear? You are not badly hurt? We must drive to the doctor's house in the carriage."

Nerissa made rueful examination of her torn and dishevelled clothing, saying quickly, "No, Mrs Pratt . . . I have no need of a doctor. I am bruised and frightened, but there is no real damage." Her voice, despite her efforts to control it, was high pitched and terrified. She turned to the coachman, who stood watching her in concern, saying earnestly, "I beg you will forgive me, sir . . . It was my own foolishness to blame, and I regret it. I regret even more putting your life into danger."

He smiled and made gentle denial, replacing the tricorne which he had been nervously fingering upon his wispy grey locks, darting a glance towards the housekeeper, and saying, "Well . . . since all has ended without real hurt, perhaps we had best make tracks for Knatchfield Grange? That is, if your errands are completed, your business here done?"

Mrs Pratt nodded assent, shaking her head in urgent warning as he made to speak further, his face awkwardly troubled. They were friends of long standing, and he knew that there was reason for her silence, and need for his own. Nerissa, shocked and terrified by the sudden violence, had been aware only of the curricle bearing down upon her. All else had been an anguish of noise and movement, too fierce to be borne. The coachman and Mrs Pratt had seen more. They had glimpsed the face of the young blade at the reins, handsome and arrogant in his certainty. A rake and a dandy, brutally contemptuous of others. A gilded youth. There were many young gentlemen such as he, feckless and heedless. Yet there was something more. Something that troubled them gravely. He had known Nerissa Pritchard, recognised her. There was no denying it. The look he had given her was of such malevolent loathing that there could be no mistake. His whipping up of the horses had been deliberate; his aim, to kill. How nearly he had succeeded.

Chapter Twelve

Richard de Granville damned himself for an imbecile. His carefully laid plans had been all but ruined by sight of that insolent chit who had so humiliated him at Holly Grove. Still shaking with rage and frustration, he drove the curricle on, whipping the horses with such fury that the delicate carriage on its slender wheels all but overturned. As he rounded the corner of a byway it swayed alarmingly and he might have been toppled into a ditch had it not suddenly righted itself. Fear for his own safety briefly sobered him and he ceased his frenzied whipping, allowing the paired horses to run at a less tortured pace. He ruefully fingered his cheek, still bruised from the fracas at Holly Grove fair, and cursed aloud and volubly. He could not believe that he had acted with such stupidity. To have endangered all, and for revenge upon a useless slut; a trollop without birth or breeding! Yet, at sight of her, all reason and caution had fled. He was filled with a white-hot hatred, bitter and all-devouring, a need to cripple and humiliate, to kill even. He would have seen her trampled beneath the horses' hooves, ground under the carriage wheels. He would have erased her from life and memory both. She had moved with such arrogant awareness of self, such damnable self-possession, as if she were a gentlewoman born and not a common hireling! What gall! And to have use of so elegant a carriage, and with that sour-faced crone acting as nervously as a chaperone . . . It was ludicrous! Beyond all enduring. His resentment still rankled, but he was aware now of the danger his hot-headedness might have wrought. The destruction might have been not only hers, but his own. A charge of wilful murder, and before reliable witnesses, would ruin all, and not all his father's influence would save him . . . It was one thing to trample and beat to death a useless poacher, a common thief, at dead of night; quite another to deliberately run down a young woman in broad daylight. A woman, moreover, in the protection and service of a gentlewoman. At least something of use had come from the chance encounter with the Pritchard girl. He knew now whereabout the chit lived, and where her mistress's house and estate lay. It should be a simple matter to insinuate himself into the unknown gentlewoman's favour. He had influence enough and presence enough to wipe out the acrimony of their first meeting. A cultivated charm and penitence seldom failed to make an impression, or to reverse an unfavourable one.

He turned his mind resolutely to the task ahead. He must see Jeremy Hardwicke at Rogerstone Manor and persuade him to return to St Samson. He did not know exactly what tactics he must use, but that was better left to chance and inspiration. He had certainly acquitted himself well and gained his father's favour by insisting that he start upon his duties to the estate that very day. It had been easy enough to deceive Sir Peter into believing that which he most wanted to hear: that his son now wished to take responsibility for the estate he must one day inherit. It had been easy, too, to leave St Samson Court early and, with use of the curricle, to call upon the tenant farmers whose needs and problems had been earlier discussed. Small matter if his visits were brief to the point of incivility, for they had no more urge for his company than he for theirs. Still, it was a duty done, and if his father proved mean-spirited enough to check it, then it would not go amiss.

Hanford had specifically asked him to stay away from Hardwicke, ordered him even! What damnable impertinence! He had advised him to be circumspect. Circumspect indeed! Hardwicke was in need not of tolerance and understanding, but firm action. He, de Granville, understood him only too well! He was a weathercock, vacillating, ineffectual, changing direction with every gust of wind that blew. Well, he would *give* him direction! It was as well, though, he reflected, that Hanford and Siberry knew nothing of his visit, or his intent . . . what the eye does not see . . .

Secure in his own cleverness, de Granville set the horses to a rhythmic trotting. The autumn air was balmy now that the frosted crispness of early morning had dissipated; the sun a gentle warmth. He was well aware of the splendid figure he cut. He was an impressive young buck to be sure; fastidiously attired, modish and indisputably handsome, despite those regrettable blemishes which might be irritatingly slow to fade. The curricle was as elegantly fashioned and stylish as he, and the horses plainly thoroughbreds. He regretted the sale of the palomino. Its distinctiveness did full justice to his own superiority of breeding and its golden colouring quite remarkably complemented his own. Together they must have proved a dramatic sight: graceful, arresting and unforgettable . . . Yet its distinctiveness was the very reason why he had been forced to sacrifice it. Perhaps, though, something might yet be salvaged from the setback.

The money from the sale of it had been delivered to him by the horse dealer who had conducted the sale at Holly Grove. The price had been just, but the buyer unknown to him. He was, it appeared, a major in the infantry, who had lately inherited a property in the neighbourhood called Knatchfield Grange. A valuable estate, lately the property of an elderly gentleman. The name of the new owner, de Granville had been informed, was Crayshaw . . . or was it Crawshay? He could not quite recall. Yet he was plainly a gentleman of substance and acumen, and a good judge of horseflesh. A call upon the major would not go amiss, for the sale of the palomino would give reason enough and make convenient introduction. To appease his father, he might even claim to try and repurchase the horse. It would make excellent diversion. Surely if Knatchfield Grange were near, then the new owner must have knowledge of the beautiful young gentlewoman at the fair and make suitable introduction? With his spirits considerably lighter and whistling tunelessly, Richard de Granville continued upon his way. That Pritchard's daughter was in the service

157

of the gentlewoman concerned troubled him not a whit. He was certain that she had not recognised him. The curricle had borne down upon her with such speed and violence that she was lucky to have escaped with her life. She would not have done so, save for the coachman's instinctive action. All those concerned were menials and of no account. They had neither status nor proof of his intent, and their word would be scathingly discounted. It would do them no credit to lay false accusation against an honest gentleman. By the time he arrived at the outskirts of Rogerstone and the limits of Sir Howard Peel's extensive estate, Richard de Granville had quite convinced himself that he was the innocent victim of calumny and spite. He was a man maligned. Misunderstood. More sinned against than sinning.

Luke Farrow and Francis Crawshay had returned to Knatchfield Grange with Francis's sickness and imminent death no longer a secret. It had, upon the hilltop, drawn them closer in companionship and understanding. Yet now, as they neared the house, the knowledge became a barrier between them. Luke had given his word that he would remain and lend his friend moral support, and he would not renege upon his promise. However, he knew that whatever decision was taken, it must be Francis's alone. His pity was as much for Arabella, whom he had grown to love and respect, and he did not know how best to treat her. Should he speak of it openly and cause her further distress, or keep up the fiction that naught was amiss? He did not know if he had strength of will enough to keep up their old familiar banter, the teasing that she so clearly enjoyed. That Arabella had courage enough to live with so cruel a prognosis and yet retain both humour and spirit chastened him. He felt humbled and inadequate, powerless to help. He did not know how he could face her or speak of the grief and sadness such a knowledge brought.

Yet it was Arabella herself who had come to the stables to greet them, deliberately seeking them out. She had put an affectionate hand to Luke's arm, saying quietly,

"Francis has told you then, as he promised. I see it in your face." As he made to reply, she urged, "No. Do not speak of it, Luke, I beg of you . . . There is naught to be said, save only that you will stay."

"I will stay," he promised.

She nodded, wordlessly.

"For as long as ever you have need of me, Arabella, and while Francis asks that I remain."

"Then we will speak no more of it." Her eyes were bright with unshed tears and she turned away abruptly that he might not pity her distress. She glanced towards Francis, who was occupied in conversation with his groom, before confessing, voice low, "I have no more tears to shed. I have wept, raged, railed at God, and others, at the cruelty of life itself. Yet to no avail, Luke, for I cannot alter the certainty of death."

Luke took her hand within his own, feeling its coldness and that same bleak coldness within himself.

"I can speak calmly of death now," she continued quietly, "for it is only a word, but I do not know how I can face the reality of what must be . . . of death itself."

"You are a loyal and courageous woman, Arabella," Luke murmured with honesty, "and a loving wife. You will find strength enough to face what comes and to give Francis ease of mind."

"Yes," she said wryly. "I shall do that. I have no qualms about nursing Francis, of tending him to the end. I shall not weaken, nor make his burden heavier by useless recrimination or open grief." Her grip upon Luke's hand tightened, as if she had need of the comfort of human flesh, the solace of another. "It is *after* his death I fear, Luke!" she exclaimed despairingly. "The loneliness. The emptiness of living. Without Francis I do not know if I shall have the will or belief to survive . . . It will be a using up of days. No more than that, for I will have died with him in all but flesh."

Luke felt her bewilderment and pain within himself, that same desolate loss, yet there was no real comfort to give and all else was a lie.

159

Francis came slowly across the yard to join them, looking enquiringly from one to the other, expression uncertain. Arabella linked her arm companionably through his and the other through Luke's arm. The smile she gave her husband was hesitant, but when she spoke her voice was carefully controlled.

"I am glad that you told Luke, my dear," she said warmly, "for now there is no need to dissemble, to keep anything secret or hid. It is better so."

"Yes," Francis agreed gravely. "It is better so. I am glad that he is here." The smile he exchanged with Luke was of open friendship, honest, and filled with gratitude.

"Then I had best be careful," Arabella teased lightly, "for I am outnumbered two to one and will have the devil's own work to keep you from argument, fisticuffs, and decently sober. Your behaviour at Holly Grove fair was quite scandalous! We will be shunned as Philistines and boors by all respectable society."

"It is a deprivation I will cheerfully survive," promised Francis.

"Especially if we are denied the company of those exquisites and dandies of yesterday," affirmed Luke. "I would sooner seek the company of their horseflesh!"

"Indeed," agreed Arabella. "They are better bred and their manners altogether more refined." Adding wickedly, "Perhaps you would have me invite the palomino and grey to the dining table and banish you gentlemen to the stables where you may give full rein to your animal spirits, and behave as outrageously as you choose?"

"An admirable suggestion, my love," Francis approved, smiling broadly, "it would give me the greatest satisfaction to offer you a frolic and bed in the hay!"

The three entered the house laughing and seemingly relaxed and Luke wondered, with a thrust of sadness, if he alone was aware of the irony of what Francis had claimed.

"I will cheerfully survive . . ." The words, uttered unthinkingly, held a new, almost unbearable, pathos. Luke would have given all he possessed to have them come true.

*　　*　　*

Arabella had left the two gentlemen to indulge themselves in a glass or two of Canary wine.

"It might fortify you," she said breezily, "to summon energy enough to change from your riding breeches into something more civilised! I'll swear, Francis," she rebuked mildly, "that you carry the smell of the stables wherever you go!"

"It is a good, wholesome smell, my love," he protested. "There is nothing on earth more natural."

"Natural it may be; fragrant it most certainly is not!"

"Would you have me scented with eau-de-cologne or lavender water, like some ninny, Arabella?" he suggested slyly. "Or perhaps you would have me preserve my complexion with milk of roses, like those pretty fellows at the fair?"

At his ridiculously affected posturing, Luke broke into irrepressible laughter, which made him posture the more.

Arabella, striving to stifle her own amusement, chided, "For heaven's sake, and my own, do not encourage his nonsense, Luke! He is contrary enough already. With encouragement he will be quite insupportable!"

"I merely said that a good, ripe animal smell has more to commend it than some dandified fal-de-ral," Francis persisted, unchastened. "Why, the smell of stables is the most normal thing in the world, Arabella . . . Animal excretions are part of the beauty and cycle of life. They make flowers bloom and flourish, vegetables grow . . ."

"I would prefer not to be reminded of it," Arabella said with finality. "And if I must, then not in my drawing room . . . You may take yourselves into the garden if you so wish, and blossom and perfume the air to your hearts' content . . . Here my scented candles and pot-pourri will give off odour enough."

Francis, smiling sheepishly, acknowledged defeat, and he and Luke withdrew to the masculine stronghold of the library, glasses in hand, while Arabella settled herself in the morning room to remedy her neglected letter writing.

She had barely seated herself at her *bonheur-de-jour*,

161

with writing materials to hand, when a sharp rapping upon the door distracted her. Her terse command to "Come!" brought in Mrs Pratt, her gaunt face flushed, manner unusually flurried.

"I would not have disturbed you, Mrs Crawshay, were it not a matter of importance, ma'am." She hesitated, blurting uncertainly, "I scarce know what to make of it. It might be of no real consequence."

Arabella, who knew her housekeeper to be the calmest and most reliable of women, said truthfully, "If it is something which so troubles you, Mrs Pratt, then it is of every consequence." She drew up a chair beside her, saying, "Sit here beside me and tell me what so vexes or distresses you. It is something to do with the household, perhaps?" she prompted gently. "A servant sick or injured?"

"No, ma'am. It was the trip to the village, the carriage ride to Knatchfield to order Miss Pritchard's clothes."

"You suffered no accident?" demanded Arabella, concerned. "There was no mishap upon the way? Hanson has made no report of it."

"No, ma'am, but he was witness, as Harold Manley, the groom. He will vouch for it."

"For *what*, Mrs Pratt?" Arabella's concern was fast giving way to exasperation. "What was it that happened? So far you have told me nothing. I cannot help unless I know what has occurred."

Mrs Pratt, who had been nervously biting at her underlip, hands clasping and unclasping irresolutely, seemed to come to a decision. "I believe, ma'am, that someone tried to kill Nerissa Pritchard!"

The accusation was defiantly blurted, her face stubbornly set, as she awaited Arabella's disbelief and curt dismissal. None came. Arabella was shocked and pale certainly, her fingers gripping hard at the edges of her chair seat as if she would physically steady herself, but there was no scornful rebuttal or reproach.

"Tell me all that occurred," she asked, voice taut. "Spare nothing."

When the housekeeper had, with much hesitation and

162

awkwardness, related what she had seen, she was painfully aware of how thin and unconvincing it sounded.

"I have no proof of it, ma'am," she said by way of apology, "but I swear that I did not invent it, nor let my imagination play me tricks. Hanson will bear me out in this."

"You have not told the others? The household staff?"

"No, ma'am, nor would I; and Hanson and Manley are reliable and discreet. 'Tis why I came first to you, thinking you would know reason for it."

"And Miss Pritchard? Nerissa?"

"She does not suspect, ma'am."

"You are certain?"

"Yes, I am certain," she said with conviction. "It was all so quick and unexpected, and her mind was upon the purchases. She saw nothing, save the curricle bearing down upon her before Hanson flung her out of the horses' path."

"She is injured, Mrs Pratt?"

"No, ma'am, but as shocked and bewildered as those who witnessed it."

Arabella nodded. "This . . . gentleman, Mrs Pratt. The driver of the curricle. Did you see him well enough to give description? Would you recognise him again?"

"Oh yes, I would know him!" She spoke with absolute conviction. "I'll own that it was the briefest glimpse that I caught, but he was unmistakable." She shivered involuntarily, confessing, "I could not easily forget that face. There was such spite and vindictiveness upon it . . . It was frenzied near to madness."

"A *young* man, Mrs Pratt?"

"Young certainly, not above two and twenty, I think, yet younger, perhaps. Handsome, and something of a dandy, for his hair was elegantly curled, and fine and golden as a child's, his clothes expensively cut." She paused to reflect, continuing uncertainly, "He was undoubtedly handsome. Yet there was something . . . something which escapes me, and not his expression alone."

As Arabella waited in silence, she exclaimed triumphantly, "Yes. That would be it. There was some disfigurement."

"A scar? A birthmark?"

"No . . . but something, a blemish of sorts. A bruising perhaps, or swelling, as if he had recently been in some accident or fight. It is little enough to go on, I know," she admitted helplessly, "for there are dozens of reckless young blades such as he, with not a pin to choose between them, and all as assured and self-centred and as blind to the feelings of others. Yet it was more than arrogance I glimpsed in him, Mrs Crawshay. It was a coldness that chilled me, an evil." Ashamed of her outburst, Mrs Pratt awkwardly smoothed down her dress then arose from her chair to declare, "I beg that you will excuse me now, Mrs Crawshay, ma'am, and if I have sounded hysterical or fanciful, that you will put it down to the shock and distress of the encounter."

Arabella put a detaining hand to the housekeeper's arm to say gently, "No. I do not think you fanciful, for I know you too well and trust your judgement implicitly. I must beg that you will speak of this to no one beyond Knatchfield Grange, Mrs Pratt, and that you will caution both Hanson and Manley to silence. Do not openly discuss it before Miss Pritchard and the servants and household staff, save as a near-accident safely averted, and one which might threaten any unfortunate upon the highway . . . You understand?"

"I do, ma'am." Mrs Pratt's reply was swift and instinctive, yet it was clear that her disquiet remained.

"I shall speak of it to Major Crawshay immediately," Arabella promised, "and tell you what transpires. I can explain no further at present, for it is a delicate matter and one which must be pursued diplomatically. It would not do to make firm accusation without proof, and the young gentleman concerned is as yet unknown to us."

"Perhaps I should not have spoken of it," Mrs Pratt declared remorsefully, "for no real harm was done, save to harass and terrify us all . . . That is not a crime, I know, and no one would think the worse of any young gentleman for a little natural wildness and high spirits. We should be made laughing stocks before all to resent it, even . . ."

"But you do not think it to be natural wildness and high spirits?"

"No, ma'am. I think it to be attempted murder!"

Arabella, deeply disturbed by Mrs Pratt's disclosures, went immediately to seek out Francis and Luke in the library. She could scarcely believe that de Granville could have behaved so callously and with such stupid recklessness, and for so trivial a cause . . . Surely he would not risk his own wretched neck to revenge himself upon a hireling at the fair? It was surely an irrational and excessive response to being humiliated . . . Unless, as Mrs Pratt suggested, he was mentally unbalanced, a declared lunatic. No, there must be a deeper, more cogent, reason than mere pique. Something well hidden.

Francis and Luke, in exuberant mood and still in their execrable riding clothes, had greeted Arabella with teasing affection, protesting that they were on their way to change at that very moment and would not allow her to detain them. Yet her obvious distress quickly sobered them to silence, and they listened with growing concern.

When she had told them all that she had learned from Mrs Pratt of Nerissa's encounter with the "young gentleman" in the curricle, Francis exclaimed furiously, "It was that imbecile, de Granville! There can be no doubt of it! Luke?"

Luke nodded agreement, saying, "I think we had best tell Arabella what we suspect, Francis. It is owed to her now. We cannot keep her in ignorance."

Arabella looked from one to the other in perplexity, as Francis gently guided her to a chair and made halting explanation. He spoke of Tom Pritchard's murder, and Luke's glimpse of his murderers and recognition of de Granville's palomino at the fair. He spoke frankly of their belief that it had not been chance alone that led de Granville and the others to Nerissa, but fear lest she held some clue to their identity, some fear which might send them to the gallows.

Arabella listened in horrified silence, too sickened to

make immediate response. When she spoke, her voice was thin and frightened.

"Nerissa is at real risk?" she demanded. "You think that he will not rest easy until she is silenced?"

"I am sure of it," Luke replied, "else he would not have shown his contempt so publicly and with such disregard for his own worthless hide!"

"Then we must give her protection!" Arabella declared. "Keep guard upon her. Let her know the danger she faces."

"No! It would serve only to terrify her and drive her away," Luke said vehemently. "Alone she would be helpless; an easier prey. Whatever is decided must be done secretly, without her knowledge."

"There is something else to be decided," Francis reminded sharply, "something of which we have not yet spoken openly."

"Arabella's part in all this," Luke agreed.

At her murmur of protest, Francis warned sharply, "You are as much at risk as she, Arabella! Consider it. You will be constantly together. Luke and I cannot always offer you protection. There are times when you and Nerissa will be driving out in the carriage to make purchases in the village . . . visiting tenants on the estate, sketching perhaps, or even strolling in the grounds."

"Francis is right," Luke interrupted firmly. "It is too great a risk. It might be better were I to accompany her to some safer place . . . see her settled elsewhere."

"And if de Granville and the others should find her? What then?" Arabella demanded with spirit. "Do you think I could rest easy knowing that I had offered her no help, no sanctuary? I would be as callous and unfeeling as they, and as culpable!"

"Then you must decide, Arabella . . . whether you will have Nerissa stay or be taken to some safer place," Francis said stiffly. "For my own part, I would not wish her to remain, lest she endanger you . . . You are my sole concern. I would protect you for as long as I am able."

Behind the stilted words lay an awkward tenderness, and Arabella and Luke, who were aware of why he had spoken

166

so harshly, shared its poignancy and were as powerless to speak of it.

Arabella rose from her chair and went to stand at Francis's side, placing a hand gently upon his arm and saying quietly, "You have asked me to decide, Francis, and I thank you, my dear, for that . . . as I thank you for your loving protection. I would choose that Nerissa stay. She has endured hurt enough. I would not offer her further rejection."

Francis studied her long and hard, his hand closing reassuringly upon hers. "If that is your wish, Arabella."

"My wish, Francis, is that you offer Nerissa that same protection, that same commitment and understanding that you have shown always to me and to others." Adding with excoriating honesty, "I would not have you changed, my dear, through fear of what must come. We will face that together, as we have faced all else."

Francis nodded, but did not speak.

"You are my rock and my strength, Francis, my love and my salvation."

Arabella's voice was so subdued by grief that Francis had to bend low to hear her. He had no need to make reply, so deep was the love between them.

Chapter Thirteen

Richard de Granville brought the horses to a halt at the outskirts of Rogerstone village and attempted to repair his dishevelment. The journey had been longer than he remembered and the roads quite appallingly neglected. To add to his discomfort, the bite upon his leg which that wretched cur at the fair had delivered had begun to throb unbearably. The wound had been attended by Matthew Siberry's father, the physician at Holly Grove, who had effectively cleansed it and applied binding and salve. Dr Siberry had pronounced it to "look healthy", for it had bled freely, adding that there had been no recent report of rabid dogs in the village, for which de Granville should feel grateful. Had there been, then he would have been forced to prescribe him a foul-tasting draught which must be taken for seven mornings, fasting, and also rubbed most painfully upon the afflicted place. De Granville had not felt grateful. Relieved, perhaps, that he had not been put to the shame of admitting that he had been savaged not by some salivating monster but by the Punch and Judy man's pathetic little whelp, but far from grateful.

Now he climbed down stiffly from the cabriolet to steady the horses and stretch his aching limb. He felt dirty and sweat stained, scarce fitted for a place in civilised society and absurdly conscious of the bruising and swelling that disfigured his usually handsome face. A fine show he would make of himself at Rogerstone Manor! Hardwicke's uncle, Sir Howard Peel, would at best think him a clumsy simpleton, at worst a vulgar brawler, ill suited to be entertained. To arrive so precipitately and without invitation would be judged the height of bad manners . . . Yet arrive he must, and with suitably convincing reason for seeking

168

Hardwicke out. He had best remain here for a moment, and fabricate some plausible excuse. He did not know how Hardwicke would react to his visit, for he was volatile and nervously unpredictable, as temperamental as those of his colouring were alleged to be. Richard de Granville was in a quandary. Should he drive brazenly through the village, then his presence would certainly be noted by the tenantry and labourers upon Sir Howard Peel's estates. The cabriolet and fine horses would attract attention, and his own appearance would not go unnoticed. If he could but see Jeremy alone and privately it would serve him better. He was in sore need of refreshment and the horses tired and needing rest and water, but that could easily enough be remedied at a convenient tavern or inn. He roused himself to lead the horses towards a boundary stone a little along the grassy verge to the roadside, and thence to the signpost marking the small crossroads beyond . . . Rogerstone Manor, he saw, could be reached by driving directly through the village, or by a quieter country route along a byway, wide enough to take a light carriage such as his own. He climbed back upon the cabriolet, cursing the painfulness of his injured leg, and set the horses to a sedate walk. He had need to think up some credible excuse, some plan of action, and must not arrive unprepared. Like it or not, Hardwicke must either be persuaded or forced to return to St Samson with him.

The byway was narrow and awkwardly twisting, bordered by high pleached hedges which screened his view, and it needed all of his considerable skill at driving to keep the carriage intact. Should he meet another such carriage or a herd of cows or flock of sheep, then one or other must yield ground, or risk disaster . . . de Granville was certain only that it was not he who would give way, and the possibility of a fracas or a dangerous encounter merely led spice to the adventure.

He had been driving for some ten minutes or more when the countryside opened up before him into a wider rolling landscape. The hedges of blackthorn were starkly scythed, and the fields and pastures for grazing flocks methodically ploughed and furrowed or set to the growing of winter vegetables. The far mountains beyond were reddened now with dying ferns, and the gentler hills before him slashed with small quarries, their grey-white limestone raggedly chiselled by man and weather . . . Here and there were crude, windowless huts for shepherds or farm labourers perhaps. They were scarcely more obtrusive than the flung boulders that dotted the hillsides or the dry-stone folds that sheltered the animals at lambing time or from marauding foxes at night. Richard de Granville was scarcely aware of the landscape through which he drove. He knew only that it was desolate and wild and that he had encountered no living creatures save the sheep grazing somnolently in the fields and the pair of predatory birds circling above, silent, with wings magnificently outspread, the masters of air and sky. He was, it seemed, the sole human to have ventured there, and he had no great wish to encounter any others of his own kind.

Yet encounter he did, a lone horseman, but set a fair distance away upon a winding hilltop path. The rider was unaware of the intrusive presence of de Granville and the carriage, for they were shielded from view by a small copse of beech trees, planted perhaps as a windbreak. In any event, the rider's thoughts were centred elsewhere, for he had dismounted with no more than a casual glance about him and was engaged in firmly tethering his mount to a sapling tree. Richard de Granville did not wish to be seen, yet to deliberately attempt concealment would, he knew, arouse the rider's open curiosity and, as like as not, his suspicions too. Before he had time to make conscious decision, the matter was settled for him. The horseman had seated himself upon a boulder beside a wide natural gully, a cleft in the hillside, and removed his high silk hat, setting it, for comfort, upon his knees. Even as he did so, the autumn sun which had been partly hidden behind a vaporous cloud, came into full view, lighting up all with a sudden, uncanny brilliance. The rider's uncovered hair shone burnished red-gold. Vivid. Unmistakable.

"By God! Hardwicke!" De Granville heard himself actually speak the words aloud. He found himself grinning absurdly at the irony of it, scarce able to credit his good fortune. To have found Hardwicke alone and away from the hearing and influence of his uncle and others. It was more than he had hoped. He carefully dismounted from the cabriolet and secured the carriage to a sturdy beech tree, allowing the horses to crop unhindered. Then, cautiously and in considerable discomfort from his injured leg, he made his way along a small bridlepath to where Hardwicke rested. The route was more precipitous and overgrown than he had thought, his leg stiffly painful and his progress irritatingly slow. He did not allow himself to be seen, approaching stealthily then appearing suddenly from behind a thicket of bramble and blackthorn at Hardwicke's side.

"Well, Hardwicke?"

Hardwicke, who had been meshed in thought, leapt to his feet as if scalded, fear and confusion disabling him, rendering him speechless.

"Have you no welcome for me? No word of greeting? I have travelled far to find you."

Jeremy Hardwicke looked about him wildly, as if searching for a way of escape. His face was as fiercely aflame as his hair as he murmured uneasily, "I had not thought to see you here . . . It was shock, surprise."

De Granville raised an eyebrow, to say sardonically, "Why should it surprise you that a friend of longstanding comes to search you out? One who has your wellbeing and interest at heart."

Hardwicke murmured something inaudible, plainly discomfited.

"I beg that you will forgive my . . . ungentlemanly appearance," de Granville said urbanely. "A slight contretemps at Holly Grove fair . . . scarce worth the bother of a mention, save that my friends were there and suffered the same . . . minor inconvenience at the hands of some ill-bred oafs, bent upon mischief."

Hardwicke turned away and kept his face deliberately averted.

"But I forgot . . ." de Granville continued with seeming indifference, "you were not there to witness it, having

171

cravenly turned tail and fled . . . Well, now is your chance to make amends, to redeem yourself."

Hardwicke turned upon him savagely hands clenched tight, to say furiously, "Damn it, de Granville! Do you take me for a fool? You were the oaf and blackguard for treating the girl so! That was the work of a craven and a bully . . . She was not deserving of it. She had done no harm."

"Then 'tis a pity you did not spring as wildly to her defence, Hardwicke, as you now spring at me! Perhaps rough words are cheaper than actions and easier to come by!"

"Damn you to hell, de Granville!" Hardwicke's face was suffused with rage, eyes engorged and bloodshot, and a small vein throbbed at his temple. "Do not unload your guilt upon me! It was you who were the instigator, the leader in hunting Pritchard down! You are murderer and coward both!"

"Then by my reckoning, Hardwicke, you are murderer too, for you were willing accomplice." De Granville's voice was coolly contemptuous. "I have come to offer you help, to talk sense into you."

"Sense?" Hardwicke was almost incoherent with rage, mouth flecked with saliva, as he spat out vindictively, "Go home, de Granville! You are too late. My mind is made up. I shall ride out to the justices directly; make full confession."

"You bloody fool!" De Granville, incensed beyond caution, had gripped Hardwicke's sleeve and dragged him round savagely to face him, demanding, "Are you mad? Have you no fear for your neck? You will end up on the gallows!"

"Then you will be beside me, as you deserve!"

De Granville, frightened now, changed his tack, saying coaxingly, "I know how this affair has disturbed you, Jeremy; set you into a nervous flux . . . You are over-wrought, not thinking as clearly as you ought."

"My mind has never been clearer, de Granville." The words were honestly uttered.

"If you have no thought for yourself," de Granville

persisted recklessly, "then have a thought for your parents, at least! It will destroy them to see you branded murderer, and hanged. It will be both sorrow and disgrace. They will barely survive it!"

"Damnation, de Granville! Do not waste your pious platitudes upon me! I am no longer an innocent . . . It is your neck, and yours alone, which concerns you. All others may go to hell! Like Pritchard, they are expendable."

"Dear God!" de Granville exclaimed despairingly. "Can I not make you see the sense in it? Confess it to a priest, if you must; beg absolution, but do not sacrifice Hanford and Siberry to your own cowardice and vanity! Give them chance to defend themselves or make escape."

"There is no escape from justice, de Granville, God's or man's."

Hardwicke turned abruptly upon his heel and strode to where his horse stood tethered, and began to unfasten it. With a cry of rage torn from his throat, de Granville was upon him, beating at him frenziedly with his fists, beside himself with terror and anguish. Hardwicke, surprised at first, had been caught cruelly off balance, but he fought back savagely and recklessly, knowing his life to be at stake. For a brief moment he believed himself to be gaining ascendancy, terror lending him strength, but de Granville hurled him away so savagely that he fell violently against a boulder, hearing the fierce crack of bone and the harsh pain as his leg shattered. He tried to crawl to safety, but white-hot pain seared him through. He could neither crawl nor protect himself as de Granville grasped him by his shirt front and half dragged, half carried him to the crevice edge. Screaming with pain and hearing his own anguished sobbing, Hardwicke tried to wrench himself from de Granville's grasp but could not, for his grip was vicelike and remorseless. He would take de Granville with him, he thought in a split second of clarity, drag him to his death as he deserved . . . but he had neither strength nor opportunity. De Granville thrust him callously and determinedly over the edge of the crevice and into the abyss beneath. Hardwicke tried to cry out, but the sound died in his throat. He felt the cold rushing of air and a

173

tightness at his ribcage, as if his lungs were bursting within him, then nothing, save a blessed deliverance from pain.

Richard de Granville did not approach the edge of the crevice. He finished untying the terrified horse and urged it to a gallop, watching it run free, reins trailing uselessly. Then, without a backward glance, he limped stiffly down the hillside to the cabriolet below.

The journey back to St Samson Court in the cabriolet had been swift and uneventful, and Richard de Granville was well pleased with himself. He felt as little remorse at killing Hardwicke as he had felt at Pritchard's murder. Indeed, he was buoyed by a sense of exhilaration, euphoria even, at his own duplicity. He had covered his tracks well by visiting the tenants upon the St Samson estates. It was, in a manner of speaking, killing two birds with one stone – an analogy that wryly amused him. By visiting the tenant farmers upon the St Samson estate, he would not only set himself in good odour with his father but provide himself with a convincing alibi, should one be needed. Yet he could not believe that any could link him with Hardwicke's death, nor even suspect his complicity. After all, Hardwicke was a friend. Or had been, de Granville amended contemptuously, until squeamishness and selfishness had turned him into an enemy. He would confide in no one, never speak of what he had been forced to do, because he could trust no one save himself.

He had believed Hardwicke to be dependable, and their secret safe. Yet weakness and remorse had destroyed him, as it had destroyed many another . . . Did Hanford and Siberry but know it, they were indebted to him. He had saved their necks, as surely as his own, and could almost delude himself that it was their safety which had prompted him to revenge. He would not call it murder, even in his thoughts, for it was no more than self-defence. Self-preservation was a right, a natural instinct, and none would blame him for rounding upon an attacker, returning blow for blow. It was a fair fight, with no advantage ceded or taken, he convinced himself, and only a coward would not have responded to Hardwicke's naked aggression.

He had brought it upon himself by his betrayal and disloyalty. He, de Granville, would never have sacrificed the others so carelessly, and to salve a guilty conscience. It was beyond belief!

Despite his attempts at self-justification and his scorn for Hardwicke, there was some unease which gnawed at the edges of de Granville's mind, something which disturbed him. What was it? As he drove the cabriolet through the pillars of St Samson Court and along the curve of the driveway, he recalled it with vexation. Of course, that damnable affair at Knatchfield, that moment of stark fury, madness even, when he had all but ridden Pritchard's daughter down. He had wanted her trapped beneath the horses' hooves, crushed by the carriage wheels . . . What lunacy had possessed him? He could scarce credit such crassness. It might have ruined all . . . and why? To humiliate a menial, a common slut! He could not believe that he had been recognised, but should he need support and alibi, then Hanford would provide it. He would tell him that his father's business affairs had taken him there, and that the encounter was the merest accident. It was no more than the truth . . . and none would connect it with Hardwicke's accidental death.

Richard de Granville climbed stiffly down from the cabriolet and put the horses and cabriolet into the care of a waiting groom and stable boy, with only the surliest recognition of their presence. His leg ached abominably from the journey, and the blows he had received from his fight with Hardwicke had left him bruised and sore fleshed. At least his injuries would cause no concern and comment, for they would be taken as being a relic of yesterday's battle. All too often such swellings and contusions looked worse before they eased and faded. As for Jeremy Hardwicke, then the violence delivered and the broken bones would be accepted without question as the result of his fall. A tragic accident. When his horse returned to Rogerstone Manor riderless, a search would immediately be made. None would doubt that he had dismounted and blundered into the crevice, or else that his horse had stumbled upon a stone and thrown him . . . There would be an inquest certainly, but none could believe it other than the cruellest misadventure.

"Dear God in heaven!" De Granville murmured the words aloud, suddenly cold with foreboding. What if Jeremy had confessed all to Sir Howard Peel? Told him of his decision to confess his part in Pritchard's murder to the justices? No! It could not be! Hardwicke had said nothing of it, made no mention of any other involved. The damnable pain in his leg was making him stupidly morbid, irrational even. He would ask that the physician from St Samson be called to attend him, for he had no desire to see Siberry's father. The man was a quack and a charlatan, and best avoided. He had put the fear of God into him with his talk of rabid dogs and the like.

Sir Peter de Granville, seeing his son so awkwardly dismounting from the carriage, and limping up the pathway, was immediately all concern and hurried out anxiously to meet him. The boy looked pallid and genuinely sick, he thought, troubled, yet he had not cavilled at visiting the tenantry but had set about his duties bravely. Perhaps he had misjudged him, and the boy was at last settling down and proving himself a man. His former wildness might have been no more than a young man's rebellion, a kicking over the traces before responsibilities bore down upon him . . . The sooner Richard was wed and safely settled, the entail ensured, the sooner he could relinquish his own obligations and cede authority to his son. He had borne the burden of the estate for too long. It would please him to hand St Samson to one young enough, and determined enough, to make good use of his inheritance. One who would hand it, intact, to the next generation of de Granville sons. A secure, unbroken line. With more paternal affection than was his usual wont, Sir Peter crossed the carriageway to meet his returning son.

Francis and Luke, although respecting Arabella's decision to let Nerissa stay, were far from sanguine at the prospect of keeping her safe at Knatchfield. Richard de Granville's crude attempt to maim or kill her by running her down in the cabriolet was further proof of his intent. Yet he was devious enough and cunning enough to ensure that even had he succeeded, it would have been judged the purest accident. Horses frightened and bolting and a carriage out of control were commonplace hazards, and none would have legally challenged his claim nor doubted his innocence. His baiting of Nerissa at the fair and his attempts to publicly humiliate her had rebounded upon him with the justice he deserved. Yet it had all too obviously set him more firmly against her, and he would not rest until the girl was destroyed.

Luke had thought of letting it be known publicly that Tom Pritchard had died without regaining consciousness, unable to name his attackers, as de Granville and his henchmen feared. The landlord at the Pilgrim's Rest would have been only too willing to help spread the message, Luke was certain, for he had little respect or liking for the young rake-hells concerned. Yet to do so might set both his livelihood and life into danger, for if they suspected collusion, he would receive the same payment as Tom Pritchard himself. Besides, Francis and Luke were agreed that de Granville and his bully boys should be kept in suspense, uncertain of what was known of the murder. Fear might make them garrulous, or more vulnerable, since murderers, like thieves, all too often fell out among themselves . . . The one thing the two friends were adamant upon was that de Granville and the rest must somehow be brought to justice. They would find a way to incriminate him, then charge him openly.

Meanwhile they would draw up a plan to protect both Nerissa and Arabella from violent harm, and take into their confidence those household staff and servants who would be necessary to their schemes. It would be enough should Hillier, the major domo, Hanson, Arabella's coachman, and Harold Manley, the young groom, be warned of some threat to Nerissa's wellbeing, and told to keep their own counsel. They were honest and reliable men, all, and Francis could vouch for their discretion. Arabella must take it upon herself to explain matters to Mrs Pratt, who had already seen evidence of de Granville's spleen and malice, and perhaps to Mrs Cobner, the cook, who would instantly be aware of any stranger trying to curry favour with the kitchen servants or arriving unheralded at the kitchen door.

Francis and Luke did not delude themselves that de Granville or his companions would perpetrate the violence. It was not their style to set themselves openly at risk. Richard de Granville's attempt upon Nerissa's life had been clumsily botched, and clearly made upon the spur of the moment, when opportunity unexpectedly came. No, the three putative "gentlemen", and the one who had turned and fled at the fair, would pay others to take action. They would pay handsomely to save their own skins, and their orders would be explicit. Nerissa Pritchard would be gravely at risk every hour of every day and must be kept unaware of it, or all would be lost. Should she learn of the vendetta, then fear would rule her life and she might flee to save Arabella from harm.

Francis's greatest concern, naturally enough, was to protect Arabella from violence for as long as he was physically able. Yet he would not see Nerissa hurt nor turned away from Knatchfield to fend for herself as best she could. He was too honest and compassionate a man. Was it asking too much of a sick, indeed a dying man to take upon himself such cruel responsibility, Luke wondered. He could not be sure. Yet knowing Francis so well, and his insatiable quest for action and adventure, he thought it might even be the catalyst for his friend's recovery or, at the very least, keep his spirits high and his determination alive.

For himself, he had no qualms about his role as protector. Nerissa Pritchard was deserving of help. She was a woman of character and spirit, as she had shown at Holly Grove fair, beautiful, certainly, and of lively and independent mind. He would stay at Knatchfield Grange for as long as he was needed, out of friendship and affection for Francis and Arabella, but for Nerissa's protection, too. He was aware of her now as a woman, and no longer thought of her as a pitiful child. Should de Granville and his henchmen attempt to harm or abduct her, then he knew that he would not rest easy until her return. He would seek them out and extract brutal revenge; kill them if need be.

Almost against his will he had become involved with her life. Fate, accident, call it what you will, had thrown them together, and their lives seemed destined always to cross . . . It would please him were Nerissa to stay with Arabella through Francis's sickness and inevitable death. It would bring the widow comfort and friendship when she was most at need. He would not admit, even to himself, that it would please him to know where Nerissa lived, and that it might one day give him opportunity to return and see her not merely as a servant, but as a friend.

Chapter Fourteen

Sir Peter de Granville had urgently summoned the physician from Knatchfield, disturbed by Richard's condition, which had worsened by the hour. The boy had never suffered a day's illness in his life, save for those childish ailments which all infants are heir to, and which were mercifully treated out of sight, in the nursery. Now he appeared to be in the severest pain from his injured leg, indeed scarce able to stand and support himself. His skin was feverishly flushed, his hair clung damply to him and his general exhaustion and distress were plain. Louisa, as disturbed as he at their son's deterioration, had ordered that he be taken to his bed at once, and would allow no one to minister to him save she, until the doctor's arrival.

Sir Peter feared that the wound in Richard's leg, from the dog bite, might have somehow become corrupted, although it had been cleaned and dressed by Dr Siberry at Holly Grove. It was true that the bruises and cuts received in some youthful scuffle, which Richard stubbornly refused to discuss, added to his general air of dejection and defeat. yet they were not severe enough, surely, to account for his present malaise? Sir Peter, while he impotently awaited Dr Munro's coming, blamed himself for his son's worsening condition, for ignoring the evidence of his own eyes. It had been obvious that the boy was far from well, yet he had unthinkingly, uncaringly even, sent him about his business upon the estate. To his credit, Richard had made neither excuse nor protest but had gone obediently about his tasks. The boy had behaved creditably, stoically even. Pricked with remorse and fearful of what the outcome of his neglect might be, Sir Peter, at the sound of the physician's curricle arriving, hurried anxiously without to greet him. A brief explanation of Richard's condition had sent Dr Munro hurrying to the sick-room, refusing all offer of refreshment and discussion until his return. With his examination made, he was escorted to the library where Sir Peter restlessly awaited him. Dr Munro's unusual gravity gave forewarning of what his prognosis might be, and Sir Peter had to keep firm grip upon his emotions as he awaited the verdict.

"I fear, sir, that your son is suffering a severe crisis; a feverish complication of the wound to his leg. It is swollen and inflamed, Sir Peter, and purulent. It has clearly become corrupted . . . infected in some way."

"But it may be treated, sir?" he demanded anxiously. "There is something to hand?"

"I will not give you false expectation, Sir Peter," the physician said quietly, "for I know that you would prefer the truth, that you may face it squarely."

"And the truth, sir?" Sir Peter's voice was harsh with alarm.

"The truth is that the corruption must be checked, sir, lest it spread through the blood and infect the whole body." He hesitated before admitting with disquiet, "I cannot yet say what damage has already occurred, for the limb is grossly distended, suppurating freely . . . Should it prove impossible to check the spread of the putrescence, then I fear that he *must* be transported to a hospital, sir, where a surgeon might see fit to amputate."

"No!" The denial was sharp with anguish. "That cannot be! I cannot give consent. The loss of a limb . . ." He broke off helplessly before confessing despairingly, "I fear, Dr Munro, that Richard would find that harder to bear than death itself. He is a young man, active . . . I *cannot* give consent!" he blurted wretchedly. "Must not . . . else he would blame me always."

Dr Munro, seeing his shock and indecision, said compassionately, "If you would have me treat him here . . . attempt to halt the contagion?"

Sir Peter nodded, murmuring, "I beg that you will first try whatever must be done, then, afterwards . . ."

"Twelve hours must suffice . . . I can delay no more,

you understand? Then the decision must be taken, and by you. Your son will be unfitted to make rational choice, nor should he be expected to."

Sir Peter promised quietly, "I shall give my decision. You have my word upon it. All that matters is that Richard should survive, and at whatever cost, whatever sacrifice. There is no other way."

The physician said briskly, to mask his sympathy, "Then I had best begin at once . . . I will cup and bleed him, apply leeches to the wound . . . use whatever purges and cures are at my command. Give bark mixture, or tartar of emetic, to lower the fever . . . You have someone reliable at hand to administer the dosage? Or would you have me find a sick-nurse?"

"My wife, sir, has vowed that she alone will nurse him . . . but if you would find a reputable aide, someone experienced, then I shall be grateful . . . with that, and the servants' help . . ." He broke off confusedly.

"I will do as you ask," the physician promised. "If you will provide me a messenger, I shall send to the apothecary for all that is needed, and ask that an aide be immediately hired to take over the more . . . arduous duties. I shall send also for my partner, Dr Brace, to relieve me. It is imperative that there is always a doctor to hand."

Sir Peter thanked him, adding stiffly, from intolerable grief, "I do not think that there is anything that my wife will not be prepared to do . . . however arduous or distressing, to ensure our son's survival."

"Nor I, sir," the physician said.

Sir Peter made no reply, for he had not heard the reassurance. His mind was filled with the prospect of failure, and the decision that must then be made.

It had been the longest twelve hours of Sir Peter de Granville's life, and he prayed to God that the wretchedness of it might never be repeated. He prayed as earnestly for his son's salvation and his own, for he knew that should Richard die, then he must bear not only the loss but the guilt of it for ever. His life had been devoted always to the de Granville estates, to keeping them intact and making them prosper. They had always come first, taking precedence over all people and all things. Even his marriage had been no more than a shrewd business transaction; a way of securing the riches and blood that would strengthen his line. He had given little thought to Louisa as a person in her own right, a woman of flesh and blood with needs and emotions. He had thought of her only as a way to obtaining an heir, a son. Now, for the first time, he was bitterly aware that his son's survival meant more to him than the de Granville name, the de Granville succession. The boy was his own flesh and blood, born of his loins, and there would be no more sons. It would be more than the end of a noble line, should Richard die. It would be the end of striving, achieving, hoping even. It would be the end of all, and he did not know if he could bear the endless burden of it . . . The question that had racked his brain was settled in his own mind. Whatever was needed for Richard's survival must be done.

When Dr Munro, tense and clearly exhausted, finally came to seek him out, Sir Peter was ready for him. He appeared coldly composed, emotionless.

"You will want my answer . . ." His voice was clipped and without inflection. "Then I give it, sir. You must do whatever is needed to save my son's life. I take full responsibility."

The physician put a compassionate hand to Sir Peter's arm, saying quietly, "I believe, sir, that the acute crisis is already past. The fever has broken and he is breathing more easily. He is not yet out of danger," he warned, "but with strict supervision and long and careful nursing, then I believe he stands a chance of recovery. I can promise no more than that."

Sir Peter hesitated only fractionally, then clasped the physician's hand fiercely in gratitude, his cold, dry touch as austere as his stilted words. Yet his expression of relief and joy spoke more eloquently than he knew.

"I will go to my wife and son now, Dr Munro, if you will allow it, to offer them what comfort I may. Louisa will be tired and in need of rest."

His eyes were preternaturally bright, and the physician,

recognising the emotional toll which the boy's sickness had taken of him, left him quietly alone. The sounds of a man's harsh, dry weeping, painful in its rawness, followed him without. Dr Munro, who was not unaware of Richard de Granville's character and reputation, felt pity for the stern, autocratic man within. He hoped that those tears shed secretly would be the last Sir Peter shed for his son. He had little enough faith that they would convert him.

Richard de Granville's return to health was as slow and tedious as Dr Munro predicted, and too often marred by minor relapses and the patient's intractability. He was bored beyond endurance by the strictness of the regime prescribed for him and by his dependence upon others. He chafed at the discipline and made the lives of those who attended him miserable with his irascible temper and petulance. Upon Dr Munro's advice, and with Sir Peter's approval, the news of the death of his friend, Jeremy Hardwicke, in a riding accident, had been kept from him. It was feared that shock and grief might unnerve him and lead to a serious collapse, for he was still physically and emotionally drained by his illness.

When Sir David Hanford and Matthew Siberry were allowed a brief visit to his bedside, the news of Hardwicke's tragic accident was gently broken to him. To the consternation of all those present Richard de Granville had been prostrated with distress, making shocked denial of it and weeping copiously. Indeed, so alarmed was Sir Peter by his grief that he summoned Dr Munro immediately, and the physician was obliged to order him a dosing of laudanum to calm his nervous agitation. His patient had been so discomposed that he had actually leapt from his bed, demanding that his clothing be brought upon the instant that he might pay his proper respects to Mrs Hardwicke, the dead man's mother. Lady Louisa de Granville had been distraught at her son's recklessness, yet touched by the undeniable selflessness of his grief. His father, too, had been impressed, and despite firmly restraining the boy, could not altogether hide his pride in him. Even Dr Munro, who looked upon his patient with no great favour, was grudgingly forced to admit that Richard de Granville was not entirely bad, only irredeemably flawed.

As they rode their horses through the pillars of St Samson Court, Sir David Hanford turned to Matthew Siberry to admit, "I'll own, Siberry, that I was surprised at de Granville's vehemence, that Hardwicke's death affected him so . . . It does not seem entirely in character. He had no great affection for him." His shrewd, dark eyes were perplexed.

"Perhaps he keeps his real feelings well hidden, Hanford?"

"Perhaps." Hanford was unconvinced.

"He has been gravely sick," Siberry reminded, striving to be fair, "no doubt he is weakened physically and emotionally . . . and has had time to reflect."

"Yes. That could well be."

"I'll readily admit, Hanford, that at news of it, the accident, I mean, I was damnably put about. Hardwicke was a good fellow and a loyal friend, for all his . . . squeamishness. There was no malice in him. He would not have hurt a fly."

"But he *did* hurt someone, Siberry, and that is the crux of it. He could never come to terms, never accept the need for it, and his own part in it."

"No more can I," Siberry confessed shamefacedly.

"Good God, Siberry! Pull yourself together!" Hanford commanded sharply. "Else you will end like Hardwicke, hurling yourself down some mine or crevice."

"You cannot believe that Hardwicke killed himself?" Siberry, white faced, had reined in his horse to the roadside verge. His expression was stricken, raw with disbelief, as Hanford reined in beside him.

"What other explanation could there be? Hardwicke was as fine a horseman as any I have seen. His mount would never have thrown him." Hanford studied him with open curiosity. "Do not tell me that it never occurred to you that it might not be an accident?"

"I had thought, perhaps, murder," Siberry admitted, voice low. "I thought de Granville might have sought him out, taken revenge." He turned abruptly in the saddle, face carefully averted, to murmur, "I was a fool to ever suspect it. An idiot. De Granville was sick," he said remorsefully, "and his grief was real. It shames me that I suspected him."

"You might as easily have suspected me." Hanford's voice was coolly accusing.

"No! For I know your movements are accounted for," Siberry mumbled awkward denial. "You are no more likely to have murdered Hardwicke than I! He was friend to us both!"

"Yet there *was* a murder done," Hanford reminded sharply.

"But to a stranger! Not one of our own kind."

Hanford stared at him for a long moment, then abruptly reined his horse away. As Siberry reluctantly followed suit, Hanford turned his head to call back, "Whatever caused Hardwicke's death, whether accident or suicide, one thing is certain."

"And that?"

"That it will save de Granville's skin and our own . . . He will not long mourn. You may depend on it!"

News of Richard de Granville's feverish illness, as a consequence of his leg wound, was greeted by Arabella and others with the scant sympathy it deserved. There had been much good-humoured bantering about Toby's tenacity and discernment, although, as Francis remarked with unusual acerbity, "The real pity would be if it were unfortunately the dog which died!" Arabella had pretended outrage at such cynicism, deploring his flippancy, but secretly she was as relieved as the men that de Granville was safely immured at St Samson Court. For the moment at least Nerissa was free of his scheming revenge, although they could not entirely discount the danger from his friends.

Nerissa herself, unaware of the fact that de Granville had tried to kill her, none the less was grateful that he had been removed from the scene. She had no wish to come across him on her carriage rides with Arabella, or to meet him accidentally upon their formal visits to acquaintances in the neighbourhood. News of Jeremy Hardwicke's death, gained from Mrs Cobner and her kitchen gossip, had grieved her more. It was true that she had barely known the young gentleman, she confided to the cook and Mrs Pratt, but he had attended her father's funeral, for Joe Protheroe of the Pilgrim's Rest had recognised him and told her his name. She had glimpsed him afterwards at Holly Grove fair, but he had taken no part in de Granville's baiting of her or the ensuing fight. He had seemed kindly and gentle mannered at her father's graveside, and genuinely distressed, yet why, she would never now discover.

"Likely Joe Protheroe will know the reason . . . the connection between them?" Henrietta Cobner suggested. "Why do you not ask one of the grooms to take you there in the waggon, when he fetches provisions? It would make a small outing upon your half-day."

"No, it is better not," Nerissa said reluctantly. "I have no wish to return to St Samson yet awhile."

Mrs Pratt cast a warning glance at the cook, who coloured and looked painfully flustered as she remembered the threat from de Granville and the others.

"It holds only unhappy memories for me," Nerissa confessed with honesty. "My father's accident and his death and all . . . Perhaps later, when all is long past and I am better able to face returning."

"Yes! Yes!" Mrs Cobner agreed. "It was foolishly perverse of me to have even suggested such a thing." Her plump face was creased with remorse. "But a visit to your friend the Punch and Judy man then, and his dog Toby? Would that not be a fine outing? You would be sure of a good welcome there."

"Yes!" Nerissa exclaimed, delighted at the prospect. "I shall go next week, if Mrs Crawshay will allow it. Mr Goliath Jones gave me open invitation, and I know where his cottage lies, for Hugh Gravelle showed me when he thatched it. It will be a rare treat to see him again, and Toby too." She hesitated. "But for this afternoon I have no plans made, save to work at my books awhile, then take a stroll in the garden, or into Knatchfield village."

Mrs Cobner exchanged a meaningful glance with the housekeeper, as Mrs Pratt offered quickly, "Then I would spend some time with you, Nerissa, my dear, if you will have me . . . I shall bring my needlework and some books of my own . . . Perhaps we might exchange some opinions upon them."

Nerissa, who knew that a lesson in reading and writing was being diplomatically offered, and so that none save she should be aware of it, was delighted.

"I shall be grateful for your company, Mrs Pratt," Nerissa replied, with the approved courtesy and formality. Yet she was unable to resist blurting impulsively, "Oh, but it will be the greatest treat. Better than any outing! I shall be on pins until our readings begin."

Mrs Pratt's thin, rather forbidding features softened into pleasure at such a spontaneous testimonial. It spoke well for her skills and company both, and although not given to the sin of pride, she was not averse to Mrs Cobner hearing it.

When Nerissa had taken her leave to attend to her duties, Mrs Cobner, glancing about her anxiously lest they be overheard, murmured, "You think that . . . business of which we spoke, the danger to her, is over, Selina?"

"With the gentleman indisposed, and likely to remain so, it would seem to be." She added cautiously, "Yet he might well employ others. We cannot relax our vigilance, Henrietta. Not yet awhile."

Mrs Cobner nodded, venturing, "She is a good-natured girl, helpful and decently bred. She is liked by everyone, from Hillier to young Bella and the rest, and treats them all with patience and respect. I cannot see why she should be so cruelly harried and set upon. It defies all reason!" Her broad, good-humoured face was creased in concern.

"The gentry . . . the so-called 'quality', are a law unto themselves!" Mrs Pratt exclaimed. "Saving our own Miss Arabella and such," she added hastily. "They show neither reason nor manners in dealing with those they consider 'inferiors', those who have somehow offended them."

"But how could she have offended him?" Mrs Cobner demanded, perplexed. "She had never set eyes upon him before the hirings at Holly Grove fair."

"Because she is proudly independent!" Mrs Pratt

exclaimed tartly, continuing less abrasively, "You your-self gave answer enough, Henrietta! She is honest and decently bred."

"But that is no reason at all!"

"It is every reason in one who aspires to being a servant to others, in one of the labouring classes, such as we . . . Nerissa has a natural dignity and ease of manner which endears her to all . . . all save those who demand subservience. Those who claim themselves to be superior by birth see excellence in others more lowly as a threat. An insolence to be curbed. It might have served her better had he been able to humiliate her publicly."

"But instead *she* humiliated him," Mrs Cobner finished wryly, "and the young 'gentleman' will not easily let her forget it. I vow, Selina, that the creature must be out of his mind, unbalanced, a candidate for Bedlam! 'Tis not normal behaviour to take violent action for such a slight, nor to bear such a grudge. 'Tis more the petulance of a spoilt child in the nursery! An infant over-indulged in his tantrums." She sniffed expressively.

"In a grown man such petulance is less easily curbed, and more brutal," Selina Pratt reminded soberly, "his hostility will not stop at words. He has means and opportunity to revenge himself."

"Perhaps his sickness has given him pause to think," Henrietta Cobner ventured timidly. "Perhaps 'twill set things into proper perspective, make him repent."

"I am no great believer in death-bed repentance," Mrs Pratt said acidly, "and less in its lasting value, should the patient recover. Human nature does not change, Henrietta!"

"Then we had best be vigilant!" the cook said briskly. "We must leave nothing to chance. See that she is watched over constantly and never left alone . . . well, save at night," she amended, adding with growing comprehen-sion, "but that is why you offered her your company, Selina!"

"I felt it my bounden duty," agreed Mrs Pratt, assuring herself that such well-intentioned prevarication could not be counted an outright lie.

"Upon my oath, Selina!" Mrs Cobner declared admiringly. "You are a clever creature! You have a good head, and that's a fact. None can beat you for intelligence."

"Or deviousness," admitted the housekeeper comfortably. "One must use whatever advantages one can muster; fight like with like." She added kindly, "There is none who can beat you at cookery, Henrietta. You have raised it to a fine art."

Mrs Cobner did not deny it.

The promised lesson in reading and writing had gone splendidly, and Selina Pratt was swift to praise Nerissa for her application and achievement, saying generously when her pupil thanked her, "Why, my dear, it is pleasure and privilege to help you. I can claim no credit, for it is due to your own hard work and enthusiasm. I'll swear that there could be no more industrious scholar, no, nor such a determined one . . . not in the whole of Christendom!"

"You think that I may, one day, be able to read and write really well, Mrs Pratt?" she asked diffidently. "Enough to write a letter, perhaps?" She flushed at her own temerity, wishing the foolish words unspoken.

"But of course," Selina Pratt said equably. "There is nothing surer."

She studied Nerissa speculatively, offering kindly, "If there is some urgency about the matter . . . something you would have me draft for you . . . something you may copy by rote?"

"No . . . I had thought a letter to my friend, Ruth, and the children, sent perhaps upon one of the company stages, just to tell her how I fare."

"But will Ruth be able to read it, my dear?" Mrs Pratt posed gently. "Will it not alarm her . . . cause her the greatest concern if she has to pay a reader to decipher it for her? It is usually news of some death or calamity that a letter brings."

"I think that if she is still in Hugh Gravelle's care, then he will reassure her . . . tell her what it contains. I know that as a master thatcher he can figure and write a little, else he would not be able to write his bills and order his reeds and such . . . but I would not like to set her at a disadvantage," Nerissa said quietly, "I would not like her to feel that I am over-proud, showing off my learning and belittling her own . . . She was a good friend to me."

"Then she will think only the best of you," Mrs Pratt said decisively. "She will be proud of your initiative and value you for what you are. Will you give her news of your new life at Knatchfield? Tell her what befell you at the fair?"

"Yes. I shall tell her that I have had the greatest good fortune. That God has been good to me." She said with quiet sincerity, "That I have found the kindest of friends, and home."

"Then it will please her greatly," Selina Pratt said matter-of-factly, "for she will have your best interests at heart, as you have hers."

"If you will help me, Mrs Pratt, then I shall count it a kindness," Nerissa said. "I had best wait until I have paid my visit to Toby and Mr Jones, that she and the children may have news of him, for he gave Sian a pup, the very spit and image of Toby, and they will remember him kindly."

"Yes, that is sensible and quite satisfactory," Selina Pratt said. "We will work upon the letter together, consider it a lesson in composition and handwriting, a test for you."

Nerissa's pretty, intelligent face was alive with delighted anticipation as she offered her thanks, her smile fading to sobriety as she asked hesitantly, "And do you think I shall one day be able to read as well as you do, Mrs Pratt? That I may pick up any book in the library, if Mrs Crawshay allows, and read it properly . . . without stumbling over the words . . . understand all?"

"There is no doubt of it! None at all!" Selina Pratt declared with formidable confidence. "Why, it will be a whole new world for you, Nerissa. A world you have never before been able to enter. You will learn the thoughts and aspirations of others, their fears and beliefs, their greatness of spirit. You will enter their very minds and hearts." Such florid hyperbole was alien to Mrs Pratt, and she reiterated quickly, to hide her embarrassment at what she had revealed of herself, "Yes. It will be a whole new world."

"It cannot be a *better* one than this, Mrs Pratt," Nerissa said with conviction. "Only different."

"Well, perhaps," agreed Mrs Pratt judicially. Then, more practically, she offered, "We had best go and sit in the garden, my dear, and blow the cobwebs from our minds. We have studied long enough for today. Bring your needlework with you and we shall sit in the garden under the peacock tree. It will be warm enough if you put on your pelisse and outdoor slippers, and I shall wrap myself well in my shawl."

They had been seated upon the wooden garden seat but a few minutes when Captain Farrow wandered without, clearly believing himself to be alone in the garden. He was smoking a post-prandial cigar and strolling without firm purpose, his mind elsewhere. Nerissa, glancing at him covertly from above her stitching, thought how distinguished and handsome he was, with his dark hair and upright, military bearing. There was an air of power and authority about him, even in relaxation, a latent energy that could not be suppressed. He glanced up idly and, seeing the two women sitting upon the garden seat, came over, smiling, to pay his compliments. The bow he made was elegantly formal, and Nerissa followed Mrs Pratt's careful acknowledgement and gracious inclination of the head, but her smile for him was wide and unfeigned, her pleasure in the meeting free of artifice.

"It is a charming garden . . ." his smile was for Nerissa, "and the better for being seen in such congenial company. You will not take cold, Mrs Pratt?" he asked solicitously. "The wind is still chill, I think, and it would not do to take some ague or rheumatic ill through dampness."

"I thank you for your concern, sir," Mrs Pratt said, straight faced, but determined to remain with Nerissa. "I am admirably equipped for the weather and would consider it a sign of weakness and self-indulgence to return indoors."

Captain Farrow's lips twitched. "Then I must congratulate you, ma'am, upon your . . . tenacity and strength of mind," he said, good-humouredly.

"And I, sir, upon your swiftness of understanding."

Nerissa, looking uncertainly from one to the other, saw to her bewilderment that they were both vastly amused and pleased with their exchanges.

"Perhaps you would care to see Miss Pritchard's needlework, Captain Farrow?" Mrs Pratt suggested primly. "Her stitching is quite exquisite . . . most expertly done. She is a most accomplished young lady."

"Nothing, ma'am, could give me greater pleasure."

The irony was not lost upon the housekeeper, who offered solicitously, "If you would have me relieve you of your cigar, sir? A temporary arrangement only. It would not do to have the . . . piece soiled or burned through lack of thought or carelessness. Such damage is often impossible to rectify afterwards."

"I would not wish that to happen, ma'am! I shall treat it with the greatest respect. You have my solemn word."

Nerissa, awkwardly flustered and with head bent low, did not see the look of shared understanding which passed between them. She was about to pass her needlework into Captain Farrow's outstretched hand when the sharp cry of his name from the doorway of the house caused him to turn and run towards Arabella, who had called out so urgently to him. Nerissa and Mrs Pratt rose too, and anxiously hurried after him.

"Francis? There is something amiss with Francis, Arabella?" His voice was sharp with fear.

Arabella, white faced and trembling, shook her head, thrusting a paper towards him, scarce able to speak coherently for shock and distress.

"No. It is Francis I seek . . ." she managed to murmur helplessly, "the letter, Luke . . . read the letter!"

"Dear God, Arabella! What madman has written this? It is obscene! Vile! Depraved beyond belief! How did you come by it? It must be put in the hands of the justices at once."

Mrs Pratt had hurried to be with her, but Luke was already at her side, taking her arm, half supporting, half carrying her within.

Francis, hearing the commotion, had run from the stables, demanding, "What is it? Is it some accident to Arabella? Is Arabella hurt?" He had lifted Arabella into his arms and carried her within and, despite her protestations, poured her a good measure of brandy and insisted that she drink it.

"For God's sake, Arabella, tell me what has occurred!" His face was as pallid and strained as her own, and Luke, although fearful, handed him the letter. Francis read it in silence and with growing incredulity.

"Dear God in heaven! It is the work of someone deranged! A lunatic!" He tore the letter savagely into fragments and hurled them into the blazing log fire. The flames curled around them, devouring, blackening, charring them to ashes. Yet they could not burn away nor cleanse memory of what had been written. Arabella's hand in Francis's was icily cold, and the rage and disgust within him colder. It would have pleased Francis to have consigned the writer to the flames and watched him burn. A foretaste of hell on earth. For now the hell was in Francis's own imagining, and in the knowledge of his own helplessness in the face of such depravity. Whatever it cost him, he must hunt the madman down, put an end to his vileness. He could not rest easy else.

Chapter Fifteen

The furore and consternation at Knatchfield Grange over the obscenely threatening letter which Arabella had received did not quickly die down. When it did, there were repercussions which none involved had foreseen. It had been an instinctive reaction on Francis's part to destroy the letter, to rid himself of its foul contamination. In burning it he felt that he had purged himself of its filthiness, its very existence. Yet it existed still in the minds of those who had read its fetid outpourings of hatred. Those crude imaginings of a sick, disordered brain, more dangerous for being by an enemy unknown.

Francis, regretting his momentary rashness, had tried to compensate by riding out at once to Lanelay Court, the house of Sir Charles Hanford, the justice. He had ridden there alone, bidding Luke stay and protect Arabella, for he would not have her left unguarded. Arabella was being ministered to by the redoubtable Mrs Pratt and Nerissa, and the two men were able to exchange a few tense words without being overheard.

"It must be that bloody lunatic, de Granville!" Francis raged impotently. "Who else would be guilty of such filth?"

"You cannot be sure of that," Luke warned, "it would be dangerous to make such accusation, for he is known to be sick and bedridden, Francis. It would do naught, save turn the justices against you, stir sympathy for him!"

"Hell and damnation, Luke!" Francis exploded. "I want him stopped. Now, before Arabella comes to harm. You cannot doubt that he is vicious enough and mindless enough to abduct and violate her as he claims!"

Luke put an arm to Crawshay's shoulder, urging, "Think

195

well on it, Francis! I have no more liking for the man than you, but he has no quarrel with Arabella. Nerissa is his quarry, and has been since Pritchard's death. It would serve no purpose for de Granville to show his hand so clumsily. He is too wary, too fearful for his own hide!"

Francis hesitated, unconvinced. "It is a ruse to deflect attention from Nerissa," he insisted stubbornly.

"A ruse?"

"By writing the letter, he could cause terror and hurt, yet provide himself an alibi . . . I am sure of it!"

Luke shook his head, declaring, "No! It would simply draw attention to him openly, and to no real purpose. His sickness gives him respite; a chance to regain control. You forget that he is not aware that we *know* of the murder."

"Perhaps."

"Besides . . . he is a bully and a coward, as we saw at the hirings and in his attempt upon Nerissa's life. He is vicious enough and depraved enough, but he will strike stealthily and at no risk to himself . . . Believe it."

Francis nodded, face bleak.

"Say nothing to the justice of Pritchard's murder and what we suspect," Luke urged firmly, "else you will only incur his enmity. Without proof, we are powerless, and he as powerless to act. It might destroy all we have tried to do."

"I will inform him of nothing save the bare facts of the letter," Francis promised curtly. "For the rest, we must make our own enquiries, and in our own way. I cannot believe that de Granville is innocent in this! He is guilty, as of all else. I will not rest until he is called to account. I will see him destroyed, his henchmen with him!"

At Lanelay Court, Sir Charles had been courteous and deeply concerned, promising that investigation would certainly be made, but reminding that in the absence of the letter itself there could be no clue as to the sender, nor firm evidence, even should he be apprehended.

"I have the evidence of my own eyes, sir!" Francis exclaimed, exasperated at his own recklessness and by the justice's apparent obtuseness. "There is also the witness of my friend, Captain Farrow, and of my wife, Arabella."

The justice made no reply.

"Each of them is reliable, intelligent and of excellent character." Francis added stiffly, "If you feel need of corroboration."

"I do not doubt your word, Major Crawshay," Sir Charles's expression was concerned, his tone sympathetic, "but you must see that in the absence of the letter, the only factual evidence, I am at a loss."

"Then I had best go, sir," Francis said abruptly. "I must apologise for unfairly taking up your time."

"Major Crawshay," Sir Charles said quietly, "I did not rebuke you for taking up my time, nor do I think that you have done so unfairly . . . I merely point out what you already know, that in destroying the letter, you have destroyed all evidence, although testimony remains." He paused, adding more kindly, "I will admit that in your situation I would have been sorely tempted to destroy the letter, to consign it to the fire where such filthy trash belongs."

Francis murmured apology, shamed by the justice's understanding and his own gracelessness.

"If you would have me return with you to Knatchfield, then I will ride with you willingly and make whatever investigation I may."

"I should be grateful, sir," Francis said, adding with raw honesty, "I am too anguished and shocked to be fitting company. I beg that you will bear with me, not judge me to be morose and uncivil."

"I am only surprised, sir, that you have remained so equable," Sir Charles said compassionately, adding firmly, "I would that we had met under kinder circumstances, Major Crawshay. It is not the introduction I would have sought."

"Nor I, sir," Francis admitted wryly.

"But since we are to be neighbours and our paths must often cross, then I hope our future meetings will be less painfully brought about, less formal." He hesitated slightly, offering his hand in friendship, and adding as

Francis took it within his own, "I will do all in my power to try and solve this disturbing business, Crawshay, to find the offender and bring him to book."

Their handclasp was firm and sealed an alliance, and Francis knew that he had found an ally whom he could trust. Sir Charles was an austere man, as spare in words as in flesh. Yet there was no doubting his resolve and integrity, his implacable will. He would see justice done, Francis was sure of it. For a brief moment Francis considered blurting out all to him, telling him of Pritchard's murder, the attempt upon Nerissa's life and his suspicion of Richard de Granville's involvement. Yet Luke's stern warning steadied him and held him back.

In the courtyard without Lanelay Court, as the justice waited impatiently for his mount and Francis's to be brought by the groom, there was a grinding of wheels upon the carriageway. A pretty, lightweight gig with a single horse drew up skilfully upon the gravel beside them, and the handsome young gentleman at the reins leapt down agiley beside them, raising his silk hat in formal acknowledgement.

"Major Crawshay, sir, I would have you meet my son, David. David, this is our new neighbour, Major Francis Crawshay of Knatchfield Grange. He has come to me on a matter of the greatest urgency."

Francis gazed stiffly into the handsome face of that arrogant gentleman, his adversary at Holly Grove fair. Yet there was little of arrogance about him now, for shock had all but robbed him of his self-possession. He seemed awkwardly deprived of wits and speech, and Sir Charles was plainly puzzled by his discomfiture.

"I believe, sir, that we have already met!" Francis's voice was clipped, incisive, rigidly under control.

Sir David Hanford made some inaudible reply, quickly surrendering the horse and gig to a nervously waiting stable boy as a groom appeared leading the two saddled mounts. Despite his contempt for Hanford's son, Francis could almost feel it in himself to be sorry for the boy, so whey faced and bewildered did he seem, body stiff with apprehension. He believes that I am here to make complaint, Francis thought incredulously. He expects me to lay formal charge against him. It is no more than he deserves! Yet I will not let him off so easily. Let him suffer and sweat a while. It will serve to chasten him, and give him pause for thought. God knows, he is in need of it!

"I will see you upon my return," Sir Charles said abruptly to his son. "There are matters which must be discussed."

"Yes, sir," his voice was low, "I shall hold myself in readiness."

What ails the boy? Sir Charles thought with rising irritation. He behaves like a nincompoop! He was scarcely civil to Major Crawshay. He swung himself into the saddle, his annoyance made plain.

With a foot in his stirrup, Francis half turned, asking conversationally, "Your friend, sir . . . Mr de Granville, was it not? He is recovered from his . . . indisposition? An infected dog bite, so I am led to believe?"

"Yes, I thank you, Major Crawshay." The reply was uttered through clenched lips. "He is much improved."

"Then I am glad to hear it! Long may it continue!"

The irony was not lost upon Hanford, who flushed deeply but made no reply.

"I beg that you will tell him of my concern for his future health and wellbeing."

"Indeed."

"It might be as well were he to avoid rabid dogs and eschew all dangerous pursuits and . . . unhealthy meeting places for a time. You will be sure to advise him?" Francis's expression was concerned and innocent of guile. "You will not forget?"

"I will not forget."

Francis mounted swiftly and with a nod and a word to Sir Charles, the two riders were away, their horses' hooves clattering noisily along the carriageway. Sir David Hanford lingered a while, gazing after them, wondering uncomfortably how much Francis Crawshay knew. At first he had believed that Crawshay had come to tell his father of the baiting of Pritchard's daughter and that fiasco of a fight at Holly Grove fair. Yet now he was not so sure . . . A matter of the greatest urgency, his father had said. Surely it could have no connection with him or de Granville? How were they involved? Francis Crawshay had given the clearest warning that he would stand no further aggression from them. He was not a man to provoke or to be taken lightly. He was a man of action. A man of his word. David Hanford only hoped that the words Crawshay used to his father would be restrained and sparing, and on some other's account. Despite his hotheadedness and careless manner, he feared his father; moreover, he respected him. It would not do to bring him grief. That cultivated charm which David Hanford used upon others to captivate or ensnare them, was lost upon Sir Charles. He was too clear sighted to be deceived. Too objective. Hanford turned disconsolately upon his heel and walked slowly into the house. It seemed to him that Major Crawshay and his father were men of the same calibre. They would, he felt certain, become firm friends. They had as much in common as he and de Granville, and would become as inexorably bound. The prospect gave him little pleasure.

Sir Charles had treated Arabella with the greatest gentleness and respect, his questioning sensitively restrained. She had taken an immediate liking to him, and from the first there had been a complete rapport between them, without a hint of self-consciousness. He had apologised for the invasion of her privacy and home, and regretted the need for it, and she in turn had answered his questions freely and with absolute honesty. His treatment of the servants, too, had been courteous, and none, not even the little serving maid, Bella, had felt intimidated. Yet his patient probing had yielded nothing of real value and he had confessed himself at a loss as to how best to proceed.

"I have learned little of real account," he confided to Francis and Luke, not attempting to hide his disappointment. "Nothing that gives me cause to feel sanguine."

"The letter, sir?" Luke asked.

"It seems that it was delivered by an under footman, one newly appointed. It was given to him by a lone horseman who accosted him when out walking in the lanes."

"A local man, Sir Charles? Someone he recognised or knew?"

"Alas, no. A stranger, it would seem, one ill dressed and roughly spoken, clearly no more than a paid messenger."

"And the message he gave?" Francis demanded.

"None, save that the letter should be delivered into Mrs Crawshay's keeping."

"Yet the footman did not deliver it into my wife's hands?"

"No . . . it seems that he placed it upon the salver in the hall, with other visiting cards and messages, forgetting to inform Hillier, your major domo. He claims that he was immediately diverted by other tasks, and the incident slipped his mind." He added dryly, "I do not think that it will as easily slip Hillier's mind, Major Crawshay, nor that such slackness will be repeated."

"You believe the footman, Sir Charles?" Luke asked. "You do not think he is involved in this? An accomplice?"

"No. From what he has told me, he was no more than an unwitting messenger . . . He appears honest and can be vouched for by the local members of your staff and by men of impeccable character and integrity in Knatchfield. His credentials are excellent."

"He has given you a description of this stranger? This messenger?" Francis demanded abruptly.

"Yes . . . but I fear, Major Crawshay, that from what he could tell me, this man is no more than the roughest vagrant, some passing traveller upon the roads. He is no more than a dupe, a pawn in the game. It is to some other we must look."

"But whom?" Francis demanded irascibly. "And where?"

"Some disgruntled servant perhaps. Someone with an imagined ill or grudge?" Luke interposed quickly to counter his friend's irritability.

"There is no such person!" Francis exclaimed abrasively. "Arabella has made no enemies. I will swear to it! It is not in her nature to antagonise others. The servants and household staff are devoted to her. Many have served her from her childhood days. No! It is not possible!"

"I am inclined to the same belief," Sir Charles confirmed

quietly. "I do not think that writing such a vitriolic and degrading letter as you have described would be a servant's way of revenge. Despite its obscenity, it was literate, or so you have assured me, Major Crawshay; the hand practised, and despite its crude offensiveness, not the work of one untutored. Would you not agree?"

Francis nodded mutely and Luke said with distaste, "Yes, I fear that you are right, Sir Charles. Despite its contents, the letter was not the work of an uneducated man."

"Or woman," Sir Charles amended.

"A woman!" Francis exclaimed incredulously. "No, I cannot believe it! No woman would be capable of such bile and filthiness. It is inconceivable."

"Unlikely, perhaps, but not inconceivable, Major Crawshay. I fear that a woman's rage and resentment can be as destructive as any man's . . . 'Hell hath no fury' has all too often proved to be true."

"Yet this was no ordinary letter," Luke reminded. "Threats were made of torture and abduction, yet others of a carnal nature, both prurient and specific." He glanced apologetically towards Francis, confiding, "I cannot believe that any woman would be so perverted, so debased."

"It would be easier to deal with a woman's violence," Francis blurted despairingly, "for they rely more heavily on the power of words, to scourge and destroy. It might go no deeper than salaciousness. A desire to shock."

His words and their implication hung heavily between them, but neither Luke nor Sir Charles spoke openly of their fears. The man they sought would not halt at mere words. He would vent his savagery and spleen in action; action that would cripple and degrade flesh and spirit. With an enemy unknown, they were powerless to act, and he would watch and wait upon it.

Sir Charles rose awkwardly from his chair, saying with compassion, "I will detain you no longer, Major Crawshay, for I know you would wish to offer comfort to your wife . . . She is a lady of the greatest intelligence and spirit and I grieve the distress that this . . . outrage has caused." He held out a hand in parting to Luke, who made suitable

202

acknowledgement, and then to Francis, declaring firmly, "I will see that your footman's background and credentials are more stringently checked, although I cannot view him as the likely culprit, or even a knowing accessory. I will have immediate enquiries made at the inns and livery stables as to the stranger who handed him the letter. If we succeed in tracing him, then his description of the man who hired him as messenger might give firm clue as to his identity."

Francis nodded, thanking him soberly.

"It is little enough," Sir Charles admitted regretfully, "but I fear that it is all I can do with so little known. Without evidence, or clue as to what prompted the threats, I am damnably shackled, impotent to act." He paused. "I have one possible line of enquiry in mind, but am not yet able to speak of it, lest it come to nothing. I would not build up false hopes."

Francis murmured, "You will tell us, should anything come to light?"

"At once, you may depend upon it."

As Francis and Luke accompanied him to the *porte-cochère* without, where his horse was saddled and waiting, Sir Charles cautioned, face grave, "Keep a strong watch upon Mrs Crawshay. Guard and protect her at all times. There is something in this which disturbs me beyond the ordinary . . . some malevolence . . . a vindictiveness I cannot fathom. There is only one thing certain – this man is near at hand."

"No." Francis's voice was raw with conviction. "The only certainty is that should he show his face here, then I will undoubtedly kill him."

Sir Charles could not doubt that he meant it.

It had been a subdued and preoccupied gathering at the dinner table at Knatchfield Grange that evening, and Francis in particular seemed uncommonly morose. Arabella, as if to defy her unknown adversary, had dressed herself with extravagant care, choosing a silk gown and slippers of clearest sapphire blue, with a necklace, bracelet and earrings of matching gemstones set into filigree gold.

Her fair hair was upswept into a pretty chignon, with cascading ringlets, and in the flickering candle flames the jewels gleaming at her throat, ears and slender wrist seemed no brighter than her vivid blue eyes. Francis, who was sunk deep into introspection, seemed not to notice his wife's unease, but Luke was painfully aware of Arabella's disquiet. It was not for her own safety she grieved, Luke thought compassionately, but for Francis and the effect of the letter upon him. He seemed diminished somehow, his old exuberance and natural authority depressed. As if to counter it, Arabella grew increasingly more loquacious, her conversation deliberately lighthearted and provocative. Luke, recognising her strain and the need to dispel it, answered in similar vein, but both were aware of its shallowness, the artificiality with which they spoke.

When dinner was ended, the two men did not linger at table over their port, but returned to the drawing room where, at Arabella's instigation, they took turns at playing her at bezique. She had won handsomely, for her opponents lacked concentration, their thoughts clearly elsewhere. Yet she persevered at trying to amuse and distract them until Francis, perturbed by her unnaturally high colour and feverish gaiety, declared that it was time that they retired to a decent night's rest. Luke had been relieved to agree, and made swift his good-nights and departure. Arabella had made no demur, but followed Francis obediently to their bedchamber.

They had undressed in near silence, each exhausted by the turmoil of the day's events, and Francis, seeing Arabella mount the bed steps to the half tester, was grieved by her air of fatigue and dejection. In the flickering light of the taper in the candlestick, her face was wan, skin delicately drawn over the high cheekbones, and he felt a stirring of remorse at his self-absorption, his neglect of her. Within the secure shelter of his arms she had soon fallen asleep, her unloosed hair spread softly upon pillow and cheeks. Francis did not sleep. Long after the taper had guttered and died, he stared wide eyed into the darkness. There would, he knew, be a greater darkness to come. A death which could not be avoided. A darkness that would be endless and absolute. Yet it was not fear of that which filled his mind but fear for Arabella. He could protect her for so little time. He could only pray that it would be enough.

Luke, who had been deeply asleep, awoke startled to find Hillier shaking him roughly into alertness. By the glow from the candle-lantern which Hillier held in his free hand, Luke could see that the servant's face was fiercely distressed, his hands trembling.

"What is it, Hillier?" he demanded urgently when he had gathered his wits. "It is not Mrs Crawshay?" he asked sharply. "Mrs Crawshay has not been harmed?"

"No, sir. It is the major . . . Major Crawshay."

"Francis?" Luke's voice was harsh. "What has occurred?"

"He has suffered some collapse . . . some fit of unconsciousness, sir, with the mistress unable to rouse him. Mrs Crawshay bids you come at once! She is all but demented, sir, with shock and fear."

Luke was already discarding his nightshirt and dragging on his clothes, demanding tensely as he dressed, "The physician has been called, Hillier?"

"Yes, sir. At once . . . as soon as ever I was alerted. Hanson has taken the carriage to bring Dr Munro to Knatchfield . . . and I have sent a groom on horseback to alert Dr Brace to the urgency, lest Dr Munro be away."

"Who is with Mrs Crawshay now? She has not been left alone?"

"No, sir. Mrs Pratt is with her. I thought it best to warn her. She has cared for Mrs Crawshay from childhood, as I, sir . . ." He broke off, too distressed to speak further.

Luke put a steadying hand to the old man's arm, saying with sincerity, "Mrs Crawshay will be grateful for your nearness, Hillier, and for the support of such loyal friends, for that is what she counts you to be."

Hillier nodded, face hollowed and gaunt in the refracted lantern light, then opening the door to the bed-chamber stood patiently aside that Luke might enter within.

Arabella, seeing him, rushed from the bedside where she and Mrs Pratt were seated and flung herself, weeping

205

distractedly, into his arms. He felt her agitated trembling and her tears wet upon his shirt front, and tried to comfort her as best he might with his own warmth and foolishly murmured endearments, but could find no comfort for himself.

Francis lay inert and frighteningly lifeless in the cavernous depths of the bed, face as colourless as the linen upon which he lay. His skin seemed waxen and cold, almost translucent, as if all blood and feeling had already drained away. His upper lip and forehead were filmed with sweat, and that and his sudden stertorous breathing were the only signs that he still clung subbornly to life.

The time of waiting before the physicians arrived seemed endless, and those attending Francis were grieved by their impotence to ease his distress. Dr Munro had arrived in the greatest haste, barely twenty minutes after Luke had been summoned by Hillier, and his partner, Dr Brace, immediately afterwards. It was plain that they were already apprised of Francis's condition and had come prepared for whatever deterioration they might find. All, including Arabella, were quickly banished from the bedchamber; her protests and cries to remain were sternly ignored. Dr Munro calmly delivered her into Mrs Pratt's care and set about the business of treating his patient, with Dr Brace as informed and willing aide.

The period of banishment had been anguished, with Arabella, tearless and stoical, refusing rest or comfort. Indeed, she seemed unaware of those around her; conscious of nothing save her own raw grief and Francis's fight to survive. Selina Pratt watched over her silently, face as tortured and bloodless as Arabella's, yet she could do nothing to ease her misery and was as powerless to mask her own.

It had been a full hour and a half before Hillier brought Dr Munro into the drawing room. Mrs Pratt would have left, and rose uncertainly from her chair, but Arabella put a restraining hand to her arm, bidding her stay. Luke took his place implacably at Arabella's side.

"Francis?" Arabella's voice was high with anxiety.

"He is resting more comfortably now."

Dr Munro glanced meaningfully towards the house-keeper then towards Hillier, his concern at their presence made plain, but Arabella said quietly, "I would have you speak openly, Dr Munro, for it is owed to Hillier and Mrs Pratt. I have kept them in ignorance for Francis's sake, and to spare them . . . His illness can no longer be hid, and I would have them hear all."

As Dr Munro still hesitated, Arabella assured with certainty, "Nothing that you speak of in confidence will be repeated beyond this room. You have my word upon it."

Dr Munro nodded, saying, "Tonight's sickness is a warning, Mrs Crawshay. A warning of what the future holds. What you must expect." He hesitated. "This disease is degenerative and progressive. It cannot be checked."

"How long?" Arabella's voice was at first low, barely audible. "How long will he survive?" she repeated more sharply.

"There may be remissions . . . periods of apparent recovery and calm."

"But there is no real hope of recovery?"

"None," he admitted, "and I can give you no time upon which you may safely rely. Much will depend upon Major Crawshay's willingness to heed advice, to stay calm and untroubled, to reserve his energy. The course of the disease is never constant. It is both volatile and unpredictable."

"As Francis himself." For the moment there was the merest glimmer of a smile upon Arabella's lips, an affectionate acknowledgement, then she said with gentle dignity, "I thank you for your honesty, Dr Munro, it is kinder so."

He nodded his understanding, but did not speak.

"It is better to be prepared." The bleakness in Arabella's voice belied the trite words, and those who listened, and loved her, knew that nothing could prepare her for such loss. It would mean the loss of all.

"If you have urgent need of me, Mrs Crawshay," Dr Munro said gently, "you have but to send word, by day or night. I shall come most willingly."

"I shall be glad of that. I thank you for what you have

done to help Francis and me this night . . . and Dr Brace too. I beg that you will tell him of my gratitude."

"Yes, ma'am, gladly." He paused, lingering uncertainly, to murmur, "It is essential that Major Crawshay is given complete rest for the next few days; that nothing is allowed to fret or harass him. You understand?"

Arabella inclined her head.

"I have left a receipt with Hillier, there, to be made up by the apothecary at Knatchfield village, and some laudanum to calm the patient's agitation, to give him ease. I shall return in the morning at ten o'clock to make a check upon his condition," promising, "as soon as ever it is light I shall send a dependable woman to nurse and watch over him."

After Dr Munro had taken his leave, Selina Pratt hurried concernedly to Arabella's side, chafing her mistress's cold hands, trying to bring life to her icy flesh, murmuring comfort as if she were still the child of old.

"You had best return to your bed, my dear, for you are all but asleep upon your feet," the housekeeper exclaimed compassionately. "You shall have a hot negus and a warm brick wrapped in flannel for your feet . . . something to take away the bitter chill."

Yet she knew, as surely as Arabella herself, that the chill lay within, and too deep for comfort. Arabella suffered Mrs Pratt to put an arm to her shoulder and to lead her, unresisting, to bed, first thanking both Hillier and Luke for their caring. She bade them a tired good-night, unaware that the night was ended and an early dawn was already breaking. At Luke's side she halted and put a hand affectionately to his arm.

"Francis will never rest meekly, Luke," she said. "It is not his way. He will live every hour to the full and with the joy and vigour of old . . . else life will not be worth a candle! I will fret and grieve and chivvy him unfairly, but I would have it no other way."

Without Knatchfield Grange, Dr Munro turned his horse towards the main highway to the village, for his house was on the farthest side. He felt suddenly old and drained of energy, emotionally spent. At the approach to a byway, he was startled into wakefulness by some movement, little more than a passing shadow, yet his mount, too, was disturbed, for it shied and all but threw him. A marauding fox, perhaps, or a sheep escaped the stone wall of a fold? He could not be sure as he struggled for control of the reins. Yet, in glancing back, he saw in the burgeoning light that it was no stray animal, but the figure of a man, secretive, fiercely intent upon not being seen. He would have returned to face the man, but tiredness and fear defeated him. The movements had been stealthy, furtive even. A poacher, perhaps, or some vagrant upon the roads seeking a barn or dry outhouse to shelter for the night? It was none of his affair. With a sigh, he set the horse to a gallop and dismissed the loiterer from his mind.

Chapter Sixteen

Upon the following morn, Francis, although pale and enervated, had visibly improved. Despite Arabella's strictures that he remain abed until Dr Munro's arrival, he was already fretting at his inactivity and demanding vociferously that his clothes be brought.

"Damn it, Arabella!" he expostulated. "I am not a confounded lily of the field!"

"You are pale and waxen enough to pass for one!" Arabella rejoined briskly, ignoring his muttered imprecations. "You will remain there, Francis, until Dr Munro gives you leave."

"Gives me leave?" Francis demanded incredulously. "How can he give me leave? He is not my gaoler, Arabella! I am neither an invalid nor a declared lunatic. This is my house, my body. I will do precisely as I choose."

"Indeed?" Arabella enquired equably. "Then you had best do it in your nightshirt, my love, since I have removed all your clothing as a precaution."

"Precaution? Against what?" he demanded irately.

"Against the petulance and stubbornness you so plainly show."

Francis, miserably outwitted, tried sweet reasonableness, then threats, and finally coaxing, but to no avail.

"You are a vixen, Arabella!" he fumed impotently. "An artful, conniving creature, sly, and not to be trusted!"

"Then we are well matched," she said, unperturbed, "for it is a trick I learned from you – desperate ills need desperate remedies. Now, settle yourself against your pillows, Francis," she advised, "for Dr Munro would not wish to see you so sulky and perverse. He is a gentleman of the sweetest disposition."

"Hell and damnation, Arabella!" Francis exclaimed in irritation. "Why should he not be? He is the one who gives the orders, who pesters and plagues me. *I* am the one who suffers!"

"Then it is certainly not in silence!" Arabella said crisply.

Francis made one last ditch attempt to persuade her to produce his clothing, but without result. She remained unmoved and unimpressed.

"Well, at least send Luke to me," he requested, aggrieved. "I should be grateful for at least some intelligent conversation and a modicum of sympathy."

"Why, certainly, my dear," Arabella promised blandly. "I will fetch him at once."

Francis relaxed visibly, and sank back against his pillows.

"But I warn you, my love," Arabella added, smiling, "that he has no notion of where your clothes are hid . . . and I fancy if you are contemplating an early morning ride that a gallop with nightshirt flying might earn you a reputation for eccentricity . . . as well as a chill."

"It would certainly startle the ladies hereabouts," Francis admitted, smiling involuntarily, good humour restored.

"As a diversion," Arabella reflected, straight faced, "I would place it a little above needlepoint, but well in advance of croquet . . . Indeed, it might well give an entirely new meaning to the phrase, 'the polite arts'." With a wickedly irrepressible smile at Francis she eased open the door and walked sedately without.

Luke, unable to sleep from concern for Francis, had arisen early and made a frugal breakfast. He had little appetite and fearful of disturbing Arabella he had put on his warm overcoat and set out for a stroll in the grounds and into the lanes beyond. The morning air was crisp and cold and by walking in solitude he felt that he might better come to terms with Francis's illness and find peace of mind. In the short time that he had been at Knatchfield Grange, the Crawshays had become more to him than friends, he thought of them now with real affection, with the closeness of blood kin. The lawns were misted still with dew, and the gravel of the carriageway beneath his feet darkened with its wetness. The small stones crunched beneath his boot soles, and that and the gentle stirring of the breeze in the leaves of the trees were the only recognisable sounds. There was, Luke thought, an almost eerie desolation about the gardens of Knatchfield Grange before the household was properly astir, as if life itself were in a state of suspended animation. There was an absence of birdsong and of birds themselves, and if there were foraging insects or small furred or cold-blooded creatures watching him, then they kept themselves silent and well hid. In the dense, overgrown shrubbery which bordered the curve of the carriageway, the dark leaves were misted with a filigree of cobwebs, silvered and drenched with dew, so that each separate droplet glittered and shone diamond bright. The effect was gauzy and delicately light, as if a soft veil had been spun over all. Luke paused for a moment, marvelling at its intricacy, its gossamer fineness. Then a sudden piercing cry and the sound of frantically hurrying footsteps sent him running to the curve of the carriageway to see what was amiss.

So blindly was the figure hurrying, and in such a panic to escape, that Luke was all but knocked off his feet by the sheer force of the impact as their bodies collided. Yet even with the breath torn from him, he somehow managed to retain a hold upon the panting, struggling creature in his grasp.

"Miss Pritchard? Nerissa?" He released her, momentarily made speechless by surprise.

"Oh, Captain Farrow, it is you, sir . . . I thought . . ." Whatever she thought, she was unable to speak of it lucidly, for she was trembling too violently, periously close, Luke thought, to a swoon.

"What is it?" he demanded urgently. "Has someone threatened you? Made attack? Wait here!" he commanded. "I will search him out."

"No!" She clung to him, terrified still. "There is no

one. It was what I saw, believed . . ." She broke off, too distraught to continue.

Luke tried to calm her, and held her close to still her trembling.

"I beg you, sir, do not leave me," she pleaded despairingly. "I will show you what it is, what made me cry out so violently."

Luke put a supporting hand to her arm, feeling the fierce agitation which still beset her, and walked with her in awkward silence towards the gates of the Grange.

"Dear God! It is monstrous! Obscene!" The cry was torn from him as he ran forward in a rage of disbelief and disgust. The crude gallows of wood was hammered firm into the grass of the lawn, the figure, in gentlewoman's clothes, dangling grotesquely from the noose. The hanged victim turned and twisted sickeningly with every twist of the breeze.

"I thought, sir, that it was real," Nerissa said, shuddering anew. "I feared that it was Mrs Crawshay, you see? I could not turn and run lest she still be alive . . . have need of me."

Luke stepped forward grimly to see the hideous figure more clearly. He was filled not only with horror at the outrage, but a murderous hate, a fury for revenge.

"There is something pinned to the sleeve," Nerissa blurted, "some writing, but I was too . . . afeared to read it. Could not," she confessed with honesty.

Luke unpinned the note, revulsion forcing gall into his throat even as he read aloud the scrawled words.

"Thief! Liar! Cheat! Go, else you will end up on the gallows! Return to me what is mine!"

"Who has written it?" Nerissa demanded in bewilderment. "And to whom?" She stared at Luke in anguish, begging, "What does it mean?"

"I do not know, Nerissa," he confessed, voice low. "I only know that we must destroy it, and this . . . this obscenity with it, else it will destroy Mrs Crawshay's peace of mind."

"The justices?" Nerissa said helplessly. "Would it not be wise to alert the justices?"

"No! You must trust me in this, for I can give no real explanation . . . You understand?"

Nerissa nodded.

"You have heard that Major Crawshay suffered a collapse in the night? That Dr Munro and Dr Brace were summoned?"

"Yes." Her voice was tight. "Mrs Pratt was greatly distressed and told me of it . . . 'tis why I sought escape, came out walking alone." She hesitated, blurting uncomfortably, "The sickness is grave, I fear, Captain Farrow, for she would not have wept else. She cares for Mrs Crawshay and the major above all others."

"That is why we must spare Mrs Crawshay the hurt of this, Nerissa. She has grief and worry enough. It would burden her needlessly, rob her of peace of mind and security."

Nerissa stared at him, but did not reply.

"Are you with me in this, Nerissa? Will you help, or at least keep the matter hid?" he implored.

"I will help, sir, and speak of it to no one. You have my solemn word."

He reached out impulsively and clasped her hand, feeling its flesh cold and lifeless within his own. Then they turned themselves grimly to the task of dismantling the grisly set-piece.

The figure which had so horrified and plagued her was no more than a scarecrow of straw, featureless, and the barest parody of human flesh. Yet in handling it Nerissa felt only revulsion, the most primitive dread, as if the evil in the mind of the monster who had created it still lived within. Its very limpness seemed the limpness of death, the elegant clothing the cruellest funeral garb. It was a caricature. Hideous. Mocking . . . but Nerissa would not allow herself to be deterred. She clung to it fiercely while Luke, with clumsy effort, wrenched the uprights of the makeshift gallows from the disordered lawn. Sickness rose in her throat, the sourness of gall, but she followed his instructions dutifully, dragging the tattered thing with her, not daring to glance at the hideously blank face, the spilled straw from its limbs. She had trailed in Luke's wake,

214

crossing the carriageway when he indicated that the coast was clear, dragging herself and the scarecrow effigy into the shelter of a copse beyond. Luke had been forced to leave her, for he had repeated journeys to make carrying the heavy spars that had made up the gallows. Although its construction had been crude through haste, the wood was solid, and its removal demanded all his concentration and effort. Nerissa applied herself stoically to dismembering the figure, her fingers oftimes trembling so painfully that she could scarce steady them to remove its bonnet and clothes. From time to time Luke returned, lugging the beams of wood, hauling them into the undergrowth, concealing them as best he could. Nerissa, absorbed in her task, was only vaguely aware of his occasional cries and the sounds of the beams being dragged across the ferny floor of the copse, their passage muffled and laboured as his breathing. So intent were they upon their respective tasks that no word passed between them, no acknowledgement of their nearness one to the other.

When all was done, Nerissa, without bidding, scattered the straw amongst the thorn and bramble of the copse and rolled the clothing into a bundle, concealing it under a heap of loose stones. Luke, his work completed, glanced about him, satisfied. His face was grimed from sweat and dirt, hands skinned raw, and his fine clothing streaked and dishevelled. Nerissa was scarcely more presentable, for her new clothing bore a scattering of fine chaff and leavings of straw, some of which had lodged in her hair and bonnet. She felt its dusty dryness thickening her throat and nostrils and sneezed with shattering violence. Her own handkerchief was so pathetically small and insubstantial that Luke smilingly handed her his own, saying, "I'll own, Miss Pritchard, that I have never before had so immediate and savage effect upon any young lady in my company."

"Nor have I, sir, ever reacted so strongly," she admitted ruefully. "I feel that my return in such a state will not pass unnoticed."

"Then you will allow me to escort you," Luke gallantly held out his arm, "and they may gossip and speculate wildly and to their hearts' content!" As she hesitated, he took her hand and placed it firmly over his own, continuing with evident amusement, "It will provide them a splendid diversion, do you not agree, Miss Pritchard?"

"I do not, sir." Nerissa's voice was subdued, her face painfully flushed, and immediately Luke was all contrition.

"I think it best, sir, if we go our separate ways, return alone," she rebuked quietly, "for then we may better slip in unseen."

He looked so awkwardly chastened that she exclaimed at once, and without artifice, "It is not your company I reject, Captain Farrow, for I would appreciate it above all else . . . but, if they speculate upon our meeting, might they also not speculate upon the damage to the lawn? They would be hard pressed to invent explanation."

Her fine blue eyes were sparkling with mischief, her mouth upturned in a smile, and Luke, brushing a piece of errant straw from the soft curve of her cheek, could not resist dropping a kiss upon the edges of her lips.

She stared at him for a long moment in curiosity, then turned abruptly upon her heel, gathering up the hem of her skirt and hurrying silently from the copse. Luke hurried after her, taking her arm, pulling her round urgently to face him.

"I beg that you will forgive what has occurred, Miss Pritchard. Nerissa," he said stiffly. "It was presumptuous of me to kiss you, and foolishly indiscreet . . . I have no excuse for taking such regrettable advantage. It was crass and over-familiar . . ." When Nerissa made no reply he blurted, "I have reason only, not excuse."

"And the reason, Captain Farrow?"

"That you have been so eager to help Mrs Crawshay . . . that I am so deeply in your debt." He floundered into strained silence.

"I need no payment for what I have done, Captain Farrow." The rebuke was sharp, her hurt plain. "My loyalty and affection for Mrs Crawshay are as deep as your own. You have already had my word, sir, that I will not speak of what we saw . . . that monstrous gallows upon the lawn." Her voice broke painfully with recollection and with the humiliation of knowing that his kiss had been no more than a gesture, meaningless, and all too soon regretted. She pulled away defiantly from Luke's restraining touch and without a backward glance lifted the hem of her skirts and ran blindly across the carriageway, through the gateway of the Grange and across the lawns and within. Hot tears stung her eyes, and shock and shame were added to her misery. It was with relief that she gained the solace of her room unseen.

Washing the treacherous tears from her face then changing her dishevelled clothing and brushing her hair into order gave her pause to think. She could not deny it. Her shame was not in allowing Captain Farrow to kiss her so negligently, like some . . . field whore or back-street doxy, but in the enjoyment it had given her. It was a sensation of the greatest pleasure, like no warmth of emotion she had ever known. Fierce. All consuming. Even to relive it in memory stirred her with longings she would not define. Had Captain Farrow but asked her, she would have gone to him gladly, offering herself openly and without false pride. The truth was that he did not want her. He had made his rejection agonisingly plain. He probably pitied her and thought to offer her consolation. There was no consoling her now. Nerissa sat down and wept for a new life that had promised so much and was as barren and loveless as the old.

Luke, gazing after her, was strangely disturbed. He would have followed her, to make proper explanation, but knew that with so much at stake he dare not arouse undue interest or suspicion. He could not regret the impulse that had made him kiss Nerissa, only that it had caused her distress. It would have surprised her had she known that Luke thought of her as a spirited young woman, intelligent and desirable. It had not entered his mind to reject her because of the disparity in their situations, but because of the danger such a liaison might cause.

Francis was sick and incapacitated and could not be told of the violence, that obscene gallows set up in the grounds to terrify and destroy. No more could he confide in

Arabella or even the servants, with the possible exception of Hillier, who could be trusted to value their safety, even above his own life. No. The justice, Sir Charles Hanford, was his only hope. He might provide guard upon the house, and do it circumspectly without arousing undue suspicion. There was proof now in the presence of the note and in the finding of the gallows. There had been no alternative but to dismantle it, yet if the justice doubted him then he could take him to where the remnants of it lay hidden. What should he do about the desecration of the lawn, Luke wondered. Perhaps he had best leave it for Sir Charles to inspect. Certainly he must first speak of it to Hillier, warn him of what had occurred and ask him to keep it well hidden from others. It could be dismissed as an act of unprovoked vandalism by some vagrant or some drunkard in his cups. Yes, that might well be accepted by the rest should it be accidentally discovered and made known before his return from Lanelay Court, for there would soon be gardeners, grooms and yard servants stirring.

Luke decided that before leaving so precipitately he would need to go within and make himself presentable, for he would make a sorry spectacle upon the roads, and ill served for formal visiting. Besides, he must make some plausible explanation to Arabella for his untimely absence and alert Hillier into keeping constant guard.

Luke, crossing the carriageway to the house, saw Nerissa's footprints dark among the silvered dew that still misted the grass and felt a stirring of affection. How small her footprints seemed, already fading, swift and transient as the dew itself. Yet how bravely she had helped him, although the terror which it caused her and the revulsion could not be hid . . . He could think of no other woman, save Arabella perhaps, who would have reacted so selflessly and with such practical courage. Nerissa was a woman of rare spirit and intelligence, a woman to trust. He could think of none among those mincing, affected gentlewomen whom he had known in the past who could hold a candle to her . . . no, not for beauty nor bravery. She was unique, distinguished in every degree . . . At another time, in another situation, he might have pursued

218

her wholeheartedly, declaring his interest openly, even making formal declaration of his intent. For the moment he could say nothing. His duty now was to Arabella and Francis. It must consume all his attention, command all his actions. He could not afford to be deflected from his need to protect them. It would cause too great a danger. Beyond that, it could lead to a violent death . . . another's, or his own.

Once safely ensconced in his room, Luke washed away the grime from his task of dismantling the mock gallows and secreting it within the wood. Then he set out his soiled clothing to be laundered by the servants. The garments would be returned in pristine condition, impeccably starched and ironed, and in the absence of a valet none would question their former disreputable state. He dressed with special care, in tight-fitting doeskin inexpressibles and hessian boots, with a shirt of finely pleated linen, extravagantly high collared and with a ruffle of lace at the cuffs. Over all he donned a favourite jacket of pearl-grey worsted, with a velvet rolled collar in a darker tone. He would tell Arabella that Sir Charles Hanford had sent a note by messenger, inviting him to take luncheon at Lanelay Court, for he had discovered by chance that they could claim a distant kinship. It was a slender enough excuse and scarcely convincing, but he could think of no other reason for leaving Knatchfield with Francis so cruelly disabled. He would assure her that he would return as soon as he decently could, and that he would tell the justice of Francis's temporary illness and find out what efforts had been made to find the writer of Arabella's threatening note.

Luke was concerned that she might consider his visit to the justice heartless and ill considered, in view of Francis's sickness. Yet it was imperative that he go, and keep her in ignorance of the latest outrage and threat to her safety.

In the event, Arabella was so absorbed in caring for Francis and awaiting Dr Munro's return, that she posed neither questions nor objection Indeed, save to remark

219

that Luke was looking extremely elegant, she made no comment at all.

"You will take care, Arabella?" he urged in leaving. "You will take no foolish risks until this affair is settled . . . the writer caught?"

"No. My greatest risk will lie in trying to keep Francis safely abed until Dr Munro calls!" she answered, smiling. "I'll swear, Luke, that it would be less wearing to nurse a raging bull! He is snorting and fuming quite outrageously. I half expect him to paw the ground and charge!"

"He is improved, then?" Luke asked gently.

"Yes. He has strength and spirit, certainly . . ."

The truth lay unspoken between them.

Luke took her hand and hesitated, biting at his lip, wondering how much he could safely tell her without adding to her alarm.

"You will take care, Arabella?" he repeated helplessly. "Promise that you will take care."

Recognising the urgency with which he spoke, Arabella said, to ease his fears, "I shall stay beside Francis, I promise, until you return. None will harm me here, not in my own house."

"I have spoken to Hillier, bidden him keep watch," Luke assured quietly. "He will allow no one to enter unchallenged."

"Then he had best make exception for Dr Munro and his nurse," Arabella reminded with an attempt at lightness, "else it will be I who will be taken to my bed, worn out with Francis's tantrums. A rest in Bedlam would serve me better!"

He smiled his understanding.

"You will see that Miss Pritchard . . . Nerissa, does not venture too far afield, Arabella?"

She looked at him with open curiosity, seeing him flush under her scrutiny.

"I will keep her close at hand," she promised, "find some excuse and useful occupation. You need have no fears for her safety, Luke."

He nodded, and took awkward leave.

Arabella, gazing after him, thought with surprise and delight, So that is the way the wind blows.

She hurried off to tell Francis of her intriguing discovery. Luke was most certainly protective towards Nerissa. If not yet enamoured, then he was undeniably susceptible to her young companion's charms. Arabella was delighted. She held no stuffy conventional theories about barriers of birth or breeding. Etiquette and social pleasantries could soon be learned and at best were no more than a veneer, a surface gloss. If Nerissa was determined and industrious enough to apply herself to conquering reading and writing, then such superficial polish could be easily acquired. Observation and imitation would suffice. Nerissa was intelligent and quick to learn, and not easily overawed, as she had shown in her dealings with Richard de Granville at Holly Grove fair. No, should Luke fall in love with her companion, then Nerissa would work devotedly at entering his world, at supporting him at whatever he chose to undertake. She was at ease with herself and would be at ease with others, whatever their rank or station in life. Luke and Nerissa had much in common: loyalty, compassion, courage and humour. It was that basic closeness, the understanding, that she and Francis had so long shared that made love and marriage an adventure. A joy to be cherished. Arabella would not allow herself to think of what lay ahead, an empty using-up of days . . . a limb torn from a living tree. She took herself to task for her morbidity and, with a defiant straightening of her shoulders and a smile carefully in place, entered Francis's bed-chamber. Already, in her mind, she was concocting schemes to bring Luke and Nerissa together, to foster the attraction between them. She greeted Francis with a kiss and settled companionably at his bedside. She would not tell him yet awhile of the romance she suspected. He would dismiss it as no more than womanly foolishness, or, worse, try to bait Luke with a heavyhandedness certain to blight or destroy.

"Are you more comfortably settled now, Francis?" she asked with wifely concern.

"Damn it, Arabella! You know full well I am not! I lie

here like a trussed chicken, with as little comfort and less to divert me."

"Dr Munro will be here soon enough," she murmured pleasantly. "He has promised to bring a reliable woman to nurse you . . . that might prove diversion?"

"She will be an ogre! A virago!" Francis expostulated furiously. "I will not have her come near me, Arabella! Be warned. I will not be wet-nursed like some puking infant!"

"Then you had best not behave like one, my love!" Arabella advised equably. "Else she might banish you to the nursery without toys and companions, where you may sulk in disgrace."

"I shall pay her off," Francis threatened. "I shall pay her most handsomely and claim that her services are no longer required."

Arabella raised her eyebrows expressively.

"I shall say that I have gaoler and dragon enough in you!"

"A pretty speech!" Arabella declared. "And it will win you no favours!" adding blandly, "Your clothes will not be forthcoming until Dr Munro gives you leave to stir from that bed."

"Then you had best stay here and try to amuse me."

"Would you have me breathe fire? Or shall I bring you an improving book from the library and flick over the pages with my tail?"

Francis's lips twitched, but he said nothing.

"I might try lighting all the candles at one blow, then set flame to your pillows for an encore," she suggested. "Will that prove diversion enough?"

"I believe," Francis said, "that I hear Dr Munro's carriage arriving. We had best defer our entertainment, Arabella . . . although it might have proved vastly amusing. The heat might have made up for the paucity of my clothing. Besides, it gives me stronger reason to persuade him that I would be wiser to stand upon my own two feet."

Arabella looked at him quizzically as he confessed, straight faced, "Any danger without could not hold a candle to the danger that lurks in my bed."

"Why, Major Crawshay, sir, I do believe that you have the audacity to flirt with me openly . . . I find that remark ungentlemanly and indelicate, sir. You are unfit company for a lady." She gave a mischievous smile. "I'll own, sir, that it is the sole reason why I married you."

Arabella heard Francis's delighted laughter follow her without as she hurried to meet Dr Munro and the gorgon.

Luke's unheralded arrival at Lanelay Court caused more commotion than he had anticipated, for it coincided with Sir Charles Hanford's climbing impatiently into his waiting carriage beneath the *porte-cochère*. His errand was clearly urgent and Luke was about to make stilted apology for his unwarranted intrusion when the justice descended in haste. Luke had barely time to swing himself from the stirrup before Sir Charles was shaking his hand feverishly, declaring, "Oh, I am exceedingly glad to see you, Captain Farrow, exceedingly glad. I was at this very moment on my way to Knatchfield Grange to see Major Crawshay on a matter of the greatest urgency . . ." He broke off, bewildered by Luke's gravity. "Is something amiss, Captain Farrow?" he asked sharply. "Mrs Crawshay has suffered no harm?"

"No, sir. I fear that it is Major Crawshay who is indisposed. He has suffered a severe collapse . . . a recurrence of an old affliction."

He did not elaborate further, and Sir Charles, plainly believing it to be the aftermath of some battlefield injury or fever, did not pursue it, save to ask, "He will recover, Captain Farrow?"

"Yes. Most certainly." Luke's hesitation had been fractional.

"I think, sir, that you had best come within," the justice ordered firmly. "I have learnt something of the gravest concern . . . something which cannot be ignored."

"The note, sir?" he asked anxiously. "It concerns the note to Mrs Crawshay . . . Arabella?"

"Yes. I fear so."

"Then, sir, I must add to your disquiet. Something occurred at Knatchfield this very morn . . . something sickening in its violence. It is why I have ridden out to apprise you."

Sir Charles took Luke by the elbow and without a wasted word steered him determinedly within. He listened to Luke's account of the finding of the gallows in near silence, before exclaiming impassionedly, "Why, it is the act of a madman! Disgusting! Obscene! I can scarce credit the grossness of such an act." He studied the note minutely, murmuring angrily beneath his breath, his words inaudible.

"I own, sir, that it made no sense to me," Luke confessed uneasily. "It was clearly meant for Arabella, and the effigy was dressed in the clothing she might have worn. The very same colours and styling. It was meant to shock and alarm, to terrify her."

"Then we had best ride out at once, Captain Farrow, before real violence is done."

"You know the culprit, sir? Have reason to suspect someone of harassing her?"

"Of resenting her, Captain Farrow, and of planning to do her harm. I have, but an hour since, seen the attorney who handled the transfer of Knatchfield Grange, a close friend of mine and legal adviser to the old gentleman who so recently died and left the property in Mrs Crawshay's keeping."

Luke looked at him in confusion.

"It was hers by right of inheritance. It is a family property, legally entailed. None can hope to challenge it, nor lay claim!"

"Yet someone has?"

He nodded. "Someone obsessed by a belief that he is the true inheritor. A man bitterly deluded and close to murder."

"Murder?" Luke's voice was raw with shock.

"I but an hour ago left the attorney's bedside. He was brutally attacked last night, savagely assaulted and left for dead. I was called to his house this morning, after he regained consciousness and pleaded that I be summoned."

"He laid complaint? Knew his assailant?"

"He named him, and I have sworn out a warrant for his arrest. Hugo Curtis is a vicious man, Captain Farrow; one who will not cavil at murder. He is beyond reason or control, and Mrs Crawshay is cruelly at risk. I have sent urgent instruction for the militia to hunt him down."

"But she is unguarded, Arabella is unguarded!" Luke exclaimed, leaping to his feet in anguish. "Francis cannot defend her, and there is none other armed."

Sir Charles pulled open a drawer of his desk and, in silence, handed Luke a pistol and a pouch of shot and powder.

"And you, sir?" Luke demanded.

"I am armed, Captain Farrow, and am prepared to use my pistol," he said quietly. "I am armed and ready. Believe it!"

Chapter Seventeen

To Arabella's relief Dr Munro had succeeded in persuading Francis that it would be crass foolishness to leave his sick-bed too soon. He should rest for the next twenty-four hours at least, he was advised, to ward off danger of relapse or further complications. After that he might gradually return to his normal activities – always with the proviso that he should not tire himself unnecessarily, nor subject himself to undue stress. Francis had reacted docilely enough in the physician's presence, indeed, he had been sweet reason itself, and Dr Munro had been agreeably surprised by his tractability. Arabella, who later bore the brunt of her husband's petulance and rising irritability, was amazed to hear Francis described as "the ideal patient". Yet, with wifely forbearance, she refrained from contradicting it. If she secretly thought that it was Dr Munro who was in need of treatment for such acute short sightedness, then she did not speak of that either. He was entitled to his euphoria. As for the "gorgon", she did indeed appear to be a grim-faced harridan. Yet, unaccountably, Francis and she took an immediate liking to each other and developed a quite extraordinary rapport.

Miss Euphemia Gibbs, as she was pleased to call herself, was hired to attend the patient for the next twenty-four hours, when he was confined to his bed with a promise that she would, thereafter, be available by day or by night to attend the patient's needs. She was, Arabella thought, all starched efficiency and brusqueness, with a backbone as rigid as her sense of decorum. Discipline was equally inflexible. Yet Francis, with his military background, seemed to thrive upon the rules and regulations

226

she enforced. Arabella, quickly deposed by this despot, was torn between relief and pique – relief that Francis was in such competent hands; pique that her services were now extraneous. Miss Euphemia Gibbs was indisputably ruler of the sick-room. Stocky, thick set and with a gnarled fist of a face, she was not a thing of beauty. Yet Arabella had hopes that she might prove a joy, if not for ever then certainly for as long as Francis had need of her services. Despite her forbidding appearance and autocratic air, her patient's every whim and need were indulged with supreme gentleness. Arabella was treated with polite reserve, her presence tolerated although not actually encouraged. She had the uncomfortable feeling that Miss Euphemia Gibbs saw her as a necessary irritant, like leeches or a mustard plaster, to be applied sparingly then quickly removed. It both amused and exasperated Arabella, but her main feeling was one of overwhelming relief that this formidably efficient creature was there to take charge. Moreover, she could be relied upon to care for Francis in future, as need and dependency deepened. Had the good woman been Medusa herself, then Arabella would unhesitatingly have embraced her. As it was, Miss Gibbs was a basically kindly creature who suffered none but Francis gladly, if at all. That Francis in turn liked and trusted her was more than Arabella had dared to hope. She was happy, for the moment, to surrender her husband to Miss Euphemia Gibbs's ministrations, and to seek out Nerissa, as Luke had asked.

With Francis still sick and abed, she reasoned, her proposed visits in the carriage might be postponed without giving offence. Those acquaintances and neighbours who were due to call formally upon her could be sent hand written notes by messenger, and their indulgence sought. For the moment she was content merely to dress warmly and venture into the garden with Nerissa for company. They would find the shelter of a garden seat beside a hedge, or else venture as far as the gazebo at the end of the rose walk, or the belvedere, for relaxation. Arabella was painfully aware of how drained of energy she felt, how low and exhausted. The menace of the note and the shock of Francis's collapse had taken harsh toll of her, physically and emotionally. She would be grateful to unwind in the tranquillity of the garden, in the clear cold air.

Nerissa, recovering from the terrible oppression which she had felt at sight of the gallows upon the lawn, and from the effects of her meeting with Luke, was only too pleased to accompany Arabella. Well wrapped in their warmest clothing, with bonnets and pelisses and sturdy shoes, they set out companionably along the carriageway. For an anxious moment Nerissa was afraid that Arabella's need for escape might take them towards the gates of Knatchfield, and the vandalism to the lawns be plainly seen.

She was nervously rehearsing some ploy in her mind, some distraction, when Arabella said, "I think, perhaps, the walled garden, Nerissa . . . the wind is keen and we will have shelter in the belvedere . . ." She hesitated, confiding, "If Francis has need of me, then I may be easily reached. I would not wish to venture too far."

Nerissa, with sickening memory of the gallows upon the lawn, murmured agreement. Had they been wise to venture out at all, she wondered uneasily. Yet surely Captain Farrow would be within call and even now watching them surreptitiously perhaps from the windows of the house.

She shivered involuntarily and Arabella said contritely, "You are cold, Nerissa. It was thoughtless of me to make you venture out. Would you rather return to the house? I shall be quite at ease alone."

"No!" Arabella looked surprised at the force of Nerissa's denial as she repeated, less vehemently, "No . . . It is a pleasure to be in the open air . . . I would sooner stay, Mrs Crawshay, if you will allow."

"I shall be glad of your company, "Arabella admitted. "It has been a long night, Nerissa, one I would be loath to repeat. Even now, with Francis recovering, I am still agitated and ill at ease. I fear that I will be poor company."

As Nerissa made to demur, Arabella continued with conviction, "I know that you have suffered grief and loss of your own and know the depths of it . . . and will understand. You will not take my silence as displeasure, or criticism of you."

228

"No . . . I will understand." The words were quietly spoken.

"There is none who can take grief from you," Arabella murmured. "Others may share, but . . ." She broke off helplessly.

"Others may share, but they cannot deaden the hurt, nor diminish it," Nerissa blurted with excoriating honesty. "It is something locked within . . . set apart, and none can know the hurt of it, or the loneliness it brings."

There was silence between them, and Nerissa, shamed by her impulsiveness, and at revealing so much of herself, flushed and would have made awkward apology, but Arabella linked her arm through her companion's, saying truthfully, "I am glad that you are here, Nerissa, for I have sore need of friendship and the support of one who understands. One to whom I may speak freely . . . It will help to ease the burden of Francis's sickness," admitting regretfully, "although it may well lay a greater burden upon you."

"There is no burden in friendship!" The denial was spontaneous and firm. "It is privilege," she added awkwardly, "as in coming to Knatchfield and all."

"You are happy here, Nerissa? You have no regrets?"

"No. I have no regrets." None save Major Crawshay's sickness, she might have added, and the sorrow that must surely come. Yet she would stay and bring whatever ease and consolation she might. She regretted, too, the menace that had come to Knatchfield Grange, the savagery of the letter, and that effigy upon the gallows, twisting and turning endlessly from the hangman's noose. She regretted more the cruelty that set her apart from Captain Farrow; the social barriers that could never be breached.

Arm in arm and deeply immersed in thought, Arabella and Nerissa took the stone-flagged pathway through the walled rose walk and thence into the secluded garden with the grassy incline that housed the belvedere. A place to find solace and peace, with naught for distraction save the glorious vista; a prospect of trees, undulating parkland and gleaming water. With a sigh of relief Arabella, with Nerissa beside her, entered the calm of the belvedere. They settled themselves companionably upon the wooden bench, the better to study the view. For the first time, the cares of the day seemed to recede, set into a wider perspective, the endless fusion of time and nature. It offered renewal and hope. An avowal of what was past and, with God's grace, a promise of what might yet be.

Hugo Curtis had kept well clear of the highway, hiding in woods and in the lee of hedges, finding shelter and concealment where he might. Now, with the coming of daylight, his position became more perilous, his need to escape more urgent . . . Yet even more vital than self-preservation was the need for revenge, the fury to see justice done. He had been cheated of what was rightfully his; his patrimony. Knatchfield Grange had been in his family's keeping for generations past. None should be allowed to wrest it from them. It was no better than common theft; a looting and sacking of another's property. It should be declared a crime and punished by law . . . Yet if the law were corrupt, and none willing to change and enforce it, then a man must right it by his own efforts. He could not stand meekly by and allow his inheritance to be plundered. They were vandals, thieves, criminals all! They should be strung from a gallows; allowed to rot . . . left prey to carrion and scavenging filth.

He dragged himself painfully from the shallow ditch where he had rested, his limbs stiffly aching, his fingers numbed by cold. It was that old man who was to blame, the one who had bought Knatchfield, taking possession as if by God-given right. As if pounds and pence were buying no more than bricks and mortar or worthless stone . . . Well, he was dead now, and might go to the devil, for it was no more than he deserved! As for that attorney, he was a liar and a cheat, a filthy scoundrel who deserved the beating he got. It had been a satisfation, a triumph even, to set about him in earnest. His sickening pleas for mercy and his craven babblings had been easy to ignore. It was to be hoped that he was dead and could violate and cheat no more, for he would have long to repent it.

Curtis glanced about him uneasily, moving stealthily

230

and with agonising slowness. He was only dimly aware of the strange figure he made, his fine clothes smeared with blood and filth, hair disordered and matted from living in the open air, always a prey to the elements. He felt no hunger, for the restless gnawing within him was stronger. He felt only a hunger and thirst for revenge, for securing what was his own. It had taken him no little effort to create the gallows and to fashion the crude straw figure and dress it in his dead wife's clothes. He had lingered near Knatchfield, waiting his chance, alert always for the right time to strike. He had almost been trapped by that bloody physician riding out, by Munro's insane curiosity, yet something had saved him from discovery and recognition. Some providence, whether divine or hellishly raised. It was said that the devil looks after his own.

Despite his fatigue and the raw ache in his flesh, Curtis could not help but smile. It was *they* who were on the devil's side, his enemies. They were the transgressors. He was the victim. His head ached, and confusion clouded his mind as he tried and failed to make sense of things. God and the devil were inextricably mixed. He could not separate them, and bewilderment so excoriated and grieved him that he found himself railing impotently, then weeping aloud. His sobs were harsh and racked his body with pain, but he would take no rest, nor pause. That bitch at Knatchfield, that thieving whore, had snatched his life from him, seduced him of what he owned . . . For a brief moment memory of the makeshift gallows and the lifeless figure upon it pierced his befuddled mind. Dead then? No. She was sly and vindictive, determined to destroy him. Kill or be killed. He was not aware that his destruction was already begun and that none could halt it. He could only await its end.

When he came again to Knatchfield Grange, it was with a sense of returning home. He felt neither triumph nor fear, only a knowledge of the inevitability of things. An ending. His mind now seemed preternaturally clear. He had come to claim his own; to take possession. His father had been forced to sell Knatchfield, crippled by the greed

231

and avarice of others, betrayed into debt. Those whom he trusted had battened upon him like predatory hawks, tearing at flesh and nerve, devouring, laying bare. It was not enough that they had destroyed him, caused his death and disgrace. They had turned their blood lust upon those who came after.

Hugo Curtis felt the tears spurt again to his eyes, hot and shaming, raw as a burn. He felt no fear for himself, but he wept for what was lost to him and could never be restored, those whose limbs and loving had fashioned him, and were no more . . . He must take care to move stealthily and not be seen. With the assault upon the attorney and his attempted murder, then the justice would have sworn a warrant. As like as not, the militia would have been called out to hunt him down, but he would not go lightly, nor surrender himself. It were better to die here, upon his own soil, than immured in some stinking prison.

He crept cautiously towards the pillared gateway of the house and peered apprehensively within. The gallows was gone. It has been discovered, taken away . . . But where, and by whom? The evidence of it remained in the torn grass and disfigured earth; an ugliness that jarred. He could only pray that it had served its purpose, brought terror and uncertainty to those within, that Arabella Crawshay knew the same fierceness of hurt that assailed him. He hoped that it pierced her through. His fingers crept involuntarily to the knife thrust into his leather belt at his waist, feeling the coldness of its metal hilt, closing exultantly upon it. If any stood in his way, then they would not live to rue it. Guilty or innocent, it was all the same. Those in her employ were traitors, tainted as she. Slowly, stealthily, and with his heart thudding so loudly at his ribs that he feared that it must burst apart, Hugo Curtis made his way through the shrubbery and to the long-neglected door to the east wing. He had spent his childhood in this house and knew every inch of it, every passage and stairway, every corner . . . hiding places that none save he had discovered. He could hide here for hours, days if need be, with none suspecting. There were priest holes and secret chambers, even an underground passage that led from a vaulted cellar to the raised turret in the garden . . . his childhood fort, the belvedere. If all else failed, it might still serve him now, as then, as a means of escape.

Luke, riding with furious concentration beside Sir Charles Hanford, felt a bleakness of despair engulf him, a sense of foreboding. Curtis was plainly deranged, a man obsessed. In his savage attack upon the attorney, he had shown that he would stop at nothing to gain revenge. Luke questioned his own wisdom now in riding out to alert the justice to the building of the gallows, the threat to Arabella. He had known it was the act of a madman, the note the ravings of a sick mind. Yet he had not wholly believed that it was more than an obscene prank; one designed to menace and terrify the mind. In attempting to murder the attorney, and callously leaving him for dead, Curtis had made threat reality. He had tried to kill once, viciously and in cold blood, and would not cavil at killing another. Had he known of Curtis's obsession with Knatchfield and his fury to regain it, then he would not have left Arabella unprotected. Francis was bed-bound and impotent to help, and Hillier, for all his loyalty and intelligence, was old, and would be unarmed. He would be no deterrent to one of Curtis's strength and resolution. The justice was no more at ease than Luke, his fear for Arabella making him gaunt faced and taciturn, ill inclined to speak. The two men rode in strained silence, urging their horses with a callousness that was alien to them. Already they were irritable and sweat streaked, their mounts lathered and ill at ease, their tortured breathing growing increasingly harsh . . . Yet they dared not slow their pace nor give them rest.

Luke exclaimed, in an anguish of frustration, "If Curtis is already at Knatchfield . . . if he finds Arabella alone and unprotected . . . ?"

"I cannot believe that he would be so foolish . . . that he would flaunt himself openly. He would be risking all!" The justice's voice held no conviction.

"If only Francis were not so damnably disabled . . . sick," Luke fumed wretchedly, "if the servants were armed."

"Then they might well prove more threat to Mrs Crawshay than Curtis himself!"

"How so?" Luke challenged abrasively.

"They might provoke violence . . . offer it carelessly."

"Perhaps."

"You are a man used to firearms, Captain Farrow, and therefore not given to rashness, impetuous action . . . If he is armed, then there will be one opportunity to halt Curtis, and one only."

"And I shall take it!" Luke said fervently.

"And without setting the lives of others in danger," the justice agreed quietly. "It would be poor victory were others to die with Curtis. He has brought violence enough!"

"And should I fail?"

"We are both armed, Captain Farrow." The promise was quietly made.

"Even should he escape, then the militia will hunt him down. They will spare him no mercy."

They rode on relentlessly and in fraught silence, the only immediate sounds those of harness and flailing hooves and the snorts and rasping breath of the horses.

The question in Luke's mind and the justice's stayed unspoken. Their fear was not that Curtis might escape the militia. They would find him. None could doubt it. They would pursue him and capture him, alive or dead. The fear was that it might already be too late.

Within Knatchfield Grange, Hillier, believing that Arabella was safely ensconced in the sick-room with Francis and Euphemia Gibbs, went conscientiously about his duties as major domo. He found that he could not set his mind entirely to his tasks, for the news which Captain Farrow had confided greatly troubled him. It was inconceivable that anyone could so hate Mrs Crawshay that he would be prepared to do her physical harm. Yet the hangman's noose and gallows, so contemptuously set up upon the lawns, was proof of some evil. Yes, "evil" was not too strong a word. It was a devilish trick, designed to intimidate and terrify, and only one corrupt and sick of mind would countenance such barbarity.

Hillier sighed and, wry faced, set out to find the head gardener, Bowles. He could not confide in him wholly, for he had promised Captain Farrow that he would tell no one of the grisly tableau that he and Miss Pritchard had discovered. It would merely serve to panic and alarm the household servants, and should Mrs Crawshay hear of it, then it would add a greater burden to the weight she already bore. Major Crawshay would not recover, that much was tragically clear. It was but a matter of time. In the face of that, all else seemed diminished, trivial even. Even the settled routine of living, the duties so painstakingly observed, were no salve. They offered no consolation. They were no more than a ritual, mechanical and without meaning. Well, life must go on, Hillier thought, and it were better that it should be ordered and disciplined than a shambles. He would concoct some story about the ravages to the lawn . . . some fallacy about scavenging foxes or human vandals. Bowles was no fool. He would suspect that some mischief was afoot and form his own conclusions. Yet he was reliable and conscientious and, above all, discreet. He would see that the damage was repaired, and, as like as not, would do the work himself, secretly, and without arousing the curiosity of others.

So deep in thought was he, and so intent upon hurrying through the maze of passageways below stairs, that he did not hear the muted click of a latch, the subdued footfalls beyond the panelled walls. Had he done so, he would have dismissed it as the scrabblings of a mouse in the wainscot, or else a rat in the cellars. As Hillier took the key from his belt and carefully unlocked the massive oak door to the garden, locking it methodically behind him, Hugo Curtis eased himself into the darkened passageway. It had been easier than he had thought, less hazardous. There was an excitement stirring within him, an exhilaration that could not be suppressed. He was home; back where all was familiar to him. He was safe here at Knatchfield, secure, as in the past. None should wrest it from him, claim it as their own. Knatchfield was his. It belonged to no other. He would fight for its present and future, as others had fought for its past. It was his God-given duty and none could defy or vanquish God. He was omnipotent. There were no sins nor crimes committed in His name, only righteousness. Justice. Whomsoever stood in the way of justice would be annihilated; cut down with the Almighty's sword of flame. He, Hugo Curtis, was the anointed sword-bearer. God's emissary. He would do proudly whatever must be done.

Hugo Curtis moved stealthily along the corridors, freezing whenever he heard a sound, concealing himself against the shadowed walls in the all-enveloping darkness. Knowledge and the dimness of light were his allies, protectively masking him from view. There were few servants using the tortuous passageways, and those scurrying through were restlessly bent upon some mission, their only desire to be quit of the dank and cold. They were ill-inclined to linger in the subterranean vaults or the grim passageways, and none was aware of Curtis's presence. Gradually, imperceptibly, he eased his way past the sculleries and kitchens, moving as cautiously and sure-footedly as a cat, and almost as soundlessly, trusting that the noise and bustle within would mask his passing. Fear and excitement lent him impetus and he felt a surge of fierce energy. He had but to mount the stairs from the basement now and the whole vista of the house lay before him. He would need to be more circumspect here, curb his impulsiveness, for the Great Hall would hold him in full view, make him vulnerable. He could not risk discovery, not with so much at stake . . .

With his heart thudding at his ribcage and a tightness at his throat, he eased himself past the door of the drawing room. Should the Crawshay woman be there, he would need to act quickly, overpower her before she could set up an alarm. He must rely upon shock and terror to first silence her, for should she cry aloud all would be lost. He could not suffer her to reach out to the bell-pull, no more must she be allowed to escape. His knife was razor sharp and its entry would be swift and soundless, its force lethal. Nervous excitement rose within him, tingling, filling him with unholy glee. He found himself laughing foolishly aloud, until caution gradually sobered him. He could not afford to rejoice too soon. Women such as she were sly and devious, cunning as serpents. He would need all his wits about him. She would twist herself about him, sinuous as a snake, poisonous, seeking to crush and destroy. Rage and self-pity consumed him. She was deliberately hiding from him, watching him unseen. Mocking. Derisory. He would not be victim! He would make attack, kill her with no word spoken, lest she disarm him with her wiles . . .

With growing anger and frustration, he moved from room to room. Where was she? Where was the bitch hiding? The Jezebel. The whore. He was trembling now, rage all but blinding him as he traversed the hall unseen and mounted the carved staircase to the bedchambers above. She need not think that she could elude him. He would find her, and soon, and by God she would rue it! The anger and resentment of years all but choked him, and spittle flecked the edges of his mouth. He could scarce breathe, scarce move. It was as though all life had fled him, all feeling. Then his hand moved instinctively towards the knob of the door and, with a cry torn deep from his throat, he flung the door wide.

It crashed upon its hinges, and Francis, eyes wide with shock, let out a curse and leapt from his bed. Curtis, startled and all but demented, ripped his knife from its sheath and lunged towards him, stabbing out wildly, slashing at Francis's raised arm. Blood spurted from the knife wound, crimson and bright, soaking his shirt sleeve. Francis, with no weapon and no way of escape, backed hard against the wall, trying to fend off the darting thrusts. If he could but drag the door of the bedside cabinet open, reach for his revolver. It was ready, and primed . . .

Even as he thought it, Curtis slashed fiercely again, then, screaming and hurling abuse, a virago attacked him. The earthenware chamber-pot crashed upon his skull, and with it a screeching, clawing frenzy of outraged flesh, irresistible, indestructible . . . For a brief moment after his skull was so brutally assaulted, Hugo Curtis had stayed upright, staring in disbelief, seemingly immune, then, with slow inevitability, had sunk to the floor.

Francis, almost as stunned as the victim by the suddenness and violence of the attack, had somehow managed to drag open the drawer and retrieve his pistol, then had collapsed gratefully upon the edge of the bed, his gun trained upon Curtis. He felt sapped of feeling, drained beyond endurance, scarce able, even, to keep the gun steady. All the while the blood dripped remorselessly from his arm, but he felt no pain from it. He felt nothing but a sense of unreality, the detachment of a dream.

"The very idea!" Euphemia Gibbs declared, outraged. "To burst into a sick-room and threaten the patient . . . The man is insane, clearly a lunatic!" Then, conscious of Francis's fatigue and pallor and the wound upon his arm, she ordered briskly, "Now, back into bed with you, Major Crawshay, lest more damage be done." As he made to protest, "At once, now!" she commanded firmly. "Do as I say! I will brook no argument!" She took the gun firmly from his unresisting hand, saying reassuringly, "You will have no need for this yet awhile. I do not think that the young . . . gentleman will be disposed towards more violence, even when he awakens." She set the pistol upon the bedside table, carelessly, as if it were a discarded dressing and of no account. "That wound upon your arm . . . "

"It is but a flesh wound," Francis protested, "and it has bled freely."

"Then that is to the good . . . but I must insist that Dr Munro be called to see it, for the knife might prove to be rusted, the blade unclean. You would not wish the flesh to fester, to become corrupt. Meanwhile, I shall clean and dress it for you . . . then I shall tidy you up, put you into a fresh nightshirt . . . "

Francis, despite his fatigue and inertia, began to laugh. The amusement began as the merest bubble within his throat, then grew and burgeoned until it exploded violently and he could scarcely check himself. His eyes filled with appreciative tears. They overflowed and ran, and his whole body shook with mirth, cleansing and quite unstoppable. When his hilarity was finally checked and died away, Euphemia Gibbs's broad, unlovely face was filled with warm humour, a gentleness that sat strangely upon her.

"Laughter is a release," she conceded fairly, "a rare healer, 'tis said. Yet I do not hold with too much of it.

238

It can weaken a body else." She set about tending his injured arm, saying with brisk reassurance, "It is the merest scratch. Scarce worth the bother of binding." When she was absorbed in tying up the wound, Hugo Curtis stirred and rose uncertainly to his feet, eyes glazed and seemingly witless. Then he stumbled towards the bedside cupboard and brought it crashing down upon himself, the gun exploding into violence as it was hurled against the floor. The bullet cracked harmlessly into the wainscot, and there was an appalled silence, then a fierce commotion without as the servants came urgently running. Euphemia Gibbs was not best pleased by the noisy invasion. She stood dour and tight lipped as Francis made garbled explanation and gave Hillier instruction to retrieve the pistol and Curtis's knife.

"You had best get him bound, Hillier, while he is still insensible . . . and set guard upon him," Francis ordered. "Then send for the justice. He will not be long in coming."

"I shall keep him in my sights, sir, with the gun trained upon him. He will not escape," Hillier promised grimly. "It is the offender you sought, sir?" he asked meaningfully.

"Yes, I am sure of it."

"Then thank God, sir!" Hillier declared fervently.

Euphemia Gibbs, who had been all but eclipsed by the surging, seething influx of bodies and the deadening cacophony of noise, suddenly came into her own. With arms akimbo and a voice like thunder, she commanded, "Out! Out, I say! I will have no more of it! This . . . this tower of Babel, this unseemly Bedlam! This is a sick-room, I will have you know. You, sir!" Her unyielding glare was upon Hillier. "Since you seem to be in charge, you will have this . . . rabble dispersed, and that creature removed elsewhere."

Sheepishly, and to awkward silence from the rest, Hillier complied.

"Now, Major Crawshay, sir, that little episode is closed," Euphemia Gibbs declared, "and I had best be about my lawful business. This place is a shambles, a veritable pig-sty, and I will not allow it! I shall send for

239

Dr Munro directly, and it would shame me should he see it thus. A sick-room should be a place of order and tranquillity, not a madhouse."

Francis surveyed the indomitable figure before him and despite his fatigue and sickness his lips curved into an irrepressible smile.

"With you beside me in battle, Miss Gibbs," he said in rueful admiration, "I would have no qualms. You are a paragon, ma'am! An inspiration. Worth any ten men."

An unbecoming blush suffused Euphemia Gibbs's face and neck as she declared primly, "I try my humble best, Major Crawshay, to do my duty." Her manner was jauntier, her intelligent eyes bright, as they exchanged a smile of complicity, a tacit understanding. "Now, I had best find you that clean nightshirt," she admonished. "I will be accused of neglecting you else."

Chapter Eighteen

Arabella and Nerissa, who had been returning from the garden that housed the belvedere, heard the sharp crack of the pistol shot as they entered the rose walk. They halted in shocked bewilderment then, realising that some violence had occurred, began running, panic stricken, towards the house.

"Dear God!" Arabella prayed aloud. "Let it not be Francis! Let Francis be safe!"

Nerissa, with memory of the gallows still raw, and the threat it posed, could scarce contain her fear. She was certain that the madman who had wrought such infamy had come seeking revenge and that Francis was his victim. She was aware of her anguished trembling and felt her limbs grow suddenly weak as she stumbled upon the pathway and all but fell. Major Crawshay was sick and vulnerable, unable to defend himself, she thought despairingly. He would make an easy target for a man deranged, one without conscience or pity. She must, in part, take blame for not revealing what she had seen . . . that hideous effigy and the hangman's noose. For a terrifying moment she feared that she would faint. Her throat grew painfully dry and her eyes misted. Such giddiness assailed her that she could barely stumble in Arabella's wake. Then, with an immense effort, she steadied herself. Anguished, tearful and with a pulse beating rawly at her throat, she entered the house at Arabella's heels. Where was Captain Farrow, she thought? Why had he not protected them? Given them warning? With a cruel intake of breath, she gave herself answer. Perhaps that was the root of it. It was not Major Crawshay who lay wounded, dead even, but Captain Farrow, Luke. The upsurge of grief all but stopped her heart, and the

241

pain was a physical blow. Should Luke Farrow die, then she knew that it was a loss from which she would never recover. She was in love with him . . . She could no more deny it, even to herself. Numbly she followed Arabella up the staircase and into the bed-chamber, not knowing if she or Arabella would be in the greater need of comfort.

Luke and Sir Charles, riding in silence and with growing apprehension through the gateway of Knatchfield Grange, heard the unmistakable sound of a pistol shot as they approached the house. They flung themselves urgently from the saddle and ran within, pistols in hand, fearful of what they might find. Luke, keenly distressed, halted indecisively upon the flagstones of the hall, gazing about him confusedly. Where would Curtis strike? he wondered impotently, and at whom? Was Arabella, or Francis, the chosen victim? He raged at himself for his uselessness, his cruel wasting of time. Arabella would surely be with Francis. Yes, he had warned her of the dangers without, and she would surely stay close to Francis. He mounted the stairs with furious recklessness, and with the justice anxiously in his wake. The hubbub and noise came from Francis's bed-chamber as, aggressively, he threw open the door, pistol cocked and primed, awaiting the well-aimed shot which might disable or kill.

In the briefest of moments his mind recorded all. It was etched in memory for all time . . . The startled faces of Francis, Arabella and Nerissa, disbelieving and with mouths agape, caught not in fear but uncontrollable laughter . . . Beyond them stood the staunch, Titan figure of some unknown woman, massively crisped and starched and all frowning disapproval. Yet it was upon Nerissa Pritchard that Luke's enquiring gaze settled, and he saw her grow uncommonly pale and sway before falling with commendable gracefulness to the floor.

With pistol in hand, he had no chance of immediately aiding her, but he thrust the weapon at Francis with a muttered word and ran to support the unconscious Nerissa. Euphemia Gibbs had taken immediate charge, but despite her strictures Luke would not be gainsaid.

242

He lifted Nerissa with the greatest tenderness, intent only upon carrying her to her own room and bed.

So it was that Nerissa tentatively opened her eyes to find herself unexpectedly in Captain Farrow's arms, his concerned face so close to her own that she could feel the soft warmth of his breath upon her cheek. For a moment she had lain inert, grateful to be so comfortingly cradled and thinking that if it were a dream, then she would be content for it to last for ever. When reality impinged, she struggled ineffectually to be free of his encircling arms, shamed and humiliated, disgraced before all. Awkwardly, she tried to make apology, but the words stuck hard in her throat. The tears squeezed beneath her closed eyelids and she prayed that she might die upon that instant, for she would never be able to face him again.

"If you will take Nerissa to her bed-chamber, Luke, then I will accompany you," Arabella invited. "I am sure that it is no more than a harmless swoon and she will soon recover." She turned to the justice, who was standing perplexed and discomfited, saying by way of apology, "I beg you will excuse us for the briefest moment, Sir Charles, while I attend to Miss Pritchard, my companion. Francis will tell you of all that has transpired, and Captain Farrow will rejoin you shortly. Miss Euphemia Gibbs has been a tower of strength, a rock, as Francis will testify. I cannot praise her too highly, nor thank her enough."

Euphemia Gibbs flushed crimson at such extraordinary praise and for a moment almost lost her composure. Then, with admirable self-possession, she said, "I am sure that you two gentlemen have much of importance to discuss. If you will excuse me, then I shall accompany Miss Pritchard to her room, render her my professional assistance. A sensitive young lady, in delicate health, should be suitably treated."

Arabella, meeting Francis's amused gaze, grinned widely and capitulated with good grace. It would not harm Luke one whit to be curbed by such a dragon. It might even spur him the more, increase his tenacity. All told, it had been a better day than she had anticipated. Francis was safe, despite the flesh wound to his arm, and the sender of the note safely captured. Her plans for Luke and Nerissa had been swiftly reinforced by no less redoubtable an ally than Euphemia Gibbs. What was more, Francis, who had claimed that he would never endure such a virago, seemed almost besotted with her. Yes, it had been a reasonably memorable day.

That debilitating sickness and collapse which had so plagued Francis gradually receded, as Dr Munro had foretold, and to Arabella's relief he seemed to regain much of his old energy and high spirits. She did not delude herself that it was more than a temporary remission. Yet it *was* a halting time, a benison, and she was grateful for that. She had learnt to live for the hour and not look beyond it. The weather had turned about and they were enjoying an Indian summer, that unexpected warmth and tranquillity which defies the seasons. It was, Arabella sometimes thought, as if, with the remission in Francis's disease, the elements, too, had lapsed into a period of calm, a time of waiting.

Miss Euphemia Gibbs had departed in a positive fanfare of glory, and with a pleasing reluctance on the part of both patient and nurse. She had made staunch promise to return immediately, should her services be required, and Arabella was grateful for such reassurance. Miss Gibbs had accepted the plaudits of the justice for her part in the capture of Hugo Curtis with fitting modesty. Dr Munro's praise had been as graciously received. She had, she insisted, done no more than was necessary to preserve her patient's wellbeing. It had been a storm in a teacup, and she could not abide storms . . . they spoiled the order of things. Like a badly made bed, they led only to discomfort. Stout, stout booted and stout hearted, Euphemia Gibbs crunched her way along the gravel of the carriageway, back ramrod stiff, straw bag clasped fiercely in hands raw-boned as hams. There was not one within Knatchfield Grange who did not admire and respect her, nor regret her leaving, nor wish her well.

It seemed as if the violence which had come to Knatchfield had served to draw those within the house closer together, to bind them more intimately. Knowledge of Francis's sickness was a shared grief, yet an encouragement, too, to make good use of those days remaining. There was perhaps a febrile gaiety to their excursions, a desire to fill each moment and to live it to the full. Picnics, outings by carriage, visits to secluded beauty spots and walks through the surrounding woods and lanes enlivened their days. Their evenings were spent playing companionably at cards, or in reading or conversation, and Nerissa was always included, her quiet presence as welcome and undemanding as Luke's.

When the two gentlemen occasionally removed themselves to the library to indulge in smoking or post-prandial drinking, or to challenge each other to billiards or chess, Arabella and Nerissa stayed contentedly together, working at their tapestry or needlework and setting the world to rights. Their talk was alternately lighthearted or deep-probing, and little by little each grew to know of the other's background, her hopes and her fears. They grew closer in understanding and liking and in depth of friendship. That their pasts and childhoods were so disparate seemed to draw them together more firmly, rather than set them apart. Nerissa truly admired Arabella for her strength of spirit in the face of Francis's grave sickness, and for her kindness and lack of arrogance. Arabella in turn admired Nerissa for overcoming the griefs and hardship of the past and for her determination to learn to read and write and make a future. Both were agreed that the chance visit to Holly Grove fair had altered their lives immeasurably.

The threat of violence had receded with Hugo Curtis's capture and incarceration, and neither gave thought to Richard de Granville. His sickness from the infected dog bite was no more than he deserved for his churlishness, and they were grateful to be rid of sight of him.

Now that Francis was recovered from his knife wound, their days were increasingly occupied, their time agreeably filled. When they were not bent upon some pleasurable outing with Francis and Luke, they were engaged in returning formal calls upon neighbours or in visiting the indigent sick upon the estate, the old and newborn, and taking gifts of warm clothing and nourishing victuals. Nerissa's compassion was inevitably aroused by the poverty and need of those visited, their patient endurance and fortitude. She had so lately escaped that same trap of deprivation that she felt their hopelessness as if it were her own, and grieved for them. That she was privileged, she knew. So much had happened in so short a time that she could scarce believe it. By God's good grace, through Arabella, she had been granted means of escape.

Yet her position in the social hierarchy was clearly defined, as she saw from the reactions of those whom Arabella and she visited. She was no more than a necessary appendage, of no particular distinction or worth. A commonplace plant, scarce worthy of cultivation. What could not be conveniently uprooted was either reluctantly tolerated or else ignored. It suited Nerissa to become invisible at such houses, to listen, learn and absorb the manners and habits of those she still thought of as her "betters". Yet she was beginning to question even that. She was beginning to think for herself, to evaluate and pass judgement, even if only in her own mind. She was reading more fluently now, her desire for knowledge insatiable. Arabella encouraged her at her lessons with Selina Pratt and gave her full use of the library at Knatchfield. She was benefiting not only from the thoughts and experiences of others, but creating her own.

She saw that in Francis and Arabella Crawshay she had found rare mentors and friends. They treated her not as a servant, but as an equal. She was aware of how radical such behaviour was, and how eccentric it would be judged by others. It challenged the recognised order of things. Those of the Crawshays' social standing, the landed gentry, would be deeply resentful of such easy familiarity, believing it deliberately perverse. It could lead only to an erosion of their privilege and power. Servants, too, would be uneasy. From the greatest to the least, they lived their lives by discipline, respecting those rigid barriers that kept them apart, never seeking to overcome them. Nerissa knew that her time at Knatchfield was the briefest idyll; time out of place. Her real milieu was not the drawing room, but the servants' quarters. Her friendship should be with those like Ruth and Hugh Gravelle, Selina Pratt or Goliath Jones and Toby over at Holly Grove. The Crawshays and Captain Farrow, for all their kindness and lack of affectation, were a breed apart, and she could never be one of them. She might study and emulate them, but it would be no more than play-acting and wholly counterfeit, convincing no one. Why, she wondered miserably, could she not be content with what she had achieved? It was more than she had ever dreamed possible. Yet, at heart, she knew the reason.

Her love for Luke Farrow, undisclosed and unreturned, was the greatest barrier of all. It had begun to fill her thoughts, overflow into every aspect of living. It was destroying even that easy familiarity that had grown between them. In his presence, she was growing increasingly self-conscious and therefore reserved, fearful that she would betray herself. It would be too great a humiliation for her and an embarrassment for him. There would be no alternative for her but to leave Knatchfield, and she could not bear to do so. Arabella had need of her now, with Francis so gravely sick, and would need her more urgently after, when all was ended. No. She must keep her affection for Captain Farrow well hid, and sacrifice all. She would not delude herself that she was sacrificing him for, save as a companion for Arabella, he was unaware that she even existed. She must satisfy her yearning with memory of how she had awakened from her shameful faint at Major Crawshay's sick-bed to find herself lifted easily in Captain Farrow's arms. His concerned face had been held tantalisingly close to her own . . . close enough to have set a kiss upon his mouth, his gravely held lips.

Nerissa chided herself bitterly for such useless imaginings. Today was her half holiday and she would be free to drive out upon the waggon to see Goliath Jones and Toby, as she had often done before. She would gain news perhaps of Ruth and the children, for a passing drover or craftsman would sometimes be entrusted to deliver messages from family or friend for the price of a tankard of ale. Yes, that was what she would do, and she did not doubt that Mrs

Cobner, who was a kindly soul, would bake Mr Jones a fine spice cake and find a well-fleshed hambone for Toby. She knew her visits were eagerly awaited by both her friends, and not only for the delectable titbits she brought them. They were as dear as kin to her, as close to family as she would ever now know. Upon her return, perhaps she might call on Joe Protheroe at the Pilgrim's Rest in St Samson. He had been kindness itself to her upon her father's death, and she had long wanted to tell him of her gratitude.

.Yet she had feared to return, grieved by sad memories and unwilling to face a surprise meeting and confrontation with Richard de Granville. Dr Munro had let fall to Major Crawshay that the young man was still indisposed, although not now confined to his bed. It would be many weeks, he hazarded, before young de Granville was restored to normal health and vigour. He would be foolish to attempt to set weight upon his injured leg, or even to ride out, save in a comfortable travelling coach. Stupid bravado before his peers would serve him ill, and he would live to regret it, for such neglect would undo all the good that had been done. Dr Brace, who was less discreet and more robust in his expression, gave it as his firm opinion that the young man in question was "spoilt and arrogant, selfish and absurdly indulged". He was, he added, "heartily sick of his insolence and tantrums". It would please him were he never to cross his path more.

There was none at Knatchfield Grange of contrary opinion. Nerissa cared for him least of all. Yet knowledge that he was still too sick and debilitated to venture abroad gave her spurious confidence. Francis, Luke and Arabella, who knew of the real savagery he had committed, his callous murder of Tom Pritchard, were lulled into a false sense of security too. So many weeks had passed since that abrasive encounter at Holly Grove, and there had been much to concern them. Francis's collapse and the affair of the menacing notes and the gallows, and finally Hugo Curtis's abortive attempt upon Francis's life, had ousted all else. Richard de Granville, too, had fought for his life. It was certain that revenge for the slights and blows suffered at the fair would be the very least of his concerns. It could scarcely be of consequence now. It would have faded from mind . . .

Francis was still determined upon bringing him to book for Tom Pritchard's murder, and Luke, he knew, would aid him. It might be the last battle he would fight, and de Granville the last enemy. Or the last before death itself. Francis knew that he would never now return to his regiment. The decision had not been his own, but forced upon him. It was that which grieved him most of all.

Richard de Granville's illness had been acute, and his convalescence long and frustratingly slow. His suffering had neither refined nor ennobled him, and it had not been borne patiently. He had found the discipline he had been forced to endure restricting, and it had been demeaning to be so absurdly dependent upon others. He missed the rakish companionship of Hanford and Siberry. He even felt the loss of Jeremy Hardwicke's company, for all he had been turncoat and traitor . . . although he did not dwell too morbidly upon his loss. It had been no more than a terrible accident, he had convinced himself, the result of Hardwicke's savage striking-out in anger, his own impetuosity. It had taken Hardwicke to his death; a terrible irony. He thought that he had tried to stop Hardwicke in his headlong fall into the crevice, tried to cling to him and save him from disaster . . . It was not quite clear; the whole scene confused and misted, and with that persistent unreality of a dream. At all events, his sickness had kept him from suspicion, provided him an unbreakable alibi. He might have admitted that he had seen him, been there at his death, had there been need or advantage. Yet it would have served no purpose, save to have grieved Hardwicke's mother the more. He had kept silent, he told himself, from necessity, to dull the suffering of others. He might easily have lauded his own efforts to save his friend, set himself in an heroic light. Yet he had not done so. Surely that was to his credit?

There had been few other advantages, save that he stood higher in his father's estimation, for having stoically completed his duties despite the anguish of his poisoned limb. His father had repeatedly spoken of it before others, praising him for his courage and stubborn adherence to duty, and he had not denied it . . . It would have been crass ingratitude to brand him a liar before others, to so publicly demean him. With his father's good favour and the benefit of his injured leg, he need not over-exert himself upon the estate, for the tenantry were plebeian, their manners uncouth, and without exception they were quite appallingly boring. Yet nothing, he thought irritably, could be more boring than the life of tedium and inertia he now endured. Thank God his leg was mending and he suffered only the slightest limp, scarce more than a hesitation in walking. Munro had declared that it would right itself in time, but the man was a quack, an ill-bred charlatan!

The accident, however, might yet be turned to advantage. It would intrigue womenfolk and elicit their sympathy, be they gentlewomen or trollops, ladies or baggages. The idea made him smile. Hanford and Siberry visited him often, but it was not the same as their forays of old. They seemed ludicrously subdued by the sick-room, scarce capable of the careless adventuring they had shared. Well, he would be rejoining them, and the stews and taverns, the inns and gaming houses would know of his coming. There was much time to be made up, much drinking and debauchery to be enjoyed.

If his mind turned to Arabella Crawshay, that beautiful, arrogant gentlewoman at the fair, then it did so with warm appreciation. He would get to know her, win her respect, make her yearn for him even. He was adamant upon it. She would not easily resist him.

As for that common trull, Tom Pritchard's daughter, she would not be allowed to forget her mistake. She would rue her insolence as painfully as her father before her. It would please him to plan his strategy for bringing her low, for humiliating her publicly. Yet it must be done with cunning and discretion so that neither suspicion nor blame fell upon him. It had been a foolishness to try and run her down in the cabriolet. It had been gauche and crude; a mistake that would not be repeated. In his vendetta against the girl, his sickness had given him pause to reflect upon his brashness and the penalty such impetuosity might exact. Moreover, it had given him a breathing space, set a distance between them. If she had been lulled into a false sense of security, then so much the better. It had helped settle the score with Tom Pritchard and Jeremy Hardwicke both. Pritchard had been no more than a thief, a filthy poacher, battening upon the flesh of the de Granville estates. The irony was that it was he who had been trapped; his flesh which had suffered. The hunter had become the hunted. There was a wry satisfaction in that. A primitive justice. Only a fool would dispute it.

Sir David Hanford's daily visit to Richard de Granville had been cursory, and little enjoyed. The sick-room bored him, made him feel restive. There was something foully debilitating about the atmosphere. The smells of lotions and herbs were nauseating, and the burning of pastilles scarce better than the burning of incense at church. Indeed, the whole caboodle was as alien and hard to take. The same low voices that scarcely rose above a reverent whisper; the sanctimonious cant; the lurking presence of those in charge. Pious. Chastening. Designed to fill with guilty unease. It was as well that de Granville was finally mending, for he did not think he could long endure such punishment. It was the injured who were supposed to endure pain, not inflict it upon others. Their talk had, as always, been desultory, inhibited by the presence of a servant or aide and, of necessity, laundered and stilted. Their old rumbustious camaraderie, their lewd exchanges, were forgone, and their innocuous social chatter all too soon exhausted, and his patience with it. His conversation with de Granville was brief and cryptic, as if they had evolved a language of their own to confound others.

"That . . . acquaintance at the fair, the gentlewoman, Hanford? She fares well?"

"It would seem so . . . She has visited my mama on several occasions, and they are due to dine formally with us on the twelfth . . ."

"Indeed? And the gentleman in attendance? The horse-buyer and pugilist?"

"Rumoured to be much improved. Siberry's father had it in confidence from Dr Munro. He is well enough to venture abroad in the carriage. He will be present at dinner."

"Then I will be glad of invitation, Hanford, if you will arrange it."

"Do you feel that is wise?"

"Wise?" de Granville echoed abrasively. "I fail to understand you, Hanford. Why should it *not* be wise?"

Hanford hesitated before saying urbanely, "I was merely concerned for your health, de Granville. You are not yet fully recovered."

"Nor shall I be if I am so ludicrously mollycoddled! I am damnably tired of my own company and that of menials . . . I shall be glad of some amusement Hanford, some intelligent conversation."

"Then I am sorry if I begin to bore you, offer you no intellectual stimulation," Hanford declared dryly. "Perhaps I had best remove myself."

"Damnation, Hanford! There is no cause to take offence . . . to be so bloody minded!" de Granville exclaimed vexedly. "You know that you and Siberry are excepted, so do not pretend otherwise!" He paused, to ask irritably, "That other creature . . . the hireling?"

"It appears that she has found safe lodging . . . indeed, she is to be seen everywhere '*en famille*' . . . No outing or expedition is taken without her."

"Hell and damnation!" de Granville erupted viciously. "It is ridiculous, farcical even . . . She is no more than a common trull!" At seeing Hanford's raised eyebrows and expressive glance towards the listening aide, he calmed himself enough to ask with apparent lightness, "How could that come about, and so soon?"

"It is rumoured that the . . . other military gentleman finds her amusing . . . is paying court."

De Granville was frankly incredulous. "It is scarcely decent," he protested. "It must be some aberration, some hole in the corner affair."

"It would seem not."

"Then it must be stopped!" de Granville insisted vehemently.

"Unless it could be turned to advantage?" Hanford reminded.

De Granville nodded, asking with unashamed curiosity, "This illness that the other suffers from? What is it? An old war wound? A fever of sorts?"

Hanford glanced towards the aide before confiding, voice low, "No, according to Siberry, it is some grave sickness . . . incurable even. He cannot long survive."

Richard de Granville's face was expressionless, his voice betraying no emotion, but he felt a quickening of excitement, a surge of triumph. Crawshay was getting no more than he deserved. He would spare him no pity, no regret. Arabella Crawshay would not long mourn him. She was young and healthy. She would be a wealthy young widow, an heiress in her own right. Could he but ingratiate himself with her, then his future would be made. She would lean on him in bereavement, allow him to console her then grow to depend upon him. Crawshay's friend, Farrow, would prove no obstacle . . . since he was said to be enamoured of the Pritchard girl . . . Oh, it was all to his advantage! A most splendid opportunity, and acquired without scheming or effort.

"You will arrange that invitation, Hanford?" he asked sharply. "See that I am not forgotten?"

"If it pleases you . . ." Hanford said languidly.

"Where do you go now?" de Granville asked plaintively. "Will you meet Siberry at the inn? What have you in mind? Gaming? Drinking? A night of cheap entertainment at some bawdy house?"

"I have some unfinished business to conclude," Hanford said, "something to our mutual advantage," he added obscurely. "I cannot tell you of it now, but it concerns an inn, certainly, and a landlord's reckoning. An account to be paid in full."

"Protheroe?" De Granville mouthed the word silently.

"The same. It seems that he is spreading malicious rumour . . . trying to revive some long-forgotten incident

. . . to link it with the affair at Knatchfield, with the attempt upon Crawshay's life."

"The devil he is!"

"He has arranged a meeting with my father, as local magistrate."

"But that is all to the good!" De Granville glanced covertly towards the aide, who was occupied at some task. "If the man, Curtis, is held to be culpable?" He shrugged expressively.

"But if he can *prove* otherwise, give convincing alibi for . . . that earlier affair, then it will serve only to reopen speculation; give cause for renewed enquiry perhaps."

"What will you do?"

"Seek explanation," Hanford said quietly, "then do whatever is necessary . . . No man is immune to persuasion, a healthy bribe, particularly when his livelihood is concerned . . . Is not the inn in your father's keeping, de Granville? Part of the St Samson estate?"

Richard de Granville nodded as Hanford continued firmly, "No man will willingly face ruination for a suspicion, a principle."

"But if he does?"

"I have already told you. I will do whatever is necessary. We are in this together."

There was a cold finality in his voice, and de Granville could not doubt that he meant it.

Chapter Nineteen

Nerissa had no doubt about what she must wear to visit Goliath Jones and Toby. She selected her prettiest gown of rose-coloured silk and with it, her matching bonnet and slippers. It was, she knew, extravagantly formal for such a visit, and a simple sprigged cotton might have served her better. Yet she knew, too, that the Punch and Judy man would be as proud as Mr Punch himself to see her so elegantly attired. He would look upon it as a tribute to their friendship and to the importance she gave to their meeting . . . as, indeed, important it was. The elegant shot-silk had the subtlest sheen, delicately iridescent and soft as a petal. It was the most exquisite thing that Nerissa had ever owned and she loved it dearly. Mrs Pinchin, the plump-breasted little dressmaker, had declared it to be "a most excellent fit, and vastly becoming". Adding with pardonable pride, "Although 'tis of my own making, I confess that none could fault it for stitching!" Goliath Jones, being a theatrical gentleman and of a more poetic turn of phrase, had declared that she looked "sweet and fresh, my dear, as a rosebud unfurling, a sight to gladden the heart," and Toby's tail had thumped eloquent agreement. Now, delightfully gowned and bonneted, and with her hooded pelisse over her arm, Nerissa descended the stairs to cross the hall, and went out into the stable yard. She had courteously declined Arabella's offer of the open carriage and Hanson to drive her, explaining that she did not know at what time she would be returning and would not have the coachman wait about in the cold air . . .

"Besides," she admitted, "I would be more at home with the waggon, if you will allow me use of it, and Mr Jones more comfortably at ease." So it was arranged.

As Nerissa walked thoughtfully across the hallway, she turned, startled, at the sound of her name.

"Miss Pritchard . . . Nerissa."

"Oh, Captain Farrow . . . " she halted, confused, "I did not see you, sir, my mind was elsewhere . . . I beg you will forgive me."

"No, ma'am. The apology should be mine. I should not have intruded, startled you so thoughtlessly."

They surveyed each other for a moment in silence, until finally Nerissa blurted uncertainly, face flushed, "There is something you require of me, Captain Farrow? Some message you would have me deliver? Some errand, perhaps, you would have me run? I am driving to Holly Grove upon the waggon."

"No, Miss Pritchard . . . rather something I would discuss with you."

"Now, sir?" she asked hesitantly.

"If you please . . . unless your visit is urgently pressing."

"It can be delayed, sir, for Mr Jones and Toby are not aware of my coming. It was to be a surprise."

"If you will be kind enough, then, to enter the library, Miss Pritchard . . . if I may escort you there . . ."

He formally held out an arm and she placed her gloved hand upon it, feeling awkwardly at a disadvantage and filled with unease. She could not for the life of her discern the purpose for this summoning. She searched her mind for sins or omissions, what she might have done to offend him, but could think of nothing.

He drew out a chair for her from beside the library table and hovered impatiently while she seated herself. His face was unusually grave, and she was filled with a sense of oppression. It must be news of Major Crawshay, she thought, fighting to control her panic. It must be news to be broken gently.

"Major Crawshay?" Her voice was thin, high pitched with alarm.

"No. Francis is well, thank God. It is on my own account that I wish to speak to you."

She stared at him in perplexity, giving him no encouragement.

256

"Dammit, Miss Pritchard . . . Nerissa," he exclaimed. "I do not know how to begin, or where! It is deucedly difficult. I do not want you to misunderstand, take offence."

"If I have said or done something to offend you, Captain Farrow," she said coldly, "then I would sooner that you told me of it. It can then be . . . rectified, set to rights."

"No, you have not offended me, ma'am. Not at any time . . . Indeed, quite the contrary."

Dear heaven! he thought, I am stuttering and posturing like an idiot, a lovesick fool. It is no wonder that she loses patience. She must think me half-witted.

"Perhaps, Captain Farrow," she suggested quietly, "it might be best were you to begin at the beginning." Her eyes glinted mischievously, "I confess I have always found it easier so."

"No, it will not be easy, Nerissa," he declared with conviction, "but it must be said, discussed between us. I would not have you misunderstand."

"Then you had best tell me, sir, that I may judge," she prompted.

"If you wish to decline, think it impossible, even, I shall think no worse of you. I shall not hold such refusal against you. It would be a business arrangement . . . for propriety's sake. A pact, you understand?"

"No, sir. I do *not* understand. Indeed, I have not the foggiest notion of what I am meant to consider . . . since you are at pains not to enlighten me. There is some business venture you would have me consider? Some errand you have in mind?"

"I would have you betrothed to me, Nerissa . . . formally engaged."

All colour had drained from Nerissa's face and she leapt to her feet in agitation, declaring, "If this is some cruel jest, Captain Farrow, some stupid wager, then I own that it gives me no pleasure to be the butt of such humour." She looked about her wildly for means of escape. "If you will excuse me, I shall ride out to Holly Grove . . . My friends there are loyal and kindly, they would not openly mock me."

"Miss Pritchard . . . damn it, Nerissa! I neither mock

nor belittle you. It is an offer made in good faith. If you will listen, and consider, hear me through, without interruption or anger."

She stared at him impassively for a moment, then nodded and seated herself rigidly upon the chair once more.

"With Arabella so bound up with Francis's wellbeing, the ravages of his sickness, we will be thrown increasingly together . . . we will be needed urgently by night or by day, expected to take the brunt of her everyday burdens . . . You understand?"

She nodded wordlessly.

"We will be spending much time together, riding out alone in the carriage perhaps, taking over her duties and responsibilities. It would be better were you to act as . . . chaperone when Arabella and I are closeted with Francis at night. She, in turn, might act as duenna to you . . . since she is a respectably married lady. You agree?"

"I do not know . . . " she admitted with awkwardness, "I do not see how it would alter things."

"You are an unmarried woman, Nerissa . . . one vulnerable to the scurrilous gossip of others, and too easily compromised. If we were seen too often together it would make your position here untenable and give Arabella added grief. It would destroy all future hope of employment as a companion, here or elsewhere, for your reputation would be tarnished, your morals suspect . . . " He took her gloved hand gently into his own, saying with understanding, "That *we* know such accusation to be false will not still the vicious tongues, I fear, nor alter the opinion of others. It is the way of the world."

"Then the world is corrupt!" Nerissa exclaimed with feeling.

"Yet we must live in it," he reminded, "whatever our misgivings. Will you not consider my proposal, Nerissa . . . give it careful thought . . . for Arabella's sake, as well as your own." As she hesitated, he added quickly, "You must not fear that things will change . . . That I will demand more of you than you will be prepared to give. I will ask nothing of you, save civility before others . . . a show of mild affection, if need should ever arise. It will not be legally binding. An engagement of convenience, not emotions . . . What do you say?"

There was the briefest hesitation.

"I say 'Yes'," Nerissa conceded reluctantly, "since you feel it to be kinder for all."

"Then it is agreed," he said with obvious relief. "I shall confide the true reason for it to Francis and Arabella . . . but to no others. They must remain convinced that it is an honest proposal, honestly made."

Nerissa's earlier pallor had given way to anguished colour, and two bright spots lay upon her cheekbones, crimson as burns. She felt nothing but shame and distress.

Luke, who thought how grave faced and dignified she looked, and how beautiful in her pretty gown and bonnet, bent instinctively to settle a light kiss upon her cheek, to seal the bargain. Nerissa turned, flustered, and his lips brushed the corner of her mouth. Her recoil had been immediate and unmistakable, and he damned himself for his clumsiness. He had been at pains to convince her that he demanded nothing of her save the old, easy friendship; that his only aim was to protect her. Then he had proceeded to treat her as if she were of no account; a demirep or a common drab.

He made clumsy apology, manner so awkward that Nerissa was further confused and humiliated. It was plain that the kiss had been carelessly given. It was meaningless. It meant no more than a handshake, a sealing of a pact. His only concern was for Francis and Arabella, and why should it not be so? Yet the pain she felt within had the force of a physical blow, a knife-thrust. She did not know if she could keep up this pretence, this show of indifference, even for Arabella's sake, and she owed her all. It was the sheerest agony to have Luke Farrow so near, and to know that she meant nothing to him. She must patiently endure his embrace and even perhaps his kisses in public, and pretend herself to be demurely compliant, emotionally unmoved. But she was neither demure nor unmoved. She was a woman, with a woman's warmth of passion, and she wanted him to take her into a real embrace, to kiss her with fervour and commitment, to love her as fiercely as she loved him. Hot tears scalded her eyes and she turned away that he might not see her shameful need for him, and feel nothing but pity. She could not bear the humiliation of that, his clumsy rejection.

Luke, to hide his own confusion of emotions, ventured quietly, "I shall ask Arabella to take the measure of your finger, Nerissa . . . so that I may visit the goldsmith tomorrow and purchase a ring." He hesitated. "Is there some particular gemstone you favour? Your birthstone, or something of special significance to you?"

She shook her head.

"Will you trust me to make choice, then?"

She nodded, unwilling to speak lest she betray herself.

"You must keep the ring . . . Take it as remembrance, proof of my friendship towards you . . . my regard."

I need no payment, Captain Farrow! The angry words sprang instinctively to mind, but she did not speak them aloud.

"I think, sir," she said, her voice held painfully steady, "that it is best that the ring be returned to your keeping . . . when all is ended. It will hold no real memories for me, or for you. We will be no more than players upon a stage . . . puppets, without thought or feeling, like . . . like Goliath Jones's."

"As you choose." Luke's voice was cold. "I had best escort you to your carriage. I will delay you no further. You will have congenial company at Holly Grove."

"Indeed. 'Tis always a pleasure to see Toby and all."

His lips curved into an involuntary smile at such honest naivety. "Would you have me drive you to Holly Grove upon the waggon?"

"No, I thank you, Captain Farrow, 'tis better not . . . since you do not wish to see me compromised, to set idle tongues wagging."

Did he see quickly suppressed amusement in her smile? He could not be sure. "Then I may, at least, escort you without?"

"Yes, Captain Farrow . . . I should be glad of that."

"Since we are soon to be engaged, Nerissa . . . formally betrothed . . . do you not think that it might be more convincing were you to address me as 'Luke'? Captain Farrow seems strangely distant."

"Yes. That will be quite in order," she agreed. "I shall do so the moment the ring is placed upon my finger, Captain Farrow. You have my word. Until then, we had best observe the formal courtesies, the . . . conventions." She brought out the word triumphantly, as if it were new to her.

Luke thought with indulgent affection that she must lately have read it but never before given it sound. He offered her his arm for support and escorted her out of the house and across the yard to where the horse and waggon awaited. Smiling, he helped her on to the platform, where she set down her pelisse beside her and took up the reins.

"You are more elegant than your equipage, ma'am," he said, smiling broadly.

She returned his smile, saying with gentle dignity, "The waggon is more luxury than I ever dreamed, Captain Farrow. For all my fine feathers, I am what I always was – simple, and without claim to be what I clearly am not. The old horse and waggon will serve me well enough. We have much in common . . . I have not changed."

"Then do not, Nerissa! Stay as you are."

With the waggon's moving, the grinding of wheels upon the cobblestones, and the clopping of hooves, he did not know if she heard his impulsively uttered words. Luke Farrow knew only that his liking for Nerissa, his protective tenderness, had grown into a deeper emotion akin to love. Yet his own future was uncharted and his commitment to Francis must take precedence over all. Nerissa was still unsettled here at Knatchfield Grange, feeling her way, and painfully vulnerable. If he declared himself too forcefully, or too soon, he was in danger of frightening her. He might lose her altogether. He must first gain her trust. Whatever his personal feelings, he must strictly honour his promise to her. Their relationship would be a charade only, emotionless, freely entered upon and as freely ended. It would be hard, damnably hard, not to declare himself. Yet it was owed to her, and to Francis and Arabella too. Sadly downcast for a nubile young gentleman who has just offered and been accepted in matrimony, Luke turned hard upon his heel and returned within.

Sir David Hanford, upon leaving St Samson Court, reined his horse towards the Pilgrim's Rest on the seaboard side of the village. There was a chill wind from the sea, sharp with the tang of iodine and salt, and refreshingly bracing. He felt vital and alert, riding easily, and only gratified to be rid of the torpidity of the sick-room, its oppressive staleness and odours. Thank God that de Granville was on the mend, he thought selfishly, for visiting him was becoming increasingly tedious. He would be glad when he was fully recovered and things returned to normality; that carefree roistering and camaraderie they had taken for granted.

A frown fleetingly disturbed his lean features as he recollected Jeremy Hardwicke's death. No. He was wrong. Things would never be as they once were. He missed Hardwicke damnably, more than he had ever thought possible. It was hard to say why, because in his lifetime he had been a constant irritant. His weakness and stubborn morality had too often set a blight over all. Perhaps it was because they no longer had a convenient whipping boy, one whom they could ridicule and berate. Yet Hardwicke had shown strength, too, a stubborn loyalty which could not be shaken . . . A sudden picture of Jeremy Hardwicke's pale-skinned face, with its stippling of freckles and thatch of red hair, came vividly to mind, and Hanford felt a pain of loss quite alien to him. Damn it if he was not growing maudlin! He was as much an old woman as Hardwicke himself. It must be the effect of de Granville's sick-room, this lingering dwelling upon death. Yes. That would be the reason, the catalyst. Death was for the old and spent, those exhausted by living. There had been no preparation for Hardwicke's death. He had simply gone; perished, as though he had never been. One did not expect such violence, such finality.

Hanford's hands tightened fiercely upon the reins and he set the horse to a gallop, as memory of the baiting and death of Tom Pritchard came inexorably to mind. He had been a thief, a filthy poacher, and the world was well rid of him and his kind. They had done the de Granville estate a service. It was no more than an organised culling, the curbing of some rogue animal . . . He had best dismiss it from mind, concentrate his thoughts upon the matter in prospect, gaining ascendancy over Joe Protheroe at the Pilgrim's Rest.

He must learn what Protheroe knew of the murder, or at least what he suspected. Had there been some witness unseen? Someone perhaps well hidden and bent upon the same mission as Pritchard himself? It would not do to confront Protheroe openly, and before others. It would arouse curiosity, set the venture at risk. His father, the justice, would hear of it and demand explanation. Sir Charles was neither a credulous peasant nor lacking in wits and intellect. He would be hard to bamboozle, harder to convince.

With no clear notion of what he might say or how he might act, Hanford rode unseen into a small coppice of willows near the inn. He tethered his horse to a tree in a grassy clearing where it might conveniently crop the grass, then he skirted the wood and crossed the byway to the Pilgrim's Rest.

Joe Protheroe had taken delivery of the barrels of ale from the brewery over towards Holly Grove. It was a rare treat he thought, to welcome the brewer's dray, the flat-topped waggon drawn by the powerful dray horses. So proud the old shires were, and so splendidly muscled, their massive strength belied by their patient temperament, their inbred gentleness. It was his custom to offer them a titbit from the pocket of his canvas apron, a piece of carrot or apple or suchlike, and he was always confounded by the gentleness of their lips, the velvety softness of their noses as they nuzzled into his outstretched palm. Oh, they were a sight to gladden the heaviest heart, for they were handsome creatures, bold of eye, and with an inbred arrogance, a certainty of their own rightness. Bill Prosser, the man who drove the dray, was as thin and wiry as they were

263

solid. He scarce looked capable of controlling them. Yet control them he did, firmly yet with a proud tenderness that he might have shown to high-spirited children, his own kin. They were groomed to within an inch of their lives, their plaited and beribboned manes brushed as devotedly as their silken tails. Their hides were polished smooth as chestnuts, gleaming as brightly as their harness and the brasses winking upon them. Their cargoes of barrels unloaded and their reward graciously given and received, Joe Protheroe stood at the entrance to the yard and watched the dray leave. My, but they were bonny horses, all rippling strength and power, the flowing hair a pale nimbus from pastern to heel, soft over gleaming hooves.

He turned away, reluctant to see them go, and turned his full attention to rolling the barrels across the cobbled yard and into the cellar below. So intent was he upon his task that he was unaware of the presence of any other until, sweat stained and with aching muscles, he straightened to ease his back. The look of astonishment he gave the elegant intruder was replaced not by one of welcome, but wary suspicion as he greeted the newcomer. Sir David Hanford was left in no doubt that he had been recognised and his mission understood.

"You would be better served within the tavern, sir." His tone was courteous but his expression surly. "There is nothing to interest you here. If you will excuse me, I must be about my business."

"As I mine, landlord."

Joe Protheroe eyed him unflinchingly, stare uncompromising.

"If you will spare me a minute, Protheroe, my business is with you."

"I cannot rightly see what we have to discuss, sir," Protheroe's broad face was stubbornly set, his body unyielding, "but whatever you have to say, it were better said indoors."

He rolled a barrel impatiently aside and made to leave the yard.

"No! What I have to say is personal . . . of interest to you alone."

264

Protheroe wiped his brawny hands upon his apron and settled himself upon a cask, regarding him steadily, saying, "Then you had best begin, sir, for I must make my living."

"Perhaps what I am about to say may help to make that easier for you."

"Indeed, sir?" Protheroe's tone was bordering upon contemptuousness. "I confess that I have never found words more rewarding than action, although they may be more cheaply made."

Hanford's dark saturnine face remained expressionless, but his gloved hand tightened involuntarily upon his riding crop and sent it stinging against the leather of his riding boots. Damn the man, he fumed impotently. Damn his insolent hide!

Protheroe, who had neither flinched at the crack of the whip upon leather nor made sound, remained obdurately unmoved.

"If you will state your business, sir . . . Sir David Hanford, is it not?"

Hanford nodded curtly.

"Then I would prefer to be about my lawful business," Protheroe said impassively.

Hanford, who was fast losing his air of languid indifference, said sharply, "I hear that you have been spreading false rumour . . . meddling in business which is none of your affair."

"And what business would that be, sir?" Protheroe's expression was guileless. "Something which perhaps concerns you?" He scratched his head, adding with irritating slowness, "I'll own that we have little in common, for we are set firmly on opposite sides."

"Opposite sides?"

"Aye . . . opposite sides of the bar."

Was the man being deliberately obtuse, Hanford wondered, or merely stupid?

"I hear that you have sought a meeting with my father, the justice," he accused, rashly showing his hand, "that you have certain information to impart."

Protheroe regarded him stonily.

"If it is of real consequence . . . usefulness, then you may bargain for a better price. You will not be the loser." It was said with supreme arrogance. "No . . . you will not be the loser."

"Will I not?" Protheroe's voice was deathly calm as he rose from the cask to tower above Hanford. "But perhaps, sir, you will . . . else why would you come here offering bribes for what might prove worthless?"

He caught Hanford angrily by the collar of his fine coat, twisting it relentlessly over his neckerchief, all but choking him. When he finally released him, Hanford, white with rage and humiliation, could barely prevent himself from slashing his whip across Protheroe's smug, self-satisfied face. Yet refrain he did, swallowing his pride as painfully as the gorge in his throat and saying with an effort, "You had best think hard, Protheroe . . . reconsider, for much is at stake."

"And what would I be risking, sir?" The landlord's voice was scornful. "The violence you have done to others? Others like Tom Pritchard, would that be?" He spat contemptuously upon the cobbles. "No, sir . . . your threats do not intimidate me. I am better equipped to defend myself. I shall make my confession before the justice and no other." He turned upon his heel.

"You fool!" Hanford's face was contorted with hate as he grasped Protheroe's arm and dragged him around to face him. "Do you not see that it is more than violence you risk? You risk losing all!"

Protheroe shook himself free impatiently, as Hanford exclaimed furiously, "You risk losing the inn . . . your livelihood! Your life, even! Think on it, man!"

Protheroe gazed at Hanford steadily. His voice, when he spoke, was all the more menacing for its quietness. "This inn is not in your keeping, but mine. None shall wrest it from me."

"Fool!" Hanford repeated scathingly. "It is in Sir Peter de Granville's keeping. Do you think you will serve him by hanging his son? He will see you crucified first!"

Protheroe stared at him for a long moment, his certainty that Pritchard had been murdered and his suspicion of who had wrought such violence confirmed beyond doubt. Yet he felt no triumph, no anger, only a weariness of spirit.

"You had best go. Go now, while you still have use of your limbs," he said bitterly to Hanford. "Get clear of my sight, else by God I swear that I will kill you!"

Hanford defiantly stood his ground, muttering threateningly, then, dropping his gaze, shuffled awkwardly across the yard.

"Do not think to return with your threats and bribes," Protheroe warned coldly. "I will not be silenced, or bought. 'Tis your father, the justice, I pity . . . for raising a runt such as you. It will grieve him. Aye, by God, it will grieve him! He is an honest man."

He turned his attention to the barrel at his feet, kicking at it violently then stooping low to haul it laboriously into his hard-muscled arms.

Hanford, crazed beyond all reason, acted by instinct, fear and humiliation laying him raw. He seized a timber from the cluttered yard and brought it crashing down upon Protheroe's skull, splitting flesh and bone, gaping it wide. With a startled cry, Protheroe lurched forward on to the cobbles and lay ominously still, a viscous pool of crimson spreading about him.

Hanford, with the timber clutched in his hand, stood shocked and vacant, hearing the barrel grating upon the cobbles, noisy, anguished, setting his teeth on edge . . . Someone must surely hear it, he thought despairingly. He must go. Leave this place. Yet his limbs were leaden and he was powerless to move. Protheroe was dead. He had killed him. Panic and terror seared him and he threw the bloodied weapon aside, shuddering so fiercely that he felt his jawbone lock.

Then suddenly his mind cleared and his trembling ceased. He must steady himself . . . give himself pause to think. He must make it look not like murder, but an accident. Protheroe was a big man, brawny and well fleshed, and he would be hard to move. Yet fear of discovery and the threat of the gallows lent Hanford superhuman strength. Dragging, pushing, hauling, he somehow manhandled the lifeless flesh to the cellar's edge then, with a vast heave that left him groaning and rasping for air, he sent him plummeting into the darkness beneath. The thud of flesh on stone all but unnerved him but he turned aside and glanced around him, anxious to make good his escape . . . Damnation, he thought, my whip! I had let fall my whip. He retrieved it with a sigh of relief from the darkening pool of blood where Protheroe had fallen. He saw, with distaste, that the whip was stained with congealing blood, his gloves darkened with it and his jacket and shirt front as disfigured and thickly coated. He must make sure that he was not seen and recognised. He would travel by the least frequented byways or keep to the shelter of hedges and woods, then enter Lanelay Court secretively and burn his clothing. He wanted nothing to incriminate him, nothing to remind him.

What he felt now as he emerged from the entrance to the inn yard was a surge of excitement, a certainty of his own skill and cunning. He had succeeded beyond his wildest dreams. None on earth could know of his involvement. He made to cross the byway to the copse where his horse was safely hidden and tethered.

The waggon slowly taking the corner to the Pilgrim's Rest came to a creaking halt upon the byway. Nerissa saw only the pale, blood-smeared face of Sir David Hanford and his blood-darkened clothes. She was aware of a feeling of terror, a sense of evil that overwhelmed her . . . She saw, too, the recognition in his eyes, the dawning horror. For a brief moment, he halted, eyes wild, and she feared that he would attack her. Then, without a word, he was gone, fleeing into the shelter of the small coppice.

She gave no alarm, but fled into the yard, heart pounding, throat dry, fearful of what she might find. At sight of the pool of blood, she felt her limbs grow weak, but urged herself forward, gazing with horrified fascination into the cellar below and upon the crumpled spreadeagled figure of Joe Protheroe. With a cry torn from her throat, she ran blindly across the cobbles and into the inn to seek help.

Nerissa could not have said afterwards why she told no one of the man she had seen fleeing. The man who had mocked and humiliated her at Holly Grove fair . . .

Joe Protheroe's murderer . . . She climbed stiffly aboard the waggon and denying all efforts of help and company drove back the long way to Knatchfield Grange. She was numbed, frozen of thought and feeling, as if it were she and not Joe Protheroe who had died. Then, when feeling returned, she felt a depth of grief for his goodness and friendship that all but broke her heart. She wept then and continued weeping through the unfamiliar lanes and byways until she came within sight of her home. Her pretty pink slippers were stained red with blood and the hem of her gown stiffly darkened. She wept for Joe Protheroe and as much for herself. Not from fear of what the murderer from Holly Grove might inflict upon her, but from knowledge that she could not bring further terror to Francis and Arabella. She must leave Knatchfield. The decision was made.

Chapter Twenty

Nerissa had managed to return to Knatchfield unseen, driving the horse and waggon through the little used north gate of the Grange unhindered, and thence to the stables and coach-house. She had delivered them into the keeping of a stable lad, grateful that she had not encountered Hanson or Manley, the groom, who would certainly have remarked on her dishevelled state and the signs of weeping. The stable lad had been no more than twelve years old, and so delighted to be held in charge that he had given all his attention to uncoupling the horse, unharnessing it and leading it within, talking to it reassuringly the while. Nerissa, painfully grieved by Joe Protheroe's murder, would have been grateful for the same kindness, the same reassurance, but knew that she could confide in no others lest they, too, be drawn into danger. She was distressingly aware of her blood-soaked slippers and the stained hems of her petticoats and gown, and was only grateful that the stable lad had been too absorbed in his tasks to notice them. She must manage now to reach her room unobserved and to change her clothing, for she could not bear the feel nor sight of it, so contaminated was it with Joe Protheroe's dying blood and the memory of his murder.

With fists clenched so tightly that her fingernails drove into her palm, and with her heart beating suffocatingly, she made her way to the servants' entrance and thence along the corridors to the staircase to her attic room. She heard the murmured voices behind closed doors and the general hubbub and clamour of the daily round but to her relief saw no one. Alone and safe in her small bed-chamber, she tried to think and plan her next move. She must leave

Knatchfield. Yet, where would she go? Who would hazard taking her in and giving her shelter? They, too, would then be at risk, in danger of murder. How would she travel the roads? She had no claim upon horse and waggon, and the little she had saved, even with Joe Protheroe's money and the purse from that unknown horseman at Scarweather Cottage, would barely purchase one. Besides, she must keep some aside for board and whatever humble lodging she might find, and to keep herself fed. She felt panic rise within her, that sense of utter desolation that she had known with her father's dying. A certainty that she was alone. Quietly, and with hands shaking, she stripped herself of her bloodied clothing and drew on the red cotton dress she had made to travel to Holly Grove fair. She would take nothing with her save what she had brought from the cottage, the contents of her shawled bundle. How poor and pathetic her treasures now seemed . . . Joe Protheroe's green clover brooch, pinned to the ribbon of her straw bonnet, was reminder of his gentleness and she began to weep anew, silently but with a grief that raked her body with hurt. She felt bruised with sadness, emptied of hope. It had been a mistake to come to Knatchfield Grange. Before, she had been contented with the little she had, for she had known no other life but one of deprivation. Here she had known true happiness. She had been granted home and sanctuary. More than that, acceptance, friendship even.

Her mind was upon Luke Farrow and the proposal that he had offered. Small matter if the promise was as empty as her future. She had believed that being with him, loving him, yet unable to declare it, would be the cruellest of ironies. Yet now she would see him no more. He would believe that she had fled Knatchfield from ingratitude, leaving Arabella and Francis to face his sickness alone. He would despise her for her cowardice, erase her from memory. She prayed that she might expunge memory of him, and knew that she could not. Joe Protheroe's green clover was not a symbol of good luck, the talisman he had intended. It had brought naught but sorrow; his own death and, in all but flesh, her own.

271

Richard de Granville and the murderous stranger from Holly Grove would be well satisfied. They had tried to shame and humiliate her, to give her true account of her worth, and she believed that they had failed. How bitterly they had succeeded now.

Luke returned from the stable yard, after seeing Nerissa drive off to Holly Grove, in a state of the utmost dejection. It was absurdly plain that she had no liking for the idea of a formal betrothal and had only agreed to it out of gratitude to Arabella and Francis. It had been foolish of him to believe that she might have grown to hold him in affection. She thought of him only as a friend of Arabella's, a surrogate brother at best. It was true that he had been willing to offer her a brotherly protectiveness, but it had been no more than an inspired means to an end. The emotion he felt for Nerissa was not brotherly love, but love of a deeper, more passionate kind. A love that needed full completion; a sharing of body and self . . . Yet all he succeeded in doing was to bind her against her will, to make her defensive and wary. The relationship between them now would have lost all of its ease. It would be fraught with embarrassed awkwardness before friends and strangers alike. He had been damnably precipitate, appallingly clumsy . . . He could think of no way to make amends.

Arabella, standing at her window and seeing him cross the yard, was surprised by his misery and hurried out to meet him and guide him within. Was it Francis's sickness which so burdened him, she wondered. Perhaps she had been guilty of asking too much of him for friendship's sake and had not thought deeply enough of the toll it would take of him. Luke was a man strong in mind and spirit as well as flesh, and would reveal little of his innermost feelings . . . a man so like Francis that she could love and understand him as if he were kin.

She walked out into the stable yard and put an arm companionably through his, saying lightly, "Nerissa is off to Holly Grove, Luke, to see Goliath Jones and Toby. Will you not come and keep me company? Francis is closeted

272

in the library with the farm bailiff and will not be free yet awhile."

"I fear that you will find me dull company, Arabella . . . as Nerissa made plain. I fear that I have made a foolish mistake, deeply offended her."

"Offended her? How, Luke?"

"By asking her to accept my proposal . . . my offer of marriage."

"Dear heaven, Luke!" Arabella exclaimed, beaming quite fatuously with surprise and delight. "I am overwhelmed! It is the last thing I was expecting to hear . . . Oh, but it is the greatest news, my dear!" In face of his misery, she broke off, crestfallen. "She has not refused you?" she asked sharply.

"No . . . she has accepted. That is the nub of it."

Arabella looked at him in bewilderment, confessing, "I swear, Luke, that I am at a loss . . . I do not understand. Surely you are not regretting it? You cannot retract such a promise, it would be too cruel. Nerissa would be humiliated beyond all reason."

"No, Arabella . . . I have not retracted, but I am regretful, sorry that I asked her to make such commitment."

"But why? Was she unwilling? Did she make demur?"

"No . . . she agreed, Arabella."

"Well, then?"

"She agreed for your sake and Francis's," he admitted quietly, "to make her position here more tenable, to prevent scurrilous gossip, since she is a woman unwed."

To Luke's complete confusion, Arabella grinned widely then broke into unrestrained laughter as her amusement grew, confessing with difficulty as she wiped her streaming eyes, "Oh, Luke, I cannot believe that you could have been so idiotic . . . so appallingly crass! You mean that you actually confided that you asked her for convention's sake and no other reason?"

"Yes," he admitted sheepishly.

"You gave her no word of affection, no yearning . . . no declaration of love? It was to be a contract only?"

"Yes. That is the crux of it."

273

"Oh, my dear Luke!" she exclaimed, amused and exasperated. "No wonder the poor girl took offence! Had Francis treated me in so cavalier a fashion, then he would not have escaped unscathed! Believe it!"

"I did not wish to alarm her . . . make proper declaration," he murmured defensively, "for fear it might confuse her."

"Confuse her? It strikes me, Luke, that you are the one confused, confused to the point of witlessness! You have convinced her that you find her undesirable, plain, unworthy of your attention, save as a convenient scapegoat . . . I do not wonder that she looked upon the proposal with disfavour . . . She must have been grossly insulted!"

Luke looked so wretchedly crestfallen that Arabella immediately took pity on him and discontinued her tirade. "Yet you say that she will tolerate such an arrangement?" she asked, puzzled. "That she will agree to a betrothal?"

"Yes . . . although," he admitted hesitantly, "more for your sake and Francis's than my own. I have told her that you will measure her finger, that I may buy her a ring . . . I told her that she might keep it afterwards," he added uncomfortably, "but she vowed that she would rather not."

"You great ninny!" Arabella exclaimed despairingly. "Can you not see the reason why? She would rather not be reminded of this . . . débâcle, this fiasco! No woman worth her salt would wish permanent reminder that she is unlovable and unloved!"

"But I *do* love her, Arabella." The confession was quietly made, but there was no doubting its sincerity.

"Then tell her so, you great lummock!"

"But if she refuses me, Arabella . . . if I drive her away?"

He looked so miserably uncertain that she all but weakened in resolve, but, "That is a risk you will have to take!" she declared brusquely. "I can give you no encouragement, no answer . . . that must be Nerissa's alone."

"But do you think that she . . . likes me, Arabella, might look favourably upon my proposal?" he probed anxiously. "You are such close companions, friends . . . Has she not confided in you?"

"Indeed, no!" Arabella's denial was immediate, her tone suitably scandalised as she tried to hide her amusement. "It would not be proper to discuss affairs of such a personal nature . . . Surely, Luke, you would not expect it?"

"No . . ." he hesitated. "No," he added more firmly. "It would be unthinkable . . . and I beg your pardon, Arabella, for suggesting it."

"It is Nerissa's pardon you should be begging!" Arabella said sharply, notwithstanding his rueful face. "You must pluck up courage to propose to her in earnest. What is more," she insisted, "you must do so this very night. She must not be allowed to suffer longer."

"But I shall be suffering, Arabella," he reminded dejectedly, "until Nerissa gives me answer."

"It will strengthen your character," Arabella said blithely. "Consider it as a spiritual challenge, a test."

She believed that she knew what Nerissa'a answer would be. Her companion was quite obviously as besotted with Luke as he with her. Only a numbskull or an innocent like Francis could be unaware of the attraction between them; their secretive glances, their covert looks and tenderly approving smiles . . . She would envy their tentative exploration, their mutual discovery of love. She had found such rare happiness with Francis, and would treasure the memory of it always. She must allow Luke to discover it unexpectedly, and alone.

Nerissa had tied up her bundle and placed it upon the bed, ready for leaving. She glanced about her dispiritedly. All was neatly tidied away, all in order. All, she thought wryly, save her treacherous emotions. Her distress could not be peremptorily tidied away nor hid. She had left a note for Arabella and was aware of how awkward and stilted it was, and ungracious. Yet in the heat of the moment she had been unable to think clearly, or to choose the right words. Reading and writing were still new to her and she had been further inhibited by the knowledge that the excuse she made for leaving was a lie. She had wondered briefly if Captain Farrow, Luke, were deserving of a letter too.

At the last she had decided against it. She was uncertain of how to address him, and what their true relationship should be. She had accepted his proposal, certainly, but it was no more than a sham, an empty promise for propriety, and for Francis's and Arabella's sakes. They would be well rid of her. She would bring them nothing but sorrow and destruction else, death even. There would be sadness enough with Major Crawshay's sickness. She could not burden them more. Her troubles were her own.

Despite her good intentions, her eyes were raw with the burn of tears, but she defied them to fall, blinking rapidly and stretching her eyelids wide. She would miss this house, and all above and below stairs, and would never know its like again. Such fortune came only once in a lifetime, if at all. She hoped that Arabella would not think too harshly of her defection and that Captain Farrow would not believe that it was from the proposed engagement that she fled. It would grieve her to believe it so.

She put on her cloak and the blue bonnet with Joe Protheroe's brooch and took up her bundle from the bed. Everything in this room had become dear to her. It was a haven, secure and reassuring. Yet with Joe Protheroe's death and the murderer knowing her, and able to identify and reach her, it would be haven no more. Nor would she find safety upon the roads, indeed anywhere on earth. The man who had killed Mr Protheroe was clearly a gentleman of means, one who would have carriage and men at his disposal, men who could be trusted to hunt her down. She could not long escape, yet should she keep her nerve she might draw them away from Knatchfield Grange, ensure the safety of Arabella and the others.

As she crept quietly down the stairs from the attic, she prayed that she would meet no one, for her tear-swollen face, old clothes and travel-worn boots would not be easily explained. When she was convinced that she was safe from prying eyes and the fear of discovery, the door to the kitchen opened and Mrs Henrietta Cobner emerged, flushed and dishevelled from the heat, plump, good-natured face alive with curiosity.

"Nerissa, my dear?" Her eyes were alert, missing nothing. "Are you set upon some excursion, alone?"

Colour flooded Nerissa's face and the cook was aware of her agitation, her urgency to be away.

"I am . . . bound for my father's grave," she blurted quickly, "to put it tidy, and such." Her voice was strained, and lacked conviction.

Mrs Cobner, who was fond of Nerissa, was strangely disturbed.

"You had best wrap up warmly, my dear," she said kindly, "for it is a long way to St Samson and the wind can be chill."

Her gentle concern made Nerissa so ashamed and guilt ridden that she could not leave her with a lie.

"I beg, Mrs Cobner, that you will ask me no more," the tears sprang painfully to her eyes, "that you will believe that what I do is from the best of motives . . . that no one will be harmed by my leaving, save me." The tears fell in earnest now.

"Leaving, you say? Glory be! I have never heard the like of it." Then, pulling herself together, she produced a vast cotton handkerchief from the folds of her voluminous apron, saying briskly, "Now, blow hard, my dear. It will help to calm you . . . there is no reason in all the world to take on so! Nothing is so bad that it cannot be mended or ended . . . and that is a fact!" Her myopic brown eyes regarded Nerissa shrewdly. " 'Tis not the visit to Mr Goliath Jones and Toby which has vexed you?" she hazarded. "Some disagreement or mishap upon the way?"

"No!" The denial was emphatic. "They are in no way involved, nor must they be! Believe me, 'tis my own decision. None has threatened nor offended me."

So painful was her distress that Mrs Cobner was afraid to question her more. Instead she held out her arms and Nerissa instinctively drew to her for comfort and was enfolded compassionately in sturdy embrace.

"There, there, my dear!" Henrietta Cobner soothed. "Let that be an end to it, 'tis your own life and your own affair. You must do what you think to be right."

Nerissa gulped and nodded, drawing away reluctantly, for she had been glad of the cook's ready kindness, her human warmth of comfort.

"Well, I will harry you no more," Mrs Cobner sniffed loudly, then wiped a floury hand across her broad nostrils. "You had best be gone."

"You will tell no one of my going, of having seen me?" Nerissa persisted anxiously.

"No. I shall tell no one. You have my solemn word."

Nerissa nodded, satisfied, to say with honesty, "I have been happy here, at Knatchfield, with you and all others . . . You will not let them believe too badly of me. I would not bring them hurt."

"No, my dear. We shall think of you kindly. Believe it."

She watched the slight, childlike figure of Nerissa Pritchard disappear into the dark length of the passage-way, then she turned regretfully away. Whatever ailed the child, it could not be easily righted nor dismissed, that much was certain. She was a brave-hearted girl, and honest, and had borne bereavement and all else bravely . . . Oh, but she would miss her sorely, for she was young and lively and filled with a joy in living. Knatchfield would be the poorer for her leaving.

Henrietta Cobner drew a brawny hand across her forehead, impatiently settling the wisps of fly away hair. As far as she knew, Nerissa Pritchard had no "followers", no romantic involvement which might have gone awry. Her leaving was certainly not of Major and Mrs Crawshay's doing, for they valued her presence, and there was not one of the household staff or servants who had cause to dislike her or to wish her ill . . . What then? Perhaps the gulf between being a cottager and a lady's companion had in the end proved too great a chasm to bridge. Whatever the reason, she hoped that Nerissa would not regret it. She had claimed, most vehemently, that her going would hurt no one, but the child's own hurt was plain to see. A life upon the roads was neither escape nor solution. It could bring only grief.

*   *   *

278

To her relief, Nerissa had seen no other in her hasty flight from Knatchfield Grange, save for the self-same stable boy. If he felt surprise at being so soon ordered to reharness the horse to the waggon, then he was careful not to show it. He completed the task efficiently, whistling tunelessly through his teeth the while. The threepence which Nerissa generously produced as payment was ecstatically received, his profuse thanks following her across the cobbled yard as the waggon trundled laboriously on to the highway. Mistress Pritchard was in a devil of a hurry, he thought, and seemed vastly impatient to be gone. Some lovers' tryst, perhaps? Yet she had looked not cheerful but painfully distressed, her eyes puffed about with weeping . . . Well, 'twas said the course of true love never did run smooth. He was only glad that he was spared all that absurd fiddle-de-dee! It was past reasoning why intelligent people should indulge in such nonsense. Horses were better company, and altogether less trouble. Best of all, they could neither scold nor harass you, for the good Lord had mercifully made them dumb. With a threepence in his pocket for ale and victuals, and work well done, there was none on God's earth he would have changed places with. Whistling cheerfully, he returned to the solace of the stables.

Nerissa, once upon the highway, could think of only one place where she would be made welcome – Goliath Jones's cottage at Holly Grove. She must tell him all, she adjured herself firmly, for that much was owed him. If he hesitated to take her into his home, then she would bear him no ill-will, for her presence would put him in the keenest danger, and Toby too. All along the sheltered byways to Holly Grove she was nervously on edge, scarce able to give the horse command for the trembling of her voice, fearful always of discovery. If Mr Jones felt unable to offer her shelter or promise of escape, then she would leave on foot and trust the horse and waggon to his care. He would see that they were returned, for he was an honest man. It grieved her that she had been forced to leave Knatchfield without taking leave of Mrs Pratt, Mr Hillier and the rest of her friends. Mrs Cobner must have thought her churlish and unfeeling to behave so, but she had promised that she would tell no one of their final meeting, and Nerissa knew that she was a woman of her word and would not break it.

Goliath Jones, eating a meal of bread, cheese and ale in his homely kitchen, with Toby demanding and receiving his fair share, was startled by the sound of a waggon halting without the gate. Upon seeing Nerissa descending, he was filled with alarm and ran anxiously without, with Toby swift at his heels.

"Nerissa, my dear?" His voice was thin with concern. "Is something amiss? Something forgot?"

Nerissa flung herself into his arms, weeping distractedly and scarce able to speak for her misery.

"What is it, my dear? You have not been harmed upon the road? Set upon by footpads or ruffians?"

"No, Mr Jones . . . 'tis worse than that!" Her words were muffled by sobs and she had buried her face against his shoulder.

Dear God! Goliath Jones thought, appalled, some brute has assaulted her, forced himself upon her . . .

"Who was it?" he demanded, stricken. "Who has done you such harm? Tell me! I swear to God that I will kill him!"

Nerissa, frightened by his rage and the grief she had brought him, said remorsefully, "None has harmed me, Mr Jones . . . 'tis Joe Protheroe at the Pilgrim's Rest. He has been murdered!"

Her weeping broke out anew and Goliath Jones put a comforting arm about her to draw her within, shock and distress for a moment silencing him. When he spoke again, his voice was raw with compassion.

"You had best come within, my dear," he said, "for I know that you were fond of him and he treated you kindly . . . 'tis plain it has unnerved you, and rightly so." He guided her gently into the cottage and settled her upon a chair at the fireside, chafing her cold hands with his own, saying, "I had best tend to the horse and waggon . . . Toby will watch over you, keep you company. Have no fear."

Toby watched him depart, gazing after him wistfully, but obedient to his command to stay. He went to sit beside Nerissa's chair, his head upon her lap, looking up at her with deep brown eyes filled with affectionate understanding. So concerned was he and so droll his expression that, despite her misery, Nerissa could not help but smile and caress him, and soon, with her face buried in the rough hair of his neck, her anguish eased. At the sound of Goliath Jones's familiar footsteps, Toby pricked up his ears and left her side, face intelligently alert as he awaited his master's coming.

"Now, Nerissa, my dear, you had best tell me all you know of this affair . . . this tragedy." He hesitated before asking anxiously, " 'Twas none of your doing? You were not involved? Did not see it happen?"

Nerissa awkwardly, and with not a few tears, told him of all that had occurred, hiding nothing, omitting nothing.

"But why did you run away? Leave Knatchfield . . . you should have told Major Crawshay. He would have sent for the justice."

"Major Crawshay is sick and not expected to recover . . . I could not burden him further, and after the attack upon his life." She broke off helplessly.

"Yes," he said quietly. "I see the reason in that . . . but I will send for the justice myself. See that he is summoned. He will not refuse. He is a fair and honest man. A man to be trusted." He broke off uncertainly to ask, "This man . . . the blood-stained murderer? You caught glimpse of him, you say? Could describe him? You would know him again?"

"He was the man at Holly Grove . . . at the fair."

"Richard de Granville? The man Toby set upon?"

"No, another . . . the dark-haired man. The thin one with the gaunt face and languid voice, dressed so stylishly. You remember," she asked anxiously, "you recall him?"

"I recall him." There was contempt in Goliath Jones's tone, but something else, akin to fear, and Nerissa looked at him perplexedly.

"I reckon, my dear, that we have small hope of the

justice's impartiality." His expression was wry. "The man you describe is his son . . . Sir David Hanford."

"But you said that the justice is a good man, and honest!"

"Indeed. In any other circumstance I would have staked my life upon it . . . but blood is thicker than water. There is not a man on earth who would be prepared to hang his own son, so there is an end to it. It were best to accept it first as last."

"Then I must take to the roads," Nerissa blurted, rising in agitation, "I will not set you and Toby into danger. He will come searching for me."

"Now, now, my dear!" Goliath Jones set an arm about her shoulder to calm her. "You shall not go alone. There is easier solution. I shall find a good neighbour to return the waggon and horse, make some plausible explanation."

"But we cannot hope to go far, and on foot. We will be tracked down."

"No. I have an old Romany waggon, a painted vardo, that Toby and I have used in times past. It served to house us on our wanderings, when I travelled the fairs with my Punch and Judy tent. 'Twill help us move fast and give us concealment. None will suspect your presence. The pony is old, I fear, and grown fat from over-indulgence, but he will do well enough to travel the byways."

"But where will we go, Mr Jones? Must we travel the roads for always? Never return to Knatchfield?"

"We will go to Talog, to your friend Ruth, and the children, who else? Hugh Gravelle will offer us protection for as long as we have need. When all is quiet here, we will return. You have my promise. What do you say?"

Nerissa, knowing how gravely he was setting himself at risk for her sake, ran to him impulsively, settling a kiss upon his gaunt cheek, hugging him close then burying her face against the roughness of his jacket.

I must not show him how grieved I am, she thought, for there will be no way of ever returning. She looked up to see him watching her intently, intelligent eyes questioning.

"What do you say?" he repeated quietly.

"I say 'Yes'." The words caught painfully in her throat,

for they were the self-same words she had used to Luke Farrow when he had asked her to marry him . . . She could have wept for the pity of it, for all that was lost, and ended, before it had even begun.

The smile which she had tried to give to Goliath Jones wavered and slipped away, and he pretended that he had not noticed, saying briskly, "Well, Toby, my lad, we had best shape our stumps, get that lazy old nag harnessed, the caravan made ready." He turned to Nerissa, saying with enthusiasm, "Oh, but 'twill be the greatest adventure, my dear . . . a life upon the roads. None can better it for joy and excitement. 'Tis freedom of the finest kind! You will relish it, you will see!"

He would keep up the pretence, he thought, for Nerissa's sake, and stay with her for as long as he was needed. To tell the truth, he felt useless and old, too exhausted for the task ahead. He and Toby were comfortable together and too set in their ways for wandering. Yet he had grown to love her like a daughter, his own child. Should harm come to her, then life would not be worth a halfpenny candle. He roused himself to go and harness the cob.

Chapter Twenty-One

Luke had dressed for dinner with scrupulous care. He intended to propose marriage once more to Nerissa, but this time a marriage of love and not mere convenience . . . but did she love him? That was a question, as Arabella had curtly reminded him, which Nerissa and no other could answer. He found himself growing increasingly perturbed and ham-fisted, scarce able to arrange his own necktie. He had dithered absurdly over the choice of style and colour and had settled at last for the one he had first chosen and discarded. Damnation! What was wrong with him? He was like a lovesick schoolboy, as nervously ill at ease. He glanced anxiously into the mirror upon his shaving stand. He looked neat enough, he supposed, his choice of toning greys respectably anonymous, yet without distinction. He did not want to be turned out like a stylish macaroni, nor yet to make Nerissa believe that he had made no great effort. He had felt this dryness of mouth and agitation before a campaign battle, the same thudding of heart and uncertainty. He supposed that this, too, was a campaign, and one which might alter the course of his life . . . a battle to win Nerissa's acceptance. More than that, Nerissa's love. He was not sanguine as to the outcome, and Arabella had given him little enough cause for optimism. He screwed his courage to the breaking point and with a quick glance at his half-hunter to make sure that he was not late, he left his bedroom for the library.

When Francis and he emerged after their pre-prandial drinks to escort the ladies to dinner, there was no sign of Nerissa, and Arabella was already looking concerned.

"We had best wait another ten minutes in the drawing room," she suggested, "for Nerissa is never late . . . there must have been some obstacle to her returning from Holly Grove."

"Would she not have sent word, my love?" Francis asked. "She is always so efficient and thoughtful. Did she mention that she would be journeying elsewhere?"

"She did not speak of it," Arabella said, troubled.

"Perhaps one of the servants might know; Mrs Pratt, or some other," Francis suggested reassuringly. "As like as not, Arabella, she has returned and is deciding what frippery to wear. She will be here directly."

But Nerissa did not come and Mrs Pratt, when summoned, could give no reason for the delay, save to suggest that perhaps Miss Pritchard had been detained at the Pilgrim's Rest, for she had made mention of seeking Joe Protheroe out, renewing their friendship.

"She has gone to St Samson?" Luke demanded abrasively. "You are sure of this? You could not be mistaken?"

Selina Pratt, alarmed at his vehemence, said, flustered, "No, sir . . . I am not mistaken. She was most insistent upon it. I am not mistaken." She glanced from one to the other, seeing by their anxious faces that they feared some accident or violence had befallen her.

"If you would have me go to her room, see if she has returned?" she ventured.

"Yes, yes, do so, please, Mrs Pratt," Francis gave instruction, "for if she has not returned, we may the sooner start searching for her." Aware of Arabella's piercing look and her extreme pallor, he added quickly, "There is some simple explanation, I do not doubt, some awkwardness with the waggon, or that the mare has cast a shoe . . . but it is as well to be certain."

Mrs Pratt, sensing some deep undercurrent of strain, hurried to Nerissa's room, her own fear rising. When she returned, it was to give Arabella the note, so laboriously written.

"Arabella? What is it?" Francis demanded sharply, fearing, as Luke, that it was some ransom note she held. "What is it, I say?"

Silently Arabella handed him the note. "Nerissa has left . . . of her own free will." Her voice was flat, face

285

painful with disbelief. "She has gone, and she will not be returning."

"Nonsense!" Luke declared harshly. "She would not go without proper reason, or bidding good-bye. It is not in her nature! I do not believe it! What reason did she give?"

"That she is forced to attend some aged relation who has fallen sick."

"Where?"

"She gives neither name nor place," Francis admitted awkwardly, "no details at all . . . save to say that it is where her duty lies, and she will not be returning to Knatchfield."

"But she has neither kith nor kin, sir!" Mrs Pratt was provoked to blurt out. "She has told me so, often."

Arabella said quickly, to mask her distress, "I had best go search her room, see what else may come to light. Whether she has left in haste. Mrs Pratt, you had best come with me."

With the two men left alone, Francis exclaimed angrily, "If the note is in Nerissa's hand, then she has gone under duress, in fear of someone or something."

"Yes. I am of the same opinion," Luke said heavily. "De Granville, do you think?"

"Or one of his minions . . . Sir David Hanford, or the other . . . Siberry's son. It bears all the hallmarks of such revenge, of abduction even."

Luke motioned him into silence at sound of Arabella's returning. Her troubled face was sign enough that some sinister proof had been found to account for Nerissa's leaving.

"She took nothing," she blurted, "nothing save the clothes she wore upon the road."

Luke's eyes were fixed in growing realisation upon what Mrs Pratt held as Francis took an agitated step forward, his exclamation of horror dying in his throat. Nerissa's rose-pink gown was crusted with a darkness of blood at bodice and hem, and the delicate slippers stiffened and congealed with it.

"Dear God!" The cry was wrenched from Luke. "What in God's name can it mean?"

*   *   *

286

Sir David Hanford had arrived back at Lanelay Court in a lather of sweat and anguish, fearful lest he be observed. His mind was in a turmoil, but he had prescience enough to abandon his mount upon the cobbles of the stable yard to await the groom's attention. He was all too aware of his blood-stained clothing and his painfully dishevelled state. He must make a bundle of his clothes and ride out to burn them unseen, else they would offer proof enough to see him strung from a gibbet. The sight of that hireling from Holly Grove, that slut of Pritchard's, had painfully unnerved him. He had all but struck her down. Indeed, he would have done so and silenced her as he had silenced Joe Protheroe, had not sanity returned and stayed his hand. He was wise not to have lingered, else discovery would have been certain. Self-preservation was his god, and it had not forsaken him! With his heart beating uncomfortably, he entered the house by a rear entrance and made his way unseen to his room.

There, he stripped off his garments and washed away all evidence of the murder, sluicing himself with cold water from his washstand jug. He would make use of his hip-bath later and summon a servant to bring him near-scalding water and a washball and towels. For the moment, a lick and a promise must suffice. It would not do to arouse his valet's suspicion. The blood upon his flesh, congealed and hardened now, filled him with disgust. His revulsion was not for the act of murder, nor because he had committed it, was culpable, but from fastidiousness alone. It offended him, as would any stain or blemish, because it marred the perfection of things, their studied elegance.

His thoughts returned again to the girl who had glimpsed him at the Pilgrim's Rest . . . she would surely not dare to speak of what she had seen, accuse him openly? She would be made a laughing stock, else considered deranged. None in St Samson was aware of his . . . altercation with Pritchard, nor could link him with Joe Protheroe, save as an infrequent visitor to the inn . . . As for alibi, he had but to state that he had been at St Samson Court with de Granville and she would be branded a scurrilous liar before all. They might even suspect her own involvement in the murder. It would be ironic indeed were she the one accused and brought to justice. The idea amused him and he smirked delightedly. And yet . . . there was a core of disquiet within him, some presentiment of danger that was hard to suppress. Hadn't de Granville sworn that she was a hazard to their safety and wellbeing and vowed to take revenge? At the time he had considered it foolishness, no more than a puerile fancy born of pique and humiliation. Yet now, all had subtly changed. Had he terrified her enough to make her flee Knatchfield? He wished he could be sure of that, or her silence . . .

There was but one thing to be done. Alone, or with de Granville's and Siberry's help, he must silence her once and for all. He would confess his murder of Joe Protheroe to no one, since it would set him more vulnerably at risk. Friends and enemies were all one when it came to a question of self-preservation, of saving their own miserable hides. He would pretend that de Granville had convinced him. His lips curved into an involuntary smile of satisfaction. That way he would keep de Granville's trust and friendship and assure him of his own. If de Granville could be counted upon to be the instrument of revenge, so much the better. In the meantime, he would keep the girl in suspense, unnerve her with a campaign of carefully planned terror. By destroying her confidence, he might destroy her certainty of what she had seen at Joe Protheroe's inn.

By fortunate chance, the Crawshays were due to dine formally at Lanelay Court in two days' time, and with them their close friend, Captain Farrow . . . Since Farrow had not mentioned their abrasive meeting at the fair to his father, the justice, and Major Crawshay had also kept silent, then it had deliberately been forgot. It would create no embarrassment at table. He had best warn de Granville, though, to hold his peace, for he too had insisted upon being invited. They must set out to charm their guests, to amuse and disarm them. That way they might learn of the Pritchard girl's movements and how to intercept her and take revenge.

Hanford resolutely stuffed his heaped and blood-stained garments into the saddle bag he had brought from below and, strapping it securely, thrust it into the base of the armoire, beneath his clothing. With a final swift look around him he sauntered without, elegant, urbane, every inch the assured gentleman, and totally in command.

Nerissa set to work with a will, cleaning the long-neglected Romany vardo in the yard, trying to make it habitable. Disuse had rendered it musty and airless, redolent of dampness and decay, and she had wrinkled her nose in distaste, vowing to scour it with a liberal helping of elbow grease.

"A little honest dust never killed anyone," Goliath Jones adjured firmly, "and we must all eat a peck of dirt before we die. You may scrub and polish to your heart's content when we are safely away from here, 'twould be small comfort to lie in a clean coffin!"

Nerissa, smiling despite her misgivings, was forced to agree. She contented herself with brushing the dirt so liberally from one place to another that Toby, as bystander, was all but asphyxiated. Indeed, so copiously did he sneeze that she was forced to desist altogether.

Goliath Jones had busied himself in making ready the old Welsh cob who, despite his pot-bellied girth and indolence, seemed delighted to be back in harness. With dry bedding brought from the house, and those few clothes and utensils which he thought indispensable, Mr Jones, with Nerissa's help, turned his attention to emptying the larder then filling some stone flagons from the well to provide them with water upon the way. Then he folded his Punch and Judy tent and placed it carefully within, together with the wooden trunk that housed the familiar characters. When all was accomplished to his satisfaction he made a brief call upon his neighbour, the apothecary, to purchase potions and herbs for the journey and to bid him return the horse and waggon to Major Crawshay at Knatchfield Grange. He gave no explanation, save that its safe return would be a favour to him, and the apothecary did not press him as to the reason why. A man's business was his own, and Jones was an honest man.

"Should any come enquiring for you," the apothecary asked, as neighbour, "what would you have me say?"

"That Toby and I will be long gone . . . journeying upon the roads. We will go wherever our fancy takes us and where we may earn a crust. I have a yearning to return to the old ways."

"There is nothing you would have me do in your absence?"

"If you would keep a close eye upon the cottage . . . see that there are no intruders." He smiled, adding dryly, "There is little of value within and naught worth the trouble of stealing, but 'tis home and shelter to Toby and me and I would not have it violated."

"Yes," the apothecary promised, "I shall do so gladly. I wish you Godspeed on your journey, neighbour, and a safe return."

"Aye. Amen to that, my friend," Goliath Jones said fervently, "amen to that."

The discovery of Nerissa's blood-stained gown and slippers at Knatchfield Grange had put the whole household in a turmoil and led to a rigorous questioning of the servants and staff. Henrietta Cobner had kept her word and maintained a stoical silence upon the matter, although speculation ran high and often wild. Once, in view of Mrs Crawshay's extreme distress, she had all but confessed to her meeting with Nerissa, but some stubbornness of pride forbade her. She at least knew that Arabella's companion had come to no actual physical harm, for all that she was emotionally distraught. Her leaving Knatchfield had been of her own volition and she had gone alone. The words Nerissa had used came vividly to mind.

"I beg, Mrs Cobner, that you will ask me no more . . . that you will believe that what I do is from the best of motives. That no one will be harmed by my leaving, save me."

So intense had been her plea, and so honestly made, that Henrietta Cobner was in no doubt as to the truth of it. Whatever had occurred to make the poor child flee, then it would stay locked within her; a secret never to be told. Mrs Cobner would betray Nerissa to no one, not even her friend and ally, Selina Pratt, for the housekeeper's allegiance was first and foremost to Major and Mrs Crawshay. Yet the anguish of divided loyalties constantly bedevilled Henrietta Cobner, excoriating, laying painfully raw. It was with relief that she heard that the stable boy had confessed that Miss Pritchard had ridden out for a second time upon the horse and waggon. He knew not whither she was bound, for it was not his place to ask her, but she had given him a threepence for his trouble and wished him well. It was all he was willing, or able, to disclose. Questions as to her possible state of mind, her appearance and whether or not she seemed terrified or at ease, were met courteously but with blankness. He was paid to tend horses, not people, and he had done so devotedly. None could fault him for that.

Francis and Luke were insistent upon riding out at once to seek Nerissa. Already it grew dark, and were she stranded somewhere alone, and victim of some accident, then she might fall prey to some marauding highwayman or thief. Arabella had begged to be allowed to ride with them, but Francis had been adamant that she remain at Knatchfield against Nerissa's possible return. Grudgingly, and only after strongest protestation, she had agreed, less from conviction than fear of causing Francis greater agitation. He would take the carriage and drive to the Pilgrim's Rest at St Samson, he declared, to question Joe Protheroe as to her whereabouts. Luke, in turn, would ride swiftly on horseback to learn what he might from Goliath Jones at Holly Grove, for she would surely have told him of her plans. The male members of the household staff and those employed in stable and yard, would take lanterns and search the surrounding lanes and highways. Mounted or on foot, they would seek urgent sighting of horse and waggon and report news of it to Hillier at Knatchfield Grange.

With this, Arabella had to content herself, for there was no more to be done. With the deepening of darkness, the fears she had tried to suppress before Francis and Luke came crowding to the surface, insistent, stark, raking her with terror. Memory of Nerissa's blood-stained gown and the blood-soaked slippers returned sickeningly to haunt her. What had Nerissa seen? Been forced to endure? What violence had driven her away? It was something so unspeakable that she had been powerless to confide it, even to those who loved and would strive to protect her. Arabella felt a coldness settle upon her that owed nothing to the chill of the night and the darkness. It was a darkness of spirit. The darkness that had come upon her with Francis's sickness. Wherever Nerissa might be, Arabella prayed that she would find comfort and escape from whatever evils threatened her. Francis and Luke would find her and bring her home. Luke loved her and would not be defeated . . . unless, like Francis, the defeat was final and irreversible, and came from death itself.

Luke's journey to Holly Grove had been constrained by darkness and the fear of what he might find. His mind returned constantly to thought of that night when he had stumbled upon the lifeless body of Tom Pritchard, flesh brutally savaged and torn. He tried to settle his mind upon other things, but the memory returned to plague him and would not be expunged. There was no profit in such macabre imaginings, he told himself harshly. That night bore no relationship to this . . . It had been a night bright with moonlight. A hunter's night. A hunter's moon, and Tom Pritchard the hunter and hunted both . . . Yet now, in the darkness, with only the pale beams of the lantern splintering light and the sound of his horse's hooves ringing clear as a tocsin, he felt the same aloneness, the same grief of loss. Then it had been at the death of a man unknown, for an evil violently done. Now the loss was deeper and more personal, the loss of the woman he loved, yet born of the flesh of one he had known only in death. How strange and tenuous the links that bind us close. Had he but turned away, or travelled by another road, he would not now be searching for Nerissa or pledged to remain at Francis's side for as long as Francis had need of him.

When he came at last to Holly Grove and the Punch

and Judy man's house, Luke was in a lather of fear and despondency. There were no lights at the windows, no visible signs of life. He was a fool to expect it, he told himself. Goliath Jones was an old man, in need of rest, and would take to his bed early. Yet as he tethered his mount at the ring set into the cottage wall and took the path to the door, he was aware of an emptiness, the sad echoing of a house deserted. Surely Toby must have heard his footsteps or his hurried arrival, and barked an alarm? But there was only the chill of darkness and an all-pervading silence. He hammered loudly upon the door, hoping to arouse those within, but to no purpose. The cottage was plainly deserted.

Yet his noisy clamouring had result, for a face appeared at the lattice of the neighbouring cottage, bathed in the flickering glow of a candle.

"What is your business, sir?" The voice was surly and thick with sleep. " 'Tis a strange hour to be calling!"

"I seek Goliath Jones."

"Are you a friend?" suspiciously.

"Indeed. One who wishes him only well."

"You had best wait there! I will descend and speak with you," he was instructed gruffly.

When he finally appeared, the unknown man seemed less disgruntled, altogether less prepossessing, dressed hurriedly as he was in the oddest assortment of clothes over his voluminous nightshirt. He carried a horn candle lantern in one hand and clutched in the other a stout stave, ready to defend himself. He held the lantern close to Luke's face then, presumably satisfied with what he saw, grunted and lowered it, saying, "You had best give account of yourself, sir. The night air is chill and I have no wish to linger."

"I am Luke Farrow, sir, a visitor from Knatchfield Grange, where I am a guest of my friends, Major and Mrs Francis Crawshay."

"Then I have a duty to discharge, sir."

"A duty?"

"Aye . . . the return of your horse and waggon . . . 'twas your friend, Goliath Jones, who charged me with it."

"He is not here?" Luke demanded anxiously.

"No, sir . . . long gone, I fear. He has taken Toby in that Romany caravan of his. 'Tis a passion of theirs to take to the roads now and again, for they relish the freedom. He will give performances upon the way, the Punch and Judy and all, and earn a bare living."

"They have gone alone? With no other?"

"Lord, sir! Who but a lunatic would travel so? There is scarce room to swing a cat within, much less swing Toby!" He laughed appreciatively at his own jest, declaring, " 'Tis my opinion he would be better housed in his Punch and Judy tent, for 'tis a rickety old contraption, and the cob winded and pot-bellied, scarce fit enough to drag it!"

"It will travel slowly, then . . . not get far?"

"That is a fact, and none will dispute it! Now, if you will excuse me, sir, I had best return to my bed, else my good wife will be screaming 'Murder'."

As Luke nodded and thanked him, he said with wry humour, "I would not be over hasty to ride after them, sir. Should you give them a full week's start, you will still overtake them at the parish boundary! Like the mills of God, its wheels grind exceeding slow."

With a swift wave of the lantern and still clutching his stave grimly, he was gone, only to call back anxiously, "The horse and waggon, sir? Will you take delivery of them? Return them to their owner at Knatchfield?"

Luke hesitated. "No. My task is not ended. Someone will collect them tomorrow, and drive them away . . . and recompense you for all your trouble."

" 'Tis no trouble to aid a neighbour, sir, and one as honest and generous as Goliath Jones, but I shall not refuse. I shall keep the money against his returning. 'Twill buy him kindling and victuals, should his showmanship or old cob fail." With a cheerful wave of his stave, and a bob of the lantern, he bade Luke "Good-night", adding, "Should you need to seek me out, you have but to ask for the apothecary. I am known so hereabouts."

Luke was certain that Goliath Jones's hurried departure and his sudden yearning to return to a wanderer's life, was not a mere whim. It must have been prompted more for Nerissa's safety than his own comfort. The waggon and horse left in the care of his obliging neighbour, the apothecary, was proof that it was to the Punch and Judy man that she had turned for support, and seemingly found it. It had been a clever solution to whatever threat or danger plagued her, for she would be safely under cover, and none would suspect her presence. Moreover, Goliath Jones, Toby and she would be free to journey where they chose, setting up the Punch and Judy tent, earning a modest living, yet arousing the suspicion of none and the gratitude of many. As he untethered his horse, Luke was in a quandary as to how best to act. It would serve no useful purpose to travel the roads at night searching for them. There were so many quiet byways and little-known drovers' trails which Goliath Jones might have taken that it would need an army to search for them. As like as not they were not even travelling the roads, but settled in some secluded field or farmyard until daybreak. Should he come upon them unawares, it would only add to their alarm. No, he would ride first to the Pilgrim's Rest at St Samson to tell Francis the little he had learned and to make plans for the morrow. Nerissa must be brought back to Knatchfield Grange, where her safety would be assured, then made to tell them what tragedy had occurred, what violence she had witnessed to make her flee so despairingly . . . As long as she remained well hidden within the Romany caravan, her whereabouts unknown, she had nothing to fear. Even so, Luke could not feel entirely sanguine. Goliath Jones, for all his stubborn loyalty, was old and slightly made, and Toby hardly more prepossessing. After the rout at Holly Grove fair, none could doubt their courage and tenacity, but that would not deter a villain more lethally armed.

Throughout the lonely ride through the darkness to the inn at St Samson, Luke was uneasy in his mind. Once, at the crossroads, he had halted his mount and all but turned back to search for her, but after a moment of painful indecision had set the horse upon the proper road again. He was, he realised, acting not with the reasoned calm of an adversary, a soldier, but with the foolish impetuosity of a lover . . . He was behaving like a man deranged. His only consolation, if it could be counted as such was that he believed he could track Nerissa down; that he had knowledge given to no other, save the unsuspecting apothecary at Holly Grove. Poor Francis, he thought fleetingly, would have had a wasted journey and would still be in ignorance of Nerissa's escape . . . It would cheer him and Arabella immeasurably to learn of Nerissa's likely whereabouts.

As he wearily approached the yard of the inn, it was to see Francis climbing into the carriage, its whale-oil lamps casting pools of flickering light upon the cobblestones. By the glow of the candle-lantern clutched in his hand, Francis's face was gaunt and anxiously drawn, a hollow death's head. For a moment, Luke felt a tightness at his throat, an anguish of fear that it was not living flesh but a skeleton he looked upon, but the fear was as swiftly passing as the light.

"Luke?" His voice was anxious. "You have heard, then?"

"Heard? No! What has occurred?" he demanded harshly.

"Joe Protheroe . . . He is dead! Murdered most foully." At Luke's cry of disbelief, he leapt from the carriage and hurried to Luke's side, reaching up and grasping his arm, warning fiercely, "No! Do not dismount! Do not question me here. Drive out beyond St Samson and I will tell you all."

When they were clear of the boundary, Francis halted the carriage noisily and Luke dismounted urgently to stand beside him.

"It was not safe to speak at the inn." Francis's face was troubled, voice bleak. "I could not afford to be overheard."

"Protheroe?"

"Savagely struck down and hurled into his own cellar!"

"Who was it? De Granville?"

Francis shook his head. "No . . . for he is not yet capable, still sick."

"Who then?"

"I swear I do not know . . . but I fear that Nerissa witnessed it, for there was a pool of blood where he lay."

"Dear God! Then she is witness . . . knows the murderer, and that is why she fled."

"Not murderer, Luke . . . although barely living. That was what I dared not reveal . . . It was confided to me by the justice, on my pledge to secrecy."

"Who else knows?" Luke asked sharply.

"Dr Munro, for he was immediately called, but he will tell no one. They plan to trap Protheroe's assailant into confession."

"Thank God that Protheroe lives!" Luke exclaimed fervently. "With his firm evidence, none can escape the gallows . . . Nerissa will be safe."

Francis was a long time in replying.

"I fear not," he said gently. "Even should Protheroe survive, the blow to his skull has all but crippled him . . . He can neither see nor make sound."

Chapter Twenty-Two

Arabella, trapped anxiously at Knatchfield, wandered with restless impatience from room to room. She found herself touching things for reassurance, lifting and replacing them without sight or volition, simply to be occupied. She could not erase from her mind the horror of finding Nerissa's blood-stained clothing and slippers, and would not allow herself to dwell upon what dangers she might face. A young woman, alone and unprotected, upon the roads was easy prey to every footpad and vandal, and now Nerissa travelled in darkness. At the welcome sound of the carriage halting without, Arabella took a lantern and hurried from the house. Even as Francis climbed down and a groom ran forward to uncouple the horses, there was the unmistakable sound of a lone rider entering upon the carriageway. Arabella glanced to Francis for reassurance, but his face was bleakly expressionless, betraying nothing.

"Nerissa? You have news of Nerissa?" she demanded.

"Luke will tell you all," fatigue and sickness thickened his voice, "but we believe her to be safe for the moment."

Arabella, alarmed by his exhaustion, made to support his arm and lead him within. Luke swiftly dismounted beside them, boot soles grating upon the scattered stones as he made to steady his mount and give it into the care of a stable lad. The horse was sweating and lathered, breath raw, and had clearly been over-ridden, and Luke, despite his own weariness, was quick to praise and gentle it, murmuring his remorse.

"Luke? You have news of Nerissa?" Arabella's voice was high pitched and querulous, her fear as much for Francis.

"Yes, my dear . . ." Unobtrusively Luke had taken hold of Francis's elbow and was assisting him gently within. "There is much to be told, much to be decided, but we had best attend first to Francis's needs."

When Francis was comfortably settled before a blazing log fire in the library and both men were warmed with generous measures of brandy, their findings were re-examined for Arabella's sake.

She listened in near-silence before exclaiming in growing horror, "Then Nerissa is not safe! She is more than ever at risk! If she recognised and can identify Joe Protheroe's assailant, he will surely track her down."

"She is safe for the moment with Goliath Jones," Luke tried to reassure her, "I am certain of it, Arabella. None would think of searching for her there."

Arabella was not wholly convinced. With memory of Hugo Curtis's violence upon Francis and the ease with which he had gained access to the house, she said vehemently, "Nerissa must be brought back . . . put under constant guard until that . . . creature who attacked Joe Protheroe is caught."

"We shall find her as soon as ever it grows light," Francis promised, "you have my word, Arabella. Luke and I will scour every field and pathway, every last trail and track. They will not have travelled far."

Luke added his firm assurance.

"But how does the justice hope to trap the man, Francis?" she asked anxiously. "What docs he propose?"

"He has demanded a meeting with Luke and me tomorrow," Francis confessed, "in order to lay proper plans . . . but they must be kept a close secret, confided to no one."

"But did he give no hint of what he intends?" she persisted.

"It seems that he will rely on the discretion of the landlord's wife . . . let no other, save Dr Munro, minister to Protheroe . . . then set a watch upon the inn, and an armed guard within the sick-room."

"But if the attacker believes that the innkeeper is dead? How will that serve?"

"Sir Charles Hanford will let news that Joe Protheroe

survives be leaked abroad, spread it through the inns and taverns, at the gaming houses and the markets and wells. What he will *not* reveal is that Protheroe is helpless as a babe, powerless to aid him, for he is robbed of both sight and speech."

"Oh, but it is horrible! Horrible!" Arabella exclaimed impassionedly, and close to tears. "To cripple an honest man deliberately . . . and to leave him for dead. What sort of a brute . . . what animal, would treat a man so? It is past believing!"

Neither Francis nor Luke made answer.

"I will go tomorrow, the very first thing, and take what comforts I may to that poor creature, Protheroe's wife. Mrs Cobner will provide some nourishing calf's-foot jelly and some fresh mutton broth . . ."

"No, Arabella! You will not go near!"

Arabella broke off, startled, staring at Francis in stupefaction as he warned tensely, "It might set the justice's plans at risk . . . Moreover, it would set you cruelly in danger! What if you were to be trapped there when the attacker returned? He would spare you as little mercy as he spared Joe Protheroe. No, Arabella, I firmly forbid it!" As Arabella made to argue, he declared with finality, "If you do not value your own life, then have a care for Protheroe and his wife. Yes, and Nerissa, too, for they will all be set at risk."

Arabella stared at him in reproach, underlip jutting mutinously, then unexpectedly capitulated, declaring grandly, "Well, I shall go as soon as ever the justice gives me leave . . . Come hell or high water, Francis, nothing shall stop me."

Despite his fatigue and irritation with her, Francis could not hide a smile as he conceded ruefully, "I would not dream of it, my love. I doubt if the army and militia combined, the entire navy and the Almighty Himself, could stay you!"

Arabella obligingly pretended outrage, but amusement defeated her as Luke intervened pertinently, "But if it were for Francis's sake, Arabella? For his sake, and mine, because we love you, and would protect you?"

"Then of course I would obey you without question!" Arabella dimpled, and kissed first Francis and then Luke, extravagantly bidding them an affectionate "good-night".

Long after she was safely abed and asleep, Francis and Luke stayed at the fireside discussing their meeting with the justice upon the morrow. Their first duty must be to seek out Nerissa and to bring her safely home to Knatchfield. Was the attack in some way connected with Tom Pritchard's death? They had discussed it endlessly, but could come to no firm conclusion. Protheroe might well have been set upon by some passing vagrant, or some drunken reveller whom he had offended. It might prove an aggravated assault for robbery or a revenge, long planned. One thing was certain, that whatever the cause, Nerissa was at risk. No, at least two things were certain, Luke corrected himself firmly as he lay abed, too restlessly disturbed to sleep . . . he loved Nerissa, and would confess it to her openly and ask her to be his wife. He had but to find her, and find her he would, even if he searched for the rest of his life.

At daybreak upon the morrow, Francis and Luke rode out separately on horseback to search for Goliath Jones's Romany caravan. Hanson, Arabella's coachman, and Manley, the groom, were also entrusted with the task of searching for the Punch and Judy man, although they were not apprised of the true nature of their quest. Should they catch glimpse of him upon the byways or encamped in some field, they were instructed to tell him that Major Crawshay would be pleased to see him at Knatchfield Grange with the valuable cargo he carried. It would be safer there. Manley, intrigued by the cryptic message, speculated that Major Crawshay no doubt wished to hire the Punch and Judy man to give Mrs Crawshay some birthday or anniversary treat, for it was rumoured that she was much taken with his performance at Holly Grove fair. Hanson, who thought he divined the true reason for the search, declared coldly that idle thoughts were no substitute for action, and Manley had best be on his way. It was not their place to question the motives of their betters. He had climbed stiffly into the gig and driven off towards the isolated drovers trail, and Manley had swung himself into the saddle of his mare and set it to the opposite direction, dwelling broodingly upon the old coachman's irascibility. The old man was growing senile, he thought. He was irritable and abrasive, all but impotent. He could not long remain in Major Crawshay's service, but should be set out to pasture, decently retired . . . Surely, if Hanson's post as coachman were to become vacant, then he would be his natural successor, the obvious choice. Much comforted and with a new elation and purpose, he set about his task of finding the Romany caravan.

The search for Goliath Jones and his decrepit horse and waggon had been thorough and painstaking, and those involved had spared no effort. Hour after hour they had patiently scoured the countryside, but to no avail. They explored every mean track which might take the caravan, combed every lane and meadow, every remote farm and cottage yard. Yet they found no trace of it nor news of its passing. None had sighted it nor showed knowledge of whom they spoke. The Punch and Judy man had disappeared, it seemed, from the face of the earth.

Francis and Luke returned disconsolately to Knatchfield Grange within ten minutes of each other to learn that Hanson and Manley had searched as fruitlessly as they. Francis was unusually pale and enervated, his disappointment plain. It was disturbingly clear that the journey had taken toll of his strength, yet none could speak of it openly nor beg him to rest for fear of eroding his confidence and sense of worth.

Arabella tried to put a brave face on her dismay, declaring that Nerissa and Goliath Jones were surely safe and settled at some village where the Punch and Judy man could test his thespian flair to the limits. As like as not, he was being fêted royally, and wined and dined as to the manner born. She did not doubt that Toby and the old cob would scarce be able to stir an inch for the titbits fed to them, and the spoiling received. Her cheerful banter soon restored Francis's spirits and, with Luke, he ate a trencherman's meal, his good humour and vitality seemingly returning.

Yet there was a new fragility about him, a transparent waxiness that gave Luke cause for deep concern, and he was painfully aware that the disease was no longer in recession, but taking stronger hold. Francis was more easily exhausted, and breathless, flesh falling inevitably away and leaving him gaunt. Luke's heart ached for Arabella, who kept up the pretence that she saw nothing amiss. Hers was a rare brand of courage; a selfless loving. He hoped that when Nerissa was finally found and brought safely to Knatchfield, their marriage might be as richly blessed with loyalty and affection . . .

Francis and Arabella were as one, and when they were riven apart by death, he feared Arabella might not survive the violence of it. It would be like a tree cleft apart, and without hope of life . . . sap withering and roots destroyed.

Francis was adamant upon returning to the search, determining to drive farther afield in the gig, and Arabella had declared her intention of travelling beside him, a decision he did not question. It had been cleverly manoeuvred, and Luke silently applauded Arabella's skill and cunning at getting her own way without causing hurt. So it was that they once more set out upon the search, travelling by different routes, and determined upon finding Nerissa.

They returned unsuccessful and woefully downcast, even Arabella unable to pretend to cheerfulness. They would, Luke declared unequivocally, have more success upon the morrow. They had searched the quieter, more inaccessible places; they had best turn their attention to the carriage roads and busier highways. Goliath Jones might well have decided that he would be better served by travelling openly, finding concealment amidst waggons and carriages and the caravans of Romanies and travelling tinkers or roving players of his own kind. Arabella made swift agreement, although she was not deceived. It seemed likely to her that Goliath Jones and Nerissa had already travelled well beyond the range of a hard day's riding. Each day took them further away, made hope of finding them more tenuous . . . Moreover, they might relax their guard, believe themselves safe; safe enough to appear openly in towns and villages, confidently setting up their Punch and Judy show. If their secret adversary proved single minded, he might well succeed in tracking them down. He had little to lose in attempting murder, since if he had already left St Samson then he believed Joe Protheroe to be dead. No, it was Nerissa and Goliath Jones who stood to lose, and if they did, then they would lose all.

Sir David Hanford, secure in the belief that Joe Protheroe was dead, knew that the only obstacle now to be removed was the witness to the murder . . . if witness she had been. She had certainly seen him fleeing, blood stained and dishevelled, from the Pilgrim's Rest and could be in little doubt as to his guilt. At least he knew who she was and where she lived, and could make opportunity to silence her. Nerissa Pritchard, the hireling at the fair, had proved more insistent an irritant than even de Granville had supposed. It seemed that, like the poor, she was destined to be always with them, and sent to try them! He was certain, he thought wryly, that he at least would not prove wanting! Nor, he was confident, would she be always with them. He permitted himself a dry smile as he made his way to the dining room, equanimity restored.

At dinner, with only he and his parents present, conversation had been sporadic, and turned inevitably to the dinner party upon the morrow. His father, although preoccupied, had declared that he would find the company of Major Crawshay and his wife, and Captain Farrow, unusually congenial. He could be sure of some intelligent conversation upon topics wide ranging, rather than the idle gossip of the parish pump.

Lady Mary had been equally enthusiastic about her guests, declaring that she found Mrs Crawshay remarkably good company, indeed, unusually civilised and cultivated . . . a pleasure to entertain. She added, in passing, "It is a pity that she has lost her companion, Miss Pritchard . . . a quiet, courteous young woman and highly regarded."

"She has left, you say?" The justice's tone was noncommital, and David Hanford, although perturbed, strove to appear disinterested.

304

"I dare say that Mrs Crawshay will survive the loss, Mama," he ventured languidly.

"Was she such a paragon, my dear?" the justice asked mildly. "And why then did she leave?"

"You may ask Mrs Crawshay tomorrow, since she dines here," his wife replied tersely. "I have only the bare facts, those which my maid related to me. It seems she simply fled."

"Fled, my dear?" the justice asked with greater animation. "How fled? You mean disappeared? Without notice, or word?"

"No. It seems she left a note explaining all."

"A note?" David Hanford asked sharply, forgetting the need for discretion. "A note, you say?"

His mother looked at him with surprise and disapproval, then softened her expression to say, "I suppose, my dear, that you are thinking that some young blade is involved . . . that it was some scandal, an affair of the heart? No such thing! She seems, by all accounts and from the little I have seen of her, to be a most intelligent and reliable young woman."

"The reason, Mama?" he reminded, tight lipped.

"Oh, as to that, I cannot say," she said lightly. "I know, and that only from hearsay, that she left in the greatest flurry and with no plans to return. Moreover, the waggon and horse upon which she left Knatchfield was collected from the apothecary at Holly Grove the very next day."

"Some sudden illness, then?" the justice suggested.

His wife raised her eyebrows expressively and inclined her head towards her son, although her face remained innocently expressionless.

"Well, my dear, it is none of our affair," the justice said curtly. "It is not ours to speculate upon the affairs of a servant."

"But it is strange, Charles, you will concur? It has the makings of an excellent mystery? A crime, even?"

"I have crimes enough of my own to solve, Mary!" he admonished. "Without inventing them! My time is already over-occupied with murder, mayhem and the rest . . . Allow me to at least eat in peace, I beg of you."

They completed their meal in strained silence. When it was ended, and David Hanford could make good his escape, he saddled his horse and instead of riding to St Samson to see de Granville, as he had intended, he rode directly to Holly Grove and the apothecary's house. He would invent some illness or demand some commonplace receipt for a toothache or suchlike . . . A man well paid would always speak more freely.

Hanford's visit to the apothecary soon provided him with the information he sought. True, he had been obliged to purchase a ludicrously expensive unguent for a putative back strain, but he considered it money well spent. What he learned seemed likely to prove a panacea for all his ills. There was no doubt in his mind that the Pritchard girl had removed herself from Knatchfield Grange with the aid of the Punch and Judy man and his caravan. If it proved as ramshackle and unreliable a conveyance as the apothecary feared, then it would not long survive upon the roads, nor could it travel at speed. It would be little trouble to intercept it upon its way and take whatever measures were necessary. There was now no great urgency to track the bitch down. As long as she was safely removed from the area she posed no immediate threat. Besides, he could be reasonably sure that the note which she had left the Crawshays did not actually incriminate him in Protheroe's murder, otherwise a hue and cry would have been called. His father, the justice, would have been the first to hear accusation against him and could not have kept such knowledge hid, even should he believe it to be false. No, for the moment he was safe enough. It would be foolhardy to search for her at night, and his prolonged absence would most certainly demand explanation. He hesitated only briefly at the apothecary's gate and reined his horse towards St Samson Court and his friend, de Granville.

His arrival had been greeted with the greatest of pleasure, for de Granville was thoroughly bored with his own company and had news of his own to impart.

306

"I have ridden abroad in the cabriolet today," he confided exuberantly, "and had the greatest excitement."

"Indeed?" Hanford murmured indifferently. "It must have been a rare adventure to travel freely again."

"No, you do not understand!" de Granville said impatiently. "The excitement lay in hearing that Joe Protheroe had been struck down by some assailant . . . That is news to you, I'll swear!" He was regarding Hanford with sly speculation.

"Yes, news indeed!" Hanford exclaimed forcefully enough to convince his friend. "How did you come by this news?"

"The village was agog with it . . . I am surprised that you have not heard. Your father did not speak of it?" he demanded.

"No. His work as justice is kept close to his chest. He will neither confide nor discuss it." He hesitated before claiming with satisfaction, "If Protheroe has been murdered by some other bearing a grudge, then it is to our advantage. He has done us a favour. I will not cavil at it!"

"No, not murdered," de Granville corrected. "Protheroe is gravely wounded, but not dead."

"Not dead?" Hanford stared at him in disbelief, mouth agape in astonishment. "You are certain of that?"

"I have it on the best authority."

"Whose?" Hanford was frankly sceptical.

"Siberry's," de Granville announced with satisfaction.

"Siberry's? How is he involved?"

"Oh, you may rest easy," de Granville said, amused. "Siberry did not strike the blow. He is in no way involved, save as an informant."

"Damnation, de Granville! Do not be so obtuse! Tell me, where did Siberry hear of it?"

"From his father, Dr Siberry. It seems that Dr Munro has been called to London on urgent business, and Dr Brace was occupied upon some other errand, so Brace was forced to send for Siberry's father and confide in him."

"And he in turn confided it to Matthew?"

"Indeed, no! He was close as the proverbial oyster! No,

307

Siberry somehow managed to eavesdrop upon their conversation and grew alarmed, fearing we were involved."

"The devil he did!"

"Well, you thought the same of him," de Granville pointed out dryly. "Anyway, the long and short of it is that Protheroe is still a danger to us . . . He will have more incentive now than ever to tell the justice all."

"Then he must be silenced," Hanford declared. "But how?"

"You are the best placed to deal with him."

"No!" Hanford's denial was angrily vehement. "With my father closely involved as justice, it would be madness . . . virtual suicide."

"Matthew Siberry, then?"

"No." The rebuttal was equally emphatic. "Siberry's father will be physician there . . . in and out at every whipstitch."

"Then it seems . . ." de Granville declared loftily, "that I have been elected . . . like it or not!"

"But you are still sick," Hanford said coldly, "barely recovered."

"It was my leg, not my wits, which was affected," de Granville reminded with wry humour. "Besides, I am better placed than any to enter legitimately. None will question my being there, should I by some mischance be discovered."

"How so?" Hanford asked brusquely.

"The inn is the property of the de Granville estate . . . I shall but be resuming my interest in it and the tenant. That will be a cause for congratulation, rather than opprobrium . . . I may even go openly if I choose, and with my father's blessing, to see how Protheroe fares."

"But you will not?"

"No. I shall go secretly and only use such excuse to protect myself, should I be challenged."

"But what will you do? How will you deal with him?" Hanford persisted.

"God knows!"

"Then it is to be hoped that He gives you inspiration," Hanford said sourly.

"You may be sure that I shall not fail," de Granville answered him smugly. "However foolish and cack-handed his would-be murderer, I shall not repeat his mistake . . . I will take whatever opportunity is offered . . . believe it!"

"And if you are caught?"

"Caught?" De Granville regarded him in absolute astonishment. "I am neither a fool nor a bungler, Hanford." He regarded him speculatively for a moment, then gave a broad grin of enlightenment. "Ah, I see," he exclaimed with relish. "It is your own hide you fear will be put at risk! You may sleep safely in your bed at night, Hanford. You need not risk your neck. I shall offer mine. You need have no nightmares about the hangman's rope."

Although he spoke lightly, there was a malicious amusement in his voice as his hands sketched out the outline of a noose then slashed a mock gash across his own throat.

Hanford, laughing sardonically, pretended to applaud, but could scarce contain the violence of anger within. What a damnable boor de Granville was, he thought abrasively, a conceited, puffed-up little coxcomb! *He* had already risked his neck, yes, and openly too . . . He had not gone sneaking to the bed of a sick man, but stood up to him, man to man, giving and allowing no quarter! Damn de Granville to hell. Damn him to little wild pieces!

"Well, will you not wish me luck, Hanford?"

"All the luck you deserve!"

It was uttered with such conviction and forcefulness that de Granville was surprised into silence. He had not realised the full extent of Hanford's fear for him, the depth of his friendship.

"Whatever befalls me," he promised with unusual gravity, "I shall not implicate you or Siberry, Hanford. You have my solemn oath upon it." He took Hanford's hand with awkwardness and clasped it tight. Hanford nodded and made his farewell.

When Francis and Luke had ridden out upon the morrow to extend their search for Nerissa and Goliath Jones, Arabella felt oddly depressed and ill at ease. She could not settle herself to the few diversions open to her. Reading

309

held no attraction, and she could work up no enthusiasm for taking her sketching block into the grounds or working at her needlework within. A strange restlessness possessed her, an anger that she was of so little use. What could she do at Knatchfield? Nothing to help in the hunt for Nerissa, nor to comfort that poor woman at St Samson, Joe Protheroe's wife. She knew well enough what the poor creature was feeling, the suffering of mind she endured. Was she not as deeply concerned for Francis, as emotionally flayed? She sometimes felt confusion about what was real and what was imagined, for it seemed that she was always hiding her emotions, playing a part. Like an actress upon a stage, she moved within a prescribed radius, her words and emotions as rigidly controlled, fearful always of revealing her true self . . . the despair she felt at Francis's dying, the rage, the grief, the unbearable hurt . . . Who better, then, to go to St Samson and share another's hurt? To Hanson's consternation, she ordered the carriage to be brought and ordered him to drive her to the Pilgrim's Rest.

"Is it wise, ma'am? With Major Crawshay away?" he mumbled uncertainly. "'Tis no place to be travelling." He broke off, confused, knowing that he had over-reached himself. He had known and loved Arabella from her childhood days, and could speak more openly than most, but could see that she was displeased at his insolence. "'Tis only your safety, ma'am, that makes me speak so," he made clumsy apology.

Arabella, who knew how stubbornly loyal the old man was, said quietly, "If you would prefer that Manley drive me, Hanson, or some other?" The rebuke was clear.

"No, Mrs Crawshay, ma'am. I shall bring the carriage to the door."

Arabella had received as little support and understanding from Mrs Pratt or Henrietta Cobner, who had furnished her with some calf's-foot jelly and other delicacies for the invalid, with a derisive sniff and a toss of the head. She had made no comment upon the outing, nor had she need to, for her expression and stance said all. She stood four square, arms akimbo, plump lips compressed – a picture of outraged misery. Selina Pratt had tentatively suggested to Arabella that she might accompany her upon the expedition, since her companion, Miss Pritchard, was absent and she had no suitable male escort.

Arabella had been courteous but firm. "Hanson will be escort enough," she declared, adding in amusement, "it is not to some . . . stew, or sordid alley that I travel to, Mrs Pratt, but a village inn in St Samson! I shall not be set upon by highwaymen nor abducted into a life of slavery!"

Mrs Pratt was shocked at such flippancy and decidedly unamused, but could not insist upon accompanying her, for Arabella was notoriously strong willed.

Arabella, climbing into the carriage, with the culinary delicacies spread carefully upon the leather seat opposite her, felt a momentary spasm of remorse at her high-handedness, but stifled it. Looking at poor Hanson's sparse locks straggling beneath his tricorne, and his frailness, she felt a pang of regret at how swiftly he had aged. He seemed skeletal almost, flesh fallen away from bone, cheeks sunken painfully. Memory of Francis rose unbidden to her mind, and she saw in him the same gauntness, the same wasting of strength and flesh, and could have wept for the grief it brought her.

Arabella had alighted at the Pilgrim's Rest with a murmured command to Hanson that when the horse and carriage were delivered into the hands of the ostler, he might refresh himself within the inn at her expense and await upon her leaving. She had entered unescorted, bearing the gifts she had brought and looking for a servant who might take her to Mrs Protheroe.

Even as she crossed the stone-flagged hall which housed the wooden staircase to the floor above, she was aware of angrily raised voices overhead, a heated exchange, sharp and acrimonious. She stepped back into the shadows, fearful of being seen. The most insistent voice was steadier now, less strident, more carefully controlled. She did not immediately recognise it, but the languid tones and affectation were familiar to her.

"My dear Dr Siberry . . . I scarce know what to say. A

311

thousand apologies . . . I would not have disturbed your patient for the world. I beg you will believe it."

There was a murmured rejoinder which she did not catch.

"I'll own, sir, that it was real concern which brought me here, not idle curiosity . . . I am scarcely recovered from my own sickness, but one must make some effort for one's tenantry!"

"Well, sir," the other speaker was plainly affronted, awkwardly at ease, "you have asked my opinion and I have given it." Then more firmly, "My patient is not to be disturbed. That is the crux of it. I can let no one enter, no one tax him."

There was an angry tirade of protest, but the physician remained unmoved, declaring, "I can make no exception. Should you wish to convey your condolences to Mrs Protheroe, then I am sure that she will accept them with the same sincerity with which they are offered. I bid you good-day, sir."

"But the patient, sir? Am I to have no account of his progress?"

"He progresses the way one would expect, given the circumstances and the severity of the assault. Now, if you will excuse me I shall return to my duties."

Arabella heard the opening and closing of a door on the landing above and footsteps descending the stairs. She was well and truly caught, she thought guiltily, as she moved impulsively from the shadows to where she could clearly be seen, her expression one of charming absentmindedness.

"Why, Mr de Granville, is it not?"

Richard de Granville, surprised and flustered, flushed like a callow schoolboy, not an assured man of the world as he would have chosen to present himself.

"Mrs Crawshay, ma'am . . . your humble servant. I had not expected to see you here."

"Nor I you, sir . . . It seems that we are bent upon the same errand."

"Indeed?" His hand went instinctively to the knife-blade in the deep pocket of his tiered cape and he could not resist a smile of amusement which Arabella was swift to observe.

"I trust, sir, that you found Mr Protheroe much improved? Were reassured?" she offered innocently. "We must all hope and pray for his swift recovery, that he might bring the guilty to justice."

He nodded curtly, saying inconsequentially, "I believe, ma'am, that we are to meet again, and soon."

"Indeed, sir? I was unaware of it!" Arabella's voice was sharp.

"We are to be fellow guests, ma'am, of the justice at Lanelay Court, tomorrow."

"Then it is to be hoped that our adventuring takes us no further, sir, than his table."

What the devil did she mean? De Granville looked at her in perplexity. What adventuring? Was she giving him open invitation to pursue her? Showing her interest in him in Crawshay's absence? Or was it some heavy-handed piece of coquetry?

Mrs Protheroe, in mob-cap and calico apron, came bustling from the kitchen, all pride and fuss to greet Arabella's coming, and de Granville rapidly made his escape. It had been a damnably close-run thing. He had not expected to see an armed guard stationed at Protheroe's bedside when he had so recklessly burst into his bed-chamber. Dr Siberry had been hostile, indeed insolent in the extreme. He was still smarting from the indignity of it and of being routed before Mrs Crawshay. For Protheroe, as for her, he could play a waiting game . . . death could conveniently deliver them both.

Chapter Twenty-Three

Goliath Jones, Nerissa and Toby had left Holly Grove by a remote and little-used track. It was known only to itinerants and passing drovers, or those who, like the Punch and Judy man, travelled with shelter and possessions, as a snail carries its home upon its back. They had seen few fellow travellers, and those, for the most part, journeymen tinkers, with their carts piled high, or paupers and vagrants seeking to barter their labour upon the farms and poor holdings. There was, Goliath Jones assured Nerissa, a brotherhood of the road, a camaraderie. It was incumbent upon those who journeyed to help each other, to treat them as if they were kin. He was a kind man, as generous in giving of himself as in providing victuals for those who were in need of them, asking nothing in return save the pleasure of their company. It seemed to Nerissa that he acted as a magnet to the weary and dispossessed, drawing them to him by the sheer force of his humanity. He drew them to his camp fire at night as he had drawn Nerissa, Ruth and the children into the all-embracing warmth of his affection. Toby, too, was as open hearted and gregarious, cheerfully indiscriminate in lavishing his welcome. If he sometimes over-reached himself by showing off his hard-learned tricks, then the visitors were well fed and indulgent, and thought no worse of him. It seemed to Nerissa that at Holly Grove fair he must have suffered a sudden rush of blood to the head in attacking de Granville, some mental aberration, for he was the most docile and tractable of creatures. It was to defend her and Goliath Jones that he had acted so violently out of character, but she did not doubt that if they were ever similarly threatened, he would repeat the performance.

314

She did not wish to dwell upon thought of Richard de Granville or the fiasco at Holly Grove, for it brought back crueller, more insistent memories of all that was lost to her . . . Knatchfield Grange and its inhabitants seemed long gone, yet they stayed vivid in her mind, Luke Farrow most painfully of all, and often, at night, her straw pillow was wet with tears. Goliath Jones could have wept himself at her awkward efforts to cry unheard, her determined cheerfulness, yet he could not show it. Toby, who had no such scruples, sometimes thrust an inquisitive nose into her fist, its cold nuzzling a well-meant comfort. Tears were often changed to laughter at his antics, and he was well satisfied. At night, he took to sleeping beside her, curled up close for warmth, and there grew a deep companionship between the pair which the Punch and Judy man was at pains to encourage.

Little by little, as the landscape changed and the miles from Holly Grove lengthened, Nerissa, for all her grief at leaving Knatchfield, seemed to grow more relaxed. She had feared boredom upon the roads, a feeling of suffocation at being so rigidly confined. Yet, as Goliath Jones had promised, there was a sense of freedom, a leisurely unfolding of time and landscape, a slowing of pace. The hours were too short for all that needed to be done . . . the constant cooking, the scouring of pots and pans, the cleaning of the caravan, the laundering in stream and pond, the welcome hospitality extended to fellow travellers . . . The lives of others added new dimensions to her own and, increasingly, she knew contentment now, but never forgetfulness. She must keep up her efforts at reading and writing, Goliath Jones declared, and soon, at some market or village fair, they might purchase old books for a few meagre pence, since few cottagers could read or write, and their daily needs were more prosaic.

"You shall learn to help me with the Punch and Judy show," he promised, and their rehearsals with Toby at the roadside proved so unexpectedly hilarious that she could scarce continue with the act, so convulsed with laughter was she at his nonsense.

In all, it was a tranquil time, an oasis as calm as the

landscape about her, with fears of the murderer of Joe Protheroe receding with every passing mile. Even Goliath Jones was lulled into a sense of security. If the justice's son meant to revenge himself upon Nerissa, he thought, he would have tracked them down by now, hunted them determinedly. The further they travelled upon the roads, the greater the prospect of safety. If he wondered when, if ever, they might return, then he never spoke openly of it. It was enough, for the present, to be alive.

His only regret was that Major Crawshay had not come seeking them or, more pertinently, the young Captain Farrow. It was transparently plain that Nerissa loved him. From what he had seen of him at Holly Grove fair, Luke Farrow was an honest man, spirited, and not lacking in compassion. Whether that would be enough to bridge the chasm between Nerissa's world and his, Goliath Jones was doubtful. "Love conquers all", someone had once given opinion . . . More like it was passion they meant; quick to flare, and as quickly extinguished. Love demanded nurturing – a fusion of time and patience, a growing together. Nerissa had been denied that. Perhaps it was in the end a kindness that she had been forced from Knatchfield Grange. The young were proud and resilient. She would forget. Better the brief anguish of a parting than the slow corrosion of disillusionment. But then he was old and had known no company save that of Toby and others of his kind. What did he know of love? Love between a man and a woman? 'Twas beyond his province and in God's alone . . . One could but leave it to the Almighty's good sense. Men showed little enough, in all conscience!

Luke and the Crawshays had little enthusiasm for attending Sir Charles Hanford's dinner party, despite their liking for the justice. All were deeply concerned at Nerissa's disappearance. They were well aware of the danger she faced, and Luke and Francis were continually frustrated in their efforts to find her, their spirits depressed. Francis, at Hillier's suggestion, had hired reliable and discreet riders to search for Goliath Jones's caravan upon the roads and to bring back news from the small towns and villages. It

316

promised to be a slow and wearisome process, with no guarantee of final success. Arabella, in addition to her fears for Nerissa, had other concerns which she tried to keep hidden. Fear for Francis and daily evidence of his deterioration were a constant grief. In addition, she was plagued by the guilty knowledge that she had defied his warning and gone to the Pilgrim's Rest to enquire about Joe Protheroe. She knew now how foolishly headstrong she had been and the risks she had faced. She had agonised long over whether she should confess her duplicity to Francis and Luke, and that she had seen Richard de Granville attempting to gain entry to Protheroe's bed-chamber. Yet what purpose would it serve? She could burden Francis no further with confirmation of her wil-fulness, the danger she had deliberately sought.

While she made preparation for an elegant appearance at Lanelay Court, her mind was occupied with thoughts of de Granville and the havoc he had already caused. Her mood was abrasive, her thoughts distinctly uncharitable. Surely he could not have intended Joe Protheroe harm? The idea was ludicrous! It seemed that he had gone quite openly to enquire as to his condition. He had done no more than she . . . It was, after all, the natural courtesy of a neighbour, one concerned at the misfortune of another. It did not equate with his treatment of Nerissa at the fair, but then, were we not all a mass of contradictions? He was arrogant and bumptious, certainly, yet no more so than many young blades of his age and social influ-ence who thought themselves God's gift to mankind! She was imputing to him all sorts of deviousness, not from evidence, but from her own instinctive dislike of him . . . Yet, was it not possible that his sickness had mellowed him? Surely his surliness at the fair did not make him irredeemable, only a boor? Francis and Luke were convinced that he had murdered Tom Pritchard, or was at least implicated in his death . . . but murder had not been proven, no more had the alleged attack upon Nerissa in the cabriolet. Hundreds of such accidents happened upon the roads, particularly when young blades were out to impress, or else in their cups. It was an immutable fact of life. Had

317

she not believed that the obscene threats upon her own life, by the lunatic Curtis, were de Granville's doing? Luke and Nerissa were as convinced that it was he who had erected the hideous gallows upon the lawns, with the threat to destroy her. Give a dog a bad name, she thought ruefully, and hang him. Of one thing she was certain, de Granville had carried no pistol and shot nor destructive weapon. He had thrown back the tiered cape he wore and from the sleek stylishness of his tailoring, he travelled unarmed, and as innocently as he claimed.

His presence at the inn still left her in a quandary. Was she deluding herself in giving him the benefit of the doubt? Was it to treat de Granville fairly or merely to set herself in a better light that she withheld all knowledge of their meeting from Francis and Luke? She suspected that it was the latter, but eased her conscience by assuring herself that it was also to spare Francis hurt. What if Richard de Granville were to speak of seeing her at the Pilgrim's Rest, make some barbed comment? It was a risk she had to take. He would scarcely behave so churlishly before others, and Mary Hanford had told her that there would be fifteen guests in all. The conversation would surely be guided into more innocuous and less contentious channels than the assault upon a local innkeeper? Francis trusted her implicitly and had never reacted jealously, for she had never given him cause. If de Granville, from pique and devilment, tried to pretend that their meeting had been prearranged, some lovers' tryst or assignation, then he and all others would be quickly disabused. She in turn would reveal his discreditable brawling at Holly Grove fair and young David Hanford's involvement . . . so they had best be circumspect!

Arabella, carefully putting the finishing touches to her toilette at the looking glass in her bed-chamber, saw a grave, slender-boned woman in a gown of muslin over eau-de-nil silk, high-breasted in the latest Regency fashion and falling from a band of embroidered silver into gentle folds. Her fair hair, swept into a chignon and falling in ringlets, was cross-laced with a matching silver riband. She fastened a necklace of aquamarines, set in filigree silver, at her throat and then a matching bracelet at her delicate wrist, with ornate aquamarine earrings as a finishing touch. She scented the pale flesh of her shoulders with lavender water and touched traces of it to the pulse spots at neck and throat and upon the inside of her wrists, then splashed it lavishly upon her lace-trimmed handkerchief. She regarded her reflection critically. Yes. She would do well enough. She would not disgrace Francis or herself. In the absence of a lady's maid, she had to depend upon her own resources. Yet she would appoint no other, but await Nerissa's return. She was firm upon it. She would not acknowledge, even to herself, that it was a superstitious dread which ruled her, a conviction that should she appoint some other in Nerissa's place then her companion would never return to Knatchfield. Arabella took up her silver reticule and the silk pelisse from her bedside chair and descended the steps to the hall, where Francis and Luke awaited her.

"You are truly beautiful, Arabella," Francis said with sincerity, eyes alight with gentle affection. "There will be none to hold a candle to you for charm and elegance."

"I heartily concur." Luke's gaze was as admiring.

"And I," Arabella responded, absurdly touched by their compliments, "will have as escorts the two most handsome and modish gentlemen in the whole of Knatchfield . . . indeed, I venture to declare, in the whole of Christendom."

"Flattery will get you everywhere, my love," Francis said, offering his arm with pardonable satisfaction.

"You are right, as always, in your assessment of our worth," Luke said, grinning broadly. "Only a churl would disagree."

"Pride goeth before a fall, sir!" Arabella reminded, taking the arm Luke courteously proffered.

As she swept out elegantly upon the arms of her two distinguished escorts, she felt a sudden chill of doubt, a presentiment. What if it were her own stupid pride and wrongheadedness which brought about a fall? The dinner at the justice's house threatened to be a trap for the unwary. She had but to hope that it was not she who was caught.

*　　*　　*

319

The distinguished arrival of the Crawshay party at Lanelay Court set the evening to a promising beginning. Their elegant travelling coach with its four perfectly matched chestnut horses, was a sight to gladden the most jaundiced eye and to excite admiration among the gentlemen. The ladies assembled were, quite naturally, less interested in the quality of the horseflesh than in the quality of Arabella's dressmaker, the estimated worth of her jewels. Like her equipage and her horses, Arabella passed handsomely on all counts. She was every whit as beautiful and stylish as her elegant conveyance, and her modishly dressed escorts did her full sartorial justice. Both gentlemen were exceedingly presentable, and with fine military bearing, although Major Crawshay appeared a little too gaunt and pallid in features, and easily exhausted. It was rumoured that he suffered from some wasting sickness, but it was as likely that it was as a result of some hard-fought battle or the constant deprivation of a soldier in the field. In any event, he was a most intelligent and amusing guest, witty, and immensely knowledgeable and well travelled, and his friend, Captain Farrow, as amenable.

There had been the slightest degree of frostiness when Major Crawshay was introduced to young Richard de Granville, as fellow guest, and a momentary awkwardness in his greeting. It was so quickly resolved that some were not even aware of it, and Major Crawshay had recovered his self-possession and urbanity almost at once. It seemed that they were already slightly acquainted, having previous dealings in horseflesh. Sir Charles Hanford, their host, who had seen Major Crawshay's discomfiture, thought it likely that young de Granville had reneged upon some promise, not kept strictly to his part of the bargain. That would be explanation enough for the reserve between them, a reserve apparently shared by Captain Farrow and Arabella Crawshay . . . Well, it was none of his affair. Francis Crawshay was more than able to deal with the young jackanapes and teach him his manners, that much was certain.

Sir Charles had no great liking for Richard de Granville,

whom he considered lightweight and arrogantly insensitive. The boy had neither the intellect nor the morality of his father, and lacked his seriousness of purpose. Indeed, the same accusation might fairly be laid against his own son, David. They were two of a kind, impetuous, bent solely upon pleasure, absurdly self-indulgent. Still, he had hopes that in his son's case it was no more than immaturity, a young man's kicking over the traces. Yet, in all honesty, he could not recall that he had ever been as hot-headed, so little interested in the estate and tenantry. Carefully hiding his displeasure, he assumed the mask of archetypal host, concerned, genially expansive, then, with the greatest of pleasure, escorted Arabella gallantly into the dining room.

It was a carefully selected, convivial gathering, which did full honour to the elegance of their surroundings. The guests sparkled and glittered as remorselessly as the candlelit chandeliers and the exquisite array of silver and crystal. The napery was as pristine and fresh as the garlanded ivy leaves and hot-house blooms which swathed the table. They trailed and spilled as freely from gleaming epergnes, profuse and exotic amidst the silver candelabra, the whole bathed in the soft glow of candlelight. It flickered and shone upon the animated faces and bejewelled flesh, the starched shirt frills and brocaded waistcoats, the careful panoply of the rich. The conversation shone as pleasantly: sometimes muted, sometimes lively and coruscating, always amusing, scandalous or designed to intrigue. Agreeably sated with wine and victuals, the company grew relaxed and carefree.

Mary Hanford, pleased with the evident success of her artistry, grew flushed and excited, exclaiming unwisely to any who would hear, "What a relief it is to see Charles so relaxed and happy! He has been so completely harassed of late. The attempted murder of that poor creature at St Samson . . . the innkeeper at the Pilgrim's Rest."

There was an immediate and awkward silence, with Sir Charles frowning his displeasure at such tactlessness and trying to change the course of the conversation. His guests were not to be so easily diverted.

"Protheroe, was it not? The landlord of the inn?" an elderly, bewigged gentleman in kneebreeches demanded abruptly. "A damned good fellow, by all accounts."

The rest of the gentlemen guests made muted agreement.

"A tenant of yours, de Granville, was he not?" the bluff-voiced gentleman demanded.

"Was, sir, and *is*, I am pleased to say, for I called at the Pilgrim's Rest but yesterday to enquire as to his progress . . . It appears that he is holding his own."

There was a grunt of disbelief from the old gentleman, a shrug of impatience as he declared sententiously, "I fear that you have been misinformed, sir. I am assured, on the best authority, that the poor wretch is scarce breathing . . . that he were better dead. He is no more than a vegetable, blind, deaf, unable to speak a word."

There was a shocked gasp from Luke and murmurs of distress from the ladies. The justice, forgetting his role as host, sprang up abruptly, chair scraping and overturning in his haste. He brought a fist crashing upon the table, to declare forcefully, "That is arrant nonsense, sir! Begging your forgiveness," he added stiffly, "I, sir, *am* the best authority. What you have heard is no more than tittle-tattle; chaff to be discarded!" Recalling himself with an effort, he ran a hand across his lips, murmuring in apology. "My anger is not with you, sir, I would have you believe, but with those who spread such rumour, such calumny. They cannot know what distress they cause."

The old gentleman was not to be easily mollified, demanding mutinously, "What harm is there, sir, in telling the truth? It will not change things . . . alter their ending! I stand by what I say. The potman at the Pilgrim's Rest, who resides there and has news of him daily, assures me that he can give no evidence against his assailant, his would-be murderer."

The justice, wry faced with anger, kept his gaze averted from Francis and Luke, but he did not miss the swift look of triumph which passed between de Granville and David Hanford. In his awkward distress, he took it as proof of their desire to see him outfaced, to be made

322

a laughing stock before his guests. The pettiness of it grieved him.

With a laudable effort, he regained control of himself, and with admirable *élan* turned the conversation to talk of books and art, skilfully drawing out opinion from the more reticent of the ladies. They blossomed under his attention and grew amusingly bold, and the whole company relaxed again, grateful that order and equanimity had been restored. The evening proceeded pleasantly enough, yet there was a certain reserve among some of the guests, a feeling of restraint that was palpable. The ubiquitous games of cards and the musical entertainment drew to an early close, and the carriages were summoned.

Sir Charles urged Francis and Luke to remain at Lanelay Court, after the other guests had departed, for there was a private matter which he would discuss with them. They had cordially agreed to his request, and none of their fellow guests could have suspected the gravity of their meeting, or the real reason for it.

While they awaited Sir Charles's return in the well-furnished library of the Court, Arabella was occupied in conversation with Mary Hanford, congratulating her upon the excellence of the arrangements and the pleasure which the evening had brought. Mary Hanford's indiscretion as hostess had apparently been forgotten by her, for she preened delightedly under Arabella's approval, growing more pinkly flustered by the moment. They were laughing companionably at some shared reminiscence when David Hanford and Richard de Granville came and stood beside them, waiting courteously until their conversation was ended. Arabella, despite her mistrust of the two young men, could not help but admire their elegance, their stylish possession. They were certainly most strikingly handsome. Each was a perfect foil for the other; one cleanly complexioned, blue eyed and with a careless clustering of fair curls, the other saturnine and lean, but as darkly arresting.

"Mrs Crawshay, your servant, ma'am."

Even as de Granville addressed her, Mary Hanford, with a murmured apology moved away to bid farewell to an elderly dowager, declaring reassuringly, "David and his friend, Richard, will entertain you, Arabella, of that I am sure."

Arabella was less convinced, but could not openly dispute it.

"Mrs Crawshay, ma'am," he repeated with a lavish bow.

"Mr de Granville," she returned coldly, to David Hanford's sly amusement. Arabella, intercepting his mother's anxious glance from across the hall, could not deliver the snub she intended for fear of offending her. Mary Hanford was a kindly soul and she did not wish to appear overtly discourteous.

"Our meeting at the Pilgrim's Rest was fortuitous, ma'am," de Granville ventured with a smug smile.

"Indeed, sir? I do not consider an assault upon an honest gentleman like Joe Protheroe fortuitous."

"Gentleman, ma'am?" Hanford asked with languid condescension.

"Yes, gentleman, sir," Arabella reiterated. "It would be foolish to judge a man's worth by the cut of his clothes. One is all too often mistaken."

Hanford flushed, although he steadfastly kept his pose of cultivated boredom as de Granville intervened smoothly, "As you say, ma'am, a tragedy that the poor . . . creature was so vilely assaulted. Some ruffian, perhaps, or labourer in his cups? Intemperance is the curse of the masses."

"Indeed, sir? I'll own that I have observed it in others more obviously advantaged. It is not peculiar to the rabble at fairs and such." The implication was plain.

"Your . . . serving girl, ma'am, your . . . hireling," Hanford's drawl was deliberately provocative, "my mama tells me that she has quit your service. Fled."

"Not 'fled', sir, but taken leave with my expressed approval and permission." Two spots of colour burned high in her cheeks and Arabella was painfully aware of his derisive scrutiny.

"Fled . . . taken leave . . . it is all one, ma'am, whichever euphemism one uses. I fear that the peasantry, the illiterate classes, have neither a sense of responsibility towards their betters, nor pride."

"Then I venture to suggest, sir, that you have pride enough, arrogance even, to compensate for any deficiency."

"Touché!"

Hanford raised his eyebrows, smiling sardonically as Arabella continued with cutting rudeness, "I require no lesson in semantics from you, sir! You might be more usefully employed in mending your manners. Your parents are too courteous and sensitive to the needs of others to allow me to believe that you were never taught."

Sir David Hanford made a deliberately mocking bow, but risked no further exchange, for he saw his mother returning.

Richard de Granville, dismayed by the abrasiveness of the meeting, and seeing advantage slipping away from him, blurted inanely, "Your husband, Major Crawshay, ma'am? His health is improving? It must be a distress that he is so . . . enervated, that he cannot return to his regiment, fulfil his approved duties."

Arabella was at first too shocked and disgusted by his impertinence to speak. When she did, it was with such chilling finality that he was cowed. "I do not think, Mr de Granville, that you need have any fears for my husband's fitness to serve his regiment. As for his ill health, he will face it as courageously and resolutely as all else, for that is the true mark of a soldier and a man. As for fulfilling his duty, he will always do that as conscientiously and remorselessly as all else. Believe it!"

Smarting with humiliation as he was, de Granville could not but be aware of the implied threat. As Lady Hanford smilingly approached, he said earnestly, to hide his chagrin, "I may hope, Mrs Crawshay, that you will forgive my brashness. Sickness has all but robbed me of my wits and courtesy." His smile was apologetic, meant to disarm, as he confided ingenuously, "I meant no offence, ma'am."

"Nor could you provide me any, Mr de Granville."

He heard Hanford's ill-concealed snigger and all but turned upon him viciously, but with an effort controlled himself, to say humbly, "I trust that we may meet again, ma'am, that I may undo the harm . . . set the matter straight."

"I think not, Mr de Granville . . . our past meetings have given me little cause for optimism . . . There! I believe that sets the matter straight enough! As for undoing the harm done, then surely that is a matter for your conscience and yours alone. However . . .?"

Confident of a softening of her attitude, de Granville expectantly awaited her surrender.

"However . . . it would seem to me that it were better not to behave as a graceless boor and a bully boy in the first place. To act as a gentleman, one who never knowingly or unthinkingly gives mindless hurt to others. Should you still be in any doubt as to how to behave, you might well take my husband, Major Crawshay, for example . . ."

Mary Hanford, warmed by the success of the evening's entertainment, returned with a gracious smile to Arabella's side, casting an affectionate glance at her son and his friend, Richard de Granville. How handsome they were, she thought indulgently. There was a fierce vitality about them; that glowing arrogance of all things young. They believed themselves invincible, indestructible. If only such spirit and confidence endured . . . Young de Granville was unusually flushed and animated. A result of his sickness, she wondered, or was he enamoured of Arabella Crawshay? Surely not? It was unthinkable . . . Yet, was it? Major Crawshay was known to be gravely sick, and a young widow, and an heiress, particularly one of Arabella's birth and breeding, would make an elegant mistress for St Samson Court. So that is the way the wind blows, she thought with secret amusement. Well, the de Granvilles might fare worse. Sir Peter would be elated at such a prospect, consider her a prize indeed. She was a beautiful and intelligent creature, amusing and self-willed, and young enough for child-bearing, for the de Granvilles would dearly wish to secure an heir.

Aware that she had been distracted by her thoughts, Mary Hanford put on the smile of a concerned and accomplished hostess to ask, "The young gentlemen have kept you amused, Mrs Crawshay?"

"Vastly amused, Lady Hanford. Indeed, they have offered every whit as much entertainment as Holly Grove fair . . ."

Mary Hanford smiled vaguely, completely oblivious to what Arabella meant, although her son and de Granville looked oddly discomfited. David had a decidedly hang-dog air, which she recognised of old. Curious . . . Perhaps they had been up to some rakish adventure, some youthful nonsense of which she was unaware.

"They have not been boring you, then?"

"Indeed, no . . . We have come to a closer understanding. We have learned much of each other. It has been enlightening, gentlemen, has it not?" she enquired brightly.

"Yes, ma'am." Hanford's reply was subdued, barely audible.

"Yes, ma'am." Richard de Granville's was bolder. "It is to be hoped that it is but a prelude to a closer knowledge, a more intimate understanding."

Mary Hanford saw Arabella's colour rise. Young de Granville is overplaying his hand, she thought ruefully, but that is the folly and arrogance of youth. He will learn. Yes, assuredly, he will learn.

Chapter Twenty-Four

Sir Charles Hanford did not attempt to hide his fury over the indiscretion of the potman at the Pilgrim's Rest.

"The man is a fool!" he declared contemptuously. "An addle-pated donkey! Who knows what mischief he has caused? He was sworn to secrecy, as all others at the inn."

"There is bound to be rumour . . . speculation," Francis ventured judiciously. "Perhaps none will believe it to be more than that."

Sir Charles was unconvinced. "You heard for yourself how eagerly it was accepted and believed," he rebutted indignantly. "Less as rumour than Holy Writ! No, I tell you, Crawshay, that it has set all my plans awry . . . that damned imbecile of a potman will live to rue it, I swear!"

"Perhaps your spirited denial to those at table might halt the rot, sir," Luke suggested, to appease him.

"Unlikely, Captain Farrow! I do not think that our would-be murderer is likely to be an accredited member of the *haut ton*," he observed, not without humour. "No. The taverns and inns will be afire with news of Joe Protheroe's condition, and an official denial will serve only to fan the flames."

"What will you do, sir? Will you take the armed guard from Protheroe's bedside?" Francis asked, concerned. "You cannot be sure that his assailant has knowledge of the landlord's state . . . If he is in hiding, or has fled for the moment . . .?"

"No. I shall not relax vigilance, withdraw Protheroe's protection," he said heavily. "While there is the faintest hope of recovery or sign of life, he remains in danger. My care must be first for him." He shook his head wearily.

"That confounded potman's gossip will cost him dear! You have my oath on it!"

There was an uneasy silence until Luke ventured hesitantly, "Unless the man who assaulted Protheroe declares his hand, then there is little to do save wait."

"Yes. I very much fear so," Sir Charles agreed dispiritedly. "If only there had been some witness . . . a servant at the inn, a passing vagrant even," he amended, adding ruefully, "if there were, then Protheroe's attacker would surely have known and already wrought vengeance."

Francis and Luke remained mute, each sedulously avoiding the other's glance.

"Well, gentlemen . . . there is little I can add to what has already been said, save to offer you my humblest apologies for the . . . débâcle at the inn. My own incompetence."

"Not incompetence, sir. Trust. Belief in others," Francis said firmly.

"That has been the ruin of many an honest man," the justice said dryly. "I trust, Major Crawshay, that with God's grace it will not prove mine."

The return journey in the coach to Knatchfield Grange seemed long and tiresome for the highway was rough, the whale-oil lamps barely scything the darkness. The clopping of hooves and the swaying of the carriage were strangely soporific and Francis, fatigued by sickness and strain, fell asleep as suddenly as a babe, his head resting innocently upon Arabella's shoulder.

She did not attempt to awaken him nor to settle herself more comfortably, saying quietly to Luke, "It is better that he sleeps. The tiredness comes upon him suddenly, without respite or warning . . . I fear, Luke, that he should not have been at Lanelay Court. It has taken too heavy a toll. Yet I did not dissuade him lest he think I believed him to be failing . . . growing steadily worse."

Luke said gently, "He would not choose to be confined within four walls, Arabella, nor to show weakness before others. It is his way. He knows no other. Francis has always been a man of action, and restrictions forced upon him would grieve him the more."

329

"Yes. I am sure that it is so . . . Oh, but I grieve for him, Luke!" she said simply. "If I could take his suffering upon myself, I would do so willingly. I sometimes feel that my heart is breaking within me, so raw is the anguish of it."

Luke reached over and took her gloved hand, saying, "It will not break, Arabella, for you will not allow it. You have a strength and spirit to match Francis's own." He put up his hand to touch her cheek with tenderness and felt the wetness of her tears, and could have wept as uselessly.

"You will stay, Luke? You will not forsake us?"

It was the self-same plea that Francis had made.

"No, my dear. I will stay for as long as ever you have need."

Francis stirred and murmured uneasily in sleep, and they fell into silence. The evening at Lanelay Court had done nothing to ease their fears for Nerissa's safety, nor brought fresh hope for her return. Arabella still smarted from her acrimonious exchange with David Hanford and de Granville, yet dared not speak of it openly. Luke, in turn, grieved Nerissa's absence and held out little hope that Joe Protheroe's attacker would betray himself by returning openly to the Pilgrim's Rest. Too much was at stake. As the justice had agreed, there was little to do but wait . . . Luke would do so for Arabella's and Nerissa's sakes, as he had promised. For Francis, deliverance might come too late.

David Hanford and de Granville stood in silence under the *porte-cochère* of Lanelay Court, watching the Crawshay coach take the drive of the carriage way and gradually disappear from view. The edges of the path had been illumined by lanterns driven into the earth upon poles, and they flickered fitfully now, glowing like fireflies against the darkness of night. Sir Charles and Lady Hanford had bidden de Granville a courteous "good-night" and returned gratefully within, for the air was chill, and there was much to mull over and discuss.

"You believe what that old fellow said of Joe Protheroe? That he is helpless and unable to speak?" de Granville asked sharply.

"I am sure of it." Hanford's voice was languid, faintly

amused. "He certainly set the cat amongst the pigeons. My poor papa was quite overwrought. I have rarely seen him in such a taking! Yes. You may be sure that the potman told the truth."

"Then we have nothing to fear."

"Nothing, save the testimony of the Pritchard girl . . ."

"How so?" de Granville demanded. "She is far removed from here. She can do us no harm."

"Can she not?" Hanford asked bitterly. "Do you think that Protheroe would not have confided in her the evidence of her father's death?"

"What evidence?"

"God knows what evidence!" Hanford exclaimed irritably. "Suspicion, then . . . but enough to swear an oath before my father. He would not do that lightly, believe it!"

"But . . ." For a moment de Granville was awkwardly at a loss, only to recover himself and say briskly, "Then we had best set about finding her, and quickly. You claim that she is with that odious Punch and Judy man and his cur?"

"I have it from the apothecary at Holly Grove. They are travelling the roads in some Romany caravan, a painted waggon."

"Then it should not be beyond our wit and resources to find her!" de Granville muttered. "We must do so before Crawshay and his friend, Farrow, succeed. It has been rumoured that they have hired riders to search the roads, and even ridden out themselves, but to no purpose."

"Then we are one step ahead," Hanford answered jubilantly, face alive with satisfaction.

"One step ahead?" de Granville asked, mystified.

"You do not think that I would allow them to get the better of us? If they believe us disinterested, or credulous fools, then that is to our advantage."

"For God's sake, speak plainly!" de Granville exclaimed impatiently. "You talk in riddles, Hanford! It is late and I am in no mood for idle chit-chat!"

"Then you had best come with me to the stables . . . straight to the horse's mouth." Hanford could not control his amusement and laughed aloud, setting the lantern

331

he carried into de Granville's hands and pushing him across the carriageway then along the pathway into the stable yard.

"It is damnably dark, Hanford!" de Granville exclaimed, disgruntled. "I hope that this is not some stupid prank of yours . . . a jest. My leg aches damnably and I am not yet steady upon my pins . . . Should I fall, then I shall hold you culpable!"

"I think, my friend, that you will find the expedition worthwhile," Hanford declared enigmatically. "Yes, you may be assured of it."

He took the lantern from de Granville's grasp and left him standing upon the cobbles, the glow from the stable lantern settling a rainbow of splintered light all about, then disappeared into the darkness. There was an awkward shuffling and confusion of sound from within, and de Granville felt certain that he had been hoodwinked. If Hanford merely wanted him to inspect some new bloodstock, give opinion on his purchase, he thought resentfully, then he would feel the rough edge of his wrath and tongue. It had been a disaster of an evening from start to finish, with the sole exception of learning of Joe Protheroe's plight! Arabella Crawshay had treated him like a nonentity, a petulant child. He was still fuming impotently and trying to quell his humiliation when Hanford ordered him peremptorily within.

He entered grudgingly as Hanford held the lantern aloft, calling out urgently, "Capel? Here! I would have you stand here!"

The animal sounds of the horses coughing and fidgeting uneasily in their stalls hid any answer, but within seconds a dark-haired imp of a man appeared in the lantern light. He was gaunt faced and dark of jowl, a small, sunken creature, scarce bigger than a twelve-year-old child. There was an air of cunning about him, a sly cupidity, which Richard de Granville deplored. Worse, the fellow actually stank! The reek of the stables and the animal smells of the horses were at least tolerable, but the stench of human sweat and accumulated filth decidedly was not! The creature was no more than an unkempt vagrant, part of that tide of human

332

dereliction that surged endlessly upon the roads . . . What in God's name could Hanford be thinking of? It was past all reason!

"Capel has news for us, de Granville." Hanford's voice was taut with triumph. "He sent word through a servant that he had come seeking me out . . . I gave him leave to wait here, unseen." He held the lantern before Capel's face, illumining the sharp bones and hollows, the small rapacious eyes, the reptilian mouth. "Speak, man! You have found her? Know of her whereabouts?"

"Yes, sir." Capel's face was sly with greedy cunning. "I can lead you to her."

Richard de Granville, driving the cabriolet home through the darkness, felt a sense of warm satisfaction, euphoria even. The evening had suddenly turned around, setting disaster into triumph. That Pritchard whore was within their sights. They had but to pull the trigger . . . then the whole damnable misadventure could be forgotten. They were in the clear. He felt a glow of pride that Hanford, generally so cynical and aloof, had unbent enough to volunteer, although stiffly, "It is as well that you went to try and silence Protheroe, de Granville."

"Yet I did not succeed," he admitted shamefacedly, regretting his failure.

"It is of no account! You took the risk . . . that is what matters. Neither Siberry nor I could have done so without arousing comment, suspicion even. It took courage, de Granville. Real nerve." He had clasped de Granville's shoulder with unusual warmth, declaring, "You are a true friend. I would trust you with my life."

Richard de Granville felt heat flood his face at the memory of it and began whistling cheerfully in the dark, his anger and humiliation briefly forgotten. He was not sure that he trusted Capel, that little sly-faced weasel of a creature, but Hanford had paid him handsomely.

When he had given voice to his reservations, complaining that the fellow was crafty and avaricious and would sell his own soul to the highest bidder, Hanford had chided lightly, "Would we not all, de Granville? Admit it, we

333

have much in common! Besides, he has *sold* to the highest
bidder. There is no more to be said. We will make excuse
and set off in search of her tomorrow, on horseback, for
that way we shall be less conspicuous." He paused. "You
are fit enough to ride?" he demanded with real concern.
"It will not over-tax you?"

Richard de Granville was firm upon it. "I will ride beside
you and shall not prove hindrance . . . What of Siberry?"

"He had best remain in ignorance. He has as little
stomach for adventure as poor Jeremy Hardwicke! It is
best that he remains in ignorance . . . that we go alone.
We trust each other implicitly. That is our best weapon,
our best defence."

Richard de Granville turned the cabriolet and drove it
skilfully between the familiar pillars of St Samson Court.
It was high time that he stopped his careless adventuring,
he thought, and turned his attention to the future and the
St Samson estates . . . With the Pritchard girl silenced,
there should be no impediment. He could not believe
that Arabella Crawshay had meant to treat him in so
high-handed and abrasive a manner. Yet, in another's
house, and with her husband close by, it would have
been foolhardy to have behaved otherwise. She was a
gentlewoman by birth and breeding, and no breath of
scandal or suspicion should be allowed to touch her
name. No. Women were notoriously fickle creatures,
temperamental and unpredictable. She had treated him
less circumspectly at the Pilgrim's Rest . . . indeed, given
him open encouragement, invitation even. He had not
misread the signals. She was merely playing the devoted
wife as convincingly in company as she would play the
grieving widow. Francis Crawshay would not long survive,
Siberry had heard Dr Munro confide it to his father. It
was but a matter of months, weeks even . . . for a prize
as rich as Arabella Crawshay he could afford to wait
until the approved period of mourning was over, her
public grieving ended. Yes. He would claim her then.
She would make a fine chatelaine for St Samson Court
and the estates, and a spirited wife. He would have the
greatest pleasure in taming her. Tomorrow would see an

end to the Pritchard whore's challenge. It would all be ended. He would begin anew.

Upon the morrow, Richard de Granville had arisen early, leaving word for his parents that he intended to ride out to visit a tenant farmer and to supervise some building work upon the estate.

Louisa de Granville was immediately all maternal concern, claiming, "The boy is scarce fitted to ride, Peter! You drive him unfairly. Such recklessness will undo all the good that has been done. Dr Munro would never allow it. You had best send a messenger after him, bidding him return at once."

"I will do no such thing, Louisa! The boy is of an age to act upon his own initiative. God knows I have castigated him enough in the past for his fecklessness. If he wishes to prove himself, then I am in no mind to hinder him! I am grateful that he has finally come to his senses."

Louisa de Granville continued to scold and chivvy him unfairly, but to no effect. Sir Peter remained phlegmatic and austerely aloof, seemingly disinterested. Yet within he felt a quickening of pride that his son had thrown off his past indolence and was devoting himself to the St Samson estates. Moreover, Richard was prepared to set himself painfully at risk to do so. It was more than he had ever believed possible, and he would not deter him, but look upon it as a God-given bounty.

"I would not strip him of his dignity, Louisa," he declared with finality. "It would demean him before the tenants to send for him, to order his return like a foolish schoolboy!"

With that she had to be content.

Upon his arrival at Lanelay Court, Richard de Granville had found Hanford already mounted and impatiently awaiting him. They had ridden out immediately, with scarcely a word exchanged until they were safely out of earshot of the groom and stable lads.

As they approached the elegantly ornate gateway to the Court, preparing to ride out, they were alerted by the

335

sound of a light carriage upon the highway and reined in their horses to await its passing. Yet it did not pass, but drove through the pillared entrance, almost brushing them in its hurry to negotiate the carriageway. They watched it take the curve in a flurry of noise and flung stones, then heard the sound of its halting, unseen, beneath the *porte-cochère*.

"Munro! I'll swear it was Munro, returned from his visit," de Granville declared. "Has he been summoned here, Hanford? Is one of your parents sick? A servant, perhaps?"

Hanford shrugged deprecatingly. "Not to my knowledge . . . It is more likely that it is some crime or villainy that he has come to report, an assault or murder. There is skullduggery everywhere, my friend." He smiled broadly and urged on his horse, with de Granville in pursuit.

"Perhaps . . . Joe Protheroe is dead?" de Granville suggested when he had drawn abreast of him.

"Very likely," Hanford answered languidly. "In any event, it is of no concern. Alive or dead, it makes no matter. Our duty is plain, de Granville. We had best concentrate upon that." He hesitated before goading, "Surely you have none of Hardwicke's yellow streak? You will have no squeamishness about what must be done?"

Angry colour flared into de Granville's face, emphasising his translucent fairness, his paleness of skin, as he declared scathingly, "You will not find me timid or wanting, Hanford! Look to yourself! I'll wager you twenty guineas that I am the one who strikes first blow."

"And I the last!" Hanford's hand closed upon the pistol hidden beneath his cape. "I will cover your wager, de Granville."

"And pay it promptly?" he taunted.

"If there is need."

They grinned at each other in friendly complicity and rode on with good humour restored.

Hillier, awakened early by a curt message from Hanson at the stables, took the unusual step of rousing Francis Crawshay, who dressed swiftly and hurried below. Arabella, who had heard the garbled exchange but had been too tired to awaken fully, dragged herself remorselessly from sleep. Some visitor, Hillier had said, someone demanding immediate audience . . . Had she misheard? She could have sworn that the meeting place was the coach-house beyond the stable yard. Concern for Francis spurred her to dress with haste and hurry below, unwashed and with hair barely combed. This was no ordinary meeting, for it was a ludicrously early hour and the visitor unwelcome within the house . . . Who then? Someone bringing news of the prisoner, Curtis? Surely he had not escaped custody? Yet what else could cause such activity and alarm? Without even halting to put on her cloak, Arabella hurried out into the cold morning air and across the cobbled yard.

The man with Francis was a wizened little gnome of a fellow, grainy jowled and furtive in manner, and Arabella felt an immediate antipathy which she made no attempt to hide. The man greeted her with an unctuousness which pleased her little better than his appearance, and her acknowledgement was barely civil.

"Francis?" She demanded explanation of this intrusion.

"The details need not concern you, my dear," Francis said cryptically, "but we had business to discuss . . . payment to be made."

"Payment, Francis?" she asked abruptly, fearful that it was of blackmail he spoke. "Payment for what? You had best tell me. I have a right to know."

"Capel here has come with news of Nerissa's where-abouts."

"She is safe, Francis?" Arabella demanded anxiously, gripping his arm.

"Safe, my dear, and well . . . thank God!"

Arabella, despite her revulsion for the sly-eyed stranger, could almost have forced herself to embrace him in her relief.

"Thank God!" She echoed Francis's words as fervently. Then, "Luke! I had best tell Luke," she exclaimed, scarce able to contain her excitement. "Oh, my dear, how pleased he will be." Her grip upon Francis's arm relaxed and she made to hurry back to the house, pausing briefly to say,

337

"I will see that an early breakfast is set out for you and the carriage made ready."

"No!" Francis's denial was curt. "A carriage would only serve to hinder us, if the byways are narrow. No. We shall go on horseback."

"But Francis!" It was a cry from the heart. "What of me?"

"You, my dear?" he asked in bewilderment.

"If you will not take the carriage, then I shall ride my grey," adding stubbornly, "whatever comes, I will ride beside you and Luke."

"No, Arabella!" His voice was harsh. "You will not stir from Knatchfield!" He glanced at Capel, who was listening intently, to say warningly, "We will discuss this matter within . . . for you know full well what else is at stake."

Arabella, although seething, nodded cold compliance. It would achieve nothing to declare open mutiny, she thought, save to embarrass Francis and amuse that fox-faced messenger, who was already regarding her with sly satisfaction.

"I will see you within, Francis," she said tersely, nodding dismissal at Capel and turning upon her heel.

As she walked, stiff backed, across the cobbled yard, she heard Francis demand, "You have confided this to no other, Capel? You have come straight to me, as I commanded?"

"As God is my judge, sir. I have breathed it to no other. I have kept silent as the grave. I would not renege upon a promise."

Even his voice held a sly oiliness, Arabella thought, a self-effacing whine which changed to cupidity as Francis counted out a generous reward in gold coins. Capel was a disgusting creature and Francis was well rid of him. Yet she could not begrudge the payment made to him. Indeed she would willingly have paid it twice over for news of Nerissa's safety, the certainty that her friend and companion now had nothing to fear. With a lighter step and delight at being so propitious a messenger, Arabella entered the house to find Luke.

*   *   *

338

There seemed no immediate urgency to ride out and find Goliath Jones's house on wheels, for they were assured of Nerissa's safety and knew exactly where she might be found. Capel, it transpired, had spent an evening in their presence and had been as wholeheartedly welcomed at the Punch and Judy man's fireside as all other travellers upon the roads. He had, he confided to Francis, been most generously victualled and refreshed, with no fee demanded save his company. Yes, he had been right royally entertained, and that was a fact that he could not deny. He was beholden to Goliath Jones for his gentleness of spirit. Such innocent unworldliness was all too seldom found, for it was a grasping, fevered world, with every man out for his own ends.

If Francis was unimpressed by this fulsome praise, then he did not show it. "You went there alone, you say?" he demanded.

"Yes, sir . . . You have my oath upon it. None saw them save me. You may rest easy on that account."

"You did not tell them of my concern for them? My searching?"

Capel's face took on a wily look as he murmured unctuously, "Lord bless you, sir! Your reason for searching is your affair, and none of mine! I would not presume to make mention of it to any other . . . that is not my way. I am an honest man, trying to earn an honest penny."

Since Francis had already paid him handsomely in gold, his show of indignation was not wholly convincing, but there was no discernible reason why he should have lied. It would gain him nothing. Francis dismissed him courteously, if without regret, then walked thoughtfully within.

Luke and Francis made a scant and hurried breakfast, for they were impatient to be away. Arabella was as eager for Nerissa to return to Knatchfield, but her care was also for Francis's wellbeing, and for Luke's, so she would brook no argument. Francis had won his battle to deter her from riding with them, declaring that he would be easier in his mind should she await their return. She had conceded

339

reluctantly and with little grace, aware that the added responsibility of her presence would weigh heavily upon him. He still had fears about Joe Protheroe's assailant, and she could not deny that even riding out to find Nerissa might prove more physically taxing than he could endure. She would not add to his unease. Their mounts were already saddled and waiting beneath the *porte-cochère*, and they would have mounted and ridden away had not the sound of a horse being hard-ridden upon the carriageway halted them.

Arabella, who was standing upon the steps to the house, started nervously and looked alarmed, taking an involuntary step backwards. Her alarm turned to concern as she saw that it was the justice who reined in his lathered mount beside her, his face wrenched in such an agony of grief that Arabella felt terror rise within her . . . a certainty of disaster. Dear God, she thought helplessly, what is amiss? Nerissa is injured, dead even! He has come to bring news of it, or of Joe Protheroe's death.

Francis, seeing the justice's pained despair and bloodlessness, ran to assist him from the saddle, but Sir Charles waved away his supporting arm, trying vainly to gain control of himself. He stood awkwardly for a moment, an austere man, used to authority. Yet now all authority was fled. He seemed confused, diminished, stripped of all power and confidence, scarce aware of where he was or those around him. He stumbled and all but fell, and Arabella was immediately at his side, taking his hand within her own, urging with gentleness, "Come within, sir, I beg of you."

"No, ma'am! There is no time. I must be away upon the instant . . . there is not a moment to be lost."

His voice faltered and died in his throat, Luke took a step forward to aid him, but was quelled by Arabella's warning glance before she murmured compassionately, "What you have to say may better be said within . . . I beg, sir, that you will not refuse me, but enter the house."

He shook his head as Luke, unable to control himself longer, blurted harshly, "You have news of Joe Protheroe, sir? Protheroe is dead?"

The justice stared at him unseeingly, then, "No . . . not dead, Captain Farrow, not dead. Recovered enough to speak, to bear witness."

"Against whom, sir?"

"Against his would-be murderer . . . my son."

The words were quietly spoken, but with such a wealth of pain that Arabella felt his hurt as rawly as if it were her own. He was a man excoriated, ripped of all pride. A man destroyed . . . There was no comfort that she or any other could give him.

"I have ridden out . . . to Sir Peter de Granville's house at St Samson," he began haltingly. "He awaits us at your gates."

"But why did he not enter, sir?" Arabella asked in bewilderment. "He would have been made welcome here."

The justice wiped a hand tiredly across his lips to confess wryly, "I fear, Mrs Crawshay, that he is as grieved and shamed as I . . . scarce fitted for company. He would not impose himself upon you, or others, you understand?"

"His son is involved in this, sir?" she asked sharply.

"Yes . . . as deeply as . . . as my own son, and young Siberry." He paused, face a mask of pain. "It was my sad duty to tell him of Richard's involvement in the murder of the cottager, Tom Pritchard." There was a tense silence as he continued, "I have come here with de Granville and Dr Siberry, to beg your help in this, Major Crawshay."

"My help, Sir Charles?"

"Yes . . . I come at Joe Protheroe's urging . . . to prevent another such murder."

"Nerissa?" Luke's voice was harsh with anger. "You believe that they will kill Nerissa? That they have knowledge of her whereabouts?"

"I fear so, Captain Farrow . . . God knows, I would rather not believe it!" he exclaimed wretchedly. "Yet I cannot deny the evidence."

"The evidence?" Francis asked curtly.

"That my son had a visitor last night . . . at the stables of my house. They met secretly, my coachman would have me believe, for he delivered word of this man's arrival.'

"The man, sir?" Francis asked tautly.

"One Jed Capel . . . a rogue and wastrel, one who lives by his wits. He is well known to me from my dealings as justice."

"He told your son and de Granville of Nerissa's whereabouts?" Arabella demanded, horrified.

"My coachman will swear to it . . . for the fellow was handsomely paid, and boasted openly of it in some drunken roistering at the inn. He bragged as crudely of preying soon upon some other . . . of being paid twice over . . . Yet, whether it was drink or lies . . .?" He broke off, face aflame.

"No lies," Francis admitted without rancour. "It was here he came."

"Yes, I suspected as much." The justice's voice was low. "That is why I have come to beg that you ride with us, to prevent what bloodshed we may." His mouth twisted in pain as he confessed, "It is not my son's blood I would spare, Major Crawshay, but the blood of those innocent . . . Too much has already been spilled. I will do whatever must be done."

Francis nodded, unspeaking.

"You will need to come armed, Major Crawshay, and provide Captain Farrow a pistol."

He climbed stiffly into the saddle, tall, austere, a man of indomitable purpose. One who could neither be bought nor swayed. If his purpose was to hunt down his own son, then none doubted that he would do it. Francis and Luke returned within to take up their pistols, and Arabella, watching Sir Charles riding, stiff backed and forbidding, felt an ache of grief. Her fears were for Nerissa, Francis and Luke, but her pity was for that proud man and those who awaited him at the gates. With God's help, Nerissa and Luke might begin anew. Yet for the rest, the future held neither hope nor promise . . . only a certainty of death.

Chapter Twenty-Five

The exchanges between the tense little company gathered at the gates of Knatchfield Grange and those within were brief and awkwardly made. There was no time to be lost, and action was crucial. Luke and Francis were bitterly aware that delay could cost Nerissa her life, and rode with a fierce concentration that excluded all else. The justice and his companions were equally withdrawn, equally committed, yet there was already about them an air of defeat. Their aim now must be to save further bloodshed, to protect those unfamiliar and unknown. In doing so, they might salve their own consciences, make restitution for the wrongs of others. Beyond that there was nothing. No future. No hope. Luke, attention briefly deflected from the road, glanced back to see Hanford and de Granville riding abreast of each other, faces determinedly set. Some trick of light and the swirling dust stirred by the horses' hooves distorted his vision. For a split second, the dark and fair figures blurred as if seen through water, and it was not the justice or Peter de Granville but their sons he saw. His breath caught raggedly in his throat and he heard the harsh sound of it as his mare awkwardly stumbled. Francis turned in the saddle to look at him in open curiosity, but stayed silent as Luke gentled his horse to obedience. Against his will, Luke felt a stirring of pity for the two men and for Dr Siberry, lagging, whey faced, behind them. They were honest men all, proud and strong minded, their emotions kept sternly hidden. Yet grief was in every line of their flesh, deep scored and indelible, beyond their power to ease. He did not know if his own uncertainty, or their own certainty of what must come, was the harder to bear. He knew only that those they sought had not the makings of such men. They were no more than pale shadows of the flesh and spirit that had sired them. Richard de Granville, Hanford and young Siberry had much to answer for, much to atone. They must pay with their lives for the murder done, but others would pay a harsher price and would go on paying all of their lives, and death would not deliver them.

He urged on his mare and drew abreast of Francis, who gave him a cursory nod but stayed silent. Already, Luke thought remorsefully, Francis looked fatigued and fine drawn, his eyes bruised about with dark shadows. It was not only fear for Nerissa that he had to face, but the ravages of sickness, the slow encroachment of decay. It was as well that Arabella had been persuaded to remain at Knatchfield, for Francis's sake and her own. She would be spared the hurt of seeing him so debilitated, and he the knowledge of her pity for him, and his fears for her safety. It would grieve him the more should he be powerless to protect her, to fail her before others.

Luke prayed that he himself would be able to defend Nerissa and Goliath Jones, for the old man would be as gravely at risk. Richard de Granville and his accomplices could not let him live, for he would be witness to their abduction of her, her murder even. White-hot rage rose within him as he forced his horse onwards, a picture of Nerissa's face, innocently vulnerable, vivid in his mind. Should de Granville or any other harm a hair of her head, then he would kill as savagely and mercilessly as they. He would demand their lives as forfeit and take whatever punishment he was called upon to endure. Without Nerissa, there could be no life for him, no future. He would welcome the ease of death and count it friend.

His mind returned to Arabella and the grief she so patiently endured, a daily crucifixion. Whatever befell, she had strength and will enough to bear it, of that he was sure . . . as Francis would bear the rigours of the day and whatever lay ahead.

The countryside blurred about him, a misted greenness, and he aware of nothing save the sound of the horses' hooves and his own heartbeats, thudding as one. Mile

344

after mile, hour after hour, with scarce a word spoken. They rode without slowing or rest, their horses fevered and restless as they, their throats an aching dryness. They would come upon that poor ramshackle waggon soon now. It could not be far ahead. Yet when they approached it, it would not be with relief but in terror of what they might find.

The justice had said that he would do whatever must be done. Luke did not doubt him, for he was an honest man. What he doubted was his own capacity for forgiveness, his willingness to deliver the murderer to the full justice of the law. He feared that his own justice would prove savage and immediate, a bloody revenge. An eye for an eye; a tooth for a tooth. A death for a death. The justice had said in despair that too much blood had been spilled. Too much innocent blood. The blood of the guilty would not serve to wipe out the stain of it, nor would it make full restitution for the savagery done. A man has but one life. When stripped of all else, it is the only thing he may claim as uniquely his own. That, and in death, his immortal soul . . . But that was in God's keeping. His vengeance would be terrible, beyond the imagining of men . . . but the vengeance of men gives comfort on earth. Sometimes it is the only comfort they have.

Arabella could settle to nothing after Luke and Francis had ridden out with the justice and the others. Her mind was in a turmoil. She did not know how she could endure the agony of waiting for their return, not knowing whether Nerissa was alive or dead. She felt riddled with guilt and apprehension. Had she told Francis of her visit to the Pilgrim's Rest and of seeing de Granville trying to gain access to Joe Protheroe's room, would it have alerted them to the danger sooner? No, surely Dr Siberry would have reported the incident to the justice? Sir Charles could not have remained in ignorance of the visit. Yet perhaps he had taken it at face value, as the concern of a landowner for a tenant, a mark of Christian charity. Had she not done so herself? What if Nerissa felt that she had betrayed and abandoned her? What if Francis fell sick upon the

345

way? They had taken neither carriage nor spare horses and would be forced to leave him to survive as best he could . . . They would be riding hard, not sparing themselves nor their mounts, and an invalid could only hinder them . . . Arabella was trapped in a maelstrom of conflicting emotions; swirled, sucked, dragged insistently down, feeling the remorseless whirlpool grip . . .

Then, as suddenly, she was released. Free. She knew exactly what she must do. She must take the gig and bring Francis home. She could not hope to catch them now, for they were long gone and would have the advantage of their horsemanship and the urgency with which they rode . . . Yet even if she arrived too late to witness the confrontation with de Granville, then she might persuade Francis to return beside her in the carriage, with his mount tethered behind. She could plead nervousness at driving alone, or feign ignorance of the way. She did not doubt that he would be infuriated at her disobedience. He would accuse her of wilfully setting herself and others at risk. Yet however fierce his anger it would be easier to bear than the uncertainty of remaining at Knatchfield, ignorant of the dangers and impotent to help. Without dwelling upon the wisdom of such defiance, she summoned the gig to be brought. Then, firmly rejecting Hanson's anxious offer to drive her in the coach to wherever she meant to journey, she demanded to know the shortest carriage route to Fair Oaks village.

"Is it wise, ma'am," he ventured tentatively, "to drive there alone? There are rogues and footpads aplenty, aye, and likely highwaymen too, waiting to prey upon the unwary." He lapsed into awkward silence.

"Highwaymen might prove the least of my worries, Hanson!" Arabella chided with spirited humour. Then, seeing that the old coachman was genuinely distressed, she added contritely, "I shall be safe, Hanson, never fear."

"I do not think, ma'am, that Major Crawshay . . . " He floundered into silence, gnarled hands gripping the reins so tightly that the knuckles shone white. "I do not think, ma'am," he persisted stubbornly, "that the major would be . . . at ease in his mind."

"And I, Hanson, would be less at ease, were I to stay. It is to fetch Major Crawshay that I go. He may turn his anger upon me if he chooses, but it will save his face before others should he be forced to accompany me home because of my wilful stupidity. To return in full fig, with a liveried coachman in attendance, would scarce higher his standing before others . . . I would not humble him so . . . You understand?"

"Yes, ma'am, I understand."

He delivered the reins into the care of a waiting stable lad and helped Arabella into the gig. He understood more than she knew, he thought, for there was little in the stables or in the house itself that escaped him although, save for Manley, the groom, whom he could trust, he confided in no other. Hanson stood stock still and watched Mrs Crawshay drive off, warmly clad and elegant in her hooded travelling cape and firmly in control of the horse and gig. He called out sharply to the stable boy to tell Manley to see to the horses and to make ready the coach without delay.

"Whither is it bound, sir?" the boy asked rashly, eyes aglow with enthusiasm.

" 'Tis none of your business, lad! You had best attend to your own, else you will know the rough edge of my tongue! Curiosity killed the cat!"

"The cat, sir?" The boy looked at him perplexed. "One of the stable cats, Mr Hanson, sir?"

"Aye . . . a nosy, cheeky-faced varmint like you, lad! Idle and slow witted! Be off with you now, else a clout will surely hasten you!"

The boy was off like greased lightning, scarce pausing to take breath, and Hanson's face relaxed into a smile of amused indulgence . . . Aye. The lad would do well enough. He was quick to act and willing, and his curiosity would serve him well, for it showed an eagerness to learn. Still, like an unbroken horse, he must be tutored and curbed by those older and more experienced. It was all of fifty years since he had first arrived, naive and trusting, eager to learn his trade. Half a century and more of mucking out stables, tending to horses, running every which way at some other's command . . .

347

Yet now it was he who was in command. He must act on his own initiative. Major Crawshay had confided his fears for Miss Arabella . . . charged him to see that she came to no harm. In Major Crawshay's absence, he must keep her well within his sights, ensure that she was protected. She would not thank him for his interference, of that Hanson was sure, for she was proudly high spirited. None the less, he would risk her wrath, else he would have neither peace of mind nor self-respect. His loyalty was to Major and Mrs Crawshay both; more than that, his honest affection. He owed them more than mere duty.

Harold Manley brought the coach skilfully to rest alongside the *porte-cochère*, with another groom and stable lad in anxious attendance. He waited impassively for the old coachman to climb onto his perch and take over the reins. He did not need to ask whither they were bound, for the conversation between Major Crawshay and the justice had been faithfully memorised, and discussed privately between them.

The old man climbed up stiffly, bones as gnarled and twisted as a wind-formed tree, skin as deeply weathered. Beneath his proud tricorne his sparse hair escaped, silvered as thistledown, and his eyes, although faded, were intelligently bright. As Manley made to surrender the reins, Hanson said gruffly, "No . . . you have earned the right."

Manley simply nodded, but his strong-boned face was glowingly flushed at the honour done to him, as he confided, "I do not know, Mr Hanson, if we will be able to keep apace with Mrs Crawshay, sir . . . or intercept her. The gig is light and will travel quickly. We cannot take the smaller roads and byways."

"No more will she," declared the coachman with pardonable satisfaction. "I have given her explicit direction . . . she will travel along the main carriageway, and I shall know where she is for every last inch of the way. We will stay close enough to save her from any unforeseen hazard, yet remain discreetly out of sight. I leave it to your skill and expertise, Harold. 'Twill be valuable experience."

348

His opaque-ringed eyes were innocent of guile, his face expressionless.

A baptism of fire, indeed! thought Manley, amused despite himself. By God, he is a sly old fox. There is not much that escapes him! He knows how eagerly I am waiting to step into his shoes as coachman.

"Aye, it will be good experience," repeated Hanson firmly. "It will stand you in good stead, for the immediate future."

"The future, Mr Hanson?"

"Aye. The future, lad." He sniffed loudly and took a pinch of snuff from the tin box in his pocket, placing it upon the back of his hand and inhaling it with noisy relish. "Since we are both doomed to be dismissed for this adventure, 'tis as well to be prepared." He sneezed violently and with every evidence of enjoyment, then began whistling tunelessly through his teeth.

Nerissa, Goliath Jones and Toby had moved on from the village of Fair Oaks, where Jem Capel had found them, and had halted the waggon in a meadow on the fringe of the hamlet of Rushfield, some three miles away. Their leaving had been a matter of regret to them and to the cottagers, for they had been welcomed most cordially there. The arrival of the Punch and Judy show had brought honest delight to countryfolk who had few worldly comforts and whose lives were spent in unremitting labour upon the land. The children, who had never before witnessed or imagined such a miracle, were at first overawed. Emboldened, they rapidly grew vociferous, their excited shouts of warning and screams of laughter and fear as much a joy to the audience as the play itself.

Nerissa had quickly adapted to the needs of the enterprise, her roles as diverse as those of the characters. She cheerfully accompanied Toby in collecting the farthings and halfpence demanded as entrance fee, washed and mended the puppets' worn clothing and Toby's ruffs, and stitched new costumes to add to her myriad chores. To her surprise and pleasure, she found that she had a natural aptitude both for performing and manipulating

349

the characters from within the booth. Soon, with Goliath Jones's encouragement, she was playing the parts of Judy and the infant and, occasionally, the voracious crocodile. She was grateful for the anonymity that let her give full rein to her emotions, uninhibited by the censure of others or crippling self-consciousness. Yet it was the secret view from within the small tent which she enjoyed above all, for the gleeful faces of the children and adults and their rapt attention were payment enough. Indeed, since the performance was inevitably in some open meadow, pasture or empty barn, it was often the only payment. Those too poor to gain official entrance crept in unhindered, and none berated them nor offered complaint.

Urchins and sweeping boys, paupers and stable lads, mingled unobtrusivley with their neighbours, united by the rare luxury of laughter and brief forgetting. It was, as Goliath Jones proudly claimed, "The best of occupations, and the most rewarding. Why," he declared to Nerissa, "travelling these roads, a beggar might live as a king, but in that small space beneath the canvas, he *becomes* one. In that moment, he rules the world. Who else can stir others to laughter and tears or give them ease from heartache? Oh, it is a rare gift, my dear, and one to be cherished."

Toby had thumped his tail in cheerful agreement, and Nerissa, for all her grief at leaving Knatchfield, could not dispute it. If she were to be forever exiled from the Grange, the Crawshays and Luke Farrow, whom she loved, then she could think of no other way of life that she would choose above it. Her affection for Goliath Jones and Toby grew by the hour, and she knew that they loved her as deeply and that whatever came, she could count on their protection. She believed now that the threat from de Granville and the justice's son was over. She had fled, as they expected, and was no more a danger to them. They had no more need to pursue her.

She was washing her clothes in the small stream that flowed through the meadow, scrubbing them upon a rough stone, when she felt the first stirring of apprehension. She glanced about her nervously, certain that she was being watched. It was foolishness, she knew, for Goliath and Toby were but forty yards away in the waggon beside the small copse that gave them shelter from the cold north-easterly wind . . . She had but to call upon them and they would come running. She chided herself for her foolishness and returned to her washing, yet the feeling of being secretly watched persisted and she could not dispel it. She was conscious of the fine hairs at the nape of her neck prickling in alarm, a feeling of such unease that she all but fled back to the shelter of the waggon, begging Goliath to move on, away from this place.

Common sense and shame at her own cowardice restrained her. The people at Rushfield must not be denied their entertainment, for they had little to amuse and divert them else . . . Every child, from the youngest babe in arms, was certain to be brought, and their disappointment would be acute if they found that she, Goliath and Toby had deserted them. It would be a betrayal too cruel to be borne.

With calm deliberation she gathered her washing, wringing it out with care and placing it in the wickerwork basket upon the ground. Then, without a backward glance, she began walking slowly towards the painted waggon, telling herself that her disquiet was imagination and no more . . . Yet even as she walked she could feel her heart beating suffocatingly at her ribs and a sense of panic enfolding her. She longed to cry out her alarm to Goliath Jones, to send Toby rushing protectively to her side. With throat dry and a rawness at her breastbone, she ran the last few paces to the waggon. Its very familiarity brought relief, and never had she been so pleased to see its garish colours and the placid, overfed cob cropping the grass contentedly beside it.

"Well, my dear, 'twas quickly done," Goliath Jones said mildly from the painted steps of the waggon. "We had best set out our tent in readiness, for the children will be here soon, in less than an hour by the sun's reckoning." He paused, concerned by her nervousness and pallor. "All is well?" he asked sharply "No one has harassed you? Set you in a flux? You have seen no strangers?"

"No," she said truthfully. "I have seen no one."

Toby, who had been pushing fiercely at his master's legs, trying vainly to force a way to Nerissa, finally succeeded, all but toppling Goliath Jones to the ground.

"Drat the animal! What in heaven's name ails him?" he exclaimed impatiently as Toby's hackles rose and he ran, barking furiously, towards the far hedge beside the stream.

The growls in his throat were strangely menacing now and no more than a low grumbling, unlike any sound that Nerissa had ever heard. In one anguished movement, he had hurled himself bodily at the hedge, a snarling fury of noisy violence. Then, conscious of his master's increased shouts and his own shameful disobedience, he slunk back, crouched and repentant, tail wagging apologies.

"You might well cower and creep, you varmint!" Goliath Jones chided good humouredly. "'Tis naught but a harmless rabbit or a field-mouse. A fine watchdog you are, to be sure! We can all make a clamour when nothing threatens!" He turned, still smiling and shaking his head indulgently, to say to Nerissa, "'Tis the artistic temperament, my dear . . . Take no account of his nonsense! He fancies himself a thespian, and must make a drama of all! Come within, for I have only this moment made a fresh pot of tea. It will strengthen and relax us all."

Toby, who had been listening with head cocked intently, needed no second bidding. He was first within.

Goliath Jones had kept firm watch over Nerissa at Fair Oaks, still fearful that the justice's son might come searching for her. He had begged the local innkeeper, Tim Clegg, to let him know if any strangers came seeking them out, and to disclaim all knowledge of their future whereabouts. Tim Clegg, a bluff good-natured man, and as solidly rotund as one of his own rum kegs, had willingly agreed to the deception. He had asked no questions, muttering that it was not in his nature to pry. A man's desire for solitude was his own affair, and he had a God-given right to choose his own friends . . . If he privately thought that the Punch and Judy man was escaping his creditors or fleeing from justice, then he kept his own counsel. There were many behind the bars of debtors' prisons undeserving of such punishment, and as many riding boldly in their carriages who should not be free. Whatever crime Goliath Jones had committed, he had absolved himself a hundred times over for the pleasure he brought to others. There was to be but one exception to the rule, Goliath Jones had declared firmly. Should a military gentleman come seeking them, giving his name as Major Crawshay and that of his companion as Captain Farrow, then he might tell them the route they planned to take to Talog in Carmarthenshire.

"'Tis a fair old journey," the innkeeper mused, "but I wish you joy of it, and a good welcome at its ending, my friend. Aye, and safe passage, too."

"Amen to that," the Punch and Judy man said fervently.

"At least your way will be measured with laughter, not tears," Tim Clegg reminded. "'Tis a good testimonial . . . an epitaph many would gladly choose were they to write their own!"

"Indeed," Goliath Jones agreed, smiling broadly. "Yet I hope, sir, that an epitaph may not be needed yet awhile."

"Amen to that, too," the innkeeper exclaimed delightedly. "Amen to that, too, sir!"

Richard de Granville had ridden hard to keep up with Hanford and was feeling the results of it in his crippled leg. He would not admit to it openly, nor beg for rest, for it would shame and humiliate him to be found wanting. He had always claimed himself to be a more vigorous rider than Hanford, and competition between them was keen. Neither would cede to the other. No quarter was asked and no quarter given. The pain in de Granville's leg was growing agonising and he could scarce bear to stay in the saddle, but he gritted his teeth and suffered it stoically. He had been foolishly sanguine about the journey, he thought disconsolately, and should have let Hanford ride out alone. Yet to have done so would have admitted defeat, confirmed Hanford's superiority as a rider. God! . . . But the ache in his leg and his spine was killing him. He could barely stay upright in the saddle. He felt as though his flesh was being torn apart, his muscles wrenched asunder. He had not realised how the sickness had debilitated him, how his nerves and sinews had weakened from lack of use . . . He could bear it no longer! He must find excuse to halt.

"That inn, Hanford," he ventured. "It might be a good place to pause."

"I have neither time¯nor inclination," Hanford replied sharply. "I would sooner we were on our way. We can refresh ourselves at leisure when our work is done."

"The horses?" de Granville mumbled awkwardly. "What of the horses?"

"They will survive, never fear."

"It is Fair Oaks inn," de Granville said with sudden inspiration, "this is the place we seek, Hanford! Where better to find out the Pritchard whore's whereabouts? The innkeeper will surely know!"

Hanford, forced to agree, dismounted with ill grace and led his mount into the stable yard, and de Granville climbed stiffly down beside him, trying to suppress a cry at the white-hot pain that seared him, and grimacing painfully as he followed in Hanford's wake. He was conscious of dragging his leg, his gait stiff and ungainly as a cripple's, and he could have wept with vexation and rage. His catechism of the innkeeper when he could be summoned was more than usually abrasive.

"We seek a Romany caravan . . . a painted waggon," he declared irritably.

"Then I fear you have come to the wrong place, sir . . . You have been misinformed. I have none to sell."

"Damnation, man! Are you deaf or merely an imbecile? I said we *seek* a caravan . . . I made no mention of buying one!"

The landlord's plump, bucolic face did not relax its smiling composure. "There are always Romanies hereabouts, didicoys and travelling tinkers, sir." He scratched his head in puzzlement. "Was it some pots and pans you were in need of mending? There is a man in the village whose work I can recommend. Or was it horseflesh you were after?"

Richard de Granville, plagued by pain and infuriated

at the man's crassness, struck his whip savagely against his leather riding boot and could scarce restrain himself from slashing it across the innkeeper's smiling face. But for Hanford's swift intervention, he might well have done so.

"It is a Punch and Judy man we seek . . . a travelling showman," Hanford declared smoothly. "We wish to hire his services. He will be well paid for his efforts, as you, sir, if you are able to assist us in this. It will be to your mutual advantage. He will thank you for it."

He produced a gold coin from the pocket of his breeches and held it out invitingly.

"Indeed, sir, I would aid you if I were able," the landlord shook his head ruefully, "'tis my misfortune that he did not pass this way. I would surely have heard of it else . . . Perhaps it was to Little Fair Oaks he was headed? 'Tis no more than three miles from here, along a forest track used by woodcutters and such. There is oft confusion, for the names are so alike. It was a foolishness to name them so. If you will take my advice, sir . . ."

"We do not take advice from menials!" de Granville interrupted curtly, not troubling to hide his contempt. Then, to Hanford, "We had best be gone! Time is wasting!"

Without waiting for a reply, he set his foot into the stirrup and swung himself irritably into the saddle, sending his mount clattering wildly across the cobbled yard.

Hanford, piqued by his friend's surliness, thrust the gold coin towards the innkeeper, saying, "You have earned this, landlord."

Tim Clegg's florid face was a mask of servility as he touched his forelock, thanking him unctuously. He watched in respectful silence as Hanford mounted and rode away. Then he examined the coin and thrust it into the pocket of his breeches, grinning broadly. Yes, he had earned it fairly. It was as well that the more obnoxious of the two so-called gentlemen had not taken his advice. It would have sent them even deeper into the surrounding woods; a very labyrinth of trails, known only to the woodcutters and poachers. However they fared, their adventure would certainly delay them by an hour or more. With luck, they might even abandon their search and return whence they came, confused and disheartened. His fingers closed hard upon the gold coin . . . No doubt he should have told them about the marshy lands, the bogs hidden by a surface crust of lichens and mosses, and set innocently amidst the rushes. As far as he knew, the swamplands had claimed nothing larger than a lost ewe or a terrified jack-rabbit. Yet who knew what had disappeared without trace? It would be a shame were such stylish macaronis to stumble and ruin their fine clothing. It was not the place for jackanapes and dandies. No, not a fit place at all. Humming contentedly to himself, he sauntered across the yard to the inn.

Hanford and de Granville had fared badly. They were irritable and abrasive, scarce able to exchange a civil word, each blaming the other for their predicament. Fatigue and pain made de Granville more than usually volatile and irascible, and Hanford grew increasingly resentful. To add to their discomfort, their boots were disgustingly mud caked, their usually pristine clothing sticky with filth and sweat. Their horses had fared little better, and despite all their attempts to extricate themselves by following the sun they were most certainly lost. Splashing through mire and bog had not noticeably improved their dispositions, and in a rage of frustration they had all but abandoned their quest, damning the landlord vehemently, each other and the whole human race.

Only a chance meeting with an obliging woodcutter had set them upon the right track with an assurance that the waggon they sought was at Rushfield, a hamlet some two miles away. He was sure of it, he insisted, for he was of a mind to walk there himself when the day's work was ended.

"'Tis a spectacle, they say, and well worth the halfpenny charged, sirs. You will find it a fine entertainment. You should not miss it."

"You may be assured that we *will* not miss it!"

De Granville's irony was lost upon him, but the sneer in his voice was not. The woodcutter, fearful lest he had over-reached himself, made mumbled apology before relapsing into awkward silence. A sixpence unexpectedly thrust at him lifted his spirits and he pocketed it without delay.

When de Granville and Hanford came at last to Rushfield, following the trail he had described, they tethered their horses in a copse and went stealthily on foot to where the caravan lay. They wanted no witnesses to what they were about to do and none remaining to identify them. It was a mistake that they had once made, and they were in no mood to repeat it. That damnable cur of the Punch and Judy man had all but betrayed them by his vicious barking, and they had been poised to flee, but he had mercifully subsided without arousing suspicion. Their conversation had been urgently whispered, their plan agreed. Both were well armed and must strike now, before the audience of cottagers came. Hanford would stand watch in the narrow approaches to the meadow and de Granville would shoot first the girl, then the old man. Should Hanford's aid be needed, then de Granville had but to call out to him.

Toby heard the muted footfalls upon the grass of the meadow and scented de Granville's approach. His hackles rose warningly and a growl started low in his throat as he hurled himself at the door of the waggon in a fury to repel his old adversary.

Goliath Jones, certain that disaster threatened, took up a stout hawthorn stave that he kept beside him and with a murmured warning to Nerissa to stay in the waggon, whatever occurred, flung open the door of the waggon to let Toby run free.

Seeing de Granville standing, purposeful and menacing, with pistol cocked, he tried to call the dog to heel, but the words died in his throat, a useless croak. In a moment, Toby was upon the aggressor, sinking his teeth into de Granville's boot, hanging on grimly. Terror constricted the Punch and Judy man's throat as he awaited the crack of the pistol shot, too sickened to cry out or move. Then, with a savage oath, de Granville kicked the cur aside as, with a wild scream of pain, it dragged itself upon its belly, scarce able to breathe for the anguish of its cracked ribs. It tried valiantly to rise, but could not. Goliath Jones raised

357

the stave and, without thought of retribution or fear, would have brought it crashing down upon the violator. The door of the waggon was thrown back with a grinding crash as Nerissa, unnerved by Toby's scream, stood rigid with shock at seeing de Granville with pistol raised.

For a moment the scene stayed frozen, drained of life and movement, then, "Run, Nerissa, for God's sake, run, my dear!"

Goliath Jones, anguished plea stirred her into action, and unthinkingly she fled into the copse beside the waggon, fearful with every step of catching the full blast of the pistol shot. She heard the swift crack of it but dared not turn nor halt, running frenziedly, she knew not where, until her breath caught painfully in her throat and her breastbone was raw with the hurt of it. She wept as she ran, for Toby and Goliath Jones, for their fate and her own. Even as she stumbled onwards and the tears fell unchecked, she knew that it was useless. She could never escape de Granville's vengeance. He would not let her go. In all but flesh she was already dead.

Richard de Granville would have shot her as she fled, but Goliath Jones, crazed by despair, had brought the stave crashing down upon his shoulders, the gun exploding violently then swept from his grasp to lie uselessly. With a curse, de Granville had turned upon him, wresting the stave from his hands, felling him with a blow to the head that clubbed him senseless. Hanford, hearing the shot, had run to the gate of the meadow and, seeing him felling the old man, had hurried to his side as de Granville retrieved the pistol.

"The girl, de Granville! What of the girl?" he asked harshly.

"Fled into the copse . . . she cannot long escape us!"

"By God, de Granville, I hope that you are right!" he exclaimed bitterly. "I would have done better on my own! If she sets up an alarm, we are done for . . . I should not have relied upon a fool and a cripple!"

"Hell and damnation, man, act, do not whine!" de Granville ordered, smarting with rage and humiliation.

"You have done nothing so far!" he flung at him accusingly.

"You fired the first shot, and I have promised to take the last!" Hanford reminded curtly. "I shall not fail in that!"

He ran towards the copse and de Granville followed stiffly, leg wracked with pain. Damn the bitch! Damn Hanford! he thought wryly. Wager or not, he would make the whore pay. That would be an end to it.

Even as they disappeared into the copse, Toby dragged himself painfully across the grass, moving with agonising slowness until he was at Goliath Jones's side. He lay for a while exhausted, then when he was able he stirred and licked the old man's face and huddled whimpering beside him.

Chapter Twenty-Six

When the justice and his fellow horsemen arrived at the inn at Fair Oaks, they were travel stained and exhausted, and not of a spirit to linger there. Indeed, to Luke's consternation, when Francis awkwardly dismounted to speak to the innkeeper, he was barely able to stand unsupported, so painfully enervated was he. He had steadied himself against the saddle of his mount, fatigue in every line of his body, his face gaunt and fine-drawn. Yet despite the rigours of the journey he still carried with him an air of authority, and none made the error of attempting to aid him.

"I seek news of a traveller, sir," he informed the landlord, "one who is said to be encamped close by."

"Indeed, sir?" The landlord's voice was neutral. "A Romany, would that be?"

"No . . . a travelling entertainer. A Punch and Judy man, by name, Goliath Jones."

"Then you are not alone sir," he said dryly. "Others have come seeking him before you." He hesitated, demanding sharply, "Your name, sir . . . if I might hear your name?"

"I am Francis Crawshay of Knatchfield."

"*Major* Crawshay?"

"The same."

"Then I have been charged to deliver you a message . . . to tell you Goliath Jones's whereabouts . . . I will give you direction, sir."

"These men, landlord," the justice interrupted tautly, "you say you gave them information? How long since? It is a matter of urgency!"

"Some hour since, sir."

The justice, who had not dismounted, was clutching

fiercely at the reins, face tense, and those beside him were as anxiously disturbed.

Tim Clegg's shining face was alive with satisfaction as he confided, "But I gave them false information . . . for I was afeared for Goliath Jones's safety. If you do not linger sir, you might reach Rushfield before them."

"I pray God you may be right!" Dr Siberry exclaimed fervently. "Two men, you said, landlord? You are sure of that?"

"I am sure." He regarded the small group steadily before adding firmly, "They were gentlemen, sir, such as you . . . and there could be no mistaking their kinship, for one was as dark as you, sir," his gaze was upon the justice, "and the other as fair as that gentleman riding beside you."

There was a fraught silence, which seemed to stretch interminably. The justice and Peter de Granville remained stoically expressionless, unwilling to betray emotion, and Dr Siberry tried as valiantly to hide his surge of joy that in this, at least, his son was blameless. As the justice turned his horse to ride out through the archway, Francis took a gold coin from his pocket as recompense for the landlord's trouble.

"No, sir." Tim Clegg's refusal was firm but courteous. "I will take no payment. It would put a price upon friendship, and that can neither be bought nor sold. May God go with you, sir."

As Francis made grave acknowledgement, the landlord murmured, so quietly that only Francis could hear, "It was the devil rode with the others, sir . . . within and without. There will be grief aplenty. He will demand full payment. It was ever his way."

Francis nodded, unspeaking, and made to join the others.

When they came to the meadow where the caravan was resting they realised that they had come too late . . . Goliath Jones, shocked and bloodless from his head wound, was barely conscious and at first too distressed to speak. As soon as he could answer coherently, Francis and Luke abandoned their horses and ran into the copse with

361

pistols drawn, urging the justice and Peter de Granville to keep watch upon the wood at the gate to the meadow, lest Nerissa or her attackers return. Dr Siberry was already carrying the Punch and Judy man within the waggon, searching for water and for clean linen to cleanse and bind up his wound.

"Toby, my dog, Toby," Goliath Jones murmured, and it was the justice who had gently lifted the dog and carried him tenderly within, and set him down gently beside his master. Then, stoically and in pained silence, he had gone to take up his vigil beside the wood.

When Nerissa could run no more, she sank down upon a log in a mossy clearing and awaited de Granville's coming. Fear was a burning rawness in her throat and her heart thudded with such violence that she felt it must burst within her. She knew that she could run no more . . . she had neither strength nor will. Her limbs were leaden and she ached in every tense muscle, every sinew and nerve. When she heard the crashing and stumbling in the undergrowth beyond her, she knew that all she could do was wait.

"Bitch! Whore!" De Granville stood before her, grinning, triumphant, pistol held menacingly as she struggled to her feet. It was pointed now at her breast and she was conscious only of a relief that all would soon be ended, that she would suffer no more.

So intent were they upon one another that they heard neither sound nor movement, until Luke's voice commanded, with cold anger, "Lay down your pistol, de Granville! No! Do not turn, else I will kill you, I swear! I need but an excuse to shoot you."

In a violent movement, de Granville turned about and fired wildly, his bullet thudding harmlessly into the trunk of a tree. Luke responded as instinctively, but his aim was surer, more practised, and found the flesh of de Granville's shoulder, causing him to spin around savagely with a scream of pain. For a brief moment his pistol was levelled again at Nerissa. She stood hypnotised, unable to think or move, until suddenly his pistol fell from his bloodied grasp and he blundered noisily into the denseness of scrub and bracken beyond.

In a second Luke was beside her, cradling her in his arms, holding her protectively to him, then kissing her cheeks, her eyelids, her lips, her hair, murmuring endearments.

"Oh, my dear, my darling girl . . . I feared that you were dead, that he had killed you."

If this were no more than a dream, she thought confusedly, or she were already dead, then she would want no heaven save this, with the promise that it might last for eternity. But she was not dead, she was gloriously, vibrantly alive, and her body ached for his caresses, the warm, hard pressure of his flesh against her own. She felt herself responding, at first with yielding tenderness, then increasing fierceness, until her passion matched his own. She felt neither shame nor regret at such sensual abandonment, only the calm certainty of belonging, the rightness of loving such a man. She clung to him feverishly, unwilling to let him go, and when they finally drew apart she asked, voice stricken, "Goliath and Toby, Luke? In my terror to escape, I had all but forgotten them. I was so afeared . . . They are not dead? He did not shoot them?"

She began to weep wretchedly.

"No, my love . . . they are not dead." He wiped the tears from her cheeks with gentle fingertips and held her close. "They are hurt, but will mend, never fear."

"Then I must go to them . . . I will find my way alone."

"No! De Granville and Hanford are still at large, and a danger. Hanford is armed and will not hesitate to shoot. He has nothing now to lose." He stopped to pick up de Granville's pistol, saying quietly, "I must join Francis in his search for them, Nerissa, but first I will see you safely returned. Dr Siberry is caring for Goliath and Toby, and the justice will stand guard to protect you."

"Why? How are they involved in this?" she asked sharply. "Tell me, Luke!" When he hesitated to reply she exclaimed in growing horror, "He knows, then, that his son is Joe Protheroe's murderer?"

"Not murderer . . . Joe Protheroe lives."

"Thank God!" The cry was torn from her. Memory of

the savagery of his wounds and the face of the blood-stained murderer still had such power to haunt her, to rake her through with terror, that she stumbled and all but fell.

Luke's arm came out to steady her as he said, "Joe Protheroe named his attacker."

"But de Granville and Hanford are not aware of it?"

"No."

She was riven with cold certainty, the knowledge that Hanford was near and would not rest until he had destroyed her. When de Granville had found her, she was past all caring, so long hunted that she would have welcomed an ending, even the ease of death. Now all was changed. Luke had found her and would not let her go. There would be a joy in living, new purpose, and she would not willingly forgo it.

Luke set de Granville's pistol into her hand before taking up his own, saying, "You will need this for protection . . . I will walk ahead of you, make certain that the way is clear . . . Should Hanford call out, do not hesitate nor try to support me. You understand? You must run, Nerissa. For God's sake, and mine, you must run!"

He settled a brief kiss upon her cheek, feeling its numbed coldness, and she did not try to hold him close. There was much to be explained, much to be said between them. For the moment they were together, and she was certain of his love. It was enough to sustain her, and more than she had dared to hope.

Hanford was determined that he, and not de Granville, would hunt down the Pritchard slut first and silence her. With Joe Protheroe powerless to speak and name his attacker, or even dead from the blow inflicted, the girl was all that threatened him now. If he could get to her before de Granville, then none would know Protheroe's attacker and he could rest easy. It would have shown admirable cunning to incite de Granville to kill her, to let him shoulder all blame, for it would have given him a hold over his friend. It would have forced de Granville's future co-operation and bought his silence and loyalty. Yet self-preservation was the main concern. Survival was all. The only way to secure it and remove the threat of the gallows was to kill the girl then return to silence that impotent old half-wit who sheltered her . . . He was unlikely to be in any fit state to summon help, for de Granville had struck him a blow that must have cracked his skull.

Hanford, unlike de Granville's noisy blundering, moved slowly and with a catlike stealth through the undergrowth of bracken and bramble, pistol held ready. He was confident of his strategy. A soft approach then a confrontation when least expected would have the element of surprise which de Granville's crude rampaging lacked. Yet he could not altogether condemn such tactics, for they gained him advantage. The girl would surely flee from the path of such bungling incompetence, terrified out of her wits. He had but to tread warily and await his chance. The edges of the wood perhaps, since panic would send her running blindly into the open, making her an easy target? It was as well, he thought smugly, that de Granville's leg wound rendered him clumsy, blunted the sharp edge of his rivalry. Fatigue and pain would hamper him, making him irritably impetuous, over-quick to react. If, by some mischance, de Granville reached her first, then even that might be turned to advantage. He would scarce be in a mood to listen to her pleas and persuasion. He would fire in cold blood and without warning. There was much to be gained from de Granville's crippled state, humiliated as he was by his useless incompetence. It made him reckless, and a reckless man was a danger not only to others but to himself. He had wagered that although de Granville might take the first shot, then he himself would certainly claim the last. The irony was that the shot would be aimed at de Granville . . . A man could trust himself, and no other. A scene of carnage such as that in the meadow could be put down to the violence of a crazed man who had killed savagely and for no apparent reason, then turned his gun upon himself. It would take no great effort to carry the girl's body to the waggon and set the stage. None knew of his presence here save de Granville . . . and although enquiries would certainly be made, the innkeeper could have no knowledge of him or his whereabouts . . . No, he was safe enough.

Two shots exploded at the far side of the wood, their harsh cracks a violence that sent a wood pigeon whirring from the undergrowth so forcefully that Hanford actually cried aloud. He steadied himself with an effort, damning his stupidity. She was dead, then? De Granville had killed her, as he promised. With an oath and a rising anger that he had been so unfairly betrayed, robbed of his prize, Hanford, dark saturnine face set mutinously, hurried to investigate.

Luke's and Nerissa's cautious return through the wood had been in awkward near-silence, their senses pricked painfully alert for sign or sound of Hanford or de Granville. Luke moved warily ahead, with pistol cocked for swift firing, and Nerissa stumbled uneasily in his wake. She, too, clutched the pistol which Luke had given her for protection, the firearm which de Granville's shattered shoulder had forced him to let fall. It brought her no comfort to be holding it, for it was viscous still with his congealing blood and she could scarce bear to handle it. Yet it gave her a kind of spurious courage, a sense that she was involved in this with Luke. He trusted her, yet she did not know if she could ever bring herself to use it, whatever threatened. Her father had nurtured a poacher's hatred of firearms, for they were the mark of authority and the law. Would the law now be on her side? Would the justice take her word and Joe Protheroe's above that of his own son? She had to believe it, and that judgement was the same for all, else it was not worth a corpse's candle. She was trapped now as never before between two worlds. If she survived, then she must choose between them. Yet she knew, even as she pushed onwards, with briar thorn tearing remorselessly, that the way was already made. Luke would guide and protect her, whatever came. Neither de Granville's blood nor his hatred had the power to halt her. She would see that he paid for the agony he had wrought. Then the future, unlike the past, would have no power to hurt her.

When they emerged, dishevelled and awkwardly daz-
zled by the suddenness of the light, into the open meadow,
guns in hand, the justice hurried, grave faced, to question them.

"You are safe, ma'am? Not harmed?" he demanded
anxiously.

"No, sir. I have suffered no harm . . . but I must go to
the waggon to tend to Mr Jones, to tell him that I am safe."
She hesitated, blurting anguishedly, "He tried to defend
me . . . took the full force of the blows. I am the cause,
and to blame!"

"No, ma'am. You are in no way to blame . . . You are
the innocent victim, as he . . ." He glanced up, face stiff
with vicarious pain, as Peter de Granville came quietly to
stand beside them.

"The shots, sir? Those we heard in the wood?" he
demanded of Luke, face tense. "Was it my son?" His
gaze fell on the pistol in Nerissa's hand and the blood
upon it, and he reached out for it in horrified recognition
as Nerissa wordlessly surrendered it. "He is dead, then?
Richard is dead?" His voice was dulled with acceptance.

"No . . . he is alive, sir, but disarmed . . . seeking
escape."

"The blood . . .?"

"He is wounded. I was forced to shoot, to protect Miss
Pritchard. He suffered a shoulder wound. I did not aim
to kill."

Peter de Granville's austere, etiolated face showed
neither relief nor condemnation. It was as coldly expressionless as his voice.

"Then we had best search for him . . . bring him to
book."

He turned abruptly on his heel and made for the woods,
thrusting his son's pistol away savagely as he walked, as if
he would rid himself of all trace of him.

"You had best go with him, Farrow," the justice
instructed wearily. "God knows how he might react
should they come face to face . . . There is a limit to
every man's endurance, the amount he can safely bear."

As Luke briefly hesitated, glancing towards Nerissa, the

367

justice said wryly, "I shall protect Miss Pritchard, never fear . . . whoever comes. She has suffered persecution enough."

Nerissa nodded to Luke but spoke no word. Fear that he might be wounded or killed all but crippled her, but she could not let him see the depths of her distress for him. It would serve only to weaken and hinder him. Her fear was all for Luke, and for Francis, but she felt an ache of pity too. In the battle already fought, she, Goliath Jones and Joe Protheroe had neither won nor lost, they were innocent survivors. In the battle ahead, David Hanford and Richard de Granville could not hope for even the poor comfort of that. Death must surely come, if not now then ignominiously upon the gallows . . . It would be an ending, and none could question the morality of it . . . For Sir Peter de Granville and the justice, it would be an ending too. An ending of hope and a beginning of grief, with none to staunch the hurt of it. Slowly, and with head bent, she made her way to the waggon, to Goliath Jones and Toby.

Francis, hearing the shots at the far side of the wood, hesitated, then moved cautiously towards the sound. He had been skirting the perimeter of the copse hoping that de Granville or Hanford would break cover and make a run for it. Yet now his concern was all for Nerissa . . . Had one of her pursuers found her? He was taut with fear and cold anger, trembling uncontrollably as the sickness took hold of him. If de Granville had harmed a hair of her, then he would bear the brunt of Luke's fury and his own. He needed but the shadow of an excuse to kill him for the violence he had already wrought. Anger, he knew, was destructive, for it sapped a man's energy, made him careless and therefore vulnerable to his enemies. He would not make that mistake. The coldness of long training reasserted itself, the caution of those in command of the lives of others. He would move circumspectly, doing nothing upon impulse. When the time was right, he would strike cleanly and with calm certainty. He had little to lose. His life was almost at an end, the thought of a lingering helplessness more threatening than death itself.

When he reached that small clearing from whence the shots had come, he moved with practised caution, keeping himself well hid, alert always for attack from others. There were the signs of a recent confrontation, the undergrowth trampled and the faint smell of cordite still pungent upon the air . . . Traces of blood, yet none dead . . . someone injured then, yet still able to flee. Nerissa or de Granville? By the signs of blundering escape and the footprints, it was de Granville. Purposefully, Francis set out in pursuit of him. He would not let him win and evade the justice he deserved. He must be wary always of threat from Hanford. Together they might plan to lure him into a trap. Yet the fear remained that it was Nerissa who had been shot and that de Granville or Hanford had abducted her, dragging or carrying her with them. The exhaustion and despair which plagued Francis were lost in his fury to find Nerissa and to deal out the punishment Hanford and de Granville deserved. They had killed Tom Pritchard, savagely and without remorse. Now the hunters were the hunted. It was a retribution that God Himself might devise.

Hanford, unaware that any save de Granville and he were in the wood, in search of the Pritchard whore, was certain that de Granville must have killed her. Two shots had been fired. It was but further proof of de Granville's bungling, his pitiful inadequacy. Hanford would have needed one bullet, and one alone. He would have killed her cleanly, competently, and without remorse, knowing that it was the means to his own salvation . . . Where was de Granville now? Returned to the waggon, most likely, to make sure that the old man was dead . . . And the girl? There was no apparent sign of her . . . de Granville must have dragged her body deep into the undergrowth to keep her well hidden . . . That might prove a problem, an obstacle to his plans. Yet it was not insurmountable. He had but to question de Granville casually, ask him to show him the exact spot where she lay. Praise and flattery would serve to disarm him and rid him of all suspicion, for de Granville was ludicrously susceptible to both.

Even as he began to retrace his steps to seek him out, he

369

heard a noisy commotion ahead, the sound of a crashing through the undergrowth and voices raised in anger. Cautiously, and with pistol raised, he crept forward to investigate, keeping himself well hidden behind a thicket of thorn and bramble. Poachers, perhaps? Or cottagers arriving early for the show in the meadow? Hell and damnation! he thought vexedly. It would put paid to all his plans . . . Yet what he saw disturbed and dismayed him more. The confrontation was between de Granville, Farrow and de Granville's own father! It made no sense! His every instinct was to flee, yet some compulsion stayed him, some perversity of mind. What had occurred? He could not even begin to fathom it. Certainly de Granville was unarmed, worse, he was painfully wounded, his shoulder shattered and useless. Who, then, had fired the shots? The two men held their pistols steady, stolid, implacable.

"Do not attempt to move, de Granville . . . You are in my sights . . . I shall not hesitate to shoot!" The voice was that of Captain Farrow, controlled and icily contemptuous.

Richard de Granville stared wildly from one to the other, seeking some sign of weakness, bent upon escape.

"Father . . .?" His voice was stricken, raw with appeal, and for a moment Hanford saw Peter de Granville's pistol waver, grief ravage his face.

"Do not attempt to escape . . . for if Captain Farrow fails to halt you, then I will not." The words were clipped, brutal in their curtness, and Richard de Granville knew they were beyond appeal.

Limping awkwardly, and with a hand to his wounded shoulder, he tried to summon his old insouciance, his devil-may-care pride, but he succeeded only in looking ridiculous. Worse than that, an object of derision and pity. He was, Hanford thought disgustedly, a poor apology of a creature, already cowering and beaten. Well, let him shoulder the blame . . . His own way was clear now, there was naught to delay him. He would find a path to where the horses were tethered and make good his escape. He would deny all involvement, pay some willing tenant or innkeeper to provide alibi . . . His father, the justice,

370

would not see him sacrificed. He had but to keep his nerve. He felt sickness rise in his throat, the sour taste of gall, as sweat broke out at his nape and beaded his lips and hairline. Yes. He had but to keep his nerve.

Richard de Granville, forced humiliatingly into the open at the point of Luke's pistol, acted a scornful indifference which he did not feel. He was sick with terror within, and as terrified that he might break down and weep like a mewling infant before all. His shoulder pained him abominably, and exhaustion and the ache in his crippled leg were more than he could bear. Even harder to bear was his father's cold indifference. There was rejection in every line and hollow of his father's sternly autocratic face, a disgust that could not be hidden. He was bitterly alone now and with none to whom he might make excuse or appeal . . . Hanford! Perhaps Hanford would find solution. He was a friend, the only real friend he had known . . . Yes, Hanford was clever and would not desert him. He would find a way.

The door to the waggon was flung open with a jarring suddenness and that bitch, that Pritchard whore, had come out, standing brazenly on the painted step. Rage and frustration had so overwhelmed him that he had lunged at her furiously, until the cold steel of Farrow's pistol had forced reason . . . Yet there was a red mist before his eyes, vivid as blood, and his every instinct was to lash out and destory her. To his chagrin, Dr Siberry had followed her into the doorway of the waggon, supporting that wretched creature, the old man, whom he had clubbed with his own stave and left for dead. Siberry's father had surrendered the man to her keeping and hurried across the green to where de Granville stood.

"Richard . . . my dear boy." His face was as compassionate as his tone. "Come within . . . I will tend to your shoulder, your gun wound. It must not be neglected."

"I have no need of your services, sir!" de Granville said contemptuously. "You had best serve those peasants best suited to your skills."

Dr Siberry flushed but held his ground, saying quietly, "You have no quarrel with me, sir . . . I have done you no harm." He hesitated, pleading with painful appeal, "My son, Matthew . . . he is not with you? He is not involved in this?"

"Oh yes, sir," de Granville sneered exultantly, "he is involved in the murder of Tom Pritchard, as in all else."

Luke heard the cry which Nerissa made and was powerless to comfort her, but Goliath Jones put an arm protectively about her, comforter and comforted both.

Dr Siberry, pale faced and close to collapse, persisted despairingly. "I have only your word on Matthew's guilt . . . his involvement. Why is he not here today? I beg you will tell me, give reason for it."

"Because, sir, he is a coward and a fool," he sneered. "He has neither the wits nor the stomach for it! Is that plain enough? I should have killed him, as I killed Jeremy Hardwicke! They are useless carrion, scavengers all!" He spat contemptuously at the ground where Dr Siberry stood, transfixed.

The blow across his mouth all but sent him stumbling to his knees as Peter de Granville said thickly, "By God! I should kill you . . . I feel shame that I have spawned you. You are no son of mine!"

Even as he spoke, there was a fierce shout from Francis at the edge of the wood as Hanford emerged with pistol held aloft and ran towards the carriageway beyond.

Francis, pursuing him at a distance, stumbled and all but fell, but recovered to let off a random shot that went wide as Hanford flung himself aside then ripped a way through the hedge on to the highway beyond.

The justice, stationed alongside the gate to the meadow, heard the carriage approaching and tried to shout warning, certain that his son would be dragged remorselessly beneath its wheels. For a moment he froze, impotent to act. Before he could leap to wrench the reins from Arabella's grasp and bring the horse to a halt, his son had dragged Arabella from her perch and was thrusting her before him, eyes crazed, a pistol held hard at her neck.

"Stand back!" Hanford's voice was shrill, thin with hysteria. "Stand back, I say, or by God I will kill her!"

The pistol was thrust deeper into Arabella's flesh and the justice, clinging despairingly to the reins, was forced to relinquish them and stand aside, pistol still clasped uselessly in his hand.

"For God's sake, David . . . let her go free!" The cry was wrung from him. "Cause no grief. There has been hurt enough."

"Stand aside!" Hanford's face was wrenched in fury, hand upon the gun trembling violently. The horse, sweating and lathered, shied nervously and Hanford stared about him, wild eyed, thrusting Arabella viciously towards the gig.

"Climb on board!"

The pistol still menaced her. As she hesitated, he struck her a blow that sent her reeling against the carriage, and the justice's cry was more violent than her own as she sought to steady herself. For the first time terror, rather than anger, raked her through as, with mouth dry and her heart beating suffocatingly, she did as he bade. Fear made her clumsy, and he let out a stream of oaths as he thrust her savagely aside and climbed up beside her.

"Take up the reins!"

"No!" The shout was from the justice as he surged forward, pistol raised high. "For pity's sake, stop now before it is too late!"

Hanford, crazed beyond reason, picked up the horse-whip and sent it stinging against his father's face, the lash lacerating, drawing blood.

The justice, shocked and raw with pain, stumbled and all but fell . . . then forced himself upright, finger closing upon the trigger of his pistol.

"Drive on!" Hanford screamed, and Arabella obeyed instinctively, turning the gig as the justice's shot tore into Hanford's sleeve.

The horse reared violently and plunged away and Arabella, losing control of the reins, shut her eyes in horror. Hanford, cursing volubly, tried vainly to regain control, lurching and stumbling awkwardly as the gig rattled and swayed. Then there was the sharp bone-crack of a second shot, a vicious explosion of sound as he screamed aloud and fell heavily across Arabella, then awkwardly to the roadside. Arabella, blind with terror and with the breath wrenched from her body, could do nothing but let the horse run free. The gig was out of control now and she clung on feverishly, eyes clenched tight, awaiting the crash that must inevitably come, bracing herself against the fall.

All was noise and anguished movement, a confusion of shouting and pain as the gig came to a juddering halt that she felt in every raw nerve and bone of her body. When she plucked up the courage to open her eyes and look about her, she saw Manley clinging fast to the reins, face reddened with sweat and effort, and the coach, with Hanson smilingly atop it, draw up beyond. She did not try to make sense of this miracle, nor of anything else, for weakness and shock overcame her and she began to weep painfully. She was aware that someone had climbed up beside her on the box and put a comforting arm about her . . . but her eyes were too blurred with tears to make sense of it.

"There, my love . . . my little dear," Francis said gently, kissing away her tears. "I would not let him harm you . . . you are safe now."

"Is he dead? Did the justice shoot him?" Her voice was shaken with horror and pity.

"No." His answer was low, scarce audible. "I could not let him kill his own son, Arabella."

Arabella saw that Francis's eyes were blurred with anguish of hurt, his exhaustion even deeper than her own, and in a moment she was the comforter and he the comforted.

They clung together wordlessly until Francis said, "We had best go and give the justice what comfort we may. He has lost more than a son, Arabella; he has lost his pride in his son . . . his reason for living."

The justice was on the grass verge of the roadside, cradling his son's head in his arms. He was staring before him, dry eyed and unmoving, and Nerissa thought that never had she seen a face so etched in suffering, such grief of loss. He did not look up as they approached to stand awkwardly beside him. Indeed, he seemed unaware of their presence, as of all else save the enormity of his own hurt. There was no need to ask if David Hanford was dead. The justice was trying to make sense of the words he had murmured, but could not, for the blood that choked his son's throat and bubbled obscenely at the corner of his mouth, like a babe's first dribbling attempts at speech. He had bent low to hear what was it that the boy was trying to say. For a moment, his dark eyes were bright again with amusement, mouth tugged into a rictus of a smile.

"The last shot . . ."

"I did not fire it!" The justice, wracked with guilt, tried to explain, to make pitiful amends.

"No . . ." He shook his head savagely, breath harsh in his throat. "I won."

The justice had stared at him in bewilderment, trying to comprehend. "You won?"

"Tell him." His son's nails dug deep into the justice's palm.

"Tell him it *was* mine."

Sir Charles Hanford sat there now, unmoving, his face as drained of colour and as lifeless as his son's, and Arabella saw with pity that his cuffs and coat sleeve were soaked through with blood, dark and stiffly congealing, and that her own gown and cloak were splashed with it. Already those in the meadow were hurrying towards them, alerted by the gunfire, and Francis said haltingly, "I will keep them clear, sir . . . explain . . . You had best take our coach, make use of it for your son's return."

If the justice was aware of the tragic irony of it, then he gave no sign. "I thank you, Major Crawshay, for that." His tone was flat, emotionless. "It would be better so."

Francis blurted impulsively, "I beg you to believe, sir, that I was forced to it . . . Arabella was at risk . . . There was no other way."

Arabella placed a compassionate hand on her husband's shoulder and led him wordlessly away.

"Major Crawshay?"

Francis turned. "Sir?"

"It was kinder . . . for all. Yes. It was kinder so."

The reunion between Nerissa and Arabella had been

warmly tearful, with much hugging and kissing, explanations given and promises made. Yet within each of those present there lay a core of pity and regret for lives violently torn asunder or wasted, and for those with private wounds excoriated, emotions laid bare.

None was of a mind to linger, and arrangements were swiftly made and as swiftly carried out. The justice and his dead son were to be transported to Lanelay Court in the coach, with Hanson at the reins. Sir Peter de Granville, it was agreed, would travel with them and beside him, with hands humiliatingly bound, his son.

Richard de Granville had shown no emotion upon hearing of the death of David Hanford and had expressed neither remorse nor pity for the violence he had done. His father had stood gaunt faced before him, pistol trained upon him, and they had exchanged barely a word.

Arabella had insisted that Goliath Jones and Toby were to be driven in the waggon to Knatchfield Grange, where they must remain under Dr Siberry's care. She was firm upon it, she declared, and would brook no argument, and Goliath Jones was in no mind to disagree. He surrendered with handsome courtesy, and even Toby, lying grieved and disconsolate in his willow basket, rallied enough to lick Arabella's hand, an accolade which, to the confusion of the men, had Arabella and Nerissa laughing then weeping quite shamelessly.

Harold Manley, the groom, was to first ride to the inn at Fair Oaks and apprise the landlord of where Hanford's and Richard de Granville's horses were tethered, with a message that Tim Clegg might collect and keep them in payment for his services, for neither the justice nor Sir Peter wished further reminder of the day . . . The rest of the horses were to be tied behind the coach and the waggon, to be later reclaimed.

The justice, with the aid of Francis and Luke, had watched his son's body lifted into the coach and had climbed in, stoical and stiff backed, to be beside him . . . Richard de Granville, hands bound and standing scornfully at Sir Peter's side, had remained silent, a contemptuous sneer upon his handsome face.

376

Sir Peter, who had not spoken while the body was carried within, turned coldly upon his son, saying through stiff lips, "By God, sir, you have done a fine thing this day! You have much to be proud of."

Richard de Granville kept obdurately silent.

"Sir Charles has lost a son," his father continued scathingly, "and I wish to God that it might have been you! His grief and shame are ending . . . Mine begin . . . One death is more than enough to bear."

Luke and Francis had watched the coach with its tragic passengers move away, then parted, chastened and unspeaking. Francis had climbed into the gig beside Arabella and let her take the reins, too exhausted and saddened to make protest.

"We will soon be home, my dear," she said gently.

"Yes." His hand reached out to cover hers upon the reins.

There were those who would never return, and the knowledge lay heavily between them, although no word of it was spoken. The future, too, was uncertain, and the promise of death a darkness.

"We are together . . ." Arabella said, "and safe."

"Yes," he said quietly. "That is all that I dared to hope, and more than I dared to ask."

If he saw the shine of tears upon Arabella's lashes, then it was but a part of living and loving. Joy and sadness are so close as to be one and the same, and neither could exist without the other.

Manley had returned to take up the reins of the waggon, first tethering the horses behind it and smiling ruefully at the pot-bellied cob that ambled before it. As the caravan moved off, in all its painted garishness, he could not help but laugh aloud at the ludicrous spectacle he presented in his bewigged and gilded livery.

Within the waggon, Dr Siberry, intent upon making his patient comfortable, glanced up at the sound of such free infectious laughter and met Goliath Jones's gaze.

" 'Twill mend, sir," Jones said quietly. " 'Twill ease . . . your hurt, I mean, like Toby and me, and all else . . .

377

Another's happiness is cold comfort for grief, but 'tis enough that it exists. 'Tis why I cherish the life I have chosen."

Dr Siberry nodded and said quietly, "And I mine, sir . . . and I mine." He turned his attention to Toby, face intent.

Nerissa was seated beside Luke, her head resting comfortably upon his breast and his arm embracing her.

"I beg, Miss Pritchard, ma'am, that you will marry me," he said, eyes alight with mischief, "for we are sorely compromised."

"Indeed, sir, I am of a mind to refuse you," she responded, straight faced. "I fear that you make a habit of such proposals . . . It is scarcely flattering to a lady."

"And are you a lady, Miss Pritchard?"

"I have aspirations, sir."

"Then I fear that I shall be disappointed, ma'am, for I looked forward to a lifetime of unrelieved depravity." He grinned, adding wickedly, "And would you fancy a travelling life, Miss Pritchard? A life upon the roads?"

"Indeed, sir . . . 'tis my joy to go adventuring."

"But with me, Miss Pritchard? Would you come with me?"

"Why . . . 'twould be very heaven on earth, Captain Farrow," she said. "I accept, sir, and gladly."

Goliath Jones, who had been eavesdropping shamelessly, smiled as broadly as Luke.